MODERN STORIES IN ENGLISH

Second Edition

Edited by

W.H. NEW
H.J. ROSENGARTEN

UNIVERSITY OF BRITISH COLUMBIA

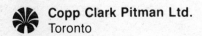

Copp Clark Pitman Ltd.
Toronto

ISBN 0 7730 4564-3

Canadian Cataloguing in Publication Data
Main entry under title:
Modern stories in English

Includes bibliographies.
ISBN 0-7730-4564-3

1. Short stories, English — 20th century.
2. Short stories, Canadian (English) — 20th century.*
I. New, W.H. (William Herbert), 1938–
II. Rosengarten, Herbert.

PR1309.S5M62 1986   823'.01'08   C86-093016-5

47,500

Editing/Margaret Larock, Barbara Tessman
Design/Doug Frank
Typesetting/Compeer Typographic Services Limited
Printing and Binding/Webcom Ltd.

Cover Painting:
Used by permission "Zing Green" by Jack Bush
© The Estate of Jack Bush

Copp Clark Pitman Ltd.
495 Wellington Street West
Toronto, Ontario
M5V 1E9

Printed and bound in Canada

TABLE OF CONTENTS

THEMATIC TABLE OF CONTENTS

CHILDHOOD, INITIATION, AND GROWTH

LOVE, MARRIAGE, AND THE ROLES OF MEN AND WOMEN

IDENTITY AND ALIENATION

DEATH

NATURE, TOWNS, AND CITIES

SOCIAL CONFLICT: RACE, WAR, CLASS, AND CIVIL UNREST

RELIGIOUS AND MORAL VALUES

ART AND REALITY

CHRONOLOGICAL TABLE OF CONTENTS

INTRODUCTION

Good stories entertain us: this is the main reason we listen to them or read them. But "entertainment" comes in many guises. For some listeners and readers, narrative is everything — they like a quick-moving tale, a thrilling plot, mystery, adventure, suspense. Some want to identify with the characters of a story, perhaps to share their experiences vicariously, or perhaps because such empathy enlarges their understanding of the complexities of human behavior. For other readers, plot and character are subordinate to a story's educational purpose or moral point; they want fiction to teach a lesson about life. A different group of readers is less interested in a separable "moral" or "subject" than in the manner by which the story is told, by its formal qualities; for them, the form that the story takes — meaning the cadences and textures of its language, as well as its structure — constitutes a "subject" in its own right. Readers look in a story variously for escape, for instruction, for a mirror of the world, for a work of artifice.

Just as there is a multiplicity of readers, so the modern short story draws on a multitude of forms that have long been a part of narrative tradition: myths, legends, fables, folk tales, ballads, fairy tales, and moral "exempla." Since the first half of the nineteenth century, when authors like Edgar Allan Poe and Nathaniel Hawthorne began producing models of narrative suspense and psychological drama in short-story form, American writers have been among the short story's foremost practitioners. But the same era saw the development of short fiction elsewhere as well, in France, Germany, England, Russia, China, Spain, Italy; and the new perspectives brought by these different cultures and traditions gave additional vigor to the short story, strengthening its claim to be regarded as a fictional form in its own right. Such cross-fertilization has continued into our own time. Twentieth-century writers in English have been influenced not only by their own cultures, but also by innovative writers in other languages: by the folk writers of Asia and India, for example, and the Gothic authors of Quebec, the political fabulists from Czechoslovakia and the "magic realists" of Latin America.

Yet in English alone there is a rich variety, reflected by the stories in this collection. They display diverse views and contrasting styles; they are representative of the century's main technical developments in short fiction; they also come from many different parts of the world: mostly from the United States, Britain, and Canada, but also from Ireland, Africa, the Caribbean, and the South Pacific. They have in common the English language; to make this assertion, however, is to cover a wealth of specific differences, for in the relation between language and culture something happens that affects the shape and substance of stories. The way writers use images, for example, derives not so much from literary or linguistic precedent and example (though these play their part), as from the way they see their own world — from their particular experience, their own observations of places and people. Joyce's Dublin and Faulkner's South, Naipaul's Trinidad and Achebe's Nigeria: these are fictional locales, rooted in specific cultural and political observations. The worlds of the Irish Catholic and the Trinidad Hindu, the social patterns of American and Nigerian families, are not the same. Comparing stories from different cultures, therefore, can provide an opportunity to study ethnic differences, and to delight in the linguistic variety to which such differences have given rise. It can also reveal elements of social disparity and inequity, even while it underlines the common humanity of the experiences that the writers have depicted.

There are many shared human experiences — love, hate, work, war, birth, death, dreams — which recur from author to author, from country to country, in all forms of literature. The function of the Thematic Table of Contents in this anthology is to guide readers to some of these points of comparison. The number of stories about growing up, for example, or about the relations between men and women, testifies to the similarity of everyday life around the world. Stories about political or racial oppression ("Brother," "Dry September"), or about the problems arising out of modern scientific progress ("The Dog Explosion," "Report") can awaken comparable responses in readers from a wide range of backgrounds. But even here a reader must be sensitive to differences, and avoid making facile connections. The roles of men and women vary from society to society, as they have varied within a single society over time; attitudes to communal and individual values differ (individualism is not universally regarded as socially desirable or necessary); and generational conflict in a culture that reveres tradition will obviously carry different overtones from those it possesses in a society committed to novelty and change.

Although all the writers in this anthology have in common the cultural and linguistic heritage of English, that heritage has been altered by time and place. During the twentieth century, many national literatures founded on English patterns and traditions moved away from them in order to reclaim older indigenous traditions, or because new experiences, landscapes, and cultural mixes led to a need for different words and different ways of using them. Walt Whitman's efforts in the mid-nineteenth century to articulate a new language for the United States provided something of a model; Whitman wanted American English to mirror his "new" nation's expansionist, democratic, colloquial politics. The American writers in this book, from Faulkner and Hemingway to Cheever and Vonnegut, convey the characteristic sounds and rhythms of the language that subsequently evolved. In Africa and the Caribbean, where the tradition of oral storytelling developed into a sophisticated folk art, the tensions of modern life are still couched in a characteristically "oral" form. Achebe and Naipaul rely extensively for their effects on the rhythms of speech and the contrasts between different orders of vernacular fluency. Achebe's "Civil Peace" deals with the collapse of communal solidarity during the Nigerian civil war, while Naipaul's "My Aunt Gold Teeth" affirms the value of a tradition the narrator admires even while he can no longer participate in it; in both cases, it is the oral character of the culture which preserves the values and forms of a civilization once strong and now lost. And in Albert Wendt's "A Resurrection," the persistence of tradition and ritual in twentieth-century Samoa finds expression in part through the story's use of oral idioms belonging to an older way of life.

As with patterns of speech, so with thematic concerns. In Australia and New Zealand, writers found new subjects in responding to a set of social preoccupations born out of their separate South Pacific contexts and their relations with the colonizing power, Britain. Katherine Mansfield's deliberate, class-conscious individualism in "The Doll's House" looks back to a time when English conventions were still strong, while the broadly absurdist satire of Peter Carey's "Crabs" emphasizes the radical changes in a society losing its traditional identity in the face of contemporary materialism. Canadians have also sought their own voice: though living in an environment in many respects similar to that of their American neighbors, they have determinedly celebrated the differences that distinguish their social organization and social values from those that pertain in Britain and the United States — in the process developing a lively rhetoric of regional identities. Both Sinclair Ross and Alice Munro, for example (Ross in "Cornet at Night," about a prairie boy's imaginative break from farm routine, and Munro in "Thanks for the Ride," describing adolescent initiation and social decay in a small Ontario town), vividly record the sounds and sights of particular locales, emphasizing how their characters' lives and language are inextricably intertwined with their environment. Similarly, Margaret Laurence's "The Merchant of Heaven" and Barry Dempster's "The Burial" place characters in cross-cultural circumstances in order to reveal the constraints of speech and the presumptions of culture. All these stories evoke the language of place, some in dialogue, some through narration or description, some in transformations of everyday speech into political or social symbol.

In one way or another then, whether through setting or subject or language, a sense of place pervades all the stories in this collection. In many, however, that awareness is rooted in feelings of exile or alienation from an older tradition. Such exile has, during this century, proved to be an opportunity to discover freedom on the one hand, and an experience that is spiritually debilitating on the other. People have chosen to emigrate, or been driven to do so; they have willingly embraced a different kind of life, or had one forced upon them. Whichever the case, such moves inevitably brought with them a sense of something left behind, something lost. Katherine Mansfield reveals this divided consciousness: she rejected what she considered the provinciality of New

Zealand, and yet her stories sometimes look back wistfully to a colonial childhood. V. S. Naipaul experienced a twofold alienation: from his Indian heritage, and from his Trinidadian upbringing. For Ernest Hemingway, exile was a deliberate choice, dictated by a need to find fresh values; working in Paris in the 1920s, he sought to break away from outworn modes and empty rhetoric, to give literature new force and meaning by portraying life in starkly realistic terms. In this he only partly succeeded, for he could never wholly shed the ideal of heroic individualism that marks the American tradition.

The experience of alienation is not restricted to individuals. The native Indian writer George Clutesi, for instance, observes that Indians and Inuit in North America are dispossessed without even moving from their homeland. Writers from ethnic minorities (Alice Walker, Clark Blaise), using or responding to the language of the "majority" culture around them, live with an isolation of a related kind. For many writers, therefore, fiction becomes a way of challenging or subverting social conventions, a means to shape in artifice an alternative vision of the world. Feminist writers (Lessing, Thomas, Walker) have attempted to combat the presumptive values inherent in linguistic conventions as well as in social ones. And there is another kind of alienation — intellectual and artistic, such as we find detailed in Rudy Wiebe's "Where Is the Voice Coming From?" which dramatizes the struggle by a member of one culture to reach some understanding of another, and to find ordered utterance for his confused and painful impressions.

The language of the modern short story, then, can be not only a means of reporting on experience, but also a way of charting alternative perceptions of experience. Whatever the goal, the writer can call on a multitude of devices through which he or she may pattern the experience: through realistic description, for example, or through fantasy, through satire, through myth. In stories like Hemingway's "Hills Like White Elephants," for example, the writer's intention is to make us believe we are direct observers of the action; he creates the illusion of reality by focusing on dialogue, so that we have the sense that we are listening in on a real conversation. Such stories move us from the page to the world; we recognize the action as a comment on or description of life, a projection of psychological disturbance or a dramatization of social conflict. But other writers (Barth most clearly) ask readers to look at the *word* as much as at the *world*. Writers like Barthelme and Vonnegut (writing "reports"), Helprin (writing "letters"), and Wiebe (copying out phrases from historical archives) adopt forms that, in part, paradoxically stress the limitations of documentary realism. Their stories challenge readers to acknowledge the empirical world and then to use their imagination to transcend its obvious restrictions. They ask readers to be co-creators of the story. They are celebrants of language-in-process, taking pleasure in language at play, exploring its boundaries.

Language takes narrative shape in other, more traditional ways. For writers like Cheever, Callaghan, and Bowles, a concern with moral behavior takes the form of parable or fable. In stories such as those by Jacobs, Forster, and Carey, it is the pattern of fantasy or myth that structures experience; the reader enters the world of dream or nightmare, with its associative leaps of logic and its symbolic or psychological implications. For writers of satire — Joyce, White, Nowlan, and others — the story is patterned by a comic irony that exposes the flaws and foibles of people who live their lives in two dimensions, blinkered to other possibilities and unaware of their own follies.

Several stories in this anthology incorporate elements of myth as a structuring device, either the kind of myth that articulates directly a society's moral tradition, or the kind that is used as a literary means to sound "archetypes," to arouse in the reader a recognition of enduring patterns of human experience. Both kinds of myth can serve didactic purposes. Clutesi's "Ko-ishin-mit and the Shadow People" comes from a tradition in which such tales were designed (in the author's own words) "to teach the young the many wonders of nature; the importance of all living things, no matter how small and insignificant." In contrast, Bowles's "Allal" merges the conventions of myth with those of realism to produce a social fable that comments on modern human beings. It is ironic, oblique, spare; its eye is on contemporary behavior all the while it seems to be concerned with events of pure fantasy. We are asked to believe in the truth of what the story tells us but not necessarily in the reality of the events it portrays — they are a means to a different end.

Other stories that employ fantasy in like fashion, to make us look afresh at the "real" world, include Yates's bizarre picture of suburban domesticity in "The Sinking of the Northwest Passage," Jackson's "The Tooth," with its surreal images of sea and sand in a New York street, Carey's "Crabs," an absurdist vision of a violent future that may already exist in the present. That such stories are in one way or another "fantastic" does not make them any less relevant to our own daily lives; it simply makes us more conscious of the artifice which characterizes all works of literature, and by means of which writer and reader are able to share the pleasures of the imagination.

CHINUA ACHEBE

Born in Ogidi, Nigeria, in 1930 and educated at Umuahia, Ibadan, and London, Chinua Achebe has become established not only as an editor and publisher, but also as one of the most respected literary voices in contemporary Africa. He has written verse, books for juveniles, two books of short stories, and four novels, of which the first three won particularly enthusiastic reviews. *Things Fall Apart* (1958), *No Longer at Ease* (1961), and *Arrow of God* (1964) render different aspects of the conflict between European and African civilizations. The powerlessness of the traditional culture to remain intact in the face of European enslavement and colonization, the inability of a modern young African to reconcile his family attachments with his sense of independence and his observation of political corruption, the incapacity of both the lay African society and the European colonial bureaucracy to understand the role and identity of a traditional priest: these are Achebe's topics. His aim is openly political and didactic. In "The Novelist as Teacher," he asserts: "Here, then, is an adequate revolution for me to espouse — to help my society regain its belief in itself and put away the complexes of the years of denigration and self-denigration." In so doing he fulfills one of the traditional roles of the writer in African society: to educate the young to an appreciation of the moral truths of their own culture. His method, too, derives from traditional techniques; he relies on simple narrative structures and on the functional patterns of Igbo proverbs. "As long as one people sit on another and are deaf to their cry," he writes, "so long will understanding elude all of us."

"Civil Peace" is the concluding story of *Girls at War and other stories* (1972), a volume which reflects the civil war that disrupted Nigerian life in the late 1960s. Though the fatalistic ironies that permeate the story are not untouched by humor, the work is fundamentally serious and reveals Achebe's continuing account of his deeply held commitment to freedom. In exploring its nature, in attempting both to communicate to a national audience and to reach across cultural and racial boundaries, he shows himself to be an acute and humane observer of human behavior.

FOR FURTHER READING

Chinua Achebe, "The Novelist as Teacher," *Morning Yet on Creation Day* (London: Heinemann, 1975), pp. 42–45.

David Carroll, *Chinua Achebe* (New York: Twayne, 1970).

G.D. Killam, *The Novels of Chinua Achebe* (London: Heinemann, 1969).

Margaret Laurence, *Long Drums and Cannons* (London: Macmillan, 1968).

CIVIL PEACE

Jonathan Iwegbu counted himself extra-ordinarily lucky. "Happy survival!" meant so much more to him than just a current fashion of greeting old friends in the first hazy days of peace. It went deep to his heart. He had come out of the war with five inestimable blessings — his head, his wife Maria's head and the heads of three out of their four children. As a bonus he also had his old bicycle — a miracle too but naturally not to be compared to the safety of five human heads.

The bicycle had a little history of its own. One day at the height of the war it was commandeered "for urgent military action." Hard as its loss would have been to him he would still have let it go without a thought had he not had some doubts about the genuineness of the officer. It wasn't his disreputable rags, nor the toes peeping out of one blue and one brown canvas shoes, nor yet the two stars of his rank done obviously in a hurry in biro, that troubled Jonathan; many good and heroic soldiers looked the same or worse. It was rather a certain lack of grip and firmness in his manner. So Jonathan, suspecting he might be amenable to influence, rummaged in his raffia bag and produced the two pounds with which he had been going to buy firewood which his wife, Maria, retailed to camp officials for extra stock-fish and corn meal, and got his bicycle back. That night he buried it in the little clearing in the bush where the dead of the camp, including his own youngest son, were buried. When he dug it up again a year later after the surrender all it needed was a little palm-oil greasing. "Nothing puzzles God," he said in wonder.

He put it to immediate use as a taxi and accumulated a small pile of Biafran money ferrying camp officials and their families across the four mile stretch to the nearest tarred road. His standard charge per trip was six pounds and those who had the money were only glad to be rid of some of it in this way. At the end of a fortnight he had made a small fortune of one hundred and fifteen pounds.

Then he made the journey to Enugu and found another miracle waiting for him. It was unbelievable. He rubbed his eyes and looked again and it was still standing there before him. But, needless to say, even that monumental blessing must be accounted also totally inferior to the five heads in the family. This newest miracle was his little house in Ogui Overside. Indeed nothing puzzles God! Only two houses away a huge concrete edifice some wealthy contractor had put up just before the war was a mountain of rubble. And here was Jonathan's little zinc house of no regrets built with mud blocks quite intact! Of course the doors and windows were missing and five sheets off the roof. But what was that? And anyhow he had returned to Enugu early enough to pick up bits of old zinc and wood and soggy sheets of cardboard lying around the neighbourhood before thousands more came out of their forest holes looking for the same things. He got a destitute carpenter with one old hammer, a blunt plane and a few bent and rusty nails in his tool bag to turn this assortment of wood, paper and metal into door and window shutters for five Nigerian shillings or fifty Biafran pounds. He paid the pounds, and moved in with his overjoyed family carrying five heads on their shoulders.

His children picked mangoes near the military cemetery and sold them to soldiers' wives for a few pennies — real pennies this time — and his wife started making breakfast akara balls for neighbours in a hurry to start life again. With his family earnings he took his bicycle to the villages around and brought fresh palm-wine which he mixed generously in his rooms with the water which had recently started running again in the public tap down the road, and opened up a bar for soldiers and other lucky people with good money.

At first he went daily, then every other day and finally once a week, to the offices of the Coal Corporation where he used to be a miner, to find out what was what. The only thing he did find out in the end was that that little house of his was even a greater blessing than he had thought. Some of his fellow ex-miners who had nowhere to return at the end of the day's waiting just slept outside the doors of the offices and cooked what meal they could scrounge together in Bournvita tins. As the weeks lengthened and still nobody could say what was what Jonathan discontinued his weekly visits altogether and faced his palm-wine bar.

But nothing puzzles God. Came the day of the windfall when after five days of endless scuffles in queues and counter-queues in the sun outside the Treasury he had twenty pounds counted into his palms as ex-gratia award for the rebel money he had turned in. It was like Christmas for him and for many others like him when the payments began. They called it (since few could manage its proper official name) *egg-rasher.*

As soon as the pound notes were placed in his palm Jonathan simply closed it tight over them and buried fist and money inside his trouser pocket. He had to be extra careful because he had seen a man a couple of days earlier collapse into near-madness in an instant before that oceanic crowd because no sooner had he got his twenty pounds than some heartless ruffian picked it off him. Though it was not right that a man in such an extremity of agony should be blamed yet many in the queues that day were able to remark quietly on the victim's carelessness, especially after he pulled out the innards of his pocket and revealed a hole in it big enough to pass a thief's head. But of course he had insisted that the money had been in the other pocket, pulling it out to show its comparative wholeness. So one had to be careful.

Jonathan soon transferred the money to his left hand and pocket so as to leave his right free for shaking hands should the need arise, though by fixing his gaze at such an elevation as to miss all approaching human faces he made sure that the need did not arise, until he got home.

He was normally a heavy sleeper but that night he heard all the neighbourhood noises die down one after another. Even the night watchman who knocked the hour on some metal somewhere in the distance had fallen silent after knocking one o'clock. That must have been the last thought in Jonathan's mind before he was finally carried away himself. He couldn't have been gone for long, though, when he was violently awakened again.

"Who is knocking?" whispered his wife lying beside him on the floor.

"I don't know," he whispered back breathlessly.

The second time the knocking came it was so loud and imperious that the rickety old door could have fallen down.

"Who is knocking?" he asked then, his voice parched and trembling.

"Na* tief-man and him people," came the cool reply. "Make you hopen de door." This was followed by the heaviest knocking of all.

Maria was the first to raise the alarm, then he followed and all their children.

"Police-o! Thieves-o! Neighbours-o! Police-o! We are lost! We are dead! Neighbours, are you asleep? Wake up! Police-o!

This went on for a long time and then stopped suddenly. Perhaps they had scared the thief away. There was total silence. But only for a short while.

"You done finish?" asked the voice outside. "Make we help you small. Oya, everybody!"

"Police-o! Tief-man-o! Neighbours-o! We done loss-o! Police-o! . . ."

There were at least five other voices besides the leader's.

Jonathan and his family were now completely paralysed by terror. Maria and the children sobbed inaudibly like lost souls. Jonathan groaned continuously.

The silence that followed the thieves' alarm vibrated horribly. Jonathan all but begged their leader to speak again and be done with it.

"My frien," said he at long last, "we don try our best for call dem but I tink say dem all done sleep-o . . . So wetin we go do now? Sometaim you wan call soja? Or you wan make we call dem for you? Soja better pass police. No be so?"

"Na so!" replied his men. Jonathan thought he heard even more voices now than before and groaned heavily. His legs were sagging under him and his throat felt like sand-paper.

"My frien, why you no de talk again. I de ask you say you wan make we call soja?"

"No."

"Awrighto. Now make we talk business. We no be bad tief. We no like for make trouble. Trouble done finish. War done finish and all the katakata wey de for inside. No Civil War again. This time na Civil Peace. No be so?"

*Na = it is.

"Na so!" answered the horrible chorus.

"What do you want from me? I am a poor man. Everything I had went with this war. Why do you come to me? You know people who have money. We . . ."

"Awright! We know you say no get plenty money. But we sef no get even anini. So derefore make you open dis window and give us one hundred pound and we go commot. Orderwise we de come for inside now to show you guitar-boy like dis . . ."

A volley of automatic fire rang through the sky. Maria and the children began to weep aloud again.

"Ah, missisi de cry again. No need for dat. We done talk say we na good tief. We just take our small money and go nwayorly. No molest. Abi we de molest?"

"At all!" sang the chorus.

"My friends," began Jonathan hoarsely. "I hear what you say and I thank you. If I had one hundred pounds . . ."

"Lookia my frien, no be play we come play for your house. If we make mistake and step for inside you no go like am-o. So derefore . . ."

"To God who made me; if you come inside and find one hundred pounds, take it and shoot me and shoot my wife and children. I swear to God. The only money I have in this life is this twenty-pounds *egg-rasher* they gave me today . . ."

"OK. Time de go. Make you open dis window and bring the twenty pound. We go manage am like dat."

There were now loud murmurs of dissent among the chorus: "Na lie de man de lie; e get plenty money . . . Make we go inside and search properly well . . . Wetin be twenty pound? . . ."

"Shurrup!" rang the leader's voice like a lone shot in the sky and silenced the murmuring at once. "Are you dere? Bring the money quick!"

"I am coming," said Jonathan fumbling in the darkness with the key of the small wooden box he kept by his side on the mat.

At the first sign of light as neighbours and others assembled to commiserate with him he was already strapping his five-gallon demijohn to his bicycle carrier and his wife, sweating in the open fire, was turning over akara balls in a wide clay bowl of boiling oil. In the corner his eldest son was rinsing out dregs of yesterday's palm wine from old beer bottles.

"I count it as nothing," he told his sympathizers, his eyes on the rope he was tying. "What is *egg-rasher*? Did I depend on it last week? Or is it greater than other things that went with the war? I say, let *egg-rasher* perish in the flames! Let it go where everything else has gone. Nothing puzzles God."

MARGARET ATWOOD

Margaret Atwood's international reputation stems from the forceful, witty, analytic character of her style, from the intellectual substance of her feminist argument, from the literary tension she establishes between the humane and the sardonic, and from her sheer productivity. Between 1961, when her first book of poems (*Double Persephone*) appeared, and 1985, she published ten volumes of poetry, five novels (including *The Edible Woman*, 1969, and *Bodily Harm*, 1981), three books of stories, two books of criticism (including the influential *Survival*, 1972), a new edition of the Oxford anthology of English-Canadian verse (1982), children's books, lectures, articles, and more. Born in Ottawa in 1939, she moved early to Sault Ste. Marie and Toronto; a graduate of Victoria College (Toronto) and Radcliffe College (Harvard), she has taught and has been writer-in-residence at a number of universities, an editor for the House of Anansi, a cartoonist for *This Magazine*, president of the Writers' Union of Canada, and an active supporter of Amnesty International. She now lives in Toronto.

"Scarlet Ibis" comes from her third book of stories, *Bluebeard's Egg* (1983), and like *Bodily Harm* is set in the Caribbean, where (for the Canadian visitors) cultural differences variously seem terrifying experiences or simply curious encounters. The author's interest, however, is more in the reaction to experience than in the experience itself; Atwood fastens on the reasons people are satisfied with superficiality and plastic culture, and on the ways (wit and anecdote, masks against others and walls against the world) in which they distance themselves from both the horrors around them and the horrors they are reluctant to recognize in themselves. As Rosemary Sullivan writes, in the *Oxford Companion to Canadian Literature*, Atwood has, in her stories, "designs on our psyches — we are to be instructed through the underdarkness so that we can become saner and more resilient."

FOR FURTHER READING

Margaret Atwood, *Second Words* (Toronto: Anansi, 1982).

Frank Davey, *Margaret Atwood: A Feminist Poetics* (Vancouver: Talonbooks, 1984).

Jerome H. Rosenberg, *Margaret Atwood* (Boston: Twayne, 1984).

SCARLET IBIS

Some years ago now, Christine went with Don to Trinidad. They took Lilian, their youngest child, who was four then. The others, who were in school, stayed with their grandmother.

Christine and Don sat beside the hotel pool in the damp heat, drinking rum punch and eating strange-tasting hamburgers. Lilian wanted to be in the pool all the time — she could already swim a little — but Christine didn't think it was a good idea, because of the sun. Christine rubbed sun block on her nose, and on the noses of Lilian and Don. She felt that her legs were too white and that people were looking at her and finding her faintly ridiculous, because of her pinky-white skin and the large hat she wore. More than likely, the young black waiters who brought the rum punch and the hamburgers, who walked easily through the sun without paying any attention to it, who joked among themselves but were solemn when they set down the glasses and plates, had put her in a category; one that included fat, although she was not fat exactly. She suggested to Don that perhaps he was tipping too much. Don said he felt tired.

"You felt tired before," Christine said. "That's why we came, remember? So you could get some rest."

Don took afternoon naps, sprawled on his back on one of the twin beds in the room — Lilian had a fold-out cot — his mouth slightly open, the skin of his face pushed by gravity back down towards his ears, so that he looked tauter, thinner, and more aquiline in this position than he did when awake. Deader, thought Christine, taking a closer look. People lying on their backs in coffins usually — in her limited experience — seemed to have lost weight. This image, of Don encoffined, was one that had been drifting through her mind too often for comfort lately.

It was hopeless expecting Lilian to have an afternoon nap too, so Christine took her down to the pool or tried to keep her quiet by drawing with her, using Magic Markers. At that age Lilian drew nothing but women or girls, wearing very fancy dresses, full-skirted, with a lot of decoration. They were always smiling, with red, curvy mouths, and had abnormally long thick eyelashes. They did not stand on any ground — Lilian was not yet putting the ground into her pictures — but floated on the page as if it were a pond they were spread out on, arms outstretched, feet at the opposite sides of their skirts, their elaborate hair billowing around their heads. Sometimes Lilian put in some birds or the sun, which gave these women the appearance of giant airborne balloons, as if the wind had caught them under their skirts and carried them off, light as feathers, away from everything. Yet, if she were asked, Lilian would say these women were walking.

After a few days of all this, when they ought to have adjusted to the heat, Christine felt they should get out of the hotel and do something. She did not want to go shopping by herself, although Don suggested it; she felt that nothing she tried on helped her look any better, or, to be more precise, that it didn't much matter how she looked. She tried to think of some other distraction, mostly for the sake of Don. Don was not noticeably more rested, although he had a sunburn — which, instead of giving him a glow of health, made him seem angry — and he'd started drumming his fingers on tabletops again. He said he was having trouble sleeping: bad dreams, which he could not remember. Also the air-conditioning was clogging up his nose. He had been under a lot of pressure lately, he said.

Christine didn't need to be told. She could feel the pressure he was under, like a clenched mass of something, tissue, congealed blood, at the back of her own head. She thought of Don as being encased in a sort of metal carapace, like the shell of a crab, that was slowly tightening on him, on all parts of him at once, so that something was sure to burst, like a thumb closed slowly in a car door. The metal skin was his entire body, and Christine didn't know how to unlock it for him and let him out. She felt as if all her ministrations — the cold washcloths for his headaches, the trips to the drugstore for this or that bottle of pills, the hours of tiptoeing around, intercepting the phone, keeping Lilian quiet, above all the mere act of witnessing him, which was so draining — were noticed by him hardly at all: moths beating on the outside of a lit window, behind which someone important was thinking about something of major significance that had nothing to do with moths. This vacation, for instance, had been her idea, but Don was only getting redder and redder.

Unfortunately, it was not carnival season. There were restaurants, but Lilian hated sitting still in them, and one thing Don did not need was more food and especially more drink. Christine wished Don had a sport, but considering the way he was, he would probably overdo it and break something.

"I had an uncle who took up hooking rugs," she'd said to him one evening after dinner. "When he retired. He got them in kits. He said he found it very restful." The aunt that went with that uncle used to say, "I said for better or for worse, but I never said for lunch."

"Oh, for God's sake, Christine," was all Don had to say to that. He'd never thought much of her relatives. His view was that Christine was still on the raw side of being raw material. Christine did not look forward to the time, twenty years away at least, when he would be home all day, pacing, drumming his fingers, wanting whatever it was that she could never identify and never provide.

In the morning, while the other two were beginning breakfast, Christine went bravely to the hotel's reception desk. There was a thin, elegant brown girl behind it, in lime green, Rasta beads, and *Vogue* make-up, coiled like spaghetti around the phone. Christine, feeling hot and porous, asked if there was any material on things to do. The girl, sliding her eyes over and past Christine as if she were a minor architectural feature, selected and fanned an assortment of brochures, continuing to laugh lightly into the phone.

Christine took the brochures into the ladies' room to preview them. Not the beach, she decided, because of the sun. Not the boutiques, not the night clubs, not the memories of Old Spain.

She examined her face, added lipstick to her lips, which were getting thin and pinched together. She really needed to do something about herself, before it was too late. She made her way back to the breakfast table. Lilian was saying that the pancakes weren't the same as the ones at home. Don said she had to eat them because she had ordered them, and if she was old enough to order for herself she was old enough to know that they cost money and couldn't be wasted like that. Christine wondered silently if it was a bad pattern, making a child eat everything on her plate, whether she liked the food or not: perhaps Lilian would become fat, later on.

Don was having bacon and eggs. Christine had asked Don to order yoghurt and fresh fruit for her, but there was nothing at her place.

"They didn't have it," Don said.

"Did you order anything else?" said Christine, who was now hungry.

"How was I supposed to know what you want?" said Don.

"We're going to see the Scarlet Ibis," Christine announced brightly to Lilian. She would ask them to bring back the menu, so she could order.

"What?" said Don. Christine handed him the brochure, which showed some red birds with long curved bills sitting in a tree; there was another picture of one close up, in profile, one demented-looking eye staring out from its red feathers like a target.

"They're very rare," said Christine, looking around for a waiter. "It's a preservation."

"You mean a preserve," said Don, reading the brochure. "In a swamp? Probably crawling with mosquitoes."

"I don't want to go," said Lilian, pushing scraps of a pancake around in a pool of watery syrup. This was her other complaint, that it wasn't the right kind of syrup.

"Imitation maple flavouring," Don said, reading the label.

"You don't even know what it is," said Christine. "We'll take some fly dope. Anyway, they wouldn't let tourists go there if there were that many mosquitoes. It's a *mangrove* swamp; that isn't the same as our kind."

"I'm going to get a paper," said Don. He stood up and walked away. His legs, coming out of the bottoms of his Bermuda shorts, were still very white, with an overglaze of pink down the backs. His body, once muscular, was losing tone, sliding down towards his waist and buttocks. He was beginning to slope. From the back, he had the lax, demoralized look of a man who has been confined in an institution, though from the front he was brisk enough.

Watching him go, Christine felt the sickness in the pit of her stomach that was becoming familiar to her these days. Maybe the pressure he was under was her. Maybe she was a weight. Maybe he wanted her to lift up, blow away somewhere, like a kite, the children hanging on behind her in a long string. She didn't know when she had first noticed this feeling; probably after it had been there some time, like a knocking on the front door when you're asleep. There had been a shifting of forces, unseen, unheard, underground, the sliding against each other of giant stones; some tremendous damage had occurred between them, but who could tell when?

"Eat your pancakes," she said to Lilian, "or your father will be annoyed." He would be annoyed anyway: she annoyed him. Even when they made love, which was not frequently any more, it was perfunctory, as if he were listening for something else, a phone call, a footfall. He was like a man scratching himself. She was like his hand.

Christine had a scenario she ran through often, the way she used to run through scenarios of courtship, back in high school: flirtation, pursuit, joyful acquiescence. This was an adult scenario, however. One evening she would say to Don as he was getting up from the table after dinner, "Stay there." He would be so surprised by her tone of voice that he would stay.

"I just want you to sit there and look at me," she would say.

He would not say, "For God's sake, Christine." He would know this was serious.

"I'm not asking much from you," she would say, lying.

"What's going on?" he would say.

"I want you to see what I really look like," she would say. "I'm tired of being invisible." Maybe he would, maybe he wouldn't. Maybe he would say he was coming on with a headache. Maybe she would find herself walking on nothing, because maybe there was nothing there. So far she hadn't even come close to beginning, to giving the initial command: "Stay," as if he were a trained dog. But that was what she wanted him to do, wasn't it? "Come back" was more like it. He hadn't always been under pressure.

Once Lilian was old enough, Christine thought, she could go back to work full time. She could brush up her typing and shorthand, find something. That would be good for her; she wouldn't concentrate so much on Don, she would have a reason to look better, she would either find new scenarios or act out the one that was preoccupying her. Maybe she was making things up, about Don. It might be a form of laziness.

Christine's preparations for the afternoon were careful. She bought some mosquito repellant at a drugstore, and a chocolate bar. She took two scarves, one for herself, one for Lilian, in case it was sunny. The big hat would blow off, she thought, as they were going to be in a boat. After a short argument with one of the waiters, who said she could only have drinks by the glass, she succeeded in buying three cans of Pepsi, not chilled. All these things she packed into her bag; Lilian's bag, actually, which was striped in orange and yellow and blue and had a picture of Mickey Mouse on it. They'd used it for the toys Lilian brought with her on the plane.

After lunch they took a taxi, first through the hot streets of the town, where the sidewalks were too narrow or nonexistent and the people crowded onto the road and there was a lot of honking, then out through the cane fields, the road becoming bumpier, the driver increasing speed. He drove with the car radio on, the left-hand window open, and his elbow out, a pink jockey cap tipped back on his head. Christine had shown him the brochure and asked him if he knew where the swamp was; he'd grinned at her and said everybody knew. He said he could take them, but it was too far to go out and back so he would wait there for them. Christine knew it meant extra money, but did not argue.

They passed a man riding a donkey, and two cows wandering around by the roadside, anchored by ropes around their necks which were tied to dragging stones. Christine pointed these out to Lilian. The little houses among the tall cane were made of cement blocks, painted light green or pink or light blue; they were built up on open-work foundations, almost as if they were on stilts. The women who sat on the steps turned their heads, unsmiling, to watch their taxi as it went by.

Lilian asked Christine if she had any gum. Christine didn't. Lilian began chewing on her nails, which she'd taken up since Don had been under pressure. Christine told her to stop. Then Lilian said she wanted to go for a swim. Don looked out the window. "How long did you say?" he asked. It was a reproach, not a question.

Christine hadn't said how long because she didn't know; she didn't know because she'd forgotten to ask. Finally they turned off the main road onto a smaller, muddier one, and parked beside some other cars in a rutted space that had once been part of a field.

"I meet you here," said the driver. He got out of the car, stretched, turned up the car radio. There were other drivers hanging around, some of them in cars, others sitting on the ground drinking from a bottle they were passing around, one asleep.

Christine took Lilian's hand. She didn't want to appear stupid by having to ask where they were supposed to go next. She didn't see anything that looked like a ticket office.

"It must be that shack," Don said, so they walked towards it, a long shed with a tin roof; on the other side of it was a steep bank and the beginning of the water. There were wooden steps leading down to a wharf, which was the same brown as the water itself. Several boats were tied up to it, all of similar design: long and thin, almost like barges, with rows of bench-like seats. Each boat had a small outboard motor at the back. The names painted on the boats looked East Indian.

Christine took the scarves out of her bag and tied one on her own head and one on Lilian's. Although it was beginning to cloud over, the sun was still very bright, and she knew about rays coming through overcast, especially in the tropics. She put sun block on their noses, and thought that the chocolate bar had been a silly idea. Soon it would be a brown puddle at the bottom of her bag, which luckily was waterproof. Don paced behind them as Christine knelt.

An odd smell was coming up from the water: a swamp smell, but with something else mixed in. Christine wondered about sewage disposal. She was glad she'd made Lilian go to the bathroom before they'd left.

There didn't seem to be anyone in charge, anyone to buy the tickets from, although there were several people beside the shed, waiting, probably: two plumpish, middle-aged men in T-shirts and baseball caps turned around backwards, an athletic couple in shorts with outside pockets, who were loaded down with cameras and binoculars, a trim grey-haired woman in a tailored pink summer suit that must have been far too hot. There was another woman off to the side, a somewhat large woman in a floral print dress. She'd spread a Mexican-looking shawl on the weedy grass near the shed and was sitting down on it, drinking a pint carton of orange juice through a straw. The others looked wilted and dispirited, but not this woman. For her, waiting seemed to be an activity, not something imposed: she gazed around her, at the bank, the brown water, the line of sullen mangrove trees beyond, as if she were enjoying every minute.

This woman seemed the easiest to approach, so Christine went over to her. "Are we in the right place?" she said. "For the birds."

The woman smiled at her and said they were. She had a broad face, with high, almost Slavic cheekbones and round red cheeks like those of an old-fashioned wooden doll, except that they were not painted on. Her taffy-coloured hair was done in waves and rolls, and reminded Christine of the pictures on the Toni home-permanent boxes of several decades before.

"We will leave soon," said the woman. "Have you seen these birds before? They come back only at sunset. The rest of the time they are away, fishing." She smiled again, and Christine thought to herself that it was a pity she hadn't had bands put on to even out her teeth when she was young.

This was the woman's second visit to the Scarlet Ibis preserve, she told Christine. The first was three years ago, when she stopped over here on her way to South America with her husband and children. This time her husband and children had stayed back at the hotel: they hadn't seen a swimming pool for such a long time. She and her husband were Mennonite missionaries, she said. She herself didn't seem embarrassed by this, but Christine blushed a little. She had been raised Anglican, but the only vestige of that was the kind of Christmas cards she favoured: prints of mediaeval or Renaissance old masters. Religious people of any serious kind made her nervous: they were like men in raincoats who might or might not be flashers. You would be going along with them in the ordinary way, and then there could be a swift movement and you would look down to find the coat wide open and nothing on under it but some pant legs held up by rubber bands. This had happened to Christine in a train station once.

"How many children do you have?" she said, to change the subject. Mennonite would explain the wide hips: they liked women who could have a lot of children.

The woman's crooked-toothed smile did not falter. "Four," she said, "but one of them is dead."

"Oh," said Christine. It wasn't clear whether the four included the one dead, or whether that was extra. She knew better than to say, "That's too bad." Such a comment was sure to produce something about the will of God, and she didn't want to deal with that. She looked to make sure Lilian was still there, over by Don. Much of the time Lilian was a given, but there were moments at which she was threatened, unknown to herself, with sudden disappearance. "That's my little girl, over there," Christine said, feeling immediately that this was a callous comment; but the woman continued to smile, in a way that Christine now found eerie.

A small brown man in a Hawaiian-patterned shirt came around from behind the shed and went quickly down the steps to the wharf. He climbed into one of the boats and lowered the outboard motor into the water.

"Now maybe we'll get some action," Don said. He had come up behind her, but he was talking more to himself than to her. Christine sometimes wondered whether he talked in the same way when she wasn't there at all.

A second man, East Indian, like the first, and also in a hula-dancer shirt, was standing at the top of the steps, and they understood they were to go over. He took their money and gave each of them a business card in return; on one side of it was a coloured picture of an ibis, on the other a name and a phone number. They went single file down the steps and the first man handed them into the boat. When they were all seated— Don, Christine, Lilian, and the pink-suited woman in a crowded row, the two baseball-cap men in front of them, the Mennonite woman and the couple with the cameras at the very front — the second man cast off and hopped lightly into the bow. After a few tries the first man got the motor started, and they putt-putted slowly towards an opening in the trees, leaving a wispy trail of smoke behind them.

It was cloudier now, and not so hot. Christine talked with the pink-suited woman, who had blonde hair elegantly done up in a French roll. She was from Vienna, she said; her husband was here on business. This was the first time she had been on this side of the Atlantic Ocean. The beaches were beautiful, much finer than those of the Mediterranean. Christine complimented her on her good English, and the woman smiled and told her what a beautiful little girl she had, and Christine said Lilian would get conceited, a word that the woman had not yet added to her vocabulary. Lilian was quiet; she had caught sight of the woman's bracelet, which was silver and lavishly engraved. The woman showed it to her. Christine began to enjoy herself, despite the fact that the two men in front of her were talking too loudly. They were drinking beer, from cans they'd brought with them in a paper bag. She opened a Pepsi and shared some with Lilian. Don didn't want any.

They were in a channel now; she looked at the trees on either side, which were all the same, dark-leaved, rising up out of the water, on masses of spindly roots. She didn't know how long they'd been going.

It began to rain, not a downpour but heavily enough, large cold drops. The Viennese woman said, "It's raining," her eyes open in a parody of surprise, holding out her hand and looking up at the sky like someone in a child's picture book. This was for the benefit of Lilian. "We will get wet," she said. She took a white embroidered handkerchief out of her purse and spread it on the top of her head. Lilian was enchanted with the handkerchief and asked Christine if she could have one, too. Don said they should have known, since it always rained in the afternoons here.

The men in baseball caps hunched their shoulders, and one of them said to the Indian in the bow, "Hey, we're getting wet!"

The Indian's timid but closed expression did not change; with apparent reluctance he pulled a rolled-up sheet of plastic out from somewhere under the front seat and handed it to the men. They spent some time unrolling it and getting it straightened out, and then everyone helped to hold the plastic overhead like a roof, while the boat glided on at its unvarying pace, through the mangroves and the steam or mist that was now rising around them.

"Isn't this an adventure?" Christine said, aiming it at Lilian. Lilian was biting her nails. The rain pattered down. Don said he wished he'd brought a paper. The men in baseball caps began to sing, sounding oddly like boys at a summer camp who had gone to sleep one day and awakened thirty years later, unaware of the sinister changes that had taken place in them, the growth and recession of hair and flesh, the exchange of their once-clear voices for the murky ones that were now singing off-key, out of time:

"They say that in the army,
   the girls are rather fine,
They promise Betty Grable,
   they give you Frankenstein . . ."

They had not yet run out of beer. One of them finished a can and tossed it overboard, and it bobbed beside the boat for a moment before falling behind, a bright red dot in the borderless expanse of dull green and dull grey. Christine felt virtuous: she'd put her Pepsi can carefully into her bag, for disposal later.

Then the rain stopped, and after some debate about whether it was going to start again or not, the two baseball-cap men began to roll up the plastic sheet. While they were doing this there was a jarring thud. The boat rocked violently, and the one man who was standing up almost pitched overboard, then sat down with a jerk.

"What the hell?" he said.

The Indian at the back reversed the motor.

"We hit something," said the Viennese woman. She clasped her hands, another classic gesture.

"Obviously," Don said in an undertone. Christine smiled at Lilian, who was looking anxious. The boat started forward again.

"Probably a mangrove root," said the man with the cameras, turning half round. "They grow out under the water." He was the kind who would know.

"Or an alligator," said one of the men in baseball caps. The other man laughed.

"He's joking, darling," Christine said to Lilian.

"But we are sinking," said the Viennese woman, pointing with one outstretched hand, one dramatic finger.

Then they all saw what they had not noticed before. There was a hole in the boat, near the front, right above the platform of loose boards that served as a floor. It was the size of a small fist. Whatever they'd hit had punched right through the wood, as if it were cardboard. Water was pouring through.

"This tub must be completely rotten," Don muttered directly to Christine this time. This was a role she was sometimes given when they were among people Don didn't know: the listener. "They get like that in the tropics."

"Hey," said one of the men in baseball caps. "You up front. There's a hole in the goddamned boat."

The Indian glanced over his shoulder at the hole. He shrugged, looked away, began fishing in the breast pocket of his sports shirt for a cigarette.

"Hey. Turn this thing around," said the man with the camera.

"Couldn't we get it fixed, and then start again?" said Christine, intending to conciliate. She glanced at the Mennonite woman, hoping for support, but the woman's broad flowered back was towards her.

"If we go back," the Indian said patiently — he could understand English after all — "you miss the birds. It will be too dark."

"Yeah, but if we go forward we sink."

"You will not sink," said the Indian. He had found a cigarette, already half-smoked, and was lighting it.

"He's done it before," said the largest baseball cap. "Every week he gets a hole in the goddamned boat. Nothing to it."

The brown water continued to come in. The boat went forward.

"Right," Don said, loudly, to everyone this time. "He thinks if we don't see the birds, we won't pay him."

That made sense to Christine. For the Indians, it was a lot of money. They probably couldn't afford the gas if they lost the fares. "If you go back, we'll pay you anyway," she called to the Indian. Ordinarily she would have made this suggestion to Don, but she was getting frightened.

Either the Indian didn't hear her or he didn't trust them, or it wasn't his idea of a fair bargain. He didn't smile or reply.

For a few minutes they all sat there, waiting for the problem to be solved. The trees went past. Finally Don said, "We'd better bail. At this rate we'll be in serious trouble in about half an hour."

"I should not have come," said the Viennese woman, in a tone of tragic despair.

"What with?" said the man with the cameras. The men in baseball caps had turned to look at Don, as if he were worthy of attention.

"Mummy, are we going to sink?" said Lilian.

"Of course not, darling," said Christine. "Daddy won't let us."

"Anything there is," said the largest baseball-cap man. He poured the rest of his beer over the side. "You got a jack-knife?" he said.

Don didn't, but the man with the cameras did. They watched while he cut the top out of the can, knelt down, moved a loose platform board so he could get at the water, scooped, dumped brown water over the side. Then the other men started taking the tops off their own beer cans, including the full ones, which they emptied out. Christine produced the Pepsi can from her bag. The Mennonite woman had her pint juice carton.

"No mosquitoes, at any rate," Don said, almost cheerfully.

They'd lost a lot of time, and the water was almost up to the floor platform. It seemed to Christine that the boat was becoming heavier, moving more slowly through the water, that the water itself was thicker. They could not empty much water at a time with such small containers, but maybe, with so many of them doing it, it would work.

"This really *is* an adventure," she said to Lilian, who was white-faced and forlorn. "Isn't this fun?"

The Viennese woman was not bailing; she had no container. She was making visible efforts to calm herself. She had taken out a tangerine, which she was peeling, over the embroidered handkerchief which she'd spread out on her lap. Now she produced a beautiful little pen-knife with a mother-of-pearl handle. To Lilian she said, "You are hungry? Look, I will cut in pieces, one piece for you, then one for me, *ja*?" The knife was not really needed, of course. It was to distract Lilian, and Christine was grateful.

There was an audible rhythm in the boat: scrape, dump; scrape, dump.

The men in baseball caps, rowdy earlier, were not at all drunk now. Don appeared to be enjoying himself, for the first time on the trip.

But despite their efforts, the level of the water was rising.

"This is ridiculous," Christine said to Don. She stopped bailing with her Pepsi can. She was discouraged and also frightened. She told herself that the Indians wouldn't keep going if they thought there was any real danger, but she wasn't convinced. Maybe they didn't care if everybody drowned; maybe they thought it was Karma. Through the hole the brown water poured, with a steady flow, like a cut vein. It was up to the level of the loose floor boards now.

Then the Mennonite woman stood up. Balancing herself, she removed her shoes, placing them carefully side by side under the seat. Christine had once watched a man do this in a subway station; he'd put the shoes under the bench where she was sitting, and a few minutes later had thrown himself in front of the oncoming train. The two shoes had remained on the neat yellow-tiled floor, like bones on a plate after a meal. It flashed through Christine's head that maybe the woman had become unhinged and was going to leap overboard; this was plausible, because of the dead child. The woman's perpetual smile was a fraud then, as Christine's would have been in her place.

But the woman did not jump over the side of the boat. Instead she bent over and moved the platform boards. Then she turned around and lowered her large flowered rump onto the hole. Her face was towards Christine now; she continued to smile, gazing over the side of the boat at the mangroves and their monotonous roots and leaves as if they were the most interesting scenery she had seen in a long time. The water was above her ankles; her skirt was wet. Did she look a little smug, a little clever or self-consciously heroic? Possibly, thought Christine, though from that round face it was hard to tell.

"Hey," said one of the men in baseball caps, "now you're cooking with gas!" The Indian in the bow looked at the woman; his white teeth appeared briefly.

The others continued to bail, and after a moment Christine began to scoop and pour with the Pepsi can again. Despite herself, the woman impressed her. The water probably wasn't that cold but it was certainly filthy, and who could tell what might be on the other side of the hole? Were they far enough south for piranhas? Yet there was the Mennonite woman plugging the hole with her bottom, serene as a brooding hen, and no doubt unaware of the fact that she was more than a little ridiculous. Christine could imagine the kinds of remarks the men in baseball caps would make about the woman afterwards. "Saved by a big butt." "Hey, never knew it had more than one use." "Finger in the dike had nothing on her." That was the part that would have stopped Christine from doing such a thing, even if she'd managed to think of it.

Now they reached the long aisle of mangroves and emerged into the open; they were in a central space, like a lake, with the dark mangroves walling it around. There was a chicken-wire fence strung across it, to keep any boats from going too close to the Scarlet Ibis' roosting area: that was what the sign said, nailed to a post that was sticking at an angle out of the water. The Indian cut the motor and they drifted towards the fence; the other Indian caught hold of the fence, held on, and the boat stopped, rocking a little. Apart from the ripples they'd caused, the water was dead flat calm; the trees doubled in it appeared black, and the sun, which was just above the western rim of the real trees, was a red disk in the hazy grey sky. The light coming from it was orangy-red and tinted the water. For a few minutes nothing happened. The man with the cameras looked at his watch. Lilian was restless, squirming on the seat. She wanted to draw; she wanted to swim in the pool. If Christine had known the whole thing would take so long she wouldn't have brought her.

"They coming," said the Indian in the bow.

"Birds ahoy," said one of the men in baseball caps, and pointed, and then there were the birds all right, flying through the reddish light, right on cue, first singly, then in flocks of four or five, so bright, so fluorescent that they were like painted flames. They settled into the trees, screaming hoarsely. It was only the screams that revealed them as real birds.

The others had their binoculars up. Even the Viennese woman had a little pair of opera glasses. "Would you look at that," said one of the men. "Wish I'd brought my movie camera."

Don and Christine were without technology. So was the Mennonite woman. "You could watch them forever," she said, to nobody in particular. Christine, afraid that she would go on to say something embarrassing, pretended not to hear her. *Forever* was loaded.

She took Lilian's hand. "See those red birds?" she said. "You might never see one of those again in your entire life." But she knew that for Lilian these birds were no more special than anything else. She was too young for them. She said, "Oh," which was what she would have said if they had been pterodactyls or angels with wings as red as blood. Magicians, Christine knew from Lilian's last birthday party, were a failure with small children, who didn't see any reason why rabbits shouldn't come out of hats.

Don took hold of Christine's hand, a thing he had not done for some time; but Christine, watching the birds, noticed this only afterwards. She felt she was looking at a picture, of exotic flowers or of red fruit growing on trees, evenly spaced, like the fruit in the gardens of mediaeval paintings, solid, clear-edged, in primary colours. On the other side of the fence was another world, not real but at the same time more real than the one on this side, the men and women in their flimsy clothes and aging bodies, the decrepit boat. Her own body seemed fragile and empty, like blown glass.

The Mennonite woman had her face turned up to the sunset; her body was cut off at the neck by shadow, so that her head appeared to be floating in the air. For the first time she looked sad; but when she felt Christine watching her she smiled again, as if to reassure her, her face luminous and pink and round as a plum. Christine felt the two hands holding her own, mooring her, one on either side.

Weight returned to her body. The light was fading, the air chillier. Soon they would have to return in the increasing darkness, in a boat so rotten a misplaced foot would go through it. The water would be black, not brown; it would be full of roots.

"Shouldn't we go back?" she said to Don.

Lilian said, "Mummy, I'm hungry," and Christine remembered the chocolate bar and rummaged in her bag. It was down at the bottom, limp as a slab of bacon but not liquid. She brought it out and peeled off the silver paper, and gave a square to Lilian and one to Don, and ate one herself. The light was pink and dark at the same time, and it was difficult to see what she was doing.

When she told about this later, after they were safely home, Christine put in the swamp and the awful boat, and the men singing and the suspicious smell of the water. She put in Don's irritability, but only on days when he wasn't particularly irritable. (By then, there was less pressure; these things went in phases, Christine decided. She was glad she had never said anything, forced any issues.) She put in how good Lilian had been even though she hadn't wanted to go. She put in the hole in the boat, her own panic, which she made amusing, and the ridiculous bailing with the cans, and the Indians' indifference to their fate. She put in the Mennonite woman sitting on the hole like a big fat hen, making this funny, but admiring also, since the woman's solution to the problem had been so simple and obvious that no one else had thought of it. She left out the dead child.

She put in the rather hilarious trip back to the wharf, with the Indian standing up in the bow, beaming his heavy-duty flashlight at the endless, boring mangroves, and the two men in the baseball caps getting into a mickey and singing dirty songs.

She ended with the birds, which were worth every minute of it, she said. She presented them as a form of entertainment, like the Grand Canyon: something that really ought to be seen, if you liked birds, and if you should happen to be in that part of the world.

JOHN BARTH

Born in 1930 and raised in Cambridge, Maryland, John Barth was educated at the Juilliard School of Music and Johns Hopkins University.
After a period of teaching at Pennsylvania State University, he moved
to the State University of New York at Buffalo, and then to Johns Hopkins, where he is a professor of English. His first novel, *The Floating
Opera* (1956), though composed in relatively conventional form, raised
questions about existence, identity, and artifice which have occupied
him in all his subsequent writings. In *The End of the Road* (1958) and
The Sot-Weed Factor (1960), through a bizarre mixture of allegory, parody, and Rabelaisian comedy, Barth began to turn his back on formal
realism as being inadequate to convey his vision; in his view the way
to deal "with the discrepancy between art and the Real Thing is to
affirm the artificial element in art (you can't get rid of it anyhow), and
make the artifice part of your point instead of working for higher and
higher fi with a lot of literary woofers and tweeters." In subsequent
works, Barth has continued to explore the connection between fiction
and reality, and the interaction of writer, text, and reader; his latest
novel, *Sabbatical* (1982), is in part a record of its own composition.
Barth's rejection of literary convention does not mean that his work is
incomprehensibly fragmentary or obscure; commenting on the novel
Giles Goat-Boy (1966), a reviewer described his style as "the most literate, controlled prose since Joyce."

Disturbed by "the arbitrariness of physical facts," Barth challenges
conventional notions of reality, history, and human personality, in literary forms which themselves come under scrutiny. "Title" is one of
several fictions in Barth's collection *Lost in the Funhouse: Fiction for
print, tape, live voice* (1968), which deal with the relation between word
and meaning, between story and storyteller. In an "Author's Note,"
Barth comments: " 'Title' makes somewhat separate but equally valid
senses in several media: print, monophonic recorded authorial voice,
stereophonic ditto in dialogue with itself, live authorial voice, live ditto
in dialogue with monophonic ditto aforementioned, and live ditto inter-
locutory with stereophonic et cetera, my own preference; it's been
'done' in all six."

FOR FURTHER READING

John Enck, "John Barth: An Interview," *Wisconsin Studies in Con-
temporary Literature* 6 (Winter/Spring 1965): 3–14.
Edgar H. Knapp, "Found in the Barthhouse: Novelist as Savior,"
Modern Fiction Studies 14 (Winter 1968/1969): 446–51.
David Morrell, *John Barth: An Introduction* (University Park: Penn-
sylvania State University Press, 1976).

TITLE

Beginning: in the middle, past the middle, nearer three-quarters done, waiting for the end. Consider how dreadful so far: passionlessness, abstraction, pro, dis. And it will get worse. Can we possibly continue?

Plot and theme; notions vitiated by this hour of the world but as yet not successfully succeeded. Conflict, complication, no climax. The worst is to come. Everything leads to nothing; future tense; past tense; present tense. Perfect. The final question is, Can nothing be made meaningful? Isn't that the final question? If not, the end is at hand. Literally, as it were. Can't stand any more of this.

I think she comes. The story of our life. This the final test. Try to fill the blank. Only hope is to fill the blank. Efface what can't be faced or else fill the blank. With words or more words, otherwise I'll fill in the blank with this noun here in my prepositional object. Yes, she already said that. And I think. What now. Everything's been said already, over and over; I'm as sick of this as you are; there's nothing to say. Say nothing.

What's new? Nothing.

Conventional startling opener. Sorry if I'm interrupting the Progress of Literature, she said, in a tone that adjective clause suggesting good-humored irony but in fact defensively and imperfectly masking a taunt. The conflict is established though as yet unclear in detail. Standard conflict. Let's skip particulars. What do you want from me? What'll the story be this time? Same old story. Just thought I'd see if you were still around. Before. What? Quit right here. Too late. Can't we start over? What's past is past. On the contrary, what's forever past is eternally present. The future? Blank. All this is just fill in. Hang on.

Still around. In what sense? Among the gerundive. What is that supposed to mean? Did you think I meant to fill in the blank? Why should I? On the other hand, why not? What makes you think I wouldn't fill in the blank instead? Some conversation this is. Do you want to go on, or shall we end it right now? Suspense. I don't care for this either. It'll be over soon enough in any case. But it gets worse and worse. Whatever happens, the ending will be deadly. At least let's have just one real conversation. Dialogue or monologue? What has it been from the first? Don't ask me. What is there to say at this late date? Let me think; I'm trying to think. Same old story. Or. Or? Silence.

This isn't so bad. Silence. There are worse things. Name three. This, that, the other. Some choices. Who said there was a choice?

Let's try again. That's what I've been doing; I've been thinking while you've been blank. Story of Our Life. However, this may be the final complication. The ending may be violent. That's been said before. Who cares? Let the end be blank; anything's better than this.

It didn't used to be so bad. It used to be less difficult. Even enjoyable. For whom? Both of us. To do what? Complicate the conflict. I am weary of this. What, then? To complete this sentence, if I may bring up a sore subject. That never used to be a problem. Now it's impossible; we just can't manage it. You can't fill in the blank; I can't fill in the blank. Or won't. Is this what we're going to talk about, our obscene verbal problem? It'll be our last conversation. Why talk at all? Are you paying attention? I dare you to quit now! Never dare a desperate person. On with it, calmly, one sentence after another, like a recidivist. A what? A common noun. Or another common noun. Hold tight. Or a chronic forger, let's say; committed to the pen for life. Which is to say, death. The point, for pity's sake! Not yet. Forge on.

We're more than halfway through, as I remarked at the outset; youthful vigor, innocent exposition, positive rising action — all that is behind us. How sophisticated we are today. I'll ignore her, he vowed, and went on. In this dehuman, exhausted, ultimate adjective hour, when every humane value has become untenable, and not only love, decency, and beauty but even compassion and intelligibility are no more than one or two subjective complements to complete the sentence. . . .

This is a story? It's a story, he replied equably, or will be if the author can finish it. Without interruption I suppose you mean? she broke in. I can't finish anything; that is my final word, Yet it's these interruptions that make it a story. Escalate the conflict further. Please let me start over.

Once upon a time you were satisfied with incidental felicities and niceties of technique; the unexpected image, the refreshingly accurate word-choice, the memorable simile that yields deeper and subtler significances upon reflection, like a memorable simile. Somebody please stop me. Or arresting dialogue, so to speak. For example?

Why do you suppose it is, she asked, long participial phrase of the breathless variety characteristic of dialogue attributions in nineteenth-century fiction, that literate people such as we talk like characters in a story? Even supplying the dialogue-tags, she added with wry disgust. Don't put words in her mouth. The same old story, an old-fashioned one at that. Even if I should fill in the blank with my idle pen? Nothing new about that, to make a fact out of a figure. At least it's good for something. Every story is penned in red ink, to make a figure out of a fact. This whole idea is insane.

And might therefore be got away with.

No turning back now, we've gone too far. Everything's finished. Name eight. Story, novel, literature, art, humanism, humanity, the self itself. Wait: the story's not finished. And you and I, Howard?, whispered Martha, her sarcasm belied by a hesitant alarm in her glance, flickering as it were despite herself to the blank instrument in his hand. Belied indeed; put that thing away! And what does flickering modify? A person who can't verb adverb ought at least to speak correctly.

A tense moment in the evolution of the story. Do you know, declared the narrator, one has no idea, especially nowadays, how close the end may be, nor will one necessarily be aware of it when it occurs. Who can say how near this universe has come to mere cessation? Or take two people, in a story of the sort it once was possible to tell. Love affairs, literary genres, third item in exemplary series, fourth — everything blossoms and decays, does it not, from the primitive and classical through the mannered and baroque to the abstract, stylized, dehumanized, unintelligible, blank. And you and I, Rosemary? Edward. Snapped! Patience. The narrator gathers that his audience no longer cherishes him. And conversely. But little does he know of the common noun concealed for months in her you name it, under her eyelet chemise. This is a slip. The point is the same. And she fetches it out nightly as I dream, I think. That's no slip. And she regards it and sighs, a quantum grimlier each night it may be. Is this supposed to be amusing? The world might end before this sentence, or merely someone's life. And/or someone else's. I speak metaphorically. Is the sentence ended? Very nearly. No telling how long a sentence will be until one reaches the stop It sounds as if somebody intends to fill in the blank. What *is* all this nonsense about?

It may not be nonsense. Anyhow it will presently be over. As the narrator was saying, things have been kaput for some time, and while we may be pardoned our great reluctance to acknowledge it, the fact is that the bloody century for example is nearing the three-quarter mark, and the characters in this little tale, for example, are similarly past their prime, as is the drama. About played out. Then God damn it let's ring the curtain. Wait wait. We're left with the following three possibilities, at least in theory. Horseshit. Hold onto yourself, it's too soon to fill in the blank. I hope this will be a short story.

Shorter than it seems. It seems endless. Be thankful it's not a novel. The novel is predicate adjective, as is the innocent anecdote of by-gone days when life made a degree of sense and subject joined to complement by copula. No longer are hese things the case, as you have doubtless remarked. There was I believe some mention of possibilities, three in number. The first is rejuvenation: having become an exhausted parody of itself, perhaps a form — Of what? Of anything — may rise neoprimitively from its own ashes. A tiresome prospect. The second, more appealing I'm sure but scarcely likely at this advanced date, is that moribund what-have-yous will be supplanted by vigorous new: the demise of the novel and short story, he went on to declare, needn't be the end of narrative art, nor need the dissolution of a used-up blank fill in the blank. The end of one road might be the beginning of another. Much good that'll do me. And you may not find the revolution as bloodless as you think, either. Shall we try it? Never dare a person who is fed up to the ears.

The final possibility is a temporary expedient, to be sure, the self-styled narrator of this so-called story went on to admit, ignoring the hostile impatience of his audience, but what is not, and every sentence completed is a step closer to the end. That is to say, every day gained is

a day gone. Matter of viewpoint, I suppose. Go on. I am. Whether anyone's paying attention or not. The final possibility is to turn ultimacy,
exhaustion, paralyzing self-consciousness and the adjective weight of
accumulated history. . . . Go on. Go on. To turn ultimacy against itself
to make something new and valid, the essence whereof would be the
impossibility of making something new. What a nauseating notion. And
pray how does it bear upon the analogy uppermost in everyone's mind?
We've gotten this far, haven't we? Look how far we've come together.
Can't we keep on to the end? I think not. Even another sentence is too
many. Only if one believes the end to be a long way off; actually it might
come at any moment; I'm surprised it hasn't before now. Nothing does
when it's expected to.

Silence. There's a fourth possibility, I suppose. Silence. General anes-
thesia. Self-extinction. Silence.

Historicity and self-awareness, he asseverated, while ineluctable and
even greatly to be prized, are always fatal to innocence and spontane-
ity. Perhaps adjective period Whether in a people, an art, a love affair,
or a fourth term added not impossibly to make the third less than ultimate. In the name of suffering humanity cease this harangue. It's over.
And the story? Is there a plot here? What's all this leading up to?

No climax. There's the story. Finished? Not quite. Story of our lives.
The last word in fiction, in fact. I chose the first-person narrative viewpoint in order to reflect interest from the peculiarities of the technique
(such as the normally unbearable self-consciousness, the abstraction, and
the blank) to the nature and situation of the narrator and his companion, despite the obvious possibility that the narrator and his companion
might be mistaken for the narrator and his companion. Occupational
hazard. The technique is advanced, as you see, but the situation of the
characters is conventionally dramatic. That being the case, may one of
them, or one who may be taken for one of them, make a longish speech
in the old-fashioned manner, charged with obsolete emotion? Of course.

I begin calmly, though my voice may rise as I go along. Sometimes it
seems as if things could instantly be altogether different and more admirable. The times be damned, one still wants a man vigorous, confident,
bold, resourceful, adjective, and adjective. One still wants a woman
spirited, spacious of heart, loyal, gentle, adjective, adjective. That man
and that woman are as possible as the ones in this miserable story, and
a good deal realer. It's as if they live in some room of our house that we
can't find the door to, though it's so close we can hear echoes of their
voices. Experience has made them wise instead of bitter; knowledge
has mellowed instead of souring them; in their forties and fifties, even
in their sixties, they're gayer and stronger and more authentic than they
were in their twenties; for the twenty-year-olds they have only affectionate sympathy. So? Why aren't the couple in this story that man and
woman, so easy to imagine? God, but I am surfeited with clever irony!
Ill of sickness! Parallel phrase to wrap up series! This last-resort idea,

it's dead in the womb, excuse the figure. A false pregnancy, excuse the figure. God damn me though if that's entirely my fault. Acknowledge your complicity. As you see, I'm trying to do something about the present mess; hence this story. Adjective in the noun! Don't lose your composure. You tell me it's self-defeating to talk about it instead of just up and doing it; but to acknowledge what I'm doing while I'm doing it is exactly the point. Self-defeat implies a victor, and who do you suppose it is, if not blank? That's the only victory left. Right? Forward! Eyes open.

No. The only way to get out of a mirror-maze is to close your eyes and hold out your hands. And be carried away by a valiant metaphor, I suppose, like a simile.

There's only one direction to go in. Ugh. We must make something out of nothing. Impossible. Mystics do. Not only turn contradiction into paradox, but *employ* it, to go on living and working. Don't bet on it. I'm betting my cliché on it, yours too. What is that supposed to mean? On with the refutation; every denial is another breath, every word brings us closer to the end.

Very well: to write this allegedly ultimate story is a form of artistic fill in the blank, or an artistic form of same, if you like. I don't. What I mean is, same idea in other terms. The storyteller's alternatives, as far as I can see, are a series of last words, like an aging actress making one farewell appearance after another, or actual blank. And I mean literally fill in the blank. Is this a test? But the former is contemptible in itself, and the latter will certainly become so when the rest of the world shrugs its shoulders and goes on about its business. Just as people would do if adverbial clause of obvious analogical nature. The fact is, the narrator has narrated himself into a corner, a state of affairs more tsk-tsk than boo-hoo, and because his position is absurd he calls the world absurd. That some writers lack lead in their pencils does not make writing obsolete. At this point they were both smiling despite themselves. At this point they were both flashing hatred despite themselves. Every woman has a blade concealed in the neighborhood of her garters. So disarm her, so to speak, don't geld yourself. At this point they were both despite themselves. Have we come to the point at last? Not quite. Where there's life there's hope.

There's no hope. This isn't working. But the alternative is to supply an alternative. That's no alternative. Unless I make it one. Just try; quit talking about it, quit talking, quit! Never dare a desperate man. Or woman. That's the one thing that can drive even the first part of a conventional metaphor to the second part of same. Talk, talk, talk. Yes yes, go on, I believe literature's not likely ever to manage abstraction successfully, like sculpture for example, is that a fact, what a time to bring up that subject, anticlimax, that's the point, do set forth the exquisite reason. Well, because wood and iron have a native appeal and first-order reality, whereas words are artificial to begin with, invented specifically to represent. Go on, please go on. I'm going. Don't you dare. Well, well, weld iron rods into abstract patterns, say, and you've still got real iron, but arrange words into abstract patterns and you've got nonsense. Nonsense is right. For example. On, God damn it; take linear plot, take resolution of conflict, take third direct object, all that business, they may very well be obsolete notions, indeed they are, no doubt untenable at this late date, no doubt at all, but in fact we still lead our lives by clock and calendar, for example, and though the seasons recur our mortal human time does not; we grow old and tired, we think of how things used to be or might have been and how they are now, and in fact, and in fact we get exasperated and desperate and out of expedients and out of words.

Go on. Impossible. I'm going, too late now, one more step and we're done, you and I. Suspense. The fact is, you're driving me to it, the fact is that people still lead lives, mean and bleak and brief as they are, briefer than you think, and people have characters and motives that we divine more or less inaccurately from their appearance, speech, behavior, and the rest, you aren't listening, go on then, what do you think I'm doing, people still fall in love, and out, yes, in and out, and out and in, and they please each other, and hurt each other, isn't that the truth, and they do these things in more or less conventionally dramatic fashion, unfashionable or not, go on, I'm going, and what goes on between them is still not only the most interesting but the most important thing in the bloody murderous world, pardon the adjectives. And that my dear is what writers have got to find ways to write about in this adjective adjective hour of the ditto ditto same noun as above, or their, that is to say our, accursed self-consciousness will lead them, that is to say us, to here it comes, say it straight out, I'm going to, say it in plain English for once, that's what I'm leading up to, me and my bloody anticlimactic noun, we're pushing each other to fill in the blank.

Goodbye. Is it over? Can't you read between the lines? One more step. Goodbye suspense goodbye.

Blank.

Oh God comma I abhor self-consciousness. I despise what we have come to; I loathe our loathesome loathing, our place our time our situation, our loathesome art, this ditto necessary story. The blank of our lives. It's about over. Let the *dénouement* be soon and unexpected, painless if possible, quick at least, above all soon. Now now! How in the world will it ever

DONALD BARTHELME

Born in Philadelphia in 1931, Donald Barthelme was educated in Texas. After graduating from the University of Houston, he worked for a time as a museum director, and also as an editor of *Location*, a journal concerned with art and literature; this interest in the visual arts, including the cinema, is reflected in all his writing. The title of his first collection of short stories, *Come Back, Dr. Caligari* (1964), alludes to an early German film, which employed expressionistic and surrealistic techniques; and Barthelme's extraordinary mixture and manipulation of styles at times seems to approximate film more closely than traditional literary modes. The rejection of literary convention, as a means of conveying the writer's sense of absurdity or meaninglessness in life, is itself a convention which Barthelme inherits from Rabelais, Sterne, and Joyce; but his more immediate literary antecedents are Poe and Kafka. Like them, he conveys a sense of purposeless evil underlying the surface of our lives; his stories are amusing and yet macabre, turning sense into non-sense, and disturbing our notions of reality. In his novel *Snow White* (1967), and such collections of stories as *City Life* (1971), *Great Days* (1979), and *Overnight to Many Distant Cities* (1983), he moves still further away from conventional methods of narration, sometimes combining typographical devices and pictures with his text, to create a dizzying series of surreal and cryptic images. "Report," from *Unspeakable Practices, Unnatural Acts* (1968), is not experimental in terms of technique; but by his adaptation and imitation of scientific jargon, Barthelme projects a bizarre picture of the human potential for self-destruction, in an age when technology seems to have deprived us of the capacity for natural feeling.

FOR FURTHER READING

Critique 16, no. 3 (1975): special Barthelme issue.
Francis Gillen, "Donald Barthelme's City: A Guide," *Twentieth Century Literature* 18 (January/October 1972): 37–44.
Lois Gordon, *Donald Barthelme* (Boston: Twayne, 1981).

REPORT

Our group is against the war. But the war goes on. I was sent to Cleveland to talk to the engineers. The engineers were meeting in Cleveland. I was supposed to persuade them not to do what they are going to do. I took United's 4:45 from LaGuardia arriving in Cleveland at 6:13. Cleveland is dark blue at that hour. I went directly to the motel, where the engineers were meeting. Hundreds of engineers attended the Cleveland meeting. I noticed many fractures among the engineers, bandages, traction. I noticed what appeared to be fracture of the carpal scaphoid in six examples. I noticed numerous fractures of the humeral shaft, of the os calcis, of the pelvic girdle. I noticed a high incidence of clay-shoveller's fracture. I could not account for these fractures. The engineers were making calculations, taking measurements, sketching on the blackboard, drinking beer, throwing bread, buttonholing employers, hurling glasses into the fireplace. They were friendly.

They were friendly. They were full of love and information. The chief engineer wore shades. Patella in Monk's traction, clamshell fracture by the look of it. He was standing in a slum of beer bottles and microphone cable. "Have some of this chicken à la Isambard Kingdom Brunel the Great Ingineer," he said. "And declare who you are and what we can do for you. What is your line, distinguished guest?"

"Software," I said. "In every sense. I am here representing a small group of interested parties. We are interested in your thing, which seems to be functioning. In the midst of so much dysfunction, function is interesting. Other people's things don't seem to be working. The State Department's thing doesn't seem to be working. The U.N.'s thing doesn't seem to be working. The democratic left's thing doesn't seem to be working. Buddha's thing —"

"Ask us anything about our thing, which seems to be working," the chief engineer said. "We will open our hearts and heads to you, Software Man, because we want to be understood and loved by the great lay public, and have our marvels appreciated by that public, for which we daily unsung produce tons of new marvels each more life-enhancing than the last. Ask us anything. Do you want to know about evaporated thin-film metallurgy? Monolithic and hybrid integrated-circuit processes? The algebra of inequalities? Optimization theory? Complex high-speed micro-miniature closed and open loop systems? Fixed variable mathematical cost searches? Epitaxial deposition of semi-conductor materials? Gross interfaced space gropes? We also have specialists in the cuckoo-flower, the doctorfish, and the dumdum bullet as these relate to aspects of today's expanding technology, and they do in the damnedest ways."

I spoke to him then about the war. I said the same things people always say when they speak against the war. I said that the war was wrong. I said that large countries should not burn down small countries. I said that the government had made a series of errors. I said that these errors once small and forgivable were now immense and unforgivable. I said that the government was attempting to conceal its original errors under layers of new errors. I said that the government was sick with error, giddy with it. I said that ten thousand of our soldiers had already been killed in pursuit of the government's errors. I said that tens of thousands of the enemy's soldiers and civilians had been killed because of various errors, ours and theirs. I said that we are responsible for errors made in our name. I said that the government should not be allowed to make additional errors.

"Yes, yes," the chief engineer said, "there is doubtless much truth in what you say, but we can't possibly *lose* the war, can we? And stopping is losing, isn't it? The war regarded as a process, stopping regarded as an abort? We don't know *how* to lose a war. That skill is not among our skills. Our array smashes their array, that is what we know. That is the process. That is what is.

"But let's not have any more of this dispiriting downbeat counter-productive talk. I have a few new marvels here I'd like to discuss with you just briefly. A few new marvels that are just about ready to be gaped at by the admiring layman. Consider for instance the area of realtime online computer-controlled wish evaporation. Wish evaporation is going to be crucial in meeting the rising expectations of the world's peoples, which are as you know rising entirely too fast."

I noticed then distributed about the room a great many transverse fractures of the ulna. "The development of the pseudo-ruminant stomach for underdeveloped peoples," he went on, "is one of our interesting things you should be interested in. With the pseudo-ruminant stomach they can chew cuds, that is to say, eat grass. Blue is the most popular color worldwide and for that reason we are working with certain strains of your native Kentucky *Poa pratensis,* or bluegrass, as the staple input for the p/r stomach cycle, which would also give a shot in the arm to our balance-of-payments thing don't you know. . . ." I noticed about me then a great number of metatarsal fractures in banjo splints. "The kangaroo initiative . . . eight hundred thousand harvested last year . . . highest percentage of edible protein of any herbivore yet studied. . . ."

"Have new kangaroos been planted?"

The engineer looked at me.

"I intuit your hatred and jealousy of our thing," he said. "The ineffectual always hate our thing and speak of it as anti-human, which is not at all a meaningful way to speak of our thing. Nothing mechanical is alien to me," he said (amber spots making bursts of light in his shades), "because I am human, in a sense, and if I think it up, then 'it' is human too, whatever 'it' may be. Let me tell you, Software Man, we have been damned forbearing in the matter of this little war you declare yourself to be interested in. Function is the cry, and our thing is functioning like crazy. There are things we could do that we have not done. Steps we could take that we have not taken. These steps are, regarded in a certain light, the light of our enlightened self-interest, quite justifiable steps. We could, of course, get irritated. We could, of course, *lose patience.*

"We could, of course, release thousands upon thousands of self-powered crawling-along-the-ground lengths of titanium wire eighteen inches long with a diameter of .0005 centimetres (that is to say, invisible) which, scenting an enemy, climb up his trouser leg and wrap themselves around his neck. We have developed those. They are within our capabilities. We could, of course, release in the arena of the upper air our new improved pufferfish toxin which precipitates an identity crisis. No special technical problems there. That is almost laughably easy. We could, of course, place up to two million maggots in their rice within twenty-four hours. The maggots are ready, massed in secret staging areas in Alabama. We have hypodermic darts capable of piebalding the enemy's pigmentation. We have rots, blights, and rusts capable of attacking his alphabet. Those are dandies. We have a hut-shrinking chemical which penetrates the fibres of the bamboo, causing it, the hut, to strangle its occupants. This operates only after 10 P.M., when people are sleeping. Their mathematics are at the mercy of a suppurating surd we have invented. We have a family of fishes trained to attack their fishes. We have the deadly testicle-destroying telegram. The cable companies are cooperating. We have a green substance that, well, I'd rather not talk about. We have a secret word that, if pronounced, produces multiple fractures in all living things in an area the size of four football fields."

"That's why —"

"Yes. Some damned fool couldn't keep his mouth shut. The point is that the whole structure of enemy life is within our power to *rend, vitiate, devour,* and *crush.* But that's not the interesting thing."

"You recount these possibilities with uncommon relish."

"Yes I realize that there is too much relish here. But *you* must realize that these capabilities represent in and of themselves highly technical and complex and interesting problems and hurdles on which our boys have expended many thousands of hours of hard work and brilliance. And that the effects are often grossly exaggerated by irresponsible victims. And that the whole thing represents a fantastic series of triumphs for the multi-disciplined problem solving team concept."

"I appreciate that."

"We *could* unleash all this technology at once. You can imagine what would happen then. But that's not the interesting thing."

"What is the interesting thing?"

"The interesting thing is that we have *a moral sense.* It is on punched cards, perhaps the most advanced and sensitive moral sense the world has ever known."

"Because it is on punched cards?"

"It considers all considerations in endless and subtle detail," he said. "It even quibbles. With this great new moral tool, how can we go wrong? I confidently predict that, although we *could* employ all this splendid new weaponry I've been telling you about, *we're not going to do it.*"

"We're not going to do it?"

I took United's 5:44 from Cleveland arriving at Newark at 7:19. New Jersey is bright pink at that hour. Living things move about the surface of New Jersey at that hour molesting each other only in traditional ways. I made my report to the group. I stressed the friendliness of the engineers. I said, It's all right. I said, We have a moral sense. I said, *We're not going to do it.* They didn't believe me.

CLARK BLAISE

Associated in the 1960s with a group called the Montreal Story Teller, Clark Blaise has moved repeatedly between Canada and the United States. Born to Canadian parents in Fargo, North Dakota in 1940, he grew up in Manitoba, on the urban American east coast, and in the rural South, and was educated in Ohio and Iowa. His work reflects this mobility, asserts his French heritage and his American upbringing, and focuses on the problems of alienation that in various ways beset modern men and women. His widely praised short-story collection *A North American Education* (1973), expresses even by its title the continental range of his background; and the stories themselves, cast as personal narratives, draw readers into an intensely immediate world. The second-person narrative technique of "Eyes" enforces such a reaction, and the story's sombre tone — the watchfulness it suggests — skilfully links method with meaning. But the immediacy rises from the author's intention as well.

   In an essay on the short-story form — "To Begin, To Begin," the title a quotation from Donald Barthelme — Blaise asserts that theme is of secondary importance to the writer who is undergoing the process of writing a story. Narrative climax and the elegant contrivance of resolution, however important, are also of less moment than the mysteries of genesis. A good story, he says, is made by its first sentence and by the embellishments which the first paragraph gives it. The first sentence must imply its own opposite — "a good sensuous description of May sets up the possibility of a May disaster"; it must start the story neither too late nor too soon; it must disrupt and reorder the reader's sense of how things are; and it must have a rhythm all its own. The moment plot appears, in "the simple terrifying adverb: *Then*," the characters start to realize the implications of the initial mysteries; such a moment "is the cracking of the perfect, smug egg of possibility." But what preceded it is what allowed it; in the beginning is the identity that the story seems later to acquire or reveal. And in realizing and appreciating this identity, readers engage themselves with the artist in the creation of the story's own truths.

FOR FURTHER READING

Clark Blaise, "On Ending Stories," *Canadian Forum* 62 (September 1982): 7, 37.

Clark Blaise, "Portrait of the Artist as Young Pup," *Canadian Literature*, no. 100 (Spring 1984): 35–41.

Clark Blaise, "To Begin, To Begin," in *The Narrative Voice*, ed. John Metcalf (Toronto: McGraw-Hill Ryerson, 1972), pp. 22–26.

Robert Lecker, *On the Line* (Toronto: ECW Press 1982).

EYES

You jump into this business of a new country cautiously. First you choose a place where English is spoken, with doctors and bus lines at hand, and a supermarket in a *centre d'achats* not too far away. You ease yourself into the city, approaching by car or bus down a single artery, aiming yourself along the boulevard that begins small and tree-lined in your suburb but broadens into the canyoned aorta of the city five miles beyond. And by that first winter when you know the routes and bridges, the standard congestions reported from the helicopter on your favorite radio station, you start to think of moving. What's the good of a place like this when two of your neighbors have come from Texas and the French paper you've dutifully subscribed to arrives by mail two days late? These French are all around you, behind the counters at the shopping center, in a house or two on your block; why isn't your little boy learning French at least? Where's the nearest *maternelle*?* Four miles away.

In the spring you move. You find an apartment on a small side street where dogs outnumber children and the row houses resemble London's, divided equally between the rundown and remodeled. Your neighbors are the young personalities of French television who live on delivered chicken, or the old pensioners who shuffle down the summer sidewalks in pajamas and slippers in a state of endless recuperation. Your neighbors pay sixty a month for rent, or three hundred; you pay two-fifty for a two-bedroom flat where the walls have been replastered and new fixtures hung. The bugs *d'antan* remain, as well as the hulks of cars abandoned in the fire alley behind, where downtown drunks sleep in the summer night.

Then comes the night in early October when your child is coughing badly, and you sit with him in the darkened nursery, calm in the bubbling of a cold-steam vaporizer while your wife mends a dress in the room next door. And from the dark, silently, as you peer into the ill-lit fire alley, he comes. You cannot believe it at first, that a rheumy, pasty-faced Irishman in slate-gray jacket and rubber-soled shoes has come purposely to *your* small parking space, that he has been here before and he is not drunk (not now, at least, but you know him as a panhandler on the main boulevard a block away), that he brings with him a crate that he sets on end under your bedroom window and raises himself to your window ledge and hangs there nose-high at a pencil of light from the ill-fitting blinds. And there you are, straining with him from the uncurtained nursery, watching the man watching your wife, praying silently that she is sleeping under the blanket. The man is almost smiling, a leprechaun's face that sees what you cannot. You are about to lift the

Maternelle = nursery school.

window and shout, but your wheezing child lies just under you; and what of your wife in the room next door? You could, perhaps, throw open the window and leap to the ground, tackle the man before he runs and smash his face into the bricks, beat him senseless then call the cops . . . Or better, find the camera, afix the flash, rap once at the window and shoot when he turns. Do nothing and let him suffer. *He is at your mercy*, no one will ever again be so helpless — but what can you do? You know, somehow, he'll escape. If you hurt him, he can hurt you worse, later, viciously. He's been a regular at your window, he's watched the two of you when you prided yourself on being young and alone and masters of the city. He knows your child and the park he plays in, your wife and where she shops. He's a native of the place, a man who knows the city and maybe a dozen such windows, who knows the fire escapes and alleys and roofs, knows the habits of the city's heedless young.

And briefly you remember yourself, an adolescent in another country slithering through the mosquito-ridden grassy fields behind a housing development, peering into those houses where newlyweds had not yet put up drapes, how you could spend five hours in a motionless crouch for a myopic glimpse of a slender arm reaching from the dark to douse a light. Then you hear what the man cannot; the creaking of your bed in the far bedroom, the steps of your wife on her way to the bathroom, and you see her as you never have before: blond and tall and rangily built, a north-Europe princess from a constitutional monarchy, sensuous mouth and prominent teeth, pale, tennis-ball breasts cupped in her hands as she stands in the bathroom's light.

"How's Kit?" she asks. "I'd give him a kiss except that there's no blind in there," and she dashes back to bed, nude, and the man bounces twice on the window ledge.

"You coming?"

You find yourself creeping from the nursery, turning left at the hall and then running to the kitchen telephone; you dial the police, then hang up. How will you prepare your wife, not for what is happening, but for what has already taken place?

"It's stuffy in here," you shout back, "I think I'll open the window a bit." You take your time, you stand before the blind blocking his view if he's still looking, then bravely you part the curtains. He is gone, the crate remains upright. "Do we have any masking tape?" you ask, lifting the window a crack.

And now you know the city a little better. A place where millions come each summer to take pictures and walk around must have its voyeurs too. And that place in all great cities where rich and poor co-exist is especially hard on the people in-between. It's health you've been seeking, not just beauty; a tough urban health that will save you money in the bargain, and when you hear of a place twice as large at half the rent, in a part of town free of Texans, English, and French, free of young actors and stewardesses who deposit their garbage in pizza boxes, you move again.

It is, for you, a city of Greeks. In the summer you move you attend a movie at the corner cinema. The posters advertise a war movie, in Greek, but the uniforms are unfamiliar. Both sides wear mustaches, both sides handle machine guns, both leave older women behind dressed in black. From the posters outside there is a promise of sex; blond women in slips, dark-eyed peasant girls. There will be rubble, executions against a wall. You can follow the story from the stills alone: mustached boy goes to war, embraces dark-eyed village girl. Black-draped mother and admiring young brother stand behind. Young soldier, mustache fuller, embraces blond prostitute on a tangled bed. Enter soldiers, boy hides under sheets. Final shot, back in village. Mother in black; dark-eyed village girl in black. Young brother marching to the front.

You go in, pay your ninety cents, pay a nickel in the lobby for a wedge of *halvah*-like sweets. You understand nothing, you resent their laughter and you even resent the picture they're running. Now you know the Greek for "Coming Attractions," for this is a gangster movie at least thirty years old. The eternal Mediterranean gangster movie set in Athens instead of Naples or Marseilles, with smaller cars and narrower roads, uglier women and more sinister killers. After an hour the movie flatters you. No one knows you're not a Greek, that you don't belong in this theater, or even this city. That, like the Greeks, you're hanging on.

Outside the theater the evening is warm and the wide sidewalks are clogged with Greeks who nod as you come out. Like the Ramblas in Barcelona, with children out past midnight and families walking back and forth for a long city block, the men filling the coffeehouses, the women left outside, chatting. Not a blond head on the sidewalk, not a blond head for miles. Greek music pours from the coffeehouses, flies stumble on the pastry, whole families munch their *torsades molles** as they walk. Dry goods are sold at midnight from the sidewalk, like New York fifty years ago. You're wandering happily, glad that you moved, you've rediscovered the innocence of starting over.

Then you come upon a scene directly from Spain. A slim blond girl in a floral top and white pleated skirt, tinted glasses, smoking, with bad skin, ignores a persistent young Greek in a shiny Salonika suit. "Whatsamatta?" he demands, slapping a ten-dollar bill on his open palm. And without looking back at him she drifts closer to the curb and a car makes a sudden squealing turn and lurches to a stop on the cross street. Three men are inside, the back door opens and not a word is exchanged as she steps inside. How? What refinement of gesture did we immigrants miss? You turn to the Greek boy in sympathy, you know just how he feels, but he's already heading across the street, shouting some-

torsades molles = soft, twisted rolls.

thing to his friends outside a barbecue stand. You have a pocketful of bills and a Mediterranean soul, and money this evening means a woman, and blond means whore and you would spend it all on another blond with open pores; all this a block from your wife and tenement. And you hurry home.

Months later you know the place. You trust the Greeks in their stores, you fear their tempers at home. Eight bathrooms adjoin a central shaft, you hear the beatings of your son's friends, the thud of fist on bone after the slaps. Your child knows no French, but he plays cricket with Greeks and Jamaicans out in the alley behind Pascal's hardware. He brings home the oily tires from the Esso station, plays in the boxes behind the appliance store. You watch from a greasy back window, at last satisfied. None of his friends is like him, like you. He is becoming Greek, becoming Jamaican, becoming a part of this strange new land. His hair is nearly white; you can spot him a block away.

On Wednesdays the butcher quarters his meat. Calves arrive by refrigerator truck, still intact but for their split-open bellies and sawed-off hooves. The older of the three brothers skins the carcass with a small thin knife that seems all blade. A knife he could shave with. The hide rolls back in a continuous flap, the knife never pops the membrane over the fat.

Another brother serves. Like yours, his French is adequate. *"Twa lif* d'hamburger,"* you request, still watching the operation on the rickety sawhorse. Who could resist? It's a Levantine treat, the calf's stumpy legs high in the air, the hide draped over the edge and now in the sawdust, growing longer by the second.

The store is filling. The ladies shop on Wednesday, especially the old widows in black overcoats and scarves, shoes and stockings. Yellow, mangled fingernails. Wednesdays attract them with boxes in the window, and they call to the butcher as they enter, the brother answers, and the women dip their fingers in the boxes. The radio is loud overhead, music from the Greek station.

"Une et soixante, m'sieur. Du bacon, jambon?"

And you think, taking a few lamb chops but not their saltless bacon, how pleased you are to manage so well. It is a Byzantine moment with blood and widows and sides of dripping beef, contentment in a snowy slum at five below.

The older brother, having finished the skinning, straightens, curses, and puts away the tiny knife. A brother comes forward to pull the hide away, a perfect beginning for a gameroom rug. Then, bending low at the rear of the glistening carcass, the legs spread high and stubby, the butcher digs in his hands, ripping hard where the scrotum is, and pulls on what seems to be a strand of rubber, until it snaps. He puts a single

Twa lif = trois livres (3 pounds).

glistening prize in his mouth, pulls again and offers the other to his brother, and they suck.

The butcher is singing now, drying his lips and wiping his chin, and still he's chewing. The old black-draped widows with the parchment faces are also chewing. On leaving, you check the boxes in the window. Staring out are the heads of pigs and lambs, some with the eyes lifted out and a red socket exposed. A few are loose and the box is slowly dissolving from the blood, and the ice beneath.

The women have gathered around the body; little pieces are offered to them from the head and entrails. The pigs' heads are pink, perhaps they've been boiled, and hairless. The eyes are strangely blue. You remove your gloves and touch the skin, you brush against the grainy ear. How the eye attracts you! How you would like to lift one out, press its smoothness against your tongue, then crush it in your mouth. And you cannot. Already your finger is numb and the head, it seems, has shifted under you. And the eye, in panic, grows white as your finger approaches. You would take that last half inch but for the certainty, in this world you have made for yourself, that the eye would blink and your neighbors would turn upon you.

PAUL BOWLES

Born in New York in 1910, Paul Bowles won acclaim as a writer after he had already secured recognition for his contributions to film and the performing arts. After a short period at the University of Virginia, he travelled to Europe, then studied music with the celebrated American composers Aaron Copland and Virgil Thomson. Subsequently he entered upon a successful career as a composer of film scores, operas, and ballets, and wrote incidental music for such plays as Tennessee Williams's *Summer and Smoke*. In 1941 his musical accomplishments were rewarded with a Guggenheim Fellowship. While still a young man, Bowles left America to travel extensively in Europe, central America, India, and North Africa, and although his work frequently took him back to the United States, he and his wife (the writer Jane Bowles) eventually settled in Morocco. His fascination with the exotic has borne fruit in travel essays, as well as in numerous translations from works in French, Arabic, Spanish, and Italian. He has published several novels, including *The Sheltering Sky* (1949) and *Let It Come Down* (1952), and his *Collected Stories 1939–1976* appeared in 1979.

The unusual and exotic settings of Bowles's stories arise naturally from his easy familiarity with many foreign cultures, but they reflect also his dissatisfaction with Western life and manners. Some of his characters are Americans or Europeans who find themselves isolated or alienated in an environment that rejects the materialism and sophistication of the modern West. What they learn offers little consolation: they are met by hostility, even violence, from a way of life that spurns them. Bowles does not offer solutions; he seems to suggest that the search for values is ultimately futile. Despite the bleakness of his vision, however, he is a fine storyteller, with the ability to realize a scene in sharp physical detail while investing it with a sense of mystery. "Allal" (1976) is a transformation tale that blends reality and fantasy in a manner suggestive of the folk tale, dramatically portraying the violence latent in all forms of life. Its Gothic quality is reminiscent of Poe's tales, and it is worth noting that Bowles's first short story collection, *The Delicate Prey* (1950), was dedicated to his mother "who first read me the stories of Poe."

FOR FURTHER READING

Paul Bowles, *Without Stopping: An Autobiography* (New York: Putnam, 1972).

Daniel Halpern, "Interview with Paul Bowles," *TriQuarterly* 33 (1975): 159–77.

L.D. Stewart, *Paul Bowles: The Illumination of North Africa* (Carbondale, Illinois: Southern Illinois University Press, 1974).

ALLAL

He was born in the hotel where his mother worked. The hotel had only three dark rooms which gave on a courtyard behind the bar. Beyond was another smaller patio with many doors. This was where the servants lived, and where Allal spent his childhood.

The Greek who owned the hotel had sent Allal's mother away. He was indignant because she, a girl of fourteen, had dared to give birth while she was working for him. She would not say who the father was, and it angered him to reflect that he himself had not taken advantage of the situation while he had had the chance. He gave the girl three months' wages and told her to go home to Marrakech. Since the cook and his wife liked the girl and offered to let her live with them for a while, he agreed that she might stay on until the baby was big enough to travel. She remained in the back patio for a few months with the cook and his wife, and then one day she disappeared, leaving the baby behind. No one heard of her again.

As soon as Allal was old enough to carry things, they set him to work. It was not long before he could fetch a pail of water from the well behind the hotel. The cook and his wife were childless, so that he played alone.

When he was somewhat older he began to wander over the empty table-land outside. There was nothing else up here but the barracks, and they were enclosed by a high blind wall of red adobe. Everything else was below in the valley: the town, the gardens, and the river winding southward among the thousands of palm trees. He could sit on a point of rock far above and look down at the people walking in the alleys of the town. It was only later that he visited the place and saw what the inhabitants were like. Because he had been left behind by his mother they called him a son of sin, and laughed when they looked at him. It seemed to him that in this way they hoped to make him into a shadow, in order not to have to think of him as real and alive. He awaited with dread the time when he would have to go each morning to the town and work. For the moment he helped in the kitchen and served the officers from the barracks, along with the few motorists who passed through the region. He got small tips in the restaurant, and free food and lodging in a cell of the servants' quarters, but the Greek gave him no wages. Eventually he reached an age when this situation seemed shameful, and he went of his own accord to the town below and began to work, along with other boys of his age, helping to make the mud bricks people used for building their houses.

Living in the town was much as he had imagined it would be. For two years he stayed in a room behind a blacksmith's shop, leading a life without quarrels, and saving whatever money he did not have to spend to keep himself alive. Far from making any friends during this time, he formed a thorough hatred for the people of the town, who never allowed him to forget that he was a son of sin, and therefore not like others, but *meskhot* — damned. Then he found a small house, not much more than a hut, in the palm groves outside the town. The rent was low and no one lived nearby. He went to live there, where the only sound was the wind in the trees, and avoided the people of the town when he could.

One hot summer evening shortly after sunset he was walking under the arcades that faced the town's main square. A few paces ahead of him an old man in a white turban was trying to shift a heavy sack from one shoulder to the other. Suddenly it fell to the ground, and Allal stared as two dark forms flowed out of it and disappeared into the shadows. The old man pounced upon the sack and fastened the top of it, at the same time beginning to shout: Look out for the snakes! Help me find my snakes!

Many people turned quickly around and walked back the way they had come. Others stood at some distance, watching. A few called to the old man: Find your snakes fast and get them out of here! Why are they here? We don't want snakes in this town!

Hopping up and down in his anxiety, the old man turned to Allal. Watch this for me a minute, my son. He pointed at the sack lying on the earth at his feet, and snatching up a basket he had been carrying, went swiftly around the corner into an alley. Allal stood where he was. No one passed by.

It was not long before the old man returned, panting with triumph. When the onlookers in the square saw him again, they began to call out, this time to Allal: Show that berrani the way out of the town! He has no right to carry those things in here. Out! Out!

Allal picked up the big sack and said to the old man: Come on.

They left the square and went through the alleys until they were at the edge of town. The old man looked up then, saw the palm trees black against the fading sky ahead, and turned to the boy beside him.

Come on, said Allal again, and he went to the left along the rough path that led to his house. The old man stood perplexed.

You can stay with me tonight, Allal told him.

And these? he said, pointing first at the sack and then at the basket. They have to be with me.

Allal grinned. They can come.

When they were sitting in the house Allal looked at the sack and the basket. I'm not like the rest of them here, he said.

It made him feel good to hear the words being spoken. He made a contemptuous gesture. Afraid to walk through the square because of a snake. You saw them.

The old man scratched his chin. Snakes are like people, he said. You have to get to know them. Then you can be their friends.

Allal hesitated before he asked: Do you ever let them out?

Always, the old man said with energy. It's bad for them to be inside like this. They've got to be healthy when they get to Taroudant, or the man there won't buy them.

He began a long story about his life as a hunter of snakes, explaining that each year he made a voyage to Taroudant to see a man who bought them for the Aissaoua snake-charmers in Marrakech. Allal made tea while he listened, and brought out a bowl of kif paste to eat with the tea. Later, when they were sitting comfortably in the midst of the pipe-smoke, the old man chuckled. Allal turned to look at him.

Shall I let them out?

Fine!

But you must sit and keep quiet. Move the lamp nearer.

He untied the sack, shook it a bit, and returned to where he had been sitting. Then in silence Allal watched the long bodies move cautiously out into the light. Among the cobras were others with markings so delicate and perfect that they seemed to have been designed and painted by an artist. One reddish-gold serpent, which coiled itself lazily in the middle of the floor, he found particularly beautiful. As he stared at it, he felt a great desire to own it and have it always with him.

The old man was talking. I've spent my whole life with snakes, he said. I could tell you some things about them. Did you know that if you give them majoun you can make them do what you want, and without saying a word? I swear by Allah!

Allal's face assumed a doubtful air. He did not question the truth of the other's statement, but rather the likelihood of his being able to put the knowledge to use. For it was at that moment that the idea of actually taking the snake first came into his head. He was thinking that whatever he was to do must be done quickly, for the old man would be leaving in the morning. Suddenly he felt a great impatience.

Put them away so I can cook dinner, he whispered. Then he sat admiring the ease with which the old man picked up each one by its head and slipped it into the sack. Once again he dropped two of the snakes into the basket, and one of these, Allal noted, was the red one. He imagined he could see the shining of its scales through the lid of the basket.

As he set to work preparing the meal Allal tried to think of other things. Then, since the snake remained in his mind in spite of everything, he began to devise a way of getting it. While he squatted over the fire in a corner, he mixed some kif paste in a bowl of milk and set it aside.

The old man continued to talk. That was good luck, getting the two snakes back like that, in the middle of the town. You can never be sure what people are going to do when they find out you're carrying snakes. Once in El Kelaa they took all of them and killed them, one after the other, in front of me. A year's work. I had to go back home and start all over again.

Even as they ate, Allal saw that his guest was growing sleepy. How will things happen? he wondered. There was no way of knowing beforehand precisely what he was going to do, and the prospect of having to handle the snake worried him. It could kill me, he thought.

Once they had eaten, drunk tea and smoked a few pipes of kif, the old man lay back on the floor and said he was going to sleep. Allal sprang up. In here! he told him, and led him to his own mat in an alcove. The old man lay down and swiftly fell asleep.

Several times during the next half hour Allal went to the alcove and peered in, but neither the body in its burnous nor the head in its turban had stirred.

First he got out his blanket, and after tying three of its corners together, spread it on the floor with the fourth corner facing the basket. Then he set the bowl of milk and kif paste on the blanket. As he loosened the strap from the cover of the basket the old man coughed. Allal stood immobile, waiting to hear the cracked voice speak. A small breeze had sprung up, making the palm branches rasp one against the other, but there was no further sound from the alcove. He crept to the far side of the room and squatted by the wall, his gaze fixed on the basket.

Several times he thought he saw the cover move slightly, but each time he decided he had been mistaken. Then he caught his breath. The shadow along the base of the basket was moving. One of the creatures had crept out from the far side. It waited for a while before continuing into the light, but when it did, Allal breathed a prayer of thanks. It was the red and gold one.

When finally it decided to go to the bowl, it made a complete tour around the edge, looking in from all sides, before lowering its head toward the milk. Allal watched, fearful that the foreign flavor of the kif paste might repel it. The snake remained there without moving.

He waited a half hour or more. The snake stayed where it was, its head in the bowl. From time to time Allal glanced at the basket, to be certain that the second snake was still in it. The breeze went on, rubbing the palm branches together. When he decided it was time, he rose slowly, and keeping an eye on the basket where apparently the other snake still slept, he reached over and gathered together the three tied corners of the blanket. Then he lifted the fourth corner, so that both the snake and the bowl slid to the bottom of the improvised sack. The snake moved slightly, but he did not think it was angry. He knew exactly where he would hide it: between some rocks in the dry river bed.

Holding the blanket in front of him he opened the door and stepped out under the stars. It was not far up the road, to a group of high palms, and then to the left down into the oued. There was a space between the boulders where the bundle would be invisible. He pushed it in with care, and hurried back to the house. The old man was asleep.

There was no way of being sure that the other snake was still in the basket, so Allal picked up his burnous and went outside. He shut the door and lay down on the ground to sleep.

Before the sun was in the sky the old man was awake, lying in the alcove coughing. Allal jumped up, went inside, and began to make a fire in the mijmah. A minute later he heard the other exclaim: They're loose again! Out of the basket! Stay where you are and I'll find them.

It was not long before the old man grunted with satisfaction. I have the black one! he cried. Allal did not look up from the corner where he crouched, the old man came over, waving a cobra. Now I've got to find the other one.

He put the snake away and continued to search. When the fire was blazing, Allal turned and said: Do you want me to help you look for it?

No, No! Stay where you are.

Allal boiled the water and made the tea, and still the old man was crawling on his knees, lifting boxes and pushing sacks. His turban had slipped off and his face ran with sweat.

Come and have tea, Allal told him.

The old man did not seem to have heard him at first. Then he rose and went into the alcove, where he rewound his turban. When he came out he sat down with Allal, and they had breakfast.

Snakes are very clever, the old man said. They can get into places that don't exist. I've moved everything in this house.

After they had finished eating, they went outside and looked for the snake between the close-growing trunks of the palms near the house. When the old man was convinced that it was gone, he went sadly back in.

That was a good snake, he said at last. And now I'm going to Taroudant.

They said good-bye, and the old man took his sack and basket and started up the road toward the highway.

All day long as he worked, Allal thought of the snake, but it was not until sunset that he was able to go to the rocks in the oued and pull out the blanket. He carried it back to the house in a high state of excitement.

Before he untied the blanket, he filled a wide dish with milk and kif paste, and set it on the floor. He ate three spoonfuls of the paste himself and sat back to watch, drumming on the low wooden tea-table with his fingers. Everything happened just as he had hoped. The snake came slowly out of the blanket, and very soon had found the dish and was drinking the milk. As long as it drank he kept drumming; when it had finished and raised its head to look at him, he stopped, and it crawled back inside the blanket.

Later that evening he put down more milk, and drummed again on the table. After a time the snake's head appeared, and finally all of it, and the entire pattern of action was repeated.

That night and every night thereafter, Allal sat with the snake, while with infinite patience he sought to make it his friend. He never attempted to touch it, but soon he was able to summon it, keep it in front of him for as long as he pleased, merely by tapping on the table, and dismiss it at will. For the first week or so he used the kif paste; then he tried the routine without it. In the end the results were the same. After that he fed it only milk and eggs.

Then one evening as his friend lay gracefully coiled in front of him, he began to think of the old man, and formed an idea that put all other things out of his mind. There had not been any kif paste in the house for several weeks, and he decided to make some. He bought the ingredients the following day, and after work he prepared the paste. When it was done, he mixed a large amount of it in a bowl with milk and set it down for the snake. Then he himself ate four spoonfuls, washing them down with tea.

He quickly undressed, and moving the table so that he could reach it, stretched out naked on a mat near the door. This time he continued to tap on the table, even after the snake had finished drinking the milk. It lay still, observing him, as if it were in doubt that the familiar drumming came from the brown body in front of it.

Seeing that even after a long time it remained where it was, staring at him with its stony yellow eyes, Allal began to say to it over and over: Come here. He knew it could not hear his voice, but he believed it could feel his mind as he urged it. You can make them do what you want, without saying a word, the old man had told him.

Although the snake did not move, he went on repeating his command, for by now he knew it was going to come. And after another long wait, all at once it lowered its head and began to move toward him. It reached his hip and slid along his leg. Then it climbed up his leg and lay for a time across his chest. Its body was heavy and tepid, its scales wonderfully smooth. After a time it came to rest, coiled in the space between his head and his shoulder.

By this time the kif paste had completely taken over Allal's mind. He lay in a state of pure delight, feeling the snake's head against his own, without a thought save that he and the snake were together. The patterns forming and melting behind his eyelids seemed to be the same ones that covered the snake's back. Now and then in a huge frenzied movement they all swirled up and shattered into fragments which swiftly became one great yellow eye, split through the middle by the narrow vertical pupil that pulsed with his own heartbeat. Then the eye would recede, through shifting shadow and sunlight, until only the designs of the scales were left, swarming with renewed insistence as they merged and separated. At last the eye returned, so huge this time that it had no edge around it, its pupil dilated to form an aperture almost wide enough for him to enter. As he stared at the blackness within, he understood that he was being slowly propelled toward the opening. He put out his hands to touch the polished surface of the eye on each side, and as he did this he felt the pull from within. He slid through the crack and was swallowed by darkness.

On awakening Allal felt that he had returned from somewhere far away. He opened his eyes and saw, very close to him, what looked like the flank of an enormous beast, covered with coarse stiff hair. There was a repeated vibration in the air, like distant thunder curling around the edges of the sky. He sighed, or imagined that he did, for his breath made no sound. Then he shifted his head a bit, to try and see beyond the mass of hair beside him. Next he saw the ear, and he knew he was looking at his own head from the outside. He had not expected this; he had hoped only that his friend would come in and share his mind with him. But it did not strike him as being at all strange; he merely said to himself that now he was seeing through the eyes of the snake, rather than through his own.

Now he understood why the serpent had been so wary of him: from here the boy was a monstrous creature, with all the bristles on his head and his breathing that vibrated inside him like a far-off storm.

He uncoiled himself and glided across the floor to the alcove. There was a break in the mud wall wide enough to let him out. When he had pushed himself through, he lay full length on the ground in the crystalline moonlight, staring at the strangeness of the landscape, where shadows were not shadows.

He crawled around the side of the house and started up the road toward the town, rejoicing in a sense of freedom different from any he had ever imagined. There was no feeling of having a body, for he was perfectly contained in the skin that covered him. It was beautiful to caress the earth with the length of his belly as he moved along the silent road, smelling the sharp veins of wormwood in the wind. When the voice of the muezzin floated out over the countryside from the mosque, he could not hear it, or know that within the hour the night would end.

On catching sight of a man ahead, he left the road and hid behind a rock until the danger had passed. But then as he approached the town there began to be more people, so that he let himself down into the seguia, the deep ditch that went along beside the road. Here the stones and clumps of dead plants impeded his progress. He was still struggling along the floor of the seguia, pushing himself around the rocks and through the dry tangles of matted stalks left by the water, when dawn began to break.

The coming of daylight made him anxious and unhappy. He clambered up the bank of the seguia and raised his head to examine the road. A man walking past saw him, stood quite still, and then turned and ran back. Allal did not wait; he wanted now to get home as fast as possible.

Once he felt the thud of a stone as it struck the ground somewhere behind him. Quickly he threw himself over the edge of the seguia and rolled squirming down the bank. He knew the terrain here: where the road crossed the oued, there were two culverts not far apart. A man stood at some distance ahead of him with a shovel, peering down into the seguia. Allal kept moving, aware that he would reach the first culvert before the man could get to him.

The floor of the tunnel under the road was ribbed with hard little waves of sand. The smell of the mountains was in the air that moved through. There were places in here where he could have hidden, but he kept moving, and soon reached the other end. Then he continued to the second culvert and went under the road in the other direction, emerging once again into the seguia. Behind him several men had gathered at the entrance to the first culvert. One of them was on his knees, his head and shoulders inside the opening.

He now set out for the house in a straight line across the open ground, keeping his eye on the clump of palm beside it. The sun had just come up, and the stones began to cast long bluish shadows. All at once a small boy appeared from behind some nearby palms, saw him, and opened his eyes and mouth wide with fear. He was so close that Allal went straight to him and bit him in the leg. The boy ran wildly toward the group of men in the seguia.

Allal hurried on to the house, looking back only as he reached the hole between the mud bricks. Several men were running among the trees toward him. Swiftly he glided through into the alcove. The brown body still lay near the door. But there was no time, and Allal needed time to get back to it, to lie close to its head and say: Come here.

As he stared out into the room at the body, there was a great pounding on the door. The boy was on his feet at the first blow, as if a spring had been released, and Allal saw with despair the expression of total terror in his face, and the eyes with no mind behind them. The boy stood panting, his fists clenched. The door opened and some of the men peered inside. Then with a roar the boy lowered his head and rushed through the doorway. One of the men reached out to seize him, but lost his balance and fell. An instant later all of them turned and began to run through the palm grove after the naked figure.

Even when, from time to time, they lost sight of him, they could hear the screams, and then they would see him, between the palm trunks, still running. Finally he stumbled and fell face downward. It was then that they caught him, bound him, covered his nakedness, and took him away, to be sent one day soon to the hospital at Berrechid.

That afternoon the same group of men came to the house to carry out the search they had meant to make earlier. Allal lay in the alcove, dozing. When he awoke, they were already inside. He turned and crept to the hole. He saw the man waiting out there, a club in his hand.

The rage always had been in his heart; now it burst forth. As if his body were a whip, he sprang out into the room. The men nearest him were on their hands and knees, and Allal had the joy of pushing his fangs into two of them before a third severed his head with an axe.

MORLEY CALLAGHAN

Morley Callaghan, author of twelve novels, many stories, and an important memoir of Paris in the 1920s, *That Summer in Paris* (1963), enjoyed
a reputation outside Canada before he became a national literary figure. One of Ernest Hemingway's co-workers at *The Toronto Star*, he
published in Ezra Pound's avant-garde magazine *exile*, as well as in
Transition, Scribner's, The New Yorker and other journals. A gathering
of his work appeared in 1959 under the title *Morley Callaghan's Stories*. Yet from the 1930s until Edmund Wilson rediscovered him in
1960 — "a writer whose work may be mentioned without absurdity
in association with Chekhov's and Turgenev's" — he was virtually
unknown. With English critics responding warmly to his work in the
1970s, his fortunes again altered; throughout, however, Callaghan himself remained fiercely committed to a sense of artistic independence.

Born in Toronto in 1903 and (though he has never practised law) the
recipient of an Osgoode Hall law degree in 1928, he has won several
Canadian literary prizes. Yet his style and literary intention were shaped
less by the cultural milieu in Toronto than by what he refers to as his
own "North American" consciousness; Hemingway, Scott Fitzgerald,
and particularly Sherwood Anderson were his guides. He worked at
paring from his style any words that might draw attention away from
his protagonists; he was concerned with focusing on moral dilemmas
and with presenting clearly the forces that turn ordinary events in
ordinary lives into momentous drama. The result can more easily be
termed parable than naturalism. If his stories are realistic, they are
so only within their own terms; at their best they have the power of
truth without the interference of petty detail, and the credibility that
accompanies intense conviction. The impact of "Two Fishermen" (*Now
that April's here and other stories*, 1936) derives from the tension between
deeply held moral convictions and the placid surface style. Where the
story leads is into a contemplation of the ways in which abstract
principles — justice, for example — take real and imperfect forms, and
so rake the lives of the people for whom they still have meaning.

FOR FURTHER READING

Morley Callaghan, "An Ocean Away," *Times Literary Supplement*, 4
June 1964, p. 493.
Fraser Sutherland, *The Style of Innocence* (Toronto: Clarke, Irwin,
1972).
Edmund Wilson, *O Canada* (New York: Farrar, Straus & Giroux, 1965).

TWO FISHERMEN

The only reporter on the town paper, the *Examiner*, was Michael Foster, a tall, long-legged, eager young fellow, who wanted to go to the city some day and work on an important newspaper.

The morning he went into Bagley's Hotel, he wasn't at all sure of himself. He went over to the desk and whispered to the proprietor, Ted Bagley, "Did he come here, Mr. Bagley?"

Bagley said slowly, "Two men came here from this morning's train. They're registered." He put his spatulate forefinger on the open book and said, "Two men. One of them's a drummer. This one here, T. Woodley. I know because he was through this way last year and just a minute ago he walked across the road to Molson's hardware store. The other one . . . here's his name, K. Smith."

"Who's K. Smith?" Michael asked.

"I don't know. A mild, harmless-looking little guy."

"Did he look like the hangman, Mr. Bagley?"

"I couldn't say that, seeing as I never saw one. He was awfully polite and asked where he could get a boat so he could go fishing on the lake this evening, so I said likely down at Smollet's place by the power-house."

"Well, thanks. I guess if he was the hangman, he'd go over to the jail first," Michael said.

He went along the street, past the Baptist church to the old jail with the high brick fence around it. Two tall maple trees, with branches drooping low over the sidewalk, shaded one of the walls from the morning sunlight. Last night, behind those walls, three carpenters, working by lamplight, had nailed the timbers for the scaffold. In the morning, young Thomas Delaney, who had grown up in the town, was being hanged: he had killed old Mathew Rhinehart whom he had caught molesting his wife when she had been berrypicking in the hills behind the town. There had been a struggle and Thomas Delaney had taken a bad beating before he had killed Rhinehart. Last night a crowd had gathered on the sidewalk by the lamppost, and while moths and smaller insects swarmed around the high blue carbon light, the crowd had thrown sticks and bottles and small stones at the out-of-town workmen in the jail yard. Billy Hilton, the town constable, had stood under the light with his head down, pretending not to notice anything. Thomas Delaney was only three years older than Michael Foster.

Michael went straight to the jail office, where Henry Steadman, the sheriff, a squat, heavy man, was sitting on the desk idly wetting his long moustaches with his tongue. "Hello, Michael, what do you want?" he asked.

"Hello, Mr. Steadman, the *Examiner* would like to know if the hangman arrived yet."

"Why ask me?"

"I thought he'd come here to test the gallows. Won't he?"

"My, you're a smart young fellow, Michael, thinking of that."

"Is he in there now, Mr. Steadman?"

"Don't ask me. I'm saying nothing. Say, Michael, do you think there's going to be trouble? You ought to know. Does anybody seem sore at me? I can't do nothing. You can see that."

"I don't think anybody blames you, Mr. Steadman. Look here, can't I see the hangman? Is his name K. Smith?"

"What does it matter to you, Michael? Be a sport, go on away and don't bother us any more."

"All right, Mr. Steadman," Michael said very competently, "just leave it to me."

Early that evening, when the sun was setting, Michael Foster walked south of the town on the dusty road leading to the powerhouse and Smollet's fishing pier. He knew that if Mr. K. Smith wanted to get a boat he would go down to the pier. Fine powdered road dust whitened Michael's shoes. Ahead of him he saw the power-plant, square and low, and the smooth lake water. Behind him the sun was hanging over the blue hills beyond the town and shining brilliantly on square patches of farm land. The air around the power-house smelt of steam.

Out of the jutting, tumbledown pier of rock and logs, Michael saw a little fellow without a hat, sitting down with his knees hunched up to his chin, a very small man with little gray baby curls on the back of his neck, who stared steadily far out over the water. In his hand he was holding a stick with a heavy fishing-line twined around it and a gleaming copper spoon bait, the hooks brightened with bits of feathers such as they used in the neighbourhood when trolling for lake trout. Apprehensively Michael walked out over the rocks toward the stranger and called, "Were you thinking of going fishing, mister?" Standing up, the man smiled. He had a large head, tapering down to a small chin, a birdlike neck and a very wistful smile. Puckering his mouth up, he said shyly to Michael, "Did you intend to go fishing?"

"That's what I came down here for. I was going to get a boat back at the boat-house there. How would you like if we went together?"

"I'd like it first rate," the shy little man said eagerly. "We could take turns rowing. Does that appeal to you?"

"Fine. Fine. You wait here and I'll go back to Smollet's place and ask for a row-boat and I'll row around here and get you."

"Thanks. Thanks very much," the mild little man said as he began to untie his line. He seemed very enthusiastic.

When Michael brought the boat around to the end of the old pier and invited the stranger to make himself comfortable so he could handle the line, the stranger protested comically that he ought to be allowed to row.

Pulling strongly at the oars, Michael was soon out in the deep water and the little man was letting his line out slowly. In one furtive glance, he had noticed that the man's hair, gray at the temples, was inclined to curl to his ears. The line was out full length. It was twisted around the little man's forefinger, which he let drag in the water. And then Michael looked full at him and smiled because he thought he seemed so meek and quizzical. "He's a nice little guy," Michael assured himself and he said, "I work on the town paper, the *Examiner*."

"Is it a good paper? Do you like the work?"

"Yes. But it's nothing like a first-class city paper and I don't expect to be working on it long. I want to get a reporter's job on a city paper. My name's Michael Foster."

"Mine's Smith. Just call me Smitty."

"I was wondering if you'd been over to the jail yet."

Up to this time the little man had been smiling with the charming ease of a small boy who finds himself free, but now he became furtive and disappointed. Hesitating, he said, "Yes, I was over there first thing this morning."

"Oh, I just knew you'd go there," Michael said. They were a bit afraid of each other. By this time they were far out on the water which had a mill-pond smoothness. The town seemed to get smaller, with white houses in rows and streets forming geometric patterns, just as the blue hills behind the town seemed to get larger at sundown.

Finally Michael said, "Do you know this Thomas Delaney that's dying in the morning?" He knew his voice was slow and resentful.

"No. I don't know anything about him. I never read about them. Aren't there any fish at all in this old lake? I'd like to catch some fish," he said rapidly. "I told my wife I'd bring her home some fish." Glancing at Michael, he was appealing, without speaking, that they should do nothing to spoil an evening's fishing.

The little man began to talk eagerly about fishing as he pulled out a small flask from his hip pocket. "Scotch," he said, chuckling with delight. "Here, take a swig." Michael drank from the flask and passed it back. Tilting his head back and saying, "Here's to you, Michael," the little man took a long pull at the flask. "The only time I take a drink," he said still chuckling, "is when I go on a fishing trip by myself. I usually go by myself," he added apologetically as if he wanted the young fellow to see how much he appreciated his company.

They had gone far out on the water but they had caught nothing. It began to get dark. "No fish tonight, I guess, Smitty," Michael said.

"It's a crying shame," Smitty said. "I looked forward to coming up here when I found out the place was on the lake. I wanted to get some fishing in. I promised my wife I'd bring her back some fish. She'd often like to go fishing with me, but of course, she can't because she can't travel around from place to place like I do. Whenever I get a call to go some place, I always look at the map to see if it's by a lake or on a river, then I take my lines and hooks along."

"If you took another job, you and your wife could probably go fishing together," Michael suggested.

"I don't know about that. We sometimes go fishing together anyway."
He looked away, waiting for Michael to be repelled and insist that he
ought to give up the job. And he wasn't ashamed as he looked down at
the water, but he knew that Michael thought he ought to be ashamed.
"Somebody's got to do my job. There's got to be a hangman," he said.

"I just meant that if it was such disagreeable work, Smitty."

The little man did not answer for a long time. Michael rowed steadily
with sweeping, tireless strokes. Huddled at the end of the boat, Smitty
suddenly looked up with a kind of melancholy hopelessness and said
mildly, "The job hasn't been so disagreeable."

"Good God, man, you don't mean you like it?"

"Oh, no," he said, to be obliging, as if he knew what Michael expected
him to say. "I mean you get used to it, that's all." But he looked down
again at the water, knowing he ought to be ashamed of himself.

"Have you got any children?"

"I sure have. Five. The oldest boy is fourteen. It's funny, but they're
all a lot bigger and taller than I am. Isn't that funny?"

They started a conversation about fishing rivers that ran into the lake
farther north. They felt friendly again. The little man, who had an
extraordinary gift for story-telling, made many quaint faces, puckered
up his lips, screwed up his eyes and moved around restlessly as if he
wanted to get up in the boat and stride around for the sake of more
expression. Again he brought out the whiskey flask and Michael stopped
rowing. Grinning, they toasted each other and said together, "Happy
days." The boat remained motionless on the placid water. Far out, the
sun's last rays gleamed on the water-line. And then it got dark and they
could only see the town lights. It was time to turn around and pull for
the shore. The little man tried to take the oars from Michael, who shook
his head resolutely and insisted that he would prefer to have his friend
catch a fish on the way back to the shore.

"It's too late now, and we may have scared all the fish away," Smitty
laughed happily. "But we're having a grand time, aren't we?"

When they reached the old pier by the power-house, it was full night
and they hadn't caught a single fish. As the boat bumped against the
rocks Michael said, "You can get out here. I'll take the boat around to
Smollet's."

"Won't you be coming my way?"

"Not just now. I'll probably talk with Smollet a while."

The little man got out of the boat and stood on the pier looking down
at Michael. "I was thinking dawn would be the best time to catch some
fish," he said. "At about five o'clock. I'll have an hour and a half to
spare anyway. How would you like that?" He was speaking with so
much eagerness that Michael found himself saying, "I could try. But if
I'm not here at dawn, you go on without me."

"All right. I'll walk back to the hotel now."

"Good night, Smitty."

"Good night, Michael. We had a fine neighbourly time, didn't we?"

As Michael rowed the boat around to the boat-house, he hoped that Smitty wouldn't realize he didn't want to be seen walking back to town with him. And later, when he was going slowly along the dusty road in the dark and hearing all the crickets chirping in the ditches, he couldn't figure out why he felt so ashamed of himself.

At seven o'clock next morning Thomas Delaney was hanged in the town jail yard. There was hardly a breeze on that leaden gray morning and there were no small whitecaps out over the lake. It would have been a fine morning for fishing. Michael went down to the jail, for he thought it his duty as a newspaperman to have all the facts, but he was afraid he might get sick. He hardly spoke to all the men and women who were crowded under the maple trees by the jail wall. Everybody he knew was staring at the wall and muttering angrily. Two of Thomas Delaney's brothers, big, strapping fellows with bearded faces, were there on the sidewalk. Three automobiles were at the front of the jail.

Michael, the town newspaperman, was admitted into the courtyard by old Willie Mathews, one of the guards, who said that two newspapermen from the city were at the gallows on the other side of the building. "I guess you can go around there, too, if you want to," Mathews said, as he sat down slowly on the step. White-faced, and afraid, Michael sat down on the step with Mathews and they waited and said nothing.

At last the old fellow said, "Those people outside there are pretty sore, ain't they?"

"They're pretty sullen, all right. I saw two of Delaney's brothers there."

"I wish they'd go," Mathews said. "I don't want to see anything. I didn't even look at Delaney. I don't want to hear anything. I'm sick." He put his head back against the wall and closed his eyes.

The old fellow and Michael sat close together till a small procession came around the corner from the other side of the yard. First came Mr. Steadman, the sheriff, with his head down as though he were crying, then Dr. Parker, the physician, then two hard-looking young newspapermen from the city, walking with their hats on the backs of their heads, and behind them came the little hangman, erect, stepping out with military precision and carrying himself with a strange cocky dignity. He was dressed in a long black cutaway coat with gray striped trousers, a gates-ajar collar and a narrow red tie, as if he alone felt the formal importance of the occasion. He walked with brusque precision till he saw Michael, who was standing up, staring at him with his mouth open.

The little hangman grinned and as soon as the procession reached the doorstep, he shook hands with Michael. They were all looking at Michael. As though his work were over now, the hangman said eagerly to Michael, "I thought I'd see you here. You didn't get down to the pier at dawn?"

"No. I couldn't make it."

"That was tough, Michael. I looked for you," he said. "But never mind. I've got something for you." As they all went into the jail, Dr. Parker glanced angrily at Michael, then turned his back on him. In the office, where the doctor prepared to sign a certificate, Smitty was bending down over his fishing-basket which was in the corner. Then he pulled out two good-sized salmon-bellied trout, folded in a newspaper, and said, "I was saving these for you, Michael. I got four in an hour's fishing." Then he said, "I'll talk about that later, if you'll wait. We'll be busy here, and I've got to change my clothes."

Michael went out to the street with Dr. Parker and the two city newspapermen. Under his arm he was carrying the fish, folded in the newspaper. Outside, at the jail door, Michael thought that the doctor and the two newpapermen were standing a little apart from him. Then the small crowd, with their clothes all dust-soiled from the road, surged forward, and the doctor said to them, "You might as well go home, boys. It's all over."

"Where's old Steadman?" somebody demanded. "We'll wait for the hangman," somebody else shouted.

The doctor walked away by himself. For a while Michael stood beside the two city newspapermen, and tried to look as nonchalant as they were looking, but he lost confidence in them when he smelled whiskey. They only talked to each other. Then they mingled with the crowd, and Michael stood alone. At last he could stand there no longer looking at all those people he knew so well, so he, too, moved out and joined the crowd.

When the sheriff came out with the hangman and two of the guards, they got half-way down to one of the automobiles before someone threw an old boot. Steadman ducked into one of the cars, as the boot hit him on the shoulder, and the two guards followed him. Those in the car must have thought at first that the hangman was with them for the car suddenly shot forward, leaving him alone on the sidewalk. The crowd threw small rocks and sticks, hooting at him as the automobile backed up slowly towards him. One small stone hit him on the head. Blood trickled from the side of his head as he looked around helplessly at all the angry people. He had the same expression on his face, Michael thought, as he had had last night when he had seemed ashamed and had looked down steadily at the water. Only now, he looked around wildly, looking for someone to help him as the crowd kept pelting him. Farther and farther Michael backed into the crowd and all the time he felt dreadlully ashamed as though he were betraying Smitty, who last night had had such a good neighbourly time with him. "It's different now, it's different," he kept thinking, as he held the fish in the newspaper tight under his arm. Smitty started to run toward the automobile, but James Mortimer, a big fisherman, shot out his foot and tripped him and sent him sprawling on his face.

Mortimer, the big fisherman, looking for something to throw, said to Michael, "Sock him, sock him."

Michael shook his head and felt sick.

"What's the matter with you, Michael?"

"Nothing. I got nothing against him."

The big fisherman started pounding his fists up and down in the air. "He just doesn't mean anything to me at all," Michael said quickly. The fisherman, bending down, kicked a small rock loose from the road bed and heaved it at the hangman. Then he said, "What are you holding there, Michael, what's under your arm? Fish. Pitch them at him. Here, give them to me." Still in a fury, he snatched the fish, and threw them one at a time at the little man just as he was getting up from the road. The fish fell in the thick dust in front of him, sending up a little cloud. Smitty seemed to stare at the fish with his mouth hanging open, then he didn't even look at the crowd. That expression on Smitty's face as he saw the fish on the road made Michael hot with shame and he tried to get out of the crowd.

Smitty had his hands over his head, to shield his face as the crowd pelted him, yelling, "Sock the little rat. Throw the runt in the lake." The sheriff pulled him into the automobile. The car shot forward in a cloud of dust.

PETER CAREY

Born in Bacchus Marsh, Victoria in 1943, and now a resident of Sydney, Peter Carey is one of a half dozen contemporary stylists who have been refashioning short fiction in Australia. Like the others — among them Murray Bail, Frank Moorhouse, and Michael Wilding, with whom he is often compared — Carey is a social iconoclast, working in fantasy. Elements of the fantastic are everywhere in his work, yet they do not provide escapist entertainment; paradoxically the fantastic serves instead to expose the ordinary cruelties that people tend passively to accept in their society. Writing in his introduction to *New Australian Short Stories* (1981), Craig Munro refers to Carey's "uncanny flair for significant settings and events." The significance derives from the associative resonances of his settings; the reader supplies it, recognizing the degree of overlap between the fictional exaggerations and ordinary life. The stories, Munro adds, "seem to fuse the past, present, and future into super-real scenarios in which the gap between the observed and the imagined disappears."

Carey has published two short-story collections, *The Fat Man in History* (1974), in which "Crabs" appeared, and *War Crimes* (1979). His novel *Bliss* appeared in 1981; *Illywacket*, in 1985. Set in the future/present setting of a drive-in movie lot, "Crabs" explores the implicit violence of a world whose only realities are egomania and make-believe. It is a world which is all the more devastating insofar as it is also exclusive, leaving Carey's character caught between equal forms of spiritual death: a mindless security and an aimless freedom.

FOR FURTHER READING

Teresa Dovey, "An Infinite Onion: Narrative Structure in Peter Carey's Fiction," *Australian Literary Studies* 11, no. 2 (October 1983): 195–204.

Van Ikin, "Peter Carey: the stories," *Science Fiction* 1 (June 1977): 19–29.

Craig Munro, Interview with Peter Carey, *Australian Literary Studies* 8 (1977): 182–87.

Elizabeth Webby, "Australian Short Fiction from *While the Billy Boils* to *The Everlasting Secret Family*," *Australian Literary Studies* 10 (1981): 147–64.

CRABS

Crabs is very neat in everything he does. His movements are almost fussy, but he has so much fight in his delicate frame that they're not fussy at all. Lately he has been eating. When Frank eats one steak, Crabs eats two. When Frank has a pint of milk, Crabs drinks two. He spends a lot of time lying on his bed, groaning, because of the food. But he's building up. At night he runs five miles to Clayton. He always means to run back, but he always ends up on the train, hot and sweating and sticking to the seat. His aim is to increase his weight and get a job driving for Allied Panel and Towing. Already he has his licence but he's too small, not tough enough to beat off the competition at a crash scene.

Frank drives night shift. He tells Crabs to get into something else, not the tow truck game, but Crabs has his heart set on the tow trucks. In his mind he sees himself driving at 80 m.p.h. with the light flashing, arriving at the scene first, getting the job, being interviewed by the guy from 3UZ's Night Watch.

At the moment Crabs weighs eight stone and four pounds, but he's increasing his weight all the time.

He is known as Crabs because of the time last year when he claimed to have the Crabs and everyone knew he was bullshitting. And then Frank told Trev that Crabs was still a virgin and so they called him Crabs. He doesn't mind it so much now. He's not a virgin now and he's more comfortable with the name. It gives him a small distinction, character is how he looks at it.

Crabs appears to be very small behind the wheel of this 1956 Dodge. He sits on two cushions so he can see properly. Carmen sits close beside him, a little shorter, because of the cushions, and around them is the vast empty space of the car — leopard skin stretching everywhere, taut and beautiful.

The night is sweet, filled with the red tail lights of other cars, sweeping headlights, flickering neon signs. Crab drives fast, keeping the needle on the 70 mark, sweating with fear and excitement as he chops in and out of the traffic. He keeps his small dark eyes on the rear-vision mirror, half hoping for the flashing blue lights that will announce the arrival of the cops. Maybe he'll accelerate, maybe he'll pull over. He doesn't know, but he dreams of that sweet moment when he will plant his foot and all the power of this hotted-up Dodge will roar to life and he will leave the cops behind. The papers will say: "An early model American car drew away from police at 100 m.p.h."

Beside him Carmen is quiet. She keeps using the cigarette lighter because she likes to use it. She thinks he doesn't see her, the way she throws away her cigarettes after a few drags, so she can use the cigarette lighter again. The cigarette lighter and the leopard skin upholstery make her feel great.

The leopard skin upholstery is why they're going to a drive-in tonight. Because Carmen whispered in his ear that she'd like to do it on the leopard skin upholstery. She was shy. It pleased him, those small hot words blowing on his ear. She blushed when he looked at her. He liked that.

He didn't tell Frank about the leopard skin. He didn't think it was good for Frank to know how Carmen felt about it. Anyway Frank hates the leopard skin. He normally keeps it covered with a couple of old grey blankets. He didn't tell Frank about the drive-in either because of the Karboys.

The Karboys have come about slowly and become more famous as the times have got worse. With every strike they seem to grow in strength. And now that imports are restricted and most of the car factories are closed down they've got worse. A year ago you only had to worry if your car broke down on the highway or in a tough suburb. They'd come and strip down your car and leave you with nothing but the picked bones. Now it's different. If you buy a used car part (and you try and get a *new* carbie, say, for a 1956 Dodge) it's sure to come from some Karboy gang or other and who's to say they didn't kill the poor bastard who owned the Dodge it came off. Everytime Frank buys a part he crosses himself. It 's a big joke with Frank, crossing himself. Crabs too. They both have this big thing going about crossing themselves. It's a joke they have. Carmen doesn't get it, but she never was a Catholic anyway.

The official word is not to resist the Karboys, to give them all your car if you have to, but you don't see a man giving his car away that easily. So a lot of drivers are carrying guns, mostly sawn off .22s. And if you've got any sense you keep your doors locked and windows up and you keep your car in good nick, so you don't get stranded anywhere. The insurance companies have altered the wars and civil disturbances clauses to cover themselves, so you take good care of your car because you'll never get another one if you lose it.

And you don't go to drive-ins. Drive-ins are bad news. You get the odd killing. The cops are there but they don't help much. Last week a cop shot another cop who was knocking off a bumper bar. He thought the cop was a Karboy but he was only supplementing his income.

So Crabs hasn't told Frank what he's doing tonight. And he's got some of Frank's defensive gear out of the truck. This is a sharpened bike chain and a heavy duty spanner. He's got them under the front seat and he's half hoping for a little trouble. He's scared, but he's hoping. Carmen hasn't said anything about the Karboys and Crabs wonders if she even knows about them. There's so much she doesn't know about. She spends all day reading papers but she never takes anything in. He wonders what she thinks about when she reads.

There are more cars at the drive-in than he expected and he drives around until he finds the cop car. He plans on parking nearby, just to be on the safe side. But Carmen is very edgy about the police, because she is only just sixteen and her mother is still looking for her, and she makes Crabs park somewhere else. In the harsh lights her small face seems very pale and frightened. So Crabs finds a lonely spot up in the back corner and combs his thick black hair with a tortoise-shell comb while he waits for the lights to go out. Carmen arranges the blankets over the windows. Frank has got this all worked out, from the times when he went to drive-ins. There are little hooks around the tops of all the windows so they can be curtained with towels or blankets. Frank is ingenious. In the old days he used to remove all the inside door handles too, just in case his girl friends wanted to run away.

They put down the layback seats and Carmen unpins her long red hair. She only pinned it up because Crabs said how he liked her unpinning it. He sits like a small Italian buddha in the back seat and watches her, watches her hair fall.

She says, you're neat, you know that, very neat.

When she says that he doesn't know how to take it. She means that he is almost dainty. She says, you're sort of . . . She is going to say "graceful" but she doesn't.

Crabs says, shut-up, and begins to struggle with the buckle of his motorcycle boots. Crabs never had a motorbike, but he bought the boots off Frank who was driving one night when there was a bike in a prang. He got them from the ambulance driver for a packet of fags. Crabs bought them for three packets of Marlborough. There was a bit of blood, but he covered it up with raven oil.

Crabs really likes heavy things. Also he dislikes laces. All his shoes have zips, buckles, or slip on. When he was at the tech they used to tie him to the chain wire fence by his shoe laces, every lunch time. They tied him to the fence right in front of the Principal's window and the only way he could ever get out was to break the laces, because he couldn't bend down—if he bent down they kicked him in the arse. Crabs's father was always coming up to see the Principal and complaining about the shoe laces but it never did any good. Once Crabs came to school with zip-up boots and they stole them from him so he had to wear the laces, for his own protection.

The first film is crackling through the loud speaker and Carmen sits up near the front window with only her black pants on, her hair down, covered with a heavy sweet perfume she always wears. Crabs shyly eyes her breasts which are small and tight. He would like her to have big boobs, like the girls in *Playboy*. That is the only way he would like to improve her, for her to have big boobs, but he never says anything about this, even to himself. He says, help me with my boot. He is embarrassed to ask her. He knew this would happen and it was worrying him. He says, just pull. Normally Frank pulls off his boots for him. The boots are one size too small but they don't hurt too much.

Crabs lies back with his shirt off, his black jeans down, and one sock off while Carmen pulls at the second boot. Crabs is coming on fuzzy as he watches Carmen stretched back, her face screwed up with concentration and effort. He watches the small soft muscle on the inside of her thigh and the small soft hollow it has, just where it disappears into her pants.

She says, hey careful. The boot is still half on the foot.

He is on top of her and she, giggling and groaning, manoeuvres sweetly below him, reciting nursery rhymes with her arse. He thinks, for the hundredth time, of the change that comes over her when she screws. Until now she is nothing much, talking dumb or sleeping or listening to the serials on the radio. It is only now she wakes up. And you could never guess, no matter how much you knew, that this girl would turn on like this. She sits around all day eating peanut butter and honey sandwiches or reading the *Women's Weekly* or reading the Tatt's results or the grocery advertisements. Crabs feels he is drowning in a sea of honey. He says, "humpty-dumpty." Carmen, swerving, swaying, singing beneath him says, "Wha?"

Crabs says, bang, bang-bang-bang.

Carmen, her mascara-smudged eyes blinking beneath his mascara-smudged lips giggles, groans, arches like a cat.

Crabs says, bang, bang, bang-bang.

Carmen arches. Crabs thinks she will break in half. Him too. She falls. He rolls and keeps rolling down to the left hand side of the car. He says shit, oh *shit!*

The car is on one side, listing sharply. Carmen lies on her back, smiling at the ceiling. She says, mmm.

Crabs says, Jesus Christ, someone's knocked off the wheels, Jesus CHRIST.

Carmen turns on her side and says, the Karboys. So she knew about them all the time. She sounds pleased.

Crabs says, you'll stain the upholstery. He searches for the other boot and the bike chain.

He runs through the cars. He doesn't know what he is looking for, just those two wheels, one will do because he has the spare. His white jacket is weighed down by the chain. He runs through the cars. Sometimes he stops. He knocks on windows but no-one will answer. Everyone's too scared.

He rounds the back of a late model Chevvy and comes face to face with the cop car. One of the cops is putting something in the boot. Crabs is convinced that it's the wheels. He keeps going past the car, walks round the perimeter of the drive-in and returns to the Dodge. Carmen has taken the blankets down and is watching the film. He tells her his theory about the cops and she says, shh, watch.

The manager fills out the two forms and gives them meal tickets. He is a slow fat man with a worn grey cardigan. He explains the meal ticket system — the government will supply them with ten dollars' worth of tickets each week, these tickets can be spent at the Ezy-Eatin right here on the drive-in. If they run out of tickets, that's too bad, because it's all they'll get. If they want blankets they have to sign for them now. Carmen asks about banana fritters. The manager looks at her feet and slowly raises his half-shut eyes until they meet hers. He says that banana fritters are only made at night, but she can purchase anything sold in the cafeteria.

The manager then asks if there's anyone they want to notify. Crabs begins to give him Frank's name and then stops. The manager waits and licks the stubby pencil he is using. Crabs says, it doesn't matter. The manager says, that's your decision. Crabs says, no it doesn't matter, forget it. He can see Frank when he gets the notification, when he learns that his Dodge has lost two wheels, when he learns Crabs took it to a drive-in. He'd come out and kill them both.

Carmen says, we'll walk home next Saturday.

The manager sighs loudly and scratches his balls. Crabs wonders if he should hit him. He's got the chain in his jacket. The manager is saying, "Now this time listen to what I tell you. First, you ain't got no public transport . . ."

Carmen says, "I didn't *mean* public transport. I . . ."

". . . you don't have a bus or a train because buses and trains don't come to the Star Drive-in. They've got no reason to, do they? Secondly, you can't walk down that highway, young lady, because it's an 'S' road. And if you know the laws of the land you ain't permitted to walk on or near an 'S' road."

He looks across at Crabs and says, "And dogs aren't allowed on 'S' roads, or bicycles or learner drivers. So we're not allowed to let you out of that gate until this bloody government finds a bus that they can spare to get you all home. There are now seventy-three people in your situation. I don't like it either. I don't make a profit from you so don't think I want you around. So we'll all have to wait until something is done. And we all pray to God that something's done soon." He crosses himself absently and Carmen laughs.

The manager stares at her blankly. Crabs would like to lay that chain across his fat face. The man says, "You want me to notify your mother?" and Carmen becomes very quiet and smoothes her skirt with great concentration. She says "no" very quietly.

The manager is standing up. He shakes them both by the hand. He advises them to sign for blankets but they say no, they have some. He has become very fatherly. At the door he shakes their hands again and says he hopes they can make themselves comfortable.

It is bright sunlight outside. Carmen says, he seemed nice.

Crabs says, he's a bastard. I'll get him.

Carmen says, for what?

Crabs says, for being a bastard.

Carmen takes his hand and they walk to the Ezy-Eatin, dodging in and out of the temporary clothes lines that have sprung up since last night. There are about thirty cars scattered throughout the drive-in. Some kids are playing on the swings beneath the screen. In front of the Ezy-Eatin a blonde woman of about forty is hanging out her washing and wearing a grey blanket like a cape. She smiles at them. Crabs scowls. When they pass she calls out, "Honey-mooners," and a man laughs. Crabs takes his hand out of Carmen's but she grabs it back.

The woman at the Ezy-Eatin explains to Carmen about the banana fritters, that they only have them at night, so she has an ice cream sundae instead. Crabs has a chocolate malted with double malt. The woman takes the coupons. Carmen says, isn't it lovely, like a picnic.

It takes him a week to collect the bricks for the back wheel. When he has enough he chocks them under the rear axle and then puts the spare on the front. Carmen reads comics and listens to the music they play through the speakers. Crabs goes looking for another Dodge to get a wheel from. There aren't any.

At night he wanders round the drive-in tapping on car windows. He plans to get a lift out, get a wheel somehow, and return. But no-one will open their windows.

He begins to collect petrol caps and hub caps, just to keep himself occupied. When he has enough he'll find a Karboy to swap his lot for a wheel. He feels heavy and dull and spends a lot of time sleeping. Carmen seems happy. She eats banana fritters at night and watches the movie. Crabs strips down the engine and puts it together again. A lot of the day he spends balancing the flow through the twin carbies, until, one afternoon at about four o'clock, he runs out of petrol.

There is no way out. Carmen tells him this every day. Each day she comes back from the Ladies' with new reasons why there is no way out. At the Ladies' they know everything. They stand and squat for hours on end, their arms folded, holding up their breasts. At the Men's it is the same. But Crabs shits in silence with his ears disconnected. He has no wish to know why there is no way out.

He is waiting for the arrival of a 1956 Dodge. He eats little, saving his coupons to exchange for a wheel and hubcap he will need. There are dozens of other wheels he could use, but he wants to return Frank's Dodge in perfect condition. So he waits, lying on the leopard skin upholstery he has come to hate. He tries not to think of Frank but he has nothing else to think of. He is not used to this, doing nothing. He has always been busy before, getting fit, or going to the pictures or out in the truck with Frank. And all day he has worked, delivering engravers' proofs in the Mini Minor. He hated that Mini. He misses that hate. He misses driving it, knocking shit out of its piddling little engine, revving it hard enough to burst, waiting for the day when he would work at Allied Panel and Towing.

But his mind keeps coming back to Frank and every day the pain is worse. He tries to think of reasons why Frank will forgive him. He can't think of any. He tries to make Frank's big spud face smile at him and say, forget it, mate, it happens to the best of us. But the face contorts, the big knobbly jaw juts and he sees Frank take out his teeth, ready for a fight. Or he sees Frank's hand holding the shifting wrench.

Frank said, you get a nice car, people respect you when you got a nice car. You go somewhere, a motel, and you got a nice car, they look after you. Frank looked after Crabs. Frank said, you build up your body, then you can stand up for yourself anywhere. You build up your body and you can walk in anywhere and know how to look after yourself. He gave him the chest expanders and an old photo he had of Charles Atlas. Frank said, that man is a genius.

Crabs hid in the Dodge and tried to keep his mind free of all these things. He tried to keep his mind free by keeping busy with Carmen but she didn't like doing it in the daylight.

Carmen lies on the roof, sunbaking while Crabs hides in the Dodge. He makes plans for getting out and he tells them to Carmen. But the wire is now electrified. But the drive-in is closed to visitors. But the security cars circle the perimeter all night.

Crabs walks through the drive-in each morning after breakfast, looking for the Dodge he is sure will arrive, somehow, one night. He picks his way through the clothes lines, around the temporary toilet facilities, skirts round the rubbish disposal holes, edges by the card games and temporary cricket pitches. It is like the beach when he was a kid. Everybody is doing something. He would like to blow them all up.

He looks at Carmen's face and tries to see exactly what has happened to it. It is older. Her sweater is covered with small "pills" of wool. Her hair is pulled back and done in a plait but doesn't hold in her ears which seem to stick out. She has got fatter. Her mouth is full of hamburger while she tells him. He knows. He has seen it. He watched it all. She knows he saw it. She wipes her mouth clean of hamburger grease with the arm of her sweater, and tells him about what happened last night.

He says, I know, I saw.

But she tells him, because she feels he sees nothing. She has told everyone at the Ladies' about him and they've come to gaze at him, individually and in groups. He puts up the blankets to keep out their stares, but Carmen invites them in. Their husbands come and invite him to cricket or two-up. He thinks of Frank and the Dodge that will come.

He says, I saw.

He saw, last night, the convoy of trucks come in through the main gate of the drive-in. Everybody went to look. Crabs went afterwards and stood on the edge of the crowd. For some reason they cheered, they cheered the trucks and the drivers as if they were liberating troops. But the trucks only held more cars, cars without wheels, cars without engines, crippled cars, cars unable to move. Crabs watched silently, wondering what it meant.

He watched while the huge mobile crane shifted the cars from the trucks to the ground. He watched the new cars being arranged in lines, in vacant spaces. And when everyone else had lost interest he still watched. He saw the prefabricated Nissen huts come on a huge Mercedes low-loader. He watched the Nissen huts unloaded under the harsh glare of searchlights that had been mounted on top of the old projection room, on top of the Ezy-Eatin.

And he was still there at dawn, when the low-loaders, the cranes, and the other trucks had gone, he was there when the buses began to arrive.

He was there, removing two wheels from a 1956 Dodge.

Everybody goes to stare at the arrivals. Carmen is frantic, she begs him to come. He has never seen her so happy, so angry. Her eyes are sharp and clear. He would like to screw her but he is busy. He would love to hold her, to calm her, warm her, cool her. But he has two wheels from a 1956 Dodge and he is busy. In the corner of his eyes he sees exotic things: cloaks, robes, dark skin, swarthy complexions. He hears voices he doesn't understand, he thinks of the tower of Babel and then he thinks of the Sunday School where he heard about the tower of Babel and then he thinks about peppercorn trees and then he thinks of the two wheels and he tells Carmen, soon, I'll come soon.

The jack is in good shape. He has kept it in good shape. He jacks up the back of the car and removes the bricks. Then he puts on the new wheel. The tyre is a little flat. He guesses at about fifteen pounds per square inch, but it is good enough. Then he removes the front wheel, and puts it back in the spare compartment, and then he puts on the new front wheel.

He will need petrol. Maybe oil too.

He feels as if he is alive again. He will bring the car back to Frank. He will tell a story to him, a fantastic story. He was driving in the country. He was forced off the road by a Mercedes low-loader, and cut off by a jeep. They lifted the Dodge onto the low-loader with Crabs and Carmen inside, and drove off to a country rendezvous. There was a gang. Crabs joined the gang. At night they drove off with the low-loaders. Crabs drove one of them, a Leyland. They stole cars from off the highway. Made the drivers walk home. Crabs became their leader after a fight. He regained the Dodge. Rebuilt it. Then he escaped and brought it back here, to you, Frank.

He is happy. There is tumult around him. He will need to check the oil and petrol. He lifts the bonnet and has the dip stick half out when he notices the carbies are missing. He stops, frozen. Then, slowly he begins the check. The generator is gone. The distributor also. The fan and fan belt. The battery together with the leads. Both radiator hoses and the air cleaner.

Something inside him goes very taut. Some invisible string is taken in one more notch.

He walks, very slowly, back to the newly arrived Dodge. There are people in it. He ignores them. He opens the door and tugs the bonnet release catch. Someone pulls at his clothing. He knocks them off. He opens the bonnet and looks in, looking for the parts he will salvage. There is nothing there. No engine. A dirty piece of plywood has been placed inside to give the engine compartment a floor. Some small chickens, very young, are drinking water from a bowl in the middle.

He lies back on the leopard skin and gazes at the sights outside. Carmen is beside him. She is snuggled up against him. She is saying a lot. Slowly Crabs begins to see what his eyes see.

A large group of Indians, dressed in saris, are gathered around a battered blue Ford Falcon. One of them, an old man, squats on the roof. The Ford Falcon was delivered last night. A group of men, possibly Italians, lean against the front of Frank's Dodge. They are laughing. They seem to be playing a game, taking turns to throw a small stone so that it lands near the front wheel of a bright yellow Holden Monaro. Small children, black, with swollen bellies run past shouting, chased by a small English child with spectacles.

Carmen is crying. She is saying, they are everywhere. They stare at me. They want to rape me.

Crabs has been thinking. He has been thinking very deeply. Things have been occurring to him and he has reached a conclusion. He has formed the conclusion into a sentence and he tells Carmen the sentence.

Crabs says, to be free, you must be a motor car or vehicle in good health.

Carmen is crying. She says, you are mad, mad. They all said you were going mad.

Crabs says, no, not mad, think about the words — to be free, you . . .

She puts her hand over his mouth. She says, it stinks. It stinks. The whole place stinks of filthy wogs. They're dirty, filthy, everything is horrible.

Crabs sees a car moving along the lane that separates this line of cars from the next. It is a 1954 Austin Sheerline. Inside is the manager, he sits behind the wheel stiffly, looking neither left nor right. It is moving. Crabs is excited for a moment, wondering if he can buy the car with his meal tickets. The car narrowly misses the Indian family and, as it passes in front of him, he sees that the Austin is being pushed by an English family, a man, a woman, and three young boys.

Crabs says, a motor car or vehicle in good health.

Flags, some of them ragged and dirty, flutter in the evening breeze. With every step Crabs smells a different smell, a different dish, a dif-

ferent excretion. He walks slowly along the dusty lanes filled with bus-
tling people. Carmen is in the Dodge. He left her with the bicycle chain
and the doors locked.

The situation has become such that no progress is possible. Crabs is
now formulating a different direction. Movement is essential, it is the
only thing he has ever believed. Only a motor car can save him and he
is now manufacturing one. Crabs has decided to become a motor vehicle in good health.

As yet, as he walks, he is unsure of what he will be. Not a Mini Minor.
He would like something larger, stronger. He begins to manufacture
the tyres, they are large and fat with heavy treads. He can feels them,
he feels the way they roll along the dusty lanes. He feel them roll over
an empty can and squash into the dust. Then the bumper bars, huge thick
pieces of roughly welded steel to protect him in case of collision. Mud
guards, large and curving. They feel cool and smooth in the evening
breeze. There is something that feels like a tray, a tray at the back. He
can feel, with his nerve ends, an apparatus, but as yet he doesn't know
what the apparatus is. The engine is a V8, a Ford, he feels the rhythm of
its engine, the warm, strong vibratings. A six-speed gearbox and another
lever to operate the towing rig. That is what the apparatus is, a towing rig.

He feels whole. For the first time in his life Crabs feels complete. He
shifts into low gear and cruises slowly between the lanes of wrecked
cars, between the crowds, the families preparing their evening meals.

And he knows he can leave.

He has forgotten Carmen. He is complete. He changes into second
and turns on the lights, turning from one lane into the next, driving
carefully through the maze of cars and Nissen huts, looking for the gate.
The drive-in seems to have been extended because he drives for several miles in the direction of the south fence. He turns, giving up, and
shifting into third looks for the west fence where the gate was.

It is late when he finds it. His headlights pick up the entry office.
No-one seems to be on guard. As he comes closer he sees that the gates
are open. He changes down to second, accelerates, and leaves the drive-in
behind in a cloud of dust.

On the highway he accelerates. He feels the light on top of him flashing and, for the pure joy of it, he turns on the siren. The truck has no
governor and he sits it on 92 m.p.h., belting down the dark highway
with the air blasting into the radiator, the cool radiator water cooling
his hot engine.

He has gone for an hour when he realizes that the road is empty. He
is the only motor vehicle around. He drives through empty suburbs.
There are no neon signs. No lights in the houses. A strong headwind is
blowing. He begins to take sideroads. To turn at every turn he sees. He
feels sharp pains as his tyres grate, squeal, and battle for grip on the
cold hard roads. He has no sense of direction.

He has been travelling for perhaps three hours. His speed is down now, hovering around thirty. He turns a corner and enters a large highway. In the distance he can see lights.

He feels better, warmer already. The highway takes him towards the lights, the only lights in the world. They are closer. They are here. He turns off the highway and finds himself separated from the lights by a high wire fence. Inside he sees people moving around, laughing, talking. Some are dancing. He drives around the perimeter of the wire, driving over rough unmade roads, through paddocks until, at last, he comes to a large gate. The gate is locked and reinforced with heavy duty steel.

Above the gate is a faded sign with peeling paint. It says, "Star Drive-in Theatre. Please turn off your lights."

JOHN CHEEVER

Born in Quincy, Massachusetts, John Cheever (1912–1982) began his writing career at the age of seventeen, when he turned the experience of his dismissal from Thayer Academy into a short story which appeared in *The New Republic*. Subsequently Cheever wrote over two hundred stories, many of them for *The New Yorker*, and writing was the main source of his income throughout his life (working for *The New Yorker*, he said, gave him "enough money to feed the family and buy a new suit every other year"). Toward the end of his life, his pre-eminence as a writer of short fiction was acknowledged by a Pulitzer Prize, a National Book Critics Circle Award, and an American Book Award, all bestowed on *The Stories of John Cheever* (1978). He also wrote five novels, including *The Wapshot Chronicle* (1957), which won a National Book Award, and *The Wapshot Scandal* (1964), winner of a Howells Medal. For the novel *Falconer* (1977), he drew on his experiences as a teacher at Sing Sing Prison in the early seventies, as well as on his own battle with alcoholism. Cheever's last work, the novella *Oh What a Paradise It Seems*, was published in 1982 shortly before his death from cancer.

The principal subject of Cheever's fiction is suburbia: the manners and mores of the affluent American upper-middle class. Seemingly insulated by their wealth from the social and political problems that afflict the majority, they nevertheless find their lives boring, frustrating, or even frightening, as they look beneath the surface comforts of domestic life and find an unsettling emptiness. Though Cheever mocks the pretensions and vanities of this society, he recognizes the common humanity of its members; they may live in large houses or belong to exclusive golf clubs, but their fears and failings are not restricted to any social class. "The Angel of the Bridge" (*The Brigadier and the Golf Widow*, 1964) presents a typical member of Cheever's society: a wealthy, middle-aged businessman, sure of his own success and importance, who is suddenly confronted by doubts and fears that emerge from his subconscious to challenge his self-assured view of the world.

FOR FURTHER READING

Samuel Coale, *John Cheever* (New York: Frederick Ungar, 1977).
Annette Grant, "The Art of Fiction LXII: John Cheever," *Paris Review* 17 (Fall 1976): 39–66.
Lynne Waldeland, *John Cheever* (Boston: Twayne, 1979).

THE ANGEL OF
THE BRIDGE

You may have seen my mother waltzing on ice skates in Rockefeller Center. She's seventy-eight years old now but very wiry, and she wears a red velvet costume with a short skirt. Her tights are flesh-colored, and she wears spectacles and a red ribbon in her white hair, and she waltzes with one of the rink attendants. I don't know why I should find the fact that she waltzes on ice skates so disconcerting, but I do. I avoid that neighborhood whenever I can during the winter months, and I never lunch in the restaurants on the rink. Once when I was passing that way, a total stranger took me by the arm and, pointing to Mother, said, "Look at that crazy old dame." I was very embarrassed. I suppose I should be grateful for the fact that she amuses herself and is not a burden to me, but I sincerely wish she had hit on some less conspicuous recreation. Whenever I see gracious old ladies arranging chrysanthemums and pouring tea, I think of my own mother, dressed like a hat-check girl, pushing some paid rink attendant around the ice, in the middle of the third biggest city of the world.

My mother learned to figure-skate in the little New England village of St. Botolphs, where we come from, and her waltzing is an expression of her attachment to the past. The older she grows, the more she longs for the vanishing and provincial world of her youth. She is a hardy woman, as you can imagine, but she does not relish change. I arranged one summer for her to fly to Toledo and visit friends. I drove her to the Newark airport. She seemed troubled by the airport waiting room, with its illuminated advertisements, vaulted ceiling, and touching and painful scenes of separation played out to an uproar of continuous tango music. She did not seem to find it in any way interesting or beautiful, and compared to the railroad station in St. Botolphs it was indeed a strange background against which to take one's departure. The flight was delayed for an hour, and we sat in the waiting room. Mother looked tired and old. When we had been waiting half an hour, she began to have some noticeable difficulty in breathing. She spread a hand over the front of her dress and began to gasp deeply, as if she was in pain. Her face got mottled and red. I pretended not to notice this. When the plane was announced, she got to her feet and exclaimed, "I want to go home! If I have to die suddenly, I don't want to die in a flying machine." I cashed in her ticket and drove her back to her apartment, and I have never mentioned this seizure to her or to anyone, but her capricious, or perhaps neurotic, fear of dying in a plane crash was the first insight I had into how, as she grew older, her way was strewn with invisible rocks and lions and how eccentric were the paths she took, as the world seemed to change its boundaries and become less and less comprehensible.

At the time of which I'm writing, I flew a great deal myself. My business was in Rome, New York, San Francisco, and Los Angeles, and I sometimes traveled as often as once a month between these cities. I liked the flying. I liked the incandescence of the sky at high altitudes. I liked all eastward flights where you can see from the ports the edge of night move over the continent and where, when it is four o'clock by your California watch, the housewives of Garden City are washing up the supper dishes and the stewardess in the plane is passing a second round of drinks. Toward the end of the flight, the air is stale. You are tired. The gold thread in the upholstery scratches your cheek, and there is a momentary feeling of forlornness, a sulky and childish sense of estrangement. You find good companions, of course, and bores, but most of the errands we run at such high altitudes are humble and terrestrial. That old lady, flying over the North Pole, is taking a jar of calf's-foot jelly to her sister in Paris, and the man beside her sells imitation-leather inner soles. Flying westward one dark night — we had crossed the Continental Divide, but we were still an hour out of Los Angeles and had not begun our descent, and were at such an altitude that the sense of houses, cities, and people below us was lost — I saw a formation, a trace of light, like the lights that burn along a shore. There was no shore in that part of the world, and I knew I would never know if the edge of the desert or some bluff or mountain accounted for this hoop of light, but it seemed, in its obscurity — and at that velocity and height — like the emergence of a new world, a gentle hint at my own obsolescence, the lateness of my time of life, and my inability to understand the things I often see. It was a pleasant feeling completely free of regret, of being caught in some observable mid-passage, the farther reaches of which might be understood by my sons.

I liked to fly, as I say, and had none of my mother's anxieties. It was my older brother — her darling — who was to inherit her resoluteness, her stubbornness, her table silver, and some of her eccentricities. One evening, my brother — I had not seen him for a year or so — called and asked if he could come for dinner. I was happy to invite him. We live on the eleventh floor of an apartment house, and at seven-thirty he telephoned from the lobby and asked me to come down. I thought he must have something to tell me privately, but when we met in the lobby he got into the automatic elevator with me and we started up. As soon as the doors closed, he showed the same symptoms of fear I had seen in my mother. Sweat stood out on his forehead, and he gasped like a runner.

"What in the world is the matter?" I asked.

"I'm afraid of elevators," he said miserably.

"But what are you afraid of?"

"I'm afraid the building will fall down."

I laughed — cruelly, I guess. For it all seemed terribly funny, his vision of the buildings of New York banging against one another like ninepins as they fell to the earth. There has always been a strain of jealousy in our feelings about one another, and I am aware, at some obscure level, that he makes more money and has more of everything than I, and to see him humiliated — crushed — saddened me but at the same time and in spite of myself made me feel that I had taken a stunning lead in the race for honors that is at the bottom of our relationship. He is the oldest, he is the favorite, but watching his misery in the elevator I felt that he was merely my poor old brother, overtaken by his worries. He stopped in the hallway to recover his composure, and explained that he had been suffering from this phobia for over a year. He was going to a psychiatrist, he said. I couldn't see that it had done him any good. He was all right once he got out of the elevator, but I noticed that he stayed away from the windows. When it was time to go, I walked him out to the corridor. I was curious. When the elevator reached our floor, he turned to me and said, "I'm afraid I'll have to take the stairs." I led him to the stairway, and we climbed slowly down the eleven flights. He clung to the railing. We said goodbye in the lobby, and I went up in the elevator, and told my wife about his fear that the building might fall down. It seemed strange and sad to her, and it did to me, too, but it also seemed terribly funny.

It wasn't terribly funny when, a month later, the firm he worked for moved to the fifty-second floor of a new office building and he had to resign. I don't know what reasons he gave. It was another six months before he could find a job in a third-floor office. I once saw him on a winter dusk at the corner of Madison Avenue and Fifty-ninth Street, waiting for the light to change. He appeared to be an intelligent, civilized, and well-dressed man, and I wondered how many of the men waiting with him to cross the street made their way as he did through a ruin of absurd delusions, in which the street might appear to be a torrent and the approaching cab driven by the angel of death.

He was quite all right on the ground. My wife and I went to his house in New Jersey, with the children, for a weekend, and he looked healthy and well. I didn't ask about his phobia. We drove back to New York on Sunday afternoon. As we approached the George Washington Bridge, I saw a thunder storm over the city. A strong wind struck the car the moment we were on the bridge, and nearly took the wheel out of my hand. It seemed to me that I could feel the huge structure swing. Halfway across the bridge, I thought I felt the roadway begin to give. I could see no signs of a collapse, and yet I was convinced that in another minute the bridge would split in two and hurl the long lines of Sunday traffic into the dark water below us. This imagined disaster was terrifying. My legs got so weak that I was not sure I could brake the car if I needed to. Then it became difficult for me to breathe. Only by opening my mouth and gasping did I seem able to take in any air. My blood pressure was affected and I began to feel a darkening of my vision. Fear has alway seemed to me to run a course, and at its climax the body and perhaps the spirit defend themselves by drawing on some new and fresh source of strength. Once over the center of the bridge, my pain and terror began to diminish. My wife and the children were admiring the storm, and they did not seem to have noticed my spasm. I was afraid both that the bridge would fall down and that they might observe my panic.

I thought back over the weekend for some incident that might account for my preposterous fear that the George Washington Bridge would blow away in a thunderstorm, but it had been a pleasant weekend, and even under the most exaggerated scrutiny I couldn't uncover any source of morbid nervousness or anxiety. Later in the week, I had to drive to Albany, and, although the day was clear and windless, the memory of my first attack was too keen; I hugged the east bank of the river as far north as Troy, where I found a small, old-fashioned bridge that I could cross comfortably. This meant going fifteen or twenty miles out of my way, and it is humiliating to have your travels obstructed by barriers that are senseless and invisible. I drove back from Albany by the same route, and next morning I went to the family doctor and told him I was afraid of bridges.

He laughed. "You, of all people," he said scornfully. "You'd better take hold of yourself."

"But Mother is afraid of airplanes," I said. "And Brother hates elevators."

"Your mother is past seventy,'" he said, "and one of the most remarkable women I've ever known. I wouldn't bring her into this. What you need is a little more backbone."

This was all he had to say, and I asked him to recommend an analyst. He does not include psychoanalysis in medical science, and told me I would be wasting my time and money, but, yielding to his obligation to be helpful, he gave me the name and address of a psychiatrist, who told me that my fear of bridges was the surface manifestation of a deep-seated anxiety and that I would have to have a full analysis. I didn't have the time, or the money, or, above all, the confidence in the doctor's methods to put myself in his hands, and I said I would try and muddle through.

There are obviously areas of true and false pain, and my pain was meretricious, but how could I convince my lights and vitals of this? My youth and childhood had their deeply troubled and their jubilant years, and could some repercussions from this past account for my fear of heights? The thought of a life determined by hidden obstacles was unacceptable, and I decided to take the advice of the family doctor and ask more of myself. I had to go to Idlewild later in the week, and rather than take a bus or a taxi, I drove the car myself. I nearly lost consciousness on the Triborough Bridge. When I got to the airport I ordered a cup of coffee, but my hand was shaking so I spilled the coffee on the counter. The man beside me was amused and said that I must have put in quite a night. How could I tell him that I had gone to bed early and sober but that I was afraid of bridges?

I flew to Los Angeles late that afternoon. It was one o'clock by my watch when we landed. It was only ten o'clock in California. I was tired and took a taxi to the hotel where I always stay, but I couldn't sleep. Outside my hotel window was a monumental statue of a young woman, advertising a Las Vegas night club. She revolves slowly in a beam of light. At 2 A.M. the light is extinguished, but she goes on restlessly turning all through the night. I have never seen her cease her turning, and I wondered, that night, when they greased her axle and washed her shoulders. I felt some affection for her since neither of us could rest, and I wondered if she had a family — a stage mother, perhaps, and a compromised and broken-spirited father who drove a municipal bus on the West Pico line? There was a restaurant across the street, and I watched a drunken woman in a sable cape being led out to a car. She twice nearly fell. The crosslights from the open door, the lateness, her drunkenness, and the solicitude of the man with her made the scene, I thought, worried and lonely. Then two cars that seemed to be racing down Sunset Boulevard pulled up at a traffic light under my window. Three men piled out of each car and began to slug one another. You could hear the blows land on bone and cartilage. When the light changed, they got back into their cars and raced off. The fight, like the hoop of light I had seen from the plane, seemed like the signs of a new world, but in this case an emergence of brutality and chaos. Then I remembered that I was to go to San Francisco on Thursday, and was expected in Berkeley for lunch. This meant crossing the San Francisco–Oakland Bay Bridge, and I reminded myself to take a cab both ways and leave the car I rented in San Francisco in the hotel garage. I tried again to reason out my fear that the bridge would fall. Was I the victim of some sexual dislocation? My life has been promiscuous, carefree, and a source of immense pleasure, but was there some secret here that would have to be mined by a professional? Were all my pleasures impostures and evasions, and was I really in love with my old mother in her skating costume?

Looking at Sunset Boulevard at three in the morning, I felt that my terror of bridges was an expression of my clumsily concealed horror of what is becoming of the world. I can drive with composure through the outskirts of Cleveland and Toledo — past the birthplace of the Polish Hot Dog, the Buffalo Burger stands, the used-car lots, and the architectural monotony. I claim to enjoy walking down Hollywood Boulevard on a Sunday afternoon. I have cheerfully praised the evening sky hanging beyond the disheveled and expatriated palm trees on Doheny Boulevard, stuck up against the incandescence, like rank upon rank of wet mops. Duluth and East Seneca are charming, and if they aren't, just look away. The hideousness of the road between San Francisco and Palo Alto is nothing more than the search of honest men and women for a decent place to live. The same thing goes for San Pedro and all that coast. But the height of bridges seemed to be one link I could not forge or fasten in this hypocritical chain of acceptances. The truth is, I hate freeways and Buffalo Burgers. Expatriated palm trees and monotonous housing developments depress me. The continuous music on special-fare trains exacerbates my feelings. I detest the destruction of familiar landmarks, I am deeply troubled by the misery and drunkenness I find among my friends, I abhor the dishonest practices I see. And it was at the highest point in the arc of a bridge that I became aware suddenly of the depth and bitterness of my feelings about modern life, and of the profoundness of my yearning for a more vivid, simple, and peaceable world.

But I couldn't reform Sunset Boulevard, and until I could, I couldn't drive across the San Francisco–Oakland Bay Bridge. What *could* I do? Go back to St. Botolphs, wear a Norfolk jacket, and play cribbage in the firehouse? There was only one bridge in the village, and you could throw a stone across the river there.

I got home from San Francisco on Saturday, and found my daughter back from school for the weekend. On Sunday morning, she asked me to drive her to the convent school in Jersey where she is a student. She had to be back in time for nine-o'clock Mass, and we left our apartment in the city a little after seven. We were talking and laughing, and I had approached and was in fact on the George Washington Bridge without having remembered my weakness. There were no preliminaries this time. The seizure came with a rush. The strength went out of my legs, I gasped for breath, and felt the terrifying loss of sight. I was, at the same time, determined to conceal these symptoms from my daughter. I made the other side of the bridge, but I was violently shaken. My daughter didn't seem to have noticed. I got her to school in time, kissed her good-bye, and started home. There was no question of my crossing the George Washington Bridge again, and I decided to drive north to Nyack and cross on the Tappan Zee Bridge. It seemed, in my memory, more gradual and more securely anchored to its shores. Driving up the parkway on the west shore, I decided that oxygen was what I needed, and I opened all the windows of the car. The fresh air seemed to help, but only momentarily. I could feel my sense of reality ebbing. The roadside and the car itself seemed to have less substance than a dream. I had some friends in the neighborhood, and I thought of stopping and asking them for a drink, but it was only a little after nine in the morning, and I could not face the embarrassment of asking for a drink so early in the day, and of explaining that I was afraid of bridges. I thought I might feel better if I talked to someone, and I stopped at a gas station and bought some gas, but the attendant was laconic and sleepy, and I couldn't explain to him that his conversation might make the difference between life and death. I had got onto the Thruway by then, and I wondered what alternatives I had if I couldn't cross the bridge. I could call my wife and ask her to make some arrangements for removing me, but our relationship involves so much self-esteem and face that to admit openly to this foolishness might damage our married happiness. I could call the garage we use and ask them to send up a man to chauffeur me home. I could park the car and wait until one o'clock, when the bars opened, and fill up on whiskey, but I had spent the last of my money for gasoline. I decided to take a chance, and turned onto the approach to the bridge.

All the symptoms returned, and this time they were much worse than ever. The wind was knocked out of my lungs as by a blow. My equilibrium was so shaken that the car swerved from one lane into another. I drove to the side and pulled on the hand brake. The loneliness of my predicament was harrowing. If I had been miserable with romantic love, racked with sickness, or beastly drunk, it would have seemed more dignified. I remembered my brother's face, sallow and greasy with sweat in the elevator, and my mother in her red skirt one leg held gracefully aloft as she coasted backward in the arms of a rink attendant, and it seemed to me that we were all three characters in some bitter and sordid tragedy, carrying impossible burdens and separated from the rest of mankind by our misfortunes. My life was over, and it would never come back, everything that I loved — blue-sky courage, lustiness, the natural grasp of things. It would never come back. I would end up in the psychiatric ward of the county hospital, screaming that the bridges, all the bridges in the world, were falling down.

Then a young girl opened the door of the car and got in. "I didn't think anyone would pick me up on the bridge," she said. She carried a cardboard suitcase and — believe me — a small harp in a cracked waterproof. Her straight light-brown hair was brushed and brushed and grained with blondness and spread in a kind of cape over her shoulders. Her face seemed full and merry.

"Are you hitchhiking?" I asked.

"Yes."

"But isn't it dangerous for a girl your age?"

"Not at all."

"Do you travel much?"

"All the time. I sing a little. I play the coffeehouses."

"What do you sing?"

"Oh, folk music, mostly. And some old things — Purcell and Dowland. But mostly folk music. . . . 'I gave my love a cherry that had no stone,' " she sang in a true and pretty voice. " 'I gave my love a chicken that had no bone/I told my love a story that had no end/I gave my love a baby with no cryin'.' "

She sang me across a bridge that seemed to be an astonishingly sensible, durable, and even beautiful construction designed by intelligent men to simplify my travels, and the water of the Hudson below us was charming and tranquil. It all came back — blue-sky courage, the high spirits of lustiness, an ecstatic sereneness. Her song ended as we got to the toll station on the east bank, and she thanked me, said goodbye, and got out of the car. I offered to take her wherever she wanted to go, but she shook her head and walked away, and I drove on toward the city through a world that, having been restored to me, seemed marvelous and fair. When I got home, I thought of calling my brother and telling him what had happened, on the chance that there was also an angel of the elevator banks, but the harp — that single detail — threatened to make me seem ridiculous or mad, and I didn't call.

I wish I could say that I am convinced that there will always be some merciful intercession to help me with my worries, but I don't believe in rushing my luck, so I will stay off the George Washington Bridge, although I can cross the Triborough and the Tappan Zee with ease. My brother is still afraid of elevators, and my mother, although she's grown quite stiff, still goes around and around and around on the ice.

GEORGE CLUTESI

Born in 1906, George Clutesi, a member of the Tse-Shaht band of the Pacific coast, is one of Canada's foremost Indian artists. A painter as well as a writer, he has shown his work internationally; a forty-foot mural, designed for the world's fair Expo 67, is now on display at Montreal's permanent "Man and His World" exhibition, and his own designs illustrate *Son of Raven, Son of Deer* (1967), from which "Ko-ishin-mit and the Shadow People" is taken. Contact with the "European" bureaucracies of the Canadian government — particularly in regard to Indian affairs — led Clutesi to become a teacher of native culture, confident that it has significant meaning for both Indians and others.

"Ko-ishin-mit and the Shadow People," like all folk tales, emerges directly from a specific culture; though it can often be related to parallel stories from other cultures, it reflects its own society's structure, beliefs, superstitions, and values, and draws its particular language, its metaphors and analogies, from the local landscape. Primarily an oral art, the folk tale generally served a moral purpose and functioned as the didactic medium through which traditional values were handed from generation to generation. In his introduction to *Son of Raven, Son of Deer*, Clutesi notes that it was "Nan-is," the grandparent, who told such tales to the "ka-coots" (grandchildren), and that this pattern of behavior not only gave the aged a respected position within society but also gave the young a sense of security. He criticizes such tales as "Henny Penny" and "Little Jack Horner," both for their implicit violence and for the gap between the child behavior that society expects and approves, and the models hallowed by the stories themselves. The Indian stories, by contrast, assert the closeness between human beings and nature, focus on the interpenetration between mythic stories and moral truths, and give expression (in Clutesi's own words) to the "imaginative, romantic and resourceful" capacities of the Indian mind.

FOR FURTHER READING

J.W. Chalmers, "When You Tell a Story," *Canadian Author and Bookman* (Fall 1971), p. 5.

KO-ISHIN-MIT AND
THE SHADOW PEOPLE

"Finders keepers — losers weepers."
Most of you, no doubt, have heard this old saying. To the non-Indian
way of life it means that if anyone finds anything it is his to keep, while
the one who has lost it may as well cry because it is lost to him, even
though someone may have found it. This did not apply to the Indian
way of life.

Ko-ishin-mit, the Son of Raven, was a very selfish and greedy person.
He was always longing to own other people's possessions and coveted
everything that was not his. Oh, he was greedy!

One fine day, early in the spring of the year, when the sun was shining and smiling with warmth, Ko-ishin-mit overheard a group of menfolk talking about a strange place where you could see everything you
could think of lying about, with never a person in sight.

"What kind of things? Where is this place? How far is it from here?"
Ko-ishin-mit demanded in a high state of excitement. He was hopping
up and down and his voice became croaky as he kept asking where to
find the place.

The menfolk ignored his frantic questions and the speaker, a grey-
haired, wizened old man, kept on with his story.

"There are canoes," he told, "big ones and small ones, paddles, fishing gear, tools, all sorts of play things and food galore. Oh, there is lots
and lots of food, and the food is always fresh, even though no one is
ever seen in the place."

Ko-ishin-mit became more and more excited and his voice was raspy
as he screamed, "Who owns all these things? Where? How can I find
them?"

The storyteller continued with his tale. "It is said that this strange
place is on a little isle around the point and across the bay. The secret is
that one must get there by sundown, and one must leave before sunup.
It is said, too, that the first person who finds this place may keep
everything."

Ko-ishin-mit ran all the way home. "I must find this strange place
first," he kept repeating to himself. "I must find the place first. I must.
I must."

He flitted into his little house, and because he was out of breath he
rasped and croaked, "Pash-hook, Pash-hook, Pash-hook, nah, my dear,
get ready quickly. We are going out. Make some lunch. We may be gone
all night," he croaked.

Pash-hook, the Daughter of Dsim-do the squirrel, scurried about. She
did not need to be coaxed for she was always a fast and frisky little
person. She never questioned her husband's wishes. Whatever her hus-

band said had always been good enough for her and she was always eager to please him. So she hurried and she hurried.

Ko-ishin-mit grew more and more excited as he flitted here and hopped there inside his little house. He got out two paddles. He hopped down to the beach and pulled and tugged at his canoe until he had it to the water, a feat he had never before done alone.

Flitting back to the house he pressed and coaxed his little wife. "Hurry, hurry! Pash-hook, hurry! We must get there first. Hurry before we are too late. We must get there first. Oh, let us be first," he kept repeating, mostly to himself.

The sun was setting when they paddled into the bay of the little isle around the point. It was a beautiful little isle with small clumpy spreading spruce trees growing from mossy green hills. The little bay was ringed with white sandy beaches. The tide was out and the green sea-grass danced and waved at them to come ashore and rest awhile. This is what Pash-hook imagined as she eased her paddling and glided their little canoe towards the glistening beach. Pash-hook was the dreamer.

"Paddle harder! Paddle harder!" Ko-ishin-mit commanded his little wife.

Straight for the beach they glided. Ko-ishin-mit flitted out onto the wet sand. "Pull the canoe up," he ordered as he hopped up the beach, looking about to see if there was anyone else there ahead of him. He could see long rows of beautiful canoes, big and small, pulled up well above the high-water mark. They all had pretty canoe mats covering them from the heat of the day and the cool of the night. There was no one in sight. Ko-ishin-mit was hopping up the beach. He did not wait to help his small wife with their canoe.

"I got here first!" he rasped as he hopped and flitted up to the neat row of houses on the grassy knoll that lay just below the spreading and clumpy spruce trees.

"I got here first!" the greedy Ko-ishin-mit croaked as he flitted swiftly to the biggest of the great houses. The huge door was shut and he pushed it open and hopped inside. He did not look back to see if his little wife Pash-hook was following. "I got here first," he chanted. Ko-ishin-mit, Son of Raven, was very, very greedy.

No one was to be seen. There was not a sound to be heard other than, "I got here first." Ko-ishin-mit's beady little black eyes grew even smaller in his greed to grab, grab, grab. "All is mine! All is mine!" his voice rasped out as he croaked, the way ravens do when they espy food.

"The whole village is mine. I got here first," he reasoned to himself. He hopped around the earthen floor of the great room. Big cedar boxes lined the walls. Ko-ishin-mit's greedy instinct told him that they would be full of dried and smoked food-stuffs. Indeed he did find smoked salmon, cured meats, oils, preserved fish eggs, dried herring roe, cured qwanis (camus bulbs), and dried berries.

"Everything, everything! All is mine. All is mine," he croaked as he flitted and hopped about opening boxes of oil, dried bulbs and fish-heads. Everything he saw he wanted. He wanted it all. His own drool spilled out of his mouth. He was very greedy.

Presently Pash-hook came into the great house. For the first time in her life she was not hurrying to do her husband's bidding. She did not scurry one little bit. Instead of helping her husband to carry out all the things and food-stuff down to their little canoe on the sandy beach, she slowly approached a small pile of embers that were still glowing on the centre hearth. There was no flame. The embers glowed warmly and invitingly. Pash-hook sat down and began to warm herself. She spread out her tiny hands. The embers still glowed warmly.

Ko-ishin-mit was so excited and so busy carrying out the food-stuff that he, for the first time in their married lives, forgot to make his wife do all the work.

"I shall never be hungry again. I shall never be hungry again," he kept repeating.

He worked hard packing, packing, packing, all he could lift and move down the long sloping beach. The tide was out and their little canoe was far down from the great houses. Pash-hook sat by the embers warming herself while Ko-ishin-mit worked at loading the canoe. At last the canoe was filled. It was so full there was hardly any room left for himself or for Pash-hook.

"One more trip. One more trip." How greedy Ko-ishin-mit was! He decided to put the last load where his wife would sit. He hopped up the high sloping beach and flitted into the now nearly empty cedar box and decided again he would put the very last load where Pash-hook would sit.

All of a sudden he remembered her. Pash-hook was still sitting by the fire warming herself at the embers.

"Come Pash-hook! Hurry! We must come back as fast as we can. We must take all. We must take all. We must come back before daylight returns. Hurry, hurry, Pash-hook!"

But Pash-hook still sat without moving, before the embers of the fire. Ko-ishin-mit lost his temper. He hopped to his wife's side demanding in his raspy voice, "What's the matter with you, woman? You have never disobeyed me like this before. Get up at once. We must go."

Pash-hook did not move. She did not speak. She did not look up at her husband.

Ko-ishin-mit was alarmed. He became very frightened.

"Get up, get up!" he croaked. In anger he grabbed Pash-hook by the shoulders and tried to pull her up. The harder he pulled the heavier she became. He could not budge the small little person. She felt like a rooted stone. Ko-ishin-mit was now trembling with fear. He hop-flitted out and down to his canoe and pushed and heaved trying to move it out to deeper water, but the harder he pulled and heaved the heavier the little canoe became.

"Something is wrong. Something is terribly wrong," he told himself. He tried to shout but only a weak croak came out. He flitted back to the great house and hopped inside. Pash-hook still sat by the embers of the fire.

Ko-ishin-mit noticed she was trying very hard to tell him something. He very gingerly approached her and bent his head towards her moving lips. Brave, gallant Pash-hook tried with all her might.

"There are strange people holding me down. I can't move," she whispered, almost out of breath. "Put back all you took," she entreated her husband.

Ko-ishin-mit flitted back to his canoe and once more tried to push it out into the stream. It would not move. He tried pulling it farther up onto the beach. It moved with hardly any effort at all. Trembling, Ko-ishin-mit grabbed the topmost bale and hauled it back to the great house. He worked very hard toting all the boxes and bales back to where he found them. When the last article had been returned to its own cedar box then only did Pash-hook stir.

"Heahh," she breathed, "I'm free," and shook herself and stood up. Her husband led her out and down the long, long beach to their canoe.

Pash-hook hopped in as her now very meek husband pushed the canoe into the stream. They both paddled with all their might and main until they were at a safe distance from the strange, strange place. When they at last stopped to rest Pash-hook spoke her first words since leaving the great house.

"Heahh, I'm free," she repeated. "There are people up there in the great house with the earthern floors. I'm sure of it. I felt hands, heavy hands, upon my shoulders holding me down. I'm certain that one of them sat on me because I felt so crushed down from above. I was very frightened. I couldn't speak. I couldn't tell you."

Ko-ishin-mit looked at his wife with great love. "Choo, choo, choo, all right, all right, Pash-hook my mate. Don't be afraid any more. We shall never go to that isle again."

It is said that all things belong to someone. The old people say it is not wise to keep anything you find.

Around the point and across the bay
There is an Isle with clumpy spruce
That stands on mossy knolls
Green with salal.
The beaches are covered with sea-shells white
When the tide runs out sea-grasses wave and beckon you in.
The shadow people live there, it is said —
Shadow people one cannot see until the sun is up
To cast their shadows on the sands of sea-shells white.

DANIEL CURLEY

Daniel Curley was born in 1918 in East Bridgewater, Massachussetts, graduated from the University of Alabama, and subsequently taught at several universities in New York and Illinois. He has also worked on the editorial staff of the literary journals *Accent* and *Ascent*. Besides poetry, criticism, plays, and several books for children, he has written two novels (*How Many Angels?* 1958, and *A Stone Man, Yes*, 1964) and published three collections of short stories, including *In the Hands of our Enemies* (1970), which won an award from the National Council on the Arts.

Curley's stories reflect his interest in experimenting with form and technique, but his themes are traditional in their focus on the problems of everyday life. His characters are beset by frustration and disillusionment as loneliness or marriage or age becomes too heavy a burden, forcing them to confront their personal failure. This is the predominant note of the collection *Love in the Winter* (1976), from which is taken "Why I Play Rugby," a story whose Oxford setting derives from Curley's visit to England as a Guggenheim Fellow in 1958/59. Like many of Curley's protagonists, the narrator is an observer, both of the world around him and of the workings of his own mind. He might be compared to the hero of "The Beast" (also from *Love in the Winter*), who, in a moment of crisis, recognizes the underlying pattern of his life: "He was never being. He wasn't even becoming. He was just waiting." But if a sense of failure seems to dog Curley's characters, he can present them, as in "Why I Play Rugby," with humor and with a sympathetic irony that exposes their faults and weaknesses, and blocks any descent into sentimental self-pity or morbidness.

FOR FURTHER READING

Leslie Lilienfeld, "Making It Through America," *Book Forum* 2 (1976): 457–59.

Gordon Weaver, ed., *The American Short Story 1945–1980: A Critical History* (Boston: Twayne, 1983), pp. 101–2.

WHY I PLAY RUGBY

The first time I saw Rugby played was in Oxford in the spring of 1959. I was slogging along a deep and dirty lane, admiring the trees, admiring the hedgerow, admiring even the rain — I think I would have been disappointed if the sun had been shining when I took my first walk through the English countryside. It was a rare moment of content. I had just seen a chaffinch. I was pleased with my stout English boots and my surplus poncho. I had even forgotten my disappointment at arriving in England too late for the Rugby season.

Although I felt myself to be a solitary figure in a landscape, I was not surprised to see a football sailing over the hedge and dropping toward me. Instinctively I held out my hands and the football settled into the basket made by my poncho. It was a football I was very glad to see, fat and ungainly like the footballs of my childhood. I worked my hands free and fondled it. Oh, it was a football.

My friend Patrick, who discovered Rugby here in the cornfields, says Rugby is a very physical game and that he plays it to unburden himself of those blows which, according to Robert Frost (Patrick says), a life of self-control requires that we spare to strike for the common good. And there must be a lot in that. All I have to do is feel that lovely football and I think of the endless games of my childhood and the twin ecstasies of smashing and being smashed, of those moments when the whole world hangs in a crunching equilibrium. And I see Patrick's face as he comes off the field after the first half. His hair and beard stand out in a ring, and his face gleams like a monstrance at the moment of truth. I hand him a section of an orange. "He's very large," I say, referring to the opposing prop. "But docile," Patrick says. "Just so," I say deferentially — Patrick is only in his middle twenties but he is a hero, a genuine Viking in spite of his Irish name. If he stepped ashore on the coast of England, the old church bells would know him and would quake in their belfries and the countryside would turn out to repel him. His face is streaming with sweat and light. His eye roves constantly as if searching out larger, less docile props. He is himself small for a prop, five foot ten, say, and a hundred ninety pounds, and his present opponent is six inches and fifty pounds bigger. "I can do what I want with him," Patrick is saying. "When I saw his size I knew I would have to be firm with him from the start." Patrick eyes a field full of varsity football players (American style) doing calisthenics across the street. "Nothing to get him angry, of course. Nothing crude. I wasn't going to swing on his beard, mind you. Can you imagine what he would be if he ever got fired up? And I wasn't about to pluck out a handful of hair from his armpit. You know all that sort of thing." I really don't, never having been a prop, but Patrick is very considerate — I'm weighing *chivalrous* against him. He sucks his orange and measures the football team. "I'd pull their beards," he says. "If they had any," I say. "So much for the worse for them," he says. I don't care to pursue that line of thought. The mysteries of the scrum are best left alone. "What friendly hint did you give your large friend?" I say at last. "In the first two scrums," Patrick says, "instead of locking shoulders with him, as he has every right to expect, I met him with my skull between his eyes. He got the message." Patrick throws down his orange skin and runs out onto the field. He waves his arms like windmills and throws himself fiercely down, bounds up, stamps out a terrible message on the earth. All about my feet the brilliant spring grass is littered violent orange. Patrick locks in for the first scrum. His head disappears. His thigh muscles stand out. The strain builds up. His shorts split up the back. His ass gleams forth. Everyone cheers. Toward the end of the match, while Patrick is lying unconscious on the sidelines, a member of the B squad donates his shorts, which are slipped onto Patrick so he can rage back into action at the first signs of life.

I climbed out of the lane and went through the hedge by a kissing gate and found myself at the edge of a sports ground. A game was in progress. I walked into the grounds unmolested, fondling the ball, my fingers remembering its slippery curves, my arms and legs remembering strength and speed. I could have sprung upstairs two at a time if there had been stairs. The smell of bruised grass and mud. The lovely tiredness of muscles. Aches and bruises just beginning gently to assert themselves. A player, hotly pursued, pivoted and kicked the ball over a hedge into the motorway. "Oh, well kicked," a man near me said. He took my ball and threw it onto the field. "Good man," his friend said and clapped him on the back, nearly falling off his crutches in his enthusiasm. There seemed to be only the three of us watching. "Got to keep them at it," the first man said. His speech was decidedly mushy, and I noticed now that he had no front teeth and that his upper lip was stitched like a baseball. "Jolly good," the man on crutches said, although I have no witnesses to it. "I'll be glad when I'm too old to play," Mushmouth said. "It's not much longer for either of us," the other said. A player, this time on the other team, pivoted and kicked the ball into the motorway. "Oh, well kicked," my companions said. "Oh, jolly good."

The rain was blowing in gray sheets across the pitch. I opened my flask under my poncho and pulled in my head like a turtle going into retirement. I suppose I must have looked remarkably like a man pretending not to be taking a drink under a poncho, but I had no information about right conduct at a Rugby match. "I'm sorry," I said when I reappeared and saw the other two staring into my shell. "Perhaps you would care—" I said. They boarded me at once. "Jolly good," one said. "Well drunk," the other said. We finished it off, turn and turn about scrupulously. Brandy, then, was definitely acceptable at a Rugby match— at least in bad weather.

In the Britannia down in back of Swiss Cottage — it was my local on one of my stays in London—on a Saturday morning—I can't remember why I happened to be in there, because drinking in the morning is not ordinarily my thing, but then, I guess you travel in order to be relieved of your thing — or something — and a couple of pints in your local at lunchtime really isn't drinking at all. The pub XV were in there, shouting and singing as usual — you should hear them on a Sunday night when they come in straight from a match. You'd think they had driven the Romans off the wall and chased them all the way to London. On that Saturday they were all of them going down to Twickenham and were even more inflamed than usual. I had a suspicion that they did not intend to visit the shrine of Alexander Pope, but it was Pope who persisted in coming into mind at each mention of Twickenham. I kept quiet and listened and sipped my Guinness, laying down in the glass a lovely tight series of foam rings that would have done credit to the most frugal old Irishman in the frugal west country. Twickenham, I eventually gathered, was Yankee Stadium. And it was Cooperstown. And it was the World Series. Revenge was the theme. Revenge against France, last year's super-champion. The XV must have liked the color of my Guinness or the cunning of my silence, because, after offering a spare ticket to everyone in the place, they asked if I'd go with them. They must have observed by then that I never had anything in particular to do.

Until that Saturday I had believed that the only place in London you could drink all day was Lord's Cricket Ground — there are many interesting things to learn in London. It was a ridiculously cheap ticket. Six shillings perhaps. I stood in the sun on the terrace with the heavy bark of ENG-LAND in one ear and in the other the light, quick chant *Allez la France, allez la France, allez*. It was marvelous being there, packed in shoulder to shoulder. The play was like the shouts, strength against quickness, but it was all very beautiful, fluid and powerful. Strength won handsomely that day, but I remember chiefly a white-haired man on the England side — my friend Patrick tells me that a prop doesn't mature until after thirty — and the drifts of wine bottles on the terraces at the end of the match. The sun, the crowd, the flowing play, and a chanticleer crowing all afternoon on someone's shoulder down in front of us. Later I read that the white-haired man was only in his twenties, but the news came too late, the picture was set by then.

Patrick tells me that he is planning to write a book about Rubgy. From what I can gather, it is to be about everything in the game and out of it that makes him a player. He's going to call it WHY I PLAY RUGBY, but he wants to wait until he is at least fifty before he begins. He hopes to attain wisdom, he says.

The rain was blowing gray along the sides of Helvellyn. Just above my head, it seemed, the white clouds were flowing over the saddle toward Patterdale. But as I came over a little rise I saw ahead of me yet another small valley with the trail going up on the other side, all but obliterated by rock slides. I had already given up the idea of reaching the top and was contenting myself with simply finding the pass and the tarn and going down to the highway on the other side. Somehow my imagination had been caught by the picture of Wordsworth saying what was to be his last goodbye to his brother near the tarn. That would satisfy me. I crossed the valley and climbed over the rocks along what remained of the old pack-horse trail. Patches of fog — clouds, should I say? — enveloped me briefly. It was very cold. Very silent. Very lonely. The wind was terrific. It would be easy to lose the trail in the fog. A fall would be nasty. However, there were cairns every few yards to keep me honest, so I advanced from cairn to cairn in the clearer moments. And after a scramble on hands and knees, I stood beside a cairn like all the others and waited for a lucid moment. When it came, I saw that this time the horizon had not skulked off a few more yards but that below me the tarn lay in a pocket and beyond that endless space.

The tarn, I saw as I walked beside it, was streaked with foam, long thin white lines from end to end. The wind was battering my body. My legs trembled. If I hadn't been so hungry, I think I might well have lain down and died on the spot. As it was, I went on as best I could. So absorbed was I in my physical self that I failed to observe a file of figures trotting toward me. They came into focus very close at hand, and I cringed against a rock to let them pass. The leader, I saw, carried a football. It was, in fact, a Rugby club, dressed as if for a match, running through the pass, silent and tireless as Indians. As I crossed the outlet to the tarn, the wind blew me off the stepping-stones into ankle-deep water, and I slogged on down the easy descent with my shoes full of water and my heart full of despair. It was only when I found a pub and sat down that I thought again of Wordsworth, of the foam-streaked tarn, and of the low white clouds, the slanting gray rain, the endless space and the quiet.

It's a sensation of power, Patrick says. A moment when you can feel the entire power of the pack focusing in your hips and thighs, and you are ready to launch yourself, to grapple — and you feel a vague dissatisfaction that your opponent is merely mortal, for you know you are yourself much more. It must be, he says, to witness that moment that the Rugby girls come out — Rugger-huggers he calls them and laughs at them but acknowledges that they are his real witnesses. And perhaps, he continues, that is also why many wives cannot come out to watch, not, as one might suppose, for fear of seeing their husbands broken up on the field but for fear of seeing them in glory, a naked display of what should be their secret joy, but what is, in fact, their secret grief. Quite probably there are many wives who know they will never have from their husbands what the husbands make a public display of time after effortless time on a Saturday afternoon. That's what Patrick talks like and that's where, in his idiom, his head is. I think he'll write a marvelous book about Rubgy. Or it may be a poem-novel like Wordsworth's

Prelude: The Growth of a Poet's Mind of A Rugby Player Finds Out Where His Head Is At.

When we got to the party, the visiting side was already puking on the lawn. "Jesus," Patrick said, "who brought them along?" This was not the Rugby party but quite a different one, intended, at least, to be very sedate. Patrick and I had left the Rugby party in full blast, we thought. It was being held in an abandoned garage that made me think of the St. Valentine's Day Massacre. The place was shaped like a shoebox, all concrete, nothing to break, the floor caked with grease and a faint smell of hot metal still in the air. Kegs of beer were scattered around strategically, but there was nothing else in the box except what I took to be two enormous white refrigerators set down very much in the way. When the visiting team tipped one over with our scrum half inside, it became quite clear that they were portable toilets. There threatened to be some unpleasantness for a while, but our side was still sober enough to understand that you might very well run up a lopsided score against those monsters, but you would do very well not to make too much of an upset toilet in an abandoned garage. They were really big. They had come over from Indianapolis, and Patrick said they looked to him like the machines that had failed to qualify for the 500.

So when we found them heaving up their guts on the lawn we were not particularly pleased. But gradually we got them stacked in the back of their van — it was a panel truck. Probably some of them had a rock group, because the van was painted in wild colors and patterns and I made out something I took to read The Vroom. About this time, a wife appeared and jumped into the back of the van and began stomping and kicking about very urgently as if to work the ball loose. Eventually she came out with the keys and scuttled around the van, giving us a dirty look as she went, and got in and drove them all off.

After that, Patrick and I, although conscious of having behaved very well, were somehow not at ease at that party, so we went back to the garage. As we went in, we held our hands to show the footballs stamped on our palms — there had been a historic fight at a party where some visiting Blacks were stamped on their palms while everyone else was being stamped on the back of their hands. Of course, the ink would show up only on the Black's palms, but they claimed discrimination and could be satisfied only by being beaten insensible. It took three weeks of debate and other persuasion for the club to adopt a rule that everyone should be stamped on the palm forevermore. So we showed our palms but there was no one there to see them.

I thought at first that the Massacre had been reenacted. But, of course, it was only the beer. "It's a massacre," Patrick said. We checked the bodies. All seemed in good shape. We checked the toilets, which were both on their sides. There was a girl asleep in the Ladies. I couldn't cope, so I gagged and closed the door. In a dark corner in the back I found a girl sitting on a beer keg with her feet tucked up out of the mess. "I knew someone would find me," she said. "I knew some prop would carry me out of here." She held out her arms toward us. "I'm sorry," Patrick said, "my wife doesn't approve of my carrying girls anywhere, period." He disappeared, pouf. "Let's get the hell out of here and go find a beer," I said. I picked her up. "You're so strong," she said. My knees were buckling, and if the garage had been ten feet longer, I'd never have made it, but as it was I set her down outside the door. I was able to control my breath and my trembling muscles, but I didn't yet trust myself to speak, so I began walking off blindly to the left with my hand firmly on her arm. "My car is this way," she said, kneading my biceps and turning me around. It was not what you would call a meaningful relationship, but it was very pleasant. I noticed that when we got to her place, I went up the stairs two at a time on the balls of my feet.

Once my flask was empty I began to feel the cold. Crutches and Mushmouth had gone all huddled and glum. They were no longer making an effort to follow the action up and down the sidelines. Water was getting inside my poncho now. My feet were either cold or wet — or both — but I was afraid it might be unsporting to go away. I looked toward the clubhouse at the end of the pitch and saw that it was now lighted. People were gathered at the windows drinking beer and watching the game. It seemed somehow very civilized. "Lucky sods," Crutches said. "We'll have our turn," Mushmouth said. "Five more years of being keen," Crutches said. "Five at the outside," Mushmouth said. "Being keen is hell," Crutches said. "Bloody hell," I said. They looked at me as if they had forgotten all about me. "But it pays off," Crutches said. "They watch," Mushmouth said. "Oh, well caught," he said. "Jolly good," Crutches said. I glanced toward the clubhouse but no one seemed to be paying much attention to anything outside.

Patrick was terrific but the snow was also terrific. Out on the field the players faded in and out like TV ghosts, and the electric orange and blue hoops of their jerseys were muted to pastels even at close range. It was a very impressionistic scene. I kept getting an image of Canterbury cathedral manifesting itself out of just such a storm at the end of a three-day mid-April walk from London.

It was a very sloppy match and very fierce. Patrick was raging up and down the field being firm. There was one time he tackled four runners one after another, flinging them down as they passed off and then collaring the receiver almost at the same time. He was a one-man pack. Nobody was saving anything that day, because it was the last match until spring, but he was letting it all go as if he planned to hibernate. Then they got him on a little up-and-under kick that dropped right into his hands. They were all around him but he broke two tackles and gave someone time to get into position to take his pass. He passed off and the play started to flow from him, and then, very late, he caught a great flying sprawling tackle. When he went down it was clear he wouldn't get up, not even Patrick. There was a terrific fight back and forth across him. Everyone on both sides was in on it. The referee was blowing his whistle like mad. The B teams were charging onto the field. I ran out along with the other two or three spectators. And then it stopped. We just stood and looked at the snow reddening around Patrick's head.

The referee looked at his watch. "Such another outbreak," he said, "and I shall abandon the match." He held the ball firmly under his arm as if he were ready to go home with it. He sent off the player who had hit Patrick, as was only right. Even I had seen that elbow come down like a club. The rest of us carried Patrick off, and even before we had crossed the touch line the game was raging again.

Patrick was obviously a hospital case. Not only had he lost some teeth but his jaw was almost certainly broken. He was showing no signs of coming around, so we began casting about for someone with a car. I was the logical one, but I made a point of never bringing my car. It gave me a good excuse to catch a ride with Patrick or somebody after the match and stop in with the players for a beer. There was a girl, however, who volunteered to drive. I said I'd go along.

Now I had noticed this girl, and I flattered myself she had noticed me. Well, she wasn't all that girlish. What — thirty — give or take a couple of years. Anyway, at the half I was measuring out a hot toddy from my thermos for Patrick and another for myself. We had taken refuge in a corner of the tennis courts where a practice wall broke the wind. I offered her a drink too. She was glad to have it. She turned out to be from New Zealand. None of your regular Rugger-huggers but a true aficionada, a little homesick. She had a brother who had been an All Black. While she was wrapping her fingers around my cup and warming them and her nose at the same time, I was bouncing a golf ball on the court. It had been lying in the corner in some leaves, lost no doubt by someone practicing on the field. I was bouncing and talking and very well pleased with myself. She was nice. She was interested. I had real hopes. But I got carried away and bounced carelessly. The ball hopped toward her. She made a motion to catch it and it landed in her cup. The toddy splashed on her hands and her coat. She was marvelous about it but I felt like a fool. Patrick thought it was very funny.

So it was this girl who volunteered to drive Patrick to the hospital and who looked toward me when someone was needed to go with her. We stuffed Patrick into her car and I got in. In two minutes she had the car at right angles to the road. The front wheels were in the ditch. I got out and tried pushing but with no luck at all. I went and got the B team and we formed in back of the car. I put my shoulder to the trunk. I felt the hard bodies of men on either side of me. I felt hands on my back, a shoulder under my butt. The entire power of the pack was focused in my hips and thighs as the car launched itself onto the road. And something went pop in my groin. She left both of us at the hospital.

The losing team ran off the field toward the clubhouse. I wanted to shout "Bad show," but my companions, Crutches and Mushmouth, were watching benignly, so I didn't presume. The losers suddenly stopped and formed a line on either side of the clubhouse door and applauded as the winners sauntered past them. "Good show," Mushmouth said. He and Crutches made their way slowly toward the clubhouse. The losers collapsed their lines and jostled on in.

The first time I saw Rugby I was already far too old to play.

BARRY DEMPSTER

Born in Scarborough, Ontario in 1952, Barry Dempster has spent his life in and around Toronto, where, as a child psychologist, he has worked for the Children's Aid Society and at the Lakeshore Psychiatric Hospital. He now works part time at the Queen Street Mental Health Centre as a member of the emergency assessment team. One of the editors for *Poetry Canada Review*, he enjoys a growing reputation as a poet and short-story writer. His books of poems include *Fables for Isolated Men* (1982) and *Globe Doubts* (1983); and he has published fiction in such journals as *Quarry* and the *University of Windsor Review*.

"The Burial" appeared in a collection called *Real Places and Imaginary Men* (1984), a title which suggests something of the quality of the stories themselves and their concern with the impact of experience upon imagination. In "The Burial," the narrator leaves Canada for India, to discover first of all his alienation from what he takes to be its "reality" (the things he identifies as dirt, stench, barbaric custom), and then to realize that he has nonetheless been touched at some other level of understanding, and has been changed by his experience. His contact with India's civilization makes him revaluate his presumptions about the "normative" character of Canadian life. This is a story about time and transformation, about racial discrimination and its effects on judgment, and about the flow of experience that changes all who surrender to it. "What you *can know*," Barry Dempster writes, "has no boundaries, no personal restrictions. The imagination can travel to India, Mars or your next-door neighbor's. Once an interest activates the mind, imagination becomes informed. A short story then can be a very real possibility of life."

FOR FURTHER READING
Clark Blaise and Bharati Mukherjee, *Days and Nights in Calcutta* (New York: Doubleday, 1977).

THE BURIAL

Sujit Mukherjee drives us to the airport in his rusty white Volvo. The lane-dividing lines on the highway are covered with snow, the wind blowing great splashes of slush across our windshield. Sujit manipulates the wheels as if he were manoeuvring the narrow lanes at a bowling-alley. Through the back window of the car just ahead, I can make out a furry shape blurred by icy glass.

"I wish I were you," Sijit says, his eyes barely straying from the road, but changing, moving back, remembering things that, to me, are as foreign and frightening as these blizzards must first have been for him, and for Ananda.

"Not even an hour after you were home," Ananda pipes up from the back seat, "you'd be dreaming about snow and ice. And how about all the pretty white faces, just think about that."

Sujit glances at me quickly, but it's too cold for me to blush; anyway, I'm getting used to being white, that is, white in the company of their brown shiny faces.

The terminal is self-consciously crowded. There's an alcove at the end of the hall, a flight to Germany, that's fairly clear. I edge toward it, just beyond the electric sign announcing the trip to Calcutta via half the world. The waiting-room is overflowing with Indians. They can't all be on the same flight, our flight. No plane is big enough for so many people. Ananda is recognized by a swarm of them and is soon surrounded. I can barely make out the top of his pink turban in the thick of the crowd. Sujit stays close to me, chatting with several men his own age, my age too, in whatever language it is they speak. I think it's Hindustani. Ananda speaks Bengali but seems to get by with a good number of dialects. His English is superb.

"Over there." Sujit is tapping me on the shoulder as he speaks. "Look over there." He's moved away from his friends and is pointing at a small cluster of people to the rear of us. In the centre stands a white girl, in her early twenties, clinging to the arm of an unusually handsome Indian. Sujit smiles and goes back to his small talk. For a moment, without thinking, my reaction is to stare, to try and make contact. But the girl doesn't notice. Still, I find myself hoping she'll be on the plane.

When the flight is called, about a quarter of the crowd move toward the gates. Most of the people left behind continue their conversations, not seeming to realize that their friends are about to disappear.

Sujit is fussing around me, warning me to be open, to forget whatever stories I might have heard, even those I heard from him.

"You must be tough," Ananda is saying to Sujit while Sujit is talking to me. "Are you listening?" he asks, slapping him on the arm. "You have to be tougher than all of them. Do you understand? You have to be better than they are."

Sujit laughs, but nods with a seriousness I know only too well. He's a happy man, he doesn't like to dwell on the facts of prejudice, although he is aware of how difficult times can be. I move forward a little, accidentally pressing my suitcase against a woman in a light green sari. She doesn't seem bothered though; she simply shoves the man in front of her.

A moment later, Ananda bumps into me. "Say goodbye," he says, gesturing toward Sujit who is fading away as we walk, his waving hand growing smaller and smaller.

The crew of the plane are all white except for one of the stewardesses, a black. I notice the white girl and her Indian lover several rows ahead of us, on the right. The girl has her head tucked into his shoulder and one of her hands resting on his thigh.

"I hope Sujit does well," Ananda keeps saying as the plane takes off. The runway is a prairie of sweeping white snow. As we pass over the highway, gradually gaining height, the cars below us seem to be crawling, weaving from lane to lane, like snakes.

"It's good to leave that behind," the black stewardess says, motioning out his window as she leans over Ananda, helping him unbuckle his seatbelt.

We land in New York in less than an hour, sitting and waiting while twenty more passengers board the plane. They're all Indians.

"It's good for us," Ananda says. "Last time I had to take a bus to New York to catch the plane. I am glad they gave us a flight," he says, referring to the airlines, the government; actually, he refers to the white man.

When I first met Ananda, at the university where he teaches a course in eastern studies, I thought him remarkably brave, worry-free, unconscious of himself. He faced the class directly, unembarrassed, his manner even a bit condescending, as if we should all be well aware of his intellectual superiority. As if he were handing out favours of wisdom in his sleep. It wasn't his nationality that might have instilled a compromise in a lesser man, but his size. He's a big man weighing close to 300 pounds, with a birth mark on his forehead that almost looks like a large red jewel. His lack of apology, of awkwardness, commanded an awesome respect; the students were blind to his bulk, seeing only what he wanted them to see.

Now, though, I notice how he worries, especially where Sujit is concerned. He is aware of prejudice, of how a classroom of wild students might translate fear or insecurity into skin colour, into race. Sujit is a graduate student, under Ananda's strong yet graceful wing. The classes he's taking over while Ananda vacations in India are his first time out alone.

We're not allowed off the plane in London but are given a free hour at Orly, in Paris. Ananda hobbles into the lobby and in less than a minute is close in conversation with another man. The white girl is leaning on her lover in the middle of the room, laughing, thumping him lightly in the stomach.

"First trip?" a young man asks me. He's been at my elbow since I first came into the room but with so many people around, I hardly took notice of him. I nod. "The first time I stepped off the plane into your country, I almost ran back into the cockpit and how do you say it, hiwacked the plane back to Calcutta."

"Hijacked." I say, not knowing why it's important to correct him. I have learned from Ananda to offhandedly pinpoint mistakes. For me though, it seems senseless.

"Hijacked then. It was like stepping out onto a cloud, all so bright and clean-looking. But the clouds had even lighter eyes, and the eyes were looking through me. I never get used to it you know, but I accept it as part of my new home. Now I feel I'm a little afraid of India, of how I'm going to feel without the clouds and the eyes, whether I will lose myself or not."

"I'm sorry," I say, meaning for the stares, the confusion.

"Oh, it is not your fault."

"I didn't mean it was," I answer quickly, still correcting. I am being made aware of an uncomfortable feeling, a fear within myself, a white fear in the midst of all the brown faces. I need Ananda's confidence now. I wish I was like the white girl, unaware of everyone but who she chooses to see. "There is a difference is all I meant to say."

"Oh, you are right. That we mustn't forget. No need to be afraid though," he says, uncannily, as if he'd read my mind.

No need. That seems naive. There must be a need for there to be so much fear. Maybe it's a need, a need gone wrong, to understand, to love, like the young woman tickling her lover in the middle of the room.

We land in Frankfurt, but only for a few minutes, to take on some extra cargo. The rain is sweeping hard outside, as if to hold us down, the plane's window steaming and stinging with a dull grey glare. I wipe away a hole in the steam, big enough for both my eyes, and watch several men moving away from the plane, their bodies hidden by clumsy raincoats; their faces, peering out of hoods, are faces like mine, white, gleaming in the storm like house lights. But these men are German. In their time, they've been hated more than any brown-skinned man or woman, yet the difference between them and myself is imperceptible to the eye. I feel warm toward them, hoping they'll find some shelter from the rain.

Ananda is good to me. Ordinarily extemely quiet, he is chatting away like a PR man when we land in Kuwait. He can see how nervous I am. We have to disembark from the plane, hauling our hand luggage with us like last links to the past: compartments of ointments and pills, note-paper and pens, maps, and matchbooks with pictures of home on their covers. As we're lining up to board another plane, the young man who talked to me in the lobby at Orly says: "Now for your first shock."

Our new plane is a jumble of human flesh and cramped corners. There are even more people on it than were on the other plane and this one is only half its size. The white crew are gone, so is the black stewardess. The young white girl and I are the only non-Indians left. The few stewardesses are dressed in soiled saris. They don't attempt any discipline, any amenities. Children run up and down the main aisle. People shove their way to favoured seats like passengers on a rush-hour bus.

"You will adapt quickly," Ananda says, reaching over and patting my hand. He looks at my face and half-smiles: "Don't worry." I'm whiter than I've ever been before, as pale as the lost Toronto snow. "You will learn quickly how to act."

In my first conversation with Ananda, he spoke a variation on these very words, "You will learn quickly." He has a heart condition and arthritis in one of his legs so badly that he can hardly walk after sitting down for any length of time. His weight aggravates both conditions. He announced after class one day that he was looking for someone interested in the position of companion, as he was unable to freely be active on his own. It meant room and board, a small salary, help with class work and some travel. I don't really remember my exact reason for applying except that my family was in Thunder Bay and I was living in the dumpiest room in the entire city, broke most of my time, with only a few convenient acquaintances who were little help in wasting a Saturday night.

His being Indian had nothing to do with it. Oh, there might have been some fantasy about my being able to understand my own feelings better if I could learn to understand his. You know, sort out whatever prejudices I might have and get rid of them. But it hasn't been that easy. The job is good, not demanding in a tedious way at all. I've grown to care about Ananda. I understand him very well. And I've discovered that I really don't have any one prejudice, one that I could hold in my hands and study before rolling it up in a ball and tossing it away. I am made up of prejudices. They're integral, like my learning that fire is hot, that when I sleep, I dream. They're reactions, constants, part of my brain. When I see a brown man on the street, I say to myself: "There's a brown man." When I see a hundred of them, I want to run away because I know they're all thinking: "There's a white man," multiplied a hundred times.

The evening is late, total darkness, when we land in Bombay, at the Santa Cruz Airport. I've been through so many different time zones that the night and my body are unrelated. Back in Toronto, Sujit must, by now, be facing much the same as what I am about to, standing at the front of a large class, the white light almost blinding him.

Ananda has said that this trip will probably be his last, a pilgrimage. He promises I will come away a better man, a richer one in spirit. Indians are always talking about spirit. As we wait for the plane doors to open, the threshold of a strange planet, I search myself for some semblance of soul, but without any success. I'm all nerves and hollows.

One of the stewardesses stands at the head of the plane and welcomes us in both English and some other language that Ananda seems to understand. Thirty-four degrees centigrade is the last thing I hear before she opens the door and a blast of heat has me gasping for breath.

The plane we catch in Bombay is about the size of an elevator, what with all the crowds and luggage. We fly across the entire width of India, Ananda dozing, a fly buzzing in and out of his nostrils. The white girl and her Indian man (her husband, they're both wearing wedding rings, shiny ones) are sitting directly in front of me. They talk about his parents, how shocked they're going to be. They haven't told anyone they're coming. A spur of the moment trip.

I cannot imagine moments in the press of brown sweaty bodies. Moments have to pass through space, preferably a field or a long deserted street. Moments should be to remember, not to survive. Moments are in a culture of wristwatches and factory whistles. A moment is one simple choice.

The landing in Calcutta is the worst I've ever endured, not that I've travelled a great deal, but with one trip to England when I was twenty and several jaunts out to Vancouver and back to visit my brother and his wife, I know a little about landings. Usually my stomach starts to spin, but we're always down and stopped before there's any danger of my head beginning to cloud, my tongue sticking to the roof of my mouth. This time though, the plane seems as if it is fighting an angry wind, moving jerkily in slow-motion, almost suspended in the air. I think about being sick, but there are no neat plastic bags and anyway, the woman across the aisle comes lurching out of her seat, falling hard on top of me. There is not time for consideration of any kind and so I manage to keep everything down.

Ananda and I wait until the other passengers have filed off, their junk under their arms or tied around their necks and waists. "Worldly possessions," Ananda says, seeing how fascinated I am with the clutter, but I don't believe him. I've heard about the poverty, but everyone has to have a place where they keep their things, a home, a hole in the side of a mountain.

I have to lug Ananda to his feet and guide him shuffling to the door of the plane. He can't raise his right leg more than half an inch off the ground. A steward helps me lift him down the steps and suddenly, we're in the thick of it.

The heat is tremendous. I've no idea of the time. There's a big clock just below a sign reading Dum Dum Airport, for the English-speaking, but the clock has no hands. From the position of the sun, I'd guess it was mid-morning, but in India, on the other side of the world, it's hard to tell.

We struggle through the crowds; this is no ordered Toronto airport with carpeted tunnels and huge empty waiting-rooms. We're pushed through a set of heavy glass doors, herded through customs, then shoved into a lobby with ceilings that brush the top of my head. A great deal of noise is centred in here, Indians running up to and embracing other Indians. The only way I can tell the travellers apart from the welcoming committees is that most of the travellers are still dressed in western clothes.

Ananda surveys the expanse of the room, his face bunched into a frown. On the third time around, his eyes light up and one stocky arm shoots into the air. He calls something that I can't understand. Several yards away I catch sight of a tiny, thin woman elbowing her way through the crowd, calling, "Ananda, Ananda," over and over again. "It is Anjali," he says to me watching her grow steadily larger as she comes closer and closer.

Anjali is much younger than Ananda, the youngest of all his brothers and sisters and the only one still living in India. She's what in Canada would be called an old maid, a woman in her forties quickly approaching old age. Even in a bright red sari, there's an aura of grey around her.

They hug, Anjali bounding off Ananda's stomach. She pats him on the head, on the back; she takes one of his hands and kisses it on the palm. Ananda introduces me, keeping one of his arms around me so I won't be swept away by the rush of people. "I have a car, I have a car," Anjali says, smiling at me. She tugs at Ananda and I follow, his arm still around me like a hook.

The car is an old black Daimler. There are men lying on the side of the road, clothes in tatters, cripples and children with fat distended bellies drawing near as we approach. The Daimler stands out in the sun like a diamond ring on a dirty finger. A man balances himself on his one remaining leg, half-leaning over the front door of the car chatting with the chauffeur. When Ananda appears, they scatter, the one-legged man hobbling over to the side of the road, crumpling into a sitting position. We climb into the car and slip away.

Halfway down the airport road, on the median strip, there's a wild, tangled garden of flowers and weeds sectioned off by chain-link fencing. All that colour in the middle of the dust and the black reflections the car makes on the road, is shocking. Like a fire in the middle of a city street.

"Is it a park?" I ask. From directly opposite, it looks like a jungle.

"Kind of," Anjali answers.

"For the people?"

"For them to look at. For show."

Ananda chuckles and slaps me on the knee. "There are ironies," he says. "You have been living too long amongst one kind to recognize any other."

The park is thick with green, the only green to be seen anywhere. Off to our left, I can make out the dim outlines of fields: a bleached-green, almost a yellow. But there are no other bursts of colour outside the park. The flowers are as bright as blood, gallant, the fingers of weeds wrapped tightly around their necks, pulling them down.

"Do you understand this?" Ananda interrupts me, both he and Anjali pointing out the window to my right. We're on the main highway, a thin strip of badly paved road divided into two winding lanes. The shoulders are narrow with people, most heading toward the city, with carts full of belongings, with animals. Cows often weave out into the road until a group of men are able to drag them back to safety. Over their heads, beyond their faded skins, there's a billboard facing us, staring down any vehicle that comes from the airport. In big, dark letters: "Man does not live by bread alone." "Is it irony?" Ananda asks, his brown face cut in two by a large, white smile.

"What does man live by here?"

"Oh, things like faith and hope, dreams they are called in Canada."

"People die here of starvation every hour. They die on the streets. Some men are even tempted to eat them," Anjali says, looking as if she were proud of herself, of her survival, her control.

"Then it's not an irony," I say, pointing back to the billboard. By now we're far ahead, although the people by the side of the road are much the same as the ones we supposedly left behind, as if it were only the billboard that was moving, retreating, back out of Calcutta. "It's a mockery, or worse, I'd call it a lie."

"It is like the Prime Minister we have in Canada, Anjali," Ananda says, enjoying himself. "He says we must learn to do without luxuries, that we must face small hardships to save the country. But there are billboards everywhere asking you to take more and more of everything. People are always complaining, Anjali, because new desires are being advertised all the time. Canada is a country of tiny ironies."

"No-one starves to death," I say, unwilling to argue or to laugh, feeling as if my very distinction was tiny. The men who are like walking bones, the stick figures, the tattered clothes, the feet bound by dirty bandages — I haven't seen any of this before, not in such profusion. It is not so much thankfulness that I feel, or patriotism, but that Canada seems less confusing, less assaultive. I cannot discern a comparison between advertising and death.

Calcutta is like the inside of an old machine. We leave the highway and turn into the city and suddenly, the car crawls, faces blearing by the window like they do in train stations, the horn honking at entire families squatting in the middle of the street. Children leap onto the back bumper, jumping up and down, chattering in almost hysterical voices. Teenagers knock on the windows and wave or hold their hands out, either begging or demonstrating how harmless they are. An old machine, having long outlived its purpose, carries on, producing noise, the complexity of rust.

I crane my neck, looking out into the street in front of me, at the wall of bodies surrounding us. I see how it doesn't end. "There is no room to move," I say, more a reaction than a statement. I'm startled when Anjali answers simply: "Life has to be much slower here."

"And noisier," Ananda adds. "I had not realized how much I missed the noise, to know that it comes from human beings, not machines, it's comforting to an old man. So much life." A human machine, I think, correcting myself. Calcutta is like the inside of a tired body.

The car comes to a stop out front of the Great Eastern Hotel. We're on a street they call Chowringhee or so Anjali says. The chauffeur comes around to open the door but is beaten to it by a grey-haired man, dressed a little better than most. He calls me Sahib as I step out, into the heat again. The crowd around me mutters Sahib, some saluting, others grinning and winking when I look at them.

The chauffeur carries our bags into the hotel, leaving the Daimler running, both passenger and driver's door wide open.

"Won't the car be stolen?" I ask, hanging back, expecting to see a dozen of the crowd throw themselves at the quietly purring car, squealing off into the distance, in search of space.

"Oh no," the chauffeur says, shaking his head furiously back and forth "Steal car?" he says, surprised.

"No-one steals cars here," Ananda says. "What for? There is nowhere else to go. Besides, no-one can eat a car."

He gives me a light shove with one of his arms, guiding me toward the hotel. I go in backwards, dizzy with the hundreds of faces in front of me, the carnival of dark-coloured, strangely dressed men and women whirling in my head. I back into the cool lobby of the hotel, turn around and am shocked by how . . . western, how Anglo-Saxon the hotel is. Like walking into a Holiday Inn off a main Toronto street, eyes tricked, for a moment, by a passing parade.

I get used to the crowds, as I did, years ago, at a fair or a circus. At first, I'd be stuck on the fringe of the fair, like snow drifted against a fence. But then, I'd perfect a style of darting in and out, of waiting for the breaks in a solid line of bodies and slipping in, defeating all obstacles as if I were in another dimension.

There are things I cannot get used to though. I don't walk down the side-streets because there are people living in corners, in every available space. I would have to step over women cooking, children having their baths, men catching a snooze in the middle of the day. There are people washing themselves out of the gutters, mothers scrubbing their children's ears with the murky water, babies dunked down up to their necks. And then farther up the street, an old man is peeing in the same gutter, a boy squatting off the edge of the sidewalk. There are sections of the gutters that are used as latrines, other sections turned into washbasins. A delicate balance of life and death.

I stick to the market places. Not that they're any cleaner, but usually no-one is living there, all the crowds just passing through. There is one, across the Maidan, near the statue of Queen Victoria, that I go to most often. A lot of tourists visit here. Ananda is busy most of the time visiting old friends, making arrangements. I meet some of the men in the evenings, at the hotel for dinner, but during the day I'm most often left alone. Even when Ananda has no engagement, he chooses to stay in his room and rest. The weather isn't agreeing with him; I don't know how he ever spent his first 40-odd years of his life in this very same city. His colour is almost grey and he has trouble keeping his food down. I hear him often in the bathroom between our rooms. I've offered him any help I can give, but he tells me that I worry like an old woman and to leave him alone.

Beggars and shopkeepers are always accosting me, as they do all white men, even though very few of them can speak any English beyond the catch phrases, "Good deal for you," or "Look, look." Even the tourists seem to be speaking different languages when I hear them talking together. A lot of Germans and French. Perhaps trips to India are at a premium this year.

On my fourth day in Calcutta, I spot the white girl I saw on the plane. She's over by a stand of jewellery, alone. While I'm considering whether I should approach her or not, a trio of overweight Germans jostle me and I'm forced to head in her direction. She's on the far side of the jewellery stall, by a group of shoeshiners. "Hello," I say, fingering a long yellow necklace.

There is no reaction.

"Hello," I say again, a little louder, jangling a few bracelets together to attract attention.

She looks up at me and with a frown on her face, says: "Leave me alone, eh." She has a distinct Maritimes accent.

"We were on the plane together, on the trip here. I saw you and your husband, but I didn't get a chance to say hello then."

"We were on the plane together?" she repeats, looking at me a bit closer.

"That's right."

"Well, so hello," she says, flinging a chain of beads down on my side of the table and walking away.

I almost follow her, apologize, at least try to explain what I felt we might have in common, but before I do anything, a voice from across the table says: "Bad luck."

One of the shoeshine boys is leaning over his little stand, smiling crookedly, pointing, with his head, after the disappearing girl.

"Sure," I say, starting to move away.

"Shoeshine, Sahib?"

"No thanks," I say without looking at him. I hold up one of my feet to show him I'm wearing sneakers.

"Fine, fine," he shouts. "I do them. Good shoes. My specially."

"You don't shine sneakers," I say, trying to sound as definite as I can, but without walking away. His English, no matter how poor, is magnetic. Shaking my head, I show him my sneakers again. I feel stronger and less confused having the opportunity to correct him.

"You American?"

"No. Canadian," I answer, wondering if a shoeshine boy in Calcutta has ever heard of Canada.

"Ah, I know," he says, sighing, then laughing a friendly kind of laugh. "Canada behind in shoeshines. Sneaker shining is new business."

I don't resist any longer. His name is Deepak. When I'm sitting above him I notice a scattering of grey hairs on his head. He is no boy. I ask him his age but he tells me he doesn't know and would hate to guess in case he's terribly wrong. I would hazard he'd be in his late thirties.

He answers all the other questions I ask him, telling me more than I want to know. He's graphic, the kind of man who would never be hired as a tour guide. He'd point out the toilets and the plaster cracks in the ancient works of art.

He seems surprised that I know so little about India after living with Ananda for over a year and through him, knowing quite a few other Indians. I try to tell him how in Canada, those from India attempt to blend in with our culture, turning themselves into good citizens, wearing good Canadian clothes, whistling at pretty Canadian girls. He doesn't understand. "We don't blend, don't believe it. There is you, Americans, Britain, all so many, all the same. Not me. Lots of us but all Indian, all Indian, all same."

I pay him, overpay him I'm sure. He even has me go across the square and buy him a few cigarettes. They sell for ten naye paise each, which is about a cent and a quarter. He lights one from a slowly burning rope that hangs at the end of the jewellery stall. These ropes hang everywhere in the market place. There are no matches.

"Tomorrow I show you around, okay? I charge little. I show you what you most want to see. How about, Sahib?"

"I don't know," I say, wondering if I'm getting clipped, whether he might be a criminal just itching to get me into a back alley. I finally decide to take him up on the offer after he pesters me for several minutes. I won't take any money other than what is essential. It will be good to see more. I'm too nervous to wander very far from the hotel on my own.

We arrange to meet in the early morning and I head back across the Maidan, my sneakers gleaming in the sun, like mirrors smudged with soap.

Anjali lives in what was once a British mansion. It's still an impressive building, even though left practically untended for over 30 years, abandoned to the elements of weather and time. But the house, inside, is crowded. Dozens and dozens of people live here, in a quarter of a room, in hallways, in nooks, in walk-in closets, in the kitchen where once a large freezer stood. Anjali lives in the space under the stairway, first floor.

Ananda and I, along with one of his closest friends, Govind, are invited to dinner. On the way, the two men laugh at me when I tell them about Deepak, my guide. Neither of them think he's dangerous, but they both warn me of how expensive he might turn out to be. I notice that Ananda's smiles are much tighter than usual. He presses his teeth painfully together and grimaces, his eyes squeezing into watery slits. He kids me about Deepak, but seems far-away at the same time, as if his soul were retreating deep into him, his life unravelling. When we get out of the car at the mansion, I help him and ask if he's all right. "Maybe a month is too long," I say, referring to the amount of time our stay is planned for. "Maybe you've got a bug," I add, thinking of the vast number of illnesses prevalent in this part of the world. He brushes me off, tells me not to act like his nurse. "But . . ." I start to say and he calls for Govind, leaving me behind.

Anjali has a large old sofa against the far wall of her makeshift room. Pillows are scattered on the floor. Near the front, where a wide piece of bright cloth, like a bedspread, hangs down like a door, she has a small table with the legs sawed off. Over in the corner is a hotplate, a kettle, a few pots and pans. Anjali says this is the best place to live in all of Calcutta for those with just a modest amount of money. She can use the giant stove in the kitchen and there's even a small ice box near the stove where she can keep cream for her tea, when she can get it. She has it in a tin canteen, a combination lock around the cap. "They steal cream here instead of cars," she says.

We sit on the pillows while we eat, in candlelight. There is no electricity. The dinner is mainly rice, with a little meat, Anjali says that it's pigeon. Govind and she do most of the talking, leaving Ananda off by himself, as if it had all been arranged. He's uncomfortable, having to squat on the pillows, his big frame almost stretching from wall to wall. He eats hardly any dinner at all. After Govind has finished eating, he glances at Ananda and then getting up, bowing to Anjali, says he'll take Ananda home. Immediately I get to my feet but Ananda puts one of his heavy hands on my shoulder, half-leaning on me, pressing me down. "Stay and keep Anjali company a while. It's not polite to eat and run," he says, chuckling a little, knowing that the cliché is something we share between us, the other two not understanding the humour at all. I persist but he tells me he would rather spend a little time alone with Govind. "We are like brothers," he says, "and you would just be a smart kid in the way."

He has a difficult time getting out of the house. His bad leg is so stiff that he's unable to lift it at all. With Govind's help, he drags himself out the front door and into the night.

"You must not worry," Anjali says later, in the face of my questions. "Ananda is in control of his own life, more so than most men."

"But he could die here."

"Is that so bad?"

"He could be saved back in Toronto. Our hospitals are modern; you don't have to die just because you're sick."

"But people die in your country too," Anjali says. Her patience with me is like a slow wave that keeps returning to the same beach.

"Only when it's hopeless," I say.

"Perhaps Ananda is hopeless."

"What do you mean?" I feel a panic, a cold hollow in my stomach, a fluttering in my chest. I'm afraid for Ananda, for myself, for all the miles that separate me from home. I'm afraid of the crowds. Ananda, in my fear, is almost a white man, the closest I can come here to a reflection of myself.

"I mean nothing," Anjali says, gently. "There is nothing to fear."

She will not return to the subject no matter how hard I try to redirect the conversation. Finally, I tell her about my meeting Deepak, asking her where I might go.

"It's hard for me to answer," she says after thinking quietly for several minutes. "I have spent my whole life here and the city is as common to me as yours would be to you. There are the Sundarbans outside of the city where you can shoot tiger, but that takes too much money. There is Trinka's, they have dancing and drinking, but you have to go there at night. The zoo is a fine place on the Howrah Station where the trains come in. It is majestic."

I decide on the train station. I like the feeling of people coming and going, the definite nature of such a place, where no-one simply wanders but must rush, each having a different destination. I hope to see another pace, a greater assuredness.

Anjali insists I take a rickshaw back to the hotel. It's too far to walk and too late to attempt it. At the front door, I ask her again about Ananda. "Leave him be. He knows his own body. Let what he wants be."

I don't understand it. There is a mystery to our trip, a sense of eerie purpose. It is as if Ananda has planned his illness to coincide with Calcutta. As if he might have created the city in order to die unseen.

Three-quarters of the way back to the hotel, I notice the rickshaw driver is an old man, his fat bony feet slapping the road like hands, his skinny body threatening to burst apart where the bones are most prevalent, dumping his life under the rickshaw's wheels. I ask him to stop, shouting above the noise of the creaking carriage, but he doesn't understand me. "Faster, faster?" he asks, willing to run the life from his body. I pay much more than the trip is worth and walk the rest of the way, running the last hundred yards. The shadows of the half-sleeping crowds have multiplied their numbers by two.

Deepak is waiting for me outside the hotel at 7:30 the next morning. Before leaving, I try to get into Ananda's room to see if he's all right, but Govind is there and won't let me in. "He is sleeping. You would only disturb him," he says, shooing me away and shutting the door.

"Why so sad?" Deepak asks.

"How far is it to the train station?"

We hurry through the busy streets, the already loud market places, the bumpy lanes of human flesh. No sign of men in business suits with shiny briefcases, no young women in colourful dresses, no buses, no sense of going anywhere at all. Just a buzz of survival, of carrying on.

Howrah Station is a set from Cecil B. De Mille. Beggars cover the platforms like abandoned luggage. People bustle in all directions, seemingly without purpose, as if, in panic, they were trapped. The trains themselves are different from any I've ever seen before: huge and ornate, with coach cars; imperial remnants of decadence and ruined money. Smoke billows in the air, separating men from light, stealing our legs and feet like a fog. There are more white men here, rich men, some with ten or fifteen servants trailing behind, toting trunks and suitcases, balancing boxes on their heads. Sellers dart in amongst the white men, carting their jewellery and fabrics with them, children hawking junk as if it were history. "It's like a bazaar," I say and Deepak nods vigorously. "Bizarre, yes, bizarre. How much you pay for seeing this?"

We wander on to a small movie house near the station. "You like to see Indian movie, Indian stars," Deepak insists, tugging at my sleeve like a child. He is so excited that I relent, imagining celluloid secrets of survival; spotlights, like tour guides, illuminating a logic of the streets. We go into the theatre, more a makeshift auditorium of chairs and benches, and sit down, visions of Satyajit Ray in my head.

For a few rupees each we watch a musical, a Busby Berkeley extravaganza, with Indian girls in short skirts and heavy makeup, with boys in tight pants, their shirt-sleeves rolled taut above their muscles. The heroine lives in a smashing apartment with lavender linoleum floors, plastic lampshades, pictures of the Eiffel Tower hanging on the walls, and space, lots of space. Her body need not touch anyone else's body, except for her hero's, a pretty young boy who drives an Italian sports car and dances like Fred Astaire. The audience cheers. They clap their hands to every song, some even singing along as if they'd seen the movie before, and when the big dance number is introduced, one woman stands up and starts to shimmy, the rest of us tapping our toes to the beat.

Outside, in the early afternoon, Deepak is quiet. As we walk away from the theatre, he keeps turning around and looking back as if he had just left home and was cherishing one last look. He seems a little drunk, stumbling over curbs. His eyes are cloudy, the world seen through the bottom of a wine glass.

"Do you like Satyajit Ray?" I ask, trying to snap him out of the movie's trance.

"Who?" he asks, not really knowing if he'd ever heard of the man or not.

"Where else will you take me?" A change of subject, a film brought forcibly to the end. "To the zoo?"

"To the river," he says finally, after another quick glance behind him. "You must go to the zoo early morning, few people. I take you to the river."

"I'm not paying for any river," I say, disappointed, urged on by all the strange things I've been seeing. A river sounds so tame.

"But the Hooghly is specially," Deepak says, watching me closely to see if my eyes light up. Ananda once said that white men are like open books, especially the ones with blue eyes, the colour changing subtly with each emotional shift. "You be surprised."

"Okay," I give in. First, a fantasy movie, now what, a magic river? On the way, I marvel at how easy I'm beginning to feel. When the extraordinary is multiplied, it comes to be what one expects. There is no longer any hint of prejudice, just an awareness of myself as someone different, which almost passes too, as if my skin, like a chameleon, was slowing turning brown. And as for the Indians, there are too many of them to think about; I accept them all.

"In monsoons, the Hooghly floods," Deepak says. "Many people are afraid, because of the dead, because the flooding of river means the dead are looking for friends."

I don't understand what he's saying and don't try to. The Indians have all sorts of strange beliefs. Water symbolizing death, it makes a crude kind of sense, especially when the people who believe it are the same ones who consider cows holy and birth marks the sign of a god. I watch Deepak instead: that remote agelessness, the dark child's eyes, the black hair hanging down onto his forehead, all the grey on top and at the back. His enthusiasm makes him young but even more than that, it's his sense of emptiness and fulfillment. He's like blown glass, shaped by each fiery day, each experience, each glowing human being, recreated by all new thoughts or sights.

We pass over the Howrah Bridge, near the train station. The river runs beneath it, but I hardly even glance at the dirty water. I'm too engrossed in Deepak and in all the other Indians we pass. Everyone shares his qualities of emptiness and joy, some in lesser amounts, few greater. There is no-one waiting to die as I would imagine I would be if I were forced to live here. No viable hierarchy of needs in Calcutta, not the same ones we study in the west and consider a rule of psychology. In the midst of needing everything, from basic shelter to basic food, the Indians don't seem to need anything extra to make them content. They are empty simply because they have nothing. A crumb will fill a stomach, a movie will fill a soul. There is literally "nothing" to envy here, and yet, their receptivity to life . . . as men and women they suffer before my eyes, as strange child-like tour guides they reflect each moment brilliantly, like water or sky.

"This is the head of the river," Deepak says. We're standing at the edge of the shore, still surrounded by the proverbial people, at the end of a little stretch of markets. "There is a burial, you are lucky," he says, motioning a few yards ahead, at a cluster of dark shapes, of softly wailing women, of small but solid men. They're holding the body of a very old man, naked, his skin the colour of melting snow. Someone is chanting. A young girl, about fourteen, is throwing grass into the river.

While watching, I make little sense out of it all, but again, I don't try to. The scene fascinates me, the discrepancies of death and dirty water, of tossed grass and moans. What will happen next? I remember, as a young teenager, being at the beach with my father on a cold day in the early fall. A man in his sixties, small but fat, dressed in what looked to be a pair of pyjamas, walked out on one of the concrete docks, stood on the tip of the stone and raising his arm high above his head, stretched, as if there were a rope several inches beyond his fingertips. Slowly, letting his arms fall back to his sides, without flinching, he fell forward into the cold lake. I was about to yell for help, to draw my father's attention away from where he was watching a cocker spaniel chasing seagulls, when the man reappeared on the shore, his pyjamas clinging to an outline of his bones. He walked back onto the concrete block and began again, without falling this time, just alternately stretching and relaxing. I never pointed him out to my father. There was nothing logical to say. We shuffled down the beach, the man growing small behind us.

Deepak mutters something beside me, a prayer perhaps, his eyes half-shut. The group of people move a little closer to the very edge of the shore and without an explanation, a eulogy or a sprinkling of dust, slide the dead man from their shoulders, down into the river. He disappears quickly, like a fish.

"Oh my God," I say, but Deepak ignores me. All I can think of is how unhealthy it is, how terrifying it would be to dive down into the belly of a dead man, or to be wading and to squish into a corpse's face as if it were mud. It's all I can think of in a city where people urinate in the gutters and cows drop their patties in the middle of the street. My stomach sways as if it were being thrown into the river as well.

"It is the burial ground," Deepak explains on our way back into the heart of the city. My legs have a rubbery feel to them; I am either bouncing or walking on air. "It is our way." He's anxious to please. He doesn't understand how he might have offended me. "It is good, no? Your dead go underground, mine underwater. It is custom," he says, meaning for me to accept without second thoughts. "It is honour. To be burned and have ashes put in the river. Or some, whole bodies. People come all the way from other countries, our people, to be buried in the Hooghly."

I see it now, a horrid vision, the last snapshot of Calcutta. Ananda's fat body turning greyer by the minute. This trip is terminal. I start to walk faster, Deepak running to keep up with me. "You have long legs," he says, trying to be funny. If I have to drag Ananda back along the highway, I will. If I have to shoot my way out of town, I will. If I have to kill him myself, he will come with me.

It isn't that I don't understand. No, Ananda, if I tried very hard, I could probably see the meaning, but I know the minute I walk off the plane in Toronto and am slapped in the face by the sweet smell of the west, the horror will strike me like a heart attack and I won't know exactly how to go on, how to face the scattering of brown faces that are slowly filling our dim white streets.

Ananda has gone from the hotel. The desk clerk explains to me in weak English that he and a friend went away for a few days, that I am not to worry.

I run all the way to Anjali's house. She is under the stairwell, sitting on her antique sofa, sewing a rip in one of her shawls. Even in the bright daylight, the cramped space has to be lit by candles.

"Where is he?" I ask, gripping the wall, dizzy from the heat.

"He is gone."

"Is he dead?" I ask.

"Soon," she answers, turning back to her sewing.

"Why?"

"He has cancer. There is now no bowel left to speak of."

"Why here? Because of the river?"

"No. Because of custom, because it is the city where he was born. Because death is not as frightening at home."

"Why me?"

"He wanted you to see his land, he thought it might make it easier for you when you are back home."

"How can it be easier? Easier because of all the filth, all the shit in your streets, all the death? What can I take back with me except a stench?" I'm crying without a trace of tears. The streets of Calcutta are teeming with my anger.

"You won't know what you take back with you until you are back. Memories are tricky." Anjali's face is empty of sorrow, of anger, of everything. She is accepting, understanding. My anger begins to fade with nothing to replace it.

"When will he be dumped into the river?" I ask, looking away.

"Sometime soon," she says.

"Will you let me know?"

"I think not. I think it better if you were to go home. You have seen a lot of Calcutta and I think it is enough."

I walk back to the hotel, my head heavy with absences, a hollow globe. Ananda's body, in my heart, is curiously light; I think I've known for a long time. Calcutta, Ananda's Calcutta, is a cruel gift. I will carry it with me, on my shoulders, for the rest of my life.

For two days I stay on at the hotel. My bill is paid up until the end of the week. I've come to terms with Ananda, dreaming farewells in my sleep.

I've come to understand that I cannot understand. Calcutta is a foreign city full of foreign things. I can see them, even touch some of them, but they remain foreign. I marvel. I'll tell stories when I'm back in Toronto, colourful tales; I'll try to believe them myself. India is different, I'll say, that's it, talking about my hotel-room with its fake Anglo style. No matter how long I lived here, I could never unconsciously shit in the streets, could never live under a staircase without remembering an entire house, could never wholeheartedly cheer at a third-rate crummy film.

I remember Ananda saying, many times, in various ways, that he couldn't understand our capitalism, our inflation of desires. "I make money though; I collect books and buy cars. Assimilation itself is an irony." The heart madly trying to trick the untrickable soul.

I walk down a street in Toronto. I pass a pair of Indians. They're my brothers, they're just like me, I say. One look in their eyes is enough to know how very far apart we are. It is a new world, this one made from pieces of different lands.

On the third day, near dusk, Deepak comes to the hotel. A porter brings me his message since he's not allowed past the front doors. A shoe-shine boy is the same as a beggar.

"I could take you somewhere," he says.

"I have no money left," I answer, standing there shifting my feet, keeping my eyes cast down. I don't make it easy for him.

"On me," he says. "I take you somewhere free."

"Nothing is free here," I say, as banal as a first impression.

"The zoo, we go to the zoo," he says, grabbing my arm. He's trying to act enthused but I can see through him, a glass face, glass eyes.

"Why are you doing this? What do you owe me?" Beggars circle us as we talk, looking at me, pleading with me to notice them. The beggars outside the Great Eastern Hotel are the cream of the crop. They've spent years training at the markets, the street corners, the train station. They're the executives of the trade.

"I just want to go to the zoo," Deepak says, trying to look sincere.

"Forget it," I say, turning around, heading for the hotel doors.

"He was buried a few days ago. I just find out. I am sorry."

For a moment I'm afraid to turn around in case he might be crying, he sounds so sad. By the time I'm facing him though, he is once again almost invisible with false enthusiasm.

"I will take you there, you like?"

"So I can throw flowers on the water?"

"No. I take you to the bridge. You can see him. Maybe time for him to rise."

I let Deepak lead me through the streets. People bump against me. Children hang onto my shirt-tails. I don't recoil, but allow them their touch. I bump off of those who bump me. I carry the clinging children, like a tide.

The Howrah Bridge is crowded, but I can't tell whether this is a special occasion or simply another aimless Calcutta evening. Deepak leads me to a spot the other side of the bridge, down by the shore, only a foot or two from the water. We stand there and wait for something.

I have planned to start the trip back in the morning. My dreams have been particularly strong the last few nights: Ananda growing smaller, still waving farewell, almost disappearing from my head. Where once, large, he waved goodbye, now he waves on, pushing me into the sky, away, far away.

"There is one," Deepak says, shaking me by the shoulder. A real enthusiasm, he can hardly stand still, beaming a big smile that is just barely reflected in the water. He points to a spot past the bridge, in the middle of the river. "I don't think it is the right one."

A body is bobbing gently in the ripples of the breezy river. A body floating downstream. It must have been under for several days, for now it has swelled and lightened in colour. Almost white. A fat and fair body buoying in the dirty brown water, like a bottle drifting by.

I stay until dark. Four more bodies come under the bridge. Any one of them could be Ananda, except for the first one, a woman. When the sunset is complete, at the point of disappearing, the corpses look like the plaster angels in Catholic churches. When the last light catches a bit of them, they almost look alive, like great white birds, or real angels, skimming the river, floating, their heads tucked away in their feathers. If I had heard a splash, I would have immediately looked up into the sky.

If Ananda is here, if he is one of the ghostly sailing figures, then, in death, he is unrecognizable from his fellow men. I can understand a little more why he wanted to die here. Death is nameless. There are no tombstones, as there are no markers for most of those living. Ananda drifts down the Hooghly River like a million before him have done, like a billion others are going to do. I think of jumping in too, being carried down with them, belonging, but I don't think of it for very long. I have been taught, over and over again, the individuality of breath, the distinctions between grains of sand.

I turn back to the hotel. Deepak has gone. I hear the buzz of people in the night, the mooing of a few cows. The moon, directly above me, is the only thing I know I'll see again.

WILLIAM FAULKNER

The main body of the fiction of William Faulkner (1897–1962) stands as a memorial to the American South, the old South of rich plantation owners and poor white trash, of slavery and sudden violence: a region not without its glories, but suffering a progressive decay from within. Faulkner was born in Oxford, Mississippi, into a family whose roots reached back into the old South; and out of this background grew the fictional city of Jefferson in Yoknapatawpha County, the history of which forms the principal subject of Faulkner's work. After service in the Canadian Flying Corps during World War I and a period at the University of Mississippi, he turned to literature as a profession, publishing his first novel, *Soldiers' Pay*, in 1926. With *Sartoris* (1929), he began his re-creation and exploration of the South, which were to continue in such works as *The Sound and the Fury* (1929), *As I Lay Dying* (1930), *Light in August* (1932), *Absalom, Absalom!* (1936), and *Go Down, Moses* (1942). In these and other works, Faulkner chronicles the fortunes of the Sartorises and the Snopeses, the Compsons and the McCaslins, characters who recur throughout his writings, sometimes at the centre, at other times at the periphery of the action; and although the novels and stories do not form a continuous series, they are linked by common themes and preoccupations: the breakdown of social traditions, the strengths and weaknesses of the old Southern code, the strained and often bloody relations between black and white in the aftermath of slavery. "Dry September," from Faulkner's first collection of stories, *These Thirteen* (1931), is a powerful evocation of the frustration, bigotry, and passion pervading a society in which old fears and hatreds die hard.

Faulkner's achievement, however, extends beyond the dramatic creation of a Southern myth; in the moral problems and the racial tensions of his imaginary community in Mississippi, he has imaged sources of guilt and conflict which beset our larger society. In his address upon receiving the Nobel Prize for literature in 1950, Faulkner spoke of the role of the artist in terms applicable to himself, exhorting young writers to depict "the old verities and truths of the heart, the old universal truths lacking which any story is ephemeral and doomed—love and honor and pity and pride and compassion and sacrifice."

FOR FURTHER READING

Malcolm Cowley, "William Faulkner's Legend of the South," *Sewanee Review* 53 (1945): 343–61.

Jean Stein, "The Art of Fiction XII: William Faulkner," *Paris Review* 12 (Spring 1956): 28–52.

J.B. Vickery, "Ritual and Theme in Faulkner's 'Dry September'," *Arizona Quarterly* 18 (Spring 1962): 5–14.

DRY SEPTEMBER

Through the bloody September twilight, aftermath of sixty-two rainless days, it had gone like a fire in dry grass — the rumor, the story, whatever it was. Something about Miss Minnie Cooper and a Negro. Attacked, insulted, frightened: none of them, gathered in the barber shop on that Saturday evening where the ceiling fan stirred, without freshening it, the vitiated air, sending back upon them, in recurrent surges of stale pomade and lotion, their own stale breath and odors, knew exactly what had happened.

"Except it wasn't Will Mayes," a barber said. He was a man of middle age; a thin, sand-colored man with a mild face, who was shaving a client. "I know Will Mayes. He's a good nigger. And I know Miss Minnie Cooper, too."

"What do you know about her?" a second barber said.

"Who is she?" the client said. "A young girl?"

"No," the barber said. "She's about forty, I reckon. She aint married. That's why I dont believe —"

"Believe, hell!" a hulking youth in a sweat-stained silk shirt said. "Wont you take a white woman's word before a nigger's?"

"I dont believe Will Mayes did it," the barber said. "I know Will Mayes."

"Maybe you know who did it, then. Maybe you already got him out of town, you damn niggerlover."

"I dont believe anybody did anything. I dont believe anything happened. I leave it to you fellows if them ladies that get old without getting married dont have notions that a man cant —"

"Then you are a hell of a white man," the client said. He moved under the cloth. The youth had sprung to his feet.

"You dont?" he said. "Do you accuse a white woman of lying?"

The barber held the razor poised above the half-risen client. He did not look around.

"It's this durn weather," another said. "It's enough to make a man do anything. Even to her."

Nobody laughed. The barber said in his mild, stubborn tone: "I aint accusing nobody of nothing. I just know and you fellows know how a woman that never —"

"You damn niggerlover!" the youth said.

"Shut up, Butch," another said. "We'll get the facts in plenty of time to act."

"Who is? Who's getting them?" the youth said. "Facts, hell! I —"

"You're a fine white man," the client said. "Aint you?" In his frothy beard he looked like a desert rat in moving pictures. "You can tell them, Jack," he said to the youth. "If there aint any white men in this town, you can count on me, even if I aint only a drummer and a stranger."

"That's right, boys," the barber said. "Find out the truth first. I know Will Mayes."

"Well, by God!" the youth shouted. "To think that a white man in this town —"

"Shut up, Butch," the second speaker said. "We got plenty of time."

The client sat up. He looked at the speaker. "Do you claim that anything excuses a nigger attacking a white woman? Do you mean to tell me you are a white man and you'll stand for it? You better go back North where you came from. The South dont want your kind here."

"North what?" the second said. "I was born and raised in this town."

"Well, by God!" the youth said. He looked about with a strained, baffled gaze, as if he was trying to remember what it was he wanted to say or to do. He drew his sleeve across his sweating face. "Damn if I'm going to let a white woman —"

"You tell them, Jack," the drummer said. "By God, if they —"

The screen door crashed open. A man stood in the floor, his feet apart and his heavy-set body poised easily. His white shirt was open at the throat; he wore a felt hat. His hot, bold glance swept the group. His name was McLendon. He had commanded troops at the front in France and had been decorated for valor.

"Well," he said, "are you going to sit there and let a black son rape a white woman on the streets of Jefferson?"

Butch sprang up again. The silk of his shirt clung flat to his heavy shoulders. At each armpit was a dark halfmoon. "That's what I been telling them! That's what I —"

"Did it really happen?" a third said. "This aint the first man scare she ever had, like Hawkshaw says. Wasn't there something about a man on the kitchen roof, watching her undress, about a year ago?"

"What?" the client said. "What's that?" The barber had been slowly forcing him back into the chair; he arrested himself reclining, his head lifted, the barber still pressing him down.

McLendon whirled on the third speaker. "Happen? What the hell difference does it make? Are you going to let the black sons get away with it until one really does it?"

"That's what I'm telling them!" Butch shouted. He cursed, long and steady, pointless.

"Here, here," a fourth said. "Not so loud. Dont talk so loud."

"Sure," McLendon said, "no talking necessary at all. I've done my talking. Who's with me?" He poised on the balls of his feet, roving his gaze.

The barber held the drummer's face down, the razor poised. "Find out the facts first, boys. I know Willy Mayes. It wasn't him. Let's get the sheriff and do this thing right."

McLendon whirled upon him his furious, rigid face. The barber did not look away. They looked like men of different races. The other barbers had ceased also above their prone clients. "You mean to tell me,"

McLendon said, "that you'd take a nigger's word before a white woman's? Why, you damn niggerloving —"

The third speaker rose and grasped McLendon's arm; he too had been a soldier. "Now, now. Let's figure this thing out. Who knows anything about what really happened?"

"Figure out hell!" McLendon jerked his arm free. "All that're with me get up from there. The ones that aint —" He roved his gaze, dragging his sleeve across his face.

Three men rose. The drummer in the chair sat up. "Here," he said, jerking at the cloth about his neck; "get this rag off me. I'm with him. I dont live here, but by God, if our mothers and wives and sisters —" He smeared the cloth over his face and flung it to the floor. McLendon stood in the floor and cursed the others. Another rose and moved toward him. The remainder sat uncomfortable, not looking at one another, then one by one they rose and joined him.

The barber picked the cloth from the floor. He began to fold it neatly. "Boys, dont do that. Will Mayes never done it. I know."

"Come on," McLendon said. He whirled. From his hip pocket protruded the butt of a heavy automatic pistol. They went out. The screen door crashed behind them reverberant in the dead air.

The barber wiped the razor carefully and swiftly, and put it away, and ran to the rear, and took his hat from the wall. "I'll be back as soon as I can," he said to the other barbers. "I cant let —" He went out, running. The two other barbers followed him to the door and caught it on the rebound, leaning out and looking up the street after him. The air was flat and dead. It had a metallic taste at the base of the tongue.

"What can he do?" the first said. The second one was saying "Jees Christ, Jees Christ" under his breath. "I'd just as lief be Will Mayes as Hawk, if he gets McLendon riled."

"Jees Christ, Jees Christ," the second whispered.

"You reckon he really done it to her?" the first said.

II

She was thirty-eight or thirty-nine. She lived in a small frame house with her invalid mother and a thin, sallow, unflagging aunt, where each morning between ten and eleven she would appear on the porch in a lace-trimmed boudoir cap, to sit swinging in the porch swing until noon. After dinner she lay down for a while, until the afternoon began to cool. Then, in one of the three or four new voile dresses which she had each summer, she would go downtown to spend the afternoon in the stores with the other ladies, where they would handle the goods and haggle over the prices in cold, immediate voices, without any intention of buying.

She was of comfortable people — not the best in Jefferson, but good people enough — and she was still on the slender side of ordinary-looking, with a bright, faintly haggard manner and dress. When she was young she had had a slender nervous body and a sort of hard vivacity which had enabled her for a time to ride upon the crest of the town's social life as exemplified by the high school party and church social period of her contemporaries while still children enough to be unclass-conscious.

She was the last to realize that she was losing ground; that those among whom she had been a little brighter and louder flame than any other were beginning to learn the pleasure of snobbery — male — and retaliation — female. That was when her face began to wear that bright, haggard look. She still carried it to parties on shadowy porticoes and summer lawns, like a mask or a flag, with that bafflement of furious repudiation of truth in her eyes. One evening at a party she heard a boy and two girls, all schoolmates, talking. She never accepted another invitation.

She watched the girls with whom she had grown up as they married and got homes and children, but no man ever called on her steadily until the children of the other girls had been calling her "aunty" for several years, the while their mothers told them in bright voices about how popular Aunt Minnie had been as a girl. Then the town began to see her driving on Sunday afternoons with the cashier in the bank. He was a widower of about forty — a high-colored man, smelling always faintly of the barber shop or of whisky. He owned the first automobile in town, a red runabout; Minnie had the first motoring bonnet and veil the town ever saw. Then the town began to say: "Poor Minnie." "But she is old enough to take care of herself," others said. That was when she began to ask her old schoolmates that their children call her "cousin" instead of "aunty."

It was twelve years now since she had been relegated into adultery by public opinion, and eight years since the cashier had gone to a Memphis bank, returning for one day each Christmas, which he spent at an annual bachelors' party at a hunting club on the river. From behind their curtains the neighbors would see the party pass, and during the over-the-way Christmas day visiting they would tell her about him, about how well he looked, and how they heard that he was prospering in the city, watching with bright, secret eyes her haggard, bright face. Usually by that hour there would be the scent of whisky on her breath. It was supplied her by a youth, a clerk at the soda fountain: "Sure; I buy it for the old gal. I reckon she's entitled to a little fun."

Her mother kept to her room altogether now; the gaunt aunt ran the house. Against that background Minnie's bright dresses, her idle and empty days, had a quality of furious unreality. She went out in the evenings only with women now, neighbors, to the moving pictures. Each afternoon she dressed in one of the new dresses and went downtown alone, where her young "cousins" were already strolling in the late afternoons with their delicate, silken heads and thin, awkward arms and conscious hips, clinging to one another or shrieking and giggling with paired boys in the soda fountain when she passed and went on along the serried store fronts, in the doors of which the sitting and lounging men did not even follow her with their eyes any more.

III

The barber went swiftly up the street where the sparse lights, insect-swirled, glared in rigid and violent suspension in the lifeless air. The day had died in a pall of dust; above the darkened square, shrouded by the spent dust, the sky was as clear as the inside of a brass bell. Below the east was a rumor of the twice-waxed moon.

When he overtook them McLendon and three others were getting into a car parked in an alley. McLendon stooped his thick head, peering out beneath the top, "Changed your mind, did you?" he said. "Damn good thing; by God, tomorrow when this town hears about how you talked tonight —"

"Now, now," the other ex-soldier said. "Hawkshaw's all right. Come on, Hawk; jump in."

"Will Mayes never done it, boys," the barber said. "If anybody done it. Why, you all know well as I do there aint any town where they got better niggers than us. And you know how a lady will kind of think things about men when there aint any reason to, and Miss Minnie anyway —"

"Sure, sure," the soldier said. "We're just going to talk to him a little; that's all."

"Talk hell!" Butch said. "When we're through with the —"

"Shut up, for God's sake!" the soldier said. "Do you want everybody in town —"

"Tell them, by God!" McLendon said. "Tell every one of the sons that'll let a white woman —"

"Let's go; let's go; here's the other car." The second car slid squealing out of a cloud of dust at the alley mouth. McLendon started his car and took the lead. Dust lay like a fog in the street. The street lights hung nimbused as in water. They drove out of town.

A rutted lane turned at right angles. Dust hung above it too, and above all the land. The dark bulk of the ice plant, where the Negro Mayes was night watchman, rose against the sky. "Better stop here, hadn't we?" the soldier said. McLendon did not reply. He hurled the car up and slammed to a stop, the headlights glaring on the blank wall.

"Listen here, boys," the barber said; "if he's here, dont that prove he never done it? Dont it? If it was him, he would run. Dont you see he would?" The second car came up and stopped. McLendon got down; Butch sprang down beside him. "Listen, boys," the barber said.

"Cut the lights off!" McLendon said. The breathless dark rushed down. There was no sound in it save their lungs as they sought air in the parched dust in which for two months they had lived; then the diminishing crunch of McLendon's and Butch's feet, and a moment later McLendon's voice:

"Will! . . . Will!"

Below the east the wan hemorrhage of the moon increased. It heaved above the ridge, silvering the air, the dust, so that they seemed to breathe, live, in a bowl of molten lead. There was no sound of nightbird nor insect, no sound save their breathing and a faint ticking of contracting metal about the cars. Where their bodies touched one another they seemed to sweat dryly, for no more moisture came. "Christ!" a voice said; "let's get out of here."

But they didn't move until vague noises began to grow out of the darkness ahead; then they got out and waited tensely in the breathless dark. There was another sound: a blow, a hissing expulsion of breath and McLendon cursing in undertone. They stood a moment longer, then they ran forward. They ran in a stumbling clump, as though they were fleeing something. "Kill him, kill the son," a voice whispered. McLendon flung them back.

"Not here," he said. "Get him into the car." "Kill him, kill the black son!" the voice murmured. They dragged the Negro to the car. The barber had waited beside the car. He could feel himself sweating and he knew he was going to be sick at the stomach.

"What is it, captains?" the Negro said. "I aint done nothing. 'Fore God, Mr John." Someone produced handcuffs. They worked busily about the Negro as though he were a post, quiet, intent, getting in one another's way. He submitted to the handcuffs, looking swiftly and constantly from dim face to dim face. "Who's here, captains?" he said, leaning to peer into the faces until they could feel his breath and smell his sweaty reek. He spoke a name or two. "What you all say I done, Mr John?"

McLendon jerked the car door open. "Get in!" he said.

The Negro did not move. "What you all going to do with me, Mr John? I aint done nothing. White folks, captains, I aint done nothing: I swear 'fore God." He called another name.

"Get in!" McLendon said. He struck the Negro. The others expelled their breath in a dry hissing and struck him with random blows and he whirled and cursed them, and swept his manacled hands across their faces and slashed the barber upon the mouth, and the barber struck him also. "Get him in there," McLendon said. They pushed at him. He ceased struggling and got in and sat quietly as the others took their places. He sat between the barber and the soldier, drawing his limbs in so as not to touch them, his eyes going swiftly and constantly from face to face. Butch clung to the running board. The car moved on. The barber nursed his mouth with his handkerchief.

"What's the matter, Hawk?" the soldier said.

"Nothing," the barber said. They regained the highroad and turned away from town. The second car dropped back out of the dust. They went on, gaining speed; the final fringe of houses dropped behind.

"Goddamn, he stinks!" the soldier said.

"We'll fix that," the drummer in front beside McLendon said. On the running board Butch cursed into the hot rush of air. The barber leaned suddenly forward and touched McLendon's arm.

"Let me out, John," he said.

"Jump out, niggerlover," McLendon said without turning his head. He drove swiftly. Behind them the sourceless lights of the second car glared in the dust. Presently McLendon turned into a narrow road. It was rutted with disuse. It led back to an abandoned brick kiln — a series of reddish mounds and weed- and vine-choked vats without bottom. It had been used for pasture once, until one day the owner missed one of his mules. Although he prodded carefully in the vats with a long pole, he could not even find the bottom of them.

"John," the barber said.

"Jump out, then," McLendon said, hurling the car along the ruts. Beside the barber the Negro spoke:

"Mr Henry."

The barber sat forward. The narrow tunnel of the road rushed up and past. Their motion was like an extinct furnace blast: cooler, but utterly dead. The car bounded from rut to rut.

"Mr Henry," the Negro said.

The barber began to tug furiously at the door. "Look out, there!" the soldier said, but the barber had already kicked the door open and swung onto the running board. The soldier leaned across the Negro and grasped at him, but he had already jumped. The car went on without checking speed.

The impetus hurled him crashing through dust-sheathed weeds, into the ditch. Dust puffed about him, and in a thin, vicious crackling of sapless stems he lay choking and retching until the second car passed and died away. Then he rose and limped on until he reached the highroad and turned toward town, brushing at his clothes with his hands. The moon was higher, riding high and clear of the dust at last, and after a while the town began to glare beneath the dust. He went on, limping. Presently he heard cars and the glow of them grew in the dust behind him and he left the road and crouched again in the weeds until they passed. McLendon's car came last now. There were four people in it and Butch was not on the running board.

They went on; the dust swallowed them; the glare and the sound died away. The dust of them hung for a while, but soon the eternal dust absorbed it again. The barber climbed back onto the road and limped on toward town.

IV

As she dressed for supper on that Saturday evening, her own flesh felt like fever. Her hands trembled among the hooks and eyes, and her eyes had a feverish look, and her hair swirled crisp and crackling under the comb. While she was still dressing the friends called for her and sat while she donned her sheerest underthings and stockings and a new voile dress. "Do you feel strong enough to go out?" they said, their eyes bright too, with a dark glitter. "When you have had time to get over the shock, you must tell us what happened. What he said and did; everything."

In the leafed darkness, as they walked toward the square, she began to breathe deeply, something like a swimmer preparing to dive, until she ceased trembling, the four of them walking slowly because of the terrible heat and out of solicitude for her. But as they neared the square she began to tremble again, walking with her head up, her hands clenched at her sides, their voices about her murmurous, also with that feverish, glittering quality of their eyes.

They entered the square, she in the center of the group, fragile in her fresh dress. She was trembling worse. She walked slower and slower, as children eat ice cream, her head up and her eyes bright in the haggard banner of her lace, passing the hotel and the coatless drummers in chairs along the curb looking around at her: "That's the one: see? The one in pink in the middle." "Is that her? What did they do with the nigger? Did they — ?" "Sure. He's all right." "All right, is he?" "Sure. He went on a little trip." Then the drug store, where even the young men lounging in the doorway tipped their hats and followed with their eyes the motion of her hips and legs when she passed.

They went on, passing the lifted hats of the gentlemen, the suddenly ceased voices, deferent, protective. "Do you see?" the friends said. Their voices sounded like long, hovering sighs of hissing exultation. "There's not a Negro on the square. Not one."

They reached the picture show. It was like a miniature fairyland with its lighted lobby and colored lithographs of life caught in its terrible and beautiful mutations. Her lips began to tingle. In the dark, when the picture began, it would be all right; she could hold back the laughing so it would not waste away so fast and so soon. So she hurried on before the turning faces, the undertones of low astonishment, and they took their accustomed places where she could see the aisle against the silver glare and the young men and girls coming in two and two against it.

The lights flicked away; the screen glowed silver, and soon life began to unfold, beautiful and passionate and sad, while still the young men and girls entered, scented and sibilant in the half dark, their paired backs in silhouette delicate and sleek, their slim, quick bodies awkward, divinely young, while beyond them the silver dream accumulated, inevitably on and on. She began to laugh. In trying to suppress it, it made more noise than ever; heads began to turn. Still laughing, her friends raised her and led her out, and she stood at the curb, laughing on a high, sustained note, until the taxi came up and they helped her in.

They removed the pink voile and the sheer underthings and the stockings, and put her to bed, and cracked ice for her temples, and sent for the doctor. He was hard to locate, so they ministered to her with hushed ejaculations, renewing the ice and fanning her. While the ice was fresh and cold she stopped laughing and lay still for a time, moaning only a little. But soon the laughing welled again and her voice rose screaming.

"Shhhhhhhhhhh! Shhhhhhhhhhhhhhh!" they said, freshening the icepack, smoothing her hair, examining it for gray; "poor girl!" Then to one another: "Do you suppose anything really happened?" their eyes darkly aglitter, secret and passionate. "Shhhhhhhhhh! Poor girl! Poor Minnie!"

V

It was midnight when McLendon drove up to his neat new house. It was trim and fresh as a birdcage and almost as small, with its clean, green-and-white paint. He locked the car and mounted the porch and entered. His wife rose from a chair beside the reading lamp. McLendon stopped in the floor and stared at her until she looked down.

"Look at that clock," he said, lifting his arm, pointing. She stood before him, her face lowered, a magazine in her hands. Her face was pale, strained, and weary-looking. "Haven't I told you about sitting up like this, waiting to see when I come in?"

"John," she said. She laid the magazine down. Poised on the balls of his feet, he glared at her with his hot eyes, his sweating face.

"Didn't I tell you?" He went toward her. She looked up then. He caught her shoulder. She stood passive, looking at him.

"Dont, John. I couldn't sleep . . . The heat; something. Please, John. You're hurting me."

"Didn't I tell you?" He released her and half struck, half flung her across the chair, and she lay there and watched him quietly as he left the room.

He went on through the house, ripping off his shirt, and on the dark, screened porch at the rear he stood and mopped his head and shoulders with the shirt and flung it away. He took the pistol from his hip and laid it on the table beside the bed, and sat on the bed and removed his shoes, and rose and slipped his trousers off. He was sweating again already, and he stooped and hunted furiously for the shirt. At last he found it and wiped his body again, and, with his body pressed against the dusty screen, he stood panting. There was no movement, no sound, not even an insect. The dark world seemed to lie stricken beneath the cold moon and the lidless stars.

E.M. FORSTER

Edward Morgan Forster (1879–1970) was born into a London family connected with the group of wealthy Evangelicals known as the Clapham Sect. His upbringing and education (Tonbridge School and King's College, Cambridge) were solidly middle class; yet despite this background, Forster turned a critical and satirical eye on the snobbery and superficiality of English society. After leaving Cambridge in 1901, he travelled through Italy and Greece, and in the Mediterranean temperament he perceived qualities of passion and responsiveness very different from the coldness and reserve of the English character. In his novels *Where Angels Fear to Tread* (1905), *The Longest Journey* (1907), and *Howards End* (1910), he exposes middle-class illusions, and sets the deadening force of social convention against the liberating power of feeling, a conflict enacted on both the spiritual and the sexual level. This opposition between social pressures and individual feeling is often expressed as a clash between the rational faculties and the imagination, and it takes on a broader significance in *A Passage to India* (1924), in which two cultures meet but do not merge: the Englishman and the Indian are symbolically parted at the end of that novel, as if to emphasize how the Western mind has lost touch with the deeper springs of intuitive awareness and the sources of natural harmony.

These concerns also find expression in Forster's short stories, collected in *The Celestial Omnibus* (1911) and *The Eternal Moment* (1928), where he gives freer rein to allegorical and mythical tendencies. In "The Road from Colonus" (*The Celestial Omnibus*), Forster juxtaposes the shallowness of contemporary English values with the spirit of life in an ancient land. The title alludes to the story of Oedipus, who, old and blind, was transfigured by his experience in the sacred grove at Colonus, and enabled to meet his death with pride and dignity.

FOR FURTHER READING

E.M. Forster, *Aspects of the Novel* (London: Edward Arnold, 1927; reprinted by Penguin Books, 1962).
F.P.W. McDowell, "Forster's 'Natural Supernaturalism': The Tales," *Modern Fiction Studies 7* (1961): 271–83.
Lionel Trilling, *E.M. Forster*, 2d ed. (New York: New Directions, 1964).

THE ROAD FROM COLONUS

I

For no very intelligible reason, Mr Lucas had hurried ahead of his party. He was perhaps reaching the age at which independence becomes valuable, because it is so soon to be lost. Tired of attention and consideration, he liked breaking away from the younger members, to ride by himself, and to dismount unassisted. Perhaps he also relished that more subtle pleasure of being kept waiting for lunch, and of telling the others on their arrival that it was of no consequence.

So, with childish impatience, he battered the animal's sides with his heels, and made the muleteer bang it with a thick stick and prick it with a sharp one, and jolted down the hill sides through clumps of flowering shrubs and stretches of anemones and asphodel, till he heard the sound of running water, and came in sight of the group of plane trees where they were to have their meal.

Even in England those trees would have been remarkable, so huge were they, so interlaced, so magnificently clothed in quivering green. And here in Greece they were unique, the one cool spot in that hard brilliant landscape, already scorched by the heat of an April sun. In their midst was hidden a tiny Khan or country inn, a frail mud building with a broad wooden balcony in which sat an old woman spinning, while a small brown pig, eating orange peel, stood beside her. On the wet earth below squatted two children, playing some primaeval game with their fingers; and their mother, none too clean either, was messing with some rice inside. As Mrs Forman would have said, it was all very Greek, and the fastidious Mr Lucas felt thankful that they were bringing their own food with them, and should eat it in the open air.

Still, he was glad to be there—the muleteer had helped him off—and glad that Mrs Forman was not there to forestall his opinions — glad even that he should not see Ethel for quite half an hour. Ethel was his youngest daughter, still unmarried. She was unselfish and affectionate, and it was generally understood that she was to devote her life to her father, and be the comfort of his old age. Mrs Forman always referred to her as Antigone, and Mr Lucas tried to settle down to the role of Oedipus, which seemed the only one that public opinion allowed him.

He had this in common with Oedipus, that he was growing old. Even to himself it had become obvious. He had lost interest in other people's affairs, and seldom attended when they spoke to him. He was fond of talking himself but often forgot what he was going to say, and even when he succeeded, it seldom seemed worth the effort. His phrases and gestures had become stiff and set, his anecdotes, once so successful, fell flat, his silence was as meaningless as his speech. Yet he had led a healthy, active life, had worked steadily, made money, educated his children. There was nothing and no one to blame: he was simply growing old.

At the present moment, here he was in Greece, and one of the dreams of his life was realized. Forty years ago he had caught the fever of Hellenism, and all his life he had felt that could he but visit that land, he would not have lived in vain. But Athens had been dusty, Delphi wet, Thermopylae flat, and he had listened with amazement and cynicism to the rapturous exclamations of his companions. Greece was like England: it was a man who was growing old, and it made no difference whether that man looked at the Thames or the Eurotas. It was his last hope of contradicting that logic of experience, and it was failing.

Yet Greece had done something for him, though he did not know it. It had made him discontented, and there are stirrings of life in discontent. He knew that he was not the victim of continual ill-luck. Something great was wrong, and he was pitted against no mediocre or accidental enemy. For the last month a strange desire had possessed him to die fighting.

"Greece is the land for young people," he said to himself as he stood under the plane trees, "but I will enter into it, I will possess it. Leaves shall be green again, water shall be sweet, the sky shall be blue. They were so forty years ago, and I will win them back. I do mind being old, and I will pretend no longer."

He took two steps forward, and immediately cold waters were gurgling over his ankle.

"Where does the water come from?" he asked himself. "I do not even know that." He remembered that all the hill sides were dry; yet here the road was suddenly covered with flowing streams.

He stopped still in amazement, saying: "Water out of a tree—out of a hollow tree? I never saw nor thought of that before."

For the enormous plane that leant towards the Khan was hollow—it had been burnt out for charcoal—and from its living trunk there gushed an impetuous spring, coating the bark with fern and moss, and flowing over the mule track to create fertile meadows beyond. The simple country folk had paid to beauty and mystery such tribute as they could, for in the rind of the tree a shrine was cut, holding a lamp and a little picture of the Virgin, inheritor of the Naiad's and Dryad's joint abode.

"I never saw anything so marvellous before," said Mr Lucas. "I could even step inside the trunk and see where the water comes from."

For a moment he hesitated to violate the shrine. Then he remembered with a smile his own thought — "the place shall be mine; I will enter it and possess it" — and leapt almost aggressively on to a stone within.

The water pressed up steadily and noiselessly from the hollow roots and hidden crevices of the plane, forming a wonderful amber pool ere it spilt over the lip of bark on to the earth outside. Mr Lucas tasted it and it was sweet, and when he looked up the black funnel of the trunk he saw sky which was blue, and some leaves which were green; and he remembered, without smiling, another of his thoughts.

Others had been before him — indeed he had a curious sense of companionship. Little votive offerings to the presiding Power were fastened on to the bark — tiny arms and legs and eyes in tin, grotesque models of the brain or the heart — all tokens of some recovery of strength or wisdom or love. There was no such thing as the solitude of nature, for the sorrows and joys of humanity had pressed even into the bosom of a tree. He spread out his arms and steadied himself against the soft charred wood, and then slowly leant back, till his body was resting on the trunk behind. His eyes closed, and he had the strange feeling of one who is moving, yet at peace — the feeling of the swimmer, who, after long struggling with chopping seas, finds that after all the tide will sweep him to his goal.

So he lay motionless, conscious only of the stream below his feet, and that all things were a stream, in which he was moving.

He was aroused at last by a shock — the shock of an arrival perhaps, for when he opened his eyes, something unimagined, indefinable, had passed over all things, and made them intelligible and good.

There was meaning in the stoop of the old woman over her work, and in the quick motions of the little pig, and in her diminishing globe of wool. A young man came singing over the streams on a mule, and there was beauty in his pose and sincerity in his greeting. The sun made no accidental patterns upon the spreading roots of the trees, and there was intention in the nodding clumps of asphodel, and in the music of the water. To Mr Lucas, who, in a brief space of time, had discovered not only Greece, but England and all the world and life, there seemed nothing ludicrous in the desire to hang within the tree another votive offering — a little model of an entire man.

"Why, here's papa, playing at being Merlin."

All unnoticed they had arrived — Ethel, Mrs Forman, Mr Graham, and the English-speaking dragoman. Mr Lucas peered out at them suspiciously. They had suddenly become unfamiliar, and all that they did seemed strained and coarse.

"Allow me to give you a hand," said Mr Graham, a young man who was always polite to his elders.

Mr Lucas felt annoyed. "Thank you, I can manage perfectly well by myself," he replied. His foot slipped as he stepped out of the tree, and went into the spring.

"Oh papa, my papa!" said Ethel, "what are you doing? Thank goodness I have got a change for you on the mule."

She tended him carefully, giving him clean socks and dry boots, and then sat him down on the rug beside the lunch basket, while she went with the others to explore the grove.

They came back in ecstasies, in which Mr Lucas tried to join. But he found them intolerable. Their enthusiasm was superficial, commonplace, and spasmodic. They had no perception of the coherent beauty that was flowering around them. He tried at least to explain his feelings, and what he said was:

"I am altogether pleased with the appearance of this place. It impresses me very favourably. The trees are fine, remarkably fine for Greece, and there is something very poetic in the spring of clear running water. The people too seem kindly and civil. It is decidedly an attractive place."

Mrs Forman upbraided him for his tepid praise.

"Oh, it is a place in a thousand!" she cried, "I could live and die here! I really would stop if I had not to be back at Athens! It reminds me of the Colonus of Sophocles."

"Well, *I* must stop," said Ethel. "I positively must."

"Yes, do! You and your father! Antigone and Oedipus. Of course you must stop at Colonus!"

Mr Lucas was almost breathless with excitement. When he stood within the tree, he had believed that his happiness would be independent of locality. But these few minutes' conversation had undeceived him. He no longer trusted himself to journey through the world, for old thoughts, old wearinesses might be waiting to rejoin him as soon as he left the shade of the planes, and the music of the virgin water. To sleep in the Khan with the gracious, kind-eyed country people, to watch the bats flit about within the globe of shade, and see the moon turn the golden patterns into silver — one such night would place him beyond relapse, and confirm him for ever in the kingdom he had regained. But all his lips could say was: "I should be willing to put in a night here."

"You mean a week, papa! It would be sacrilege to put in less."

"A week then, a week," said his lips, irritated at being corrected, while his heart was leaping with joy. All through lunch he spoke to them no more, but watched the place he should know so well, and the people who would so soon be his companions and friends. The inmates of the Khan only consisted of an old woman, a middle-aged woman, a young man and two children, and to none of them had he spoken, yet he loved them as he loved everything that moved or breathed or existed beneath the benedictory shade of the planes.

"*En route!*" said the shrill voice of Mrs Forman. "Ethel! Mr. Graham! The best of things must end."

"To-night," thought Mr Lucas, "they will light the little lamp by the shrine. And when we all sit together on the balcony, perhaps they will tell me which offerings they put up."

"I beg your pardon, Mr Lucas," said Graham, "but they want to fold up the rug you are sitting on."

Mr Lucas got up, saying to himself: "Ethel shall go to bed first, and then I will try to tell them about my offering too — for it is a thing I must do. I think they will understand if I am left with them alone."

Ethel touched him on the cheek. "Papa! I've called you three times. All the mules are here."

"Mules? What mules?"

"Our mules. We're all waiting. Oh, Mr Graham, do help my father on."

"I don't know what you're talking about, Ethel."

"My dearest papa, we must start. You know we have to get to Olympia tonight."

Mr Lucas in pompous, confident tones replied: "I always did wish, Ethel, that you had a better head for plans. You know perfectly well that we are putting in a week here. It is your own suggestion."

Ethel was startled into impoliteness. "What a perfectly ridiculous idea. You must have known I was joking. Of course I meant I wished we could."

"Ah! if we could only do what we wished!" sighed Mrs Forman, already seated on her mule.

"Surely," Ethel continued in calmer tones, "you didn't think I meant it."

"Most certainly I did. I have made all my plans on the supposition that we are stopping here, and it will be extremely inconvenient, indeed, impossible for me to start."

He delivered this remark with an air of great conviction, and Mrs Forman and Mr Graham had to turn away to hide their smiles.

"I am sorry I spoke so carelessly; it was wrong of me. But, you know, we can't break up our party, and even one night here would make us miss the boat at Patras."

Mrs Forman, in an aside, called Mr Graham's attention to the excellent way in which Ethel managed her father.

"I don't mind about the Patras boat. You said that we should stop here, and we are stopping."

It seemed as if the inhabitants of the Khan had divined in some mysterious way that the altercation touched them. The old woman stopped her spinning, while the young man and the two children stood behind Mr Lucas, as if supporting him.

Neither arguments nor entreaties moved him. He said little, but he was absolutely determined, because for the first time he saw his daily life aright. What need had he to return to England? Who would miss him? His friends were dead or cold. Ethel loved him in a way, but, as was right, she had other interests. His other children he seldom saw. He had only one other relative, his sister Julia, whom he both feared and hated. It was no effort to struggle. He would be a fool as well as a coward if he stirred from the place which brought him happiness and peace.

At last Ethel, to humour him, and not disinclined to air her modern Greek, went into the Khan with the astonished dragoman to look at the rooms. The woman inside received them with loud welcomes, and the young man, when no one was looking, began to lead Mr Lucas' mule to the stable.

"Drop it, you brigand!" shouted Graham, who always declared that foreigners could understand English if they chose. He was right, for the man obeyed, and they all stood waiting for Ethel's return.

She emerged at last, with close-gathered skirts, followed by the dragoman bearing the little pig, which he had bought at a bargain.

"My dear papa, I will do all I can for you, but stop in that Khan — no."

"Are there — fleas?" asked Mrs Forman.

Ethel intimated that "fleas" was not the word.

"Well, I am afraid that settles it," said Mrs Forman, "I know how particular Mr Lucas is."

"It does not settle it," said Mr Lucas. "Ethel, you go on. I do not want you. I don't know why I ever consulted you. I shall stop here alone."

"That is absolute nonsense," said Ethel, losing her temper. "How can you be left alone at your age? How would you get your meals or your bath? All your letters are waiting for you at Patras. You'll miss the boat. That means missing the London operas, and upsetting all your engagements for the month. And as if you could travel by yourself!"

"They might knife you," was Mr Graham's contribution.

The Greeks said nothing; but whenever Mr Lucas looked their way, they beckoned him towards the Khan. The children would even have drawn him by the coat, and the old woman on the balcony stopped her almost completed spinning, and fixed him with mysterious appealing eyes. As he fought, the issue assumed gigantic proportions, and he believed that he was not merely stopping because he had regained youth or seen beauty or found happiness, but because in that place and with those people a supreme event was awaiting him which would transfigure the face of the world. The moment was so tremendous that he abandoned words and arguments as useless, and rested on the strength of his mighty unrevealed allies: silent men, murmuring water, and whispering trees. For the whole place called with one voice, articulate to him, and his garrulous opponents became every minute more meaningless and absurd. Soon they would be tired and go chattering away into the sun, leaving him to the cool grove and the moonlight and the destiny he foresaw.

Mrs Forman and the dragoman had indeed already started, amid the piercing screams of the little pig, and the struggle might have gone on indefinitely if Ethel had not called in Mr Graham.

"Can you help me?" she whispered. "He is absolutely unmanageable."

"I'm no good at arguing — but if I could help you in any other way — " and he looked down complacently at his well-made figure.

Ethel hesitated. Then she said: "Help me in any way you can. After all, it is for his good that we do it."

"Then have his mule led up behind him."

So when Mr Lucas thought he had gained the day, he suddenly felt himself lifted off the ground, and sat sideways on the saddle, and at the same time the mule started off at a trot. He said nothing, for he had nothing to say, and even his face showed little emotion as he felt the shade pass and heard the sound of the water cease. Mr Graham was running at his side, hat in hand, apologizing.

"I know I had no business to do it, and I do beg your pardon awfully. But I do hope that some day you too will feel that I was — damn!"

A stone had caught him in the middle of the back. It was thrown by the little boy, who was pursuing them along the mule track. He was followed by his sister, also throwing stones.

Ethel screamed to the dragoman, who was some way ahead with Mrs Forman, but before he could rejoin them, another adversary appeared. It was the young Greek, who had cut them off in front, and now dashed down at Mr Lucas' bridle. Fortunately Graham was an expert boxer, and it did not take him a moment to beat down the youth's feeble defence, and to send him sprawling with a bleeding mouth into the asphodel. By this time the dragoman had arrived, the children, alarmed at the fate of their brother, had desisted, and the rescue party, if such it is to be considered, retired in disorder to the trees.

"Little devils!" said Graham, laughing with triumph. "That's the modern Greek all over. Your father meant money if he stopped, and they consider we were taking it out of their pocket."

"Oh, they are terrible — simple savages! I don't know how I shall ever thank you. You've saved my father."

"I only hope you didn't think me brutal."

"No," replied Ethel with a little sigh. "I admire strength."

Meanwhile the cavalcade reformed, and Mr Lucas, who, as Mrs Forman said, bore his disappointment wonderfully well, was put comfortably on to his mule. They hurried up the opposite hillside, fearful of another attack, and it was not until they had left the eventful place far behind that Ethel found an opportunity to speak to her father and ask his pardon for the way she had treated him.

"You seemed so different, dear father, and you quite frightened me. Now I feel that you are your old self again."

He did not answer, and she concluded that he was not unnaturally offended at her behaviour.

By one of those curious tricks of mountain scenery, the place they had left an hour before suddenly reappeared far below them. The Khan was hidden under the green dome, but in the open there still stood three figures, and through the pure air rose up a faint cry of defiance or farewell.

Mr Lucas stopped irresolutely, and let the reins fall from his hand. "Come, father dear," said Ethel gently.

He obeyed, and in another moment a spur of the hill hid the dangerous scene for ever.

II

It was breakfast time, but the gas was alight, owing to the fog. Mr Lucas was in the middle of an account of a bad night he had spent. Ethel, who was to be married in a few weeks, had her arms on the table, listening.

"First the door bell rang, then you came back from the theatre. Then the dog started, and after the dog the cat. And at three in the morning a young hooligan passed by singing. Oh yes: then there was the water gurgling in the pipe above my head."

"I think that was only the bath water running away," said Ethel, looking rather worn.

"Well, there's nothing I dislike more than running water. It's perfectly impossible to sleep in the house. I shall give it up. I shall give notice next quarter. I shall tell the landlord plainly, 'The reason I am giving up the house is this: it is perfectly impossible to sleep in it.' If he says — says — well, what has he got to say?"

"Some more toast, father?"

"Thank you, my dear." He took it, and there was an interval of peace.

But he soon recommenced. "I'm not going to submit to the practising next door as tamely as they think. I wrote and told them so — didn't I?"

"Yes," said Ethel, who had taken care that the letter should not reach. "I have seen the governess, and she has promised to arrange it differently. And Aunt Julia hates noise. It will sure to be all right."

Her aunt, being the only unattached member of the family, was coming to keep house for her father when she left him. The reference was not a happy one, and Mr Lucas commenced a series of half articulate sighs, which was only stopped by the arrival of the post.

"Oh, what a parcel!" cried Ethel. "For me! What can it be! Greek stamps. This is most exciting!"

It proved to be some asphodel bulbs, sent by Mrs Forman from Athens for planting in the conservatory.

"Doesn't it bring it all back! You remember the asphodels, father. And all wrapped up in Greek newspapers. I wonder if I can read them still. I used to be able to, you know."

She rattled on, hoping to conceal the laughter of the children next door — a favourite source of querulousness at breakfast time.

"Listen to me! 'A rural disaster.' Oh, I've hit on something sad. But never mind. 'Last Tuesday at Plataniste, in the province of Messenia, a shocking tragedy occurred. A large tree' — aren't I getting on well? — 'blew down in the night and' — wait a minute — oh, dear! 'crushed to death the five occupants of the little Khan there, who had apparently been sitting in the balcony. The bodies of Maria Rhomaides, the aged proprietress, and of her daughter, aged forty-six, were easily recognizable, whereas that of her grandson' — oh, the rest is really too horrid; I wish I had never tried it, and what's more I feel to have heard the name

Plataniste before. We didn't stop there, did we, in the spring?''

"We had lunch," said Mr Lucas, with a faint expression of trouble on his vacant face. "Perhaps it was where the dragoman bought the pig."

"Of course," said Ethel in a nervous voice. "Where the dragoman bought the little pig. How terrible!"

"Very terrible!" said her father, whose attention was wandering to the noisy children next door. Ethel suddenly started to her feet with genuine interest.

"Good gracious!" she exclaimed. "This is an old paper. It happened not lately but in April — the night of Tuesday the eighteenth — and we — we must have been there in the afternoon."

"So we were," said Mr Lucas. She put her hand to her heart, scarcely able to speak.

"Father, dear father, I must say it: you wanted to stop there. All those people, those poor half savage people, tried to keep you, and they're dead. The whole place, it says, is in ruins, and even the stream has changed its course. Father, dear, if it had not been for me, and if Arthur had not helped me, you must have been killed."

Mr Lucas waved his hand irritably. "It is not a bit of good speaking to the governess, I shall write to the landlord and say, 'The reason I am giving up the house is this: the dog barks, the children next door are intolerable, and I cannot stand the noise of running water.'"

Ethel did not check his babbling. She was aghast at the narrowness of the escape, and for a long time kept silence. At last she said: "Such a marvellous deliverance does make one believe in Providence."

Mr Lucas, who was still composing his letter to the landlord, did not reply.

NADINE GORDIMER

A native of Springs, Transvaal, where she was born in 1923, Nadine Gordimer focuses almost exclusively in her work on the impact of South Africa on the individual consciousness. Though she has been a visiting lecturer at several American universities (Harvard, Princeton, Northwestern, Michigan, Columbia), and has lived for short periods in England, the world outside South Africa enters her fictional world only through the experience of exiles, émigrés, and foreign travellers. Yet the appeal of her work is not diminished by this restriction in locale. She is not a polemical writer, even though she does respond morally to such questions as justice and apartheid in her country. Writing should not, she observes in an interview with Alan Ross, be put at the service of a cause, although a cause may itself become the topic of a story. "I write about . . . private selves," she adds; but these, "even in the most private situations, . . . are what they are because . . . lives are regulated and . . . mores formed by the political situation. You see, in South Africa, society *is* the political situation. To paraphrase, one might say . . . , politics is character."

This relation between society and individual behavior is one which she has variously probed in the many novels and volumes of short stories published between 1949 and 1985. *A World of Strangers* (1958), for example, examines the inability of a young Englishman to reconcile his attraction to South Africa with his rejection of the racial divisions he finds there. *The Late Bourgeois World* (1966) presents the paralysis of will that affects one level of white society in the country — a world in which a clock ticking "afraid, alive, afraid, alive . . . " renders the moral tension in a single terse image. "No Place Like," which originally appeared in *The Southern Review* and then was collected in *Livingstone's Companions* (1971), demonstrates the same talent for trenchant observation. Details of setting and style — the fragmentary phrases, the tone, the repetitiousness, and the point of view — all contribute to the story's effect. Momentary experiences are made into the arenas where the mind can discover or fail to discover significant meaning in life, and ideas about human behavior and human potential are distilled into exact images and precisely rendered scenes.

FOR FURTHER READING

Thomas H. Gullason, "The Short Story: an Underrated Art," *Studies in Short Fiction* 2 (Fall 1964): 13–31.

Robert F. Haugh, *Nadine Gordimer* (New York: Twayne, 1974).

Ezekiel Mphahlele, *The African Image* (London: Faber, 1962).

Alan Ross, "A Writer in South Africa: Nadine Gordimer," *London Magazine* 5 (May 1965): 12–28.

Michael Wade, *Nadine Gordimer* (London: Evans Brothers, 1978).

NO PLACE LIKE

The relief of being down, out, and on the ground after hours in the plane was brought up short for them by the airport building: dirty, full of up-ended chairs like a closed restaurant. *Transit? Transit?* Some of them started off on a stairway but were shooed back exasperatedly in a language they didn't understand. The African heat in the place had been cooped up for days and nights; somebody tried to open one of the windows but again there were remonstrations from the uniformed man and the girl in her white gloves and leopard-skin pillbox hat. The windows were sealed, anyway, for the air-conditioning that wasn't working; the offender shrugged. The spokesman that every group of travellers produces made himself responsible for a complaint; at the same time some of those sheep who can't resist a hole in a fence had found a glass door unlocked on the far side of the transit lounge — they were leaking to an open passage-way: grass, bougainvillea trained like standard roses, a road glimpsed there! But the uniformed man raced to round them up and a cleaner trailing his broom was summoned to bolt the door.

The woman in beige trousers had come very slowly across the tarmac, putting her feet down on this particular earth once more, and she was walking even more slowly round the dirty hall. Her coat dragged from the crook of her elbow, her shoulder was weighed by the strap of a bag that wouldn't zip over a package of duty-free European liquor, her bright silk shirt opened dark mouths of wet when she lifted her arms. Fellow-glances of indignance or the seasoned superiority of a sense of humour found no answer in her. As her pace brought her into the path of the black cleaner, the two faces matched perfect indifference: his, for whom the distance from which these people came had no existence because he had been nowhere outside the two miles he walked from his village to the airport; hers, for whom the distance had no existence because she had been everywhere and arrived back.

Another black man, struggling into a white jacket as he unlocked wooden shutters, opened the bar, and the businessmen with their hard-top briefcases moved over to the row of stools. Men who had got talking to unattached women — not much promise in that now; the last leg of the journey was ahead — carried them glasses of gaudy synthetic fruit juice. The Consul who had wanted to buy her a drink with dinner on the plane had found himself a girl in red boots with a small daughter in identical red boots. The child waddled away and flirtation took the form of the two of them hurrying after to scoop it up, laughing. There was a patient queue of ladies in cardigans waiting to get into the lavatories. She passed — once, twice, three times in her slow rounds — a woman who was stitching petit-point. The third time she made out that the subject was a spaniel dog with orange-and-black-streaked ears. Beside the needle-woman was a husband of a species as easily identifiable as the breed of dog — an American, because of the length of bootlace, slotted through some emblem or badge, worn in place of a tie. He sighed and his wife looked up over her glasses as if he had made a threatening move.

The woman in the beige trousers got rid of her chit for Light Refreshment in an ashtray but she had still the plastic card that was her authority to board the plane again. She tried to put it in the pocket of the coat but she couldn't reach, so she had to hold the card in her teeth while she unharnessed herself from the shoulder-bag and the coat. She wedged the card into the bag beside the liquor packages, leaving it to protrude a little so that it would be easy to produce when the time came. But it slipped down inside the bag and she had to unpack the whole thing — the hairbrush full of her own hair, dead, shed; yesterday's newspaper from a foreign town; the book whose jacket tore on the bag's zip as it came out; wads of pink paper handkerchiefs, gloves for a cold climate, the quota of duty-free cigarettes, the Swiss pocket-knife that you couldn't buy back home, the wallet of travel documents. There at the bottom was the shiny card. Without it, you couldn't board the plane again. With it, you were committed to go on to the end of the journey, just as the passport bearing your name committed you to a certain identity and place. It was one of the nervous tics of travel to feel for the reassurance of that shiny card. She had wandered to the revolving stand of paperbacks and came back to make sure where she had put the card: yes, it was there. It was not a bit of paper; shiny plastic, you couldn't tear it up — indestructible, it looked, of course they use them over and over again. *Tropic of Capricorn, Kamasutra, Something of Value.* The stand revolved and brought round the same books, yet one turned it again in case there should be a book that had escaped notice, a book you'd been wanting to read all your life. If one were to find such a thing, here and now, on this last stage, this last stop . . . She felt strong hope, the excitation of weariness and tedium perhaps. They came round — *Something of Value, Kamasutra, Tropic of Capricorn.*

She went to the seat where she had left her things and loaded up again, the coat, the shoulder-bag bearing down. Somebody had fallen asleep, mouth open, bottom fly-button undone, an Austrian hat with plaited cord and feather cutting into his damp brow. How long had they been in this place? What time was it where she had left? (Some airports had a whole series of clockfaces showing what time it was everywhere.) Was it still yesterday, there? — Or tomorrow. And where she was going? She thought, I shall find out when I get there.

A pair of curio vendors had unpacked their wares in a corner. People stood about in a final agony of indecision: What would he do with a thing like that? Will she appreciate it, I mean? A woman repeated as she must have done in bazaars and shops and marketplaces all over the world, I've seen them for half the price. . . . But this was the last stop of all, the last chance *to take back something.* How else stake a claim? The last place of all the other places of the world.

Bone bracelets lay in a collapsed spiral of overlapping circles. Elephant hair ones fell into the pattern of the Olympic symbol. There were the ivory paper-knives and the little pictures of palm trees, huts and dancers on black paper. The vendor, squatting in the posture that derives from the necessity of the legless beggar to sit that way and has become as much a mark of the street professional, in such towns as the one that must be somewhere behind the airport, as the hard-top briefcase was of the international businessman drinking beer at the bar, importuned her with the obligation to buy. To refuse was to upset the ordination of roles. He was there to sell "ivory" bracelets and "African" art; they — these people shut up for him in the building — had been brought there to buy. He had a right to be angry. But she shook her head, she shook her head, while he tried out his few words of German and French (*bon marché, billig*) as if it could only be a matter of finding the right cue to get her to play the part assigned to her. He seemed to threaten, in his own tongue, finally, his head in its white skullcap hunched between jutting knees. But she was looking again at the glass case full of tropical butterflies under the President's picture. The picture was vivid, and new; a general successful in coup only months ago, in full dress uniform, splendid as the dark one among the Magi. The butterflies, relic of some colonial conservationist society, were beginning to fall away from their pins in grey crumbs and gauzy fragments. But there was one big as a bat and brilliantly emblazoned as the general: something in the soil and air, in whatever existed out there — whatever "out there" there was — that caused nature and culture to imitate each other . . . ?

If it were possible to take a great butterfly. Not take back; just take. But she had the Swiss knife and the bottles, of course. The plastic card. It would see her onto the plane once more. Once the plastic card was handed over, nowhere to go but across the tarmac and up the stairway into the belly of the plane, no turning back past the air hostess in her leopard-skin pillbox, past the barrier. It wasn't allowed; against regulations. The plastic card would send her to the plane, the plane would arrive at the end of the journey, the Swiss knife would be handed over for a kiss, the bottles would be exchanged for an embrace — she was shaking her head at the curio vendor (he had actually got up from his knees and come after her, waving his pictures), *no thanks, no thanks.* But he wouldn't give up and she had to move away, to walk up and down once more in the hot, enclosed course dictated by people's feet, the up-ended chairs and tables, the little shored-up piles of hand-luggage. The Consul was swinging the child in red boots by its hands, in an arc. It was half-whimpering, half-laughing, yelling to be let down, but the larger version of the same model, the mother, was laughing in a way to make her small breasts shake for the Consul, and to convey to everyone how marvellous such a distinguished man was with children.

There was a gritty crackle and then the announcement in careful, African-accented English, of the departure of the flight. A kind of concerted shuffle went up like a sigh: at last! The red-booted mother was telling her child it was silly to cry, the Consul was gathering their things together, the woman was winding the orange thread for her needlework rapidly round a spool, the sleepers woke and the beer-drinkers threw the last of their foreign small change on the bar counter. No queue outside the Ladies' now and the woman in the beige trousers knew there was plenty of time before the second call. She went in and, once more, unharnessed herself among the crumpled paper towels and spilt powder. She tipped all the liquid soap containers in turn until she found one that wasn't empty; she washed her hands thoroughly in hot and then cold water and put her wet palms on the back of her neck, under her hair. She went to one of the row of mirrors and looked at what she saw there a moment, and then took out from under the liquor bottles, the Swiss knife and the documents, the hairbrush. It was full of hair; a web of dead hairs that bound the bristles together so that they could not go through a head of live hair. She raked her fingers slowly through the bristles and was aware of a young Indian woman at the next mirror, moving quickly and efficiently about an elaborate toilet. The Indian backcombed the black, smooth hair cut in Western style to hang on her shoulders, painted her eyes, shook her ringed hands dry rather than use the paper towels, sprayed French perfume while she extended her neck, repleated the green and silver sari that left bare a small roll of lavender-grey flesh between waist and *choli*.

This is the final call for all passengers.

The hair from the brush was no-colour, matted and coated with fluff. Twisted round the forefinger (like the orange thread for the spaniel's ears) it became a fibrous funnel, dusty and obscene. She didn't want the Indian girl to be confronted with it and hid it in her palm while she went over to the dustbin. But the Indian girl saw only herself, watching her reflection appraisingly as she turned and swept out.

The brush went easily through the living hair, now. Again and again, until it was quite smooth and fell, as if it had a memory, as if it were cloth that had been folded and ironed a certain way, along the lines in which it had been arranged by professional hands in another hemisphere. A latecomer rushed into one of the lavatories, sounded the flush and hurried out, plastic card in hand.

The woman in the beige trousers had put on lipstick and run a nail-file under her nails. Her bag was neatly packed. She dropped a coin in the saucer set out, like an offering for some humble household god, for the absent attendant. The African voice was urging all passengers to proceed immediately through Gate B. The voice had some difficulty with *l*'s, pronouncing them more like *r*'s; a pleasant, reasoning voice, asking only for everyone to present the boarding pass, avoid delay, come quietly.

She went into one of the lavatories marked "Western-type toilet" that bolted automatically as the door shut, a patent device ensuring privacy;

there was no penny to pay. She had the coat and bag with her and arranged them, the coat folded and balanced on the bag, on the cleanest part of the floor. She thought what she remembered thinking so many times before: not much time, I'll have to hurry. That was what the plastic card was for — surety for not being left behind, never. She had it stuck in the neck of the shirt now, in the absence of a convenient pocket; it felt cool and wafer-stiff as she put it there but had quickly taken on the warmth of her body. Some tidy soul determined to keep up Western-type standards had closed the lid and she sat down as if on a bench — the heat and the weight of the paraphernalia she had been carrying about were suddenly exhausting. She thought she would smoke a cigarette; there was no time for that. But the need for a cigarette hollowed out a deep sigh within her and she got the pack carefully out of the pocket of her coat without disturbing the arrangement on the floor. All passengers delaying the departure of the flight were urged to proceed immediately through Gate B. Some of the words were lost over the echoing intercommunication system and at times the only thing that could be made out was the repetition, Gate B, a vital fact from which all grammatical contexts could fall away without rendering the message unintelligible. Gate B. If you remembered, if you knew Gate B, the key to mastery of the whole procedure remained intact with you. Gate B was the converse of the open sesame; it would keep you, passing safely through it, in the known, familiar, and inescapable, safe from caves of treasure and shadow. *Immediately. Gate B. Gate B.*

She could sense from the different quality of the atmosphere outside the door, and the doors beyond it, that the hall was emptying now. They were trailing, humping along under their burdens—the petit-point, the child in red boots—to the gate where the girl in the leopard skin pillbox collected their shiny cards.

She took hers out. She looked around the cell as one looks around for a place to set down a vase of flowers or a note that mustn't blow away. It would not flush down the outlet; plastic doesn't disintegrate in water. As she had idly noticed before, it wouldn't easily tear up. She was not at all agitated; she was simply looking for somewhere to dispose of it, now. She heard the voice (was there a shade of hurt embarrassment in the rolling *r*-shaped *l*'s) appealing to the passenger who was holding up flight so-and-so to please . . . She noticed for the first time that there was actually a tiny window, with the sort of pane that tilts outwards from the bottom, just above the cistern. She stood on the seat-lid and tried to see out, just managing to post the shiny card like a letter through the slot.

Gate B, the voice offered, *Gate B*. But to pass through Gate B you had to have a card, without a card Gate B had no place in the procedure. She could not manage to see anything at all, straining precariously from up there, through the tiny window; there was no knowing at all where the card had fallen. But as she half-jumped, half-clambered down again, for a second the changed angle of her vision brought into sight something like a head — the top of a huge untidy palm tree, up in the sky, rearing perhaps between buildings or above shacks and muddy or dusty streets where there were donkeys, bicycles and barefoot people. She saw it only for that second but it was so very clear, she saw even that it was an old palm tree, the fronds rasping and sharpening against each other. And there was a crow — she was sure she had seen the black flap of a resident crow.

She sat down again. The cigarette had made a brown aureole round itself on the cistern. In the corner what she had thought was a date-pit was a dead cockroach. She flicked the dead cigarette butt at it. Heel-taps clattered into the outer room, an African voice said, Who is there? Please, are you there? She did not hold her breath or try to keep particularly still. There was no one there. All the lavatory doors were rattled in turn. There was a high-strung pause, as if the owner of the heels didn't know what to do next. Then the heels rang away again and the door of the Ladies' swung to with the heavy sound of fanned air.

There were bursts of commotion without, reaching her muffledly where she sat. The calm grew longer. Soon the intermittent commotion would cease; the jets must be breathing fire by now, the belts fastened and the cigarettes extinguished, although the air-conditioning wouldn't be working properly yet, on the ground, and they would be patiently sweating. They couldn't wait forever, when they were so nearly there. The plane would be beginning to trundle like a huge perambulator, it would be turning, winking, shuddering in summoned power.

Take off. It was perfectly still and quiet in the cell. She thought of the great butterfly; of the general with his beautiful markings of braid and medals. Take off.

So that was the sort of place it was: crows in old dusty palm trees, crows picking the carrion in open gutters, legless beggars threatening in an unknown tongue. Not Gate B, but some other gate. Suppose she were to climb out that window, would they ask her for her papers and put her in some other cell, at the general's pleasure? The general had no reason to trust anybody who did not take Gate B. No sound at all, now. The lavatories were given over to their own internal rumblings; the cistern gulped now and then. She was quite sure, at last, that flight so-and-so had followed its course; was gone. She lit another cigarette. She did not think at all about what to do next, not at all; if she had been inclined to think that, she would not have been sitting wherever it was she was. The butterfly, no doubt, was extinct and the general would dislike strangers; the explanations (everything has an explanation) would formulate themselves, in her absence, when the plane reached its destination. The duty-free liquor could be poured down the lavatory, but there remained the problem of the Swiss pocket-knife. And yet — through the forbidden doorway: grass, bougainvillea trained like standard roses, a road glimpsed there!

GRAHAM GREENE

In a writing career spread over forty years (his first novel, *The Man Within*, appeared in 1929), Graham Greene has published over thirty volumes of fiction, essays, plays, and poetry, and has written a number of film scripts, including the screenplays of some of his own novels. Born in 1904, he has been a journalist, a film critic, an intelligence officer (in Africa from 1941 to 1943), and an indefatigable traveller. His fictional writings reflect the breadth of his experience, and may be divided into three main groups: adventure stories, which Greene calls "entertainments," usually about spies or criminals, books such as *A Gun for Sale* (1936) or *The Third Man* (1950); "political" thrillers dramatizing ideological conflicts, as *England Made Me* (1935) or *The Quiet American* (1955); and "Catholic" novels which reflect Greene's preoccupation with sin, damnation, and the struggle between good and evil (Greene converted to Catholicism in 1926). The works in the last-named group (for example, *Brighton Rock*, 1938, *The Power and the Glory*, 1940) are primarily concerned with the spiritual state of their protagonists, but they also make use of the conventions of the thriller: pursuit, betrayal, capture, violent death (sometimes self-inflicted). Even in his "entertainments," Greene is an essentially serious writer, always exploring questions of conduct and belief. The world of Greeneland — a world stretching from Brighton to Saigon, from Vienna to Haiti — is populated by priests and murderers; gangsters and revolutionaries, who live on the fringe of society; outcasts or rebels, whose spiritual and moral crises epitomize the modern search for values in an anarchic world.

"Brother" (1935; in *Collected Stories*, 1973) presents one of Greene's favorite themes, that of trust and betrayal. It deals with the political agitation of a restless Europe in the 1930s, and reflects his sympathy for leftist causes. Greene has always rejected comfortable orthodoxies in favor of a questioning spirit; he believes that the task of the storyteller is "to act as the devil's advocate, to elicit sympathy and a measure of understanding for those who lie outside the boundaries of State approval."

FOR FURTHER READING

Robert O. Evans, ed., *Graham Greene: Some Critical Considerations* (Lexington: University of Kentucky Press, 1963).

David Lodge, *Graham Greene* (New York: Columbia University Press, 1966).

Martin Shuttleworth and Simon Raven, "The Art of Fiction: III. Graham Greene," *Paris Review* 1 (Autumn 1953): 24–41.

Peter Wolfe, *Graham Greene: The Entertainer* (Carbondale, Illinois: Southern Illinois University Press, 1972).

BROTHER

The Communists were the first to appear. They walked quickly, a group of about a dozen, up the boulevard which runs from Combat to Ménilmontant; a young man and a girl lagged a little way behind because the man's leg was hurt and the girl was helping him along. They looked impatient, harassed, hopeless, as if they were trying to catch a train which they knew already in their hearts they were too late to catch.

The proprietor of the café saw them coming when they were still a long way off; the lamps at that time were still alight (it was later that the bullets broke the bulbs and dropped darkness all over that quarter of Paris), and the group showed up plainly in the wide barren boulevard. Since sunset only one customer had entered the café, and very soon after sunset firing could be heard from the direction of Combat; the Métro station had closed hours ago. And yet something obstinate and undefeatable in the proprietor's character prevented him from putting up the shutters; it might have been avarice; he could not himself have told what it was as he pressed his broad yellow forehead against the glass and stared this way and that, up the boulevard and down the boulevard.

But when he saw the group and their air of hurry he began immediately to close his café. First he went and warned his only customer, who was practising billiard shots, walking round and round the table, frowning and stroking a thin moustache between shots, a little green in the face under the low diffused lights.

"The Reds are coming," the proprietor said, "you'd better be off. I'm putting up the shutters."

"Don't interrupt. They won't harm me," the customer said. "This is a tricky shot. Red's in baulk. Off the cushion. Screw on spot." He shot his ball straight into a pocket.

"I knew you couldn't do anything with that," the proprietor said, nodding his bald head. "You might just as well go home. Give me a hand with the shutters first. I've sent my wife away." The customer turned on him maliciously, rattling the cue between his fingers. "It was your talking that spoilt the shot. You've cause to be frightened, I dare say. But I'm a poor man. I'm safe. I'm not going to stir." He went across to his coat and took out a dry cigar. "Bring me a bock." He walked round the table on his toes and the balls clicked and the proprietor padded back into the bar, elderly and irritated. He did not fetch the beer but began to close the shutters; every move he made was slow and clumsy. Long before he had finished the group of Communists was outside.

He stopped what he was doing and watched them with furtive dislike. He was afraid that the rattle of the shutters would attract their attention. If I am very quiet and still, he thought, they may go on, and he remembered with malicious pleasure the police barricade across the Place de la République. That will finish them. In the meanwhile I must be very quiet, very still, and he felt a kind of warm satisfaction at the idea that worldly wisdom dictated the very attitude most suited to his nature. So he stared through the edge of a shutter, yellow, plump, cautious, hearing the billiard balls crackle in the other room, seeing the young man come limping up the pavement on the girl's arm, watching them stand and stare with dubious faces up the boulevard towards Combat.

But when they came into the café he was already behind the bar, smiling and bowing and missing nothing, noticing how they had divided forces, how six of them had begun to run back the way they had come.

The young man sat down in a dark corner above the cellar stairs and the others stood round the door waiting for something to happen. It gave the proprietor an odd feeling that they should stand there in his café not asking for a drink, knowing what to expect, when he, the owner, knew nothing, understood nothing. At last the girl said ''Cognac,'' leaving the others and coming to the bar, but when he had poured it out for her, very careful to give a fair and not a generous measure, she simply took it to the man sitting in the dark and held it to his mouth.

''Three francs,'' the proprietor said. She took the glass and sipped a little and turned it so that the man's lips might touch the same spot. Then she knelt down and rested her forehead against the man's forehead and so they stayed.

''Three francs,'' the proprietor said, but he could not make his voice bold. The man was no longer visible in his corner, only the girl's back, thin and shabby in a black cotton frock, as she knelt, leaning forward to find the man's face. The proprietor was daunted by the four men at the door, by the knowledge that they were Reds who had no respect for private property, who would drink his wine and go away without paying, who would rape his women (but there was only his wife, and she was not there), who would rob his bank, who would murder him as soon as look at him. So with fear in his heart he gave up the three francs as lost rather than attract any more attention.

Then the worst that he contemplated happened.

One of the men at the door came up to the bar and told him to pour out four glasses of cognac. ''Yes, yes,'' the proprietor said, fumbling with the cork, praying secretly to the Virgin to send an angel, to send the police, to send the Gardes Mobiles, now, immediately, before the cork came out, ''that will be twelve francs.''

''Oh, no,'' the man said, ''we are all comrades here. Share and share alike. Listen,'' he said, with earnest mockery, leaning across the bar, ''all we have is yours just as much as it's ours, comrade,'' and stepping back a pace he presented himself to the proprietor, so that he might take his choice of stringy tie, of threadbare trousers, of starved features.

"And it follows from that, comrade, that all you have is ours. So four cognacs. Share and share alike."

"Of course," the proprietor said, "I was only joking." Then he stood with bottle poised, and the four glasses tingled upon the counter. "A machine-gun," he said, "up by Combat," and smiled to see how for the moment the men forgot their brandy as they fidgeted near the door. Very soon now, he thought, and I shall be quit of them.

"A machine-gun," the Red said incredulously, "they're using machine-guns?"

"Well," the proprietor said, encouraged by this sign that the Gardes Mobiles were not very far away, "you can't pretend that you aren't armed yourselves." He leant across the bar in a way that was almost paternal. "After all, you know, your ideas — they wouldn't do in France. Free love."

"Who's talking of free love?" the Red said.

The proprietor shrugged and smiled and nodded at the corner. The girl knelt with her head on the man's shoulder, her back to the room. They were quite silent and the glass of brandy stood on the floor beside them. The girl's beret was pushed back on her head and one stocking was laddered and darned from knee to ankle.

"What, those two? They aren't lovers."

"I," the proprietor said, "with my bourgeois notions would have thought . . ."

"He's her brother," the Red said.

The men came clustering round the bar and laughed at him, but softly as if a sleeper or a sick person were in the house. All the time they were listening for something. Between their shoulders the proprietor could look out across the boulevard; he could see the corner of the Faubourg du Temple.

"What are you waiting for?"

"For friends," the Red said. He made a gesture with open palm as if to say, You see, we share and share alike. We have no secrets.

Something moved at the corner of the Faubourg du Temple.

"Four more cognacs," the Red said.

"What about those two?" the proprietor asked.

"Leave them alone. They'll look after themselves. They're tired."

How tired they were. No walk up the boulevard from Ménilmontant could explain the tiredness. They seemed to have come farther and fared a great deal worse than their companions. They were more starved; they were infinitely more hopeless, sitting in their dark corner away from the friendly gossip, the amicable desperate voices which now confused the proprietor's brain, until for a moment he believed himself to be a host entertaining friends.

He laughed and made a broad joke directed at the two of them; but they made no sign of understanding. Perhaps they were to be pitied, cut off from the camaraderie round the counter; perhaps they were to be envied for their deeper comradeship. The proprietor thought for no reason at all of the bare grey trees of the Tuileries like a series of exclamation marks drawn against the winter sky. Puzzled, disintegrated, with all his bearings lost, he stared out through the door towards the Faubourg.

It was as if they had not seen each other for a long while and would soon again be saying good-bye. Hardly aware of what he was doing he filled the four glasses with brandy. They stretched out worn blunted fingers for them.

"Wait," he said. "I've got something better than this"; then paused, conscious of what was happening across the boulevard. The lamplight splashed down on blue steel helmets; the Gardes Mobiles were lining out across the entrance to the Faubourg, and a machine-gun pointed directly at the café windows.

So, the proprietor thought, my prayers are answered. Now I must do my part, not look, not warn them, save myself. Have they covered the side door? I will get the other bottle. Real Napoleon brandy. Share and share alike.

He felt a curious lack of triumph as he opened the trap of the bar and came out. He tried not to walk quickly back towards the billiard room. Nothing that he did must warn these men; he tried to spur himself with the thought that every slow casual step he took was a blow for France, for his café, for his savings. He had to step over the girl's feet to pass her; she was asleep. He noted the sharp shoulder blades thrusting through the cotton, and raised his eyes and met her brother's, filled with pain and despair.

He stopped. He found he could not pass without a word. It was as if he needed to explain something, as if he belonged to the wrong party. With false bonhomie he waved the corkscrew he carried in the other's face. "Another cognac, eh?"

"It's no good talking to them," the Red said. "They're German. They don't understand a word."

"German?"

"That's what's wrong with his leg. A concentration camp."

The proprietor told himself that he must be quick, that he must put a door between him and them, that the end was very close, but he was bewildered by the hopelessness in the man's gaze. "What's he doing here?" Nobody answered him. It was as if his question were too foolish to need a reply. With his head sunk upon his breast the proprietor went past, and the girl slept on. He was like a stranger leaving a room where all the rest are friends. A German. They don't understand a word; and up, up through the heavy darkness of his mind, through the avarice and the dubious triumph, a few German words remembered from very old days climbed like spies into the light: a line from the *Lorelei* learnt at school, *Kamerad* with its war-time suggestion of fear and surrender, and oddly from nowhere the phrase *mein Bruder*. He opened the door of the billiard room and closed it behind him and softly turned the key.

"Spot in baulk," the customer explained and leant across the great green table, but while he took aim, wrinkling his narrow peevish eyes, the firing started. It came in two bursts with a rip of glass between. The girl cried out something, but it was not one of the words he knew. Then feet ran across the floor, the trap of the bar slammed. The proprietor sat back against the table and listened and listened for any further sound; but silence came in under the door and silence through the keyhole.

"The cloth. My God, the cloth," the customer said, and the proprietor looked down at his own hand which was working the corkscrew into the table.

"Will this absurdity ever end?" the customer said. "I shall go home."

"Wait," the proprietor said. "Wait." He was listening to voices and footsteps in the other room. These were voices he did not recognize. Then a car drove up and presently drove away again. Somebody rattled the handle of the door.

"Who is it?" the proprietor called.

"Who are you? Open that door."

"Ah," the customer said with relief, "the police. Where was I now? Spot in baulk." He began to chalk his cue. The proprietor opened the door. Yes, the Gardes Mobiles had arrived; he was safe again, though his windows were smashed. The Reds had vanished as if they had never been. He looked at the raised trap, at the smashed electric bulbs, at the broken bottle which dripped behind the bar. The café was full of men, and he remembered with odd relief that he had not had time to lock the side door.

"Are you the owner?" the officer asked. "A bock for each of these men and a cognac for myself. Be quick about it."

The proprietor calculated: "Nine francs fifty," and watched closely with bent head the coins rattle down upon the counter.

"You see," the officer said with significance, "we pay." He nodded towards the side door. "Those others: did they pay?"

No, the proprietor admitted, they had not paid, but as he counted the coins and slipped them into the till, he caught himself silently repeating the officer's order — "A bock for each of these men." Those others, he thought, one's got to say that for them, they weren't mean about the drink. It was four cognacs with them. But, of course, they did not pay. "And my windows," he complained aloud with sudden asperity, "what about my windows?"

"Never you mind," the officer said, "the government will pay. You have only to send in your bill. Hurry up now with my cognac. I have no time for gossip."

"You can see for yourself," the proprietor said, "how the bottles have been broken. Who will pay for that?"

"Everything will be paid for," the officer said.

"And now I must go to the cellar to fetch more."

He was angry at the reiteration of the word pay. They enter my café, he thought, they smash my windows, they order me about and think that all is well if they pay, pay, pay. It occurred to him that these men were intruders.

"Step to it," the officer said and turned and rebuked one of the men who had leant his rifle against the bar.

At the top of the cellar stairs the proprietor stopped. They were in darkness, but by the light from the bar he could just make out a body half-way down. He began to tremble violently, and it was some seconds before he could strike a match. The young German lay head downwards, and the blood from his head had dropped on to the step below. His eyes were open and stared back at the proprietor with the old despairing expression of life. The proprietor would not believe that he was dead. "Kamerad," he said bending down, while the match singed his fingers and went out, trying to recall some phrase in German, but he could only remember, as he bent lower still, "mein Bruder." Then suddenly he turned and ran up the steps, waved the match-box in the officer's face, and called out in a low hysterical voice to him and his men and to the customer stooping under the low green shade, "Cochons. Cochons."

"What was that? What was that?" the officer exclaimed. "Did you say that he was your brother? It's impossible," and he frowned incredulously at the proprietor and rattled the coins in his pocket.

MARK HELPRIN

Born in 1947 and educated at Harvard College and at Harvard's Center for Middle Eastern Studies, Mark Helprin served in the British Merchant Navy and in the Israeli Army and Air Force. His military experience has provided him with much material for his fiction; his first novel, *Refiner's Fire* (1977), is a picaresque narrative depicting the adventures of a young American caught up in Israel's conflict with its neighbors. Helprin is a frequent contributor to *The New Yorker*, and his stories, collected in *A Dove of the East* (1975) and *Ellis Island & other stories* (1981), have a breadth of subject and setting that reflects the diversity of his experience. *Ellis Island & other stories* won the 1982 National Jewish Book Award for fiction.

Whether focusing on a Middle-Eastern battlefield, mountain climbing in the Alps, or scullers racing on the River Charles in Boston, Helprin's writing is grounded in sharp, realistic detail born of careful observation. At the same time, his characters spring from a more romantic tradition; moved by a mixture of idealism and doubt, they have an awareness of inexplicable forces at work within themselves as well as in the external environment, and like classical heroes they struggle to make an assertion of self over the physical limits of their existence. These tensions are sometimes conveyed through an injection of fantasy (a prominent element of Helprin's 1981 novel *Winter's Tale*), through which he can give his characters and situations an archetypal dimension. In "Letters from the *Samantha*" (*Ellis Island & other stories*), a story cast in traditional epistolary form, he has produced a variation on the theme of Coleridge's "Rime of the Ancient Mariner"; a ship's captain must try to maintain the orderly values of the civilized society he represents in the face of an unexpected and a threatening presence. As in the tales of Joseph Conrad, the shipboard setting becomes an arena of moral conflict in which the protagonist must make a crucial decision affecting others as well as himself.

FOR FURTHER READING

Anne Duchene, "Out of the Icebox," *Times Literary Supplement*, 13 March 1981, p. 278.

Gerald Locklin, Review of *Ellis Island & other stories*. *Studies in Short Fiction* 18 (Summer 1981): 339–40.

LETTERS FROM
THE *SAMANTHA*

These letters were recovered in good condition from the vault of the sunken *Samantha*, an iron-hulled sailing ship of one thousand tons, built in Scotland in 1879 and wrecked during the First World War in the Persian Gulf off Basra.

20 August, 1909, 20° 14′ 18″ S,
43° 51′ 57″ E
Off Madagascar

DEAR SIR:

Many years have passed since I joined the Green Star Line. You may note in your records and logs, if not, indeed, by memory, the complete absence of disciplinary action against me. During my command, the *Samantha* has been a trim ship on time. Though my subordinates sometimes complain, they are grateful, no doubt, for my firm rule and tidiness. It saves the ship in storms, keeps them healthy, and provides good training — even though they will be masters of steamships.

No other vessel of this line has been as punctual or well run. Even today we are a week ahead and our Madagascar wood will reach Alexandria early. Bound for London, the crew are happy, and though we sail the Mozambique Channel, they act as if we had just caught sight of Margate. There are no problems on this ship. But I must in conscience report an irregular incident for which I am ready to take full blame.

Half a day out of Androka, we came upon a sea so blue and casual that its waters seemed fit to drink. Though the wind was slight and we made poor time, we were elated by perfect climate and painter's colors, for off the starboard side Madagascar rose as green and tranquil as a well-watered palm, its mountains engraved by thrashing freshwater streams which beat down to the coast. A sweet up-welling breeze blew steadily from shore and confounded our square sails. Twenty minutes after noon, the lookout sighted a tornado on land. In the ship's glass I saw it, horrifying and enormous. Though at a great distance, its column appeared as thick as a massive tree on an islet in an atoll, and stretched at least 70 degrees upward from the horizon.

I have seen these pipes of windy fleece before. If there is sea nearby, they rush to it. So did this. When it became not red and black from soil and debris but silver and green from the water it drew, I began to tighten ship. Were the typhoon to have struck us directly, no preparation would have saved us. But what a shame to be swamped by high waves, or to be dismasted by beaten sea and wind. Hatches were battened as if for storm, minor sails furled, and the mainsail driven down half.

It moved back and forth over the sea in illegible patterning, as if tacking to changing winds. To our dismay, the distance narrowed. We were afraid, though every man on deck wanted to see it, to feel it, perhaps to ride its thick swirling waters a hundred times higher than our mast — higher than the peaks inland. I confess that I have wished to be completely taken up by such a thing, to be lifted into the clouds, arms and legs pinned in the stream. The attraction is much like that of phosphorescent seas, when glowing light and smooth swell are dangerously magnetic even for hardened masters of good ships. I have wanted to surrender to plum-colored seas, to know what one might find there naked and alone. But I have not, and will not.

Finally, we began to run rough water. The column was so high that we bent our heads to see its height, and the sound was greater than any engine, causing masts and spars to resonate like cords. Waves broke over the prow. Wind pushed us on, and the curl of the sea rushed to fill the depression of the waters. No more than half a mile off the starboard bow, the column veered to the west, crossing our path to head for Africa as rapidly as an express. Within minutes, we could not even see it.

As it crossed our bows, I veered in the direction from which it had come. It seemed to communicate a decisiveness of course, and here I took opportunity to evade. In doing so we came close to land. This was dangerous not only for the presence of reefs and shoals but because of the scattered debris. Trees as tall as masts and much thicker, roots sucked clean, lay in puzzlement upon the surface. Brush and vines were everywhere. The water was reddish brown from earth which had fallen from the cone. We were meticulously careful in piloting through this fresh salad, as a good ram against a solid limb would have been the end. Our cargo is hardwoods, and would have sunk us like granite. I myself straddled the sprit stays, pushing aside small logs with a boat hook and calling out trim to the wheel.

Nearly clear, we came upon a clump of tangled vegetation. I could not believe my eyes, for floating upon it was a large monkey, bolt upright and dignified. I sighted him first, though the lookout called soon after. On impulse, I set trim for the wavy mat and, as we smashed into it, offered the monkey an end of the boat hook. When he seized it I was almost pulled in, for his weight is nearly equal to mine. I observed that he had large teeth, which appeared both white and sharp. He came close, and then took to the lines until he sat high on the topgallant. As he passed, his foot cuffed my shoulder and I could smell him.

My ship is a clean ship. I regretted immediately my gesture with the hook. We do not need the mysterious defecations of such a creature, or the threat of him in the rigging at night. But we could not capture him to throw him back into the sea and, even had we collared him, might not have been able to get him overboard without danger to ourselves. We are now many miles off the coast. It is dark, and he sits high off the deck. The night watch is afraid and requests that I fell him with my rifle. They have seen his sharp teeth, which he displays with much screaming and gesticulating when they near him in the rigging. I think he is merely afraid, and I cannot bring myself to shoot him. I realize that no animals are allowed on board and have often had to enforce this rule when coming upon a parrot or cat hidden belowdecks where some captains do not go. But this creature we have today removed from the sea is like a man, and he has ridden the typhoon. Perhaps we will pass a headland and throw him overboard on a log. He must eventually descend for want of food. Then we will have our way. I will report further when the matter is resolved, and assure you that I regret this breach of regulations.

Yours & etc.,
SAMSON LOW
MASTER, S/V SAMANTHA

23 August, 1909, 10° 43′ 3″ S,
49° 5′ 27″ E
South of the Seychelles

DEAR SIR:

We have passed the Channel and are heading north-northeast, hoping to ride the summer monsoon. It is shamefully hot, though the breeze is less humid than usual. Today two men dropped from the heat but they resumed work by evening. Because we are on a homeward tack, morale is at its best, or rather would be were it not for that damned ape in the rigging. He has not come down, and we have left behind his island and its last headland. He will have to have descended by the time we breach passage between Ras Asir and Jazirat Abd al-Kuri. The mate has suggested that there we throw him into the sea on a raft, which the carpenter has already set about building. He has embarked upon this with my permission, since there is little else for him to do. It has been almost an overly serene voyage and the typhoon caused no damage.

The raft he designed is very clever and has become a popular subject of discussion. It is about six feet by three feet, constructed of spare pine dunnage we were about to cast away when the typhoon was sighted. On each side is an outrigger for stability in the swell. In the center is a box, in which is a seat. Flanking this box are several smaller ones for fruit, biscuit, and a bucket of fresh water, in case the creature should drift a long time on the sea. This probably will not be so; the currents off Ras Asir drive for the beach, and we have noted that dunnage is quickly thrown upon the strand. Nevertheless, the crew have added their own touch — a standard distress flag flying from a ten-foot switch. They do not know, but I will order it replaced by a banner of another color, so that a hapless ship will not endanger itself to rescue a speechless monkey.

The crew have divided into two factions — those who wish to have the monkey shot, and those who would wait for him to descend and then put him in his boat. I am with the latter, since I would be the huntsman, and have already mentioned my lack of enthusiasm for this. A delegation of the first faction protested. They claimed that the second faction comprised those who stayed on deck, that the creature endangered balance in the rigging, and that he produced an uncanny effect in his screeching and bellicose silhouettes, which from below are humorous but which at close range, they said, are disconcerting and terrifying.

Since I had not seen him for longer than a moment and wanted to verify their complaint, I went up. Though sixty years of age, I did not use the bosun's chair, and detest those masters who do. It is pharaonic, and smacks of days in my father's youth when he saw with his own eyes gentlemen in sedan chairs carried about the city. The sight of twenty men laboring to hoist a ship's rotund captain is simply Egyptian, and I will not have it. Seventy feet off the deck, a giddy height to which I have not ascended in years, I came even with the ape. The ship was passing a boisterous sea and had at least a twenty-degree roll, which flung the two of us from side to side like pendula.

I am not a naturalist, nor have we on board a book of zoology, so the most I can do is to describe him. He is almost my height (nearly five feet ten inches) and appears to be sturdily built. Feet and hands are human in appearance except that they have a bulbous, skew, arthritic look common to monkeys. He is muscular and covered with fine reddish-brown hair. One can see the whiteness of his tendons when he stretches an arm or leg. I have mentioned the sharp, dazzling white teeth, set in rows like a trap, canine and pointed. His face is curiously delicate, and covered with orange hair leading to a snow-white crown of fur. My breath nearly failed when I looked into his eyes, for they are a bright, penetrating blue.

At first, he began to scream and swing as if he would come at me. If he had, I would have fared badly. The sailors fear him, for there is no man on board with half his strength, no man on the sea with a tenth his agility in the ropes, and if there is a man with the glacierlike pinnacled teeth, then he must be in a Scandinavian or Eastern European circus, for there they are fond of such things. To my surprise, he stopped his pantomine and, with a gentle and quizzical tilt of his head, looked me straight in the eyes. I had been sure that as a man I could answer his gaze as if from infallibility, and I calmly looked back. But he had me. His eyes unset me, so that I nearly shook. From that moment, he has not threatened or bared his teeth, but merely rests near the top of the foremast. The crew have attributed his conversion to my special power. This is flattering, though not entirely, as it assumes my ability to commune with an ape. Little do they suspect that it is I and not the monkey who have been converted, although to what I do not know. I am still thoroughly ashamed of my indiscretion and the troubles arising from it. We will get him and put him adrift off Ras Asir.

This evening, the cook grilled up some beef. I had him thoroughly vent the galley and use a great many herbs. The aroma was maddening. I sat in near-hypnotic ease in a canvas chair on the quarterdeck, a glass of wine in hand, as the heat fell to a cool breeze. We are all sunburnt and have been working hard, as the ape silently watches, to trim regularly and catch the best winds. We are almost in the full swift of the monsoon, and shortly will ride it in all its speed. It was wonderful to sit on deck and smell the herb-laden meat. The sea itself must have been jealous. I had several men ready with cargo net and pikes, certain that he would come down. We stared up at him as if he were the horizon, waiting. He smelled the food and agitated back and forth. Though he fretted, he did not descend. Even when we ate we saw him shunting to and fro on a yardarm. We left a dish for him away from us but he did not venture to seize it. If he had, we would have seized him.

From his impatience, I predict that tomorrow he will surrender to his stomach. Then we will catch him and this problem will be solved. I truly regret such an irregularity, though it would be worthwhile if he could only tell us how far he was lifted inside the silvered cone, and what it was like.

Yours & etc.,
SAMSON LOW

25 August, 1909, 2° 13′ 10″ N,
51° 15′ 17″ E
Off Mogadishu

DEAR SIR:
Today he came down. After the last correspondence, it occurred to me that he might be vegetarian, and that though he was hungry, the meat had put him off. Therefore, I searched my memory for the most aromatic vegetable dish I know. In your service as a fourth officer, I called at Jaffa port, in Palestine, in January of 1873. We went up to Sfat, a holy town high in the hills, full of Jews and Arabs, quiet and mystical. There were so many come into that freezing velvet dome of stars that all hostelries were full. I and several others paid a small sum for private lodging and board. At two in the morning, after we had returned from Mt. Jermak, the Arabs made a hot lively fire from bundles of dry cyprus twigs, and in a great square pan heated local oil and herbs, in which they fried thick sections of potato. I have never eaten so well. Perhaps it was our hunger, the cold, the silence, being high in the mountains at Sfat, where air is like ether and all souls change. Today I made the cook follow that old receipt.

We had been in the monsoon for several hours, and the air was littered with silver sparks — apparitions of heat from a glittering afternoon. Though the sun was low, iron decks could not be tread. In the rigging, he appeared nearly finished, limp and slouching, an arm hanging without energy, his back bent. We put potatoes in a dish on the forecastle. He descended slowly, finally touching deck lightly and ambling to the bows like a spider, all limbs brushing the planks. He ate his fill, and we threw the net over him. We had expected a ferocious struggle, but his posture and expression were so peaceful that I ordered the net removed. Sailors stood ready with pikes, but he stayed in place. Then I approached him and extended my hand as if to a child.

In imitation, he put out his arm, looking much less fearsome. Without a show of teeth, in his tired state, crouched on all fours to half our heights, he was no more frightening than a hound. I led him to the stern and back again while the crew cheered and laughed. Then the mate took him, and then the entire hierarchy of the ship, down to the cabin boys, who are smaller than he and seemed to interest him the most. By dark, he had strolled with every member of the crew and was miraculously tame. But I remembered his teeth, and had him chained to his little boat.

He was comfortable there, surrounded by fruit and water (which he ate and drank methodically) and sitting on a throne of sorts, with half a dozen courtiers eager to look in his eyes and hold his obliging wrist. Mine is not the only London post in which he will be mentioned. Those who can write are describing him with great zeal. I have seen some of these letters. He has been portrayed as a "mad baboon," a "man-eating gorilla of horrible colors, muscled but as bright as a bird," a "pygmy man set down on the sea by miracle and typhoon," and as all manner of Latin names, each different from the others and incorrectly spelled.

Depending on the bend of the monsoon and whether it continues to run strongly, we will pass Ras Asir in three days. I thought of casting him off early but was implored to wait for the Cape. I relented, and in doing so was made to understand why those in command must stay by rules. I am sure, however, that my authority is not truly diminished, and when the ape is gone I will again tighten discipline.

I have already had the distress flag replaced by a green banner. It flies over the creature on his throne. Though in splendor, he is in chains and in three days' time will be on the sea once more.

Yours & etc.,
SAMSON LOW

28 August, 1909, 12° 4' 39" N,
50° 1' 2" E
North of Ras Asir

DEAR SIR:

A most alarming incident has occurred. I must report, though it is among the worst episodes of my command. This morning, I arose, expecting to put the ape over the side as we rounded Ras Asir at about eleven. (The winds have been consistently excellent and a northward breeze veering off the monsoon has propelled us as steadily as an engine.) Going out on deck, I discovered that his boat was nowhere to be seen. At first, I thought that the mate had already disposed of him, and was disappointed that we were far from the coast. Then, to my shock, I saw him sitting unmanacled atop the main cargo hatch.

I screamed at the mate, demanding to know what had happened to the throne (as it had come to be called). He replied that it had gone overboard during the twelve-to-four watch. I stormed below and got that watch out in a hurry. Though sleepy-eyed, they were terrified. I told them that if the guilty one did not come forth I would put them all in irons. My temper was short and I could have struck them down. Two young sailors, as frightened as if they were surrendering themselves to die, admitted that they had thrown it over. They said they did not want to see the ape put to drift.

They are in irons until we make Suez. Their names are Mulcahy and Esper, and their pay is docked until they are freed. As we rounded the Cape, cutting close in (for the waters there are deep), we could see that though the creature would have been immediately cast up on shore, the shore itself was barren and inhospitable, and surely he would have died there. My Admiralty chart does not detail the inland topography of this area and shows only a yellow tongue marked "Africa" thrusting into the Gulf of Aden.

I can throw him overboard now or later. I do not want to do it. I brought him on board in the first place. There is nothing with which to fashion another raft. We have many tons of wood below, but not a cubic foot of it is lighter than water. The wind is good and we are making for the Bab al-Mandab, where we will pass late tomorrow afternoon — after that, the frustrating run up the Red Sea to the Canal.

The mate suggests that we sell him to the Egyptians. But I am reluctant to make port with this in mind, as it would be a victory for the two in chains and in the eyes of many others. And we are not animal traders. If he leaves us at sea the effects of his presence will be invalidated, we will touch land with discipline restored, and I will have the option of destroying these letters, though everything here has been entered in short form in the log. I have ordered him not to be fed, but they cast him scraps. I must get back my proper hold on the ship.

Yours & etc.,
SAMSON LOW

30 August, 1909, 15° 49′ 30″ N,
41° 5′ 32″ E
Red Sea off Massawa

DEAR SIR:

I have been felled by an attack of headaches. Never before has this happened. There is pressure in my skull enough to burst it. I cannot keep my balance; my eyes roam and I am drunk with pain. For the weary tack up the Red Sea I have entrusted the mate with temporary command, retiring to my cabin with the excuse of heat prostration. I have been in the Red Sea time and again but have never felt apprehension that death would follow its heat. We have always managed. To the east, the mountains of the Hijaz are so dry and forbidding that I have seen sailors look away in fright.

The ape has begun to suffer from the heat. He is listless and ignored. His novelty has worn off (with the heat as it is) and no one pays him any attention. He will not go belowdecks but spends most of the day under the canvas sun shield, chewing slowly, though there is nothing in his mouth. It is hot there — the light so white and uncompromising it sears the eyes. I have freed his champions from irons and restored their pay. By this act I have won over the crew and caused the factions to disappear. No one thinks about the ape. But I dare not risk a recurrence of bad feeling and have decided to cast him into the sea. Where we found him, a strong seaward current would have carried him to the open ocean. Here, at least, he can make the shore, although it is the most barren coast on earth. But who would have thought he might survive the typhoon? He has been living beyond his time. To be picked up and whirled at incomprehensible speed, carried for miles above the earth where no man has even been, and thrown into the sea is a death sentence. If he survived that, perhaps he can survive Arabian desert.

His expression is neither sad nor fierce. He looks like an old man, neutral to the world. In the last two days he has become the target of provocation and physical blows. I have ordered this stopped, but a sailor will sometimes throw a nail or a piece of wood at him. We shall soon be rid of him.

Yesterday we came alongside another British ship, the *Stonepool*, of the Dutch Express Line. On seeing the ape, they were envious. What is it, their captain asked, amazed at its coloring. I replied that he was a Madagascar ape we had fished from the sea, and I offered him to them, saying he was as tame as a dog. At first, they wanted him. The crew cried out for his acceptance, but the captain demurred, shaking his head and looking into my eyes as if he were laughing at me. "Damn!" I said, and went below without even a salute at parting.

My head aches. I must stop. At first light tomorrow, I will toss him back.

Yours & etc.,
SAMSON LOW

3 September 1909
Suez

DEAR SIR:

The morning before last I went on deck at dawn. The ape was sitting on the main hatch, his eyes upon me from the moment I saw him. I walked over to him and extended my arm, which he would not take in his customary manner. I seized his wrist, which he withdrew. However, as he did this I laid hold of the other wrist, and pulled him off the hatch. He did not bare his teeth. He began to scream. Awakened by this, most of the crew stood in the companionways or on deck, silently observing.

He was hard to drag, but I towed him to the rail. When I took his other arm to hoist him over, he bared his teeth with a frightening shriek. Everyone was again terrified. The teeth must be six inches long.

He came at me with those teeth, and I could do nothing but throttle him. With my hands on his throat, his arms were free. He grasped my side. I felt the pads of his hands against my ribs. I had to tolerate that awful sensation to keep hold of his throat. No man aboard came close. He shrieked and moaned. His eyes reddened. My response was to tighten my hold, to end the horror. I gripped so hard that my own teeth were bared and I made sounds similar to his. He put his hands around my neck as if to strangle me back, but I had already taken the inside position and, despite his great strength, lessened the power of his grip merely by lifting my arms against his. Nevertheless he choked me. But I had a great head start. We held this position for long minutes, sweating, until his arms dropped and his body convulsed. In rage, I threw him by the neck into the sea, where he quickly sank.

Some of the crew have begun to talk about him as if he were about to be canonized. Others see him as evil. I assembled them as the coasts began to close on Suez and the top of the sea was white and still. I made my views clear, for in years of command in a life on the sea I have learned much. I felt confident of what I told them.

He is not a symbol. He stands neither for innocence nor for evil. There is no parable and no lesson in his coming and going. I was neither right nor wrong in bringing him aboard (though it was indeed incorrect) or in what I later did. We must get on with the ship's business. He does not stand for a man or men. He stands for nothing. He was an ape, simian and lean, half sensible. He came on board, and now he is gone.

Yours & etc.,
SAMSON LOW

ERNEST HEMINGWAY

Perhaps the most widely read and influential writer of his generation, Ernest Hemingway (1899–1961) embodied the vigor, the restlessness, and the despair of the twentieth century, in his life as well as his writings. The son of a physician, he was born in Oak Park, near Chicago, and spent his boyhood in Illinois and Michigan. After leaving school in 1917 and working briefly as a reporter for the *Kansas City Star*, he joined the Red Cross, and drove an ambulance on the Italian front until he was wounded. After the war, he became a reporter for *The Toronto Star*, in company with Morley Callaghan. Then Hemingway began to produce novels and stories about the waste and sterility that marked the postwar period, and which led his friend Gertrude Stein to remark, "You are all a lost generation." *In Our Time* appeared in 1924, followed by *The Sun Also Rises* (1926), and *Men Without Women* (1927); in these works Hemingway revealed an originality of plot and a striking economy of style which quickly established him as a major writer. *A Farewell to Arms* (1929) was inspired by his war experiences in Italy; and *For Whom the Bell Tolls* (1940) grew out of the period he spent in Spain in 1937 during the Spanish Civil War. Between 1941 and 1945 he was a war correspondent in Europe and the Far East. His last major work was *The Old Man and the Sea* (1952), which brought him the Pulitzer Prize in 1953; and in 1954 he was awarded the Nobel Prize for literature. In his last years Hemingway suffered periods of illness and depression; and while in Idaho in July 1961 he committed suicide with a shotgun.

Hemingway's life was filled with action and adventure; and his preoccupation with the physical aspect of existence, particularly its violence, is reflected in most of his writing. Whether his subject is the horror of war, or the struggle between human beings and nature, Hemingway draws a picture of a world where the only certainties are pain, deprivation, or death. Whatever their hopes or ideals may have been, his characters learn that life is a futile ordeal; to counter this, they must develop a protective shell of toughness, or endure their fate with numb resignation. Even in "Hills Like White Elephants" (*Men Without Women*), a story far removed from the brutalities of war or the bullring, there is an undercurrent of emotional violence. The dialogue is terse and laconic; but Hemingway's spare style conveys hidden tensions with admirable understatement, hinting at the sterility and breakdown of a whole way of life.

FOR FURTHER READING

Jackson J. Benson, *The Short Stories of Ernest Hemingway: Critical Essays* (Durham, N.C.: Duke University Press, 1975).

Joseph Defalco, *The Hero in Hemingway's Short Stories* (Pittsburgh: University of Pittsburgh Press, 1963).

Leo Gurko, *Ernest Hemingway and the Pursuit of Heroism* (New York: T.Y. Crowell, 1968).

Eusebio L. Rodrigues, " 'Hills Like White Elephants': An Analysis," *Literary Criterion* 5 (1962): 105–9.

HILLS LIKE WHITE ELEPHANTS

The hills across the valley of the Ebro were long and white. On this side there was no shade and no trees and the station was between two lines of rails in the sun. Close against the side of the station there was the warm shadow of the building and a curtain, made of strings of bamboo beads, hung across the open door into the bar, to keep out flies. The American and the girl with him sat at a table in the shade, outside the building. It was very hot and the express from Barcelona would come in forty minutes. It stopped at this junction for two minutes and went on to Madrid.

"What should we drink?" the girl asked. She had taken off her hat and put it on the table.

"It's pretty hot," the man said.

"Let's drink beer."

"Dos cervezas," the man said into the curtain.

"Big ones?" a woman asked from the doorway.

"Yes. Two big ones."

The woman brought two glasses of beer and two felt pads. She put the felt pads and the beer glasses on the table and looked at the man and the girl. The girl was looking off at the line of hills. They were white in the sun and the country was brown and dry.

"They look like white elephants," she said.

"I've never seen one," the man drank his beer.

"No, you wouldn't have."

"I might have," the man said. "Just because you say I wouldn't have doesn't prove anything."

The girl looked at the bead curtain. "They've painted something on it," she said. "What does it say?"

"Anis del Toro. It's a drink."

"Could we try it?"

The man called "Listen" through the curtain. The woman came out from the bar.

"Four reales."

"We want two Anis del Toro."

"With water?"

"Do you want it with water?"

"I don't know," the girl said. "Is it good with water?"

"It's all right."

"You want them with water?" asked the woman.

"Yes, with water."

"It tastes like licorice," the girl said and put the glass down.

"That's the way with everything."

"Yes," said the girl. "Everything tastes of licorice. Especially all the things you've waited so long for, like absinthe."

"Oh, cut it out."

"You started it," the girl said. "I was being amused. I was having a fine time."

"Well, let's try and have a fine time."

"All right. I was trying. I said the mountains looked like white elephants. Wasn't that bright?"

"That was bright."

"I wanted to try this new drink. That's all we do, isn't it — look at things and try new drinks?"

"I guess so."

The girl looked across at the hills.

"They're lovely hills," she said. "They don't really look like white elephants. I just meant the coloring of their skin through the trees."

"Should we have another drink?"

"All right."

The warm wind blew the bead curtain against the table.

"The beer's nice and cool," the man said.

"It's lovely," the girl said.

"It's really an awfully simple operation, Jig," the man said. "It's not really an operation at all."

The girl looked at the ground the table legs rested on.

"I know you wouldn't mind it, Jig. It's really not anything. It's just to let the air in."

The girl did not say anything.

"I'll go with you and I'll stay with you all the time. They just let the air in and then it's all perfectly natural."

"Then what will we do afterward?"

"We'll be fine afterward. Just like we were before."

"What makes you think so?"

"That's the only thing that bothers us. It's the only thing that's made us unhappy."

The girl looked at the bead curtain, put her hand out and took hold of two of the strings of beads.

"And you think then we'll be all right and be happy."

"I know we will. You don't have to be afraid. I've known lots of people that have done it."

"So have I," said the girl. "And afterward they were all so happy."

"Well," the man said, "if you don't want to you don't have to. I wouldn't have you do it if you didn't want to. But I know it's perfectly simple."

"And you really want to?"

"I think it's the best thing to do. But I don't want you to do it if you don't really want to."

"And if I do it you'll be happy and things will be like they were and you'll love me?"

"I love you now. You know I love you."

"I know. But if I do it, then it will be nice again if I say things are like white elephants, and you'll like it?"

"I'll love it. I love it now but I just can't think about it. You know how I get when I worry."

"If I do it you won't ever worry?"

"I won't worry about that because it's perfectly simple."

"Then I'll do it. Because I don't care about me."

"What do you mean?"

"I don't care about me."

"Well, I care about you."

"Oh, yes. But I don't care about me. And I'll do it and then everything will be fine."

"I don't want you to do it if you feel that way."

The girl stood up and walked to the end of the station. Across, on the other side, were fields of grain and trees along the banks of the Ebro. Far away, beyond the river, were mountains. The shadow of a cloud moved across the field of grain and she saw the river through the trees.

"And we could have all this," she said. "And we could have everything and every day we make it more impossible."

"What did you say?"

"I said we could have everything."

"We can have everything."

"No, we can't."

"We can have the whole world."

"No, we can't."

"We can go everywhere."

"No, we can't. It isn't ours any more."

"It's ours."

"No, it isn't. And once they take it away, you never get it back."

"But they haven't taken it away."

"We'll wait and see."

"Come on back in the shade," he said. "You mustn't feel that way."

"I don't feel any way," the girl said. "I just know things."

"I don't want you to do anything that you don't want to do —"

"Nor that isn't good for me," she said. "I know. Could we have another beer?"

"All right. But you've got to realize —"

"I realize," the girl said. "Can't we maybe stop talking?"

They sat down at the table and the girl looked across at the hills on the dry side of the valley and the man looked at her and at the table.

"You've got to realize," he said, "that I don't want you to do it if you don't want to. I'm perfectly willing to go through with it if it means anything to you."

"Doesn't it mean anything to you? We could get along."

"Of course it does. But I don't want anybody but you. I don't want any one else. And I know it's perfectly simple."

"Yes, you know it's perfectly simple."

"It's all right for you to say that, but I do know it."

"Would you do something for me now?"

"I'd do anything for you."

"Would you please please please please please please please stop talking?"

He did not say anything but looked at the bags against the wall of the station. There were labels on them from all the hotels where they had spent nights.

"But I don't want you to," he said. "I don't care anything about it."

"I'll scream," the girl said.

The woman came out through the curtains with two glasses of beer and put them down on the damp felt pads. "The train comes in five minutes," she said.

"What did she say?" asked the girl.

"That the train is coming in five minutes."

The girl smiled brightly at the woman, to thank her.

"I'd better take the bags over to the other side of the station," the man said. She smiled at him.

"All right. Then come back and we'll finish the beer."

He picked up the two heavy bags and carried them around the station to the other tracks. He looked up the tracks but could not see the train. Coming back, he walked through the barroom, where people waiting for the train were drinking. He drank an Anis at the bar and looked at the people. They were all waiting reasonably for the train. He went out through the bead curtain. She was sitting at the table and smiled at him.

"Do you feel better?" he asked.

"I feel fine," she said. "There's nothing wrong with me. I feel fine."

JACK HODGINS

Jack Hodgins was born in 1938 in Merville, at the north end of Vancouver Island, where he lived until he left for Vancouver to go to university in 1956. After training there to be a teacher, he returned to the
Island to teach in Nanaimo; some years later he left to teach at the
University of Ottawa, then returned once more, this time to Victoria,
where he now teaches Creative Writing at the University of Victoria.
The North Island community, where Hodgins's family were loggers
for two generations, is still a rural one. His memories of this rural
life — its anecdotal dialogues, its penchant for tall tales and grand gestures — give much of his writing its vigorous character. His stories teem
with incidents and individuals, and yet the exaggeration which gives
them their comic quality also serves as a reminder of the chance dreams
and stern realities that generate the exaggeration in the first place. It is
a process of transformation. As W.J. Keith observes, such points of
transformation constitute the narrative heart of Hodgins's fiction; comedy, says Keith, is always teetering on the edge of something else —
tragedy, perhaps, or a recognition of the sadness of the unattainable.
It is this recognition which turns "his local backyard into an image of
the whole creative universe."

"Mr. Pernouski's Dream" — the bittersweet story of a real estate
salesman's come-uppance and downfall — amply illustrates this art of
"subtle interconnection." It comes from Hodgins's fourth book of
fiction, *The Barclay Family Theatre* (1981). Earlier books include *The
Invention of the World* (1977) and the Governor-General's Award-
winning novel *The Resurrection of Joseph Bourne* (1979). Influencing
all these narratives are several other coherent worlds of fiction — those
of Faulkner's Yoknapatawpha County, Steinbeck's Salinas Valley,
Gabriel Garcia Marquez's Macondo, and Al Capp's Dogpatch — but
Hodgins makes "the Island" recognizably his own.

FOR FURTHER READING

Geoff Hancock, "An Interview with Jack Hodgins," *Canadian Fiction
Magazine*, nos. 32/33 (1979/80): 33–63.
David L. Jeffrey, "Jack Hodgins and the Island Mind," *Book Forum*
4 (1980): 70–78.
W.J. Keith, "Jack Hodgins' Island World," *Canadian Forum* 61
(September/October 1981): 30–31.

MR. PERNOUSKI'S DREAM

No wonder this woman couldn't take her eyes off Mr. Pernouski. With her knees almost touching his, he knew she could hardly fail to notice his tremendous size. He'd come to expect this kind of attention from strangers; he'd come to depend on it. Perhaps she'd never seen a person like him before, perhaps he was the fattest man this grey-haired lady had seen. Mr. Pernouski believed himself to be the largest person ever to ride these ferries. He hoped he was. Only a few minutes before, he'd made a joke for the young woman who'd sold him his ticket: "Maybe I should sit close to the centre of the boat, in order to keep things in balance?" The young woman had laughed, and said no, that it wasn't necessary, but if the ferry sank they would know who they ought to blame.

And he didn't sit in the middle, he sat here in a window seat on the starboard side, facing this elderly couple with the mess of cigarette butts on the carpet around their feet. The gentleman wore a hat with a wide felt brim and took several pictures of the waves that splashed against the ferry below the window, but the woman lit one cigarette off the butt of another and watched Mr. Pernouski out of pale blue eyes that squinted against her smoke. She watched him finish a can of diet cola and begin a second. She watched him riffle through a newspaper he'd found abandoned on his seat. She watched him toss back several handfuls of salted peanuts. Then, because Mr. Pernouski believed that a ninety-minute ferry ride across the Strait of Georgia was wasted time if you didn't make some useful contacts with people, he washed the last of the peanuts down with diet cola and sat back to level a long hard squint of his own in the woman's direction. She neither flinched nor turned away; she wrapped one long narrow leg around the other and hugged herself while she sucked at her cigarette. Did she think if she stared at him hard enough she would discover the key to his size?

"You see that little sailboat out there, with the bright green hull?" he said. "Got one exactly like it at home but I never have time to use her. She's been in the water just once in more than a year."

She frowned, peered out the window at the tiny boat that leaned its narrow sail away from the ferry, and shuddered. "I wouldn't trust my life to a thing like that. For me, this tub we're *riding* on is bad enough. I'd have felt safer in a plane." She stuck the cigarette in the middle of her mouth, sucked noisily, then jerked it out like a plug while she inhaled.

"You folks are new to this part of the country, aren't you? Tourists. Myself, I'm just returning to the Island from a convention." And then, in case she thought of him in robes and an Arab's hat: "Of salesmen."

He took her small nod as permission to continue. "You expect outrageous things to happen at conventions. Sometimes that's why you attend — because you know outrageous things will happen there." Mr. Pernouski chuckled to himself, then told the woman about poor old Swampy Grogan, who'd got so drunk last night that he'd passed right out. A number of his friends — Mr. Pernouski included — had carried him up to his room, which overlooked the harbour and had seagulls screeching and swooping around the balcony. "We stripped him down to the skin and laid him out on the bed. Then we opened the sliding glass doors to the balcony — this was Mr. Pimlott's idea — and made a trail of peanuts from out there across the carpet to the bed. We also left peanuts scattered on Swampy's bed and all over his sleeping body. When he woke up this morning . . ."

"Mmmmfff," the woman said, and closed her eyes.

"Well, I can see I don't have to tell you the rest."

She removed the cigarette from her mouth and held it between two long stained fingers. "Your colours," she said, "are rude."

Mr. Pernouski knew that she couldn't be referring to the colour of his suit, which was a conservative grey, so he lifted one foot to check on his socks. They too were grey. If she meant the orange of the vinyl seats on this ferry he was prepared to agree, but he saw no reason why he should take the blame.

"No no," she said. "I mean your colours." She gestured with the cigarette in the direction of the window, where her husband was aiming his camera. "Your greens are too green. Your blues. It's gaudy here, people must go blind. The trees are unnatural, and look — look at those mountains."

Mr. Pernouski glanced at the mountains of the island they were approaching, but they looked to him the same as they'd always looked — like mountains. They were part of his own back yard. Something more important than an attitude towards nature's colour scheme had been uncovered here, however, and he felt his instincts pounce. "You're from the prairies," he said.

The man put down his camera and looked at Mr. Pernouski. His wife permitted the smallest smile to flicker across her lips.

"Because of the way you keep taking pictures of the waves."

The man, who had not taken off his hat, stuck out his bottom lip. "We could be from the Yukon."

"And because of the skin," Mr. Pernouski added. "In my business you learn these things. The dry skin always gives them away. You've lived all your life in Saskatchewan."

The woman puffed out another cloud of smoke, and raised her chin. "But I was born in Nebraska."

"And because, sir," Mr. Pernouski said to the gentleman with the camera, "your wife has smoked seven cigarettes in a row, sitting directly under the No Smoking sign."

The elderly couple, apparently so impressed with Mr. Pernouski that they did not challenge his logic, looked at the carpet where the woman had been grinding her cigarette stubs and matches under her heel. The gentleman pushed his hat back and looked up at the sign that hung from the ceiling above him. His wife took another cigarette from her package and lit it off the butt in her hand. "Silly rule," she said, and added the new butt to the mess at her feet.

Mr. Pernouski explained that the reason he had been so quick to recognize they were from the prairie provinces was that he was in real estate. He said that he saw thousands of people like them every year. They'd left farms behind, or shops. They'd finally retired, or sold everything, and could hardly wait to find a little house on the coast, or some property to build on, in order to escape the winters back home. He himself, he said, had been personally responsible for finding many of them the little retirement place they'd dreamed of. It was one of the rewards of his job. As a matter of fact, it was because he had an appointment this afternoon with a charming couple from Calgary that he was returning a day earlier than the rest of the conventioners.

"Now what type of home were you folks hoping to find?" he said. "I probably have just the thing."

The woman unwrapped her left leg from around her right and pointed her toes. "We're visiting," she said. "We have friends here. We'll never stay."

The gentleman lifted his camera to his eye and took a picture of Mr. Pernouski. People all over the lounge turned to see why there'd been a flash. The gentleman leaned forward and shook Mr. Pernouski's hand. "The name's Eckhart."

"The name's Pernouski," Mr. Pernouski said, and reached for one of his cards. "Eden Realty. You might say, without fear of contradiction, that I'm the biggest man in real estate on the Island."

While Mr. Eckhart stared at the little white card, Mr. Pernouski said he always offered to pay double when he rode the ferries, on account of his size. He patted his belly to show what he meant. "The girl in the window told me they have different fares for the various sizes of automobiles, but lucky for me only one for humans." Since the elderly couple seemed reluctant to show an interest in his bulk, he decided to tell them that he understood perfectly why so many prairie people fell in love with this part of the world and refused to leave. He'd been everywhere himself, he said, and knew exactly what this island had to offer. He'd been to Saskatoon and Regina and Thunder Bay. He'd also been to Greece once, would you believe it, not long ago. He'd won the trip by selling the most houses that year of anyone in the office. He'd been down to Florida, and Mexico, and over to whatsit, Taiwan. He knew what the rest of the world was like so he also knew precisely why everyone everywhere would give a leg to live on this island they were approaching. Climate was only half of it.

"We haven't been to many places ourselves," said Mr. Eckhart, but his wife was quick to add: "Well, there was Montana." She sounded annoyed, as if she resented telling this stranger even that much about themselves. In case the little couple thought he was bragging when he told about all the places he'd been, Mr. Pernouski remarked that he wasn't the only member of his family who travelled. His wife Christina, in fact, had been to far more places than he had. She was in Africa right this minute, on a buying trip. Or more precisely — he glanced at his watch — she'd started home but was stopping for a few days in Toronto where she'd been asked to make a speech. Because they looked as if they expected to hear even more, Mr. Pernouski explained that shortly before she married him, a widower with three growing children, his wife had bought an import shop once owned by the husband of one of her sisters and become a successful retailer on her own. Even after their marriage, while caring for his children, she expanded her business in a dramatic fashion until she owned a string of shops right across the country and had to travel abroad in order to select the merchandise herself. She was so successful that groups of businesswomen paid her to stop on her way through their towns and cities to make speeches on the secrets of her success.

Mr. Echkart said he must be married to a most remarkable woman, but his wife pulled a small hardcover book out of her purse, and said she was going to read. She opened the book to where she'd turned a corner down and settled back in her seat. With eyes shifting back and forth across the pages, she kept her nose in the book while Mr. Pernouski and her husband talked about the price of homes and the differences in weather between the coast and the prairies. She didn't look up again until a voice came out of the ceiling to warn them they would soon be docking. Mr. Pernouski rode down the three flights of escalators with the Eckharts in order to help them find their car, which turned out to be an expensive late-model sedan with suitcases and cardboard boxes piled high in the back seat. He estimated that they would be in the market for something substantial when they came around, waterfront maybe, or a view home high up a hill. Mrs. Eckhart looked to him like the kind of woman who would demand that her husband buy her only the best. "You've got my card," he said. "You know where you can find me if you want." Before he shut the little woman's door, however, he asked them if he couldn't have the address of their friends, in case he needed to get in touch with *them* for some reason or other in the next few days. Mrs. Eckhart laughed and said she couldn't imagine what reason he might have for wanting to contact them, and shut her door herself.

Nevertheless you'll be seeing me again, Mr. Pernouski thought. He had no doubts about that. For him it was a matter of principle that no ninety-minute ferry ride across the strait be wasted time. He didn't intend to let today be any exception. While he hurried forward up the ramp and into a light gusting rain, he sorted in his mind through various list-ings he was responsible for, in search of the one which would be exactly right for the Eckharts.

Mr. Pernouski's determination was not something he could easily explain to his son, who had only recently got into the business of selling real estate himself and had much to learn. The boy insisted he had no desire to be Number One Salesman of Anywhere like his father, he simply liked his work. He claimed that he enjoyed the company of the people he met and the satisfaction of finding them what they wanted. It was clear to Mr. Pernouski that the boy hadn't learned a thing from his father's example.

Still, he spent most of dinner telling his family about the convention. You can always count on something outrageous to happen, he said, and told them about sprinkling peanuts all over Swampy Grogan's body in his hotel room so the seagulls would come in while he was sleeping.

"EEEeeeeee!" The twins pulled faces at one another and squealed. They wanted to know if he had a shower before he came down to breakfast.

"Of course he did, but boy was he ever mad!"

Mr. Pernouski's son said that Swampy Grogan must be one hell of a grouch. No sense of humour at all. "A real son-of-a-bitch, eh, not to think it was funny to have seagull shit on his body and smeared all over his face."

Mr. Pernouski had learned long ago to ignore the sarcasm in his son's voice. He said he didn't know why Swampy Grogan ever went to these things since he certainly wasn't any great shakes as a salesman. "If he ever sells a house it's just because no other salesman's around and the customer's begging for it." Mr. Pernouski's son said he ought to be glad of that, at least there was no danger of Swampy Grogan pushing him out of the Number One spot in the foreseeable future.

Mr. Pernouski said that this year every person in that convention hall recognized him without an introduction. Even old Pimlott from West Vancouver forgot his snootiness and treated him like the star he was. They couldn't ignore him now. When you were Number One Salesman on the Island, even mainlanders had to sit up and take notice. Everybody wanted to congratulate him, as if they'd only now discovered he'd held the position for five years in a row. Everybody wanted to know his secret. He was a hero. Naturally he enjoyed every minute of the convention and nothing short of an appointment with a potential buyer from Calgary could have pulled him away.

Without looking up from his plate, his son said he was sure all of Calgary was grateful for the fantastic goddam sacrifice that had been made.

Mr. Pernouski's voice took on an impatient edge. "Look. That's exactly the difference between Number One and all those others." While he was over here selling a hundred-thousand-dollar house to a retired druggist from Calgary, he said, Number Two and Number Three-hundred-and-two were still over there having a good time.

"Oh wow!" His son pushed away from the table and took his dishes to the sink. "I imagine we can count on you to let Number Two and Number Three-hundred-and-two know what stupid assholes they've been."

Rather than call him back for an argument, Mr. Pernouski reminded himself that this was the same person who'd run away to live in a commune for six months only a couple of years ago. His first job after that had been on a tugboat hauling barges up and down the strait, where he'd turned himself into a legend by regularly stripping to the skin and parading around the deck of his boat in sunlight playing a flute. How much did you expect from a boy who behaved like that? He still smoked an incredible amount of something he liked to call "the green stuff" which he grew in an attic window. That such a boy should agree to try a job like selling real estate was something in itself to be grateful for, and Mr. Pernouski knew better than to push his luck too far. As his wife was fond of saying, you didn't count on miracles to happen overnight, you just went on trying to set a good example.

He was reminded, now, that this was the day his wife was to make her big speech. "Think of me when I'm in Toronto," she'd written. "You know how nervous I get." While the twins washed up the dishes, Mr. Pernouski found her most recent letter and carried it into his bedroom where he sat to reread it. Her plane had been delayed by a dust storm off the Sahara, she wrote, but she'd arrived safely in Kano and spent her day wandering amongst the colourful market stalls. In all Nigeria, this promised to be her most rewarding stop. Calabashes. Carvings. Talking drums. Thornwood figures. Brilliantly dyed cloth. The place, of course, had been invaded by tourists but if you knew how to shop you could still get some bargains. The dust, the heat, were terrible! She might even adopt the local women's custom of wearing a huge colourful rag around their heads — if it didn't keep you cool, at least it would keep the dust out of your hair. She'd been nearly run down by a snub-nosed truck with bicycles and bedsprings roped to the sides and at least twenty people standing jam-packed in the back of it, in their robes, laughing at her with their huge white teeth. NO STANDING were the words painted on the sign that flapped just below their elbows. She enclosed a postcard showing the local emir on a white horse, the man so wrapped in white that only his eyes were showing. Mr. Pernouski didn't know what an emir was but he could guess this fellow was some kind of prince. The men who surrounded him in their brilliant robes, she wrote on the back, were supposed to be his eunuchs. Whether they were or not she hadn't found out for herself. "Think of me when I'm in Toronto," she added. "You know how nervous I get."

He knew how nervous she got before these things but he also knew she could handle it. She even enjoyed it. She looked forward to working herself up into a high-strung nervous state, like an actress. She would stand in the middle of her hotel room and holler at the top of her voice, over and over, that she was terrific, that she was marvellous, that she was fantastic, and that she was going to knock them dead. He knew, too, just what she was going to tell those women, all those young Christinas who came lusting after her kind of success. She'd practised several times in front of him. Up there behind her lectern she would give her secrets away, her top ten requirements for the successful modern woman of business. Necessities, she liked to call them. Pride in yourself was one, you could get nowhere at all without it. Flexibility too. Understanding the workings of your business. Each of these she developed in detail for several minutes. Independence — it came natural to her. Caring for others. Tenacity. Planning. Honesty. Clearsightedness. These were her first nine. She had several others that she used for her tenth, depending on the audience and the circumstances. The woman loved it. When she'd explained all ten of the necessities they begged for more; she couldn't possibly make all the speeches she was asked to make, not if she wanted to keep her own business growing, and pay a little attention to her family.

Mr. Pernouski wondered if sometimes, in front of those audiences so eager for secrets, his wife was tempted to use him as an example of what you could do. It wasn't impossible. That he was Number One in his line of work was indisputable. Five wooden plaques on the wall of his office proclaimed him Salesman of the Year. Last spring, with over one and a half million dollars' worth of business, he'd won a trip to New Zealand. Three years in a row his own company had awarded him a trip to the World Real Estate Convention — last year in Greece. Once, he'd won a station wagon for the largest volume of sales in just this district — his wife still drove it — another time a mobile home for the largest volume of sales in the mid-Island region. And if the plaques on his office wall weren't proof enough, there was his healthy bank account to consider, his accumulated investments in properties that would boom some day, and this comfortable house with the spectacular view of the strait. And of course (most important of all) there was the long list of buyers, sellers, and businessmen who refused to do business with anybody else but him. If that wasn't proof of success, what was?

A more important question he liked to ask himself was, how did he do it? He could list the ways. He'd often done so, in fact, for the benefit of his son, but liked to go over the list in his head once a day in case he came up with anything new. Most obvious, of course, was his high profile. He was noticeable. When he was travelling as a private individual, Mr. Pernouski wore conservative grey suits to offset the attention his bulk quite naturally drew, but when he was on duty he wore a red-and-white tartan jacket and white pants and shoes, in order to take advantage of his size. People could hardly avoid him. Dressed up like that he became a presence in the town — everyone knew him. Other salesmen, who believed you should wear three-piece suits in order to improve the public image of the profession, called him the Plaid Tank. Mr. Pernouski was always prepared to tell a joke about his appearance. He had to wear brighter clothes than most, he said, so he wouldn't get lost in the crowd, a tiny fellow like him. He said he bought his suit from Brown's Tent and Awning and rented it out to circuses on weekends when he wasn't working.

Of course there was seldom a time when he wasn't working — and that was part of the secret too. Energy. Enthusiasm. He never let up. If you turned your back or closed your eyes or put your feet up for a rest, somebody else (his eye on the Number One plaque) would grab those clients away from you. He couldn't blame them, it was part of the job, in fact he would be happy to show respect for any man or woman who deposed him as Number One, any man or woman who equalled his talent for sales and salesmanship.

Even as he drifted off to sleep that night, Mr. Pernouski was aware that despite the difference in time his wife would be still performing for those women in Toronto. Her speech would be over by now but they would be pressing themselves on her for more, touching her, praising her success and her speaking ability and the remarkable flair with which she carried everything off. In the crowd, she would be the tallest, the most poised, by far the most tastefully dressed. One of the women, the one who was the most like Christina, would be standing back from the rest, with her eyes narrowed, thinking *Just you wait*. In his sleep this woman walked into his head and lit a cigarette and squinted at him through clouds of smoke out of Mrs. Eckhart's face.

Exactly the way Mrs. Eckhart was looking at him in real life the next morning when Mr. Pernouski stepped into the coffee shop for his break and discovered the couple sitting at the booth nearest the door. They didn't seem at all surprised. Mrs. Eckhart took a Kleenex out of her purse, blew her nose, and put the Kleenex back. "My nose has been running since I arrived," she said. "It's your damp air."

Mr. Pernouski squeezed into the bench on the facing side of their table and ordered his usual from the waitress, who looked up from behind the counter and smiled. Three doughnuts and a glass of diet cola. "A beautiful day out there," he said, unwilling to let this woman get away with her jibes. "The sun is going to break through those clouds any minute, you wait and see."

Mrs. Eckhart drew her eyebrows together in a frown. "What will people do, if it does come out? Will they hide, or fall down and worship it?" Through his laughter her husband explained to Mr. Pernouski that prairie people believed that folks out here dried up and shrivelled away like a jellyfish on the beach if it ever stopped raining.

When Mr. Pernouski had finished the last of his doughnuts, he insisted on paying for the Eckhart's coffee and buying Mrs. Eckhart a package of cigarettes. Out on the sidewalk she looked at the package as if she couldn't quite believe they sold her brand in this part of the country. "And now, since it's obviously Providence that we should meet this second time," Mr. Pernouski said, "I insist on being allowed to take you on a scenic drive of the area."

Mrs. Eckhart's head jerked up. "No!" By the look on her face it was clear that she smelled a plot. Her eyes shifted to her husband for support. "We've got things to do! Shopping! And there's Nellie's . . . you know."

Mr. Eckhart shook his head, as if to say he regretted everything, everything. "A half-hour's drive, Mr. Pernouski, would be pleasant. But after that, I'm afraid my wife is correct. There are things that must be done. We have friends here, you see, who are expecting us."

Mrs. Eckhart allowed herself to be helped into the back seat but she slouched in one corner where her clouds of smoke could escape through the open window and made it clear, almost immediately, that she intended to make a nuisance of herself. Was there an art gallery in the town, she wanted to know. Mr. Pernouski laughed. With all this beautiful scenery to look at, he said, why would anyone want to look at pictures? When he stopped his car in front of a small waterfront home with his company's sign on the front lawn so that they might admire the view of the strait and a few little islands, she blew her nose again and wanted to know what you could do with a view after you've looked at it twice. She hated views. "After a week of living along this stretch these people probably couldn't tell you whether their windows looked out on the strait or the city dump. The eyes adjust to anything." When Mr. Pernouski drove them down the lane of a small hobby farm he'd been trying to sell for a year and a half, she wanted to know what kind of tree that was whose ratty bark was peeling off like the hide of a mangy dog.

In a new subdivision high on a hill behind town he insisted they all get out of the car and admire the panorama. He led them to the edge of the gravel and remained silent while they took it in: the sharp treed slope beneath them, the town laid out around the harbour with its little islands and cluster of sailboats, the strait and the purple mountains of the mainland and the moving clouds in the sky. "And all that," Mr. Pernouski said, "is what I'm offering you."

Mrs. Eckhart seemed to find something amusing in what he'd said. "You offer us that?" She moved closer, prepared to laugh. Just by the amused and squinting look on her face she made him feel that he didn't understand a thing. "You offer us that?" she repeated, and jabbed her cigarette in the general direction of the view, laughing. "If we *what*? If we *what*? If we hurl ourselves down this cliff? If we sign away our souls to you?"

"Doris," Mr. Eckhart warned.

"I meant it only in a manner of speaking, of course," Mr. Pernouski said. "For the price of the lot behind us."

"Oh." Was she satisfied or disappointed? In either case she twitched her nose and shifted her attention to a crow which was making a racket in a fir.

Perhaps it was the altitude. Perhaps it was the sense he had that he'd just put the Eckhart woman in her place. Whatever the reason, Mr. Pernouski decided to risk a confidence and tell Mr. Eckhart his special dream. He saw all the rest of the world made up of broken-hearted people, he said, whose own dreams had failed them. Millions and millions out there who lived in squalor and ignorance and hunger and backward cultures, looking for something better. He saw mothers and fathers and hopeful children, he saw old people and sick people and tired people, all living amongst the ruins of plans that had come to nothing — wars and dead civilizations and outdated languages and old-fashioned buildings and meaningless religions. All of them, he said, dreamed of a place where they could start over again — a place that was green and clean and still uncluttered by the ruins of other people's mistakes. He saw himself — oh, he knew this was a romantic notion but wasn't it still worthwhile? — he saw himself as a person whose job it was to make all those dreams come true, to gather all those tear-stained faces full of worry lines onto this island and give them the chance they needed, provide them with a home. Nothing made him happier than to hear that a new family had landed in from India, say, so he could start looking around for a nice house painted blue with a basement large enough for all the relatives who were bound to follow soon, and of course in a neighbourhood where they would be surrounded by relatives who had already arrived before them. Prairie people were his favourites, because he knew that by the time they put themselves into his hands most of them were panting for what he had to offer. It was an impossible dream, he knew that! There wasn't enough room for the whole world here, he just wished the Island were a little bigger so that everyone who deserved to live in this place could find the room. Sometimes he felt he was offering a little piece of paradise to anyone out there who needed it!

Mr. Eckhart made appreciative muttering noises and pushed back his hat and looked out over the strait as if he could see all those homeless broken-hearted people heading this way right now. He lifted his camera and snapped a picture, perhaps to capture Mr. Pernouski's vision on film.

His wife, however, was trembling. "Sir!" She puffed her cigarette and narrowed her eyes at Mr. Pernouski. He hadn't noticed before how noisily she sucked on her smoke, how impatiently she blew it out. "Do I understand . . .?" She seemed unable to find the words she wanted. "Do I understand that you . . . that you think you're in a position . . . to offer us paradise?"

"Doris," her husband said, his face colouring. "Is that any way . . .?"

Mr. Pernouski, who hadn't even realized the woman had been listening to him, thought she must be working up to some bitter joke, in her manner. But she hunched over her crossed arms and paced along the gravel shoulder of the road and came back to squint up angrily at him through her smoke. "When you are more likely the proprietor of . . .," her eyes searched for the word amongst stones by her feet, ". . . of hell." From her sudden smile, you might think she expected to receive congratulations for her daring.

Mr. Pernouski decided he would tell his family at the dinner table that after all these years he had finally met an honest-to-goodness mad-woman, something right out of a loony-bin, or a book. "No more meat on her bones than a cat," he would say, "but she's as crazy as they come."

He would be sorry, though, that he'd mentioned her at all. Mr. Pernouski's son threw himself back in his chair and laughed. "She said you were the proprietor of *where!*" This struck him as so funny that he had to leave the table and get himself a drink of water from the kitchen sink to keep from choking on his peas. Shit, he wished he could have met this babe, he said. She must be really something.

Mr. Pernouski did not add that she'd gone on to accuse him of wearing a jacket that made her think of a mobile billboard, a lurid advertisement for the attractions of his native land. And by his native land, she said, jabbing her cigarette into the air all around her, she did not mean this. He knew what she meant but he saw no point in taking advantage of the woman's mental illness for the sake of an easy laugh.

There was no harm in reporting what the husband had said to him once the woman was back in the car, however. He said she was a saint, a real saint — could you believe it? He said this little display of anger was as much a surprise to him as it was to Mr. Pernouski. He said he'd never seen anyone bring out the vicious side of her the way Mr. Pernouski had. Back home she was one of those saintly people who quietly go about looking after everybody that needed looking after in their town. She was loved, he said, by everyone.

She was also, Mr. Eckhart added — as if it were an obvious fact — the wisest woman in the world. A respected professor of fine arts in Regina.

Mr. Pernouski did not need to remind his family of how realtors looked on clients who were teachers: the bottom of the list, to be avoided wherever possible, or foisted off on some unsuspecting beginner. They were impossible to get along with. Thought they knew everything. Mr. Pernouski said he also doubted very much that she was the wisest woman in the world since she wasn't smart enough to know an arbutus tree when she was faced with one. If he had any sense he would forget about her right now. But the thing that made it impossible for him to do that was this — the husband had admitted it was only his wife who was keeping him from buying a little place and settling here. Like everyone else he had dreamed of it for years, but his wife just wouldn't budge.

"Which means?" his son said.

"Which means," Mr. Pernouski explained, "that tomorrow I'm going to sell something to those people, you just watch."

To Mr. Pernouski's surprise, this simple announcement led to an instant row. His son said it was typical of these bloody high-pressure gougers to act as if people didn't mean it when they said they didn't want to buy; and Mr. Pernouski said that some people just didn't have the sense to know what was best for them. His son said that if a product didn't bloody well sell itself, a salesman had no right to try and change a person's mind, or trick him into thinking he wanted something he didn't want. He wished to know if Mr. Pernouski was afraid this one old lady teacher would prevent him from being the Number One Salesman for the sixth year in a row, and Mr. Pernouski said that with an attitude like that his son would be on welfare within the year, he'd never last. Because if you weren't aggressive in this business you might as well give the country back to the Indians and let it sit, just going to waste. Mr. Pernouski's son became very red in the face and scraped back his chair to stand up. "Maybe that woman's right, did you think of that? Maybe there's more in what she called you than you think." He left the room before Mr. Pernouski could find an appropriate response.

But the Eckharts were not in the coffee shop the next day, or any other place in town that Mr. Pernouski could see. He neglected several clients — forfeited them, in fact, to a panting novice on the staff — while he went in search of them. Shops, restaurants, business offices were full of people, many of them quite likely visitors from out of town, but none delivered up the missing Eckhart couple. No hotels admitted to the name on their list of guests. Mr. Pernouski felt ill at the thought that the Eckharts might have left the Island prematurely, or driven on to another town. When his son at the dinner table asked if he'd found his crazy lady off the ferry yet, Mr. Pernouski said he could curse himself for not insisting on the names of their friends in town while he had the chance. Would he have to knock on doors? His son suggested that a month of knocking ought to be enough — aside from digging up his ladyfriend it would give him a chance to ram expensive mortgages down the throats of sixty thousand innocent people who might otherwise never even have thought of coming to him for the pleasure.

When Mr. Pernouski's wife telephoned from Toronto, his son picked up the receiver and told her that Mr. Pernouski had fallen in love. He was sick like a boy for the love of a wild crazy-woman out of a bloody madhouse, he said, and he wouldn't relax until he'd tracked her down and brought her home to sleep between them in the bed.

"Get out of the way," Mr. Pernouski said, and took the receiver out of his hand. A client, he said, was driving him crazy. Even at dinner, while he was talking to the children, his mind continued to walk the streets, looking for her. And her husband. He peered into shops, knocked on doors, surveyed the cars waiting at traffic lights. They'd become a damned obsession.

"Sounds like a normal day in a salesman's life," Christina Pernouski said. As for herself, she'd had a busy, wonderful day in Toronto. This woman who was herself very successful in the retail business invited her to her home for lunch today, to a lovely brick house in Rosedale with ivy growing all up the face of it and lovely Eskimo sculptures inside. They had eaten salads, which were brought in by a maid, and sipped sherry. And afterwards the woman had taken her on a walk through a park, down by a ravine, and told her she could do anything she wanted, anything. The woman told her she could spend all her time making those wonderful speeches and forget her own business if she wanted. The woman told Christina Pernouski that she was an inspiration to every modern woman in the country, an inspiration and at the same time a challenge.

"Yes," Mr. Pernouski agreed. "I'm sure it's the truth."

"She said I was a genius," Christina Pernouski said. "I've been invited to stay for a few more days. I'm afraid there are several more groups who want me to speak to them while I'm here." She added that she'd been interviewed by several magazines that day, they were really making a fuss over her back there. "Including *Maclean's*," she said. "They said I was probably one of the three best-known businesswomen in the country already, especially amongst other women, and it was about time they did a feature on me. *Chatelaine* asked me to condense my speeches into an article for them." She said a couple more days ought to wrap things up and she could get back to the Coast, she hoped, at least as far as Vancouver, where she would have to look in on her shop. She said she hoped everything else was going well at home, she missed the kids, and missed him too.

His son leaned close to the phone to say she'd better get home in a hurry, that Mr. Pernouski was so much in love with the crazy-woman he was wasting away to a shadow. Sorrowing over this wild impetuous love affair had shrunk him to skin and bones, he said. Down to four hundred pounds, he'd had to take several great big tucks in the plaid jacket. He would soon start losing interest in his job and sink to position three-hundred-and-two amongst the salesmen of the Island.

"A position just above your own," Mr. Pernouski said, waving his son out of the way. Laughing, his wife said he could fool around if he wanted, see if she cared, but he'd better have that woman out of her bed by the time she got home.

The notion was ludicrous, of course, and she must have known it. Mr. Pernouski seldom considered another woman seriously in that way, she knew that by now. His obsession with the Eckhart woman had nothing to do with that. It had little to do with real estate, for that matter, either. It had something to do with this feeling he had whenever he thought of her with that schoolteacher look on her face. He was sure she believed herself capable of doing him damage. He intended to show her she was capable of no such thing. Nor any other man or woman in this world.

Mr. Pernouski himself could hardly believe he was becoming so obsessed. All his life he'd been a sensible man, his only obsession the healthy drive to be Number One. When he'd fallen in love with the first Mrs. Pernouski it had been a quiet unremarkable affair, just as he'd expected it to be. Their marriage had been a sensible unremarkable relationship, without rifts or ructions, as both of them desired. When she'd died, quite unexpectedly, Christina Barclay had come into his life, quietly, a little older than he was, but wonderfully attractive to him and very kind to his children. She'd been recently divorced from a runaway beachcomber named Speedy Maclean who preferred to live on his boat. A mother herself, of a daughter who'd grown up and left home, she saw no reason why her remarkable success in the business world should stop her from having a second marriage, a second family, and a second home. In seven years they'd never had a fight, or any serious interference in their life together.

Of course, it helped that Mr. Pernouski had always been a sensible, reasonable, and even predictable man. He'd never even been one to lie awake at night worrying about his children, or to become a raving maniac when they defied their parents — not even when his son had run away from home to join that commune. Whatever it was this prairie woman was bringing out in him, a streak of some kind he hadn't suspected he had, he knew he couldn't rest, or carry on with his job, or care again about the only ambition that meant anything in his life, until he'd cornered her somewhere, and stared her down, and showed her he could sell her a piece of land, or a house, despite her determination to defy him. He dreamed at night that she was watching him from just beyond the rim of his vision, and laughing while she filled the air with her smoke. In the mornings his son reported that the sound of him grinding his teeth carried easily through the wall.

After several days of searching, Mr. Pernouski caught sight of Mr. Eckhart's hat at a service station, where the little man was putting air in his tires. He looked at Mr. Pernouski as if he had some difficulty imagining why this enormous red-and-white jacket had swooped down on him to shake his hand and slap his back and inquire about his wife.

"Pernouski," Mr. Pernouski said, "Remember?"

"Yes, yes, of course I remember."

But nothing had changed. They were catching a ferry back to the mainland in an hour, he was getting the car ready, and no, his wife hadn't changed her mind about anything. She seldom did. Mr. Eckhart admitted that he himself would give much to buy a little place here before going home, something he could look forward to returning to, but — too bad — it was far too late now, it would probably never happen.

"She's a stubborn woman," he said. "And who knows but that she may be right in the end?"

"You'll give up your dream just like that, because of her stubbornness?"

Mr. Eckhart laughed and dragged the hose around to another tire. "I've never met a man so desperate to sell me something."

"You've never met a man so used to getting his way. I've got places to show you that even she won't want to leave behind. Just give me the chance, I'll turn her around."

Mr. Eckhart said it was too bad they didn't have time to look at some undeveloped property. His wife would never say yes to a house, but if he could convince her that buying a piece of land was a good investment, she might agree. He could try and convince her later to let him build a little house on it, a place they could come and stay in a while each year.

"You have an hour? Then give me half of it. Go pick her up and give me half an hour to show you something. A piece of . . ." Mr. Pernouski's mind went through his files. "A piece of waterfront. The perfect investment. You can't lose."

When Mr. Eckhart continued to look doubtful, Mr. Pernouski said he'd make it easier for him. He got into the front seat of the car. "Are you prepared to try pushing me out? Let's go, we're wasting time, we've got to pick up your wife and tramp over your brand-new piece of the world!"

No wonder Mr. Pernouski's heart was pounding. No wonder his palms were sweaty, his enormous stomach churning with excitement. His chance had come at last, she wouldn't escape him now. The showdown, so to speak, was imminent. He was about to demonstrate to that Mrs. Eckhart just what it was he was made of. The thing was to make the best possible choice, to show them a piece of land that would sell itself, something that not even the little madwoman could stand to let go. If he could show them something they would fall in love with right away, then there was nothing left to be done but sign the papers.

Whether he'd made the perfect choice was not immediately clear. This was the best piece of waterfront property he had, with a spectacular view. But it was steep. Now that he was looking at it, it appeared to be nearly vertical. A sudden plunge down from the road to the beach. Maybe not the wisest choice for people who loved their flat prairie, but he hadn't been given much time to make his choice, he'd operated on instincts only and forgotten about the slope.

He'd also forgotten about the isolation. There was no sign of life around, except for a couple of half-finished houses on neighbouring lots. Once Mrs. Eckhart had dismissed the view of the pale blue strait dotted with fishing boats and the curve of shoreline that lay beneath them, she said a person living in a place like this would have to grow one leg longer than the other just to keep herself upright. "You want to turn us into cliff-dwellers — like birds?" The cliff-dwellers of Arizona, she added, had the sense to build their houses inside the cracks and caves of the hill. Getting out of the car, she smiled at Mr. Pernouski. "They had ladders they could retract — whenever they heard the real estate developers planning to descend."

Determined to recover what he could from his mistake in judgement, Mr. Pernouski gave the place a history. "All this used to be part of a colony," he said, indicating with his hand that he meant the whole stretch of land around the bay, not just this lot. "A bunch of religious fanatics from Australia that put up some shacks and a big high fence around them to keep out the world. After their leader blew his own brains out, the rest of them moved away and some hippies took over. To do whatever hippies do when they get together."

His own son had lived among them for a while, Mr. Pernouski admitted. That was how he'd come to hear about the place and found out who owned the land and convinced his boss to make them an offer. "They practically gave it to us. Those types don't have any business sense to know what something's worth, they're just as well off up in the mountains or wherever they went."

Mrs. Eckhart looked as if she were prepared to return to the car. "You claim it was the rest of the world that lived in the rubble of failed dreams," she said. "This paradise of yours was supposed to be fresh and new."

"Oh, that's all right," Mr. Pernouski said. "We bulldozed all the buildings down and burned them. We cleaned the place right up. You won't find a trace of any of that left here."

Mrs. Eckhart squinted at him through the cigarette smoke but said nothing.

Mr. Eckhart stood up on a stump and took a picture of a fishing boat that was throbbing by. The voices of men on board carried hollowly in to shore. "If you lived here," Mr. Pernouski suggested, "you could have your own boat. Fishing's supposed to be wonderful out where you can see those specks. I talked to a man last week who caught something that weighed twenty pounds."

"He can't swim," Mrs. Eckhart said. "He's afraid of the water."

Mr. Eckhart's face coloured. He jumped off the stump and aimed his camera down the curve of the coastline. "Maybe that's only because I never had the chance to learn," he said. "If I lived here, things might be different."

"If you lived here, things would be different," Mrs. Eckhart said. "You'd be living alone." Using her cigarette butt as a light, she puffed a new one noisily to life. "Now, Mr. Pernouski, do you intend us to tramp over this paradise of yours like genuine customers . . . or are you going to cut us loose to catch our ferry?"

Mr. Pernouski considered the slope beneath him. There was no question that he had to get them down to the lower edge, to the beach, if he had any hope of salvaging something from this big mistake. "What you are about to witness," he said, "is an act of pure faith. For a man of my size and weight to go down that slope is asking for trouble. I may never get back up again."

This was the first time that Mrs. Eckhart had shown amusement at one of Mr. Pernouski's jokes about himself. "A true act of faith," she said, "would be to throw yourself in that . . . that water down there. And *then* see." She turned and snatched a sweater off the seat of the car.

He saw what her grin meant. It wasn't amusement at all. Having chosen foolishly, having brought her here, he should now be prepared to surrender — this was what she was thinking. Having come this far, to the top of this slope, they both understood that it had nothing to do with real estate, or with selling. Having brought him here — how could he pretend he had anything to do with it? — she expected him now to concede, or jump in the sea.

Mr. Pernouski felt there wasn't all that much difference between jumping into the ocean and what he was about to do. They were equally foolish. To plunge down into this steep jungle of thick wet underbrush seemed not unlike a dive into dark bottomless sea. There was no way for him to enter it but to hold his breath and leap, all at once, and to hope that he didn't disappear altogether, or break an ankle, or go rolling out of control. The thud, when he landed, jarred bones up as far as his neck, and made his ears sing. With salal and tangled vines up to his elbows he turned and waved them down: "Come in, the water's fine."

Above him, the Eckharts gaped, apparently unwilling to accept his invitation. Mrs. Eckhart edged herself along the gravel until she'd found a gentler entry, and told him about it. "There's something of a trail over here . . . where you won't have to dog-paddle through that mess." She all but disappeared herself, except for her head, but when he'd waded through to her (his pants and jacket soaked, from the rainy leaves) she was standing in a narrow clearing where the ground had been dug up, or pounded bare. Below her a narrow path slashed downhill at an angle . . . why hadn't he noticed it? . . . a deer's trail, he supposed, since he hadn't heard there were mountain sheep in the area. Mr. Pernouski decided it would be best if he led the way, since a woman like Mrs. Eckhart was only too willing to snatch control away from you, and turn it into her own show.

"What's this?"

Mr. Pernouski held onto the limb of a small tree to help himself come to a stop, and turned to see what Mrs. Eckhart was up to. Bent over, with her face down around her knees, she was scraping around in the dirt with her hands. Fingers pried up something lumpy out of the ground.

"They had children," she said, looking at the object with a sense of wonder on her face. "Those people had children."

Mr. Pernouski saw that it was a small metal car of some kind, rusted and squished flat. "I don't know about that Australian bunch," he said, "but the hippies had dozens of kids, swarming all over the place. Dirty and smelly and completely wild, a pack of savages."

Mrs. Eckhart looked from the small toy to Mr. Pernouski without changing the expression on her face. "The child who played with this thing may have been your grandson, Mr. Pernouski." She stuck her cigarette between her lips and squinted through the smoke while she brushed the dirt away to get at the metal.

Mr. Pernouski turned his back to her and led the way still farther down this damnable cliff. Even holding onto the bunches of small trees and the twisted roots of dug-up stumps he felt as if he were climbing precariously down the side of something. The weight of his own body threatened to send him hurtling down the slope at any moment. Maybe once he'd got to the beach at the bottom he'd feel less insecure.

But there was nothing when you got there that you could call a beach. The water slapped against slabs of rock, which were scarred by glacier marks and cracked in a checkered pattern like old paint and in places crumbled away to a pile of stones. No sand, no gravel, no gradual slope; hardly anything even here that was close to level, where you could feel you weren't about to fall off and crack your head on the bottom. There were a few places where you could find a spot to sit, and natural steps where you might climb around the jagged lumps, and a sharp V where a small rowboat might be tied up out of the wind. A row of tangled weeds and chips and feathers and slimy kelp had been left behind by the sea. When Mr. Pernouski's shoe, with its slippery sole, slid out from under him, he was saved from crashing by Mr. Eckhart, whose hand shot out to grab his arm. For a moment, the two of them teetered above the spray. Mrs. Eckhart, behind, said, "My Lord, look how far we've come down!"

The car, when Mr. Pernouski could bear to look up, was a small bump on the sky. Everything between him and it was a green jungle wall, which could as easily have been leaning towards him as away. Only his presence here could convince him that trail was something you could walk on and not just a dark scar scratched into the side of a cliff.

"You'll never sell this lot to anyone," Mrs. Eckhart said. "Where could you tell a person to perch his house?"

Mr. Eckhart looked at Mr. Pernouski for help. Perhaps he'd been thinking the same himself.

"You get a bulldozer, Mrs. Eckhart," Mr. Pernouski said. "Have a look at those houses on either side. You get a bulldozer and make a shelf to build your house on. This is the modern world, the landscape can be altered to suit your needs."

Mrs. Eckhart jerked herself upright to look at him. "Would *your* wife agree to that?" she said. "Or your children? If you consult them." Before Mr. Pernouski had time to protest she glanced at her watch. "Well, I've seen all I need to see, let's go. We've got a ferry to catch."

Just like that? Mr. Pernouski would have thought she had plans for a shouting match, at least, here at the bottom. Or a discussion of philosophies. Having brought him down here, was she simply going to turn around and leave? "Just hold it a minute," he said. "Have you any idea just how much the value of this property will go up in the next few years? You're passing up a wonderful investment."

No talk of investments, no talk of resale profits could stop her. When he tried to paint a picture of the summer cabin they might build there some day, with a cantilevered patio over the rocks where she could plan her lectures accompanied by the background sounds of waves, she said she couldn't imagine anything worse. Right now, she said, she was thinking of all the other cars that were getting ahead of them in the ferry line-up. With her narrow legs jabbing into the slope, she found it easier going up than coming down.

Behind her, Mr. Eckhart, after only a few feet of the climb, had to stop and puff. "There wasn't really much of a chance," he panted down at Mr. Pernouski. "Though I thought that, maybe . . ."

If coming down for Mr. Pernouski had been a matter of abandoning himself to gravity, except for a restraining hand on well-rooted trees to keep from falling, going up soon proved to be impossible. He'd have had better hopes of surfacing from Mrs. Eckhart's suggested plunge in the sea. His body, after just a very few steps, refused to rise. His heart pounded dangerously, his knees seemed prepared to buckle under his weight, the sweat that poured out of his skin felt hot and greasy inside his clothes. His vision blurred. Hoisting this bulk would do some terrible damage. He couldn't move.

He sat, and tried to laugh it off. What a ridiculous figure he was proving himself to be!

"You can't stay there," Mr. Eckhart called down. He sounded as if he believed Mr. Pernouski were just being stubborn. He came down to sit beside him on the log. "You can't just sit here."

Mr. Pernouski fanned his face with his hand. "I should have known better in the first place. I'll never get up."

"Well, you've got to try," Mr. Eckhart said. "We have that ferry. If I pulled on you . . ."

It was worth an attempt. Mr. Pernouski stood up and let Mr. Eckhart show him how they could grasp each other's elbow for a steady grip. Mr. Eckhart grunted, leaning back, and Mr. Pernouski strained forward, eager to help all he could. But his foot pushed dirt from under itself and he fell to his knee.

"If I got behind you and pushed!" Mrs. Eckhart shouted down.

Mr. Pernouski sat on his wet log with his knees far apart, panting, and imagined Mrs. Eckhart beneath him, pushing, while her husband pulled on his arm. Laughter bubbled up in his throat. If he fell, she could be ironed out, like a piece of cardboard, on the rocks. He felt his whole body heaving with laughter.

"Well then, if you crawled!"

Mr. Pernouski roared, and threw out his arms. If it hadn't been too undignified, he might have pedalled his feet in the air. "Crawled!" Like a great fat baby, he could get down on all fours and drag himself up the hill, from bush to bush.

He took off his jacket and tossed it over a twisted root. He hauled his shirt up out of his belt and used the wide wrinkled tail of it to wipe the tears and sweat off his face. "I can't. It would take forever."

"Yes, crawl!" Even at this distance he could hear her mouth sucking impatiently at smoke, blowing it out. Mrs. Eckhart had come down a little closer to squat on her heels. She wasn't laughing, nor was her husband, who made sympathetic noises in his mouth. "It's the only way. Otherwise we'll have to flag down a boat." She stood up straight and stuck her cigarette in her mouth and waved her arms about over her head. But all the fishing boats were tiny dots, miles away.

"My son has a boat," Mr. Pernouski said, almost before he realized he was going to say it. It sobered him up. There was nothing funny now.

"But your son isn't here, is he?" Mrs. Eckhart said.

"We could call him," Mr. Eckhart said. "We could find a phone."

Would it really come to that? A rescue mission from the sea, when he was only a hundred feet or so from the road? There were those who might still find some humour in the situation, he supposed, but Mr. Pernouski felt the first stabs of panic. It would be like his son to bring a whole flotilla with him — dozens of boats filling up the bay, dozens of people to laugh. "If I have the choice," he said, "I would rather you didn't." The truth of the matter was that he'd rather perish in great agony on this slope than live to see the grin on his son's face as he hopped out of his boat to rescue him.

It wasn't something, though, that he was willing to share with a woman like Mrs. Eckhart. Mr. Pernouski considered the alternatives. If up was impossible here, then how about *along*? It seemed a reasonable thought, but when Mr. Pernouski looked at the coastline on either side he realized that there would be at least four miles of stumbling over this rocky obstacle course before he'd get to an access road that could lead him gently uphill to the world.

"If I had a rope in the trunk of the car," Mr. Eckhart said.

"There's no rope in the car," Mrs. Eckhart said. "We took everything out before we packed."

"I helped this fellow pull a tractor that had gone over a bank, once. We could've put a loop around your chest, under your arms see, and pulled you up with the car."

"Surely someone in one of those houses . . .," Mrs. Eckhart proposed, from above.

But there was no one around to help. On Sundays, builders were at home, or out on picnics.

"Walter," Mrs. Eckhart said. "If we don't *move*."

Mr. Eckhart glanced at his watch and took off his hat for the first time. He was bald. "We can't miss it, Mr. Pernouski. There are people on the other side, expecting us."

Mr. Pernouski might have suggested they phone their friends on the other side, since they'd seemed so eager to phone someone. Tell them they'd be a ferry later than expected. One missed ferry was not a tragedy. But he could think of no practical use these two might be to him if they stayed. All they could offer was company and the sound of her puffing — filling the air with the smoke of her impatient righteousness. It would be better, in fact, to have Mrs. Eckhart some place where she couldn't watch him helpless like this, a fat fool. Like a cow on its back, bloating up. Or an overturned bug, wiggling its useless legs. Go ahead, go ahead, he told them. Someone was bound to come along sooner or later. Someone with a rope in his trunk, as Mr. Eckhart had already suggested. Or one of those fishing boats coming in at the end of the day, if it came to that.

Mr. Eckhart stood up and looked all around, as if in search of some alternative which hadn't occurred to anyone yet. He shook his head, sadly, and put a hand on Mr. Pernouski's wet shoulder. "When we get to the ferry dock we'll call your home. I'll tell your son to come help you out of here."

Mr. Pernouski closed his eyes and thought of his wife — his nationally famous wife — being interviewed by magazines in Toronto. "Call my office," he said. "Call my office. They'll make jokes but they'll send someone to come pick me up." Maybe, he added, they could even get some publicity out of it — good for business. He tried to laugh. "The Plaid Tank Scuttled". He saw it in terms of headlines. "By Prairie Guerrillas". Then he put his hand over his eyes. "Don't bother my family, though. Don't phone them."

When he removed his hand from his eyes, he saw that Mrs. Eckhart had come farther down the slope to squat on her heels just above him. He knew when he looked up at her face that it would be a miracle if any phone call at all was made. "In the meantime," she said, "you'll have your paradise all to yourself." She reached for the damp tail of his shirt and wiped his forehead with it. "And you can think about things, while you're waiting to be rescued. I should imagine, at a time like this, a man has no shortage of things to contemplate. I imagine you will think, for instance, about your family, and the kind of success you have been as a family man. You will think about your career, I'm sure, and estimate its importance to you."

"Please go," Mr. Pernouski said.

She smiled. This woman who'd been described by her husband as a saint. And turned to hoist herself up the hill.

Mr. Pernouski watched the ferry approach the Island from out in the strait and then, a half-hour later, nose out into the open water again from behind the point of land. Without moving from his spot on the damp log he continued to watch, until it had become a tiny white dot in the haze. Then he put his jacket on, took a deep breath, and started to crawl up the slope. Chuckling at the picture he would make if anyone saw. And whimpering. By grabbing onto the thicker salal stems, and chunks of roots sticking out of the ground, he was able to drag himself uphill a foot, a couple of feet, maybe even three, before collapsing, heaving for air, on his side. His hands already were bleeding. It would take forever. His knees and the rocks, between them, had already torn holes into the flapping tail of his shirt. How was it possible, he wondered, to get yourself into such a mess? When he had bounced, so stupidly, down this same slope.

By the time he'd reached a point which he estimated to be about a third of the way up, Mr. Pernouski imagined that the ferry had docked and that Mr. and Mrs. Eckhart were taking off their sweaters and making themselves at home in the living room of their friends. It struck him that this might become one of those jokes he could tell on himself — a fat man without the sense to avoid going to the bottom of a hill he wasn't able to climb up. "They waited until they got to the mainland before they phoned," he would say. "And naturally, they didn't phone my office, they phoned my house. I had crawled half-way to the top, three-quarters of the way to the top, already ten pounds lighter just from the sweat I'd lost, when my son's motor boat rounded the point and roared across the bay towards me. Hey Dad, he yelled, and I staggered down to the beach to embrace him. Thank God you found me, I said, but he pushed me away. Never mind that, he said, did you make the goddam sale?"

The light had begun to fade from the sky before it occurred to Mr. Pernouski that they might not have telephoned at all, this saint and her husband. They could not possibly have forgotten such a thing, but they were capable of discussing it on the ferry and of deciding that there would be no real harm in it, that he was bound to be rescued sooner or later, if only by accident, and a little bit of a scare never killed anyone. The woman would be thinking there was some lesson in it for him undoubtedly. For the Number One Salesman of the Island. Who knew what a woman like her intended? Or even whether this indignity was intended just for him, or for everyone who lived in this place she hated, everyone who lived on this island.

When dark made it impossible for him to see where he was going, Mr. Pernouski curled up under his jacket against a charred stump and thought of his wife, Christina. Perhaps she was in her hotel room, already beginning to work on a condensed version of her speeches for the women who read *Chatelaine*. Maybe she was dreaming of that *Maclean's* article and wondering if they would put her on the front cover. Or considering the Toronto woman's suggestion — that she sell her string of import shops and spend all her time travelling, making her speeches for the hungry crowds of women who desired to emulate her example. Eventually, despite sharp stones that dug into his flesh and the wet leaves that brushed his face, he fell asleep and dreamt that rescuers came from every direction for him. Dozens of fishing boats and yachts and pleasure craft crowded into the bay, while wrecking trucks and police cars and wailing ambulances lined up along the road at the top of the hill. It was a helicopter, however, that got to him first. It hovered above him, slicing the air with its blades, and lowered a man on a ladder who strapped Mr. Pernouski into a giant sling on the end of a rope. Up into the air went Mr. Pernouski, arms and legs dangling, like an elephant being rescued from a pit, or one of those polar bears he had seen on television, being flown back to the north, tranquillized, after coming south to raid garbage dumps. With the helicopter throbbing above him he rose up over the coastline, over the trees, up over the town and the strait with the small white-and-blue ferries cutting lines on the surface, and ascended — perhaps the men in the helicopter had no intention of letting him down — to become engulfed in the clouds before breaking free to clear sunny sky.

When he awoke it was a grey dawn, and there were no helicopters, no sounds at all but the soft splash of waves. He was damp, cold; his legs ached. There were no boats either, or wrecking trucks or ambulances with sirens, no police. As Mr. Pernouski grunted to a sitting position, pushing the jungle of salal out of his way, he saw that if he were to be rescued at all from this hellish slope, he would have to do it himself, in whatever way he could manage. On his knees if necessary, though it could take all this day that stretched ahead of him, it could take all his life, with the imagined sound of Mrs. Eckhart's righteous puffing all around him as he climbed.

HUGH HOOD

"I think," said Hugh Hood in an interview, "rituals and liturgies are artistic forms of group behavior, the means by which we try to preserve the culture, and acting the values of the culture over and over again, keep asserting that we want to stay together for this reason, keep asserting that the ocean won't conquer us, or that famine won't conquer us and so on." A practising Catholic, Hood posits that human assertions are men and women's only defence against the chaos of the universe. Of these, religion is one of the most complex in form and one of the most necessary for human survival. It represents an appreciation of the transcendental in everyday reality, and, as a corollary, it allows Hood to reject theories of the unconscious as explanations of the irrational and visionary in human experience.

Novels like *White Figure, White Ground* (1964) and *A Game of Touch* (1970) and his three volumes of short stories express this perspective in different ways. Born in Toronto in 1928, he now lives in Montreal, where he teaches at l'université de Montréal. His characteristic setting is the province of Quebec, and one of his collections, a unified work called *Around the Mountain: Scenes from Montreal Life* (1967), has been his most critically successful book. Currently he is writing a multi-volume fictional history of Canada's twentieth century, called *The New Age*. Other novels have employed American and African settings, and his landscapes, sharply perceived, often take on (in Hood's own words) a Fellini-like "super-realism." Sometimes his works end up as fantasies, and sometimes (as in "The Dog Explosion," from *The Fruit Man, the Meat Man & the Manager*, 1972) the fantasy catches satirically at the absurdities of modern institutions. Science, advertising, faddishness, the media, and social-reform groups all prove targets for Hood's wit, but the satire is gentle and sympathetic; it does not stridently call for reform. Fads are themselves rituals of a kind, after all, and are therefore attempts to act out a culture's values.

FOR FURTHER READING

Keith Garebian, "The Short Stories," *Hugh Hood* (Boston: Twayne, 1983), pp. 10–53.

Hugh Hood, *The Governor's Bridge Is Closed* (Ottawa: Oberon, 1973).

Robert Lecker, *On the Line* (Toronto: ECW Press, 1982).

John Metcalf, *Kicking Against the Pricks* (Toronto: ECW Press, 1982).

THE DOG EXPLOSION

For Raymond Fraser and Sharon Johnston

Not used to foreseeing consequences, a bit of a kidder, Tom Fuess sat quietly in his living-room, in a comfortable armchair in front of the fire. He thought of making mischief. His wife Connie had her legs curled up underneath her on the davenport; she was reading some book or other and looked absorbed in it. Tom looked at her thighs, then at the fireplace; the light reflected on her pantie-hose excited him. He shook out the evening paper, making plenty of noise so that Connie would look up. Then he folded the sheets back and squinted at the middle of page three, as if concentrating on the news. He spoke in a level voice:

Science Strikes at New Scare

Dogs to Cover Earth by Year 2000

Baltimore, Oct. 9, A.P. While North American and European foreign-aid programs strive to control man's threat to reproduce himself out of existence, via birth-control clinics in underdeveloped lands (see picture Page 4), an unforeseen new peril strikes at efforts to limit food-consuming populations, said Doctor Bentley French, famed animal ecologist and head of the Johns Hopkins Institute for Canine Reproduction Research, today at the second annual international conference on dog population.

"Unless steps to correct an unmistakable statistical trend are taken immediately," said Doctor French, "the balance of world food supply is gravely in danger of irreparable shock. Worse still, if present dog birth-rates are maintained, and the extension of normal canine life-expectancies continues, a drastic over-population problem will confront us in the mid-seventies."

"Congress must act immediately to appropriate funds and inaugurate programs for world dog-population surveillance. By the year 1980 these trends will be irreversible, and the dog explosion will amount to nothing less than Armageddon."

"According to latest figures obtained from all quarters of the scientific community," said Doctor French emphatically, "unless we in the free world move at once, the entire habitable living-space of the globe will be covered with dogs' bodies to a depth exceeding three feet, by the year 2000."

"Samoyedes are the worst for some reason," concluded the Johns Hopkins spokesman.

"Hmmmnn," said Tom, ostensibly to himself, "here's another item, like kind of a continuing dialogue."

Samoyede Owners Rebut French

A.S.P.C.A. "Deeply Involved" Says Prexy

"Hmmmmnn . . . rejection of any measure to extirpate man's best friend . . . dog's inalienable right to multiply his kind . . . pariah dogs on Indian sub-continent . . . give a dog a bad name . . . science no ultimate authority . . . Samoyede breeders press counter-charges against Afghans and Pomeranians."

He glanced up at Connie, who was now staring at him with electrified attention. "I'll be a son of a bitch," he said, "I always thought dogs were some kind of sacred cow."

"You!" said his wife.

"No, no."

"You made that up. You did, Tom."

"Not at all."

"Read it again."

He repeated what he had said, making slight changes in the wording. Connie got up off the davenport and came around behind his chair. "Show me where it says that," she commanded.

"Got it right here," he said, "let's see. 'Nudie shows ruled acceptable to general public.' 'Jacqueline Onassis fells cameraman with karate chop.' I tell you, it's here somewhere."

"Balls," said his wife, and he dropped the paper and started to laugh helplessly. "The dog explosion, Christ, can't you just see it?"

Connie began to get a malicious gleam in her eye. "See what?"

"It's a natural, that's all. If I went up to the university and said something about this casually to, oh, let's say, three people, it would galvanize the intellectual community. I'm willing to bet you the Montreal *Star* would have a full-page story on it within a month, anyway six weeks."

"There isn't a word of truth in it, is there?"

"Not an atom. It just came to me. Imagine the possible implications. Serious men in lab coats hunched over our four-legged friends in the small hours, seeking a way to implant anti-ovulatory capsules in the thigh at birth."

"And trying to figure out how to keep them from scratching?"

"Now you've got it. Programs of public education in the Bombay and Calcutta metropolitan areas, with pictures and easy-to-understand diagrams because, naturally, dogs can't read."

"But they sure can screw."

"You bet they can, the little buggers. Doggy diaphragms. Research into whether or not contraceptives have undesirable side-effects. High incidence of migraine among Pekingese on the pill."

"Do owners who forget the daily dose unconsciously desire their pet's pregnancy?" asked Connie.

"Or their own," said Tom. "Then there's the darker side of the program: mass neurosis, the threat to individual dog living space, the resentments of dogs in the have-not nations."

"Now you're letting your imagination run away with you."

"Well maybe, just a bit. If there's anything I can't stand, though, it's discrimination on the basis of race, colour or breed."

Connie said, "It's a good thing you don't talk to anybody but me this way. You could stir up a lot of animosity."

"All the same . . ." he said.

"You mustn't."

"It's worth a try."

"Don't say I encouraged you."

"Certainly not."

A day or two later, Tom started to circulate this rumour among faculty members chosen apparently at random: a junior lecturer known for his radicalism and espousal of all humanitarian causes; two men from the computer centre he bumped into at the coffee machines.

"It doesn't seem possible," one of them said.

"I don't know . . . I don't know," said the other, looking upset. "Remember, they laughed at Malthus. Where did you hear this?" he asked Tom.

"I read it somewhere, I think in the *Star.*"

"It's possible all right. It's all a question of the curve of progression. I never thought of it before, but you do see a hell of a lot of dogs around."

"Sure do," said Tom, finishing his coffee. He watched the two information theorists walk away agitatedly, and felt pleased with himself. The next person he inoculated was an elderly department chairman, close to retirement, a kindly man unwilling to think ill of anybody and therefore very receptive to fantasy.

"Have you heard about this dog business, sir?"

Professor Joyce gave a start. "I don't want to hear any scandal, Fuess," he said.

Tom told him his tale.

"The poor creatures, surely something can be done for them," said Professor Joyce.

"Well, you see sir, the whole problem is in the communications breakdown."

"Of course, of course."

"It's a question of getting across to them, don't you see?"

"Perfectly."

"I understand that a number of linguistics departments are trying to evolve a code for dog language." When he said this a flicker of doubt crossed Professor Joyce's face, and he went on hastily, giving the story colour, "You know, like the work they've been doing with dolphins. Apparently dolphins have a consistent system of verbal signals on regular wave-lengths, with logical structures. Now if they could only break down the language of dogs in the same way. . . ."

"I don't think there's any consistency in a dog's utterances," said the professor. "I should think the right way to tackle the problem would be to help them to retrain their impulses, I mean to begin with. Get right at the heart of the matter and alleviate misery. I don't like to think of any sentient creature suffering the pangs of hunger."

"Maybe some dogs would sooner reproduce than eat," said Tom.

"There is that," said Professor Joyce. "Tell me, do you know of any program of public education?" He fumbled around in his attaché case, and to Tom's amazement produced his cheque book.

"I don't think the public has been alerted, sir."

"Pity," said the old department chairman, letting his cheque book flap open and looking vaguely around him,"a great pity."

Tom went home and announced his results to Connie, who was already beginning to chicken out on the experiment. "You better not mess around with Joyce," she said. "For one, he's too nice, and for two, he has an awful conscience."

"That's why I picked him out."

"Do you think he'll remember that it was you?"

"I'll deny it."

"You'd better let it drop."

He really meant to take her advice, and make no further references to the dog explosion for some time, except now and then to drop the phrase into conversation as though it were one of the recognized social problems of our time, like the generation gap or the monolithic nature of the power structure. He mentioned it in a couple of classes and noticed that the students nodded wisely, as though they were wholly *au courant* dogwise. This reaction seemed promising to him, and he idled through his lectures and his daily routine, waiting for feedback.

A month later he met Professor Joyce in the cafeteria, and they had lunch together, from time to time eyeing one another with misgivings. Over dessert the professor broke a silence of some minutes by clearing his throat twice, then saying,"This dog affair is snowballing, eh?"

Tom ate two spoonfuls of caramel pudding without answering.

"The dogs, the dogs," said Joyce.

"What?" said Tom.

"You know. C.A.N.I.N.E. *Committee Against Native Instincts and Natural Energies.*"

Tom almost choked, but managed to preserve his composure. "I don't understand you," he said.

"I'm a founding member," said Professor Joyce. "I don't like the name too much. I mean generally I'm in favour of nature and energy. Lifetime of studies in Nietzsche, you know. All that. Still, they were the only words that would fit the letters, and I suppose they stick in your mind. Good advertising."

"But what is it?"

"C.A.N.I.N.E.?"

"Yes."

"It's the official relief agency to combat dog overpopulation, for this area to start with. But we hope to extend our activities internationally.

We plan to get in touch with that fellow in Baltimore, what's his name? Baldwin French?''

"Who?''

"Baldwin French, isn't that it?''

"The big dog man at Hopkins?'' said Tom, hoping to mislead. "French doesn't sound quite right to me. Might be Francis.''

"You've heard of him then,'' said the professor with relief.

"Somebody said something to me about him, when was it, might have been a month ago.''

"It wasn't you who mentioned the problem to me?''

"Me, sir? No, I've never mentioned it to a soul.'' In case this should seem heartless, he added, "I've thought about it quite a lot, naturally. You might say it's been constantly on my mind.''

Professor Joyce looked sad. "I was certain it was you, Fuess. Must have been somebody else. Sorry. Pressure of work, you know, and then I have all these committees and my work with C.A.N.I.N.E. It may have been somebody in the biology department.''

Tom got away as soon as he could, which was not too soon because the professor insisted on giving him a full rundown on animal population.

"I don't know where he got all those figures,'' he said to Connie that evening. "Do you suppose he was kidding me?''

"I don't like to think about it. That's exactly how these things get started,'' she said. She did a lot of grumbling while washing the dishes and hurried off to bed an hour earlier than usual on the pretext of a sick headache, leaving Tom to wander around downstairs. He knew that she liked old Joyce and thought that perhaps he had exceeded certain unspoken limits. He might say something about what he had done next time he saw the professor, but decided that he wouldn't go looking for him. It would be better if they just came across each other accidentally.

The old guy might look like a bumbler on the brink of senile decay, but he had terrific energy and a well-known reluctance to let anything drop, once he'd taken it up out of humanitarian impulse. Tom considered this out of line; he couldn't see why anybody had to make a Federal case out of a mere prank. After all, what he had done was harmless sport, in no way destructive, and it seemed to him kind of a shame that he would now have to embarrass himself with such a confession. Maybe nothing would come of the affair; better wait and see. Meanwhile there was Connie to placate. She upbraided him continually for his frivolity.

"A joke is one thing and malice is something else.''

"Malice?''

"You've got a nasty habit of speaking out of both sides of your mouth at once.''

"White man speak with forked tongue,'' said Tom thoughtlessly.

"Oh, cut it out!''

"Sorry.''

He came home one afternoon to find her staring morosely at the paper, and when he asked what was the matter she pointed out a tiny box on page sixty-four, next to the comics:

C.A.N.I.N.E.

All contributions gratefully accepted
Star. Box 261b. Montreal

"That's nothing," he said, but all the same he was worried. He kept seeing Professor Joyce away down at the end of a corridor or turning into somebody's office, arm-in-arm with men from the computer center. The old man would wave to him cheerily, mouthing good news at him from a distance, his pockets bulging with papers. It got so that when Tom saw dogs making love in alleys or pissing against posts, digging in garbage cans or just walking along on the end of a leash, he would snarl mentally, sometimes even mumbling curses under his breath.

Around Hallowe'en Tom and Connie were sitting in the playroom watching TV late at night when the station breaks are surrounded by commercials. The movie on the CBC station was lousy, so they switched to the NBC outlet in Burlington just as the Carson show went away for a break and a string of half-minute spots came on. They drowsed through Uncle Ben's Converted Rice, Northern New England Light and Power, and Albert's Restaurant-Hotel on the Northway, just outside of Glen's Falls. Then they came sharply awake when the familiar face of one of the great movie stars of the forties hove in view on the screen.

"Hi there, I'm X.Y.Z. (famous movie star of the forties)," he said. "Say, do you know that over seventy percent of the world's dogs kennel-up hungry every night?"

"Christ," said Tom.

The star continued. "When your Rover or Prince or Spot beds down on his warm blanket in your kitchen, do you ever stop to think about his millions of cousins in Asia and Africa and Latin America who sleep in ditches and swamps, who go hungry because they have no master to feed them, who breed irresponsibly because they just don't know any better? Are you and your neighbours aware that unless the unplanned reproduction of world dog population is brought under control now — NOT TOMORROW — NOW — that human and animal food supplies will be inadequate in five years, and at mass famine level by 1980? More dogs are alive today than in the entire previous history of the world. Ninety-five percent of all dogs ever born are alive now and the numbers are increasing hourly. Help us to avoid the crisis of the dog explosion! Write today for the free pamphlet, *From Pillar to Post,* and send your contributions to C.A.N.I.N.E., Box 500, Washington, D.C. Remember, only you can help avert disaster. Don't forget. That's C.A.N.I.N.E., Committee Against Native Instincts and Natural Energies. Post Office Box 500, Washington, D.C."

The station's call letters came on the screen; then Johnny Carson reappeared, but Tom switched the set off. He and Connie looked at each other silently for a while. Finally she said,"You must never, never admit that you had anything to do with this."

Tom said,"Half a minute on the network. Can you imagine what that cost? They've got it institutionalized now — somebody has a letter-drop in Washington and he just sits there opening envelopes with cheques in them. There's no way to stop it."

"That's right," said Mrs. Fuess.

After that whenever they saw one of that series of public-service announcements they would huddle close together as if for mutual protection, giving themselves up to apprehension and dismay.

SHIRLEY JACKSON

A native of California, Shirley Jackson (1919–1965) was educated at Syracuse University, New York, and was married to the critic Stanley Edgar Hyman. As she indicates in her amusing fictionalized memoirs *Life Among the Savages* (1953) and *Raising Demons* (1957), she led a warm and happy domestic life; but her writing reveals a much darker side, an awareness of cruelty and madness and alienation. Although her best stories are those concerned with the mysterious and the macabre, she was not simply a writer of ghost stories or Gothic tales; she firmly believed that "the genesis of any fictional work has to be human experience"; and in her own work she sought "to make stories out of things that happen, things like moving, and kittens, and Christmas concerts at the grade school, and broken bicycles." It is her power to make the ordinary seem chilling, to turn mundane reality into nightmare, that gives her fiction such impact; Dorothy Parker once called her the "leader in the field of beautifully written, quiet, cumulative shudders." Like Mrs. Spencer in "The Tooth" (*The Lottery and other stories*, 1949), Jackson's protagonists are confronted by bus drivers or shop assistants, not by ghosts or monsters; but they suffer a distortion or disturbance of vision, and the ordinary world suddenly takes on a hostile and menacing aspect. The horrors perceived by Shirley Jackson are sometimes "real" in the sense of being external to her characters; but often they are projections of inner disturbance, of a personality in the process of breaking down, one no longer able to cope with external pressures.

FOR FURTHER READING

Lenemaja Friedman, *Shirley Jackson* (Boston: Twayne, 1975).

Shirley Jackson, "Experience and Fiction," in *Come Along With Me: Part of a Novel, Sixteen Stories and Three Lectures*, ed. Stanley Edgar Hyman (New York: Viking, 1968), pp. 195–204.

THE TOOTH

The bus was waiting, panting heavily at the curb in front of the small bus station, its great blue-and-silver bulk glittering in the moonlight. There were only a few people interested in the bus, and at that time of night no one passing on the sidewalk: the one movie theatre in town had finished its show and closed its doors an hour before, and all the movie patrons had been to the drugstore for ice cream and gone on home; now the drugstore was closed and dark, another silent doorway in the long midnight street. The only town lights were the street lights, the lights in the all-night lunchstand across the street, and the one remaining counter lamp in the bus station where the girl sat in the ticket office with her hat and coat on, only waiting for the New York bus to leave before she went home to bed.

Standing on the sidewalk next to the open door of the bus, Clara Spencer held her husband's arm nervously. "I feel so funny," she said.

"Are you all right?" he asked. "Do you think I ought to go with you?"

"No, of course not," she said. "I'll be all right." It was hard for her to talk because of her swollen jaw; she kept a handkerchief pressed to her face and held hard to her husband. "Are you sure *you*'ll be all right?" she asked. "I'll be back tomorrow night at the latest. Or else I'll call."

"Everything will be fine," he said heartily. "By tomorrow noon it'll all be gone. Tell the dentist if there's anything wrong I can come right down."

"I feel so funny," she said. "Light-headed, and sort of dizzy."

"That's because of the dope," he said. "All that codeine, and the whisky, and nothing to eat all day."

She giggled nervously. "I couldn't comb my hair, my hand shook so. I'm glad it's dark."

"Try to sleep in the bus," he said. "Did you take a sleeping pill?"

"Yes," she said. They were waiting for the bus driver to finish his cup of coffee in the lunchstand; they could see him through the glass window, sitting at the counter, taking his time. "I feel so *funny*," she said.

"You know, Clara," he made his voice very weighty, as though if he spoke more seriously his words would carry more conviction and be therefore more comforting, "you know, I'm glad you're going down to New York to have Zimmerman take care of this. I'd never forgive myself if it turned out to be something serious and I let you go to this butcher up here."

"It's just a *toothache*," Clara said uneasily, "nothing very serious about a *toothache*."

"You can't tell," he said. "It might be abscessed or something; I'm sure he'll have to pull it."

"Don't even talk like that," she said, and shivered.

"Well, it looks pretty bad," he said soberly, as before. "Your face so swollen, and all. Don't you worry."

"I'm not worrying," she said. "I just feel as if I were all tooth. Nothing else."

The bus driver got up from the stool and walked over to pay his check. Clara moved toward the bus, and her husband said, "Take your time, you've got plenty of time."

"I just feel funny," Clara said.

"Listen," her husband said, "that tooth's been bothering you off and on for years; at least six or seven times since I've known you you've had trouble with that tooth. It's about time something was done. You had a toothache on our honeymoon," he finished accusingly.

"Did I?" Clara said. "You know," she went on, and laughed, "I was in such a hurry I didn't dress properly. I have on old stockings and I just dumped everything into my good pocketbook."

"Are you sure you have enough money?" he said.

"Almost twenty-five dollars," Clara said. "I'll be home tomorrow."

"Wire if you need more," he said. The bus driver appeared in the doorway of the lunchroom. "Don't worry," he said.

"Listen," Clara said suddenly, "are you *sure* you'll be all right? Mrs. Lang will be over in the morning in time to make breakfast, and Johnny doesn't need to go to school if things are too mixed up."

"I know," he said.

"Mrs. Lang," she said, checking on her fingers. "I called Mrs. Lang, I left the grocery order on the kitchen table, you can have the cold tongue for lunch and in case I don't get back Mrs. Lang will give you dinner. The cleaner ought to come about four o'clock; I won't be back so give him your brown suit and it doesn't matter if you forget but be sure to empty the pockets."

"Wire if you need more money," he said. "Or call. I'll stay home tomorrow so you can call at home."

"Mrs. Lang will take care of the baby," she said.

"Or you can wire," he said.

The bus driver came across the street and stood by the entrance to the bus.

"Okay?" the bus driver said.

"Good-bye," Clara said to her husband.

"You'll feel all right tomorrow," her husband said. "It's only a toothache."

"I'm fine," Clara said. "Don't you worry." She got on the bus and then stopped, with the bus driver waiting behind her. "Milkman," she said to her husband. "Leave a note telling him we want eggs."

"I will," her husband said. "Good-bye."

"Good-bye," Clara said. She moved on into the bus and behind her the driver swung into his seat. The bus was nearly empty and she went far back and sat down at the window outside which her husband waited.

"Good-bye," she said to him through the glass, "take care of yourself."

"Good-bye," he said, waving violently.

The bus stirred, groaned, and pulled itself forward. Clara turned her head to wave good-bye once more and then lay back against the heavy soft seat. Good Lord, she thought, what a thing to do! Outside, the familiar street slipped past, strange and dark and seen, unexpectedly, from the unique station of a person leaving town, going away on a bus. It isn't as though it's the first time I've ever been to New York, Clara thought indignantly, it's the whisky and the codeine and the sleeping pill and the toothache. She checked hastily to see if her codeine tablets were in her pocketbook; they had been standing, along with the aspirin and a glass of water, on the diningroom sideboard, but somewhere in the lunatic flight from her home she must have picked them up, because they were in her pocketbook now, along with the twenty-odd dollars and her compact and comb and lipstick. She could tell from the feel of the lipstick that she had brought the old, nearly finished one, not the new one that was a darker shade and had cost two-fifty. There was a run in her stocking and a hole in the toe that she never noticed at home wearing her old comfortable shoes, but which was now suddenly and disagreeably apparent inside her best walking shoes. Well, she thought, I can buy new stockings in New York tomorrow, after the tooth is fixed, after everything's all right. She put her tongue cautiously on the tooth and was rewarded with a split-second crash of pain.

The bus stopped at a red light and the driver got out of his seat and came back toward her. "Forgot to get your ticket before," he said.

"I guess I was a little rushed at the last minute," she said. She found the ticket in her coat pocket and gave it to him. "When do we get to New York?" she asked.

"Five-fifteen," he said. "Plenty of time for breakfast. One-way ticket?"

"I'm coming back by train," she said, without seeing why she had to tell him, except that it was late at night and people isolated together in some strange prison like a bus had to be more friendly and communicative than at other times.

"Me, I'm coming back by bus," he said, and they both laughed, she painfully because of her swollen face. When he went back to his seat far away at the front of the bus she lay back peacefully against the seat. She could feel the sleeping pill pulling at her; the throb of the toothache was distant now, and mingled with the movement of the bus, a steady beat like her heartbeat which she could hear louder and louder, going on through the night. She put her head back and her feet up, discreetly covered with her skirt, and fell asleep without saying good-bye to the town.

She opened her eyes once and they were moving almost silently through the darkness. Her tooth was pulsing steadily and she turned her cheek against the cool back of the seat in weary resignation. There was a thin line of lights along the ceiling of the bus and no other light.

Far ahead of her in the bus she could see the other people sitting; the driver, so far away as to be only a tiny figure at the end of a telescope, was straight at the wheel, seemingly awake. She fell back into her fantastic sleep.

She woke up later because the bus had stopped, the end of that silent motion through the darkness so positive a shock that it woke her stunned, and it was a minute before the ache began again. People were moving along the aisle of the bus and the driver, turning around, said, "Fifteen minutes." She got up and followed everyone else out, all but her eyes still asleep, her feet moving without awareness. They were stopped beside an all-night restaurant, lonely and lighted on the vacant road. Inside, it was warm and busy and full of people. She saw a seat at the end of the counter and sat down, not aware that she had fallen asleep again when someone sat down next to her and touched her arm. When she looked around foggily he said, "Traveling far?"

"Yes," she said.

He was wearing a blue suit and he looked tall; she could not focus her eyes to see any more.

"You want coffee?" he asked.

She nodded and he pointed to the counter in front of her where a cup of coffee sat steaming.

"Drink it quickly," he said.

She sipped at it delicately; she may have put her face down and tasted it without lifting the cup. The strange man was talking.

"Even farther than Samarkand," he was saying, "and the waves ringing on the shore like bells."

"Okay, folks," the bus driver said, and she gulped quickly at the coffee, drank enough to get her back into the bus.

When she sat down in her seat again the strange man sat down beside her. It was so dark in the bus that the lights from the restaurant were unbearably glaring and she closed her eyes. When her eyes were shut, before she fell asleep, she was closed in alone with the toothache.

"The flutes play all night," the strange man said, "and the stars are as big as the moon and the moon is as big as a lake."

As the bus started up again they slipped back into the darkness and only the thin thread of lights along the ceiling of the bus held them together, brought the back of the bus where she sat along with the front of the bus where the driver sat and the people sitting there so far away from her. The lights tied them together and the strange man next to her was saying, "Nothing to do all day but lie under the trees."

Inside the bus, traveling on, she was nothing; she was passing the trees and the occasional sleeping houses, and she was in the bus but she was between here and there, joined tenuously to the bus driver by a thread of lights, being carried along without effort of her own.

"My name is Jim," the strange man said.

She was so deeply asleep that she stirred uneasily without knowledge, her forehead against the window, the darkness moving along beside her.

Then again that numbing shock, and, driven awake, she said, frightened, "What's happened?"

"It's all right," the strange man — Jim — said immediately. "Come along."

She followed him out of the bus, into the same restaurant, seemingly, but when she started to sit down at the same seat at the end of the counter he took her hand and led her to a table. "Go and wash your face," he said. "Come back here afterward."

She went into the ladies' room and there was a girl standing there powdering her nose. Without turning around the girl said, "Costs a nickel. Leave the door fixed so's the next one won't have to pay."

The door was wedged so it would not close, with half a match folder in the lock. She left it the same way and went back to the table where Jim was sitting.

"What do you want?" she said, and he pointed to another cup of coffee and a sandwich. "Go ahead," he said.

While she was eating her sandwich she heard his voice, musical and soft, "And while we were sailing past the island we heard a voice calling us. . . ."

Back in the bus Jim said, "Put your head on my shoulder now, and go to sleep."

"I'm all right," she said.

"No," Jim said. "Before, your head was rattling against the window."

Once more she slept, and once more the bus stopped and she woke frightened, and Jim brought her again to a restaurant and more coffee. Her tooth came alive then, and with one hand pressing her cheek she searched through the pockets of her coat and then through her pocketbook until she found the little bottle of codeine pills and she took two while Jim watched her.

She was finishing her coffee when she heard the sound of the bus motor and she started up suddenly, hurrying, and with Jim holding her arm she fled back into the dark shelter of her seat. The bus was moving forward when she realized that she had left her bottle of codeine pills sitting on the table in the restaurant and now she was at the mercy of her tooth. For a minute she stared back at the lights of the restaurant through the bus window and then she put her head on Jim's shoulder and he was saying as she fell asleep, "The sand is so white it looks like snow, but it's hot, even at night it's hot under your feet."

Then they stopped for the last time, and Jim brought her out of the bus and they stood for a minute in New York together. A woman passing them in the station said to the man following her with suitcases, "We're just on time, it's five-fifteen."

"I'm going to the dentist," she said to Jim.

"I know," he said. "I'll watch out for you."

He went away, although she did not see him go. She thought to watch for his blue suit going through the door, but there was nothing.

I ought to have thanked him, she thought stupidly, and went slowly into the station restaurant, where she ordered coffee again. The counter man looked at her with the worn sympathy of one who has spent a long night watching people get off and on buses.

"Sleepy?" he asked.

"Yes," she said.

She discovered after a while that the bus station joined Pennsylvania Terminal and she was able to get into the main waiting-room and find a seat on one of the benches by the time she fell asleep again.

Then someone shook her rudely by the shoulder and said, "What train you taking, lady, it's nearly seven." She sat up and saw her pocketbook on her lap, her feet neatly crossed, a clock glaring into her face. She said, "Thank you," and got up and walked blindly past the benches and got on to the escalator. Someone got on immediately behind her and touched her arm; she turned and it was Jim. "The grass is so green and so soft," he said, smiling, "and the water of the river is so cool."

She stared at him tiredly. When the escalator reached the top she stepped off and started to walk to the street she saw ahead. Jim came along beside her and his voice went on, "The sky is bluer than anything you've ever seen, and the songs. . . ."

She stepped quickly away from him and thought that people were looking at her as they passed. She stood on the corner waiting for the light to change and Jim came swiftly up to her and then away. "Look," he said as he passed, and he held out a handful of pearls.

Across the street there was a restaurant, just opening. She went in and sat down at a table, and a waitress was standing beside her frowning. "You was asleep," the waitress said accusingly.

"I'm very sorry," she said. It was morning. "Poached eggs and coffee, please."

It was a quarter to eight when she left the restaurant, and she thought, if I take a bus, and go straight downtown now, I can sit in the drugstore across the street from the dentist's office and have more coffee until about eight-thirty and then go into the dentist's when it opens and he can take me first.

The buses were beginning to fill up; she got into the first bus that came along and could not find a seat. She wanted to go to Twenty-third Street, and got a seat just as they were passing Twenty-sixth Street; when she woke she was so far downtown that it took her nearly half-an-hour to find a bus and get back to Twenty-third.

At the corner of Twenty-third Street, while she was waiting for the light to change, she was caught up in a crowd of people, and when they crossed the street and separated to go different directions someone fell into step beside her. For a minute she walked on without looking up, staring resentfully at the sidewalk, her tooth burning her, and then she looked up, but there was no blue suit among the people pressing by on either side.

When she turned into the office building where her dentist was, it was still very early morning. The doorman in the office building was freshly shaven and his hair was combed; he held the door open briskly, as at five o'clock he would be sluggish, his hair faintly out of place. She went in through the door with a feeling of achievement; she had come successfully from one place to another, and this was the end of her journey and her objective.

The clean white nurse sat at the desk in the office; her eyes took in the swollen cheek, the tired shoulders, and she said, "You poor thing, you look worn out."

"I have a toothache." The nurse half-smiled, as though she were still waiting for the day when someone would come in and say, "My feet hurt." She stood up into the professional sunlight. "Come right in," she said. "We won't make you wait."

There was sunlight on the headrest of the dentist's chair, on the round white table, on the drill bending its smooth chromium head. The dentist smiled with the same tolerance as the nurse; perhaps all human ailments were contained in the teeth, and he could fix them if people would only come to him in time. The nurse said smoothly, "I'll get her file, doctor. We thought we'd better bring her right in."

She felt, while they were taking an X-ray, that there was nothing in her head to stop the malicious eye of the camera, as though the camera would look through her and photograph the nails in the wall next to her, or the dentist's cuff buttons, or the small thin bones of the dentist's instruments; the dentist said, "Extraction," regretfully to the nurse, and the nurse said, "Yes, doctor, I'll call them right away."

Her tooth, which had brought her here unerringly, seemed now the only part of her to have any identity. It seemed to have had its picture taken without her; it was the important creature which must be recorded and examined and gratified; she was only its unwilling vehicle, and only as such was she of interest to the dentist and the nurse, only as the bearer of her tooth was she worth their immediate and practiced attention. The dentist handed her a slip of paper with the picture of a full set of teeth drawn on it; her living tooth was checked with a black mark, and across the top of the paper was written "Lower molar; extraction."

"Take this slip," the dentist said, "and go right up to the address on this card; it's a surgeon dentist. They'll take care of you there."

"What will they do?" she said. Not the question she wanted to ask, not: What about me? or, How far down do the roots go?

"They'll take that tooth out," the dentist said testily, turning away. "Should have been done years ago."

I've stayed too long, she thought, he's tired of my tooth. She got up out of the dentist chair and said, "Thank you. Good-bye."

"Good-bye," the dentist said. At the last minute he smiled at her, showing her his full white teeth, all in perfect control.

"Are you all right? Does it bother you too much?" the nurse asked.

"I'm all right."

"I can give you some codeine tablets," the nurse said. "We'd rather you didn't take anything right now, of course, but I think I could let you have them if the tooth is really bad."

"No," she said, remembering her little bottle of codeine pills on the table of a restaurant between here and there. "No, it doesn't bother me too much."

"Well," the nurse said, "good luck."

She went down the stairs and out past the doorman; in the fifteen minutes she had been upstairs he had lost a little of his pristine morning-ness, and his bow was just a fraction smaller than before.

"Taxi?" he asked, and, remembering the bus down to Twenty-third Street, she said, "Yes."

Just as the doorman came back from the curb, bowing to the taxi he seemed to believe he had invented, she thought a hand waved to her from the crowd across the street.

She read the address on the card the dentist had given her and repeated it carefully to the taxi driver. With the card and the little slip of paper with "Lower molar" written on it and her tooth identified so clearly, she sat without moving, her hands still around the papers, her eyes almost closed. She thought she must have been asleep again when the taxi stopped suddenly, and the driver, reaching around to open the door, said, "Here we are, lady." He looked at her curiously.

"I'm going to have a tooth pulled," she said.

"Jesus," the taxi driver said. She paid him and he said, "Good luck," as he slammed the door.

This was a strange building, the entrance flanked by medical signs carved in stone; the doorman here was faintly professional, as though he were competent to prescribe if she did not care to go any farther. She went past him, going straight ahead until an elevator opened its door to her. In the elevator she showed the elevator man the card and he said, "Seventh floor."

She had to back up in the elevator for a nurse to wheel in an old lady in a wheel chair. The old lady was calm and restful, sitting there in the elevator with a rug over her knees; she said, "Nice day" to the elevator operator and he said, "Good to see the sun," and then the old lady lay back in her chair and the nurse straightened the rug around her knees and said, "Now we're not going to worry," and the old lady said irritably, "Who's worrying?"

They got out at the fourth floor. The elevator went on up and then the operator said, "Seven," and the elevator stopped and the door opened.

"Straight down the hall and to your left," the operator said.

There were closed doors on either side of the hall. Some of them said

"DDS," some of them said "Clinic," some of them said "X-Ray." One of them, looking wholesome and friendly and somehow most comprehensible, said "Ladies." Then she turned to the left and found a door with the name on the card and she opened it and went in. There was a nurse sitting behind a glass window, almost as in a bank, and potted palms in tubs in the corners of the waiting room, and new magazines and comfortable chairs. The nurse behind the glass window said, "Yes?" as though you had overdrawn your account with the dentist and were two teeth in arrears.

She handed her slip of paper through the glass window and the nurse looked at it and said, "Lower molar, yes. They called about you. Will you come right in, please? Through the door to your left."

Into the vault? she almost said, and then silently opened the door and went in. Another nurse was waiting, and she smiled and turned, expecting to be followed, with no visible doubt about her right to lead.

There was another X-ray, and the nurse told another nurse: "Lower molar," and the other nurse said, "Come this way, please."

There were labyrinths and passages, seeming to lead into the heart of the office building, and she was put, finally, in a cubicle where there was a couch with a pillow and a washbasin and a chair.

"Wait here," the nurse said. "Relax if you can."

"I'll probably go to sleep," she said.

"Fine," the nurse said. "You won't have to wait long."

She waited, probably for over an hour, although she spent the time half-sleeping, waking only when someone passed the door; occasionally the nurse looked in and smiled, once she said, "Won't have to wait much longer." Then, suddenly, the nurse was back, no longer smiling, no longer the good hostess, but efficient and hurried. "Come along," she said, and moved purposefully out of the little room into the hallways again.

Then, quickly, more quickly than she was able to see, she was sitting in the chair and there was a towel around her head and a towel under her chin and the nurse was leaning a hand on her shoulder.

"Will it hurt?" she asked.

"No," the nurse said, smiling. "You know it won't hurt, don't you?"

"Yes," she said.

The dentist came in and smiled down on her from over her head. "Well," he said.

"Will it hurt?" she said.

"Now," he said cheerfully, "we couldn't stay in business if we hurt people." All the time he talked he was busying himself with metal hidden under a towel, and great machinery being wheeled in almost silently behind her. "We couldn't stay in business at all," he said. "All you've got to worry about is telling us all your secrets while you're asleep. Want to watch out for that, you know. Lower molar?" he said to the nurse.

"Lower molar, doctor," she said.

Then they put the metal-tasting rubber mask over her face and the dentist said, "You know," two or three times absent-mindedly while she could still see him over the mask. The nurse said "Relax your hands, dear," and after a long time she felt her fingers relaxing.

First of all, things get so far away, she thought, remember this. And remember the metallic sound and taste of all of it. And the outrage.

And then the whirling music, the ringing confusedly loud music that went on and on, around and around, and she was running as fast as she could down a long horribly clear hallway with doors on both sides and at the end of the hallway was Jim, holding out his hands and laughing, and calling something she could never hear because of the loud music, and she was running and then she said, "I'm not afraid," and someone from the door next to her took her arm and pulled her through and the world widened alarmingly until it would never stop and then it stopped with the head of the dentist looking down at her and the window dropped into place in front of her and the nurse was holding her arm.

"Why did you pull me back?" she said, and her mouth was full of blood. "I wanted to go on."

"I didn't pull you," the nurse said, but the dentist said, "She's not out of it yet."

She began to cry without moving and felt the tears rolling down her face and the nurse wiped them off with a towel. There was no blood anywhere around except in her mouth; everything was as clean as before. The dentist was gone, suddenly, and the nurse put out her arm and helped her out of the chair. "Did I talk?" she asked suddenly, anxiously. "Did I say anything?"

"You said, 'I'm not afraid,' " the nurse said soothingly. "Just as you were coming out of it."

"No," she said, stopping to pull at the arm around her. "Did I *say* anything? Did I say where he is?"

"You didn't say *anything*," the nurse said. "The doctor was only teasing you."

"Where's my tooth?" she asked suddenly, and the nurse laughed and said, "All gone. Never bother you again."

She was back in the cubicle, and she lay down on the couch and cried, and the nurse brought her whisky in a paper cup and set it on the edge of the washbasin.

"God has given me blood to drink," she said to the nurse, and the nurse said, "Don't rinse your mouth or it won't clot."

After a long time the nurse came back and said to her from the doorway, smiling, "I see you're awake again."

"Why?" she said.

"You've been asleep," the nurse said. "I didn't want to wake you."

She sat up; she was dizzy and it seemed that she had been in the cubicle all her life.

"Do you want to come along now?" the nurse said, all kindness again. She held out the same arm, strong enough to guide any wavering footstep; this time they went back through the long corridor to where the nurse sat behind the bank window.

"All through?" this nurse said brightly. "Sit down a minute, then." She indicated a chair next to the glass window, and turned away to write busily. "Do not rinse your mouth for two hours," she said, without turning around. "Take a laxative tonight, take two aspirin if there is any pain. If there is much pain or excessive bleeding notify this office at once. All right?" she said, and smiled brightly again.

There was a new little slip of paper; this one said, "Extraction," and underneath, "Do not rinse mouth. Take mild laxative. Two aspirin for pain. If pain is excessive or any hemorrhage occurs, notify office."

"Good-bye," the nurse said pleasantly.

"Good-bye," she said.

With the little slip of paper in her hand, she went out through the glass door and, still almost asleep, turned the corner and started down the hall. When she opened her eyes a little and saw that it was a long hall with doorways on either side, she stopped and then saw the door marked "Ladies" and went in. Inside there was a vast room with windows and wicker chairs and glaring white tiles and glittering silver faucets; there were four or five women around the washbasins, combing their hair, putting on lipstick. She went directly to the nearest of the three washbasins, took a paper towel, dropped her pocketbook and the little slip of paper on the floor next to her, and fumbled with the faucets, soaking the towel until it was dripping. Then she slapped it against her face violently. Her eyes cleared and she felt fresher, so she soaked the paper again and rubbed her face with it. She felt out blindly for another paper towel, and the woman next to her handed her one, with a laugh she could hear, although she could not see for the water in her eyes. She heard one of the women say, "Where we going for lunch?" and another one say, "Just downstairs, prob'ly. Old fool says I gotta be back in half-an-hour."

Then she realized that at the washbasin she was in the way of the women in a hurry so she dried her face quickly. It was when she stepped a little aside to let someone else get to the basin and stood up and glanced into the mirror that she realized with a slight stinging shock that she had no idea which face was hers.

She looked into the mirror as though into a group of strangers, all staring at her or around her; no one was familiar in the group, no one smiled at her or looked at her with recognition; you'd think my own face would know me, she thought, with a queer numbness in her throat. There was a creamy chinless face with bright blonde hair, and a sharp-looking face under a red veiled hat, and a colorless anxious face with brown hair pulled straight back, and a square rosy face under a square haircut, and two or three more faces pushing close to the mirror, moving, regarding themselves. Perhaps it's not a mirror, she thought, maybe it's a window and I'm looking straight through at women washing on the other side. But there were women combing their hair and consulting the mirror; the group was on her side, and she thought, I hope I'm not the blonde, and lifted her hand and put it on her cheek.

She was the pale anxious one with the hair pulled back and when she realized it she was indignant and moved hurriedly back through the crowd of women, thinking, It isn't fair, why don't I have any color in my face? There were some pretty faces there, why didn't I take one of those? I didn't have time, she told herself sullenly, they didn't give me time to think, I could have had one of the nice faces, even the blonde would be better.

She backed up and sat down in one of the wicker chairs. It's mean, she was thinking. She put her hand up and felt her hair; it was loosened after her sleep but that was definitely the way she wore it, pulled straight back all around and fastened at the back of her neck with a wide tight barrette. Like a schoolgirl, she thought, only — remembering the pale face in the mirror — only I'm older than that. She unfastened the barrette with difficulty and brought it around where she could look at it. Her hair fell softly around her face; it was warm and reached to her shoulders. The barrette was silver; engraved on it was the name, "Clara."

"Clara," she said aloud. *"Clara?"* Two of the women leaving the room smiled back at her over their shoulders; almost all the women were leaving now, correctly combed and lipsticked, hurrying out talking together. In the space of a second, like birds leaving a tree, they all were gone and she sat alone in the room. She dropped the barrette into the ashstand next to her chair; the ashstand was deep and metal, and the barrette made a satisfactory clang falling down. Her hair down on her shoulders, she opened her pocketbook, and began to take things out, setting them on her lap as she did so. Handkerchief, plain, white, uninitialled. Compact, square and brown tortoiseshell plastic, with a powder compartment and a rouge compartment; the rouge compartment had obviously never been used, although the powder cake was half-gone. That's why I'm so pale, she thought, and set the compact down. Lipstick, a rose shade, almost finished. A comb, an opened package of cigarettes and a package of matches, a change purse, and a wallet. The change purse was red imitation leather with a zipper across the top; she opened it and dumped the money out into her hand. Nickels, dimes, pennies, a quarter. Ninety-seven cents. Can't go far on that, she thought, and opened the brown leather wallet; there was money in it but she looked first for papers and found nothing. The only thing in the wallet was money. She counted it; there were nineteen dollars. I can go a little farther on *that,* she thought.

There was nothing else in the pocketbook. No keys — shouldn't I have keys? she wondered — no papers, no address book, no identification. The pocketbook itself was imitation leather, light grey, and she looked down and discovered that she was wearing a dark grey flannel suit and a salmon pink blouse with a ruffle around the neck. Her shoes were black and stout with moderate heels and they had laces, one of which was untied. She was wearing beige stockings and there was a ragged tear in the right knee and a great ragged run going down her leg and ending in a hole in the toe which she could feel inside her shoe. She was wearing a pin on the lapel of her suit which, when she turned it around to look at it, was a blue plastic letter C. She took the pin off and dropped it into the ashstand, and it made a sort of clatter at the bottom, with a metallic clang when it landed on the barrette. Her hands were small, with stubby fingers and no nail polish; she wore a thin gold wedding ring on her left hand and no other jewelry.

Sitting alone in the ladies' room in the wicker chair, she thought, The least I can do is get rid of these stockings. Since no one was around she took off her shoes and stripped away the stockings with a feeling of relief when her toe was released from the hole. Hide them, she thought: the paper towel wastebasket. When she stood up she got a better sight of herself in the mirror; it was worse than she had thought: the grey suit bagged in the seat, her legs were bony, and her shoulders sagged. I look fifty, she thought; and then, consulting the face, but I can't be more than thirty. Her hair hung down untidily around the pale face and with sudden anger she fumbled in the pocketbook and found the lipstick; she drew an emphatic rosy mouth on the pale face, realizing as she did so that she was not very expert at it, and with the red mouth the face looking at her seemed somehow better to her, so she opened the compact and put on pink cheeks with the rouge. The cheeks were uneven and patent, and the red mouth glaring, but at least the face was no longer pale and anxious.

She put the stockings into the wastebasket and went barelegged out into the hall again, and purposefully to the elevator. The elevator operator said, "Down?" when he saw her and she stepped in and the elevator carried her silently downstairs. She went back past the grave professional doorman and out into the street where people were passing, and she stood in front of the building and waited. After a few minutes Jim came out of a crowd of people passing and came over to her and took her hand.

Somewhere between here and there was her bottle of codeine pills, upstairs on the floor of the ladies' room she had left a little slip of paper headed "Extraction"; seven floors below, oblivious of the people who stepped sharply along the sidewalk, not noticing their occasional curious glances, her hand in Jim's and her hair down on her shoulders, she ran barefoot through hot sand.

W.W. JACOBS

William Wymark Jacobs (1863–1943) was born and raised in Wapping, London, where his father was manager of a ships' wharf. Following his education at a private school in London and at Birkbeck College, he entered the Civil Service, and worked in the Savings Bank department from 1883 to 1899. During this period he began to submit stories and sketches to the popular magazines of the day, *Blackfriars*, *The Idler*, and *Strand Magazine*, with such success that by 1899 he was earning enough from his writing to enable him to give up his job and devote himself to full-time authorship. Between 1896 and 1926 Jacobs wrote over a hundred and fifty short stories, five novels, and several plays; but for the last seventeen years of his life, he retired into private life and published almost nothing at all.

Jacobs is especially remembered for his humorous tales about seafaring men and dockyard workers, gathered in such collections as *Many Cargoes* (1896) and *Odd Craft* (1904); his settings are cheap lodging houses, ships' wharves, or dock-side pubs where old sea dogs gather to swap yarns or spin tall tales. "The Monkey's Paw," from *The Lady of the Barge* (1902), is a somewhat macabre exception to Jacob's usual light comedy, though it too has the flavor of the tall tale. He introduces the supernatural into a plain domestic setting with a clarity and an economy of style that lend the plot added force and authenticity, intensifying the horror of the outcome.

FOR FURTHER READING

Hugh Greene, Introduction to W.W. Jacobs, *Selected Short Stories* (London: Bodley Head, 1975).

J.B. Priestley, "Mr. W.W. Jacobs," *Figures in Modern Literature* (London: John Lane, 1924), pp. 103–23.

THE MONKEY'S PAW

I

Without, the night was cold and wet, but in the small parlour of Laburnam Villa the blinds were drawn and the fire burned brightly. Father and son were at chess, the former, who possessed ideas about the game involving radical changes, putting his king into such sharp and unnecessary perils that it even provoked comment from the white-haired old lady knitting placidly by the fire.

"Hark at the wind," said Mr. White, who, having seen a fatal mistake after it was too late, was amiably desirous of preventing his son from seeing it.

"I'm listening," said the latter, grimly surveying the board as he stretched out his hand. "Check."

"I should hardly think that he'd come tonight," said his father, with his hand poised over the board.

"Mate," replied the son.

"That's the worst of living so far out," bawled Mr. White, with sudden and unlooked-for violence; "of all the beastly, slushy, out-of-the-way places to live in, this is the worst. Pathway's a bog, and the road's a torrent. I don't know what people are thinking about. I suppose because only two houses in the road are let, they think it doesn't matter."

"Never mind, dear," said his wife, soothingly; "perhaps you'll win the next one."

Mr. White looked up sharply, just in time to intercept a knowing glance between mother and son. The words died away on his lips, and he hid a guilty grin in this thin grey beard.

"There he is," said Herbert White, as the gate banged to loudly and heavy footsteps came toward the door.

The old man rose with hospitable haste, and opening the door, was heard condoling with the new arrival. The new arrival also condoled with himself, so that Mrs. White said, "Tut, tut!" and coughed gently as her husband entered the room, followed by a tall, burly man, beady of eye and rubicund of visage.

"Sergeant-Major Morris," he said, introducing him.

The sergeant-major shook hands, and taking the proffered seat by the fire, watched contentedly while his host got out whiskey and tumblers and stood a small copper kettle on the fire.

At the third glass his eyes got brighter, and he began to talk, the little family circle regarding with eager interest this visitor from distant parts, as he squared his broad shoulders in the chair and spoke of wild scenes and doughty deeds; of wars and plagues and strange peoples.

"Twenty-one years of it," said Mr. White, nodding at his wife and son. "When he went away he was a slip of youth in the warehouse. Now look at him."

"He don't look to have taken much harm," said Mrs. White, politely.

"I'd like to go to India myself," said the old man, "just to look round a bit, you know."

"Better where you are," said the sergeant-major, shaking his head. He put down the empty glass, and sighing softly, shook it again.

"I should like to see those old temples and fakirs and jugglers," said the old man. "What was that you started telling me the other day about a monkey's paw or something, Morris?"

"Nothing," said the soldier, hastily. "Leastways nothing worth hearing."

"Monkey's paw?" said Mrs. White, curiously.

"Well, it's just a bit of what you might call magic, perhaps," said the sergeant-major, offhandedly.

His three listeners leaned forward eagerly. The visitor absent-mindedly put his empty glass to his lips and then set it down again. His host filled it for him.

"To look at," said the sergeant-major, fumbling in his pocket, "it's just an ordinary little paw, dried to a mummy."

He took something out of his pocket and proffered it. Mrs. White drew back with a grimace, but her son, taking it, examined it curiously.

"And what is there special about it?" inquired Mr. White as he took it from his son, and having examined it, placed it upon the table.

"It had a spell put on it by an old fakir," said the sergeant-major, "a very holy man. He wanted to show that fate ruled people's lives, and that those who interfered with it did so to their sorrow. He put a spell on it so that three separate men could each have three wishes from it."

His manner was so impressive that his hearers were conscious that their light laughter jarred somewhat.

"Well, why don't you have three, sir?" said Herbert White, cleverly.

The soldier regarded him in the way that middle age is wont to regard presumptuous youth. "I have," he said, quietly, and his blotchy face whitened.

"And did you really have the three wishes granted?" asked Mrs. White.

"I did," said the sergeant-major, and his glass tapped against his strong teeth.

"And has anybody else wished?" persisted the old lady.

"The first man had his three wishes. Yes," was the reply; "I don't know what the first two were, but the third was for death. That's how I got the paw."

His tones were so grave that a hush fell upon the group.

"If you've had your three wishes, it's no good to you now, then, Morris," said the old man at last. "What do you keep it for?"

The soldier shook his head. "Fancy, I suppose," he said, slowly. "I did have some idea of selling it, but I don't think I will. It has caused enough mischief already. Besides, people won't buy. They think it's a fairy tale; some of them, and those who do think anything of it want to try it first and pay me afterward.''

''If you could have another three wishes,'' said the old man, eyeing him keenly, ''would you have them?''

''I don't know,'' said the other. ''I don't know.''

He took the paw, and dangling it between his forefinger and thumb, suddenly threw it upon the fire. White, with a slight cry, stooped down and snatched it off.

''Better let it burn,'' said the soldier, solemnly.

''If you don't want it, Morris,'' said the other, ''give it to me.''

''I won't,'' said his friend, doggedly. ''I threw it on the fire. If you keep it, don't blame me for what happens. Pitch it on the fire again like a sensible man.''

The other shook his head and examined his new possession closely. ''How do you do it?'' he inquired.

''Hold it up in your right hand and wish aloud,'' said the sergeant-major, ''but I warn you of the consequences.''

''Sounds like the *Arabian Nights*,'' said Mrs. White, as she rose and began to set the supper. ''Don't you think you might wish for four pairs of hands for me?''

Her husband drew the talisman from pocket, and then all three burst into laughter as the sergeant-major, with a look of alarm on his face, caught him by the arm.

''If you must wish,'' he said, gruffly, ''wish for something sensible.''

Mr. White dropped it back in his pocket, and placing chairs, motioned his friend to the table. In the business of supper the talisman was partly forgotten, and afterward the three sat listening in an enthralled fashion to a second instalment of the soldier's adventures in India.

''If the tale about the monkey's paw is not more truthful than those he has been telling us,'' said Herbert, as the door closed behind their guest, just in time for him to catch the last train, ''we shan't make much out of it.''

''Did you give him anything for it, father?'' inquired Mrs. White, regarding her husband closely.

''A trifle,'' said he, colouring slightly. ''He didn't want it, but I made him take it. And he pressed me again to throw it away.''

''Likely,'' said Herbert, with pretended horror. ''Why, we're going to be rich, and famous and happy. Wish to be an emperor, father, to begin with; then you can't be henpecked.''

He darted round the table, pursued by the maligned Mrs. White armed with an antimacassar.

Mr. White took the paw from his pocket and eyed it dubiously. ''I don't know what to wish for, and that's a fact,'' he said, slowly. ''It seems to me I've got all I want.''

''If you only cleared the house, you'd be quite happy, wouldn't you?''

said Herbert, with his hand on his shoulder. "Well, wish for two hundred pounds, then; that'll just do it."

His father, smiling shamefacedly at his own credulity, held up the talisman, as his son, with a solemn face, somewhat marred by a wink at his mother, sat down at the piano and struck a few impressive chords.

"I wish for two hundred pounds," said the old man distinctly.

A fine crash from the piano greeted the words, interrupted by a shuddering cry from the old man. His wife and son ran toward him.

"It moved," he cried, with a glance of disgust at the object as it lay on the floor. "As I wished, it twisted in my hand like a snake."

"Well, I don't see the money," said his son as he picked it up and placed it on the table, "and I bet I never shall."

"It must have been your fancy, father," said his wife, regarding him anxiously.

He shook his head. "Never mind, though; there's no harm done, but it gave me a shock all the same."

They sat down by the fire again while the two men finished their pipes. Outside, the wind was higher than ever, and the old man started nervously at the sound of a door banging upstairs. A silence unusual and depressing settled upon all three, which lasted until the old couple rose to retire for the night.

"I expect you'll find the cash tied up in a big bag in the middle of your bed," said Herbert, as he bade them good-night, "And something horrible squatting up on top the wardrobe watching you as you pocket your ill-gotten gains."

He sat alone in the darkness, gazing at the dying fire, and seeing faces in it. The last face was so horrible and so simian that he gazed at it in amazement. It got so vivid that, with a little uneasy laugh, he felt on the table for a glass containing a little water to throw over it. His hand grasped the monkey's paw, and with a little shiver he wiped his hand on his coat and went up to bed.

II

In the brightness of the wintry sun next morning as it streamed over the breakfast table he laughed at his fears. There was an air of prosaic wholesomeness about the room which it had lacked on the previous night, and the dirty, shrivelled little paw was pitched on the sideboard with a carelessness which betokened no great belief in its virtues.

"I suppose all old soldiers are the same," said Mrs. White. "The idea of our listening to such nonsense! How could wishes be granted in these days? And if they could, how could two hundred pounds hurt you, father?"

"Might drop on his head from the sky," said the frivolous Herbert.

"Morris said the things happened so naturally," said his father, "that you might if you so wished attribute it to coincidence."

"Well, don't break into the money before I come back," said Herbert as he rose from the table. "I'm afraid it'll turn you into a mean, avaricious man, and we shall have to disown you."

His mother laughed, and following him to the door, watched him down the road; and returning to the breakfast table, was very happy at the expense of her husband's credulity. All of which did not prevent her from scurrying to the door at the postman's knock, nor prevent her from referring somewhat shortly to retired sergeant-majors of bibulous habits when she found that the post brought a tailor's bill.

"Herbert will have some more of his funny remarks, I expect, when he comes home," she said, as they sat at dinner.

"I dare say," said Mr. White, pouring himself out some beer; "but for all that, the thing moved in my hand; that I'll swear to."

"You thought it did," said the old lady soothingly.

"I say it did," replied the other. "There was no thought about it; I have just —— What's the matter?"

His wife made no reply. She was watching the mysterious movements of a man outside, who, peering in an undecided fashion at the house, appeared to be trying to make up his mind to enter. In mental connection with the two hundred pounds, she noticed that the stranger was well dressed, and wore a silk hat of glossy newness. Three times he paused at the gate, and then walked on again. The fourth time he stood with his hand upon it, and then with sudden resolution flung it open and walked up the path. Mrs. White at the same moment placed her hands behind her, and hurriedly unfastening the strings of her apron, put that useful article of apparel beneath the cushion of her chair.

She brought the stranger, who seemed ill at ease, into the room. He gazed at her furtively, and listened in a preoccupied fashion as the old lady apologized for the appearance of the room, and her husband's coat, a garment which he usually reserved for the garden. She then waited as patiently as her sex would permit, for him to broach his business, but he was at first strangely silent.

"I—was asked to call," he said at last, and stooped and picked a piece of cotton from his trousers. "I come from 'Maw and Meggins.' "

The old lady started. "Is anything the matter?" she asked, breathlessly. "Has anything happened to Herbert? What is it? What is it?"

Her husband interposed. "There, there, mother," he said, hastily. "Sit down, and don't jump to conclusions. You've not brought bad news, I'm sure, sir;" and he eyed the other wistfully.

"I'm sorry — " began the visitor.

"Is he hurt?" demanded the mother, wildly.

The visitor bowed in assent. "Badly hurt," he said, quietly, "but he is not in any pain."

"Oh, thank God!" said the old woman, clasping her hands. "Thank God for that! Thank —— "

She broke off suddenly as the sinister meaning of the assurance dawned upon her and she saw the awful confirmation of her fears in the other's perverted face. She caught her breath, and turning to her slower-witted husband, laid her trembling old hand upon his. There was a long silence.

"He was caught in the machinery," said the visitor at length in a low voice.

"Caught in the machinery," repeated Mr. White, in a dazed fashion, "yes."

He sat staring blankly out at the window, and taking his wife's hand between his own, pressed it as he had been wont to do in their old courting-days nearly forty years before.

"He was the only one left to us," he said, turning gently to the visitor. "It is hard."

The other coughed, and rising, walking slowly to the window. "The firm wished me to convey their sincere sympathy with you in your great loss," he said, without looking round. "I beg that you will understand I am only their servant and merely obeying orders."

There was no reply; the old woman's face was white, her eyes staring, and her breath inaudible; on the husband's face was a look such as his friend the sergeant might have carried into his first action.

"I was to say that Maw and Meggins disclaim all responsibility," continued the other. "They admit no liability at all, but in consideration of your son's services, they wish to present you with a certain sum as compensation."

Mr. White dropped his wife's hand, and rising to his feet, gazed with a look of horror at his visitor. His dry lips shaped the words, "How much?"

"Two hundred pounds," was the answer.

Unconscious of his wife's shriek, the old man smiled faintly, put out his hands like a sightless man, and dropped, a senseless heap, to the floor.

III

In the huge new cemetery, some two miles distant, the old people buried their dead, and came back to a house steeped in shadow and silence. It was all over so quickly that at first they could hardly realize it, and remained in a state of expectation as though of something else to happen — something else which was to lighten this load, too heavy for old hearts to bear.

But the days passed, and expectation gave place to resignation — the hopeless resignation of the old, sometimes miscalled, apathy. Sometimes they hardly exchanged a word, for now they had nothing to talk about, and their days were long to weariness.

It was about a week after that the old man, waking suddenly in the night, stretched out his hand and found himself alone. The room was in darkness, and the sound of subdued weeping came from the window. He raised himself in bed and listened.

"Come back," he said, tenderly. "You will be cold."

"It is colder for my son," said the old woman, and wept afresh.

The sound of her sobs died away on his ears. The bed was warm, and his eyes heavy with sleep. He dozed fitfully, and then slept until a sudden wild cry from his wife awoke him with a start.

"*The paw!*" she cried widly. "The monkey's paw!"

He started up in alarm. "Where? Where is it? What's the matter?"

She came stumbling across the room toward him. "I want it," she said, quietly. "You've not destroyed it?"

"It's in the parlour, on the bracket," he replied, marvelling. "Why?"

She cried and laughed together, and bending over, kissed his cheek.

"I only just thought of it," she said, hysterically. "Why didn't I think of it before? Why didn't *you* think of it?"

"Think of what?" he questioned.

"The other two wishes," she replied, rapidly. "We've only had one."

"Was not that enough?" he demanded, fiercely.

"No," she cried, triumphantly; "we'll have one more. Go down and get it quickly, and wish our boy alive again."

The man sat up in bed and flung the bedclothes from his quaking limbs. "Good God, you are mad!" he cried, aghast.

"Get it," she panted; "get it quickly, and wish —— Oh, my boy, my boy!"

Her husband struck a match and lit the candle. "Get back to bed," he said, unsteadily. "You don't know what you are saying."

"We had the first wish granted," said the old woman, feverishly; "why not the second?"

"A coincidence," stammered the old man.

"Go and get it and wish," cried his wife, quivering with excitement.

The old man turned and regarded her, and his voice shook. "He has been dead ten days, and besides he — I would not tell you else, but — I could only recognize him by his clothing. If he was too terrible for you to see then, how now?"

"Bring him back," cried the old woman, and dragged him toward the door. "Do you think I fear the child I have nursed?"

He went down in the darkness, and felt his way to the parlour, and then to the mantelpiece. The talisman was in its place, and a horrible fear that the unspoken wish might bring his mutilated son before him ere he could escape from the room seized upon him, and he caught his breath as he found that he had lost the direction of the door. His brow cold with sweat, he felt his way round the table, and groped along the wall until he found himself in the small passage with the unwholesome thing in his hand.

Even his wife's face seemed changed as he entered the room. It was white and expectant, and to his fears seemed to have an unnatural look upon it. He was afraid of her.

"*Wish!*" she cried, in a strong voice.

"It is foolish and wicked," he faltered.

"*Wish!*" repeated his wife.

He raised his hand. "I wish my son alive again."

The talisman fell to the floor, and he regarded it fearfully. Then he sank trembling into a chair as the old woman, with burning eyes, walked to the window and raised the blind.

He sat until he was chilled with the cold, glancing occasionally at the figure of the old woman peering through the window. The candle-end, which had burned below the rim of the china candlestick, was throwing pulsating shadows on the ceiling and walls, until, with a flicker larger than the rest, it expired. The old man, with an unspeakable sense of relief at the failure of the talisman, crept back to his bed, and a minute or two afterward the old woman came silently and apathetically beside him.

Neither spoke, but lay silently listening to the ticking of the clock. A stair creaked, and a squeaky mouse scurried noisily through the wall. The darkness was oppressive, and after lying for some time screwing up his courage, he took the box of matches, and striking one, went downstairs for a candle.

At the foot of the stairs the match went out, and he paused to strike another; and at the same moment a knock, so quiet and stealthy as to be scarcely audible, sounded on the front door.

The matches fell from his hand and spilled in the passage. He stood motionless, his breath suspended until the knock was repeated. Then he turned and fled swiftly back to his room, and closed the door behind him. A third knock sounded through the house.

"*What's that?*" cried the old woman, starting up.

"A rat," said the old man in shaking tones — "a rat. It passed me on the stairs."

His wife sat up in bed listening. A loud knock resounded through the house.

"It's Herbert!" she screamed. "It's Herbert!"

She ran to the door, but her husband was before her, and catching her by the arm, held her tightly.

"What are you going to do?" he whispered hoarsely.

"It's my boy; it's Herbert!" she cried, struggling mechanically. "I forgot it was two miles away. What are you holding me for? Let go. I must open the door."

"For God's sake don't let it in," cried the old man, trembling.

"You're afraid of your own son," she cried, struggling. "Let me go. I'm coming, Herbert; I'm coming."

There was another knock, and another. The old woman with a sudden wrench broke free and ran from the room. Her husband followed to the landing, and called after her appealingly as she hurried downstairs. He heard the chain rattle back and the bottom bolt drawn slowly and stiffly from the socket. Then the old woman's voice, strained and panting.

"The bolt," she cried, loudly. "Come down. I can't reach it."

But her husband was on his hands and knees groping wildly on the floor in search of the paw. If he could only find it before the thing outside got in. A perfect fusillade of knocks reverberated through the house, and he heard the scaping of a chair as his wife put it down in the passage against the door. He heard the creaking of the bolt as it came slowly back, and at the same moment he found the monkey's paw, and frantically breathed his third and last wish.

The knocking ceased suddenly, although the echoes of it were still in the house. He heard the chair drawn back, and the door opened. A cold wind rushed up the staircase, and a long loud wail of disappointment and misery from his wife gave him courage to run down to her side, and then to the gate beyond. The street lamp flickering opposite shone on a quiet and deserted road.

JAMES JOYCE

Born in Dublin, the city which figures so largely in all his writing, James Joyce (1882-1941) was educated at two Jesuit schools, and at University College, Dublin. He early showed himself to be a rebel against tradition, rejecting his Catholic background and leaving Ireland soon after his graduation in 1902. With his lifelong companion Nora Barnacle, whom he eventually married in 1931, Joyce spent most of his life in self-imposed exile in various parts of Europe, supporting himself first by teaching, and then with the help of wealthy patrons. Though his writing career spanned forty years, Joyce published relatively little; his major works being *Dubliners* (1914), *A Portrait of the Artist as a Young Man* (1916), *Ulysses* (1922), and *Finnegan's Wake* (1939). Despite this limited output, Joyce's experiments in language and technique had an enormous influence, even in his own lifetime. But his work was also controversial: *Ulysses* was charged with obscenity on its first appearance, and banned in both England and America.

Dubliners, too, was regarded as a daring book, and Joyce fought for many years over its publication. Though it was completed initially in 1905, the publisher objected to some parts of the book (for example, to the use of the word "bloody" in several stories), and feared that publication would lead to a prosecution for indecency. Joyce fought to retain his stories intact, because, as he wrote to the publisher concerned (Grant Richards), "I believe that in composing my chapter of moral history in exactly the way I have composed it I have taken the first step towards the spiritual liberation of my country."

In "The Boarding House," as in the other stories in *Dubliners*, Joyce presents an episode in the life of his native city, turning a pitiless light on its follies and frailties. With an astonishingly small compass, he creates a vivid sense of the seedy gentility of such establishments as that run by Mrs. Mooney; and he conveys too the moral duplicity practised by mother and daughter on their helpless victim, a man made only too vulnerable by his own sense of decency. The tone of the story is drily comic; but its effect is not far removed from "the odour of ashpits and old weeds and offal" which Joyce said hung around his stories.

FOR FURTHER READING

Richard Ellmann, *James Joyce* (New York: Oxford University Press, 1959).

Hugh Kenner, *Dublin's Joyce* (Bloomington: Indiana University Press, 1956).

Bruce A. Rosenberg, "The Crucifixion in 'The Boarding House,'" *Studies in Short Fiction* 5 (1967): 44-53.

THE BOARDING HOUSE

Mrs Mooney was a butcher's daughter. She was a woman who was quite able to keep things to herself: a determined woman. She had married her father's foreman, and opened a butcher's shop near Spring Gardens. But as soon as his father-in-law was dead Mr Mooney began to go to the devil. He drank, plundered the till, ran headlong into debt. It was no use making him take the pledge: he was sure to break out again a few days after. By fighting his wife in the presence of customers and by buying bad meat he ruined his business. One night he went for his wife with the cleaver, and she had to sleep in a neighbour's house.

After that they lived apart. She went to the priest and got a separation from him, with care of the children. She would give him neither money nor food nor house-room; and so he was obliged to enlist himself as a sheriff's man. He was a shabby stooped little drunkard with a white face and a white moustache and white eyebrows, pencilled above his little eyes, which were pink-veined and raw; and all day long he sat in the bailiff's room, waiting to be put on a job. Mrs Mooney, who had taken what remained of her money out of the butcher business and set up a boarding house in Hardwicke Street, was a big imposing woman. Her house had a floating population made up of tourists from Liverpool and the Isle of Man and, occasionally, *artistes* from the music halls. Its resident population was made up of clerks from the city. She governed the house cunningly and firmly, knew when to give credit, when to be stern and when to let things pass. All the resident young men spoke of her as *The Madam*.

Mrs Mooney's young men paid fifteen shillings a week for board and lodgings (beer or stout at dinner excluded). They shared in common tastes and occupations and for this reason they were very chummy with one another. They discussed with one another the chances of favourites and outsiders. Jack Mooney, the Madam's son, who was clerk to a commission agent in Fleet Street, had the reputation of being a hard case. He was fond of using soldiers' obscenities: usually he came home in the small hours. When he met his friends he had always a good one to tell them, and he was always sure to be on to a good thing — that is to say, a likely horse or a likely *artiste*. He was also handy with the mitts and sang comic songs. On Sunday nights there would often be a reunion in Mrs Mooney's front drawing-room. The music-hall *artistes* would oblige; and Sheridan played waltzes and polkas and vamped accompaniments. Polly Mooney, the Madam's daughter, would also sing. She sang:

I'm a . . . naughty girl
You needn't sham:
You know I am.

Polly was a slim girl of nineteen; she had light soft hair and a small full mouth. Her eyes, which were grey with a shade of green through them, had a habit of glancing upwards when she spoke with anyone, which made her look like a little perverse madonna. Mrs Mooney had first sent her daughter to be a typist in a corn-factor's office, but as a disreputable sheriff's man used to come every other day to the office, asking to be allowed to say a word to his daughter, she had taken her daughter home again and set her to do housework. As Polly was very lively, the intention was to give her the run of the young men. Besides, young men like to feel that there is a young woman not very far away. Polly, of course, flirted with the young men, but Mrs Mooney, who was a shrewd judge, knew that the young men were only passing the time away: none of them meant business. Things went on so for a long time, and Mrs Mooney began to think of sending Polly back to typewriting, when she noticed that something was going on between Polly and one of the young men. She watched the pair and kept her own counsel.

Polly knew that she was being watched, but still her mother's persistent silence could not be misunderstood. There had been no open complicity between mother and daughter, no open understanding, but though people in the house began to talk of the affair, still Mrs Mooney did not intervene. Polly began to grow a little strange in her manner, and the young man was evidently perturbed. At last, when she judged it to be the right moment, Mrs Mooney intervened. She dealt with moral problems as a cleaver deals with meat: and in this case she had made up her mind.

It was a bright Sunday morning of early summer, promising heat, but with a fresh breeze blowing. All the windows of the boarding house were open and the lace curtains ballooned gently towards the street beneath the raised sashes. The belfry of George's Church sent out constant peals, and worshippers, singly or in groups, traversed the little circus before the church, revealing their purpose by their self-contained demeanour no less than by the little volumes in their gloved hands. Breakfast was over in the boarding house, and the table of the breakfast-room was covered with plates on which lay yellow streaks of eggs with morsels of bacon-fat and bacon-rind. Mrs Mooney sat in the straw arm-chair and watched the servant Mary remove the breakfast things. She made Mary collect the crusts and pieces of broken bread to help to make Tuesday's bread-pudding. When the table was cleared, the broken bread collected, the sugar and butter safe under lock and key, she began to reconstruct the interview which she had had the night before with Polly. Things were as she had suspected: she had been frank in her questions and Polly had been frank in her answers. Both had been somewhat awkward, of course. She had been made awkward by her not wishing to receive the news in too cavalier a fashion or to seem to have connived, and Polly had been made awkward not merely because allusions of that kind always made her awkward, but also because she did not wish it to be thought that in her wise innocence she had divined the intention behind her mother's tolerance.

Mrs Mooney glanced instinctively at the little gilt clock on the mantelpiece as soon as she had become aware through her reverie that the bells of George's Church had stopped ringing. It was seventeen minutes past eleven: she would have lots of time to have the matter out with Mr Doran and then catch short twelve at Marlborough Street. She was sure she would win. To begin with, she had all the weight of social opinion on her side: she was an outraged mother. She had allowed him to live beneath her roof, assuming that he was a man of honour, and he had simply abused her hospitality. He was thirty-four or thirty-five years of age, so that youth could not be pleaded as his excuse; nor could ignorance be his excuse, since he was a man who had seen something of the world. He had simply taken advantage of Polly's youth and inexperience: that was evident. The question was: What reparation would he make?

There must be reparation made in such a case. It is all very well for the man: he can go his ways as if nothing had happened, having had his moment of pleasure, but the girl has to bear the brunt. Some mothers would be content to patch up such an affair for a sum of money: she had known cases of it. But she would not do so. For her only one reparation could make up for the loss of her daughter's honour: marriage.

She counted all her cards again before sending Mary up to Mr Doran's room to say that she wished to speak with him. She felt sure she would win. He was a serious young man, not rakish or loud-voiced like the others. If it had been Mr Sheridan or Mr Meade or Bantam Lyons, her task would have been much harder. She did not think he would face publicity. All the lodgers in the house knew something of the affair; details had been invented by some. Besides, he had been employed for thirteen years in a great Catholic wine-merchant's office, and publicity would mean for him, perhaps, the loss of his job. Whereas if he agreed all might be well. She knew he had a good screw for one thing, and she suspected he had a bit of stuff put by.

Nearly the half-hour! She stood up and surveyed herself in the pier-glass. The decisive expression of her great florid face satisfied her, and she thought of some mothers she knew who could not get their daughters off their hands.

Mr Doran was very anxious indeed this Sunday morning. He had made two attempts to shave, but his hand had been so unsteady that he had been obliged to desist. Three days' reddish beard fringed his jaws, and every two or three minutes a mist gathered on his glasses so that he had to take them off and polish them with his pocket-handkerchief. The recollection of his confession of the night before was a cause of acute pain to him; the priest had drawn out every ridiculous detail of the affair, and in the end had so magnified his sin that he was almost thankful at being afforded a loophole of reparation. The harm was done. What could he do now but marry her or run away? He could not brazen it out. The affair would be sure to be talked of, and his employer would be certain to hear of it. Dublin is such a small city: everyone knows everyone else's business. He felt his heart leap warmly in his throat as he heard in his excited imagination old Mr Leonard calling out in his rasping voice: "Send Mr Doran here, please."

All his long years of service gone for nothing! All his industry and diligence thrown away! As a young man he had sown his wild oats, of course; he had boasted of his free-thinking and denied the existence of God to his companions in public-houses. But that was all passed and done with . . . nearly. He still bought a copy of *Reynolds Newspaper* every week, but he attended to his religious duties, and for nine-tenths of the year lived a regular life. He had money enough to settle down on; it was not that. But the family would look down on her. First of all there was her disreputable father, and then her mother's boarding house was beginning to get a certain fame. He had a notion that he was being had. He could imagine his friends talking of the affair and laughing. She *was* a little vulgar; sometimes she said "I seen" and "If I had've known." But what would grammar matter if he really loved her? He could not make up his mind whether to like her or despise her for what she had done. Of course he had done it too. His instinct urged him to remain free, not to marry. Once you are married you are done for, it said.

While he was sitting helplessly on the side of the bed in shirt and trousers, she tapped lightly at his door and entered. She told him all, that she had made a clean breast of it to her mother and that her mother would speak with him that morning. She cried and threw her arms round his neck, saying:

"O Bob! Bob! What am I to do? What am I to do at all?"

She would put an end to herself, she said.

He comforted her feebly, telling her not to cry, that it would be all right, never fear. He felt against his shirt the agitation of her bosom.

It was not altogether his fault that it had happened. He remembered well, with the curious patient memory of the celibate, the first casual caresses her dress, her breath, her fingers had given him. Then late one night as he was undressing for bed she had tapped at his door, timidly. She wanted to relight her candle at his, for hers had been blown out by a gust. It was her bath night. She wore a loose open combing-jacket of printed flannel. Her white instep shone in the opening of her furry slippers and the blood glowed warmly behind her perfumed skin. From her hands and wrists too as she lit and steadied her candle a faint perfume arose.

On nights when he came in very late it was she who warmed up his dinner. He scarcely knew what he was eating, feeling her beside him alone, at night, in the sleeping house. And her thoughtfulness! If the night was anyway cold or wet or windy there was sure to be a little tumbler of punch ready for him. Perhaps they could be happy together . . .

They used to go upstairs together on tiptoe, each with a candle, and on the third landing exchange reluctant good nights. They used to kiss. He remembered well her eyes, the touch of her hand and his delirium . . .

But delirium passes. He echoed her phrase, applying it to himself: "What am I to do?" The instinct of the celibate warned him to hold back. But the sin was there; even his sense of honour told him that reparation must be made for such a sin.

While he was sitting with her on the side of the bed Mary came to the door and said that the missus wanted to see him in the parlour. He stood up to put on his coat and waistcoat, more helpless than ever. When he was dressed he went over to her to comfort her. It would be all right, never fear. He left her crying on the bed and moaning softly: "O my God!"

Going down the stairs his glasses became so dimmed with moisture that he had to take them off and polish them. He longed to ascend through the roof and fly away to another country where he would never hear again of his trouble, and yet a force pushed him downstairs step by step. The implacable faces of his employer and of the Madam stared upon his discomfiture. On the last flight of stairs he passed Jack Mooney, who was coming up from the pantry nursing two bottles of *Bass*. They saluted coldly; and the lover's eyes rested for a second or two on a thick bulldog face and a pair of thick short arms. When he reached the foot of the staircase he glanced up and saw Jack regarding him from the door of the return-room.

Suddenly he remembered the night when one of the music-hall *artistes,* a little blond Londoner, had made a rather free allusion to Polly. The reunion had been almost broken up on account of Jack's violence. Everyone tried to quiet him. The music-hall *artiste,* a little paler than usual, kept smiling and saying that there was no harm meant; but Jack kept shouting at him that if any fellow tried that sort of a game on with his sister he'd bloody well put his teeth down his throat: so hc would.

Polly sat for a little time on the side of the bed, crying. Then she dried her eyes and went over to the looking-glass. She dipped the end of the towel in the water-jug and refreshed her eyes with the cool water. She looked at herself in profile and readjusted a hairpin above her ear. Then she went back to the bed again and sat at the foot. She regarded the pillows for a long time, and the sight of them awakened in her mind secret, amiable memories. She rested the nape of her neck against the cool iron bedrail and fell into a reverie. There was no longer any perturbation visible on her face.

She waited on patiently, almost cheerfully, without alarm, her memories gradually giving place to hopes and visions of the future. Her hopes and visions were so intricate that she no longer saw the white pillows on which her gaze was fixed, or remembered that she was waiting for anything.

At last she heard her mother calling. She started to her feet and ran to the banisters.

"Polly! Polly!"

"Yes, mamma?"

"Come down, dear. Mr Doran wants to speak to you."

Then she remembered what she had been waiting for.

MARGARET LAURENCE

In several of her novels and stories, Margaret Wemyss Laurence has transformed the place of her birth in 1926 — a Manitoba town called Neepawa (Cree for "land of plenty") — into a town called Manawaka. *The Stone Angel* (1964), *A Jest of God* (1966) (upon which the film *Rachel Rachel* was based), and *A Bird in the House* (1970) are all set in that rural landscape. Ukrainians and Scots and others have all emigrated there to start a new life, and though generations pass, pride and folly and other traits of human individuality continue to interfere with their happiness. Laurence is extraordinarily sensitive to this individuality and also respectful of it. It is a frame of mind that gives her both insight into the lives of the women around whom these stories revolve and perspective on them. Her characters are, by turns, bound by convention, in search of freedom, constrained by weakness, and aroused by anger, love, and pride; above all, they are separate human beings, alive and warm, needing and demanding a recognition of their distinctive selves.

Sympathy toward this need for self-expression found another outlet for Margaret Laurence in her African stories. From 1950 to 1952 she lived in Somaliland, and from 1952 to 1957 in Ghana. Out of this experience came several books, including *The Tomorrow-Tamer and other stories* (1963), in which "The Merchant of Heaven" appears. The book focuses on some of the realities of modern Africa: the enthusiasms and ideals that accompanied independence, the conflicts between indigenous and European ways of life, and the problems with expatriates. The task of making these subjects appear to be realistic segments from actual life is one of rigorous selection. "I don't think of the form as something imposed upon a novel," she wrote to Clara Thomas, "but as its bone, the skeleton which makes it possible for the flesh to move and be revealed as itself." The imagery reinforces the reader's appreciation of character and culture; the form of the storytelling embodies the angle of vision which the narrative attempts to explore.

FOR FURTHER READING

Margaret Laurence, "Ten Years' Sentences," *Canadian Literature*, no. 41 (Summer 1969): 10–16.
Patricia Morley, *Margaret Laurence* (Boston: Twayne, 1981).
W.H. New, "Text and Subtext: Laurence's 'The Merchant of Heaven'," *Journal of Canadian Studies* 13 (Fall 1978): 19–22.

THE MERCHANT
OF HEAVEN

Across the tarmac the black-and-orange dragon lizards skitter, occasionally pausing to raise their wrinkled necks and stare with ancient saurian eyes on a world no longer theirs. In the painted light of mid-day, the heat shimmers like molten glass. No shade anywhere. You sweat like a pig, and inside the waiting-room you nearly stifle. The African labourers, trundling baggage or bits of air-freight, work stripped to the waist, their torsos sleek and shining. The airport officials in their white drill uniforms are damp and crumpled as gulls newly emerged from the egg.

In this purgatorially hot and exposed steam bath, I awaited with some trepidation the arrival of Amory Lemon, proselytizer for a mission known as the Angel of Philadelphia.

Above the buildings flew the three-striped flag — red, yellow and green — with the black star of Africa in its centre. I wondered if the evangelist would notice it or know what it signified. Very likely not. Brother Lemon was not coming here to study political developments. He was coming — as traders once went to Babylon — for the souls of men.

I had never seen him before, but I knew him at once, simply because he looked so different from the others who came off the plane — ordinary English people, weary and bored after the long trip, their still-tanned skins indicating that this was not their first tour in the tropics. Brother Lemon's skin was very white and smooth — it reminded me of those sea pebbles which as a child I used to think were the eyeballs of the drowned. He was unusually tall; he walked in a stately and yet brisk fashion, with controlled excitement. I realized that this must be a great moment for him. The apostle landing at Cyprus or Thessalonica, the light of future battles already kindling in his eyes, and replete with faith as a fresh-gorged mosquito is with blood.

"Mr. Lemon? I'm Will Kettridge — the architect. We've corresponded —"

He looked at me with piercing sincerity from those astonishing turquoise eyes of his.

"Yes, of course," he said, grasping me by the hand. "I'm very pleased to make your acquaintance. It surely was nice of you to meet me. The name's Lee-*mon*. Brother Lee-*mon*. Accent on the last syllable. I really appreciate your kindness, Mr. Kettridge."

I felt miserably at a disadvantage. For one thing, I was wearing khaki trousers which badly needed pressing, whereas Brother Lemon was clad in a dove-grey suit of a miraculously immaculate material. For another, when a person interprets your selfish motive as pure altruism, what can you tactfully say?

"Fine," I said. "Let's collect your gear."

Brother Lemon's gear consisted of three large wardrobe suitcases, a pair of water skis, a box which from its label and size appeared to contain a gross of cameras but turned out to contain only a Rolleiflex and a cine-camera complete with projector and editing equipment, a carton of an anti-malarial drug so new that we in this infested region had not yet heard of it, and finally, a lovely little pigskin case which enfolded a water-purifier. Brother Lemon unlocked the case and took out a silvery mechanism. His face glowed with a boyish fascination.

"See? It works like a syringe. You just press this thing, and the water is sucked up here. Then you squirt it out again, and there you are. Absolutely guaranteed one hundred per cent pure. Not a single bacteria. You can even drink swamp water."

I was amused and rather touched. He seemed so frankly hopeful of adventure. I was almost sorry that this was not the Africa of Livingstone or Burton.

"Wonderful," I said. "The water is quite safe here, though. All properly filtered and chlorinated."

"You can't be too careful," Brother Lemon said. "I couldn't afford to get sick — I'll be the only representative of our mission, for a while at least."

He drew in a deep breath of the hot salty tar-stinking air.

"I've waited six years for this day, Mr. Kettridge," he said. "Six years of prayer and preparation."

"I hope the country comes up to your expectations, then."

He looked at me in surprise.

"Oh, it will," he said with perfect equanimity. "Our mission, you know, is based on the Revelation of St. John the Divine. We believe there is a special message for us in the words given by the Spirit to the Angel of the Church in Philadelphia ——"

"A different Philadelphia, surely."

His smile was confident, even pitying.

"These things do not happen by accident, Mr. Kettridge. When Andrew McFetters had his vision, back in 1924, it was revealed that the ancient Church would be reborn in our city of the same name, and would take the divine word to unbelievers in seven different parts of the world."

Around his head his fair hair sprouted and shone like some fantastic marigold halo in a medieval painting.

"I believe my mission has been foretold," he said with stunning simplicity. "I estimate I'll have a thousand souls within six months."

Suddenly I saw Brother Lemon as a kind of soul-purifier, sucking in the septic souls and spewing them back one hundred per cent pure.

That evening I told Danso of my vague uneasiness. He laughed, as I had known he would.

"Please remember you are an Englishman, Will," he said. "Englishmen should not have visions. It is not suitable. Leave that to Brother Lemon and me. Evangelists and Africans always get on well — did you know? It is because we are both so mystical. Did you settle anything?''

"Yes, I'm getting the design work. He says he doesn't want contemporary for the church, but he's willing to consider it for his house.''

"What did he say about money?'' Danso asked. "That's what I'm interested in.''

"His precise words were — 'the Angel of Philadelphia Mission isn't going to do this thing on the cheap.' ''

Danso was short and slim, but he made up for it in mercurial energy. Now he crouched tigerish by the chaise-longue, and began feinting with clenched fists like a bantamweight — which, as a matter of fact, he used to be, before a scholarship to an English university and an interest in painting combined to change the course of his life.

"Hey, come on, you Brother Lemon!'' he cried. "That's it, man! You got it and I want it — very easy, very simple. Bless you, Brother Lemon, benedictions on your name, my dear citric sibling.''

"I have been wondering,'' I said, "how you planned to profit from Brother Lemon's presence.''

"Murals, of course.''

"Oh, Danso, don't be an idiot. He'd never —— ''

"All right, all right, man. Pictures, then. A nice oil. Everybody wants holy pictures in a church, see?''

"He'll bring them from Philadelphia,'' I said. "Four-tone prints, done on glossy paper.''

Danso groaned. "Do you really think he'll do that, Will?''

"Maybe not,'' I said encouragingly. "You could try.''

"Listen — how about this? St. Augustine, bishop of hippos.''

"Hippo, you fool. A place.''

"I know that,'' Danso said witheringly. "But, hell, who wants to look at some fly-speckled North African town, all mudbrick and camel dung? Brother Lemon wants colour, action, you know what I mean. St. Augustine is on the river bank, see, the Congo or maybe the Niger. Bush all around. Ferns thick as a woman's hair. Palms — great big feathery palms. But very stiff, very stylized — Rousseau stuff — like this —— ''

His brown arms twined upward, became the tree trunks, and his thick fingers the palm fans, precise, sharp in the sun.

"And in the river — real blue and green river, man, all sky and scum — in that river is the congregation, only they're hippos, see — enormous fat ones, all bulging eyes, and they're singing 'Hallelujah' like the angels themselves, while old St. Augustine leads them to paradise —— ''

"Go ahead — paint it,'' I began, "and we'll —— ''

I stopped. My smile withdrew as I looked at Danso.

"Whatsamatter?'' he said. "Don't you think the good man will buy it?''

In his eyes there was an inexpressible loathing.

"Danso! How can you ——? You haven't even met him yet."

The carven face remained ebony, remained black granite.

"I have known this pedlar of magic all my life, Will. My mother always took me along to prayer meetings, when I was small."

The mask slackened into laughter, but it was not the usual laughter.

"Maybe he thinks we are short of ju-ju," Danso remarked. "Maybe he thinks we need a few more devils to exorcise."

When I first met Brother Lemon, I had seen him as he must have seen himself, an apostle. Now I could almost see him with Danso's bitter eyes — as sorcerer.

I undertook to show Brother Lemon around the city. He was impressed by the profusion and cheapness of tropical fruit; delightedly he purchased baskets of oranges, pineapples, paw-paw. He loaded himself down with the trinkets of Africa — python-skin wallets, carved elephants, miniature *dono* drums.

On our second trip, however, he began to notice other things. A boy with suppurating yaws covering nearly as much of his body as did his shreds of clothing. A loin-clothed labourer carrying a headload so heavy that his flimsy legs buckled and bent. A trader woman minding a road-side stall on which her living was spread — half a dozen boxes of cube sugar and a handful of pink plastic combs. A girl child squatting modestly in the filth-flowing gutter. A grinning penny-pleading gamin with a belly outpuffed by navel hernia. A young woman, pregnant and carrying another infant on her back, her placid eyes growing all at once proud and hating as we passed comfortably by. An old Muslim beggar who howled and shouted *sura** from the Qoran, and then, silent, looked and looked with the unclouded innocent eyes of lunacy. Brother Lemon nodded absently as I dutifully pointed out the new Post Office, the library, the Law Courts, the Bank.

We reached shanty town, where the mud and wattle huts crowded each other like fish in a net, where plantains were always frying on a thousand smoky charcoal burners, where the rhythm of life was forever that of the women's lifted and lowered wooden pestles as the cassava was pounded into meal, where the crimson portulaca and the children swarmed over the hard soil and survived somehow, at what loss of individual blossom or brat one could only guess.

"It's a crime," Brother Lemon said, "that people should have to live like this."

He made the mistake all kindly people make. He began to give money to children and beggars — sixpences, shillings — thinking it would help. He overpaid for everything he bought. He distributed largesse.

"These people are poor, real poor, Mr. Kettridge," he said seriously,

---

*Sura = a chapter from the Koran.

"and the way I figure it — if I'm able through the Angel of Philadelphia Mission to ease their lives, then it's my duty to do so."

"Perhaps," I said. "But the shilling or two won't last long, and then what? You're not prepared to take them all on as permanent dependants, are you?"

He gazed at me blankly. I guess he thought I was stony-hearted. He soon came to be surrounded by beggars wherever he went. They swamped him; their appalling voices followed him down any street. Fingerless hands reached out; half-limbs hurried at his approach. He couldn't cope with it, of course. Who could? Finally, he began to turn away, as ultimately we all turn, frightened and repelled by the outrageous pain and need.

Brother Lemon was no different from any stranger casting his tiny shillings into the wishful well of good intentions, and seeing them disappear without so much as a splash or tinkle. But unlike the rest of us, he at least could console himself.

"Salvation is like the loaves and fishes," he said. "There's enough for all, for every person in this world. None needs to go empty away."

He could hardly wait to open his mission. He frequently visited my office, in order to discuss the building plans. He wanted me to hurry with them, so construction could begin the minute his landsite was allocated. I knew there was no hurry — he'd be lucky if he got the land within six months — but he was so keen that I hated to discourage him.

He did not care for the hotel, where the bottles and glasses clinked merrily the night through, disturbing his sombre slumbers. I helped him find a house. It was a toy-size structure on the outskirts of the city. It had once (perhaps in another century) been whitewashed, but now it was ashen. Brother Lemon immediately had it painted azure. When I remonstrated with him — why spend money on a rented bungalow? — he gave me an odd glance.

"I grew up on the farm," he said. "We never did get around to painting that house."

He overpaid the workmen and was distressed when he discovered one of them had stolen a gallon of paint. The painters, quite simply, regarded Brother Lemon's funds as inexhaustible. But he did not understand and it made him unhappy. This was the first of a myriad annoyances.

A decomposing lizard was found in his plumbing. The wiring was faulty and his lights winked with persistent malice. The first cook he hired turned out to have both forged references and gonorrhoea.

Most of his life, I imagine, Brother Lemon had been fighting petty battles in preparation for the great one. And now he found even this battle petty. As he recounted his innumerable domestic difficulties, I could almost see the silken banners turn to grey. He looked for dragons to slay, and found cockroaches in his store-cupboard. Jacob-like, he came to wrestle for the Angel's blessing, and instead was bent double with cramps in his bowels from eating unwashed salad greens.

I was never tempted to laugh. Brother Lemon's faith was of a quality that defied ridicule. He would have preferred his trials to be on a grander scale, but he accepted them with humility. One thing he could not accept, however, was the attitude of his servants. Perhaps he had expected to find an African Barnabas, but he was disappointed. His cook was a decent enough chap, but he helped himself to tea and sugar.

"I pay Kwaku half again as much as the going wage — you told me so yourself. And now he does this."

"So would you," I said, "in his place."

"That's where you're wrong," Brother Lemon contradicted, so sharply that I never tried that approach again.

"All these things are keeping me from my work," he went on plaintively. "That's the worst of it. I've been in the country three weeks tomorrow, and I haven't begun services yet. What's the home congregation going to think of me?"

Then he knotted his big hands in sudden and private anguish.

"No — —" he said slowly. "I shouldn't say that. It shouldn't matter to me. The question is — what is the Almighty going to think?"

"I expect He's learned to be patient," I ventured.

But Brother Lemon hadn't even heard. He wore the fixed expression of a man beholding a vision.

"That's it," he said finally. "Now I see why I've been feeling so let down and miserable. It's because I've been putting off the work of my mission. I had to look around — oh yes, see the sights, buy souvenirs. Even my worry about the servants, and the people who live so poor and all. I let these things distract me from my true work."

He stood up, there in his doll's house, an alabaster giant.

"My business," he said, "is with the salvation of their immortal souls. That, and that alone. It's the greatest kindness I can do these people."

After that day, he was busy as a nesting bird. I met him one morning in the Post Office, where he was collecting packages of Bibles. He shook my hand in that casually formal way of his.

"I reckon to start services within a week," he said. "I've rented an empty lot, temporarily, and I'm having a shelter put up."

"You certainly haven't wasted any time recently."

"There isn't any time to waste," Brother Lemon's bell voice tolled. "Later may be too late."

"You can't carry all that lot very far," I said. "Can I give you a lift?"

"That's very friendly of you, Mr. Kettridge, but I'm happy to say I've got my new car at last. Like to see it?"

Outside, a dozen street urchins rushed up, and Brother Lemon allowed several of them to carry his parcels on their heads. We reached the appointed place, and the little boys, tattered and dusty as fallen leaves, lively as clickety-winged cockroaches, began to caper and jabber.

"Mastah — I beg you — you go dash me!"

A "dash" of a few pennies was certainly in order. But Brother Lemon gave them five shillings apiece. They fled before he could change his mind. I couldn't help commenting wryly on the sum, but his eyes never wavered.

"You have to get known somehow," Brother Lemon said. "Lots of churches advertise nowadays."

He rode off, then, in his new two-toned orchid Buick.

Brother Lemon must have been lonely. He knew no other Europeans, and one evening he dropped in, uninvited, to my house.

"I've never explained our teaching to you, Mr. Kettridge," he said, fixing me with his blue-polished eyes. "I don't know, mind you, what your views on religion are, or how you look at salvation —— "

He was so pathetically eager to preach that I told him to go ahead. He plunged into his spiel like the proverbial hart into cooling streams. He spoke of the seven golden candlesticks, which were the seven churches of Asia, and the seven stars — the seven angels of the churches. The seven lamps of fire, the heavenly book sealed with seven seals, the seven-horned Lamb which stood as it had been slain.

I had not read Revelation in years, but its weird splendour came back to me as I listened to him. Man, however, is many-eyed as the beasts around that jewelled throne. Brother Lemon did not regard the Apocalypse as poetry.

"We have positive proof," he cried, "that the Devil — he who bears the mark of the beast — shall be loosed out of his prison and shall go out to deceive the nations."

This event, he estimated, was less than half a century away. Hence the urgency of his mission, for the seven churches were to be reborn in strategic spots throughout the world, and their faithful would spearhead the final attack against the forces of evil. Every soul saved now would swell that angelic army; every soul unsaved would find the gates of heaven eternally barred. His face was tense and ecstatic. Around his head shone the terrible nimbus of his radiant hair.

"Whosoever is not found written in the book of life will be cast into the lake of fire and brimstone, and will be tormented day and night for ever and ever. But the believers will dwell in the new Jerusalem, where the walls are of jasper and topaz and amethyst, and the city is of pure gold."

I could not find one word to say. I was thinking of Danso. Danso as a little boy, in the evangel's meeting place, listening to the same sermon while the old gods of his own people still trampled through the night forests of his mind. The shadow spirits of stone and tree, the hungry gods of lagoon and grove, the fetish hidden in its hut of straw, the dark soul-hunter Sasabonsam — to these were added the dragon, the serpent, the mark of the beast, the lake of fire and the anguish of the damned. What had Danso dreamed about, those years ago, when he slept?

"I am not a particularly religious man," I said abruptly.

"Well, okay," he said regretfully. "Only — I like you, Mr. Kettridge, and I'd like to see you saved."

Later that evening Danso arrived. I had tried to keep him from meeting Brother Lemon. I felt somehow I had to protect each from the other.

Danso was dressed in his old khaki trousers and a black mammy-cloth shirt patterned with yellow diamonds. He was all harlequin tonight. He dervished into the room, swirled a bow in the direction of Brother Lemon, whose mouth had dropped open, then spun around and presented me with a pile of canvases.

Danso knew it was not fashionable, but he painted people. A globe-hipped market mammy stooped while her friends loaded a brass tray full of tomatoes onto her head. A Hausa trader, encased in his long embroidered robe, looked haughtily on while boys floated stick boats down a gutter. A line of little girls in their yellow mission school dresses walked lightfoot back from the well, with buckets on their heads.

A hundred years from now, when the markets and shanties have been supplanted by hygienic skyscrapers, when the gutters no longer reek, when pidgin English has grown from a patois into a sedate language boasting grammar texts and patriotic poems, then Africans will look nostalgically at Danso's pictures of the old teeming days, and will probably pay fabulous prices. At the moment, however, Danso could not afford to marry, and were it not for his kindly but conservative uncles, who groaned and complained and handed over a pound here, ten shillings there, he would not have been able to paint, either.

I liked the pictures. I held one of them up for Brother Lemon to see.

"Oh yes, a market scene," he said vaguely. "Say, that reminds me, Mr. Kettridge. Would you like me to bring over my colour slides some evening? I've taken six rolls of film so far, and I haven't had one failure."

Danso, slit-eyed and lethal, coiled himself up like a spitting cobra.

"Colour slides, eh?" he hissed softly. "Very fine — who wants paintings if you can have the real thing? But one trouble — you can't use them in your church. Every church needs pictures. Does it look like a church, with no pictures? Of course not. Just a cheap meeting place, that's all. Real religious pictures. What do you say, Mr. Lemon?"

I did not know whether he hoped to sell a painting, or whether the whole thing was one of his elaborate farces. I don't believe he knew, either.

Brother Lemon's expression stiffened. "Are you a Christian, Mr. Danso?"

Immediately, Danso's demeanour altered. His muscular grace was transformed into the seeming self-effacement of a spiritual grace. Even the vivid viper markings of his mammy-cloth shirt appeared to fade into something quiet as mouse fur or monk's robe.

"Of course," he said with dignity. "I am several times a Christian. I have been baptised into the Methodist, Baptist and Roman Catholic churches, and one or two others whose names I forget."

He laughed at Brother Lemon's rigid face.

"Easy, man — I didn't mean it. I am only once a Christian — that's better, eh? Even then, I may be the wrong kind. So many, and each says his is the only one. The Akan church was simpler."

"Beg pardon?"

"The Akan church — African." Danso snapped his fingers. "Didn't you know we had a very fine religion here before ever a whiteman came?"

"Idolatry, paganism," Brother Lemon said. "I don't call that a religion."

Danso had asked for it, admittedly, but now he was no longer able to hold around himself the cloak of usual mockery.

"You are thinking of fetish," he said curtly. "But that is not all. There is plenty more. Invisible, intangible — real proper gods. If we'd been left alone, our gods would have grown, as yours did, into One. It was happening already — we needed only a prophet. But now our prophet will never come. Sad, eh?"

And he laughed. I could see he was furious at himself for having spoken. Danso was a chameleon who felt it was self-betrayal to show his own hues. He told me once he sympathized with the old African belief that it was dangerous to tell a stranger all your name, as it gave him power over you.

Brother Lemon pumped the bellows of his preacher voice.

"Paganism in any form is an abomination! I'm surprised at you, a Christian, defending it. In the words of Jeremiah — 'Pour out thy fury upon the heathen!' "

"You pour it out, man," Danso said with studied languor. "You got lots to spare."

He began leafing through the Bible that was Brother Lemon's invariable companion, and suddenly he leapt to his feet.

"Here you are!" he cried. "For a painting. The throne of heaven, with all the elders in white, and the many-eyed beasts saying 'Holy, Holy' — what about it?"

He was perfectly serious. One might logically assume that he had given up any thought of a religious picture, but not so. The apocalyptic vision had caught his imagination, and he frowned in concentration, as though he were already planning the arrangement of figures and the colours he would use.

Brother Lemon looked flustered. Then he snickered. I was unprepared, and the ugly little sound startled me.

"You?" he said. "To paint the throne of heaven?"

Danso snapped the book shut. His face was volcanic rock, hard and dark, seeming to bear the marks of the violence that formed it. Then he picked up his pictures and walked out of the house.

"Well, I must say there was no need for him to go and fly off the handle like that," Brother Lemon said indignantly. "What's wrong with him, anyway?"

He was not being facetious. He really didn't know.

"Mr. Lemon," I asked at last, "don't you ever — not even for an instant — have any doubts?"

"What do you mean, doubts?" His eyes were genuinely puzzled.

"Don't you ever wonder if salvation is — well — yours to dole out?"

"No," he replied slowly. "I don't have any doubts about my religion, Mr. Kettridge. Why, without my religion, I'd be nothing."

I wondered how many drab years he must have lived, years like unpainted houses, before he set out to find his golden candlesticks and jewelled throne in far places.

By the time Danso and I got around to visiting the Angel of Philadelphia Mission, Brother Lemon had made considerable headway. The temporary meeting place was a large open framework of poles, roofed with sun-whitened palm boughs. Rough benches had been set up inside, and at the front was Brother Lemon's pulpit, a mahogany box draped with delphinium-coloured velvet. A wide silken banner proclaimed "Ye Shall Be Saved."

At the back of the hall, a long table was being guarded by muscular white-robed converts armed with gilt staves. I fancied it must be some sort of communion set-up, but Danso, after a word with one of the men, enlightened me. Those who remained for the entire service would receive free a glass of orange squash and a piece of *kenkey.* *

Danso and I stationed ourselves unobtrusively at the back, and watched the crowd pour in. Mainly women, they were. Market woman and fishwife, quail-plump and bawdy, sweet-oiled flesh gleaming brownly, gaudy as melons in trade cloth and headscarf. Young women with sleeping children strapped to their backs by the cover cloth. Old women whose unsmiling eyes had witnessed heaven knows how much death and who now were left with nothing to share their huts and hearts. Silent as sandcrabs, frightened and fascinated, women who sidled in, making themselves slight and unknown, as though apologizing for their presence on earth. Crones and destitutes, shrunken skins scarcely covering their insistent bones, dried dugs hanging loose and shrivelled.

Seven boys, splendidly uniformed in white and scarlet, turbanned in gold, fidgeted and tittered their way into the hall, each one carrying his fife or drum. Danso began to laugh.

"Did you wonder how he trained a band so quickly, Will? They're all from other churches. I'll bet that cost him a good few shillings. He said he wasn't going to do things on the cheap."

I was glad Danso was amused. He had been sullen and tense all evening, and had changed his mind a dozen times about coming.

The band began to whistle and boom. The women's voices shrilled in hymn. Slowly, regally, his bright hair gleaming like every crown in Chris-

Kenkey = a Ghanaian food made of fermented cornmeal.

tendom, Brother Lemon entered his temple. Over his orlon suit he wore a garment that resembled an academic gown, except that his was a resplendent peacock-blue, embroidered with stars, seven in number. He was followed by seven mites or sprites, somebody's offspring, each carrying a large brass candlestick complete with lighted taper. These were placed at intervals across the platform, and each attendant stood wide-eyed behind his charge, like small bedazzled genii.

Brother Lemon raised both arms. Silence. He began to speak, pausing from time to time in order that his two interpreters might translate into Ga and Twi. Although most of his listeners could not understand the words of Brother Lemon himself, they could scarcely fail to perceive his compulsive fire.

In the flickering flarelight of torches and tapers, the smoky light of the sweat-stinking dark, Brother Lemon seemed to stretch tall as a shadow, tall as the pale horseman at night when children cry in their sleep.

Beside me, Danso sat quietly, never stirring. His face was blank and his eyes were shuttered.

The sun would become black as sackcloth of hair, and the moon would become as blood. In Brother Lemon's voice the seven trumpets sounded, and the fire and hail were cast upon earth. The bitter star fell upon the fountains of waters; the locusts of hell emerged with wings like the sound of chariots. And for the unbelieving and idolatrous — plague and flagellation and sorrow.

The women moaned and chanted. The evening was hot and dank, and the wind from the sea did not reach here.

"Do you think they really do believe, though?" I whispered to Danso.

"If you repeat something often enough, someone will believe you. The same people go to the fetish priest, this man's brother."

But I looked at Brother Lemon's face. "He believes what he says."

"A wizard always believes in his own powers," Danso said.

Now Brother Lemon's voice softened. The thunders and trumpets of impending doom died, and there was hope. He told them how they could join the ranks of saints and angels, how the serpent could be quelled for evermore. He told them of the New Jerusalem, with its walls of crysolyte and beryl and jacinth, with its twelve gates each of a single pearl. The women shouted and swayed. Tears like the rains of spring moistened their parched and praising faces. I felt uneasy, but I did not know why.

"My people," Danso remarked, "drink dreams like palm wine."

"What is the harm in that?"

"Oh, nothing. But if you dream too long, nothing else matters. Listen — he is telling them that life on earth doesn't matter. So the guinea worm stays in the flesh. The children still fall into the pit latrines and die with excrement in their mouths. And women sit for all eternity, breaking building-stones with hammers for two shillings a day."

Brother Lemon was calling them up to the front. Come up, come up, all ye who would be saved. In front of the golden candlesticks of brass the women jostled and shoved, hands outstretched. Half in a trance, a woman walked stiffly to the evangel's throne, her voice keening and beseeching. She fell, forehead in the red dust.

"Look at that one," I said with open curiosity. "See?"

Danso did not reply. I glanced at him. He sat with his head bowed, and his hands were slowly clenching and unclenching, as though cheated of some throat.

We walked back silently through the humming streets.

"My mother," Danso said suddenly, "will not see a doctor. She has a lot of pain. So what can I do?"

"What's the matter with her?"

"A malignant growth. She believes everything will be all right in a very short time. Everything will be solved. A few months, maybe, a year at most —— "

"I don't see ——"

Danso looked at me.

"She was the woman who fell down," he said, "who fell down there at his feet."

Danso's deep-set eyes were fathomless and dark as sea; life could drown there.

The next morning Brother Lemon phoned and asked me to accompany him to the African market-place. He seemed disturbed, so I agreed, although without enthusiasm.

"Where are the ju-ju stalls?" he enquired, when we arrived.

"Whatever for?"

"I've heard a very bad thing," he said grimly, "and I want to see if it's true."

So I led him past the stalls piled with green peppers and tomatoes and groundnuts, past the tailors whirring on their treadle sewing machines, past trader women in wide hats of woven rushes, and babies creeping like lost toads through the centipede-legged crowd. In we went, into the recesses of a labyrinthian shelter, always shadowed and cool, where the stalls carried the fetish priests' stock-in-trade, the raw materials of magic. Dried roots, parrot beak, snail shell, chunks of sulphur and blue-stone, cowrie shells and strings of bells.

Brother Lemon's face was strained, skin stretched luminous over sharp bones. I only realized then how thin he had grown. He searched and searched, and finally he found what he had hoped not to find. At a little stall in a corner, the sort of place you would never find again once you were outside the maze, a young girl sat. She was selling crudely carved wooden figures, male and female, of the type used to kill by sorcery. I liked the look of the girl. She wasn't more than seventeen, and her eyes were almond and daylight. She was laughing, although she sold death.

I half expected Brother Lemon to speak to her, but he did not. He turned away.

"All right," he said. "We can go now."

"You know her?"

"She joined my congregation," he said heavily. "Last week, she came up to the front and was saved. Or so I thought."

"This is her livelihood, after all," I said inadequately. "Anyway, they can't all be a complete success."

"I wonder how many are," Brother Lemon said. "I wonder if any are."

I almost told him of one real success he had had. How could I? The night before I could see only Danso's point of view, yet now, looking at the evangelist's face, I came close to betraying Danso. But I stopped myself in time. And the thought of last night's performance made me suddenly angry.

"What do you expect?" I burst out. "Even Paul nearly got torn to pieces by the Ephesians defending their goddess. And who knows — maybe Diana was better for them than Jehovah. She was theirs, anyway."

Brother Lemon gazed at me as though he could hardly believe I had spoken the words. A thought of the design contract flitted through my mind, but when you've gone so far, you can't go back.

"How do you think they interpret your golden candlesticks and gates of pearl?" I went on. "The ones who go because they've tried everywhere else? As ju-ju, Mr. Lemon, just a new kind of ju-ju. That's all."

All at once I was sorrier than I could possibly say. Why the devil had I spoken? He couldn't comprehend, and if he ever did, he would be finished and done for.

"That's — not true —— " he stammered. "That's — why, that's an awful thing to say."

And it was. It was.

This city had assimilated many gods. A priest of whatever faith would not have had to stay here very long in order to realize that the competition was stiff. I heard indirectly that Brother Lemon's conversions, after the initial success of novelty, were tailing off. The Homowo festival was absorbing the energies of the Ga people as they paid homage to the ancient gods of the coast. A touring faith-healer from Rhodesia was drawing large crowds. The Baptists staged a parade. The Roman Catholics celebrated a saint's day, and the Methodists parried with a picnic. A new god arrived from the northern deserts and its priests were claiming for it marvellous powers in overcoming sterility. The oratory of a visiting *imam** from Nigeria was boosting the local strength of Islam. Allah has ninety-nine names, say the Muslims. But in this city, He must have had nine hundred and ninety-nine, at the very least. I remembered Brother Lemon's brave estimate — a thousand souls within six

*Imam = Muslim priest.

months. He was really having to scrabble for them now.

I drove over to the meeting place one evening to take some building plans. The service was over, and I found Brother Lemon, still in his blue and starred robe, frantically looking for one of his pseudo-golden candlesticks which had disappeared. He was enraged, positive that someone had stolen it.

"Those candlesticks were specially made for my mission, and each member of the home congregation contributed towards them. It's certainly going to look bad if I have to write back and tell them one's missing —— "

But the candlestick had not been stolen. Brother Lemon came into my office the following day to tell me. He stumbled over the words as though they were a matter of personal shame to him.

"It was one of my converts. He — borrowed it. He told me his wife was barren. He said he wanted the candlestick so he could touch her belly with it. He said he'd tried plenty of other — fetishes, but none had worked. So he thought this one might work."

He avoided my eyes.

"I guess you were right," he said.

"You shouldn't take it so hard," I said awkwardly. "After all, you can't expect miracles."

He looked at me, bewildered.

His discoveries were by no means at an end. The most notable of all occurred the night I went over to his bungalow for dinner and found him standing bleak and fearful under the flame tree, surrounded by half a dozen shouting and gesticulating ancients who shivered with years and anger. Gaunt as pariah dogs, bleached tatters fluttering like wind-worn prayer flags, a delegation of mendicants — come to wring from the next world the certain mercy they had not found in this?

"What's going on?" I asked.

Brother Lemon looked unaccountably relieved to see me.

"There seems to have been some misunderstanding," he said. "Maybe you can make sense of what they say."

The old men turned milky eyes to me, and I realized with a start that every last one of them was blind. Their leader spoke pidgin.

"Dis man" — waving in Brother Lemon's direction — "he say, meka we come heah, he go find we some shade place, he go dash me plenty plenty chop, he mek all t'ing fine too much, he mek we eye come strong. We wait long time, den he say 'go, you.' We no savvy dis palavah. I beg you, mastah, you tell him we wait long time."

"I never promised anything," Brother Lemon said helplessly. "They must be crazy."

Screeched protestations from the throng. They pressed around him, groping and grotesque beside his ivory height and his eyes. The tale emerged, bit by bit. Somehow, they had received the impression that the evangelist intended to throw a feast for them, at which, in the traditional African manner, a sheep would be throat-slit and sacrificed, then roasted and eaten. Palm wine would flow freely. Brother Lemon, furthermore, would restore the use of their eyes.

Brother Lemon's voice was unsteady.

"How could they? How could they think —— "

"Who's your Ga interpreter?" I asked.

Brother Lemon looked startled.

"Oh no. He wouldn't say things I hadn't said. He's young, but he's a good boy. It's not just a job to him, you know. He's really interested. He'd never —— "

"All the same, I think it would be wise to send for him."

The interpreter seemed all right, although perhaps not in quite the way Brother Lemon meant. This was his first job, and he was performing it with all possible enthusiasm. But his English vocabulary and his knowledge of fundamentalist doctrine were both strictly limited. He had not put words into Brother Lemon's mouth. He had only translated them in his own way, and the listening beggars had completed the transformation of text by hearing what they wanted to hear.

In a welter of words in two tongues, the interpreter and Brother Lemon sorted out the mess. The ancients still clung to him, though, claw hands plucking at his suit. He pulled away from them, almost in desperation, and finally they left. They did not know why they were being sent away, but they were not really surprised, for hope to them must always have been suspect. Brother Lemon did not see old men trailing eyeless out of his compound and back to the begging streets. I think he saw something quite different — a procession of souls, all of whom would have to be saved again.

The text that caused the confusion was from chapter seven of Revelation. "They shall hunger no more, neither thirst any more; neither shall the sun light on them, nor any heat. For the Lamb which is in the midst of the throne shall feed them, and shall lead them unto living fountains of waters, and God shall wipe away all tears from their eyes."

I thought I would not see Brother Lemon for a while, but a few days later he was at my office once more. Danso was in the back working out some colour schemes for a new school I was doing, and I hoped he would not come into the main office. Brother Lemon came right to the point.

"The municipal authorities have given me my building site, Mr. Kettridge."

"Good. That's fine."

"No, it's not fine," Brother Lemon said. "That's just what it's not."

"What's the matter? Where is it?"

"Right in the middle of shantytown."

"Well?"

"It's all right for the mission, perhaps, but they won't give me a separate site for my house."

"I wasn't aware that you wanted a separate site."

"I didn't think there would be any need for one," he said. "I certainly didn't imagine they'd put me there. You know what that place is like."

He made a gesture of appeal.

"It isn't that I mind Africans, Mr. Kettridge. Honest to goodness it isn't that at all. But shantytown — the people live so close together and it smells so bad, and at night the drums and that lewd dancing they do, and the idolatry. I can't — I don't want to be reminded every minute —— "

He broke off and we were silent. Then he sighed.

"They'd always be asking," he said, "for things I can't give. It's not my business, anyway. It's not up to me. I won't be kept from my work."

I made no comment. The turquoise eyes once more glowed with proselytizing zeal. He towered; his voice cymballed forth.

"Maybe you think I was discouraged recently. Well, I was. But I'm not going to let it get me down. I tell you straight, Mr. Kettridge, I intend to salvage those souls, as many as I can, if I have to give my very life to do it."

And seeing his resilient radiance, I could well believe it. But I drew him back to the matter at hand.

"It would be a lot easier if you accepted this site, Mr. Lemon. Do you think, perhaps, a wall —— "

"I can't," he said. "I — I'm sorry, but I just can't. I thought if you'd speak to the authorities. You're an Englishman —— "

I told him I had no influence in high places. I explained gently that this country was no longer a colony. But Brother Lemon only regarded me mournfully, as though he thought I had betrayed him.

When he had gone, I turned and there was Danso, lean as a leopard, draped in the doorway.

"Yes," he said, "I heard. At least he's a step further than the slavers. They didn't admit we had souls."

"It's not that simple, Danso —— "

"I didn't say it was simple," Danso corrected. "It must be quite a procedure — to tear the soul out of a living body, and throw the inconvenient flesh away like fruit rind."

"He doesn't want to live in that area," I tried ineffectually to explain, "because in some way the people there are a threat to him, to everything he is —— "

"Good," Danso said. "That makes it even."

I saw neither Danso nor Brother Lemon for several weeks. The plans for the mission were still in abeyance, and for the moment I almost forgot about them. Then one evening Danso ambled in, carrying a large wrapped canvas.

"What's this?" I asked.

He grinned. "My church picture. The one I have done for Brother Lemon."

I reached out, but Danso pulled it away.

"No, Will. I want Brother Lemon to be here. You ask him to come over."

"Not without seeing the picture," I said. "How do I know what monstrosity you've painted?"

"No — I swear it — you don't need to worry."

I was not entirely convinced, but I phoned Brother Lemon. Somewhat reluctantly he agreed, and within twenty minutes we heard the Buick scrunching on the gravel drive.

He looked worn out. His unsuccessful haggling with the municipal authorities seemed to have exhausted him. He had been briefly ill with malaria despite his up-to-date preventive drugs. I couldn't help remembering how he had looked that first morning at the airport, confidently stepping onto the alien soil of his chosen Thessalonica, to take up his ordained role.

"Here you are, Mr. Lemon," Danso said. "I painted a whole lot of stars and candlesticks and other junk in the first version, then I threw it away and did this one instead."

He unwrapped the painting and set it up against a wall. It was a picture of the Nazarene. Danso had not portrayed any emaciated mauve-veined ever sorrowful Jesus. This man had the body of a fisherman or a carpenter. He was well built. He had strong wrists and arms. His eyes were capable of laughter. Danso had shown Him with a group of beggars, sore-fouled, their mouths twisted in perpetual leers of pain.

Danso was looking at me questioningly.

"It's the best you've done yet," I said.

He nodded and turned to Brother Lemon. The evangelist's eyes were fixed on the picture. He did not seem able to look away. For a moment I thought he had caught the essential feeling of the thing, but then he blinked and withdrew his gaze. His tall frame sagged as though he had been struck and — yes — hurt. The old gods he could fight. He could grapple with and overcome every obstacle, even his own pity. But this was a threat he had never anticipated. He spoke in a low voice.

"Do many — do all of you — see Him like that?"

He didn't wait for an answer. He did not look at Danso or myself as he left the house. We heard the orchid Buick pull away.

Danso and I did not talk much. We drank beer and looked at the picture.

"I have to tell you one thing, Danso," I said at last. "The fact that you've shown Him as an African doesn't seem so very important one way or another."

Danso set down his glass and ran one finger lightly over the painting.

"Perhaps not," he admitted reluctantly. "But could anyone be shown as everything? How to get past the paint, Will?"

"I don't know."

Danso laughed and began slouching out to the kitchen to get another beer.

"We will invent new colours, man," he cried. "But for this we may need a little time."

I was paid for the work I had done, but the mission was never built. Brother Lemon did not obtain another site, and in a few months, his health — as they say — broke down. He returned whence he had come, and I have not heard anything about the Angel of Philadelphia Mission from that day to this.

Somewhere, perhaps, he is still preaching, heaven and hell pouring from his apocalyptic eyes, and around his head that aureole, hair the colour of light. Whenever Danso mentions him, however, it is always as the magician, the pedlar who bought souls cheap, and sold dear his cabbalistic word. But I can no longer think of Brother Lemon as either Paul or Elymas, apostle or sorcerer.

I bought Danso's picture. Sometimes, when I am able to see through black and white, until they merge and cease to be separate or apart, I look at those damaged creatures clustering so despairingly hopeful around the Son of Man, and it seems to me that Brother Lemon, after all, is one of them.

D.H. LAWRENCE

The son of a coal miner in Nottingham, David Herbert Lawrence (1885-1930) was brought up in a household very similar to that depicted in his novel *Sons and Lovers* (1913), in which the father's coarse sensuality struggled against the mother's finer sensibilities. With his mother's encouragement, Lawrence developed his literary abilities; and after a spell as a teacher in Croydon, near London, he made writing his full-time profession, producing a great many essays, poems, and short stories. His work, particularly his novels, often aroused controversy because of his frank treatment of sexual relations; two of his novels, *The Rainbow* (1915) and *Lady Chatterley's Lover* (1928), were declared obscene and banned in England for many years. Disgusted by the response of the press and public, Lawrence left England with his German wife in 1919, and travelled in various parts of the world for a number of years, chiefly in the United States and Mexico.

In much of his writing, Lawrence examines the tension between men and women as social creatures, hemmed in by conventions and "responsibilities," and as feeling creatures, part of a larger universe of instinctive response. "The Horse Dealer's Daughter" dramatizes this conflict through the relationship of Dr. Fergusson with Mabel Pervin. Initially both are creatures of habit and convention, cut off from true feeling and turned in upon themselves. Once relieved of their social roles, they respond to each other with almost brutal urgency, in a manner reflecting Lawrence's antiromantic ideas about love and sexual awareness. "Accept the sexual, physical being of yourself," he wrote, "and of every other creature. Don't be afraid of the physical functions. . . . Conquer the fear of sex, and restore the natural flow" ("The State of Funk").

FOR FURTHER READING

Donald Junkins, "D.H. Lawrence's 'The Horse-Dealer's Daughter'," *Studies in Short Fiction* 6 (1969): 210–12.
D.H. Lawrence, *Fantasia of the Unconscious and Psychoanalysis and the Unconscious* (Melbourne: Heinemann, 1961).
Keith Sagar, *The Life of D.H. Lawrence* (New York: Pantheon, 1980).
Mark Spilka, *The Love Ethic of D.H. Lawrence* (Bloomington: Indiana University Press, 1955).

THE HORSE DEALER'S DAUGHTER

"Well, Mabel, and what are you going to do with yourself?" asked Joe, with foolish flippancy. He felt quite safe himself. Without listening for an answer, he turned aside, worked a grain of tobacco to the tip of his tongue, and spat it out. He did not care about anything, since he felt safe himself.

The three brothers and the sister sat round the desolate breakfast table, attempting some sort of desultory consultation. The morning's post had given the final tap to the family fortune, and all was over. The dreary dining-room itself, with its heavy mahogany furniture, looked as if it were waiting to be done away with.

But the consultation amounted to nothing. There was a strange air of ineffectuality about the three men, as they sprawled at table, smoking and reflecting vaguely on their own condition. The girl was alone, a rather short, sullen-looking young woman of twenty-seven. She did not share the same life as her brothers. She would have been good-looking, save for the impressive fixity of her face, "bulldog," as her brothers called it.

There was a confused tramping of horses' feet outside. The three men all sprawled round in their chairs to watch. Beyond the dark holly bushes that separated the strip of lawn from the high-road, they could see a cavalcade of shire horses swinging out of their own yard, being taken for exercise. This was the last time. These were the last horses that would go through their hands. The young men watched with critical, callous look. They were all frightened at the collapse of their lives, and the sense of disaster in which they were involved left them no inner freedom.

Yet they were three fine, well-set fellows enough. Joe, the eldest, was a man of thirty-three, broad and handsome in a hot, flushed way. His face was red, he twisted his black moustache over a thick finger, his eyes were shallow and restless. He had a sensual way of uncovering his teeth when he laughed, and his bearing was stupid. Now he watched the horses with a glazed look of helplessness in his eyes, a certain stupor of downfall.

The great draught-horses swung past. They were tied head to tail, four of them, and they heaved along to where a lane branched off from the high-road, planting their great hoofs floutingly in the fine black mud, swinging their great rounded haunches sumptuously, and trotting a few sudden steps as they were led into the lane, round the corner. Every movement showed a massive, slumbrous strength, and a stupidity which held them in subjection. The groom at the head looked back, jerking the leading rope. And the cavalcade moved out of sight up the lane, the tail of the last horse, bobbed up tight and stiff, held out taut from the swinging great haunches as they rocked behind the hedges in a motion-like sleep.

Joe watched with glazed hopeless eyes. The horses were almost like his own body to him. He felt he was done for now. Luckily he was engaged to a woman as old as himself, and therefore her father, who was steward of a neighbouring estate, would provide him with a job. He would marry and go into harness. His life was over, he would be a subject animal now.

He turned uneasily aside, the retreating steps of the horses echoing in his ears. Then, with foolish restlessness, he reached for the scraps of bacon-rind from the plates, and making a faint whistling sound, flung them to the terrier that lay against the fender. He watched the dog swallow them, and waited till the creature looked into his eyes. Then a faint grin came on his face, and in a high, foolish voice he said:

"You won't get much more bacon, shall you, you little b ——?"

The dog faintly and dismally wagged its tail, then lowered its haunches, circled round, and lay down again.

There was another helpless silence at the table. Joe sprawled uneasily in his seat, not willing to go till the family conclave was dissolved. Fred Henry, the second brother, was erect, clean-limbed, alert. He had watched the passing of the horses with more *sang-froid*. If he was an animal, like Joe, he was an animal which controls, not one which is controlled. He was master of any horse, and he carried himself with a well-tempered air of mastery. But he was not master of the situations of life. He pushed his coarse brown moustache upwards, off his lip, and glanced irritably at his sister, who sat impassive and inscrutable.

"You'll go and stop with Lucy for a bit, shan't you?" he asked. The girl did not answer.

"I don't see what else you can do," persisted Fred Henry.

"Go as a skivvy,"* Joe interpolated laconically.

The girl did not move a muscle.

"If I was her, I should go in for training for a nurse," said Malcolm, the youngest of them all. He was the baby of the family, a young man of twenty-two, with a fresh, jaunty *museau*.†

But Mabel did not take any notice of him. They had talked at her and round her for so many years, that she hardly heard them at all.

The marble clock on the mantelpiece softly chimed the half-hour, the dog rose uneasily from the hearthrug and looked at the party at the breakfast table. But still they sat on in ineffectual conclave.

"Oh, all right," said Joe suddenly, apropos of nothing. "I'll get a move on."

He pushed back his chair, straddled his knees with a downward jerk, to get them free, in horsey fashion, and went to the fire. Still he did not

---

*Skivvy = cleaning woman.
†*Museau* = snout, face.

go out of the room; he was curious to know what the others would do or say. He began to charge his pipe, looking down at the dog and saying in a high, affected voice:

"Going wi' me? Going wi' me are ter?* Tha'rt goin' further than tha counts on just now, dost hear?"

The dog faintly wagged its tail, the man stuck out his jaw and covered his pipe with his hands, and puffed intently, losing himself in the tobacco, looking down all the while at the dog with an absent brown eye. The dog looked up at him in mournful distrust. Joe stood with his knees stuck out, in real horsey fashion.

"Have you had a letter from Lucy?" Fred Henry asked of his sister.

"Last week," came the neutral reply.

"And what does she say?"

There was no answer.

"Does she *ask* you to go and stop there?" persisted Fred Henry.

"She says I can if I like."

"Well, then, you'd better. Tell her you'll come on Monday."

This was received in silence.

"That's what you'll do then, is it?" said Fred Henry, in some exasperation.

But she made no answer. There was a silence of futility and irritation in the room. Malcolm grinned fatuously.

"You'll have to make up your mind between now and next Wednesday," said Joe loudly, "or else find yourself lodgings on the kerbstone."

The face of the young woman darkened, but she sat on immutable.

"Here's Jack Fergusson!" exclaimed Malcolm, who was looking aimlessly out of the window.

"Where?" exclaimed Joe, loudly.

"Just gone past."

"Coming in?"

Malcolm craned his neck to see the gate.

"Yes," he said.

There was a silence. Mabel sat on like one condemned, at the head of the table. Then a whistle was heard from the kitchen. The dog got up and barked sharply. Joe opened the door and shouted:

"Come on."

After a moment a young man entered. He was muffled up in overcoat and a purple woollen scarf, and his tweed cap, which he did not remove, was pulled down on his head. He was of medium height, his face was rather long and pale, his eyes looked tired.

"Hello, Jack! Well, Jack!" exclaimed Malcolm and Joe. Fred Henry merely said, "Jack."

"What's doing?" asked the newcomer, evidently addressing Fred Henry.

*Are ter = are you.

"Same. We've got to be out by Wednesday. Got a cold?"

"I have — got it bad, too."

"Why don't you stop in?"

"*Me* stop in? When I can't stand on my legs, perhaps I shall have a chance." The young man spoke huskily. He had a slight Scotch accent.

"It's a knock-out, isn't it," said Joe, boisterously, "if a doctor goes round croaking with a cold. Looks bad for the patients, doesn't it?"

The young doctor looked at him slowly.

"Anything the matter with *you*, then?" he asked sarcastically.

"Not as I know of. Damn your eyes, I hope not. Why?"

"I thought you were very concerned about the patients, wondered if you might be one yourself."

"Damn it, no, I've never been patient to no flaming doctor, and hope I never shall be," returned Joe.

At this point Mabel rose from the table, and they all seemed to become aware of her existence. She began putting the dishes together. The young doctor looked at her, but did not address her. He had not greeted her. She went out of the room with the tray, her face impassive and unchanged.

"When are you off then, all of you?" asked the doctor.

"I'm catching the eleven-forty," replied Malcolm. "Are you goin' down wi' th' trap, Joe?"

"Yes, I've told you I'm going down wi' th' trap, haven't I?"

"We'd better be getting her in then. So long, Jack, if I don't see you before I go," said Malcolm, shaking hands.

He went out, followed by Joe, who seemed to have his tail between his legs.

"Well, this is the devil's own," exclaimed the doctor, when he was left alone with Fred Henry. "Going before Wednesday, are you?"

"That's the orders," replied the other.

"Where, to Northampton?"

"That's it."

"The devil!" exclaimed Fergusson, with quiet chagrin.

And there was silence between the two.

"All settled up, are you?" asked Fergusson.

"About."

There was another pause.

"Well, I shall miss yer, Freddy, boy," said the young doctor.

"And I shall miss thee, Jack," returned the other.

"Miss you like hell," mused the doctor.

Fred Henry turned aside. There was nothing to say. Mabel came in again, to finish clearing the table.

"What are *you* going to do, then, Miss Pervin?" asked Fergusson. "Going to your sister's, are you?"

Mabel looked at him with her steady, dangerous eyes, that always made him uncomfortable, unsettling his superficial ease.

"No," she said.

"Well, what in the name of fortune *are* you going to do? Say what you mean to do," cried Fred Henry, with futile intensity.

But she only averted her head, and continued her work. She folded the white table-cloth, and put on the chenille cloth.

"The sulkiest bitch that ever trod!" muttered her brother.

But she finished her task with perfectly impassive face, the young doctor watching her interestedly all the while. Then she went out.

Fred Henry stared after her, clenching his lips, his blue eyes fixing in sharp antagonism, as he made a grimace of sour exasperation.

"You could bray her into bits, and that's all you'd get out of her," he said, in a small, narrowed tone.

The doctor smiled faintly.

"What's she *going* to do, then?" he asked.

"Strike me if *I* know!" returned the other.

There was a pause. Then the doctor stirred.

"I'll be seeing you to-night, shall I?" he said to his friend.

"Ay — where's it to be? Are we going over to Jessdale?"

"I don't know. I've got such a cold on me. I'll come round to the 'Moon and Stars', anyway."

"Let Lizzie and May miss their night for once, eh?"

"That's it — if I feel as I do now."

"All's one —"

The two young men went through the passage and down to the back door together. The house was large, but it was servantless now, and desolate. At the back was a small bricked house-yard, and beyond that a big square, gravelled fine and red, and having stables on two sides. Sloping, dank, winter-dark fields stretched away on the open sides.

But the stables were empty. Joseph Pervin, the father of the family, had been a man of no education, who had become a fairly large horse dealer. The stables had been full of horses, there was a great turmoil and come-and-go of horses and of dealers and grooms. Then the kitchen was full of servants. But of late things had declined. The old man had married a second time, to retrieve his fortunes. Now he was dead and everything was gone to the dogs, there was nothing but debt and threatening.

For months, Mabel had been servantless in the big house, keeping the home together in penury for her ineffectual brothers. She had kept house for ten years. But previously it was with unstinted means. Then, however brutal and coarse everything was, the sense of money had kept her proud, confident. The men might be foulmouthed, the women in the kitchen might have bad reputations, her brothers might have illegitimate children. But so long as there was money, the girl felt herself established, and brutally proud, reserved.

No company came to the house, save dealers and coarse men. Mabel had no associates of her own sex, after her sister went away. But she did not mind. She went regularly to church, she attended to her father. And she lived in the memory of her mother, who had died when she was fourteen, and whom she had loved. She had loved her father, too, in a different way, depending upon him, and feeling secure in him, until at the age of fifty-four he married again. And then she had set hard against him. Now he had died and left them all hopelessly in debt.

She had suffered badly during the period of poverty. Nothing, however, could shake the curious sullen, animal pride that dominated each member of the family. Now, for Mabel, the end had come. Still she would not cast about her. She would follow her own way just the same. She would always hold the keys of her own situation. Mindless and persistent, she endured from day to day. Why should she think? Why should she answer anybody? It was enough that this was the end, and there was no way out. She need not pass any more darkly along the main street of the small town, avoiding every eye. She need not demean herself any more, going into the shops and buying the cheapest food. This was at an end. She thought of nobody, not even of herself. Mindless and persistent, she seemed in a sort of ecstasy to be coming nearer to her fulfilment, her own glorification, approaching her dead mother, who was glorified.

In the afternoon she took a little bag, with shears and sponge and a small scrubbing brush, and went out. It was a grey, wintry day, with saddened, dark green fields and an atmosphere blackened by the smoke of foundries not far off. She went quickly, darkly along the causeway, heeding nobody, through the town to the churchyard.

There she always felt secure, as if no one could see her, although as a matter of fact she was exposed to the stare of every one who passed along under the churchyard wall. Nevertheless, once under the shadow of the great looming church, among the graves, she felt immune from the world, reserved within the thick churchyard wall as in another country.

Carefully she clipped the grass from the grave, and arranged the pinky white, small chrysanthemums in the tin cross. When this was done, she took an empty jar from a neighbouring grave, brought water, and carefully, most scrupulously sponged the marble headstone and the coping-stone.

It gave her sincere satisfaction to do this. She felt in immediate contact with the world of her mother. She took minute pains, went through the park in a state bordering on pure happiness, as if in performing this task she came into a subtle, intimate connection with her mother. For the life she followed here in the world was far less real than the world of death she inherited from her mother.

The doctor's house was just by the church. Fergusson, being a mere hired assistant, was slave to the country-side. As he hurried now to attend to the outpatients in the surgery, glancing across the graveyard with his quick eye, he saw the girl at her task at the grave. She seemed so intent and remote, it was like looking into another world. Some mystical element was touched in him. He slowed down as he walked, watching her as if spell-bound.

She lifted her eyes, feeling him looking. Their eyes met. And each looked away again at once, each feeling, in some way, found out by the other. He lifted his cap and passed on down the road. There remained distinct in his consciousness, like a vision, the memory of her face, lifted from the tombstone in the churchyard, and looking at him with slow, large, portentous eyes. It *was* portentous, her face. It seemed to mesmerize him. There was a heavy power in her eyes which laid hold of his whole being, as if he had drunk some powerful drug. He had been feeling weak and done before. Now the life came back into him, he felt delivered from his own fretted, daily self.

He finished his duties at the surgery as quickly as might be, hastily filling up the bottles of the waiting people with cheap drugs. Then, in perpetual haste, he set off again to visit several cases in another part of his round, before teatime. At all times he preferred to walk if he could, but particularly when he was not well. He fancied the motion restored him.

The afternoon was falling. It was grey, deadened, and wintry, with a slow, moist, heavy coldness sinking in and deadening all the faculties. But why should he think or notice? He hastily climbed the hill and turned across the dark green fields, following the black cindertrack. In the distance, across a shallow dip in the country, the small town was clustered like smouldering ash, a tower, a spire, a heap of low, raw, extinct houses. And on the nearest fringe of the town, sloping into the dip, was Oldmeadow, the Pervins' house. He could see the stables and the outbuildings distinctly, as they lay towards him on the slope. Well, he would not go there many more times! Another resource would be lost to him, another place gone: the only company he cared for in the alien, ugly little town he was losing. Nothing but work, drudgery, constant hastening from dwelling to dwelling among the colliers and the iron-workers. It wore him out, but at the same time he had a craving for it. It was a stimulant to him to be in the homes of the working people, moving, as it were, through the innermost body of their life. His nerves were excited and gratified. He could come so near, into the very lives of the rough, inarticulate, powerfully emotional men and women. He grumbled, he said he hated the hellish hole. But as a matter of fact it excited him, the contact with the rough, strongly-feeling people was a stimulant applied direct to his nerves.

Below Oldmeadow, in the green, shallow, soddened hollow of fields, lay a square, deep pond. Roving across the landscape, the doctor's quick eye detected a figure in black passing through the gate of the field, down towards the pond. He looked again. It would be Mabel Pervin. His mind suddenly became alive and attentive.

Why was she going down there? He pulled up on the path on the slope above, and stood staring. He could just make sure of the small black figure moving in the hollow of the failing day. He seemed to see her in the midst of such obscurity, that he was like a clairvoyant, seeing rather with the mind's eye than with ordinary sight. Yet he could see her positively enough, whilst he kept his eye attentive. He felt, if he looked away from her, in the thick, ugly falling dusk, he would lose her altogether.

He followed her minutely as she moved, direct and intent, like something transmitted rather than stirring in voluntary activity, straight down the field towards the pond. There she stood on the bank for a moment. She never raised her head. Then she waded slowly into the water.

He stood motionless as the small black figure walked slowly and deliberately towards the centre of the pond, very slowly, gradually moving deeper into the motionless water, and still moving forward as the water got up to her breast. Then he could see her no more in the dusk of the dead afternoon.

"There!" he exclaimed. "Would you believe it?"

And he hastened straight down, running over the wet, soddened fields, pushing through the hedges, down into the depression of callous wintry obscurity. It took him several minutes to come to the pond. He stood on the bank, breathing heavily. He could see nothing. His eyes seemed to penetrate the dead water. Yes, perhaps that was the dark shadow of her black clothing beneath the surface of the water.

He slowly ventured into the pond. The bottom was deep, soft clay, he sank in, and the water clasped dead cold round his legs. As he stirred he could smell the cold, rotten clay that fouled up into the water. It was objectionable in his lungs. Still, repelled and yet not heeding, he moved deeper into the pond. The cold water rose over his thighs, over his loins, upon his abdomen. The lower part of his body was all sunk in the hideous cold element. And the bottom was so deeply soft and uncertain, he was afraid of pitching with his mouth underneath. He could not swim, and was afraid.

He crouched a little, spreading his hands under the water and moving them round, trying to feel for her. The dead cold pond swayed upon his chest. He moved again, a little deeper, and again, with his hands underneath, he felt all around under the water. And he touched her clothing. But it evaded his fingers. He made a desperate effort to grasp it.

And so doing he lost his balance and went under, horribly, suffocating in the foul earthy water, struggling madly for a few moments. At last, after what seemed an eternity, he got his footing, rose again into the air and looked around. He gasped, and knew he was in the world. Then he looked at the water. She had risen near him. He grasped her clothing, and drawing her nearer, turned to take his way to land again.

He went very slowly, carefully, absorbed in the slow progress. He rose higher, climbing out of the pond. The water was now only about his legs; he was thankful, full of relief to be out of the clutches of the pond. He lifted her and staggered on to the bank, out of the horror of wet, grey clay.

He laid her down on the bank. She was quite unconscious and running with water. He made the water come from her mouth, he worked to restore her. He did not have to work very long before he could feel the breathing begin again in her; she was breathing naturally. He worked a little longer. He could feel her live beneath his hands; she was coming back. He wiped her face, wrapped her in his overcoat, looked round into the dim, dark grey world, then lifted her and staggered down the bank and across the fields.

It seemed an unthinkably long way, and his burden so heavy he felt he would never get to the house. But at last he was in the stable-yard, and then in the house-yard. He opened the door and went into the house. In the kitchen he laid her down on the hearthrug, and called. The house was empty. But the fire was burning in the grate.

Then again he kneeled to attend to her. She was breathing regularly, her eyes were wide open and as if conscious, but there seemed something missing in her look. She was conscious in herself, but unconscious of her surroundings.

He ran upstairs, took blankets from a bed, and put them before the fire to warm. Then he removed her saturated, earthy-smelling clothing, rubbed her dry with a towel, and wrapped her naked in the blankets. Then he went into the dining-room, to look for spirits. There was a little whisky. He drank a gulp himself, and put some into her mouth.

The effect was instantaneous. She looked full into his face, as if she had been seeing him for some time, and yet had only just become conscious of him.

"Dr. Fergusson?" she said.

"What?" he answered.

He was divesting himself of his coat, intending to find some dry clothing upstairs. He could not bear the smell of the dead, clayey water, and he was mortally afraid for his own health.

"What did I do?" she asked.

"Walked into the pond," he replied. He had begun to shudder like one sick, and could hardly attend to her. Her eyes remained full on him, he seemed to be going dark in his mind, looking back at her helplessly. The shuddering became quieter in him, his life came back to him, dark and unknowing, but strong again.

"Was I out of my mind?" she asked, while her eyes were fixed on him all the time.

"Maybe, for the moment," he replied. He felt quiet, because his strength had come back. The strange fretful strain had left him.

"Am I out of my mind now?" she asked.

"Are you?" he reflected a moment. "No," he answered truthfully, "I don't see that you are." He turned his face aside. He was afraid now, because he felt dazed, and felt dimly that her power was stronger than his, in this issue. And she continued to look at him fixedly all the time. "Can you tell me where I shall find some dry things to put on?" he asked.

"Did you dive into the pond for me?" she asked.

"No," he answered. "I walked in. But I went in overhead as well."

There was silence for a moment. He hesitated. He very much wanted to go upstairs to get into dry clothing. But there was another desire in him. And she seemed to hold him. His will seemed to have gone to sleep, and left him, standing there slack before her. But he felt warm inside himself. He did not shudder at all, though his clothes were sodden on him.

"Why did you?" she asked.

"Because I didn't want you to do such a foolish thing," he said.

"It wasn't foolish," she said, still gazing at him as she lay on the floor, with a sofa cushion under her head. "It was the right thing to do. *I* knew best, then."

"I'll go and shift these wet things," he said. But still he had not the power to move out of her presence, until she sent him. It was as if she had the life of his body in her hands, and he could not extricate himself. Or perhaps he did not want to.

Suddenly she sat up. Then she became aware of her own immediate condition. She felt the blankets about her, she knew her own limbs. For a moment it seemed as if her reason were going. She looked round, with wild eye, as if seeking something. He stood still with fear. She saw her clothing lying scattered.

"Who undressed me?" she asked, her eyes resting full and inevitable on his face.

"I did," he replied, "to bring you round."

For some moments she sat and gazed at him awfully, her lips parted.

"Do you love me, then?" she asked.

He only stood and stared at her, fascinated. His soul seemed to melt.

She shuffled forward on her knees, and put her arms round him, round his legs, as he stood there, pressing her breasts against his knees and thighs, clutching him with strange, convulsive certainty, pressing his thighs against her, drawing him to her face, her throat, as she looked up at him with flaring, humble eyes of transfiguration, triumphant in first possession.

"You love me," she murmured, in strange transport, yearning and triumphant and confident. "You love me. I know you love me, I know."

And she was passionately kissing his knees, through the wet clothing, passionately and indiscriminately kissing his knees, his legs, as if unaware of everything.

He looked down at the tangled wet hair, the wild, bare, animal shoulders. He was amazed, bewildered, and afraid. He had never thought of loving her. He had never wanted to love her. When he rescued her and restored her, he was a doctor, and she was a patient. He had had no single personal thought of her. Nay, this introduction of the personal element was very distasteful to him, a violation of his professional honour. It was horrible to have her there embracing his knees. It was horrible. He revolted from it, violently. And yet — and yet — he had not the power to break away.

She looked at him again, with the same supplication of powerful love, and that same transcendent, frightening light of triumph. In view of the delicate flame which seemed to come from her face like a light, he was powerless. And yet he had never intended to love her. He had never intended. And something stubborn in him could not give way.

"You love me," she repeated, in a murmur of deep, rhapsodic assurance. "You love me."

Her hands were drawing him, drawing him down to her. He was afraid, even a little horrifed. For he had, really, no intention of loving her. Yet her hands were drawing him towards her. He put out his hand quickly to steady himself, and grasped her bare shoulder. A flame seemed to burn the hand that grasped her soft shoulder. He had no intention of loving her: his whole will was against his yielding. It was horrible. And yet wonderful was the touch of her shoulders, beautiful the shining of her face. Was she perhaps mad? He had a horror of yielding to her. Yet something in him ached also.

He had been staring away at the door, away from her. But his hand remained on her shoulder. She had gone suddenly very still. He looked down at her. Her eyes were now wide with fear, with doubt, the light was dying from her face, a shadow of terrible greyness was returning. He could not bear the touch of her eyes' question upon him, and the look of death behind the question.

With an inward groan he gave way, and let his heart yield towards her. A sudden gentle smile came on his face. And her eyes, which never left his face, slowly, slowly filled with tears. He watched the strange water rise in her eyes, like some slow fountain coming up. And his heart seemed to burn and melt away in his breast.

He could not bear to look at her any more. He dropped on his knees and caught her head with his arms and pressed her face against his throat. She was very still. His heart, which seemed to have broken, was burning with a kind of agony in his breast. And he felt her slow, hot tears wetting his throat. But he could not move.

He felt the hot tears wet his neck and the hollows of his neck, and he remained motionless, suspended through one of man's eternities. Only now it had become indispensable to him to have her face pressed close to him; he could never let her go again. He could never let her head go away from the close clutch of his arm. He wanted to remain like that for ever, with his heart hurting him in a pain that was also life to him. Without knowing, he was looking down on her damp, soft brown hair.

Then, as it were suddenly, he smelt the horrid stagnant smell of that water. And at the same moment she drew away from him and looked at him. Her eyes were wistful and unfathomable. He was afraid of them, and he fell to kissing her, not knowing what he was doing. He wanted her eyes not to have that terrible, wistful, unfathomable look.

When she turned her face to him again, a faint delicate flush was glowing, and there was again dawning that terrible shining of joy in her eyes, which really terrifed him, and yet which he now wanted to see, because he feared the look of doubt still more.

"You love me?" she said, rather faltering.

"Yes." The word cost him a painful effort. Not because it wasn't true. But because it was too newly true, the *saying* seemed to tear open again his newly-torn heart. And he hardly wanted it to be true, even now.

She lifted her face to him, and he bent forward and kissed her on the mouth, gently, with the one kiss that is an eternal pledge. And as he kissed her his heart strained again in his breast. He never intended to love her. But now it was over. He had crossed over the gulf to her, and all that he had left behind had shrivelled and become void.

After the kiss, her eyes again slowly filled with tears. She sat still, away from him, with her face drooped aside, and her hands folded in her lap. The tears fell very slowly. There was complete silence. He too sat there motionless and silent on the hearthrug. The strange pain of his heart that was broken seemed to consume him. That he should love her? That this was love! That he should be ripped open in this way! Him, a doctor! How they would all jeer if they knew! It was agony to him to think they might know.

In the curious naked pain of the thought he looked again to her. She was sitting there drooped into a muse. He saw a tear fall, and his heart flared hot. He saw for the first time that one of her shoulders was quite uncovered, one arm bare, he could see one of her small breasts; dimly, because it had become almost dark in the room.

"Why are you crying?" he asked, in an altered voice.

She looked up at him, and behind her tears the consciousness of her situation for the first time brought a dark look of shame to her eyes.

"I'm not crying, really," she said, watching him, half frightened. He reached his hand, and softly closed it on her bare arm.

"I love you! I love you!" he said in a soft, low vibrating voice, unlike himself.

She shrank, and dropped her head. The soft, penetrating grip of his hand on her arm distressed her. She looked up at him.

"I want to go," she said. "I want to go and get you some dry things."

"Why?" he said. "I'm all right."

"But I want to go," she said. "And I want you to change your things."

He released her arm, and she wrapped herself in the blanket, looking at him rather frightened. And still she did not rise.

"Kiss me," she said wistfully.

He kissed her, but briefly, half in anger.

Then, after a second, she rose nervously, all mixed up in the blanket. He watched her in her confusion, as she tried to extricate herself and wrap herself up so that she could walk. He watched her relentlessly, as she knew. And as she went, the blanket trailing, and as he saw a glimpse of her feet and her white leg, he tried to remember her as she was when he had wrapped her in the blanket. But then he didn't want to remember, because she had been nothing to him then, and his nature revolted from remembering her as she was when she was nothing to him.

A tumbling, muffled noise from within the dark house startled him. Then he heard her voice: — "There are clothes." He rose and went to the foot of the stairs, and gathered up the garments she had thrown down. Then he came back to the fire, to rub himself down and dress. He grinned at his own appearance when he had finished.

The fire was sinking, so he put on coal. The house was now quite dark, save for the light of a street-lamp that shone in faintly from beyond the holly trees. He lit the gas with matches he found on the mantel-piece. Then he emptied the pockets of his own clothes, and threw all his wet things in a heap into the scullery. After which he gathered up her sodden clothes, gently, and put them in a separate heap on the copper-top in the scullery.

It was six o'clock on the clock. His own watch had stopped. He ought to go back to the surgery. He waited, and still she did not come down. So he went to the foot of the stairs and called:

"I shall have to go."

Almost immediately he heard her coming down. She had on her best dress of black voile, and her hair was tidy, but still damp. She looked at him — and in spite of herself, smiled.

"I don't like you in those clothes," she said.

"Do I look a sight?" he answered.

They were shy of one another.

"I'll make you some tea," she said.

"No, I must go."

"Must you?" And she looked at him again with the wide, strained, doubtful eyes. And again, from the pain of his breast, he knew how he loved her. He went and bent to kiss her, gently, passionately, with his heart's painful kiss.

"And my hair smells so horrible," she murmured in distraction. "And I'm so awful, I'm so awful! Oh, no, I'm too awful." And she broke into bitter, heart-broken sobbing. "You can't want to love me, I'm horrible."

"Don't be silly, don't be silly," he said, trying to comfort her, kissing her, holding her in his arms. "I want you, I want to marry you, we're going to be married, quickly, quickly — tomorrow if I can."

But she only sobbed terribly, and cried:

"I feel awful. I feel awful. I feel I'm horrible to you."

"No, I want you, I want you," was all he answered, blindly, with that terrible intonation which frightened her almost more than her horror lest he should *not* want her.

DORIS LESSING

Born in Kermanshah, Persia in 1919, Doris Lessing (neé Tayler) was the elder child of a banker who gave up his job for idealistic reasons and in 1925 took his family to farm in Rhodesia. It was there that she stayed until 1949, despite crop failures, other farm misfortunes, and two unsuccessful marriages. With the manuscript of her first novel, *The Grass Is Singing*, she then went to England, where it was published the following year. Like her *African Stories* (1964), it expresses a deep sense of injustice, of opposition toward the racism that has resulted so often from the European and American presences in Africa. It was that outrage, together with her observations of social inequalities (particularly those which affected the English working class), which led her to communism in 1942.

Throughout her work there persists a tension between the collective good and the individual conscience. In *The New Statesman* in 1956, she wrote: "A large number of my friends are locked out of countries and unable to return; locked into countries and unable to get out; have been deported, prohibited and banned." In context she is referring to Africa, but the phrase also makes a kind of symbolic gesture; her characters, too, are locked into or out of experience and must locate the world that can be their own. For example, the five novels about Martha Quest (the *Children of Violence* cycle) portray the growing political, marital, intellectual, and emotional freedom of a woman who is taken to typify her generation. Her science-fiction stories examine in fantasy and abstract principle the structures of power within which individual action acquires its meaning. "Our Friend Judith" (*A Man and Two Women*, 1963) focuses on some of the particular difficulties of being an independent woman in the modern world—on the double standards, petty interferences, and social pressures that disrupt her life and in so doing, it tries to distinguish between frustration and enlightenment. *The Golden Notebook* (1962) probes a similar distinction, revealing the many simultaneous impulses that direct and bedevil a writer's consciousness. The apocalyptic political visions of *The Four-Gated City* (1969) and *Briefing for a Descent into Hell* (1971) emerge from this sense of division, of commitment at once to a world of social reality and a world of private sensibility. But in rendering them both, Doris Lessing has managed to transform both social history and personal experience into art.

FOR FURTHER READING

Dorothy Brewster, *Doris Lessing* (New York: Twayne, 1969).

Doris Lessing, *Going Home* (London: Michael Joseph, 1957).

Roy Newquist, "Interview with Doris Lessing," *Counterpoint* (New York: Rand McNally, 1964), pp. 413–24.

OUR FRIEND JUDITH

I stopped inviting Judith to meet people when a Canadian woman remarked, with the satisfied fervour of one who has at last pinned a label on a rare specimen: "She is, of course, one of your typical English spinsters."

This was a few weeks after an American sociologist, having elicited from Judith the facts that she was forty-ish, unmarried, and living alone, had inquired of me: "I suppose she has given up?" "Given up what?" I asked; and the subsequent discussion was unrewarding.

Judith did not easily come to parties. She would come after pressure, not so much — one felt — to do one a favour, but in order to correct what she believed to be a defect in her character. "I really ought to enjoy meeting new people more than I do," she said once. We reverted to an earlier pattern of our friendship: odd evenings together, an occasional visit to the cinema, or she would telephone to say: "I'm on my way past you to the British Museum. Would you care for a cup of coffee with me? I have twenty minutes to spare."

It is characteristic of Judith that the word spinster, used of her, provoked fascinated speculation about other people. There are my aunts, for instance: aged seventy-odd, both unmarried, one an ex-missionary from China, one a retired matron of a famous London hospital. These two old ladies live together under the shadow of the Cathedral in a country town. They devote much time to the Church, to good causes, to letter writing with friends all over the world, to the grandchildren and the great-grand-children of relatives. It would be a mistake, however, on entering a house in which nothing has been moved for fifty years, to diagnose a condition of fossilized late-Victorian integrity. They read every book reviewed in the *Observer* or *The Times,* so that I recently got a letter from Aunt Rose inquiring whether I did not think that the author of *On the Road* was not perhaps? — exaggerating his difficulties. They know a good deal about music, and write letters of encouragement to young composers they feel are being neglected — "You must understand that anything new and original takes time to be understood." Well-informed and critical Tories, they are as likely to dispatch telegrams of protest to the Home Secretary as letters of support. These ladies, my aunts Emily and Rose, are surely what is meant by the phrase *English spinster.* And yet, once the connection had been pointed out, there is no doubt that Judith and they are spiritual cousins, if not sisters. Therefore it follows that one's pitying admiration for women who have supported manless and uncomforted lives needs a certain modification?

One will, of course, never know; and I feel now that it is entirely my fault that I shall never know. I had been Judith's friend for upwards of five years before the incident occurred which I involuntarily thought of — stupidly enough — as "the first time Judith's mask slipped."

A mutual friend, Betty, had been given a cast-off Dior dress. She was too short for it. Also she said: "It's not a dress for a married woman with three children and a talent for cooking. I don't know why not, but it isn't." Judith was the right build. Therefore one evening the three of us met by appointment in Judith's bedroom, with the dress. Neither Betty nor I was surprised at the renewed discovery that Judith was beautiful. We had both too often caught each other, and ourselves, in moments of envy when Judith's calm and severe face, her undemonstratively perfect body, succeeded in making everyone else in a room or a street look cheap.

Judith is tall, small-breasted, slender. Her light brown hair is parted in the centre and cut straight around her neck. A high straight forehead, straight nose, a full grave mouth are a setting for her eyes, which are green, large and prominent. Her lids are very white, fringed with gold, and moulded close over the eyeball, so that in profile she has the look of a staring gilded mask. The dress was of dark green glistening stuff, cut straight, with a sort of loose tunic. It opened simply at the throat. In it Judith could of course evoke nothing but classical images. Diana, perhaps, back from the hunt, in a relaxed moment? A rather intellectual wood nymph who had opted for an afternoon in the British Museum reading-room? Something like that. Neither Betty nor I said a word, since Judith was examining herself in a long mirror, and must know she looked magnificent.

Slowly she drew off the dress and laid it aside. Slowly she put on the old cord skirt and woollen blouse she had taken off. She must have surprised a resigned glance between us, for she then remarked, with the smallest of mocking smiles: "One surely ought to stay in character, wouldn't you say?" She added, reading the words out of some invisible book, written not by her, since it was a very vulgar book, but perhaps by one of us: "It does everything *for* me, I must admit."

"After seeing you in it," Betty cried out, defying her, "I can't bear for anyone else to have it. I shall simply put it away." Judith shrugged, rather irritated. In the shapeless skirt and blouse, and without make-up, she stood smiling at us, a woman at whom forty-nine out of fifty people would not look twice.

A second revelatory incident occurred soon after. Betty telephoned me to say that Judith had a kitten. Did I know that Judith adored cats? "No, but of course she would," I said.

Betty lived in the same street as Judith and saw more of her than I did. I was kept posted about the growth and habits of the cat and its effect on Judith's life. She remarked, for instance, that she felt it was good for her to have a tie and some responsibility. But no sooner was the cat out of kittenhood than all the neighbours complained. It was a tomcat, ungelded, and making every night hideous. Finally the landlord said that either the cat or Judith must go, unless she was prepared to have the cat "fixed." Judith wore herself out trying to find some person, anywhere in Britain, who would be prepared to take the cat. This person would, however, have to sign a written statement not to have the cat "fixed." When Judith took the cat to the vet to be killed, Betty told me she cried for twenty-four hours.

"She didn't think of compromising? After all, perhaps the cat might have preferred to live, if given the choice?"

"Is it likely I'd have the nerve to say anything so sloppy to Judith? It's the nature of a male cat to rampage lustfully about, and therefore it would be morally wrong for Judith to have the cat fixed, simply to suit her own convenience."

"She said that?"

"She wouldn't have to *say* it, surely?"

A third incident was when she allowed a visiting young American, living in Paris, the friend of a friend and scarcely known to her, to use her flat while she visited her parents over Christmas. The young man and his friends lived it up for ten days of alcohol and sex and marijuana, and when Judith came back it took a week to get the place clean again and the furniture mended. She telephoned twice to Paris, the first time to say that he was a disgusting young thug and if he knew what was good for him he would keep out of her way in the future; the second time to apologize for losing her temper. "I had a choice either to let someone use my flat, or to leave it empty. But having chosen that you should have it, it was clearly an unwarrantable infringement of your liberty to make any conditions at all. I do most sincerely ask your pardon." The moral aspects of the matter having been made clear, she was irritated rather than not to receive letters of apology from him — fulsome, embarrassed, but above all, baffled.

It was the note of curiosity in the letters — he even suggested coming over to get to know her better — that irritated her most. "What do you suppose he means?" she said to me. "He lived in my flat for ten days. One would have thought that should be enough, wouldn't you?"

The facts about Judith, then, are all in the open, unconcealed, and plain to anyone who cares to study them; or, as it became plain she feels — to anyone with the intelligence to interpret them.

She has lived for the last twenty years in a small two-roomed flat high over a busy West London street. The flat is shabby and badly heated. The furniture is old, was never anything but ugly, is now frankly rickety and fraying. She has an income of £200 a year from a dead uncle. She lives on this and what she earns from her poetry, and from lecturing on poetry to night classes and extra-mural University classes.

She does not smoke or drink, and eats very little, from preference, not self-discipline.

She studied poetry and biology at Oxford, with distinction.

She is a Castlewell. That is, she is a member of one of the academic upper-middle-class families, which have been producing for centuries a steady supply of brilliant but sound men and women who are the backbone of the arts and sciences in Britain. She is on cool good terms with her family who respect her and leave her alone.

She goes on long walking tours, by herself, in such places as Exmoor or West Scotland.

Every three or four years she publishes a volume of poems.

The walls of her flat are completely lined with books. They are scientific, classical and historical; there is a great deal of poetry and some drama. There is not one novel. When Judith says: "Of course I don't read novels," this does not mean that novels have no place, or a small place, in literature; or that people should not read novels; but that it must be obvious that she can't be expected to read novels.

I had been visiting her flat for years before I noticed two long shelves of books, under a window, each shelf filled with the works of a single writer. The two writers are not, to put it at the mildest, the kind one would associate with Judith. They are mild, reminiscent, vague and whimsical. Typical English *belles-lettres*, in fact, and by definition abhorrent to her. Not one of the books in the two shelves has been read; some of the pages are still uncut. Yet each book is inscribed or dedicated to her: gratefully, admiringly, sentimentally and, more than once, amorously. In short, it is open to anyone who cares to examine these two shelves, and to work out dates, to conclude that Judith from the age of fifteen to twenty-five had been the beloved young companion of one elderly literary gentleman, and from twenty-five to thirty-five, the inspiration of another.

During all that time she had produced her own poetry, and the sort of poetry, it is quite safe to deduce, not at all likely to be admired by her two admirers. Her poems are always cool and intellectual; that is their form, which is contradicted or supported by a gravely sensuous texture. They are poems to read often; one has to, to understand them.

I did not ask Judith a direct question about these two eminent but rather fusty lovers. Not because she would not have answered, or because she would have found the question impertinent, but because such questions are clearly unnecessary. Having those two shelves of books where they are, and books she could not conceivably care for, for their own sake, is publicly giving credit where credit is due. I can imagine her thinking the thing over, and deciding it was only fair, or perhaps honest, to place the books there; and this despite the fact that she would not care at all for the same attention to be paid to her. There is something almost contemptuous in it. For she certainly despises people who feel they need attention.

For instance, more than once a new emerging wave of "modern" young poets have discovered her as the only "modern" poet among their despised and well-credited elders. This is because, since she began writing at fifteen, her poems have been full of scientific, mechanical and chemical imagery. This is how she thinks, or feels.

More than once has a young poet hastened to her flat, to claim her as an ally, only to find her totally and by instinct unmoved by words like modern, new, contemporary. He has been outraged and wounded by her principle, so deeply rooted as to be unconscious, and to need no expression but a contemptuous shrug of the shoulders, that publicity seeking or to want critical attention is despicable. It goes without saying that there is perhaps one critic in the world she has any time for. He has sulked off, leaving her on her shelf, which she takes it for granted is her proper place, to be read by an appreciative minority.

Meanwhile she gives her lectures, walks alone through London, writes her poems, and is seen sometimes at a concert or a play with a middle-aged professor of Greek who has a wife and two children.

Betty and I speculated about this Professor, with such remarks as: Surely she must sometimes be lonely? Hasn't she ever wanted to marry? What about that awful moment when one comes in from somewhere at night to an empty flat?

It happened recently that Betty's husband was on a business trip, her children visiting, and she was unable to stand the empty house. She asked Judith for a refuge until her own home filled again.

Afterwards Betty rang me up to report:

"Four of the five nights Professor Adams came in about ten or so."

"Was Judith embarrassed?"

"Would you expect her to be?"

"Well if not embarrassed at least conscious there was a situation?"

"No, not at all. But I must say I don't think he's good enough for her. He can't possibly understand her. He calls her Judy."

"Good God."

"Yes. But I was wondering. Suppose the other two called her Judy — ''little Judy'' — imagine it! Isn't it awful! But it does rather throw a light on Judith?"

"It's rather touching."

"I suppose it's touching. But *I* was embarrassed — oh, not because of the situation. Because of how she was, with him. 'Judy, is there another cup of tea in that pot?' And she, rather daughterly and demure, pouring him one."

"Well yes, I can see how you felt."

"Three of the nights he went to her bedroom with her — very casual about it, because she was being. But he was not there in the mornings. So I asked her. You know how it is when you ask her a question. As if you've been having long conversations on that very subject for years and years, and she is merely continuing where you left off last. So when she says something surprising, one feels such a fool to be surprised?"

"Yes. And then?"

"I asked her if she was sorry not to have children. She said yes, but one couldn't have everything."

"One can't have everything, she said?"

"Quite clearly feeling she *has* nearly everything. She said she thought it was a pity, because she would have brought up children very well."

"When you come to think of it, she would, too."

"I asked about marriage, but she said on the whole the rôle of a mistress suited her better."

"She used the word mistress?"

"You must admit it's the accurate word."

"I suppose so."

"And then she said that while she liked intimacy and sex and everything, she enjoyed waking up in the morning alone and *her own person.*"

"Yes, *of course.*"

"Of course. But now she's bothered because the Professor would like to marry her. Or he feels he ought. At least, he's getting all guilty and obsessive about it. She says she doesn't see the point of divorce, and anyway, surely it would be very hard on his poor old wife after all these years particularly after bringing up two children so satisfactorily. She talks about his wife as if she's a kind of nice old charwoman, and it wouldn't be *fair* to sack her, you know. Anyway. What with one thing and another Judith's going off to Italy soon in order *to collect herself.*"

"But how's she going to pay for it?"

"Luckily the Third Programme's commissioning her to do some arty programmes. They offered her a choice of The Cid — El Thid, you know — and the Borgias. Well, the Borghese, then. And Judith settled for the Borgias."

"The Borgias," I said, "*Judith?*"

"Yes quite. I said that too, in that tone of voice. She saw my point. She says the epic is right up her street, whereas the Renaissance has never been on her wavelength. Obviously it couldn't be, all the magnificence and cruelty and *dirt.* But of course chivalry and a high moral code and all those idiotically noble goings-on are right on her wavelength."

"Is the money the same?"

"Yes. But is it likely Judith would let money decide? No, she said that one should always choose something new, that isn't up one's street. Well, because it's better for her character, and so on, to get herself unsettled by the Renaissance. She didn't say *that,* of course."

"Of course not."

Judith went to Florence; and for some months postcards informed us tersely of her doings. Then Betty decided she must go by herself for a holiday. She had been appalled by the discovery that if her husband was away for a night she couldn't sleep; and when he went to Australia for three weeks, she stopped living until he came back. She had discussed this with him, and he had agreed that, if she really felt the situation to be serious, he would dispatch her by air, to Italy, in order to recover her self-respect. As she put it.

I got this letter from her: "It's no use, I'm coming home. I might have known. Better face it, once you're really married you're not fit for man nor beast. And if you remember what I used to be like! *Well!* I moped around Milan. I sun-bathed in Venice, then I thought my tan was surely worth something, so I was on the point of starting an affair with another lonely soul, but I lost heart, and went to Florence to see Judith. She wasn't there. She'd gone to the Italian Riviera. I had nothing better to do, so I followed her. When I saw the place I wanted to laugh, it's so much not Judith, you know, all those palms and umbrellas and gaiety at all costs and ever such an ornamental blue sea. Judith is in an enormous stone room up on the hillside above the sea, with grape-vines all over the place. You should see her, she's got beautiful. It seems for the last fifteen years she's been going to Soho every Saturday morning to buy food at an Italian shop. I must have looked surprised, because she explained she liked Soho. I suppose because all that dreary vice and nudes and prostitutes and everything prove how right she is to be as she is? She told the people in the shop she was going to Italy, and the signora said what a coincidence, she was going back to Italy too, and she did hope an old friend like Miss Castlewell would visit her there. Judith said to me: "I felt lacking, when she used the word friend. Our relations have always been formal. Can you understand it?" she said to me. "For fifteen years," I said to her. She said: "I think I must feel it's a kind of imposition, don't you know, expecting people to feel friendship for one." *Well.* I said: "You ought to understand it, because you're like that yourself." "Am I?" she said. "Well, think about it," I said. But I could see she didn't want to think about it. Anyway, she's here, and I've spent a week with her. The widow Maria Rineiri inherited her mother's house, so she came home, from Soho. On the ground floor is a tatty little Rosticcheria patronized by the neighbours. They are all working people. This isn't tourist country, up on the hill. The widow lives above the shop with her little boy, a nasty little brat of about ten. Say what you like, the English are the only people who know how to bring up children, I don't care if that's insular. Judith's room is at the back, with a balcony. Underneath her room is the barber's shop, and the barber is Luigi Rineiri, the widow's younger brother. Yes, I was keeping him until the last. He is about forty, tall dark handsome, a great *bull*, but rather a sweet fatherly bull. He has cut Judith's hair and made it lighter. Now it looks like a sort of gold helmet. Judith is all brown. The widow Rineiri has made her a white dress and a green dress. They fit, for a change. When Judith walks down the street to the lower town, all the Italian males take one look at the golden girl and melt in their own oil like ice-cream. Judith takes all this in her stride. She sort of acknowledges the homage. Then she strolls into the sea and vanishes into the foam. She swims five miles every day. *Naturally.* I haven't asked Judith whether she has collected herself, because you can see she hasn't. The widow Rineiri is match-making. When I noticed this I wanted to laugh, but luckily I didn't, because Judith asked me, really wanting to know, Can you see me married to an Italian barber? (Not being snobbish, but stating the position, so to speak.) "Well yes," I said, "you're the only woman

I know who I can see married to an Italian barber." Because it wouldn't matter who she married, she'd always be her *own person*. "At any rate, for a time," I said. At which she said, asperously: "You can use phrases like for a time in England but not in Italy." Did you ever see England, at least London, as the home of licence, liberty and free love? No, neither did I, but of course she's right. Married to Luigi it would be the family, the neighbours, the church and the bambini. All the same she's thinking about it, believe it or not. Here she's quite different, all relaxed and free. She's melting in the attention she gets. The widow mothers her and makes her coffee all the time, and listens to a lot of good advice about how to bring up that nasty brat of hers. Unluckily she doesn't take it. Luigi is crazy for her. At mealtimes she goes to the trattoria in the upper square and all the workmen treat her like a goddess. Well, a film-star then. I said to her, you're mad to come home. For one thing her rent is ten bob a week, and you eat pasta and drink red wine till you bust for about one and sixpence. No, she said, it would be nothing but self-indulgence to stay. Why? I said. She said, she's got nothing to stay for. (Ho ho!) And besides, she's done her research on the Borghese, though so far she can't see her way to an honest presentation of the facts. What made these people tick? she wants to know. And so she's only staying because of the cat. I forgot to mention the cat. This is a town of cats. The Italians here love their cats. I wanted to feed a stray cat at the table, but the waiter said no; and after lunch, all the waiters came with trays crammed with left-over food and stray cats came from everywhere to eat. And at dark when the tourists go in to feed and the beach is empty — you know how empty and forlorn a beach is at dusk? — well, cats appear from everywhere. The beach seems to move, then you see it's cats. They go stalking along the thin inch of grey water at the edge of the sea, shaking their paws crossly at each step, snatching at the dead little fish, and throwing them with their mouths up on to the dry sand. Then they scamper after them. You've never seen such a snarling and fighting. At dawn when the fishing-boats come in to the empty beach, the cats are there in dozens. The fishermen throw them bits of fish. The cats snarl and fight over it. Judith gets up early and goes down to watch. Sometimes Luigi goes too, being tolerant. Because what he really likes is to join the evening promenade with Judith on his arm around and around the square of the upper town. Showing her off. Can you *see* Judith? But she does it. Being tolerant. But she smiles and enjoys the attention she gets, there's no doubt of it.

"She has a cat in her room. It's a kitten really, but it's pregnant. Judith says she can't leave until the kittens are born. The cat is too young to have kittens. Imagine Judith. She sits on her bed in that great stone room, with her bare feet on the stone floor and watches the cat, and tries to work out why a healthy uninhibited Italian cat always fed on the best from the Rosticcheria should be neurotic. Because it is. When it sees Judith watching it gets nervous and starts licking at the roots of its tail. But Judith goes on watching, and says about Italy that the reason why the English love the Italians is because the Italians make the English feel superior. They have no discipline. And that's a despicable reason for one nation to love another. Then she talks about Luigi and says he has no sense of guilty but a sense of sin; whereas she has no sense of sin but she has guilt. I haven't asked her if this has been an insuperable barrier, because judging from how she looks, it hasn't. She says she would rather have a sense of sin, because sin can be atoned for, and if she understood sin, perhaps she would be more at home with the Renaissance. Luigi is very healthy, she says, and not neurotic. He is a Catholic, of course. He doesn't mind that she's an atheist. His mother has explained to him that the English are all pagans, but good people at heart. I suppose he thinks a few smart sessions with the local priest would set Judith on the right path for good and all. Meanwhile, the cat walks nervously around the room, stopping to lick, and when it can't stand Judith watching it another second, it rolls over on the floor, with its paws tucked up, and rolls up its eyes, and Judith scratches its lumpy pregnant stomach and tells it to relax. It makes *me* nervous to see her, it's not like her, I don't know why. Then Luigi shouts from the barber's shop, then he comes up and stands at the door laughing, and Judith laughs, and the widow says: Children enjoy yourselves. And off they go, walking down to the town eating ice-cream. The cat follows them. It won't let Judith out of its sight, like a dog. When she swims miles out to sea, the cat hides under a beach-hut until she comes back. Then she carries it back up the hill, because that nasty little boy chases it. *Well.* I'm coming home tomorrow, thank God, to my dear old Billy, I was mad to ever leave him. There is something about Judith and Italy that has upset me, I don't know what. The point is, what on earth can Judith and Luigi *talk* about? Nothing. How can they? And, of course, it doesn't matter. So I turn out to be a prude as well. See you next week.''

It was my turn for a dose of the sun, so I didn't see Betty. On my way back from Rome I stopped off in Judith's resort and walked up through narrow streets to the upper town, where, in the square with the vine-covered trattoria at the corner, was a house with Rosticcheria written in black print on a cracked wooden board over a low door. There was a door-curtain of red beads, and flies settled on the beads. I opened the beads with my hands and looked into a small dark room with a stone counter. Loops of salami hung from metal hooks. A glass bell covered some plates of cooked meats. There were flies on the salami and on the glass bell. A few tins on the wooden shelves, a couple of pale loaves, some wine-casks and an open case of sticky pale green grapes covered with fruit flies, seemed to be the only stock. A single wooden table with two chairs stood in a corner, and two workmen sat there, eating lumps of sausage and bread. Through another bead curtain at the back came a short, smoothly fat, slender limbed woman with greying hair. I asked for Miss Castlewell, and her face changed. She said in an offended, off-hand way: "Miss Castlewell left last week." She took a white cloth from under the counter, and flicked at the flies on the glass bell. "I'm a friend of hers," I said, and she said "Si," and put her hands, palm down, on the counter and looked at me, expressionless. The workmen got up, gulped down the last of their wine, nodded and went. She ciao'd them; and looked back at me. Then, since I didn't go, she called "Luigi!" A shout came from the back room, there was a rattle of beads, and in came first a wiry sharp-faced boy, and then Luigi. He was tall, heavy shouldered, and his black rough hair was like a cap, pulled low over his brows. He looked good-natured, but at the moment, uneasy. His sister said something, and he stood beside her, an ally, and confirmed: "Miss Castlewell went away." I was on the point of giving up, when through the bead curtain that screened off a dazzling light eased a thin, tabby cat. It was ugly and it walked uncomfortably, with its back quarters bunched up. The child suddenly let out a "Sssss" through his teeth, and the cat froze. Luigi said something sharp to the child, and something encouraging to the cat, which sat down, looked straight in front of it, then began frantically licking at its flanks. "Miss Castlewell was offended with us," said Mrs Rineiri suddenly, and with dignity. "She left early one morning. We did not expect her to go." I said: "Perhaps she had to go home and finish some work."

Mrs Rineiri shrugged, then sighed. Then she exchanged a hard look with her brother. Clearly the subject had been discussed, and closed for ever.

"I've known Judith a long time," I said, trying to find the right note. "She's a remarkable woman. She's a poet." But there was no response to this at all. Meanwhile the child, with a fixed bared-teeth grin, was staring at the cat, narrowing his eyes. Suddenly he let out another "Ssssssss," and added a short, high yelp. The cat shot backwards, hit the wall, tried desperately to claw its way up the wall, came to its senses and again sat down and began its urgent, undirected licking at its fur. This time Luigi cuffed the child, who yelped in earnest, and then ran out into the street past the cat. Now that the way was clear the cat shot across the floor, up on to the counter, and bounded past Luigi's shoulder and straight through the bead curtain into the barber's shop, where it landed with a thud.

"Judith was sorry when she left us," said Mrs Rineiri uncertainly.

"She was crying."

"I'm sure she was."

"And so," said Mrs Rineiri, with finality, laying her hands down again, and looking past me at the bead curtain. That was the end. Luigi nodded brusquely at me, and went into the back. I said goodbye to Mrs Rineiri and walked back to the lower town. In the square I saw the child, sitting on the running-board of a lorry parked outside the trattoria, drawing in the dust with his bare toes, and directing in front of him a blank, unhappy stare.

I had to go through Florence, so I went to the address Judith had been at. No, Miss Castlewell had not been back. Her papers and books were still here. Would I take them back with me to England? I made a great parcel and brought them back to England.

I telephoned Judith and she said she had already written for the papers to be sent, but it was kind of me to bring them. There had seemed to be no point, she said, in returning to Florence.

"Shall I bring them over?"

"I would be very grateful, of course."

Judith's flat was chilly, and she wore a bunchy sage-green woollen dress. Her hair was still a soft gold helmet, but she looked pale and rather pinched. She stood with her back to a single bar of electric fire — lit because I demanded it — with her legs apart and her arms folded. She contemplated me.

"I went to the Rineiris' house."

"Oh. Did you?"

"They seemed to miss you."

She said nothing.

"I saw the cat too."

"Oh. Oh, I suppose you and Betty discussed it?" This was with a small unfriendly smile.

"Well, Judith, you must see we were likely to?"

She gave this her consideration and said: "I don't understand why people discuss other people. Oh — I'm not criticizing you. But I don't see why you are so interested. I don't understand human behaviour and I'm not particularly interested."

"I think you should write to the Rineiris."

"I wrote and thanked them, of course."

"I don't mean that."

"You and Betty have worked it out?"

"Yes, we talked about it. We thought we should talk to you, so you should write to the Rineiris."

"Why?"

"For one thing, they are both very fond of you."

"Fond," she said smiling.

"Judith, I've never in my life felt such an atmosphere of being let down."

Judith considered this. "When something happens that shows one there is really a complete gulf in understanding, what is there to say?"

"It could scarcely have been a complete gulf in understanding. I suppose you are going to say we are being interfering?"

Judith showed distaste. "That is a very stupid word. And it's a stupid idea. No one can interfere with me if I don't let them. No, it's that I don't understand people. I don't understand why you or Betty should care. Or why the Rineiris should, for that matter," she added with the small tight smile.

"Judith!"

"If you've behaved stupidly, there's no point in going on. You put an end to it."

"What happened? Was it the cat?"

"Yes, I suppose so. But it's not important." She looked at me, saw my ironical face, and said: "The cat was too young to have kittens. That is all there was to it."

"Have it your way. But that is obviously not all there is to it"

"What upsets me is that I don't understand at all why I was so upset then."

"What happened? Or don't you want to talk about it?"

"I don't give a damn whether I talk about it or not. You really do say the most extraordinary things, you and Betty. If you want to know, I'll tell you, what does it matter?"

"I would like to know, of course."

"*Of course!*" she said. "In your place I wouldn't care. Well, I think the essence of the thing was that I must have had the wrong attitude to that cat. Cats are supposed to be independent. They are supposed to go off by themselves to have their kittens. This one didn't. It was climbing up on to my bed all one night and crying for attention. I don't like cats on my bed. In the morning I saw she was in pain. I stayed with her all that day. Then Luigi — he's the brother, you know."

"Yes."

"Did Betty mention him? Luigi came up to say it was time I went for a swim. He said the cat should look after itself. I blame myself very much. That's what happens when you submerge yourself in somebody else."

Her look at me was now defiant; and her body showed both defensiveness and aggression. "Yes. It's true. I've always been afraid of it. And in the last few weeks I've behaved badly. It's because I let it happen."

"Well, go on."

"I left the cat and swam. It was late, so it was only for a few minutes. When I came out of the sea the cat had followed me and had had a kitten on the beach. That little beast Michele — the son, you know? — Well, he always teased the poor thing, and now he had frightened her off the kitten. It was dead, though. He held it up by the tail and waved it at me as I came out of the sea. I told him to bury it. He scooped two inches of sand away and pushed the kitten in — on the beach, where people are all day. So I buried it properly. He had run off. He was chasing the poor cat. She was terrified and running up the town. I ran too. I caught Michele and I was so angry I hit him. I don't believe in hitting children. I've been feeling beastly about it ever since."

"You were angry."

"It's no excuse. I would never have believed myself capable of hitting a child. I hit him very hard. He went off, crying. The poor cat had got under a big lorry parked in the square. Then she screamed. And then a most remarkable thing happened. She screamed just once, and all at once cats just materialized. One minute there was just one cat, lying under a lorry, and the next, dozens of cats. They sat in a big circle around the lorry, all quite still, and watched my poor cat.''

"Rather moving," I said.

"Why?''

"There is no evidence one way or the other," I said in inverted commas, "that the cats were there out of concern for a friend in trouble.''

"No," she said energetically. "There isn't. It might have been curiosity. Or anything. How do we know? However, I crawled under the lorry. There were two paws sticking out of the cat's back end. The kitten was the wrong way round. It was stuck. I held the cat down with one hand and I pulled the kitten out with the other.'' She held out her long white hands. They were still covered with fading scars and scratches. "She bit and yelled, but the kitten was alive. She left the kitten and crawled across the square into the house. Then all the cats got up and walked away. It was the most extraordinary thing I've ever seen. They vanished again. One minute they were all there, and then they had vanished. I went after the cat, with the kitten. Poor little thing, it was covered with dust — being wet, don't you know. The cat was on my bed. There was another kitten coming, but it got stuck too. So when she screamed and screamed I just pulled it out. The kittens began to suck. One kitten was very big. It was a nice fat black kitten. It must have hurt her. But she suddenly bit out — snapped, don't you know, like a reflex action, at the back of the kitten's head. It died, just like that. Extraordinary, isn't it?'' she said, blinking hard, her lips quivering. "She was its mother, but she killed it. Then she ran off the bed and went downstairs into the shop under the counter. I called to Luigi. You know, he's Mrs Rineiri's brother.''

"Yes, I know.''

"He said, she was too young, and she was badly frightened and very hurt. He took the alive kitten to her but she got up and walked away. She didn't want it. Then Luigi told me not to look. But I followed him. He held the kitten by the tail and he banged it against the wall twice. Then he dropped it into the rubbish heap. He moved aside some rubbish with his toe, and put the kitten there and pushed rubbish over it. Then Luigi said the cat should be destroyed. He said she was badly hurt and it would always hurt her to have kittens.''

"He hasn't destroyed her. She's still alive. But it looks to me as if he were right.''

"Yes, I expect he was.''

"What upset you — that he killed the kitten?''

"Oh no, I expect the cat would if he hadn't. But that isn't the point is it?''

"What is the point?''

"I don't think I really know.'' She had been speaking breathlessly, and fast. Now she said slowly: "It's not a question of right or wrong is it? Why should it be? It's a question of what one is. That night Luigi wanted to go promenading with me. For him, that was *that*. Something had to be done, and he'd done it. But I felt ill. He was very nice to me. He's a very good person," she said, defiantly.

"Yes, he looks it."

"That night I couldn't sleep. I was blaming myself. I should never have left the cat to go swimming. Well, and then I decided to leave the next day. And I did. And that's all. The whole thing was a mistake, from start to finish."

"Going to Italy at all?"

"Oh, to go for a holiday would have been all right."

"You've done all that work for nothing? You mean you aren't going to make use of all that research?"

"No. It was a mistake."

"Why don't you leave it a few weeks and see how things are then?"

"Why?"

"You might feel differently about it."

"What an extraordinary thing to say. Why should I? Oh, you mean, time passing, healing wounds — that sort of thing? What an extraordinary idea. It's always seemed to me an extraordinary idea. No, right from the beginning I've felt ill at ease with the whole business, not myself at all."

"Rather irrationally, I should have said."

Judith considered this, very seriously. She frowned while she thought it over. Then she said: "But if one cannot rely on what one feels, what can one rely on?"

"On what one thinks, I should have expected you to say."

"Should you? Why? Really, you people are all very strange. I don't understand you." She turned off the electric fire, and her face closed up. She smiled, friendly and distant and said: "I don't really see any point at all in discussing it."

KATHERINE MANSFIELD

Born Kathleen Mansfield Beauchamp, the third of five children in a prosperous New Zealand family, Katherine Mansfield (1888-1923) grew up in Wellington, was educated at Queen's College (London), and returned only briefly to New Zealand before finally settling in Europe in 1908. In England she lived what was then considered a bohemian life, one marked by its love of theatre, its urbanity, and its shifting liaisons. On the edge of several famous literary circles — Bloomsbury, Garsington, and the milieu of D.H. and Frieda Lawrence, for example — she published stories in *The New Age, Rhythm, Adelphi*, and several other periodicals. A deft satirist in her early sketches (*In a German Pension*, 1911), she drew most attention for the later stories she collected in *Bliss* (1920) and *The Garden Party* (1922). Her sharp, spare style contrasted strongly with conventional forms of storytelling; she strove to break away from plotted narrative and to evoke through image and cadence the pressures, perspectives, and insights of particular frames of mind. For her, beauty was evanescent, order a fond dream; isolation at once fed and desolated the creative imagination. In a contemporary review, the poet Walter de la Mare wrote of her work: "The pitch of mind is invariably emotional, the poise lyrical. Nonetheless that mind is absolutely tranquil and attentive in its intellectual grasp of the matter in hand. And through all, Miss Mansfield's personality, whatever its disguises, haunts her work just as its customary inmate may haunt a vacant room, its *genius* a place." More recent critics have attempted to come to terms with how and why this process happens, finding her work variously confessional, political, and technically innovative.

One of the places that haunted her was New Zealand. It was — as "The Doll's House" (*The Dove's Nest*, 1923) suggests — something of a bittersweet memory. She rejected what she saw as New Zealand's provincialism, yet was attracted to its natural beauty — a double perspective clearly shown in "The Doll's House." It is a story about children, but it is an oblique one; it is not about childlike harmony. It is a story which animates instead the chance moments of insight and the codified techniques of social violence which strafe the child's world. As some of her other stories show, they strafe the adult's world as well. But the kind of order Mansfield could craft in prose always eluded her in life. In 1923 she died in France, of tuberculosis, at the Gurdjieff Institute for the Harmonious Development of Man.

FOR FURTHER READING

Paul Delaney, "Short and Simple Annals of the Poor: Katherine Mansfield's 'The Doll's House'," *Mosaic* 10 (Fall 1976):7-17

David Dowling, "Aunt Beryl's Doll's House," *Landfall* 34 (June 1980): 148-58.

Cherry A. Hankin, *Katherine Mansfield and Her Confessional Stories* (London: Macmillan, 1983).

Clare Hanson and Andrew Gurr, *Katherine Mansfield* (London: Macmillan, 1981).

THE DOLL'S HOUSE

When dear old Mrs. Hay went back to town after staying with the Burnells she sent the children a doll's house. It was so big that the carter and Pat carried it into the courtyard, and there it stayed, propped up on two wooden boxes beside the feed-room door. No harm could come to it; it was summer. And perhaps the smell of paint would have gone off by the time it had to be taken in. For, really, the smell of paint coming from that doll's house ("Sweet of old Mrs. Hay, of course; most sweet and generous!") — but the smell of paint was quite enough to make anyone seriously ill, in Aunt Beryl's opinion. Even before the sacking was taken off. And when it was. . . .

There stood the doll's house, a dark, oily, spinach green, picked out with bright yellow. Its two solid little chimneys, glued on to the roof, were painted red and white, and the door, gleaming with yellow varnish, was like a little slab of toffee. Four windows, real windows, were divided into panes by a broad streak of green. There was actually a tiny porch, too, painted yellow, with big lumps of congealed paint hanging along the edge.

But perfect, perfect little house! Who could possibly mind the smell. It was part of the joy, part of the newness.

"Open it quickly, someone!"

The hook at the side was stuck fast. Pat prised it open with his penknife, and the whole house front swung back, and — there you were, gazing at one and the same moment into the drawing-room and dining-room, the kitchen and two bedrooms. That is the way for a house to open! Why don't all houses open like that? How much more exciting than peering through the slit of a door into a mean little hall with a hat-stand and two umbrellas! That is — isn't it? — what you long to know about a house when you put your hand on the knocker. Perhaps it is the way God opens houses at the dead of night when He is taking a quiet turn with an angel. . . .

"Oh-oh!" The Burnell children sounded as though they were in despair. It was too marvellous; it was too much for them. They had never seen anything like it in their lives. All the rooms were papered. There were pictures on the walls, painted on the paper, with gold frames complete. Red carpet covered all the floors except the kitchen; red plush chairs in the drawing-room, green in the dining-room; tables, beds with real bedclothes, a cradle, a stove, a dresser with tiny plates and one big jug. But what Kezia liked more than anything, what she liked frightfully, was the lamp. It stood in the middle of the dining-room table, an exquisite little amber lamp with a white globe. It was even filled all ready for lighting, though, of course, you couldn't light it. But there was something inside that looked like oil and moved when you shook it.

The father and mother dolls, who sprawled very still as though they had fainted in the drawing-room, and their two little children asleep upstairs, were really too big for the doll's house. They didn't look as though they belonged. But the lamp was perfect. It seemed to smile at Kezia, to say "I live here." The lamp was real.

The Burnell children could hardly walk to school fast enough the next morning. They burned to tell everybody, to describe, to — well — to boast about their doll's house before the schoolbell rang.

"I'm to tell," said Isabel,"because I'm the eldest. And you two can join in after. But I'm to tell first."

There was nothing to answer. Isabel was bossy, but she was always right, and Lottie and Kezia knew too well the powers that went with being eldest. They brushed through the thick buttercups at the road edge and said nothing.

"And I'm to choose who's to come and see it first. Mother said I might."

For it had been arranged that while the doll's house stood in the court-yard they might ask the girls at school, two at a time, to come and look. Not to stay to tea, of course, or to come traipsing through the house. But just to stand quietly in the courtyard while Isabel pointed out the beauties, and Lottie and Kezia looked pleased. . . .

But hurry as they might, by the time they had reached the tarred palings of the boys' playground the bell had begun to jangle. They only just had time to whip off their hats and fall into line before the roll was called. Never mind. Isabel tried to make up for it by looking very impor-tant and mysterious and by whispering behind her hand to the girls near her, "Got something to tell you at playtime."

Playtime came and Isabel was surrounded. The girls of her class nearly fought to put their arms round her, to walk away with her, to beam flatteringly, to be her special friend. She held quite a court under the huge pine trees at the side of the playground. Nudging, giggling together, the little girls pressed up close. And the only two who stayed outside the ring were the two who were always outside, the little Kelveys. They knew better than to come anywhere near the Burnells.

For the fact was, the school the Burnell children went to was not at all the kind of place their parents would have chosen if there had been any choice. But there was none. It was the only school for miles. And the consequence was all the children of the neighbourhood, the Judge's little girls, the doctor's daughters, the storekeeper's children, the milk-man's, were forced to mix together. Not to speak of there being an equal number of rude, rough little boys as well. But the line had to be drawn somewhere. It was drawn at the Kelveys. Many of the children, includ-ing the Burnells, were not allowed even to speak to them. They walked past the Kelveys with their heads in the air, and as they set the fashion in all matters of behaviour, the Kelveys were shunned by everybody.

Even the teacher had a special voice for them, and a special smile for the other children when Lil Kelvey came up to her desk with a bunch of dreadfully common-looking flowers.

They were the daughters of a spry, hard-working little washerwoman, who went about from house to house by the day. This was awful enough. But where was Mr. Kelvey? Nobody knew for certain. But everybody said he was in prison. So they were the daughters of a washerwoman and a gaolbird. Very nice company for other people's children! And they looked it. Why Mrs. Kelvey made them so conspicuous was hard to understand. The truth was they were dressed in "bits" given to her by the people for whom she worked. Lil, for instance, who was a stout, plain child, with big freckles, came to school in a dress made from a green art-serge tablecloth of the Burnells', with red plush sleeves from the Logans' curtains. Her hat, perched on top of her high forehead, was a grown-up woman's hat, once the property of Miss Lecky, the postmistress. It was turned up at the back and trimmed with a large scarlet quill. What a little guy she looked! It was impossible not to laugh. And her little sister, our Else, wore a long white dress, rather like a nightgown, and a pair of little boy's boots. But whatever our Else wore she would have looked strange. She was a tiny wishbone of a child, with cropped hair and enormous solemn eyes — a little white owl. Nobody had ever seen her smile; she scarcely ever spoke. She went through life holding on to Lil, with a piece of Lil's skirt screwed up in her hand. Where Lil went, our Else followed. In the playground, on the road going to and from school, there was Lil marching in front and our Else holding on behind. Only when she wanted anything, or when she was out of breath, our Else gave Lil a tug, a twitch, and Lil stopped and turned around. The Kelveys never failed to understand each other.

Now they hovered at the edge; you couldn't stop them listening. When the little girls turned round and sneered, Lil, as usual, gave her silly, shamefaced smile, but our Else only looked.

And Isabel's voice, so very proud, went on telling. The carpet made a great sensation, but so did the beds with real bedclothes, and the stove with an oven door.

When she finished Kezia broke in. "You've forgotten the lamp, Isabel."

"Oh yes," said Isabel, "and there's a teeny little lamp, all made of yellow glass, with a white globe that stands on the dining-room table. You couldn't tell it from a real one."

"The lamp's best of all," cried Kezia. She thought Isabel wasn't making half enough of the little lamp. But nobody paid any attention. Isabel was choosing the two who were to come back with them that afternoon and see it. She chose Emmie Cole and Lena Logan. But when the others knew they were all to have a chance, they couldn't be nice enough to Isabel. One by one they put their arms round Isabel's waist and walked her off. They had something to whisper to her, a secret. "Isabel's *my* friend."

Only the little Kelveys moved away forgotten; there was nothing more for them to hear.

Days passed, and as more children saw the doll's house, the fame of it spread. It became the one subject, the rage. The one question was, "Have you seen Burnells' doll's house? Oh, ain't it lovely!" "Haven't you seen it? Oh, I say!"

Even the dinner hour was given up to talking about it. The little girls sat under the pines eating their thick mutton sandwiches and big slabs of johnny cake spread with butter. While always, as near as they could get, sat the Kelveys, our Else holding on to Lil, listening too, while they chewed their jam sandwiches out of a newspaper soaked with large red blobs.

"Mother," said Kezia, "can't I ask the Kelveys just once?"

"Certainly not, Kezia."

"But why not?"

"Run away, Kezia; you know quite well why not."

At last everybody had seen it except them. On that day the subject rather flagged. It was the dinner hour. The children stood together under the pine trees, and suddenly, as they looked at the Kelveys eating out of their paper, always by themselves, always listening, they wanted to be horrid to them. Emmie Cole started the whisper.

"Lil Kelvey's going to be a servant when she grows up."

"O-oh, how awful!" said Isabel Burnell, and she made eyes at Emmie.

Emmie swallowed in a very meaning way and nodded to Isabel as she'd seen her mother do on those occasions.

"It's true — it's true — it's true," she said.

Then Lena Logan's little eyes snapped. "Shall I ask her?" she whispered.

"Bet you don't," said Jessie May.

"Pooh, I'm not frightened," said Lena. Suddenly she gave a little squeal and danced in front of the other girls. "Watch! Watch me! Watch me now!" said Lena. And sliding, gliding, dragging one foot, giggling behind her hand, Lena went over to the Kelveys.

Lil looked up from her dinner. She wrapped the rest quickly away. Our Else stopped chewing. What was coming now?

"Is it true you're going to be a servant when you grow up, Lil Kelvey?" shrilled Lena.

Dead silence. But instead of answering, Lil only gave her silly, shame-faced smile. She didn't seem to mind the question at all. What a sell for Lena! The girls began to titter.

Lena couldn't stand that. She put her hands on her hips; she shot forward. "Yah, yer father's in prison!" she hissed spitefully.

This was such a marvellous thing to have said that the little girls rushed away in a body, deeply, deeply excited, wild with joy. Some one found a long rope, and they began skipping. And never did they skip so high, run in and out so fast, or do such daring things as on that morning.

In the afternoon Pat called for the Burnell children with the buggy and they drove home. There were visitors. Isabel and Lottie, who liked visitors, went upstairs to change their pinafores. But Kezia thieved out at the back. Nobody was about; she began to swing on the big white gates of the courtyard. Presently, looking along the road, she saw two little dots. They grew bigger, they were coming towards her. Now she could see that one was in front and one close behind. Now she could see that they were the Kelveys. Kezia stopped swinging. She slipped off the gate as if she was going to run away. Then she hesitated. The Kelveys came nearer, and beside them walked their shadows, very long, stretching right across the road with their heads in the buttercups. Kezia clambered back on the gate; she had made up her mind; she swung out.

"Hullo," she said to the passing Kelveys.

They were so astounded that they stopped. Lil gave her silly smile. Our Else stared.

"You can come and see our doll's house if you want to," said Kezia, and she dragged one toe on the ground. But at that Lil turned red and shook her head quickly.

"Why not?" asked Kezia.

Lil gasped, then she said, "Your ma told our ma you wasn't to speak to us."

"Oh, well," said Kezia. She didn't know what to reply. "It doesn't matter. You can come and see our doll's house all the same. Come on. Nobody's looking."

But Lil shook her head still harder.

"Don't you want to?" asked Kezia.

Suddenly there was a twitch, a tug at Lil's skirt. She turned round. Our Else was looking at her with big, imploring eyes; she was frowning; she wanted to go. For a moment Lil looked at our Else very doubtfully. But then our Else twitched her skirt again. She started forward. Kezia led the way. Like two little stray cats they followed across the courtyard to where the doll's house stood.

"There it is," said Kezia.

There was a pause. Lil breathed loudly, almost snorted; our Else was still as stone.

"I'll open it for you," said Kezia kindly. She undid the hook and they looked inside.

"There's the drawing-room and the dining-room, and that's the — "

"Kezia!"

Oh, what a start they gave!

"Kezia!"

It was Aunt Beryl's voice. They turned round. At the back door stood Aunt Beryl, staring as if she couldn't believe what she saw.

"How dare you ask the little Kelveys into the courtyard!" said her cold, furious voice. "You know as well as I do, you're not allowed to talk to them. Run away, children, run away at once. And don't come back again," said Aunt Beryl. And she stepped into the yard and shooed them out as if they were chickens.

"Off you go immediately!" she called, cold and proud.

They did not need telling twice. Burning with shame, shrinking together, Lil huddling along like her mother, our Else dazed, somehow they crossed the big courtyard and squeezed through the white gate.

"Wicked, disobedient little girl!" said Aunt Beryl bitterly to Kezia, and she slammed the doll's house to.

The afternoon had been awful. A letter had come from Willie Brent, a terrifying, threatening letter, saying if she did not meet him that evening in Pulman's Bush, he'd come to the front door and ask the reason why! But now that she had frightened those little rats of Kelveys and given Kezia a good scolding, her heart felt lighter. That ghastly pressure was gone. She went back to the house humming.

When the Kelveys were well out of sight of Burnells', they sat down to rest on a big red drainpipe by the side of the road. Lil's cheeks were still burning; she took off the hat with the quill and held it on her knee. Dreamily they looked over the hay paddocks, past the creek, to the group of wattles where Logan's cows stood waiting to be milked. What were their thoughts?

Presently our Else nudged up close to her sister. But now she had forgotten the cross lady. She put out a finger and stroked her sister's quill; she smiled her rare smile.

"I seen the little lamp," she said softly.

Then both were silent once more.

ALICE MUNRO

For the settings of her prose fiction, Alice Munro has relied primarily on the small towns and rural landscapes of Western Ontario, where she was born in 1931. Although she started publishing short stories in such journals as *Queen's Quarterly*, *Tamarack Review*, and *The Canadian Forum* in the 1950s, she published no book until 1968, when a collection of fifteen stories appeared under the title *Dance of the Happy Shades* and immediately won critical acclaim. Like the novel which followed in 1971, *Lives of Girls and Women* — and stories in subsequent collections: *Something I've Been Meaning to Tell You* (1974), *Who Do You Think You Are?* (1978), and *The Moons of Jupiter* (1982) — her fiction explores tensions between the orderly and the uncontrollable in modern life, particularly as they affect women. The orderly manifests itself in conventions of various kinds: the moral and social structure of small-town society, the dimensions of family life, the roles accorded men and women by tradition and inertia.

Munro's dramatization of these social realities brings her characters up against the knowledge of the limits which such order imposes on them. They rebel, or they surrender, or they question their ability to escape themselves — to escape the identities which the conventions have inevitably helped create. When the father in one of her stories ("Boys and Girls"), for example, dismisses his daughter's intentional rebellion with the phrase "she's only a girl," he dismisses implicitly her capacities for intelligence and independent judgment; moreover, the girl has become so pressured by family expectations, that she acknowledges "maybe it was true." The characters in the sardonically titled "Thanks for the Ride" also are circumscribed by imposed stereotypes. Those who know what limits them do not delight in their knowledge; those who do not know are equally joyless, for their very lack of knowledge creates an emptiness in their lives. The story is one which gains its meaning not just from the characters' behavior, but also from the writer's control over setting and style, over image, allusion, and oxymoron. The unity of the whole gives evidence that the act of storytelling is both a fine art and a careful craft.

FOR FURTHER READING

Heliane Catherine Daziron, "The Preposterous Oxymoron," *Literary Half-Yearly* 24 (July 1983): 116–24.

Helen Hoy, " 'Dull, Simple, Amazing and Unfathomable': Paradox and Double Vision in Alice Munro's Fiction," *Studies in Canadian Literature*, no. 5 (1980): 100–15.

L.K. MacKenick, ed., *Probable Fictions: Alice Munro's Narrative Acts* (Toronto: ECW Press, 1983).

Alice Munro, "The Colonel's Hash Resettled," in *The Narrative Voice*, ed. John Metcalf (Toronto: McGraw-Hill Ryerson, 1972), pp. 181–83.

THANKS FOR THE RIDE

My cousin George and I were sitting in a restaurant called Pop's Cafe, in a little town close to the Lake. It was getting dark in there, and they had not turned the lights on, but you could still read the signs plastered against the mirror between the fly-speckled and slightly yellowed cut-outs of strawberry sundaes and tomato sandwiches.

"Don't ask for information," George read. "If we knew anything we wouldn't be here" and "If you've got nothing to do, you picked a hell of a good place to do it in." George always read everything out loud — posters, billboards, Burma-Shave signs, "Mission Creek. Population 1700. Gateway to the Bruce. We love our children."

I was wondering whose sense of humour provided us with the signs. I thought it would be the man behind the cash register. Pop? Chewing on a match, looking out at the street, not watching for anything except for somebody to trip over a crack in the sidewalk or have a blowout or make a fool of himself in some way that Pop, rooted behind the cash register, huge and cynical and incurious, was never likely to do. Maybe not even tﬁat; maybe just by walking up and down, driving up and down, going places, the rest of the world proved its absurdity. You see the judgment on the faces of people looking out of windows, sitting on front steps in some little towns; so deeply, deeply uncaring they are, as if they had sources of disillusionment which they would keep, with some satisfaction, in the dark.

There was only the one waitress, a pudgy girl who leaned over the counter and scraped at the polish on her fingernails. When she had flaked most of the polish off her thumbnail she put the thumb against her teeth and rubbed the nail back and forth absorbedly. We asked her what her name was and she didn't answer. Two or three minutes later the thumb came out of her mouth and she said, inspecting it: "That's for me to know and you to find out."

"All right," George said. "Okay if I call you Mickey?"

"I don't care."

"Because you remind me of Mickey Rooney," George said. "Hey, where's everybody go in this town? Where's everybody go?" Mickey had turned her back and begun to drain out the coffee. It looked as if she didn't mean to talk any more, so George got a little jumpy, as he did when he was threatened with having to be quiet or be by himself. "Hey, aren't there any girls in this town?" he said almost plaintively. "Aren't there any girls or dances or anything? We're strangers in town," he said. "Don't you want to help us out?"

"Dance hall down on the beach closed up Labour Day," Mickey said coldly.

"There any other dance halls?"

"There's a dance tonight out at Wilson's *school*," Mickey said.

"That old-time? No, no, I don't go for the old-time. *All-a-man left* and that, used to have that down in the basement of the church. Yeah, *ever' body swing* — I don't go for that. Inna basement of the *church*," George said, obscurely angered. "You don't remember that," he said to me. "Too young."

I was just out of high-school at this time, and George had been working for three years in the Men's Shoes in a downtown department store, so there was that difference. But we had never bothered with each other back in the city. We were together now because we had met unexpectedly in a strange place and because I had a little money, while George was broke. Also I had my father's car, and George was in one of his periods between cars, which made him always a little touchy and dissatisfied. But he would have to rearrange these facts a bit, they made him uneasy. I could feel him manufacturing a sufficiency of good feeling, old-pal feeling, and dressing me up as Old Dick, good kid, real character — which did not matter one way or the other, though I did not think, looking at his tender blond piggish handsomeness, the nudity of his pink mouth, and the surprised, angry creases that frequent puzzlement was beginning to put into his forehead, that I would be able to work up an Old George.

I had driven up to the Lake to bring my mother home from a beach resort for women, a place where they had fruit juice and cottage cheese for reducing, and early-morning swims in the Lake, and some religion, apparently, for there was a little chapel attached. My aunt, George's mother, was staying there at the same time, and George arrived about an hour or so after I did, not to take his mother home, but to get some money out of her. He did not get along well with his father, and he did not make much money working in the shoe department, so he was very often broke. His mother said he could have a loan if he would stay over and go to church with her the next day. George said he would. Then George and I got away and drove half a mile along the lake to this little town neither of us had seen before, which George said would be full of bootleggers and girls.

It was a town of unpaved, wide, sandy streets and bare yards. Only the hardy things like red and yellow nasturtiums, or a lilac bush with brown curled leaves, grew out of that cracked earth. The houses were set wide apart, with their own pumps and sheds and privies out behind; most of them were built of wood and painted green or grey or yellow. The trees that grew there were big willows or poplars, their fine leaves greyed with the dust. There were no trees along the main street, but spaces of tall grass and dandelions and blowing thistles — open country between the store buildings. The town hall was surprisingly large, with a great bell in a tower, the red brick rather glaring in the midst of the town's walls of faded, pale-painted wood. The sign beside the door said that it was a memorial to the soldiers who had died in the First World War. We had a drink out of the fountain in front.

We drove up and down the main street for a while, with George saying: "What a dump! Jesus, what a dump!" and "Hey, look at that! Aw, not so good either." The people on the street went home to supper, the shadows of the store buildings lay solid across the street, and we went into Pop's.

"Hey," George said, "is there any other restaurant in this town? Did you see any other restaurant?"

"No," I said.

"Any other town I ever been," George said, "pigs hangin' out the windows, practically hangin' off the trees. Not here. Jesus! I guess it's late in the season," he said.

"You want to go to a show?"

The door opened. A girl came in, walked up and sat on a stool, with most of her skirt bunched up underneath her. She had a long somnolent face, no bust, frizzy hair; she was pale, almost ugly, but she had that inexplicable aura of sexuality. George brightened, though not a great deal. "Never mind," he said. "This'll do. This'll do in a pinch, eh? In a pinch."

He went to the end of the counter and sat down beside her and started to talk. In about fve minutes they came back to me, the girl drinking a bottle of orange pop.

"This is Adelaide," George said. "Adelaide, Adeline — Sweet Adeline. I'm going to call her Sweet A, Sweet A."

Adelaide sucked at her straw, paying not much attention.

"She hasn't got a date," George said. "You haven't got a date have you, honey?"

Adelaide shook her head very slightly.

"Doesn't hear half what you say to her," George said. "Adelaide, Sweet A, have you got any friends? Have you got any nice, young little girl friend to go out with Dickie? You and me and her and Dickie?"

"Depends," said Adelaide. "Where do you want to go?"

"Anywhere you say. Go for a drive. Drive up to Owen Sound, maybe."

"You got a car?"

"Yeah, yeah, we got a car. C'mon, you must have some nice little friend for Dickie." He put his arm around this girl, spreading his fingers over her blouse. "C'mon out and I'll show you the car."

Adelaide said: "I know one girl might come. The guy she goes around with, he's engaged, and his girl came up and she's staying at his place up the beach, his mother and dad's place, and —"

"Well that is certainly int-er-esting," George said. "What's her name? Come on, let's go round and get her. You want to sit around drinking pop all night?"

"I'm finished," Adelaide said. "She might not come. I don't know."

"Why not? Her mother not let her out nights?"

"Oh, she can do what she likes," said Adelaide. "Only there's times she don't want to. I don't know."

We went out and got into the car, George and Adelaide in the back. On the main street about a block from the cafe we passed a thin, fair-haired girl in slacks and Adelaide cried: "Hey stop! That's her! That's Lois!"

I pulled in and George stuck his head out of the window, whistling. Adelaide yelled, and the girl came unhesitatingly, unhurriedly to the car. She smiled, rather coldly and politely, when Adelaide explained to her. All the time George kept saying: "Hurry up, come on, get in! We can talk in the car." The girl smiled, did not really look at any of us, and in a few moments, to my surprise, she opened the door and slid into the car.

"I don't have anything to do," she said. "My boy friend's away."

"That so?" said George, and I saw Adelaide, in the rear-vision mirror, make a cross warning face. Lois did not seem to have heard him.

"We better drive around to my house," she said. "I was just going down to get some Cokes, that's why I only have my slacks on. We better drive around to my house and I'll put on something else."

"Where are we going to go," she said, "so I know what to put on?"

I said: "Where do you want to go?"

"Okay, okay," George said. "First things first. We gotta get a bottle, then we'll decide. You know where to get one?" Adelaide and Lois both said yes, and then Lois said to me: "You can come in the house and wait while I change, if you want to." I glanced in the rear mirror and thought that there was probably some agreement she had with Adelaide.

Lois's house had an old couch on the porch and some rugs hanging down over the railing. She walked ahead of me across the yard. She had her long pale hair tied at the back of her neck; her skin was dustily freckled, but not tanned; even her eyes were light-coloured. She was cold and narrow and pale. There was derision, and also great gravity, about her mouth. I thought she was about my age or a little older.

She opened the front door and said in a clear, stilted voice: "I would like you to meet my family."

The little front room had linoleum on the floor and flowered paper curtains at the windows. There was a glossy chesterfeld with a Niagara Falls and a To Mother cushion on it, and there was a little black stove with a screen around it for summer, and a big vase of paper apple blossoms. A tall, frail woman came into the room drying her hands on a dishtowel, which she flung into a chair. Her mouth was full of blue-white china teeth, and long cords trembled in her neck. I said how-do-you-do to her, embarrassed by Lois's announcement, so suddenly and purposefully conventional. I wondered if she had any misconceptions about this date, engineered by George for such specific purposes. I did not think so. Her face had no innocence in it that I could see; it was knowledgeable, calm, and hostile. She might have done it, then, to mock me, to make me into this caricature of The Date, the boy who grins and shuffles in the front hall and waits to be presented to the nice girl's family. But that was a little far-fetched. Why should she want to embarrass me when she had agreed to go out with me without even looking into my face? Why should she care enough?

Lois's mother and I sat down on the chesterfield. She began to make conversation, giving this The Date interpretation. I noticed the smell in the house, the smell of stale small rooms, bedclothes, frying, washing, and medicated ointments. And dirt, though it did not look dirty. Lois's mother said: "That's a nice car you got out front. Is that your car?"

"My father's."

"Isn't that lovely! Your father has such a nice car. I always think it's lovely for people to have things. I've got no time for these people that's just eaten up with malice 'n envy. I say it's lovely. I bet your mother, every time she wants anything, she just goes down to the store and buys it — new coat, bedspread, pots and pans. What does your father do? Is he a lawyer or doctor or something like that?"

"He's a chartered accountant."

"Oh. That's in an office, is it?"

"Yes."

"My brother, Lois's uncle, he's in the office of the CPR in London. He's quite high up there, I understand."

She began to tell me about how Lois's father had been killed in an accident at the mill. I noticed an old woman, the grandmother probably, standing in the doorway of the room. She was not thin like the others, but as soft and shapeless as a collapsed pudding, pale brown spots melting together on her face and arms, bristles of hairs in the moisture around her mouth. Some of the smell in the house seemed to come from her. It was a smell of hidden decay, such as there is when some obscure little animal has died under the verandah. The smell, the slovenly, confiding voice — something about this life I had not known, something about these people. I thought: my mother, George's mother, they are innocent. Even George, George is innocent. But these others are born sly and sad and knowing.

I did not hear much about Lois's father except that his head was cut off.

"Clean off, imagine, and rolled on the floor! Couldn't open the coffin. It was June, the hot weather. And everybody in town just stripped their gardens, stripped them for the funeral. Stripped their spirea bushes and peenies and climbin' clemantis. I guess it was the worst accident ever took place in this town.

"Lois had a nice boy friend this summer," she said. "Used to take her out and sometimes stay here overnight when his folks weren't up at the cottage and he didn't feel like passin' his time there all alone. He'd bring the kids candy and even me he'd bring presents. That china elephant up there, you can plant flowers in it, he brought me that. He fixed the radio for me and I never had to take it into the shop. Do your folks have a summer cottage up here?"

I said no, and Lois came in, wearing a dress of yellow-green stuff —
stiff and shiny like Christmas wrappings — high-heeled shoes, rhine-
stones, and a lot of dark powder over her freckles. Her mother was
excited.

"You like that dress?" she said. "She went all the way to London and
bought that dress, didn't get it anywhere round here!"

We had to pass by the old woman as we went out. She looked at us
with sudden recognition, a steadying of her pale, jellied eyes. Her mouth
trembled open, she stuck her face out at me.

"You can do what you like with my gran'daughter," she said in her
old, strong voice, the rough voice of a country woman. "But you be
careful. And you know what I mean!"

Lois's mother pushed the old woman behind her, smiling tightly,
eyebrows lifted, skin straining over her temples. "Never mind," she
mouthed at me, grimacing distractedly. "Never mind. Second childhood." The smile stayed on her face; the skin pulled back from it. She
seemed to be listening all the time to a perpetual din and racket in her
head. She grabbed my hand as I followed Lois out. "Lois is a nice girl,"
she whispered. "You have a nice time, don't let her mope!" There was
a quick, grotesque, and, I suppose, originally flirtatious, flickering of
brows and lids. "Night!"

Lois walked stiffy ahead of me, rustling her papery skirt. I said: "Did
you want to go to a dance or something?"

"No," she said. "I don't care."

"Well you got all dressed up —"

"I always get dressed up on Saturday night," Lois said, her voice
floating back to me, low and scornful. Then she began to laugh, and I
had a glimpse of her mother in her, that jaggedness and hysteria. "Oh,
my God!" she whispered. I knew she meant what had happened in the
house, and I laughed too, not knowing what else to do. So we went
back to the car laughing as if we were friends, but we were not.

We drove out of town to a farmhouse where a woman sold us a whiskey bottle full of muddy-looking liquor, something George and I had
never had before. Adelaide had said that this woman would probably
let us use her front room, but it turned out that she would not, and that
was because of Lois. When the woman peered up at me from under the
man's cap she had on her head and said to Lois, "Change's as good as a
rest, eh?" Lois did not answer, kept a cold face. Then later the woman
said that if we were so stuck-up tonight her front room wouldn't be
good enough for us and we better go back to the bush. All the way back
down the lane Adelaide kept saying: "Some people can't take a joke,
can they? Yeah, stuck-up is right —" until I passed her the bottle to keep
her quiet. I saw George did not mind, thinking this had taken her mind
off driving to Owen Sound.

We parked at the end of the lane and sat in the car drinking. George and Adelaide drank more than we did. They did not talk, just reached for the bottle and passed it back. This stuff was different from anything I had tasted before; it was heavy and sickening in my stomach. There was no other effect, and I began to have the depressing feeling that I was not going to get drunk. Each time Lois handed the bottle back to me she said "Thank you" in a mannerly and subtly contemptuous way. I put my arm around her, not much wanting to. I was wondering what was the matter. This girl lay against my arm, scornful, acquiescent, angry, inarticulate and out-of-reach. I wanted to talk to her then more than to touch her, and that was out of the question; talk was not so little a thing to her as touching. Meanwhile I was aware that I should be beyond this, beyond the first stage and well into the second (for I had a knowledge, though it was not very comprehensive, of the orderly progression of stages, the ritual of back- and front-seat seduction). Almost I wished I was with Adelaide.

"Do you want to go for a walk?" I said.

"That's the first bright idea you've had all night," George told me from the back seat. "Don't hurry," he said as we got out. He and Adelaide were muffled and laughing together. "Don't hurry back!"

Lois and I walked along a wagon track close to the bush. The fields were moonlit, chilly and blowing. Now I felt vengeful, and I said softly, "I had quite a talk with your mother."

"I can imagine," said Lois.

"She told me about that guy you went out with last summer."

"This summer."

"It's last summer now. He was engaged or something, wasn't he?"

"Yes."

I was not going to let her go. "Did he like you better?" I said. "Was that it? Did he like you better?"

"No, I wouldn't say he liked me," Lois said. I thought, by some thickening of the sarcasm in her voice, that she was beginning to be drunk. "He liked Momma and the kids okay but he didn't like me. *Like me*," she said. "What's that?"

"Well, he went out with you —"

"He just went around with me for the summer. That's what those guys from up the beach always do. They come down here to the dances and get a girl to go around with. For the summer. They always do.

"How I know he didn't *like* me," she said, "he said I was always bitching. You have to act grateful to those guys, you know, or they say you're bitching."

I was a little startled at having loosed all this. I said: "Did you like him?"

"Oh, sure! I should, shouldn't I? I should just get down on my knees and thank him. That's what my mother does. He brings her a cheap old spotted elephant —"

"Was this guy the first?" I said.

"The first steady. Is that what you mean?"

It wasn't. "How old are you?"

She considered. "I'm almost seventeen. I can pass for eighteen or nineteen. I can pass in a beer parlour. I did once."

"What grade are you in at school?"

She looked at me, rather amazed. "Did you think I still went to school? I quit that two years ago. I've got a job at the glove-works in town."

"That must have been against the law. When you quit."

"Oh, you can get a permit if your father's dead or something."

"What do you do at the glove-works?" I said.

"Oh, I run a machine. It's like a sewing machine. I'll be getting on piecework soon. You make more money."

"Do you like it?"

"Oh, I wouldn't say I loved it. It's a job — you ask a lot of questions," she said.

"Do you mind?"

"I don't have to answer you," she said, her voice flat and small again. "Only if I like." She picked up her skirt and spread it out in her hands. "I've got burrs on my skirt," she said. She bent over, pulling them one by one, "I've got burrs on my dress," she said. "It's my good dress. Will they leave a mark? If I pull them all — slowly — I won't pull any threads."

"You shouldn't have worn that dress," I said. "What'd you wear that dress for?"

She shook the skirt, tossing a burr loose. "I don't know," she said. She held it out, the stiff, shining stuff, with faintly drunken satisfaction. "I wanted to show you guys!" she said, with a sudden small explosion of viciousness. The drunken, nose-thumbing, toe-twirling satisfaction could not now be mistaken as she stood there foolishly, tauntingly, with her skirt spread out. "I've got an imitation cashmere sweater at home. It cost me twelve dollars," she said. "I've got a fur coat I'm paying on, paying on for next winter. I've got a fur coat —"

"That's nice," I said. "I think it's lovely for people to have things."

She dropped the skirt and struck the flat of her hand on my face. This was a relief to me, to both of us. We felt a fight had been building in us all along. We faced each other as warily as we could, considering we were both a little drunk, she tensing to slap me again and I to grab her or slap her back. We would have it out, what we had against each other. But the moment of this keenness passed. We let out our breath; we had not moved in time. And the next moment, not bothering to shake off our enmity, nor thinking how the one thing could give way to the other, we kissed. It was the first time, for me, that a kiss was accomplished without premeditation, or hesitancy, or over-haste, or the usual vague ensuing disappointment. And laughing shakily against me, she began to talk again, going back to the earlier part of our conversation as if nothing had come between.

"Isn't it funny?" she said. "You know, all winter all the girls do is talk about last summer, talk and talk about those guys, and I bet you those guys have forgotten even what their names were —"

But I did not want to talk any more, having discovered another force in her that lay side by side with her hostility, that was, in *fact,* just as enveloping and impersonal. After a while I whispered: "Isn't there some place we can go?"

And she answered: "There's a barn in the next field."

She knew the countryside; she had been there before.

We drove back into town after midnight. George and Adelaide were asleep in the back seat. I did not think Lois was asleep, though she kept her eyes closed and did not say anything. I had read somewhere about *Omne animal,* and I was going to tell her, but then I thought she would not know Latin words and would think I was being — oh, pretentious and superior. Afterwards I wished that I had told her. She would have known what it meant.

Afterwards the lassitude of the body, and the cold; the separation. To brush away the bits of hay and tidy ourselves with heavy unconnected movements, to come out of the barn and find the moon gone down, but the flat stubble fields still there, and the poplar trees, and the stars. To find our same selves, chilled and shaken, who had gone that headlong journey and were here still. To go back to the car and find the others sprawled asleep. That is what it is: *triste. Triste est.*

That headlong journey. Was it like that because it was the first time, because I was a little, strangely drunk? No. It was because of Lois. There are some people who can go only a little way with the act of love, and some others who can go very far, who can make a greater surrender, like the mystics. And Lois, this mystic of love, sat now on the far side of the carseat, looking cold and rumpled, and utterly closed up in herself. All the things I wanted to say to her went clattering emptily through my head. *Come and see you again — Remember — Love —* I could not say any of these things. They would not seem even half-true across the space that had come between us. I thought: I will say something to her before the next tree, the next telephone pole. But I did not. I only drove faster, too fast, making the town come nearer.

The street lights bloomed out of the dark trees ahead; there were stirrings in the back seat.

"What time is it?" George said.

"Twenty past twelve."

"We musta finished that bottle. I don't feel so good. Oh, Christ, I don't feel so good. How do you feel?"

"Fine."

"Fine, eh? Feel like you finished your education tonight, eh? That how you feel? Is yours asleep? Mine is."

"I am not," said Adelaide drowsily. "Where's my belt? George — oh.

Now where's my other shoe? It's early for Saturday night, isn't it? We could go and get something to eat.''

''I don't feel like food,'' George said. ''I gotta get some sleep. Gotta get up early tomorrow and go to church with my mother.''

''Yeah, I know,'' said Adelaide, disbelieving, though not too ill-humoured. ''You could've anyways bought me a hamburger!''

I had driven around to Lois's house. Lois did not open her eyes until the car stopped.

She sat still a moment, and then pressed her hands down over the skirt of her dress, flattening it out. She did not look at me. I moved to kiss her, but she seemed to draw slightly away, and I felt that there had after all been something fraudulent and theatrical about this final gesture. She was not like that.

George said to Adelaide: ''Where do you live? You live near here?''

''Yeah. Half a block down.''

''Okay. How be you get out here too? We gotta get home sometime tonight.''

He kissed her and both the girls got out.

I started the car. We began to pull away, George settling down on the back seat to sleep. And then we heard the female voice calling after us, the loud, crude, female voice, abusive and forlorn:

''Thanks for the ride!''

It was not Adelaide calling; it was Lois.

V.S. NAIPAUL

A Trinidadian born in 1932, who emigrated to England in 1950, an Oxonian, a novelist, a reporter, and the winner of such prestigious awards as the Hawthornden and Booker Prizes, Vidiadhar Surajprasad Naipaul is a man of extraordinary talent and complex motivations. Profoundly influenced by both his Indian and West Indian heritages, he yet finds India and Trinidad to be constraining environments; and in his travel books (among them, *The Middle Passage*, 1962, and *An Area of Darkness*, 1964) he shrewdly observes the details of life in the two societies and broods over his own sense of alienation from them. From one vantage point, such "exile" can be seen as a reflection of the Caribbean predicament; that of societies founded by exiles and historically uncertain of their allegiances and identities: the acute consciousness of being alive and alone, the laconic acceptance of the fugitive joys and persistent sadness of life, the alternately grim and wry rendering of a society that cannot locate or cannot believe in a sustaining code of values. Naipaul's characteristically tragicomic tone catches at exactly this ambivalence.

The most lighthearted of his works are early books—the sketches of *Miguel Street* (1959) and the novel *The Mystic Masseur* (1957). But the vein of dislocating irony that occurs even here has grown larger with each succeeding work: *A House for Mr. Biswas* (1961), an inventive portrait of Trinidad domestic crises and individual pride; *A Flag on the Island* (1967), from which "My Aunt Gold Teeth" is taken; *The Mimic Men* (1967), about middle-class drive and human emptiness; *In a Free State* (1971), a collection of stories and journal entries that explores the dimensions of freedom in the mind and the modern world. Reading the present and recognizing the hand of history in shaping it constitute for him a kind of psychological burden, which his writing addresses but refuses to pretend to resolve. Accompanying this intellectual development is an increasing stylistic skill. Naipaul's incisive portraits, his intelligent understanding of human behavior, and his powers of rendering intense awareness have made him one of the most significant modern prose writers and the most accomplished to have emerged thus far from the nations of the Caribbean.

FOR FURTHER READING

Robert D. Hamner, ed. *Critical Perspectives on V.S. Naipaul* (Washington: Three Continents, 1977).

V.S. Naipaul, *The Overcrowded Barracoon and Other Articles* (London: Andre Deutsch, 1972).

V.S. Naipaul and Ian Hamilton, "Without a Place," *Times Literary Supplement*, 30 August 1971, pp. 897–98.

William Walsh, *V.S. Naipaul* (Edinburgh: Oliver & Boyd, 1973).

MY AUNT GOLD TEETH

I never knew her real name and it is quite likely that she did have one, though I never heard her called anything but Gold Teeth. She did, indeed, have gold teeth. She had sixteen of them. She had married early and she had married well, and shortly after her marriage she exchanged her perfectly sound teeth for gold ones, to announce to the world that her husband was a man of substance.

Even without her gold teeth my aunt would have been noticeable. She was short, scarely five foot, and she was very fat. If you saw her in silhouette you would have found it difficult to know whether she was facing you or whether she was looking sideways.

She ate little and prayed much. Her family being Hindu, and her husband being a pundit, she, too, was an orthodox Hindu. Of Hinduism she knew little apart from the ceremonies and the taboos, and this was enough for her. Gold Teeth saw God as a Power, and religious ritual as a means of harnessing that Power for great practical good, her good.

I may have given the impression that Gold Teeth prayed because she wanted to be less fat. The fact was that Gold Teeth had no children and she was almost forty. It was her childlessness, not her fat, that oppressed her, and she prayed for the curse to be removed. She was willing to try any means — any ritual, any prayer — in order to trap and channel the supernatural Power.

And so it was that she began to indulge in surreptitious Christian practices.

She was living at the time in a country village called Cunupia, in County Caroni. Here the Canadian Mission had long waged war against the Indian heathen, and saved many. But Gold Teeth stood firm. The Minister of Cunupia expended his Presbyterian piety on her; so did the headmaster of the Mission school. But all in vain. At no time was Gold Teeth persuaded even to think about being converted. The idea horrified her. Her father had been in his day one of the best-known Hindu pundits, and even now her husband's fame as a pundit, as a man who could read and write Sanskrit, had spread far beyond Cunupia. She was in no doubt whatsoever the Hindus were the best people in the world, and that Hinduism was a superior religion. She was willing to select, modify and incorporate alien eccentricities into her worship; but to abjure her own faith — never!

Presbyterianism was not the only danger the good Hindu had to face in Cunupia. Besides, of course, the ever-present threat of open Muslim aggression, the Catholics were to be reckoned with. Their pamphlets were everywhere and it was hard to avoid them. In them Gold Teeth read of novenas and rosaries, of squads of saints and angels. These were things she understood and could even sympathize with, and they encouraged her to seek further. She read of the mysteries and the miracles, of penances and indulgences. Her scepticism sagged, and yielded to a quickening, if reluctant, enthusiasm.

One morning she took the train for the County town of Chaguanas, three miles, two stations and twenty minutes away. The Church of St Philip and St James in Chaguanas stands imposingly at the end of the Caroni Savannah Road, and although Gold Teeth knew Chaguanas well, all she knew of the church was that it had a clock, at which she had glanced on her way to the railway station nearby. She had hitherto been far more interested in the drab ochre-washed edifice opposite, which was the police station.

She carried herself into the churchyard, awed by her own temerity, feeling like an explorer in a land of cannibals. To her relief, the church was empty. It was not as terrifying as she had expected. In the gilt and images and the resplendent cloths she found much that reminded her of her Hindu temple. Her eyes caught a discreet sign: CANDLES TWO CENTS EACH. She undid the knot in the end of her veil, where she kept her money, took out three cents, popped them into the box, picked up a candle and muttered a prayer in Hindustani. A brief moment of elation gave way to a sense of guilt, and she was suddenly anxious to get away from the church as fast as her weight would let her.

She took a bus home, and hid the candle in her chest of drawers. She had half feared that her husband's Brahminical flair for clairvoyance would have uncovered the reason for her trip to Chaguanas. When after four days, which she spent in an ecstasy of prayer, her husband had mentioned nothing, Gold Teeth thought it safe to burn the candle. She burned it secretly at night, before her Hindu images, and sent up, as she thought, prayers of double efficacy.

Every day her religious schizophrenia grew, and presently she began wearing a crucifix. Neither her husband nor her neighbours knew she did so. The chain was lost in the billows of fat around her neck, and the crucifix was itself buried in the valley of her gargantuan breasts. Later she acquired two holy pictures, one of the Virgin Mary, the other of the crucifixion, and took care to conceal them from her husband. The prayers she offered to these Christian things filled her with new hope and buoyancy. She became an addict of Christianity.

Then her husband, Ramprasad, fell ill.

Ramprasad's sudden, unaccountable illness alarmed Gold Teeth. It was, she knew, no ordinary illness, and she knew, too, that her religious transgression was the cause. The District Medical Officer at Chaguanas said it was diabetes, but Gold Teeth knew better. To be on the safe side, though, she used the insulin he prescribed and, to be even safer, she consulted Ganesh Pundit, the masseur with mystic leanings, celebrated as a faith-healer.

Ganesh came all the way from Fuente Grove to Cunupia. He came in great humility, anxious to serve Gold Teeth's husband, for Gold Teeth's husband was a Brahmin among Brahmins, *a Panday*, a man who knew all five Vedas; while he, Ganesh, was a mere *Chaubay* and knew only four.

With spotless white *koortah,*[*] his dhoti[†] cannily tied, and a tasselled green scarf as a concession to elegance, Ganesh exuded the confidence of the professional mystic. He looked at the sick man, observed his pallor, sniffed the air. "This man," he said, "is bewitched. Seven spirits are upon him."

He was telling Gold Teeth nothing she didn't know. She had known from the first that there were spirits in the affair, but she was glad that Ganesh had ascertained their number.

"But you mustn't worry," Ganesh added. "We will 'tie' the house — in spiritual bonds — and no spirit will be able to come in."

Then, without being asked, Gold Teeth brought out a blanket, folded it, placed it on the floor and invited Ganesh to sit on it. Next she brought him a brass jar of fresh water, a mango leaf and a plate full of burning charcoal.

"Bring me some ghee," Ganesh said, and after Gold Teeth had done so, he set to work. Muttering continuously in Hindustani he sprinkled the water from the brass jar around him with the mango leaf. Then he melted the ghee in the fire and the charcoal hissed so sharply that Gold Teeth could not make out his words. Presently he rose and said, "You must put some of the ash of this fire on your husband's forehead, but if he doesn't want you to do that, mix it with his food. You must keep the water in this jar and place it every night before your front door."

Gold teeth pulled her veil over her forehead.

Ganesh coughed. "That," he said, rearranging his scarf, "is all. There is nothing more I can do. God will do the rest."

He refused payment for his services. It was enough honour, he said, for a man as humble as he was to serve Pundit Ramprasad, and she, Gold Teeth, had been singled out by fate to be the spouse of such a worthy man. Gold Teeth received the impression that Ganesh spoke from a first-hand knowledge of fate and its designs, and her heart, buried deep down under inches of mortal, flabby flesh, sank a little.

"Baba," she said hesitantly, "revered Father, I have something to say to you." But she couldn't say anything more and Ganesh, seeing this, filled his eyes with charity and love.

"What is it, my child?"

"I have done a great wrong, Baba."

"What sort of wrong?" he asked, and his tone indicated that Gold Teeth could do no wrong.

"I have prayed to Christian things."

And to Gold Teeth's surprise, Ganesh chuckled benevolently. "And do you think God minds, daughter? There is only one God and differ-

---

Koortah = long shirt.
†Dhoti = loincloth.

ent people pray to Him in different ways. It doesn't matter how you pray, but God is pleased if you pray at all.''

''So it is not because of me that my husband has fallen ill?''

''No, to be sure, daughter.''

In his professional capacity Ganesh was consulted by people of many faiths, and with the licence of the mystic he had exploited the commodiousness of Hinduism, and made room for all beliefs. In this way he had many clients, as he called them, many satisfied clients.

Henceforward Gold Teeth not only pasted Ramprasad's pale forehead with the sacred ash Ganesh had prescribed, but mixed substantial amounts with his food. Ramprasad's appetite, enormous even in sickness, diminished; and he shortly entered into a visible and alarming decline that mystified his wife.

She fed him more ash than before, and when it was exhausted and Ramprasad perilously macerated, she fell back on the Hindu wife's last resort. She took her husband home to her mother. That venerable lady, my grandmother, lived with us in Port-of-Spain.

Ramprasad was tall and skeletal, and his face was grey. The virile voice that had expounded a thousand theological points and recited a hundred *puranas** was now a wavering whisper. We cooped him up in a room called, oddly, ''the pantry.'' It had never been used as a pantry and one can only assume that the architect had so designated it some forty years before. It was a tiny room. If you wished to enter the pantry you were compelled, as soon as you opened the door, to climb on to the bed: it fitted the room to a miracle. The lower half of the walls were concrete, the upper close lattice-work; there were no windows.

My grandmother had her doubts about the suitability of the room for a sick man. She was worried about the lattice-work. It let in air and light, and Ramprasad was not going to die from these things if she could help it. With cardboard, oil-cloth and canvas she made the lattice-work air-proof and light-proof.

And, sure enough, within a week Ramprasad's appetite returned, insatiable and insistent as before. My grandmother claimed all the credit for this, though Gold Teeth knew that the ash she had fed him had not been without effect. Then she realized with horror that she had ignored a very important thing. The house in Cunupia had been tied and no spirits could enter, but the house in the city had been given no such protection and any spirit could come and go as it chose. The problem was pressing.

Ganesh was out of the question. By giving his services free he had made it impossible for Gold Teeth to call him in again. But thinking in this way of Ganesh, she remembered his words: ''It doesn't matter how you pray, but God is pleased if you pray at all.''

Why not, then, bring Christianity into play again?

Puranas = Hindu scriptures.

She didn't want to take any chances this time. She decided to tell Ramprasad.

He was propped up in bed, and eating. When Gold Teeth opened the door he stopped eating and blinked at the unwonted light. Gold Teeth, stepping into the doorway and filling it, shadowed the room once more and he went on eating. She placed the palms of her hands on the bed. It creaked.

"Man," she said.

Ramprasad continued to eat.

"Man," she said in English, "I thinking about going to the church to pray. You never know, and it better to be on the safe side. After all, the house ain't tied —"

"I don't want you to pray in no church," he whispered, in English too.

Gold Teeth did the only thing she could do. She began to cry.

Three days in succession she asked his permission to go to church, and his opposition weakened in the face of her tears. He was now, besides, too weak to oppose anything. Although his appetite had returned, he was still very ill and very weak, and every day his condition became worse.

On the fourth day he said to Gold Teeth, "Well, pray to Jesus and go to church, if it will put your mind at rest."

And Gold Teeth straight away set about putting her mind at rest. Every morning she took the trolley-bus to the Holy Rosary Church, to offer worship in her private way. Then she was emboldened to bring a crucifix and pictures of the Virgin and the Messiah into the house. We were all somewhat worried by this, but Gold Teeth's religious nature was well known to us; her husband was a learned pundit and when all was said and done this was an emergency, a matter of life and death. So we could do nothing but look on. Incense and camphor and ghee burned now before the likeness of Krishna and Shiva as well as Mary and Jesus. Gold Teeth revealed an appetite for prayer that equalled her husband's for food, and we marvelled at both, if only because neither prayer nor food seemed to be of any use to Ramprasad.

One evening, shortly after bell and gong and conch-shell had announced that Gold Teeth's official devotions were almost over, a sudden chorus of lamentation burst over the house, and I was summoned to the room reserved for prayer. "Come quickly, something dreadful has happened to your aunt."

The prayer-room, still heavy with fumes of incense, presented an extraordinary sight. Before the Hindu shrine, flat on her face, Gold Teeth lay prostrate, rigid as a sack of flour. I had only seen Gold Teeth standing or sitting, and the aspect of Gold Teeth prostrate, so novel and so grotesque, was disturbing.

My grandmother, an alarmist by nature, bent down and put her ear to the upper half of the body on the floor. "I don't seem to hear her heart," she said.

We were all somewhat terrified. We tried to lift Gold Teeth but she seemed as heavy as lead. Then, slowly, the body quivered. The flesh beneath the clothes rippled, then billowed, and the children in the room sharpened their shrieks. Instinctively we all stood back from the body and waited to see what was going to happen. Gold Teeth's hand began to pound the floor and at the same time she began to gurgle.

My grandmother had grasped the situation. "She's got the spirit," she said.

At the word "spirit," the children shrieked louder, and my grandmother slapped them into silence.

The gurgling resolved itself into words pronounced with a lingering ghastly quaver. "Hail Mary, Hare Ram," Gold Teeth said, "the snakes are after me. Everywhere snakes. Seven snakes. Rama! Rama! Full of grace. Seven spirits leaving Cunupia by the four-o'clock train for Port-of-Spain."

My grandmother and my mother listened eagerly, their faces lit up with pride. I was rather ashamed at the exhibition, and annoyed with Gold Teeth for putting me into a fright. I moved towards the door.

"Who is that going away? Who is the young *caffar*, the unbeliever?" the voice asked abruptly.

"Come back quickly, boy," my grandmother whispered. "Come back and ask her pardon."

I did as I was told.

"It is all right, son," Gold Teeth replied, "you don't know. You are young."

Then the spirit appeared to leave her. She wrenched herself up to a sitting position and wondered why we were all there. For the rest of that evening she behaved as if nothing had happened, and she pretended she didn't notice that everyone was looking at her and treating her with unusual respect.

"I have always said it, and I will say it again," my grandmother said, "that these Christians are very religious people. That is why I encouraged Gold Teeth to pray to Christian things."

Ramprasad died early next morning and we had the announcement on the radio after the local news at one o'clock. Ramprasad's death was the only one announced and so, although it came between commercials, it made some impression. We buried him that afternoon in Mucurapo Cemetery.

As soon as we got back my grandmother said, "I have always said it, and I will say it again: I don't like these Christian things. Ramprasad would have got better if only you, Gold Teeth, had listened to me and not gone running after these Christian things."

Gold Teeth sobbed her assent; and her body squabbered and shook as she confessed the whole story of her trafficking with Christianity. We listened in astonishment and shame. We didn't know that a good

Hindu, and a member of our family, could sink so low. Gold Teeth beat her breast and pulled ineffectually at her long hair and begged to be forgiven. "It is all my fault," she cried. "My own fault, Ma. I fell in a moment of weakness. Then I just couldn't stop."

My grandmother's shame turned to pity. "It's all right, Gold Teeth. Perhaps it was this you needed to bring you back to your senses."

That evening Gold Teeth ritually destroyed every reminder of Christianity in the house.

"You have only yourself to blame," my grandmother said, "if you have no children now to look after you."

ALDEN NOWLAN

Born and educated in Nova Scotia, Alden Nowlan (1933–1983) moved in 1952 to the neighboring province of New Brunswick, where he became editor of the Hartland *Observer*. His Maritime roots go deep, and his insights into the stark details and laconic tempo of rural Maritime life derive from his sympathetic experience of it. Although better known as a poet and playwright than as a short-story writer, he has produced several volumes of prose: a collection of stories, *Miracle at Indian River* (1968), and a novel, *Various Persons Named Kevin O'Brien* (1973), that takes the form of loosely linked episodes in the shifting identity of the title character. Of his many volumes of poetry, *Bread, Wine and Salt* won the Governor-General's Award when it appeared in 1967.

Nowlan's characters typically are constrained by their Calvinist Maritime heritage. Life is dour; authority is firm; and joy is not to be trusted. Yet they are not without humor, nor is the writer without a strong sense of irony as he views their predicament. The portrait of the Evangelical church in "Miracle at Indian River" neither ridicules nor condemns the naïveté it discloses. Relying as heavily as it does on the techniques of the anecdote, however, the story communicates its central joke with broad humor. The exaggeration of the tall tale is there, tempered by controlled understatement. The result is a witty satire of a whole way of life, which never loses sight of the realities in which it is founded, and never takes lightly the seriousness with which those realities affect individual human lives.

FOR FURTHER READING

Sandra Djwa, "Alden Nowlan 1933–1983," *Canadian Literature*, no. 101 (Summer 1984): 181–83.

Keith Fraser, "Notes on Alden Nowlan," *Canadian Literature*, no. 45 (Summer 1970): 41–51.

Alden Nowlan, "An Interview with Alden Nowlan," *Fiddlehead* 81 (1969): 5–13.

MIRACLE AT
INDIAN RIVER

This is the story of how mates were chosen for all the marriageable young men and women in the congregation of the Fire-Baptized Tabernacle of the Living God in Indian River, New Brunswick. It is a true story, more or less, and whether it is ridiculous or pathetic or even oddly beautiful depends a good deal on the mood you're in when you read it.

Indian River is one of those little places that don't really exist, except in the minds of their inhabitants. Passing through it as a stranger you might not even notice that it is there. Or if you did notice it, you'd think it was no different from thousands of other little backwoods communities in Canada and the United States. But you'd be wrong. Indian River, like every community large and small, has a character all its own.

The inhabitants of Indian River are pure Dutch, although they don't know it. Their ancestors settled in New Amsterdam more than three hundred years ago and migrated to New Brunswick after the American Revolution. But they've always been isolated, always intermarried, so that racially they're probably more purely Dutch than most of the Dutch in Holland, even though they've long ago forgotten the language and few of them could locate the Netherlands on a map.

The village contains a railway station which hasn't been used since 1965 when the CNR discontinued passenger service in that part of northwestern New Brunswick, a one-room school that was closed five years ago when the government began using buses to carry local children to the regional school in Cumberland Centre, a general store and two churches: St. Edward's Anglican, which used to be attended by the station agent, the teacher and the store-keeper, and the Fire-Baptized Tabernacle of the Living God, attended by practically everyone else in Indian River.

The tabernacle, formerly a barracks, was bought from the Department of National Defence and brought in on a flatcar. "Jesus Saves" is painted in big red letters over the door. A billboard beside the road warns drivers to prepare to meet their God. There is an evergreen forest to the north, a brook full of speckled trout to the west and, in the east, a pasture in which a dozen Holstein cattle and a team of Clydesdale horses graze together. The pastor, Rev. Horace Zwicker, his wife, Myrtle, and their five children live in a flat behind the pulpit.

Pastor Zwicker was born in Indian River and, before he was called of God to the ministry, was a door-to-door salesman of magazine subscriptions and patent medicines, chauffeur for a chiropractor, and accordionist in a hillbilly band that toured the Maritime Provinces and Maine.

Services are held in the tabernacle Wednesday night, Sunday morning and Sunday night. During the summer evangelists arrive, usually from Alabama, Georgia or Tennessee, and then there are services every night of the week. Almost every one of the evangelists has some sort of speciality, like painting a pastel portrait of Christ as he delivers his sermon or playing "The Old Rugged Cross" on an instrument made from empty whiskey bottles. Once there was a man with a long black beard and shoulder-length hair who claimed to have gone to school with Hitler; another time a professed ex-convict named Bent-Knee Benjamin preached in striped pajamas, a ball and chain fastened to his leg.

Fire-Baptized people worry a good deal about sin — mostly innocent little rural sins like smoking, drinking, watching television and going to the movies. Fire-Baptized women, of whom there are several thousands in northwestern New Brunswick, are easy to identify on the streets of towns like Woodstock and Fredericton because they don't use cosmetics and wear their hair in a sort of Oregon Trail bun at the backs of their necks. Fire-Baptized girls are made to dress somewhat the way Elizabeth dressed before she met Philip. There is a legend, invented presumably by Anglicans and Catholics, that Fire-Baptized girls are extraordinarily agreeable and inordinately passionate.

A few years ago there happened to be an unusually large number of unmarried young men and women in Indian River.

Pastor Zwicker frequently discussed this matter with his Lord.

"Lord," he said, "You know as well as I do that it isn't good to have a pack of hot young bucks and fancy-free young females running around loose. Like Paul says, those who don't marry are apt to burn, and when they've burned long enough they'll do just about anything to put the fire out. Now, tell me straight, Lord, what do You figure I should do about it?"

The Lord offered various suggestions and Pastor Zwicker tried them all.

He had long and prayerful conversations with each young man and woman. He told Harris Brandt, for example, that Rebecca Vaneyck was not only a sweet Christian girl, pure and obedient, she made the best blueberry pie of any cook her age in Connaught County. "Never cared much for blueberries myself, Pastor," Harris said. He told Rebecca that Harris was a stout Christian youth who wouldn't get drunk, except if he were sorely tempted of the devil on election day, and wouldn't beat her unless she really deserved it. And she replied: "But, Pastor, he has such bad teeth!"

His conversations with the others were equally fruitless. The Lord advised stronger methods.

"Look here, Brother," the pastor admonished young Francis Witt's father, "it's time that young fellow of yours settled down and got himself a wife. I was talking it over with the Lord just the other night. Now, as you're well aware, Brother, the Scriptures tell us that a son should be obedient to his father. So if I was you —"

"Need the boy," replied the father. "Couldn't run this place without him. Talked to the Lord about it myself. Wife did too. Lord said maybe Francis wouldn't ever get married. Might be an old bachelor like his Uncle Ike. Nothing wrong in that, Lord said."

Other parents made other excuses. If even one couple had responded favourably to his efforts, Pastor Zwicker might have decided that he was worrying himself and the Lord needlessly. But to be met everywhere by disinterest! It was unnatural. Was the devil turning his flock into a herd of Papist celibates?

He had talked once with an escapee from a nunnery in Ireland. A tunnel to the rectory. Lecherous old men, naked under their black nightgowns. Babies' bones in the walls.

His body trembled and his soul — although he did not know this and would have been horrified had he known — made the sign of the cross. What was there left for a man of God to do?

God moves in a mysterious way His wonders to perform. The following Sunday night the power of the Holy Ghost shook the tabernacle to its very foundations. The Day of Pentecost described in the Acts of the Apostles was reenacted with more fervour than ever before in Indian River.

Pastor Zwicker had summoned a guitarist from Houlton, Maine, and a fiddler from Fredericton. He himself played the accordion and his wife the Jew's harp. Old Sister Rossa was at the piano and little Billy Wagner was sent home to fetch his harmonica and mandolin.

There was music — music even as the pastor laid aside his accordion and preached, music and singing and, as the service progressed, a Jericho dance up and down the aisle.

Later, old men said it was the best sermon they had ever heard. "Brother Zwicker just opened his mouth and let the Lord fill it," they said.

His theme was the sins of the flesh. As near as Woodstock, as near as Fredericton, as near as Presque Isle, half-naked women with painted faces and scented bodies prowled the streets seeking whom they might devour. He had looked upon their naked thighs, observed the voluptuous movements of their rumps, had noted that their nipples were visible through their blouses. In King Square in Saint John he had stepped aside to allow a young lady to precede him onto a bus and had discovered to his horrified amazement that she was not wearing drawers. Saint John was another Babylon where before long men and women would be dancing together naked in the streets.

There was much more of the same kind of thing, interspersed, of course, with many quotations from the Bible, particularly from Genesis, Leviticus and Revelation. The Bible was almost the only book that Pastor Zwicker had ever read and he knew great stretches of it by heart.

"Praise the Lord!" the people shouted. "Hallelujah! Thank you, Jesus!" Old Ike Witt stood on his chair and danced.

"Oh, diddly-doe-dum, diddly-dee-doe-dee," he sang. "Oh, too-row-lou-row-tiddly-lou-do-dee! Glory to Jesus! Diddly-day-dum! Glory to Jesus! Tiddly-lee-tum-tee!''

Matilda Rega threw herself on the floor, laughing and crying, yelling: ''Oh, Jesus! Christ Almighty! Oh, sweet Jesus! God Almighty! Oh, Jesus!''

She began crawling down the aisle toward the altar. The Jericho dancers leapt back and forth across her wriggling body:

We are marching to Zion!
Beautiful, beautiful Zion!
We are marching to Zion,
The beautiful City of God!

Kneeling before the altar, Timothy Fairvort whimpered and slapped his own face, first one cheek, then the other.

''I have sinned,'' he moaned.

SLAP!

''I have lusted in my heart.''

SLAP!

''I will burn in hell if I am not saved.''

SLAP!

''Oh, help me, Jesus.''

SLAP!

The Jericho dancers sang:

Joy, Joy, Joy, There is joy in my heart!
Joy in my heart! Joy in my heart!
Joy, Joy, Joy, There is joy in my heart!
Joy in my heart TODAY!

It was as if the midway of the Fredericton Exhibition, Hank Snow and the Rainbow Ranch Boys, Oral Roberts, Billy Graham, a Salvation Army band, Lester Flatt and Earl Scruggs, Garner Ted Armstrong and a Tory leadership convention were somehow all rolled into one and compressed into the lobby of the Admiral Beatty Hotel in Saint John.

Then it happened.

Sister Zwicker began speaking in an unknown tongue.

''Elohim!'' she yelled. ''Elohim, angaro metalani negat! Gonolariski motono etalo bene! Wanga! Wanga! Angaro talans fo do easta analandanoro!''

''Listen!'' roared the pastor. ''Listen!''

The Jericho dancers sang:

When the saints go marching in!
When the saints go marching in!
How I long to be in that company
When the saints go marching in!

"Elohim!" screamed Myrtle Zwicker. "Wanga! Ortoro ortoro clana estanatoro! Wanga!"

"Listen!" bellowed the pastor. "Listen!"

Others took up the cry. At last the Jericho dancers returned to their seats, exhausted, sweat pouring down their hot, red faces. The music faded away. Old Ike Witt climbed down from his chair. Matilda Rega lay still, quietly sobbing, at the foot of the altar. Timothy Fairvort put his jacket over his head, like a criminal in a newspaper photograph. There was silence except for the voices of the pastor and his wife.

"The Lord is talking to us!" shouted the pastor, who had by now taken off his jacket and tie and unbuttoned his shirt to the waist. "Harken to the voice of the Lord!"

"Elohim!" cried his wife. "Naro talaro eganoto wanga! Tao laro matanotalero. Wanga!"

"It is Egyptian," the pastor explained. "The Lord is addressing us in the language of Pharaoh, the tongue that Joseph spoke when he was a prisoner in the land of Egypt."

"Egyptian," murmured the congregation. "Thank you, Jesus."

"Taro wanga sundaro —"

"The Lord is telling us that His heart is saddened."

"Metizo walla toro delandonaro —"

"His heart is saddened by the disobedience of His people."

"Crena wontano meta kleva sancta danco —"

"The disobedience and perversity of His young people is heavy upon His heart."

"Zalanto wanga —"

"For they have refused to marry and multiply and be fruitful and replenish the earth, as He has commanded them."

"Toronalanta wanga —"

"In His mercy He has chosen to give them one more chance to escape the just punishment for their disobedience."

"Praise His name! Thank you, Jesus!"

"Willo morto innitaro —"

"It is His will that His handmaiden, Rebecca Vaneyck, should become the bride of —"

"Altaro mintanaro —"

"Yes, yes, the bride of Harris Brandt. This is the will of the God of Abraham and of Isaac and of Jacob, for it was He who brought you out of the land of Egypt."

"Yes, yes," chanted the congregation. "It is the Lord's will. Let it be done. Hallelujah!"

Rebecca and Harris were led to the altar. They looked at one another with dazed, wondering faces. After a moment he reached out and took her hand.

Within half an hour, three other couples stood with them. The Lord had revealed His will. Puny mortals such as they had no say in the matter.

The Jericho dancers leapt and cavorted in thanksgiving. So did Ike Witt and Timothy Fairvort, whose face was still hidden by his jacket. He stumbled blindly around the tabernacle, knocking over chairs, singing behind his jacket:

When the roll is called up yonder!
When the roll is called up yonder!
When the roll is called up yonder!
When the roll is called up yonder,
I'll be there!

Pastor Zwicker fanned himself with a copy of *The Fire-Baptized Quarterly.* Next week there would be four marriages in his tabernacle. The Lord's will had been accomplished.

"Thank you, Jesus," he murmured.

Then he remembered Ike Witt and Matilda Rega, the old bachelor and the old maid. Could it be the Lord's will that they, too, should be joined together? He would discuss it with Myrtle. Perhaps next Sunday the Lord would reveal His thoughts about the matter.

JOYCE CAROL OATES

Joyce Carol Oates was born in New York in 1938 and educated at Syracuse University and the University of Wisconsin. After a period in Canada, teaching English at the University of Windsor, she took up a post at Princeton. Her work has received wide critical acclaim, and brought her many awards, including a Guggenheim Fellowship in 1967 and an O. Henry Special Award for Continuing Achievement in 1970. She has written sixteen novels as well as several volumes of poetry and literary criticism, and has had two plays produced on the New York stage; in addition to these successes, her short stories have appeared in many journals and anthologies, and have been published in twelve collections, the most recent of which is *Last Days* (1984).

In her preoccupation with violence, emotional disturbance, and familial conflict, Oates has been likened to Faulkner; and there is undoubtedly a dark, sometimes melodramatic, quality to her writing which recalls the Gothic element in Faulkner's books; her novel *Wonderland* (1971), for example, opens with the shotgun slaying of five people. Many of her characters are ordinary people who, confronted by the apparent senselessness of life, are driven to extremes by fear or frustration; or they are stunned, like Sister Irene in "In the Region of Ice" (*The Wheel of Love*, 1970), by an awareness of human helplessness and isolation. In an exchange of letters with the American writer Joe David Bellamy, Oates wrote: "I believe that the storm of emotion constitutes our human tragedy, if anything does. It's our constant battle with nature (Nature), trying to subdue chaos outside and inside ourselves, occasionally winning small victories, then being swept along by some cataclysmic event of our own making. I feel an enormous sympathy with people who've gone under, who haven't won even the smallest victories. . . ."

FOR FURTHER READING

J.D. Bellamy, "The Dark Lady of American Letters," *Atlantic Monthly* 229 (February 1972): 63–67.

Joanne V. Creighton, *Joyce Carol Oates* (Boston: Twayne, 1979).

Joyce Carol Oates, "Building Tension in the Short Story," *Writer* 79 (June 1966): 11–12; "Background and Foreground in Fiction," *Writer* 80 (August 1967): 11–13.

IN THE REGION OF ICE

Sister Irene was a tall, deft woman in her early thirties. What one could see of her face made a striking impression — serious, hard gray eyes, a long slender nose, a face waxen with thought. Seen at the right time, from the right angle, she was almost handsome. In her past teaching positions she had drawn a little upon the fact of her being young and brilliant and also a nun, but she was beginning to grow out of that.

This was a new university and an entirely new world. She had heard — of course it was true — that the Jesuit administration of this school had hired her at the last moment to save money and to head off the appointment of a man of dubious religious commitment. She had prayed for the necessary energy to get her through this first semester. She had no trouble with teaching itself; once she stood before a classroom she felt herself capable of anything. It was the world immediately outside the classroom that confused and alarmed her, though she let none of this show — the cynicism of her colleagues, the indifference of many of the students, and, above all, the looks she got that told her nothing much would be expected of her because she was a nun. This took energy, strength. At times she had the idea that she was on trial and that the excuses she made to herself about her discomfort were only the common excuses made by guilty people. But in front of a class she had no time to worry about herself or the conflicts in her mind. She became, once and for all, a figure existing only for the benefit of others, an instrument by which facts were communicated.

About two weeks after the semester began, Sister Irene noticed a new student in her class. He was slight and fair-haired, and his face was blank, but not blank by accident, blank on purpose, suppressed and restricted into a dumbness that looked hysterical. She was prepared for him before he raised his hand, and when she saw his arm jerk, as if he had at last lost control of it, she nodded to him without hesitation.

"Sister, how can this be reconciled with Shakespeare's vision in *Hamlet*? How can these opposing views be in the same mind?"

Students glanced at him, mildly surprised. He did not belong in the class, and this was mysterious, but his manner was urgent and blind.

"There is no need to reconcile opposing views," Sister Irene said, leaning forward against the podium. "In one play Shakespeare suggests one vision, in another play another; the plays are not simultaneous creations, and even if they were, we never demand a logical —"

"We must demand a logical consistency," the young man said. "The idea of education is itself predicated upon consistency, order, sanity —"

He had interrupted her, and she hardened her face against him — for his sake, not her own, since she did not really care. But he noticed nothing. "Please see me after class," she said.

After class the young man hurried up to her.

"Sister Irene, I hope you didn't mind my visiting today. I'd heard some things, interesting things," he said. He stared at her, and something in her face allowed him to smile. "I . . . could we talk in your office? Do you have time?"

They walked down to her office. Sister Irene sat at her desk, and the young man sat facing her; for a moment they were self-conscious and silent.

"Well, I suppose you know — I'm a Jew," he said.

Sister Irene stared at him. "Yes?" she said.

"What am I doing at a Catholic university, huh?" He grinned. "That's what you want to know."

She made a vague movement of her hand to show that she had no thoughts on this, nothing at all, but he seemed not to catch it. He was sitting on the edge of the straight-backed chair. She saw that he was young but did not really look young. There were harsh lines on either side of his mouth, as if he had misused that youthful mouth somehow. His skin was almost as pale as hers, his eyes were dark and not quite in focus. He looked at her and through her and around her, as his voice surrounded them both. His voice was a little shrill at times.

"Listen, I did the right thing today — visiting your class! God, what a lucky accident it was; some jerk mentioned you, said you were a good teacher — I thought, what a laugh! These people know about good teachers here? But yes, listen, yes, I'm not kidding — you are good. I mean that."

Sister Irene frowned. "I don't quite understand what all this means."

He smiled and waved aside her formality, as if he knew better. "Listen, I got my B.A. at Columbia, then I came back here to this crappy city. I mean, I did it on purpose, I wanted to come back. I wanted to. I have my reasons for doing things. I'm on a three-thousand-dollar fellowship," he said, and waited for that to impress her. "You know, I could have gone almost anywhere with that fellowship, and I came back home here — my home's in the city — and enrolled here. This was last year. This is my second year. I'm working on a thesis, I mean I was, my master's thesis — but the hell with that. What I want to ask you is this: Can I enroll in your class, is it too late? We have to get special permission if we're late."

Sister Irene felt something nudging her, some uneasiness in him that was pleading with her not to be offended by his abrupt, familiar manner. He seemed to be promising another self, a better self, as if his fair, childish, almost cherubic face were doing tricks to distract her from what his words said.

"Are you in English studies?" she asked.

"I was in history. Listen," he said, and his mouth did something odd, drawing itself down into a smile that made the lines about it deepen like knives, "listen, they kicked me out."

He sat back, watching her. He crossed his legs. He took out a package of cigarettes and offered her one. Sister Irene shook her head, staring at his hands. They were small and stubby and might have belonged to a ten-year-old, and the nails were a strange near-violet color. It took him awhile to extract a cigarette.

"Yeah, kicked me out. What do you think of that?"

"I don't understand."

"My master's thesis was coming along beautifully, and then this bastard—I mean, excuse me, this professor, I won't pollute your office with his name—he started making criticisms, he said some things were unacceptable, he —" The boy leaned forward and hunched his narrow shoulders in a parody of secrecy. "We had an argument. I told him some frank things, things only a broad-minded person could hear about himself. That takes courage, right? He didn't have it! He kicked me out of the master's program, so now I'm coming into English. Literature is greater than history; European history is one big pile of garbage. Sky-high. Filth and rotting corpses, right? Aristotle says that poetry is higher than history; he's right; in your class today I suddenly realized that this is my field, Shakespeare, only Shakespeare is —"

Sister Irene guessed that he was going to say that only Shakespeare was equal to him, and she caught the moment of recognition and hesitation, the half-raised arm, the keen, frowning forehead, the narrowed eyes; then he thought better of it and did not end the sentence. "The students in your class are mainly negligible, I can tell you that. You're new here, and I've been here a year—I would have finished my studies last year but my father got sick, he was hospitalized, I couldn't take exams and it was a mess—but I'll make it through English in one year or drop dead. I can do it, I can do anything. I'll take six courses at once —" He broke off, breathless. Sister Irene tried to smile. "All right then, it's settled? You'll let me in? Have I missed anything so far?"

He had no idea of the rudeness of his question. Sister Irene, feeling suddenly exhausted, said, "I'll give you a syllabus of the course."

"Fine! Wonderful!"

He got to his feet eagerly. He looked through the schedule, muttering to himself, making favorable noises. It struck Sister Irene that she was making a mistake to let him in. There were these moments when one had to make an intelligent decision. . . . But she was sympathetic with him, yes. She was sympathetic with something about him.

She found out his name the next day: Allen Weinstein.

After this she came to her Shakespeare class with a sense of excitement. It became clear to her at once that Weinstein was the most intelligent student in the class. Until he had enrolled, she had not understood what was lacking, a mind that could appreciate her own. Within a week his jagged, protean mind had alienated the other students, and though he sat in the center of the class, he seemed totally alone, encased by a miniature world of his own. When he spoke of the "frenetic humanism of the High Renaissance," Sister Irene dreaded the raised eyebrows and mocking smiles of the other students, who no longer bothered to look at Weinstein. She wanted to defend him, but she never did, because there was something rude and dismal about his knowledge; he used it like a weapon, talking passionately of Nietzsche and Goethe and Freud until Sister Irene would be forced to close discussion.

In meditation, alone, she often thought of him. When she tried to talk about him to a young nun, Sister Carlotta, everything sounded gross. "But no, he's an excellent student," she insisted. "I'm very grateful to have him in class. It's just that . . . he thinks ideas are real." Sister Carlotta, who loved literature also, had been forced to teach grade-school arithmetic for the last four years. That might have been why she said, a little sharply, "You don't think ideas are real?"

Sister Irene acquiesced with a smile, but of course she did not think so: only reality is real.

When Weinstein did not show up for class on the day the first paper was due, Sister Irene's heart sank, and the sensation was somehow a familiar one. She began her lecture and kept waiting for the door to open and for him to hurry noisily back to his seat, grinning an apology toward her — but nothing happened.

If she had been deceived by him, she made herself think angrily, it was as a teacher and not as a woman. He had promised her nothing.

Weinstein appeared the next day near the steps of the liberal arts building. She heard someone running behind her, a breathless exclamation: "Sister Irene!" She turned and saw him, panting and grinning in embarrassment. He wore a dark-blue suit with a necktie, and he looked, despite his childish face, like a little old man; there was something oddly precarious and fragile about him. "Sister Irene, I owe you an apology, right?" He raised his eyebrows and smiled a sad, forlorn, yet irritatingly conspiratorial smile. "The first paper — not in on time, and I know what your rules are. . . . You won't accept late papers, I know — that's good discipline, I'll do that when I teach too. But, unavoidably, I was unable to come to school yesterday. There are many — many —" He gulped for breath, and Sister Irene had the startling sense of seeing the real Weinstein stare out at her, a terrified prisoner behind the confident voice. "There are many complications in family life. Perhaps you are unaware — I mean —"

She did not like him, but she felt this sympathy, something tugging and nagging at her the way her parents had competed for her love so many years before. They had been whining, weak people, and out of their wet need for affection, the girl she had been (her name was Yvonne) had emerged stronger than either of them, contemptuous of tears because she had seen so many. But Weinstein was different; he was not simply weak — perhaps he was not weak at all — but his strength was confused and hysterical. She felt her customary rigidity as a teacher begin to falter. "You may turn your paper in today if you have it," she said, frowning.

Weinstein's mouth jerked into an incredulous grin. "Wonderful! Marvelous!" he said. "You are very understanding, Sister Irene, I must say. I must say . . . I didn't expect, really . . ." He was fumbling in a shabby old briefcase for the paper. Sister Irene waited. She was prepared for another of his excuses, certain that he did not have the paper, when he suddenly straightened up and handed her something. "Here! I took the liberty of writing thirty pages instead of just fifteen," he said. He was obviously quite excited; his cheeks were mottled pink and white. "You may disagree violently with my interpretation — I expect you to, in fact I'm counting on it — but let me warn you, I have the exact proof, right here in the play itself!" He was thumping at a book, his voice growing louder and shriller. Sister Irene, startled, wanted to put her hand over his mouth and soothe him.

"Look," he said breathlessly, "may I talk with you? I have a class now I hate, I loathe, I can't bear to sit through! Can I talk with you instead?"

Because she was nervous, she stared at the title page of the paper: " 'Erotic Melodies in *Romeo and Juliet*' by Allen Weinstein, Jr."

"All right?" he said. "Can we walk around here? Is it all right? I've been anxious to talk with you about some things you said in class."

She was reluctant, but he seemed not to notice. They walked slowly along the shaded campus paths. Weinstein did all the talking, of course, and Sister Irene recognized nothing in his cascade of words that she had mentioned in class. "The humanist must be committed to the totality of life," he said passionately. "This is the failing one finds everywhere in the academic world! I found it in New York and I found it here and I'm no ingénu, I don't go around with my mouth hanging open — I'm experienced, look, I've been to Europe, I've lived in Rome! I went everywhere in Europe except Germany, I don't talk about Germany . . . Sister Irene, think of the significant men in the last century, the men who've changed the world! Jews, right? Marx, Freud, Einstein! Not that I believe Marx, Marx is a madman . . . and Freud, no, my sympathies are with spiritual humanism. I believe that the Jewish race is the exclusive . . . the exclusive, what's the word, the exclusive means by which humanism will be extended. . . . Humanism begins by excluding the Jew, and now," he said with a high, surprised laugh, "the Jew will perfect it. After the Nazis, only the Jew is authorized to understand humanism, its limitations and its possibilities. So, I say that the humanist is committed to life in its totality and not just to his profession! The religious person is totally religious, he is his religion! What else? I recognize in you a humanist and a religious person —"

But he did not seem to be talking to her or even looking at her.

"Here, read this," he said. "I wrote it last night." It was a long free-verse poem, typed on a typewriter whose ribbon was worn out.

"There's this trouble with my father, a wonderful man, a lovely man, but his health — his strength is fading, do you see? What must it be to him to see his son growing up? I mean, I'm a man now, he's getting old, weak, his health is bad — it's hell, right? I sympathize with him. I'd do anything for him, I'd cut open my veins, anything for a father — right? That's why I wasn't in school yesterday," he said, and his voice dropped for the last sentence, as if he had been dragged back to earth by a fact.

Sister Irene tried to read the poem, then pretended to read it. A jumble of words dealing with "life" and "death" and "darkness" and "love." "What do you think?" Weinstein said nervously, trying to read it over her shoulder and crowding against her.

"It's very . . . passionate," Sister Irene said.

This was the right comment; he took the poem back from her in silence, his face flushed with excitement. "Here, at this school, I have few people to talk with. I haven't shown anyone else that poem." He looked at her with his dark, intense eyes, and Sister Irene felt them focus upon her. She was terrified at what he was trying to do — he was trying to force her into a human relationship.

"Thank you for your paper," she said, turning away.

When he came the next day, ten minutes late, he was haughty and disdainful. He had nothing to say and sat with his arms folded. Sister Irene took back with her to the convent a feeling of betrayal and confusion. She had been hurt. It was absurd, and yet — She spent too much time thinking about him, as if he were somehow a kind of crystallization of her own loneliness; but she had no right to think so much of him. She did not want to think of him or of her loneliness. But Weinstein did so much more than think of his predicament: he embodied it, he acted it out, and that was perhaps why he fascinated her. It was as if he were doing a dance for her, a dance of shame and agony and delight, and so long as he did it, she was safe. She felt embarrassment for him, but also anxiety; she wanted to protect him. When the dean of the graduate school questioned her about Weinstein's work, she insisted that he was an "excellent" student, though she knew the dean had not wanted to hear that.

She prayed for guidance, she spent hours on her devotions, she was closer to her vocation than she had been for some years. Life at the convent became tinged with unreality, a misty distortion that took its tone from the glowering skies of the city at night, identical smokestacks ranged against the clouds and giving to the sky the excrement of the populated and successful earth. This city was not her city, this world was not her world. She felt no pride in knowing this, it was a fact. The little convent was not like an island in the center of this noisy world, but rather a kind of hole or crevice the world did not bother with, something of no interest. The convent's rhythm of life had nothing to do with the world's rhythm, it did not violate or alarm it in any way. Sister Irene tried to draw together the fragments of her life and synthesize them somehow in her vocation as a nun: she was a nun, she was recognized as a nun and had given herself happily to that life, she had a name, a place, she had dedicated her superior intelligence to the Church, she worked without pay and without expecting gratitude, she had given up pride, she did not think of herself but only of her work and her vocation, she did not think of anything external to these, she saturated herself daily in the knowledge that she was involved in the mystery of Christianity.

A daily terror attended this knowledge, however, for she sensed herself being drawn by that student, that Jewish boy, into a relationship she was not ready for. She wanted to cry out in fear that she was being forced into the role of a Christian, and what did that mean? What could her studies tell her? What could the other nuns tell her? She was alone, no one could help; he was making her into a Christian, and to her that was a mystery, a thing of terror, something others slipped on the way they slipped on their clothes, casually and thoughtlessly, but to her a magnificent and terrifying wonder.

For days she carried Weinstein's paper, marked A, around with her; he did not come to class. One day she checked with the graduate office and was told that Weinstein had called in to say his father was ill and that he would not be able to attend classes for a while. "He's strange, I remember him," the secretary said. "He missed all his exams last spring and made a lot of trouble. He was in and out of here every day."

So there was no more of Weinstein for a while, and Sister Irene stopped expecting him to hurry into class. Then, one morning, she found a letter from him in her mailbox.

He had printed it in black ink, very carefully, as if he had not trusted handwriting. The return address was in bold letters that, like his voice, tried to grab onto her: Birchcrest Manor. Somewhere north of the city. "Dear Sister Irene," the block letters said, "I am doing well here and have time for reading and relaxing. The Manor is delightful. My doctor here is an excellent, intelligent man who has time for me, unlike my former doctor. If you have time, you might drop in on my father, who worries about me too much, I think, and explain to him what my condition is. He doesn't seem to understand. I feel about this new life the way that boy, what's his name, in *Measure for Measure*, feels about the prospects of a different life; you remember what he says to his sister when she visits him in prison, how he is looking forward to an escape into another world. Perhaps you could *explain* this to my father and he would stop worrying." The letter ended with the father's name and address, in letters that were just a little too big. Sister Irene, walking slowly down the corridor as she read the letter, felt her eyes cloud over with tears. She was cold with fear, it was something she had never experienced before. She knew what Weinstein was trying to tell her, and the desperation of his attempt made it all the more pathetic; he did not deserve this, why did God allow him to suffer so?

She read through Claudio's speech to his sister, in *Measure for Measure:*

Ay but to die, and go we know not where;
To lie in cold obstruction and to rot;
This sensible warm motion to become
A kneaded clod; and the delighted spirit
To bathe in fiery floods, or to reside
In thrilling region of thick-ribbed ice,
To be imprison'd in the viewless winds
And blown with restless violence round about
The pendent world; or to be worse than worst
Of those that lawless and incertain thought
Imagines howling! 'Tis too horrible!
The weariest and most loathed worldly life
That age, ache, penury, and imprisonment
Can lay on nature is a paradise
To what we fear of death.

Sister Irene called the father's number that day. "Allen Weinstein residence, who may I say is calling?" a woman said, bored. "May I speak to Mr. Weinstein? It's urgent — about his son," Sister Irene said. There was a pause at the other end. "You want to talk to his mother, maybe?" the woman said. "His mother? Yes, his mother, then. Please. It's very important."

She talked with this strange, unsuspected woman, a disembodied voice that suggested absolutely no face, and insisted upon going over that afternoon. The woman was nervous, but Sister Irene, who was a university professor, after all, knew enough to hide her own nervousness. She kept waiting for the woman to say, "Yes, Allen has mentioned you . . ." but nothing happened.

She persuaded Sister Carlotta to ride over with her. This urgency of hers was something they were all amazed by. They hadn't suspected that the set of her gray eyes could change to this blurred, distracted alarm, this sense of mission that seemed to have come to her from nowhere. Sister Irene drove across the city in the late afternoon traffic, with the high whining noises from residential streets where trees were being sawed down in pieces. She understood now the secret, sweet wildness that Christ must have felt, giving himself for man, dying for the billions of men who would never know of him and never understand the sacrifice. For the first time she approached the realization of that great act. In her troubled mind the city traffic was jumbled and yet oddly coherent, an image of the world that was always out of joint with what was happening in it, its inner history struggling with its external spectacle. This sacrifice of Christ's, so mysterious and legendary now, almost lost in time — it was that by which Christ transcended both God and man at one moment, more than man because of his fate to do what no other man could do, and more than God because no god could suffer as he did. She felt a flicker of something close to madness.

She drove nervously, uncertainly, afraid of missing the street and afraid of finding it too, for while one part of her rushed forward to confront these people who had betrayed their son, another part of her would have liked nothing so much as to be waiting as usual for the summons to dinner, safe in her room. . . . When she found the street and turned onto it, she was in a state of breathless excitement. Here lawns were bright green and marred with only a few leaves, magically clean, and the houses were enormous and pompous, a mixture of styles: ranch houses, colonial houses, French country houses, white-bricked wonders with curving glass and clumps of birch trees somehow encircled by white concrete. Sister Irene stared as if she had blundered into another world. This was a kind of heaven, and she was too shabby for it.

The Weinstein's house was the strangest one of all: it looked like a small Alpine lodge, with an inverted-V-shaped front entrance. Sister Irene drove up the black-topped driveway and let the car slow to a stop; she told Sister Carlotta she would not be long.

At the door she was met by Weinstein's mother, a small, nervous woman with hands like her son's. "Come in, come in," the woman said. She had once been beautiful, that was clear, but now in missing beauty she was not handsome or even attractive but looked ruined and perplexed, the misshapen swelling of her white-blond professionally set hair like a cap lifting up from her surprised face. "He'll be right in. Allen?" she called, "our visitor is here." They went into the living room. There was a grand piano at one end and an organ at the other. In between were scatterings of brilliant modern furniture in conversational groups, and several puffed-up white rugs on the polished floor. Sister Irene could not stop shivering.

"Professor, it's so strange, but let me say when the phone rang I had a feeling—I had a feeling," the woman said, with damp eyes. Sister Irene sat, and the woman hovered about her. "Should I call you Professor? We don't . . . you know . . . we don't understand the technicalities that go with—Allen, my son, wanted to go here to the Catholic school; I told my husband why not? Why fight? It's the thing these days, they do anything they want for knowledge. And he had to come home, you know. He couldn't take care of himself. New York, that was the beginning of the trouble. . . . Should I call you Professor?"

"You can call me Sister Irene."

"Sister Irene?" the woman said, touching her throat in awe, as if something intimate and unexpected had happened.

Then Weinstein's father appeared, hurrying. He took long, impatient strides. Sister Irene stared at him and in that instant doubted everything—he was in his fifties, a tall, sharply handsome man, heavy but not fat, holding his shoulders back with what looked like an effort, but holding them back just the same. He wore a dark suit and his face was flushed, as if he had run a long distance.

"Now," he said, coming to Sister Irene and with a precise wave of his hand motioning his wife off, "now, let's straighten this out. A lot of confusion over that kid, eh?" He pulled a chair over, scraping it across a rug and pulling one corner over, so that its brown underside was exposed. "I came home early just for this, Libby phoned me. Sister, you got a letter from him, right?"

The wife looked at Sister Irene over her husband's head as if trying somehow to coach her, knowing that this man was so loud and impatient that no one could remember anything in his presence.

"A letter — yes — today —"

"He says what in it? You got the letter, eh? Can I see it?"

She gave it to him and wanted to explain, but he silenced her with a flick of his hand. He read through the letter so quickly that Sister Irene thought perhaps he was trying to impress her with his skill at reading. "So?" he said, raising his eyes, smiling, "so what is this? He's happy out there, he says. He doesn't communicate with us any more, but he writes to you and says he's happy — what's that? I mean, what the hell is that?"

"But he isn't happy. He wants to come home," Sister Irene said. It was so important that she make him understand that she could not trust her voice; goaded by this man, it might suddenly turn shrill, as his son's did. "Someone must read their letters before they're mailed, so he tried to tell me something by making an allusion to —"

"What?"

" — an allusion to a play, so that I would know. He may be thinking suicide, he must be very unhappy —"

She ran out of breath. Weinstein's mother had begun to cry, but the father was shaking his head jerkily back and forth. "Forgive me, Sister, but it's a lot of crap, he needs the hospital, he needs help — right? It costs me fifty a day out there, and they've got the best place in the state, I figure it's worth it. He needs help, that kid, what do I care if he's unhappy? He's unbalanced!" he said angrily. "You want us to get him out again? We argued with the judge for two hours to get him in, an acquaintance of mine. Look, he can't control himself — he was smashing things here, he was hysterical. They need help, lady, and you do something about it fast! You do something! We made up our minds to do something and we did it! This letter — what the hell is this letter? He never talked like that to us!"

"But he means the opposite of what he says —"

"Then he's crazy! I'm the first to admit it." He was perspiring, and his face had darkened. "I've got no pride left this late. He's a little bastard, you want to know? He calls me names, he's filthy, got a filthy mouth — that's being smart, huh? They give him a big scholarship for his filthy mouth? I went to college too, and I got out and knew something, and I for Christ's sake did something with it; my wife is an intelligent woman, a learned woman, would you guess she does book reviews for the little newspaper out here? Intelligent isn't crazy — crazy isn't intelligent. Maybe for you at the school he writes nice papers and gets an A, but out here, around the house, he can't control himself, and we got him committed!"

"But —"

"We're fixing him up, don't worry about it!" He turned to his wife. "Libby, get out of here, I mean it. I'm sorry, but get out of here, you're making a fool of yourself, go stand in the kitchen or something, you and the goddamn maid can cry on each other's shoulders. That one in the kitchen is nuts too, they're all nuts. Sister," he said, his voice lowering,"I thank you immensely for coming out here. This is wonderful, your interest in my son. And I see he admires you — that letter there. But what about that letter? If he did want to get out, which I don't admit — he was willing to be committed, in the end he said okay himself—if he wanted out I wouldn't do it. Why? So what if he wants to come back? The next day he wants something else, what then? He's a sick kid, and I'm the first to admit it."

Sister Irene felt that sickness spread to her. She stood. The room was so big it seemed it must be a public place; there had been nothing personal or private about their conversation. Weinstein's mother was standing by the fireplace, sobbing. The father jumped to his feet and wiped his forehead in a gesture that was meant to help Sister Irene on her way out. "God, what a day," he said, his eyes snatching at hers for understanding, "you know — one of those days all day long? Sister, I thank you a lot. There should be more people in the world who care about others, like you. I mean that."

On the way back to the convent, the man's words returned to her, and she could not get control of them; she could not even feel anger. She had been pressed down, forced back, what could she do? Weinstein might have been watching her somehow from a barred window, and he surely would have understood. The strange idea she had had on the way over, something about understanding Christ, came back to her now and sickened her. But the sickness was small. It could be contained.

About a month after her visit to his father, Weinstein himself showed up. He was dressed in a suit as before, even the necktie was the same. He came right into her office as if he had been pushed and could not stop.

"Sister," he said, and shook her hand. He must have seen fear in her because he smiled ironically. "Look, I'm released. I'm let out of the nut house. Can I sit down?"

He sat. Sister Irene was breathing quickly, as if in the presence of an enemy who does not know he is an enemy.

"So, they finally let me out. I heard what you did. You talked with him, that was all I wanted. You're the only one who gave a damn. Because you're a humanist and a religious person, you respect . . . the individual. Listen," he said, whispering, "it was hell out there! Hell Birchcrest Manor! All fixed up with fancy chairs and *Life* magazines lying around — and what do they do to you? They locked me up, they gave me shock treatments! Shock treatments, how do you like that, it's discredited by everybody now — they're crazy out there themselves, sadists. They locked me up, they gave me hypodermic shots, they didn't treat me like a human being! Do you know what that is," Weinstein demanded savagely, "not to be treated like a human being? They made me an animal — for fifty dollars a day! Dirty filthy swine! Now I'm an outpatient because I stopped swearing at them. I found somebody's bobby pin, and when I wanted to scream I pressed it under my fingernail and it stopped me — the screaming went inside and not out — so they gave me good reports, those sick bastards. Now I'm an outpatient and I can walk along the street and breathe in the same filthy exhaust from the buses like all you normal people! Christ," he said, and threw himself back against the chair.

Sister Irene stared at him. She wanted to take his hand, to make some gesture that would close the aching distance between them. "Mr. Weinstein —"

"Call me Allen!" he said sharply.

"I'm very sorry — I'm terribly sorry —"

"My own parents committed me, but of course they didn't know what it was like. It was hell," he said thickly, "and there isn't any hell except what other people do to you. The psychiatrist out there, the main shrink, he hates Jews too, some of us were positive of that, and he's got a bigger nose than I do, a real beak." He made a noise of disgust. "A dirty bastard, a sick, dirty, pathetic bastard — all of them. Anyway, I'm getting out of here, and I came to ask you a favor."

"What do you mean?"

"I'm getting out. I'm leaving. I'm going up to Canada and lose myself. I'll get a job, I'll forget everything, I'll kill myself maybe — what's the difference? Look, can you lend me some money?"

"Money?"

"Just a little! I have to get to the border, I'm going to take a bus."

"But I don't have any money —"

"No money?" He stared at her. "You mean — you don't have any? Sure you have some!"

She stared at him as if he had asked her to do something obscene. Everything was splotched and uncertain before her eyes.

"You must . . . you must go back," she said, "you're making a —"

"I'll pay it back. Look, I'll pay it back, can you go to where you live or something and get it? I'm in a hurry. My friends are sons of bitches: one of them pretended he didn't see me yesterday — I stood right in the middle of the sidewalk and yelled at him, I called him some appropriate names! So he didn't see me, huh? You're the only one who understands me, you understand me like a poet, you —"

"I can't help you, I'm sorry — I . . ."

He looked to one side of her and flashed his gaze back, as if he could control it. He seemed to be trying to clear his vision.

"You have the soul of a poet," he whispered, "you're the only one. Everybody else is rotten! Can't you lend me some money, ten dollars maybe? I have three thousand in the bank, and I can't touch it! They take everything away from me, they make me into an animal. . . . You know I'm not an animal, don't you? Don't you?"

"Of course," Sister Irene whispered.

"You could get money. Help me. Give me your hand or something, touch me, help me — please. . . ." He reached for her hand and she drew back. He stared at her and his face seemed about to crumble, like a child's. "I want something from you, but I don't know what — I want something!" he cried. "Something real! I want you to look at me like I was a human being, is that too much to ask? I have a brain, I'm alive, I'm suffering — what does that mean? Does that mean nothing? I want something real and not this phony Christian love garbage — it's all in the books, it isn't personal — I want something real — look. . . ."

He tried to take her hand again, and this time she jerked away. She got to her feet. "Mr. Weinstein," she said, "please —"

"You! You nun!" he said scornfully, his mouth twisted into a mock grin. "You nun! There's nothing under that ugly outfit, right? And you're not particularly smart even though you think you are; my father has more brains in his foot than you —"

He got to his feet and kicked the chair.

"You bitch!" he cried.

She shrank back against her desk as if she thought he might hit her, but he only ran out of the office.

Weinstein: the name was to become disembodied from the figure, as time went on. The semester passed, the autumn drizzle turned into snow. Sister Irene rode to school in the morning and left in the afternoon, four days a week, anonymous in her black winter cloak, quiet and stunned. University teaching was an anonymous task, each day dissociated from the rest, with no necessary sense of unity among the teachers: they came and went separately and might for a year just miss a colleague who left his office five minutes before they arrived, and it did not matter.

She heard of Weinstein's death, his suicide by drowning, from the English Department secretary, a handsome white-haired woman who kept a transistor radio on her desk. Sister Irene was not surprised; she had been thinking of him as dead for months. "They identifed him by some special television way they have now," the secretary said. "They're shipping the body back. It was up in Quebec. . . ."

Sister Irene could feel a part of herself drifting off, lured by the plains of white snow to the north, the quiet, the emptiness, the sweep of the Great Lakes up to the silence of Canada. But she called that part of herself back. She could only be one person in her lifetime. That was the ugly truth, she thought, that she could not really regret Weinstein's suffering and death; she had only one life and had already given it to someone else. He had come too late to her. Fifteen years ago, perhaps, but not now.

She was only one person, she thought, walking down the corridor in a dream. Was she safe in this single person, or was she trapped? She had only one identity. She could make only one choice. What she had done or hadn't done was the result of that choice, and how was she guilty? If she could have felt guilt, she thought, she might at least have been able to feel something.

FLANN O'BRIEN

"Flann O'Brien" (1911–1966) was a pseudonym of Brian O'Nuallain (sometimes written Nolan or O'Nolan), who was born in Northern Ireland but spent most of his life in the Irish Republic. He graduated from University College, Dublin, and spent many years as a civil servant in the Ministry of Local Government. He was best known to his compatriots as "Myles na Gopaleen" ("Myles of the ponies"), another pseudonym under which he wrote a regular column for the *Irish Times* from 1940 to 1966.

O'Brien was a student of Celtic language and literature, and in his stories, plays, and novels he drew extensively on Irish literary tradition. He has been compared to Joyce and Beckett in his cavalier disregard for narrative conventions and in the mixture of learning, satire, and fantasy in his writings. His first novel, *At Swim-Two Birds* (1939), has (somewhat belatedly) won critical acclaim as one of the great comic works of the century; in this and other works of fiction, O'Brien anticipated writers like Barth and Nabokov with his parody of novelistic conventions and modern critical pedantry. In "John Duffy's Brother" (1941; *Stories and Plays*, 1973), he sets the ordinary and the absurd side by side in such a way as to challenge our preconceptions about the nature of "normality," at the same time casting a characteristically whimsical eye on the conventions of fictional realism. The story is not merely an example of the author at play, however; it also offers a sardonic comment on the entrapment of human consciousness by the mechanistic concepts of time and work developed in an industrial society.

FOR FURTHER READING

Robert Martin Adams, *Afterjoyce: Studies in Fiction After* Ulysses (New York: Oxford University Press, 1977).

Anne Clissman, *Flann O'Brien: A critical introduction to his writings* (Dublin: Gill and Macmillan, 1975).

Vivian Mercier, *The Irish Comic Tradition* (Oxford: Clarendon Press, 1962).

JOHN DUFFY'S BROTHER

Strictly speaking, this story should not be written or told at all. To write it or to tell it is to spoil it. This is because the man who had the strange experience we are going to talk about never mentioned it to anybody, and the fact that he kept his secret and sealed it up completely in his memory is the whole point of the story. Thus we must admit that handicap at the beginning — that it is absurd for us to tell the story, absurd for anybody to listen to it and unthinkable that anybody should believe it.

We will, however, do this man one favour. We will refrain from mentioning him by his complete name. This will enable us to tell his secret and permit him to continue looking his friends in the eye. But we can say that his surname is Duffy. There are thousands of these Duffys in the world; even at this moment there is probably a new Duffy making his appearance in some corner of it. We can even go so far as to say that he is John Duffy's brother. We do not break faith in saying so, because if there are only one hundred John Duffys in existence, and even if each one of them could be met and questioned, no embarrassing enlightenments would be forthcoming. That is because the John Duffy in question never left his house, never left his bed, never talked to anybody in his life and was never seen by more than one man. That man's name was Gumley. Gumley was a doctor. He was present when John Duffy was born and also when he died, one hour later.

John Duffy's brother lived alone in a small house on an eminence in Inchicore. When dressing in the morning he could gaze across the broad valley of the Liffey to the slopes of the Phoenix Park, peacefully. Usually the river was indiscernible but on a sunny morning it could be seen lying like a long glistening spear in the valley's palm. Like a respectable married man, it seemed to be hurrying into Dublin as if to work.

Sometimes, recollecting that his clock was fast, John Duffy's brother would spend an idle moment with his father's spy glass, ranging the valley with an eagle eye. The village of Chapelizod was to the left and invisible in the depth but each morning the inhabitants would erect, as if for Mr Duffy's benefit, a lazy plume of smoke to show exactly where they were.

Mr Duffy's glass usually came to rest on the figure of a man hurrying across the uplands of the Park and disappearing from view in the direction of the Magazine Fort. A small white terrier bounced along ahead of him but could be seen occasionally sprinting to overtake him after dallying behind for a time on private business.

The man carried in the crook of his arm an instrument which Mr Duffy at first took to be a shotgun or patent repeating rifle, but one morning the man held it by the butt and smote the barrels smartly on the ground as he walked, and it was then evident to Mr Duffy — he felt some disappointment — that the article was a walking-stick.

It happened that this man's name was Martin Smullen. He was a retired stationary-engine-driver and lived quietly with a delicate sister at Number Four, Cannon Row, Parkgate. Mr Duffy did not know his name and was destined never to meet him or have the privilege of his acquaintance, but it may be worth mentioning that they once stood side by side at the counter of a public-house in Little Easter Street, mutually unrecognised, each to the other a black stranger. Mr Smullen's call was whiskey, Mr Duffy's stout.

Mr Smullen's sister's name was not Smullen but Goggins, relict of the late Paul Goggins, wholesale clothier. Mr Duffy had never even heard of her. She had a cousin by the name of Leo Corr who was not unknown to the police. He was sent up in 1924 for a stretch of hard labour in connection with the manufacture of spurious currency. Mrs Goggins had never met him, but heard that he had emigrated to Labrador on his release.

About the spy glass. A curious history attaches to its owner, also a Duffy, late of the Mercantile Marine. Although unprovided with the benefits of a University education — indeed, he had gone to sea at the age of sixteen as a result of an incident arising out of an imperfect understanding of the sexual relation — he was of a scholarly turn of mind and would often spend the afternoons of his sea-leave alone in his dining-room thumbing a book of Homer with delight or annotating with erudite sneers the inferior Latin of the Angelic Doctor. On the fourth day of July, 1927, at four o'clock, he took leave of his senses in the dining-room. Four men arrived in a closed van at eight o'clock that evening to remove him from mortal ken to a place where he would be restrained for his own good.

It could be argued that much of the foregoing has little real bearing on the story of John Duffy's brother, but modern writing, it is hoped, has passed the stage when simple events are stated in the void without any clue as to the psychological and hereditary forces working in the background to produce them. Having said so much, however, it is now permissible to set down briefly the nature of the adventure of John Duffy's brother.

He arose one morning — on the 9th of March, 1932 — dressed and cooked his frugal breakfast. Immediately afterwards, he became possessed of the strange idea that he was a train. No explanation of this can be attempted. Small boys sometimes like to pretend that they are trains, and there are fat women in the world who are not, in the distance, without some resemblance to trains. But John Duffy's brother was certain that he *was* a train — long, thunderous and immense, with white steam escaping noisily from his feet and deep-throated bellows coming rhythmically from where his funnel was.

Moreover, he was certain that he was a particular train, the 9.20 into Dublin. His station was the bedroom. He stood absolutely still for twenty minutes, knowing that a good train is equally punctual in departure as in arrival. He glanced often at his watch to make sure that the hour should not go by unnoticed. His watch bore the words "Shockproof" and "Railway Timekeeper."

Precisely at 9.20 he emitted a piercing whistle, shook the great mass of his metal ponderously into motion and steamed away heavily into town. The train arrived dead on time at its destination, which was the office of Messrs Polter and Polter, Solicitors, Commissioners for Oaths. For obvious reasons, the name of this firm is fictitious. In the office were two men, old Mr Cranberry and young Mr Hodge. Both were clerks and both took their orders from John Duffy's brother. Of course, both names are imaginary.

"Good morning, Mr Duffy," said Mr Cranberry. He was old and polite, grown yellow in the firm's service.

Mr Duffy looked at him in surprise. "Can you not see I am a train?" he said. "Why do you call me Mr Duffy?"

Mr Cranberry gave a laugh and winked at Mr Hodge who sat young, neat and good-looking, behind his typewriter.

"Alright, Mr Train," he said. "That's a cold morning, sir. Hard to get up steam these cold mornings, sir."

"It is not easy," said Mr Duffy. He shunted expertly to his chair and waited patiently before he sat down while the company's servants adroitly uncoupled him. Mr Hodge was sniggering behind his roller.

"Any cheap excursions, sir?" he asked.

"No," Mr Duffy replied. "There are season tickets, of course."

"Third class and first class, I suppose, sir?"

"No," said Mr Duffy. "In deference to the views of Herr Marx, all class distinctions in the passenger rolling-stock have been abolished."

"I see," said Mr Cranberry.

"That's communism," said Mr Hodge.

"He means," said Mr Cranberry, "that it is now first-class only."

"How many wheels has your engine?" asked Mr Hodge. "Three big ones?"

"I am not a goods train," said Mr Duffy acidly. "The wheel formation of a passenger engine is four-four-two — two large driving wheels on each side, coupled, of course, with a four-wheel bogey in front and two small wheels at the cab. Why do you ask?"

"The platform's in the way," Mr Cranberry said. "He can't see it."

"Oh, quite," said Mr Duffy, "I forgot."

"I suppose you use a lot of coal?" Mr Hodge said.

"About half a ton per thirty miles," said Mr Duffy slowly, mentally checking the consumption of that morning. "I need scarcely say that frequent stopping and starting at suburban stations takes a lot out of me."

"I'm sure it does," said Mr Hodge, with sympathy.

They talked like that for half an hour until the elderly Mr Polter arrived and passed gravely into his back office. When that happened, conversation was at an end. Little was heard until lunch-time except the scratch of pens and the fitful clicking of the typewriter.

John Duffy's brother always left the office at one thirty and went home to his lunch. Consequently he started getting steam up at twelve forty-five so that there should be no delay at the hour of departure. When the "Railway Timekeeper" said that it was one thirty, he let out another shrill whistle and steamed slowly out of the office without a word or a look at his colleagues. He arrived home dead on time.

We now approach the really important part of the plot, the incident which gives the whole story its significance. In the middle of his lunch John Duffy's brother felt something important, something queer, momentous and magical taking place inside his brain, an immense tension relaxing, clean light flooding a place which had been dark. He dropped his knife and fork and sat there for a time wild-eyed, a filling of potatoes unattended in his mouth. Then he swallowed, rose weakly from the table and walked to the window, wiping away the perspiration which had started out on his brow.

He gazed out into the day, no longer a train, but a badly frightened man. Inch by inch he went back over his morning. So far as he could recall he had killed no one, shouted no bad language, broken no windows. He had only talked to Cranberry and Hodge. Down in the roadway there was no dark van arriving with uniformed men infesting it. He sat down again desolately beside the unfinished meal.

John Duffy's brother was a man of some courage. When he got back to the office he had some whiskey in his stomach and it was later in the evening than it should be. Hodge and Cranberry seemed preoccupied with their letters. He hung up his hat casually and said:

"I'm afraid the train is a bit late getting back."

From below his downcast brows he looked very sharply at Cranberry's face. He thought he saw the shadow of a smile flit absently on the old man's placid features as they continued poring down on a paper. The smile seemed to mean that a morning's joke was not good enough for the same evening. Hodge rose suddenly in his corner and passed silently into Mr Polter's office with his letters. John Duffy's brother sighed and sat down wearily at his desk.

When he left the office that night, his heart was lighter and he thought he had a good excuse for buying more liquor. Nobody knew his secret but himself and nobody else would ever know.

It was a complete cure. Never once did the strange malady return. But to this day John Duffy's brother starts at the rumble of a train in the Liffey tunnel and stands rooted to the road when he comes suddenly on a level-crossing — silent, so to speak, upon a peak in Darien.

KATHERINE ANNE PORTER

Katherine Anne Porter (1890–1980) was born in Texas, and her formal education was limited to girls' schools in the South; but she learned much from her own reading, and early formed the desire to be a writer. Her first collection of short stories, *Flowering Judas and other stories* (1930; augmented edition, 1935), won immediate critical praise for her smooth, spare prose, and for the psychological insights of such stories as "He." The success of *Flowering Judas and other stories* brought her a Guggenheim Fellowship, which enabled her to travel; and her subsequent voyage to Europe in 1931 provided the material for her longest work, the novel *Ship of Fools* (1962). The many awards and distinctions conferred upon her include a Pulitzer Prize, which she received in 1966.

In her introduction to the 1940 edition of *Flowering Judas and other stories*, Porter described how she sought "to understand the logic of this majestic and terrible failure of the life of man in the Western world"; and to a greater or lesser extent, this concern is reflected in all her work. She dramatizes the human struggle for contact and communication in the face of all fears, prejudices, and frustrations which alienate people from each other. Like the protagonist in her long story "The Leaning Tower" (1944), many of her characters confront a society in the process of disintegration, or experience "an infernal desolation of the spirit, the chill and the knowledge of death. . . ." Porter's stories reflect her sense of the confusion that characterizes human life; she investigates "self-betrayal and self-deception — the way that all human beings deceive themselves about the way they operate. . . . Everyone takes his stance, asserts his own rights and feelings, mistaking the motives of others, and his own . . ." (*Paris Review* interview, 1963). In "He," Mrs. Whipple succeeds for a while in shutting away the truth about her feelings for her son; but the author passes no harsh judgment on her self-delusion and insincerity, and portrays with compassion the dawning horror of her final recognition of failure.

FOR FURTHER READING

George Hendrick, *Katherine Anne Porter* (New York: Twayne, 1965).
M.M. Libermann, *Katherine Anne Porter's Fiction* (Detroit: Wayne State University Press, 1971).
Barbara Thompson, "The Art of Fiction XXIX: Katherine Anne Porter," *Paris Review* 8 (Winter/Spring 1963): 87–114.

HE

Life was very hard for the Whipples. It was hard to feed all the hungry mouths, it was hard to keep the children in flannels during the winter, short as it was. "God knows what would become of us if we lived north," they would say; keeping them decently clean was hard. "It looks like our luck won't never let up on us," said Mr Whipple, but Mrs Whipple was all for taking what was sent and calling it good, anyhow when the neighbours were in earshot. "Don't ever let a soul hear us complain," she kept saying to her husband. She couldn't stand to be pitied. "No, not if it comes to it that we have to live in a wagon and pick cotton around the country," she said, "nobody's going to get a chance to look down on us."

Mrs Whipple loved her second son, the simple-minded one, better than she loved the other two children put together. She was for ever saying so, and when she talked with certain of her neighbours, she would even throw in her husband and her mother for good measure.

"You needn't keep on saying it around," said Mr Whipple, "you'll make people think nobody else has any feelings about Him but you."

"It's natural for a mother," Mrs Whipple would remind him. "You know yourself it's more natural for a mother to be that way. People don't expect so much of fathers, some way."

This didn't keep the neighbours from talking plainly among themselves. "A Lord's pure mercy if He should die," they said. "It's the sins of the fathers," they agreed among themselves. "There's bad blood and bad doings somewhere, you can bet on that." This behind the Whipples' backs. To their faces everybody said, "He's not so bad off. He'll be all right yet. Look how He grows!"

Mrs Whipple hated to talk about it, she tried to keep her mind off it, but every time anybody set foot in the house, the subject always came up, and she had to talk about Him first, before she could get on to anything else. It seemed to ease her mind. "I wouldn't have anything happen to Him for all the world, but it just looks like I can't keep Him out of mischief. He's so strong and active, He's always into everything; He was like that since He could walk. It's actually funny sometimes the way He can do anything; it's laughable to see Him up to His tricks. Emly has more accidents; I'm for ever tying up her bruises, and Adna can't fall a foot without cracking a bone. But He can do anything and not get a scratch. The preacher said such a nice thing once when he was here. He said, and I'll remember it to my dying day, 'The innocent walk with God—that's why He don't get hurt.'" Whenever Mrs Whipple repeated these words, she always felt a warm pool spread in her breast, and the tears would fill her eyes, and then she could talk about something else.

He did grow and He never got hurt. A plank blew off the chicken house and struck Him on the head and He never seemed to know it. He had learned a few words, and after this He forgot them. He didn't whine for food as the other children did, but waited until it was given Him; He ate squatting in the corner, smacking and mumbling. Rolls of fat covered Him like an overcoat, and He could carry twice as much wood and water as Adna. Emly had a cold in the head most of the time — ''she takes that after me,'' said Mrs Whipple — so in bad weather they gave her the extra blanket off His cot. He never seemed to mind the cold.

Just the same, Mrs Whipple's life was a torment for fear something might happen to Him. He climbed the peach trees much better than Adna and went skittering along the branches like a monkey, just a regular monkey. ''Oh, Mrs Whipple, you hadn't ought to let Him do that. He'll lose His balance sometime. He can't rightly know what He's doing.''

Mrs Whipple almost screamed out at the neighbour. ''He *does* know what He's doing! He's as able as any other child! Come down out of there, you!'' When He finally reached the ground she could hardly keep her hands off Him for acting like that before people, a grin all over His face and her worried sick about Him all the time.

''It's the neighbours,'' said Mrs Whipple to her husband. ''Oh, I do mortally wish they would keep out of our business. I can't afford to let Him do anything for fear they'll come nosing around about it. Look at the bees, now. Adna can't handle them, they sting him so. I haven't got time to do everything, and now I don't dare let Him. But if He gets a sting He don't really mind.''

''It's just because He ain't got sense enough to be scared of anything,'' said Mr Whipple.

''You ought to be ashamed of yourself,'' said Mrs Whipple, ''talking that way about your own child. Who's to take up for Him if we don't, I'd like to know? He sees a lot that goes on, He listens to things all the time. And anything I tell Him to do He does it. Don't never let anybody hear you say such things. They'd think you favoured the other children over Him.''

''Well, now I don't, and you know it, and what's the use of getting all worked up about it? You always think the worst of everything. Just let Him alone, He'll get along somehow. He gets plenty to eat and wear, don't He?'' Mr Whipple suddenly felt tired out. ''Anyhow, it can't be helped now.''

Mrs Whipple felt tired too; she complained in a tired voice: ''What's done can't never be undone, I know that good as anybody; but He's my child, and I'm not going to have people say anything. I get sick of people coming around saying things all the time.''

In the early autumn Mrs Whipple got a letter from her brother saying he and his wife and two children were coming over for a little visit next Sunday week. ''Put the big pot in the little one,'' he wrote at the end. Mrs Whipple read this part out loud twice, she was so pleased. Her brother was a great one for saying funny things. ''We'll just show him that's no joke," she said, "we'll just butcher one of the sucking pigs."

"It's a waste and I don't hold with waste the way we are now," said Mr Whipple. "That pig'll be worth money by Christmas."

"It's a shame and a pity we can't have a decent meal's vittles once in a while when my own family comes to see us," said Mrs Whipple. "I'd hate for his wife to go back and say there wasn't a thing in the house to eat. My God, it's better than buying up a great chance of meat in town. There's where you'd spend the money!"

"All right, do it yourself then," said Mr Whipple. "Christamighty, no wonder we can't get ahead!"

The question was how to get the little pig away from his ma, a great fighter, worse than a Jersey cow. Adna wouldn't try it: "That sow'd rip my insides out all over the pen." "All right, old fraidy," said Mrs Whipple, "*He's* not scared. Watch *Him* do it." And she laughed as though it was all a good joke and gave Him a little push towards the pen. He sneaked up and snatched the pig right away from the teat and galloped back and was over the fence with the sow raging at His heels. The little black squirming thing was screeching like a baby in a tantrum, stiffening its back and stretching its mouth to the ears. Mrs Whipple took the pig with her face stiff and sliced its throat with one stroke. When He saw the blood He gave a great jolting breath and ran away. "But He'll forget and eat plenty, just the same," thought Mrs Whipple. Whenever she was thinking, her lips moved, making words. "He'd eat it all if I didn't stop Him. He'd eat up every mouthful from the other two if I'd let Him."

She felt badly about it. He was ten years old now and a third again as large as Adna, who was going on fourteen. "It's a shame, a shame," she kept saying under her breath, "and Adna with so much brains!"

She kept on feeling badly about all sorts of things. In the first place it was the man's work to butcher; the sight of the pig scraped pink and naked made her sick. He was too fat and soft and pitiful-looking. It was simply a shame the way things had to happen. By the time she had finished it up, she almost wished her brother would stay at home.

Early on Sunday morning Mrs Whipple dropped everything to get Him all cleaned up. In an hour He was dirty again, with crawling under fences after an opossum, and straddling along the rafters of the barn looking for eggs in the hayloft. "My lord, look at you now after all my trying! And here's Adna and Emly staying so quiet. I get tired trying to keep you decent. Get off that shirt and put on another; people will say I don't half dress you!" And she boxed Him on the ears, hard. He blinked and blinked and rubbed His head, and His face hurt Mrs Whipple's feelings. Her knees began to tremble, she had to sit down while she buttoned His shirt. "I'm just all gone before the day starts."

The brother came with his plump healthy wife and two great roaring hungry boys. They had a grand dinner, with the pig roasted to a crackling in the middle of the table, full of dressing, a pickled peach in his mouth and plenty of gravy for the sweet potatoes.

"This looks like prosperity all right," said the brother; "you're going to have to roll me home like I was a barrel when I'm done."

Everybody laughed out loud; it was fine to hear them laughing all at once around the table. Mrs Whipple felt warm and good about it. "Oh, we've got six more of these; I say it's as little as we can do when you come to see us so seldom."

He wouldn't come into the dining-room and Mrs Whipple passed it off very well. "He's timider than my other two," she said. "He'll just have to get used to you. There isn't everybody He'll make up with, you know how it is with some children, even cousins." Nobody said anything out of the way.

"Just like my Alfy here," said the brother's wife. "I sometimes got to lick him to make him shake hands with his own grandmammy."

So that was over, and Mrs Whipple loaded up a big plate for Him first, before everybody. "I always say He ain't to be slighted, no matter who else goes without," she said, and carried it to Him herself.

"He can chin Himself on the top of the door," said Emly, helping along.

"That's fine, He's getting along fine," said the brother.

They went away after supper. Mrs Whipple rounded up the dishes, sent the children to bed, and sat down and unlaced her shoes. "You see?" she said to Mr Whipple. "That's the way my whole family is. Nice and considerate about everything. No out-of-the-way remarks — they *have* got refinement. I get awfully sick of people's remarks. Wasn't that pig good?"

Mr Whipple said, "Yes, we're out three hundred pounds of pork, that's all. It's easy to be polite when you come to eat. Who knows what they had in their minds all along?"

"Yes, that's like you," said Mrs Whipple. "I don't expect anything else from you. You'll be telling me next that my own brother will be saying around that we made Him eat in the kitchen! Oh, my God!" She rocked her head in her hands, a hard pain started in the very middle of her forehead. "Now it's all spoiled, and everything was so nice and easy. All right, you don't like them and you never did — all right, they'll not come here again soon, never you mind! But they *can't* say He wasn't dressed every lick as good as Adna — oh, honest, sometimes I wish I was dead!"

"I wish you'd let up," said Mr Whipple. "It's bad enough as it is."

It was a hard winter. It seemed to Mrs Whipple that they hadn't ever known anything but hard times, and now to cap it all a winter like this. The crops were about half of what they had a right to expect; after the cotton was in it didn't do much more than cover the grocery bill. They swapped off one of the plough horses, and got cheated, for the new one died of the heaves. Mrs Whipple kept thinking all the time it was terrible to have a man you couldn't depend on not to get cheated. They cut down on everything, but Mrs Whipple kept saying there are things you can't cut down on, and they cost money. It took a lot of warm clothes for Adna and Emly, who walked four miles to school during the three-months session. "He sets around the fire a lot, He won't need so much," said Mr Whipple. "That's so," said Mrs Whipple, "and when He does the outdoor chores He can wear your tarpaulin coat. I can't do no better, that's all."

In February He was taken sick, and lay curled up under His blanket looking very blue in the face and acting as if He would choke. Mr and Mrs Whipple did everything they could for Him for two days, and then they were scared and sent for the doctor. The doctor told them they must keep Him warm and give Him plenty of milk and eggs. "He isn't as stout as He looks, I'm afraid," said the doctor. "You've got to watch them when they're like that. You must put more cover on Him, too."

"I just took off His big blanket to wash," said Mrs Whipple, ashamed. "I can't stand dirt."

"Well, you'd better put it back on the minute it's dry," said the doctor, "or He'll have pneumonia."

Mr and Mrs Whipple took a blanket off their own bed and put His cot in by the fire. "They can't say we didn't do everything for Him," she said, "even to sleeping cold ourselves on His account."

When the winter broke He seemed to be well again, but He walked as if His feet hurt Him. He was able to run a cotton planter during the season.

"I got it all fixed up with Jim Ferguson about breeding the cow next time," said Mr Whipple. "I'll pasture the bull this summer and give Jim some fodder in the autumn. That's better than paying out money when you haven't got it."

"I hope you didn't say such a thing before Jim Ferguson," said Mrs Whipple. "You oughtn't to let him know we're so down as all that."

"Godamighty, that ain't saying we're down! A man has got to look ahead sometimes. *He* can lead the bull over today. I need Adna on the place."

At first Mrs Whipple felt easy in her mind about sending Him for the bull. Adna was too jumpy and couldn't be trusted. You've got to be steady around animals. After He was gone she started thinking, and after a while she could hardly bear it any longer. She stood in the lane and watched for Him. It was nearly three miles to go and a hot day, but He oughtn't to be so long about it. She shaded her eyes and stared until coloured bubbles floated in her eyeballs. It was just like everything else in life, she must always worry and never know a moment's peace about anything. Afer a long time she saw Him turn into the side lane, limping. He came on very slowly, leading the big hulk of an animal by a ring in the nose, twirling a little stick in His hand, never looking back or sideways, but coming on like a sleepwalker with His eyes half shut.

Mrs Whipple was scared sick of bulls; she had heard awful stories about how they followed on quietly enough, and then suddenly pitched on with a bellow and pawed and gored a body to pieces. Any second now that black monster would come down on Him. My God, He'd never have sense enough to run.

She mustn't make a sound nor a move; she mustn't get the bull started. The bull heaved his head aside and horned the air at a fly. Her voice burst out of her in a shriek, and she screamed at Him to come on, for God's sake. He didn't seem to hear her clamour, but kept on twirling His switch and limping on, and the bull lumbered along behind him as gently as a calf. Mrs Whipple stopped calling and ran towards the house, praying under her breath: "Lord, don't let anything happen to Him. Lord, you *know* people will say we oughtn't to have sent Him. You *know* they'll say we didn't take care of Him. Oh, get Him home, safe home, safe home, and I'll look out for Him better! Amen."

She watched from the window while He led the beast in and tied him up in the barn. It was no use trying to keep up, Mrs Whipple couldn't bear another thing. She sat down and rocked and cried with her apron over her head.

From year to year the Whipples were growing poorer and poorer. The place just seemed to run down of itself, no matter how hard they worked. "We're losing our hold," said Mrs Whipple. "Why can't we do like other people and watch for our best chances? They'll be calling us poor white trash next."

"When I get to be sixteen I'm going to leave," said Adna. "I'm going to get a job in Powell's grocery store. There's money in that. No more farm for me."

"I'm going to be a school teacher," said Emly. "But I've got to finish the eighth grade, anyhow. Then I can live in town. I don't see any chances here."

"Emly takes after my family," said Mrs Whipple. "Ambitious every last one of them, and they don't take second place for anybody."

When autumn came Emly got a chance to wait at table in the railroad eating-house in the town near by, and it seemed such a shame not to take it when the wages were good and she could get her food too, that Mrs Whipple decided to let her take it, and not bother with school until the next session. "You've got plenty of time," she said. "You're young and smart as a whip."

With Adna gone too, Mr Whipple tried to run the farm with just Him to help. He seemed to get along fine, doing His work and part of Adna's without noticing it. They did well enough until Christmas time, when one morning He slipped on the ice coming up from the barn. Instead of getting up He thrashed round and round, and when Mr Whipple got to Him, He was having some sort of fit.

They brought Him inside and tried to make Him sit up, but He blubbered and rolled, so they put Him to bed and Mr Whipple rode to town for the doctor. All the way there and back he worried about where the money was to come from: it sure did look like he had about all the troubles he could carry.

From then on He stayed in bed. His legs swelled up double their size, and the fits kept coming back. After four months the doctor said, "It's no use, I think you'd better put Him in the County Home for treatment right way. I'll see about it for you. He'll have good care there and be off your hands."

"We don't begrudge Him any care, and I won't let Him out of my sight," said Mrs Whipple. "I won't have it said I sent my sick child off among strangers."

"I know how you feel," said the doctor. "You can't tell me anything about that, Mrs Whipple. I've got a boy of my own. But you'd better listen to me. I can't do anything more for Him, that's the truth."

Mr and Mrs Whipple talked it over a long time that night after they went to bed. "It's just charity," said Mrs Whipple, "that's what we've come to, charity! I certainly never looked for this."

"We pay taxes to help to support the place just like everybody else," said Mr Whipple, "and I don't call that taking charity. I think it would be fine to have Him where He'd get the best of everything . . . and besides, I can't keep up with these doctor's bills any longer."

"Maybe that's why the doctor wants us to send Him — he's scared he won't get his money," said Mrs Whipple.

"Don't talk like that," said Mr Whipple, feeling pretty sick, "or we won't be able to send Him."

"Oh, but we won't keep Him there long," said Mrs Whipple. "Soon's He's better we'll bring Him right back home."

"The doctor has told you, and told you time and again, He can't ever get better, and you might as well stop talking," said Mr Whipple.

"Doctors don't know everything," said Mrs Whipple, feeling almost happy. "But anyhow, in the summer Emly can come home for a vacation, and Adna can get down for Sundays: we'll all work together and get on our feet again, and the children will feel they've got a place to come to."

All at once she saw it full summer again, with the garden going fine, and new white roller shades up all over the house, and Adna and Emly home, so full of life; all of them happy together. Oh, it could happen, things would ease up on them.

They didn't talk before Him much, but they never knew just how much He understood. Finally the doctor set the day and a neighbour who owned a double-seated carryall offered to drive them over. The hospital would have sent an ambulance, but Mrs Whipple couldn't stand to see Him going away looking so sick as all that. They wrapped Him in blankets, and the neighbour and Mr. Whipple lifted Him into the back seat of the carryall beside Mrs Whipple, who had on her black shirt-waist. She couldn't stand to go looking like charity.

"You'll be all right, I guess I'll stay behind," said Mr Whipple. "It don't look like everybody ought to leave the place at once."

"Besides, it ain't as if He was going to stay for ever," said Mrs Whipple to the neighbour. "This is only for a little while."

They started away, Mrs Whipple holding to the edges of the blankets to keep Him from sagging sideways. He sat there blinking and blinking. He worked His hands out and began rubbing His nose with His knuckles, and then with the end of the blanket. Mrs Whipple couldn't believe what she saw; He was scrubbing away big tears that rolled out of the corners of His eyes. He snivelled and made a gulping noise. Mrs Whipple kept saying, "Oh, honey, you don't feel so bad, do you? You don't feel so bad, do you?" for He seemed to be accusing her of something. Maybe He remembered that time she boxed His ears; maybe He had been scared that day with the bull; maybe He had slept cold and couldn't tell her about it; maybe He knew they were sending Him away for good and all because they were too poor to keep Him. Whatever it was, Mrs Whipple couldn't bear to think of it. She began to cry, frightfully, and wrapped her arms tightly round him. His head rolled on her shoulder: she had loved Him as much as she possibly could; there were Adna and Emly who had to be thought of too, there was nothing she could do to make up to Him for His life. Oh, what a mortal pity He was ever born.

They came in sight of the hospital, with the neighbour driving very fast, not daring to look behind him.

SINCLAIR ROSS

Born in Shellbrook, Saskatchewan in 1908, Sinclair Ross grew up on the Canadian prairies. He worked as a banker there and in Montreal before retiring to live in Greece and Spain, and subsequently in Vancouver. The author of several novels, he is particularly known for his first, *As for Me and My House*, which appeared in 1941. Like many of his short stories, most of which were collected in 1968 under the title *The Lamp at Noon and other stories*, it deals with the realities of rural prairie life during the drought and depression of the 1930s.

Ross's art displays the chief characteristics of literary regionalism: scrupulous fidelity to the geographical realities of a place and time, sensitivity to the details of speech, habit, and social convention, and a vital interest in the connections between a landscape and its people. He attempts not only to invoke these connections but also to elicit from the reader an appreciation of the way in which they give a particular cast to a universal human dilemma. Recurrently Ross dramatizes the tensions between human beings and nature, integrates them with Calvinist mores, and then qualifies his response to the Protestant ethic by the importance he attaches to artistic freedom. In the world he draws, nature and society exert uncompromising demands; beauty and art are ephemeral things, and against the pressures of day-to-day survival they seem to have peripheral value—to be sentimental, impractical, and (in the language of that culture) "womanish." At the same time, they are extraordinarily important. As "Cornet at Night" suggests, the characters who appreciate artistry will be all the more frustrated by their immediate environment because of their sensitivity. But in recognizing the limitations of their surroundings they also discover resources upon which less fortunate individuals cannot draw.

FOR FURTHER READING

Keath Fraser, "Futility at the Pump: the Short Stories of Sinclair Ross," *Queen's Quarterly* 77 (Spring 1970): 72–80.

Lorraine McMullen, *Sinclair Ross* (Boston: Twayne, 1979).

Donald Stephens, ed., *Writers of the Prairies* (Vancouver: University of British Columbia, 1973).

CORNET AT NIGHT

The wheat was ripe and it was Sunday. "Can't help it — I've got to cut," my father said at breakfast. "No use talking. There's a wind again and it's shelling fast."

"Not on the Lord's Day," my mother protested. "The horses stay in the stables where they belong. There's church this afternoon and I intend to ask Louise and her husband home for supper."

Ordinarily my father was a pleasant, accommodating little man, but this morning his wheat and the wind had lent him sudden steel. "No, today we cut," he met her evenly. "You and Tom go to church if you want to. Don't bother me."

"If you take the horses out today I'm through — I'll never speak to you again. And this time I mean it."

He nodded. "Good — if I'd known I'd have started cutting wheat on Sundays years ago."

"And that's no way to talk in front of your son. In the years to come he'll remember."

There was silence for a moment and then, as if in its clash with hers his will had suddenly found itself, my father turned to me.

"Tom, I need a man to stook for a few days and I want you to go to town tomorrow and get me one. The way the wheat's coming along so fast and the oats nearly ready too I can't afford the time. Take old Rock. You'll be safe with him."

But ahead of me my mother cried, "That's one thing I'll not stand for. You can cut your wheat or do anything else you like yourself, but you're not interfering with him. He's going to school tomorrow as usual."

My father bunched himself and glared at her. "No, for a change he's going to do what I say. The crop's more important than a day at school."

"But Monday's his music lesson day — and when will we have another teacher like Miss Wiggins who can teach him music too?"

"A dollar for lessons and the wheat shelling! When I was his age I didn't even get to school."

"Exactly," my mother scored, "and look at you today. Is it any wonder I want him to be different?"

He slammed out at that to harness his horses and cut his wheat, and away sailed my mother with me in her wake to spend an austere half-hour in the dark, hot, plushy little parlour. It was a kind of vicarious atonement, I suppose, for we both took straight-backed leather chairs, and for all of the half-hour stared across the room at a big pansy-bordered motto on the opposite wall: *As for Me and My House We Will Serve the Lord.*

At last she rose and said, "Better run along and do your chores now, but hurry back. You've got to take your bath and change your clothes, and maybe help a little getting dinner for your father."

There was a wind this sunny August morning, tanged with freedom and departure, and from his stall my pony Clipper whinnied for a race with it. Sunday or not, I would ordinarily have had my gallop anyway, but today a sudden welling-up of social and religious conscience made me ask myself whether one in the family like my father wasn't bad enough. Returning to the house, I merely said that on such a fine day it seemed a pity to stay inside. My mother heard but didn't answer. Perhaps her conscience too was working. Perhaps after being worsted in the skirmish with my father, she was in no mood for granting dispensations. In any case I had to take my bath as usual, put on a clean white shirt, and change my overalls for knicker corduroys.

They squeaked, those corduroys. For three months now they had been spoiling all my Sundays. A sad, muted, swishing little squeak, but distinctly audible. Every step and there it was, as if I needed to be oiled. I had to wear them to church and Sunday-school; and after service, of course, while the grown-ups stood about gossiping, the other boys discovered my affliction. I sulked and fumed, but there was nothing to be done. Corduroys that had cost four-fifty simply couldn't be thrown away till they were well worn-out. My mother warned me that if I started sliding down the stable roof, she'd patch the seat and make me keep on wearing them.

With my customary little bow-legged sidle I slipped into the kitchen again to ask what there was to do. "Nothing but try to behave like a Christian and a gentleman," my other answered stiffly. "Put on a tie, and shoes and stockings. Today your father is just about as much as I can bear."

"And then what?" I asked hopefully. I was thinking that I might take a drink to my father, but dared not as yet suggest it.

"Then after you can stay quiet and read—and afterwards practise your music lesson. If your Aunt Louise should come she'll find that at least I bring my son up decently."

It was a long day. My mother prepared the midday meal as usual, but, to impress upon my father the enormity of his conduct, withdrew as soon as the food was served. When he was gone, she and I emerged to take our places at the table in an atmosphere of unappetizing righteousness. We didn't eat much. The food was cold, and my mother had no heart to warm it up. For relief at last she said, "Run along and feed the chickens while I change my dress. Since we aren't going to service today we'll read Scripture for a while instead."

And Scripture we did read, Isaiah, verse about, my mother in her black silk dress and rhinestone brooch, I in my corduroys and Sunday shoes that pinched. It was a very august afternoon, exactly like the tone that had persisted in my mother's voice since breakfast time. I think I might have openly rebelled, only for the hope that by compliance I yet might win permission for the trip to town with Rock. I was inordinately proud that my father had suggested it, and for his faith in me forgave him even Isaiah and the plushy afternoon. Whereas with my mother, I decided, it was a case of downright bigotry.

We went on reading Isaiah, and then for a while I played hymns on the piano. A great many hymns — even the ones with awkward sharps and accidentals that I'd never tried before — for, fearing visitors, my mother was resolved to let them see that she and I were uncontaminated by my father's sacrilege. But among these likely visitors was my Aunt Louise, a portly, condescending lady married to a well-off farmer with a handsome motor-car, and always when she came it was my mother's vanity to have me play for her a waltz or reverie, or *Holy Night* sometimes with variations. A man-child and prodigy might eclipse the motor-car. Presently she roused herself, and pretending mild reproof began, ''Now, Tommy, you're going wooden on those hymns. For a change you'd better practise *Sons of Liberty*. Your Aunt Louise will want to hear it, anyway.''

There was a fine swing and vigour in this piece, but it was hard. Hard because it was so alive, so full of youth and head-high rhythm. It was a march, and it did march. I couldn't take time to practise at the hard spots slowly till I got them right, for I had to march too. I had to let my fingers sometimes miss a note or strike one wrong. Again and again this afternoon I started carefully, resolving to count right through, the way Miss Wiggins did, and as often I sprang ahead to lead my march a moment or two all dash and fire, and then fall stumbling in the bitter dust of dissonance. My mother didn't know. She thought that speed and perseverance would eventually get me there. She tapped her foot and smiled encouragement, and gradually as the afternoon wore on began to look a little disappointed that there were to be no visitors, after all. ''Run along for the cows,'' she said at last, ''while I get supper ready for your father. There'll be nobody here, so you can slip into your overalls again.''

I looked at her a moment, and then asked: ''What am I going to wear to town tomorrow? I might get grease or something on the corduroys.''

For while it was always my way to exploit the future, I liked to do it rationally, within the limits of the sane and probable. On my way for the cows I wanted to live the trip to town tomorrow many times, with variations, but only on the explicit understanding that tomorrow there was to be a trip to town. I have always been tethered to reality, always compelled by an unfortunate kind of probity in my nature to prefer a barefaced disappointment to the luxury of a future I have no just claims upon.

I went to town the next day, though not till there had been a full hour's argument that paradoxically enough gave all three of us the victory. For my father had his way: I went; I had my way: I went; and in return for her consent my mother wrung a promise from him of a pair of new plush curtains for the parlour when the crop was threshed, and for me the metronome that Miss Wiggins declared was the only way I'd ever learn to keep in time on marching pieces like the *Sons of Liberty*.

It was my first trip to town alone. That was why they gave me Rock, who was old and reliable and philosophic enough to meet motor-cars and the chance locomotive on an equal and even somewhat supercilious footing.

"Mind you pick somebody big and husky," said my father as he started for the field. "Go to Jenkins' store, and he'll tell you who's in town. Whoever it is, make sure he's stooked before."

"And mind it's somebody who looks like he washes himself," my mother warned, "I'm going to put clean sheets and pillowcases on the bunkhouse bed, but not for any dirty tramp or hobo."

By the time they had both finished with me there were a great many things to mind. Besides repairs for my father's binder, I was to take two crates of eggs each containing twelve dozen eggs to Mr. Jenkins' store and in exchange have a list of groceries filled. And to make it complicated, both quantity and quality of some of the groceries were to be determined by the price of eggs. Thirty cents a dozen, for instance, and I was to ask for coffee at sixty-five cents a pound. Twenty-nine cents a dozen and coffee at fifty cents a pound. Twenty-eight and no oranges. Thirty-one and bigger oranges. It was like decimals with Miss Wiggins, or two notes in the treble against three in the bass. For my father a tin of special blend tobacco, and my mother not to know. For my mother a box of face powder at the drugstore, and my father not to know. Twenty-five cents from my father on the side for ice-cream and licorice. Thirty-five from my mother for my dinner at the Chinese restaurant. And warning, of course, to take good care of Rock, speak politely to Mr. Jenkins, and see that I didn't get machine oil on my corduroys.

It was three hours to town with Rock, but I don't remember them, I remember nothing but a smug satisfaction with myself, an exhilarating conviction of importance and maturity—and that only by contrast with the sudden sag to embarrassed insignificance when finally old Rock and I drove up to Jenkins' store.

For a farm boy is like that. Alone with himself and his horse he cuts a fine figure. He is the measure of the universe. He foresees a great many encounters with life, and in them all acquits himself a little more than creditably. He is fearless, resourceful, a bit of a brag. His horse never contradicts.

But in town it is different. There are eyes here, critical, that pierce with a single glance the little bubble of his self-importance, and leave him dwindled smaller even than his normal size. It always happens that way. They are so superbly poised and sophisticated, these strangers, so completely masters of their situation as they loll in doorways and go sauntering up and down Main Street. Instantly he yields to them his place as measure of the universe, especially if he is a small boy wearing squeaky corduroys, especially if he has a worldly-wise old horse like Rock, one that knows his Main Streets, and will take them in nothing but his own slow philosophic stride.

We arrived all right. Mr. Jenkins was a little man with a freckled bald head, and when I carried in my two crates of eggs, one in each hand, and my legs bowed a bit, he said curtly, "Well, can't you set them down? My boy's delivering, and I can't take time to count them now myself."

"They don't need counting," I said politely. "Each layer holds two dozen, and each crate holds six layers. I was there. I saw my mother put them in."

At this a tall, slick-haired young man in yellow shoes who had been standing by the window turned around and said, "That's telling you, Jenkins — he was there." Nettled and glowering, Jenkins himself came round the counter and repeated, "So you were there, were you? Smart youngster! What did you say was your name?"

Nettled in turn to preciseness I answered, "I haven't yet. It's Thomas Dickson and my father's David Dickson, eight miles north of here. He wants a man to stook and was too busy to come himself."

He nodded, unimpressed, and then putting out his hand said, "Where's your list? Your mother gave you one, I hope?"

I said she had and he glowered again. "Then let's have it and come back in half an hour. Whether you were there or not, I'm going to count your eggs. How do I know that half of them aren't smashed?"

"That's right," agreed the young man, sauntering to the door and looking at Rock. "They've likely been bouncing along at a merry clip. You're quite sure, Buddy, that you didn't have a runaway?"

Ignoring the impertinence I staved off Jenkins. "The list, you see, has to be explained. I'd rather wait and tell you about it later on."

He teetered a moment on his heels and toes, then tried again. "I can read too. I make up orders every day. Just go away for a while — look for your man — anything."

"It wouldn't do," I persisted. "The way this one's written isn't what it really means. You'd need me to explain —"

He teetered rapidly. "Show me just one thing I don't know what it means."

"Oranges," I said, "but that's only oranges if eggs are twenty-nine cents or more — and bigger oranges if they're thirty-one. You see, you'd never understand —"

So I had my way and explained it all right then and there. What with eggs at twenty-nine and a half cents a dozen and my mother out a little in her calculations, it was somewhat confusing for a while; but after arguing a lot and pulling away the paper from each other that they were figuring on, the young man and Mr. Jenkins finally had it all worked out, with mustard and soap omitted altogether, and an extra half-dozen oranges thrown in. "Vitamins," the young man overruled me, "they make you grow" — and then with a nod towards an open biscuit box invited me to help myself.

I took a small one, and started up Rock again. It was nearly one o'clock now, so in anticipation of his noonday quart of oats he trotted off, a little more briskly, for the farmers' hitching-rail beside the lumber-yard. This was the quiet end of town. The air drowsed redolent of pine and tamarack, and resin simmering slowly in the sun. I poured out the oats and waited till he had finished. After the way the town had treated me it was comforting and peaceful to stand with my fingers in his mane, hearing him munch. It brought me a sense of place again in life. It made me feel almost as important as before. But when he finished and there was my own dinner to be thought about I found myself more of an alien in the town than ever, and felt the way to the little Chinese restaurant doubly hard. For Rock was older than I. Older and wiser, with a better understanding of important things. His philosophy included the relishing of oats even within a stone's throw of sophisticated Main Street. Mine was less mature.

I went, however, but I didn't have dinner. Perhaps it was my stomach, all puckered and tense with nervousness. Perhaps it was the restaurant itself, the pyramids of oranges in the window and the dark green rubber plant with the tropical-looking leaves, the indolent little Chinaman behind the counter and the dusky smell of last night's cigarettes that to my prairie nostrils was the orient itself, the exotic atmosphere about it all with which a meal of meat and vegetables and pie would have somehow simply jarred. I climbed onto a stool and ordered an ice-cream soda.

A few stools away there was a young man sitting. I kept watching him and wondering.

He was well-dressed, a nonchalance about his clothes that distinguished him from anyone I had ever seen, and yet at the same time it was a shabby suit, with shiny elbows and threadbare cuffs. His hands were slender, almost a girl's hands, yet vaguely with their shapely quietness they troubled me, because, however slender and smooth, they were yet hands to be reckoned with, strong with a strength that was different from the rugged labour-strength I knew.

He smoked a cigarette, and blew rings towards the window.

Different from the farmer boys I knew, yet different also from the young man with the yellow shoes in Jenkins' store. Staring out at it through the restaurant window he was as far away from Main Street as was I with plodding old Rock and my squeaky corduroys. I presumed for a minute or two an imaginary companionship. I finished my soda, and to be with him a little longer ordered lemonade. It was strangely important to be with him, to prolong a while this companionship. I hadn't the slightest hope of his noticing me, nor the slightest intention of obtruding myself. I just wanted to be there, to be assured by something I had never encountered before, to store it up for the three hours home with old Rock.

Then a big, unshaven man came in, and slouching onto the stool beside me said, "They tell me across the street you're looking for a couple of hands. What's your old man pay this year?"

"My father," I corrected him, "doesn't want a couple of men. He just wants one."

"I've got a pal," he insisted, "and we always go together."

I didn't like him. I couldn't help making contrasts with the cool, trim quietness of the young man sitting farther along. "What do you say?" he said as I sat silent, thrusting his stubby chin out almost over my lemonade. "We're ready any time."

"It's just one man my father wants," I said aloofly, drinking off my lemonade with a flourish to let him see I meant it. "And if you'll excuse me now — I've got to look for somebody else."

"What about this?" he intercepted me, and doubling up his arm displayed a hump of muscle that made me, if not more inclined to him, at least a little more deferential. "My pal's got plenty, too. We'll set up two stooks any day for anybody else's one."

"Not both," I edged away from him. "I'm sorry — you just wouldn't do."

He shook his head contemptuously. "Some farmer — just one man to stook."

"My father's a good farmer," I answered stoutly, rallying to the family honour less for its own sake than for what the young man on the other stool might think of us. "And he doesn't need just one man to stook. He's got three already. That's plenty other years, but this year the crop's so big he needs another. So there!"

"I can just see the place," he said, slouching to his feet and starting towards the door. "An acre or two of potatoes and a couple of dozen hens."

I glared after him a minute, then climbed back onto the stool and ordered another soda. The young man was watching me now in the big mirror behind the counter, and when I glanced up and met his eyes he gave a slow, half-smiling little nod of approval. And out of all proportion to anything it could mean, his nod encouraged me. I didn't flinch or fidget as I would have done had it been the young man with the yellow shoes watching me, and I didn't stammer over the confession that his amusement and appraisal somehow forced from me. "We haven't three men — just my father — but I'm to take one home today. The wheat's ripening fast this year and shelling, so he can't do it all himself."

He nodded again and then after a minute asked quietly, "What about me? Would I do?"

I turned on the stool and stared at him.

"I need a job, and if it's any recommendation there's only one of me."

"You don't understand," I started to explain, afraid to believe that perhaps he really did. "It's to stook. You have to be in the field by seven o'clock and there's only a bunkhouse to sleep in — a granary with a bed in it —"

"I know — that's about what I expect." He drummed his fingers a minute, then twisted his lips into a kind of half-hearted smile and went on, ''They tell me a little toughening up is what I need. Outdoors, and plenty of good hard work — so I'll be like the fellow that just went out.''

The wrong hands: white slender fingers, I knew they'd never do — but catching the twisted smile again I pushed away my soda and said quickly, ''Then we'd better start right away. It's three hours home, and I've still some places to go. But you can get in the buggy now, and we'll drive around together.''

We did. I wanted it that way, the two of us, to settle scores with Main Street. I wanted to capture some of old Rock's disdain and unconcern; I wanted to know what it felt like to take young men with yellow shoes in my stride, to be preoccupied, to forget them the moment that we separated. And I did. ''My name's Philip,'' the stranger said as we drove from Jenkins' to the drugstore. ''Philip Coleman — usually just Phil,'' and companionably I responded, ''Mine's Tommy Dickson. For the last year, though, my father says I'm getting big and should be called just Tom.''

That was what mattered now, the two of us there, and not the town at all. ''Do you drive yourself all the time?'' he asked, and nonchalant and off-hand I answered, ''You don't really have to drive old Rock. He just goes, anyway. Wait till you see my chestnut three-year-old. Clipper I call him. Tonight after supper if you like you can take him for a ride.''

But since he'd never learned to ride at all he thought Rock would do better for a start, and then we drove back to the restaurant for his cornet and valise.

''Is it something to play?'' I asked as we cleared the town. ''Something like a bugle?''

He picked up the black leather case from the floor of the buggy and held it on his knee. ''Something like that. Once I played a bugle too. A cornet's better, though.''

''And you mean you can play the cornet?''

He nodded. ''I play in a band. At least I did play in a band. Perhaps if I get along all right with the stooking I will again some time.''

It was later that I pondered this, how stooking for my father could have anything to do with going back to play in a band. At the moment I confided, ''I've never heard a cornet — never even seen one. I suppose you still play it sometimes — I mean at night, when you've finished stooking.''

Instead of answering directly he said, ''That means you've never heard a band either.'' There was surprise in his voice, almost incredulity, but it was kindly. Somehow I didn't feel ashamed because I had lived all my eleven years on a prairie farm, and knew nothing more than Miss Wiggins and my Aunt Louise's gramophone. He went on, ''I was younger than you are now when I started playing in a band. Then I was with an orchestra a while — then with the band again. It's all I've done ever since.''

It made me feel lonely for a while, isolated from the things in life that mattered, but, brightening presently, I asked, "Do you know a piece called *Sons of Liberty*? Four flats in four-four time?"

He thought hard a minute, and then shook his head. "I'm afraid I don't — not by name anyway. Could you whistle a bit of it?"

I whistled two pages, but still he shook his head. "A nice tune, though," he conceded. "Where did you learn it?"

"I haven't yet," I explained. "Not properly, I mean. It's been my lesson for the last two weeks, but I can't keep up to it."

He seemed interested, so I went on and told him about my lessons and Miss Wiggins, and how later on they were going to buy me a metronome so that when I played a piece I wouldn't always be running away with it, "Especially a march. It keeps pulling you along the way it really ought to go until you're all mixed up and have to start at the beginning again. I know I'd do better if I didn't feel that way, and could keep slow and steady like Miss Wiggins."

But he said quickly, "No, that's the right way to feel — you've just got to learn to harness it. It's like old Rock here and Clipper. The way you are, you're Clipper. But if you weren't that way, if you didn't get excited and wanted to run sometimes, you'd just be Rock. You see? Rock's easier to handle than Clipper, but at his best he's a sleepy old plow-horse. Clipper's harder to handle — he may even cost you some tumbles. But finally get him broken in and you've got a horse that amounts to something. You wouldn't trade him for a dozen like Rock."

It was a good enough illustration, but it slandered Rock. And he was listening. I know — because even though like me he had never heard a cornet before, he had experience enough to accept it at least with tact and manners.

For we hadn't gone much farther when Philip, noticing the way I kept watching the case that was still on his knee, undid the clasps and took the cornet out. It was a very lovely cornet, shapely and eloquent, gleaming in the August sun like pure and mellow gold. I couldn't restrain myself. I said, "Play it — play it now — just a little bit to let me hear." And in response, smiling at my earnestness, he raised it to his lips.

But there was only one note — only one fragment of a note — and then away went Rock. I'd never have believed he had it in him. With a snort and plunge he was off the road and into the ditch — then out of the ditch again and off at a breakneck gallop across the prairie. There were stones and badger holes, and he spared us none of them. The egg-crates full of groceries bounced out, then the tobacco, then my mother's face powder. "Whoa, Rock!" I cried, "Whoa, Rock!" but in the rattle and whir of wheels I don't suppose he even heard. Philip couldn't help much because he had his cornet to hang on to. I tried to tug on the reins, but at such a rate across the prairie it took me all my time to keep from following the groceries. He was a big horse, Rock, and once under way had to run himself out. Or he may have thought that if he gave us a thorough shaking-up we would be too subdued when it was over to feel like taking him seriously to task. Anyway, that was how it worked out. All I dared to do was run round to pat his sweaty neck and say, "Good Rock, good Rock — nobody's going to hurt you."

Besides there were the groceries to think about, and my mother's box of face powder. And his pride and reputation at stake, Rock had made it a runaway worthy of the horse he really was. We found the powder smashed open and one of the egg-crates cracked. Several of the oranges had rolled down a badger hole, and couldn't be recovered. We spent nearly ten minutes sifting raisins through our fingers, and still they felt a little gritty. "There were extra oranges," I tried to encourage Philip, "and I've seen my mother wash her raisins." He looked at me dubiously, and for a few minutes longer worked away trying to mend the egg-crate.

We were silent for the rest of the way home. We thought a great deal about each other, but asked no questions. Even though it was safely away in its case again I could still feel the cornet's presence as if it were a living thing. Somehow its gold and shapeliness persisted, transfiguring the day, quickening the dusty harvest fields to a gleam and lustre like its own. And I felt assured, involved. Suddenly there was a force in life, a current, an inevitability, carrying me along too. The questions they would ask when I reached home — the difficulties in making them understand that faithful old Rock had really run away — none of it now seemed to matter. This stranger with the white, thin hands, this gleaming cornet that as yet I hadn't even heard, intimately and enduringly now they were my possessions.

When we reached home my mother was civil and no more. "Put your things in the bunkhouse," she said, "and then wash here. Supper'll be ready in about an hour."

It was an uncomfortable meal. My father and my mother kept looking at Philip and exchanging glances. I told them about the cornet and the runaway, and they listened stonily. "We've never had a harvest-hand before that was a musician too," my mother said in a somewhat thin voice. "I suppose, though, you do know how to stook?"

I was watching Philip desperately and for my sake he lied, "Yes, I stooked last year. I may have a blister or two by this time tomorrow, but my hands will toughen up."

"You don't as a rule do farm work?" my father asked.

And Philip said, "No, not as a rule."

There was an awkward silence, so I tried to champion him. "He plays his cornet in a band. Ever since he was my age — that's what he does."

Glances were exchanged again. The silence continued.

I had been half-intending to suggest that Philip bring his cornet into the house to play it for us, I perhaps playing with him on the piano, but the parlour with its genteel plushiness was a room from which all were excluded but the equally genteel — visitors like Miss Wiggins and the minister — and gradually as the meal progressed I came to understand that Philip and his cornet, so far as my mother was concerned, had failed to qualify.

So I said nothing when he finished his supper, and let him go back to the bunkhouse alone. "Didn't I say to have Jenkins pick him out?" my father stormed as soon as he had gone. "Didn't I say somebody big and strong?"

"He's tall," I countered, "and there wasn't anybody else except two men, and it was the only way they'd come."

"You mean you didn't want anybody else. A cornet player! Fine stooks he'll set up." And then, turning to my mother, "It's your fault — you and your nonsense about music lessons. If you'd listen to me sometimes, and try to make a man of him."

"I do listen to you," she answered quickly. "It's because I've had to listen to you now for thirteen years that I'm trying to make a different man of him. If you'd go to town yourself instead of keeping him out of school — and do your work in six days a week like decent people. I told you yesterday that in the long run it would cost you dear."

I slipped away and left them. The chores at the stable took me nearly an hour; and then, instead of returning to the house, I went over to see Philip. It was dark now, and there was a smoky lantern lit. He sat on the only chair, and in a hospitable silence motioned me to the bed. At once he ignored and accepted me. It was as if we had always known each other and long outgrown the need of conversation. He smoked, and blew rings towards the open door where the warm fall night encroached. I waited, eager, afraid lest they call me to the house, yet knowing that I must wait. Gradually the flame in the lantern smoked the glass till scarcely his face was left visible. I sat tense, expectant, wondering who he was, where he came from, why he should be here to do my father's stooking.

There were no answers, but presently he reached for his cornet. In the dim, soft darkness I could see it glow and quicken. And I remember still what a long and fearful moment it was, crouched and steeling myself, waiting for him to begin.

And I was right: when they came the notes were piercing, golden as the cornet itself, and they gave life expanse that it had never known before. They floated up against the night, and each for a moment hung there clear and visible. Sometimes they mounted poignant and sheer. Sometimes they soared and then, like a bird alighting, fell and brushed earth again.

It was *To the Evening Star*. He finished it and told me. He told me the names of all the other pieces that he played: an Ave *Maria*, *Song of India*, a serenade — all bright through the dark like slow, suspended lightning, chilled sometimes with a glimpse of the unknown. Only for Philip there I could not have endured it. With my senses I clung hard to him — the acrid smell of his cigarettes, the tilted profile daubed with smoky light.

Then abruptly he stood up, as if understanding, and said, "Now we'd better have a march, Tom—to bring us back where we belong. A cornet can be good fun, too, you know. Listen to this one and tell me."

He stood erect, head thrown back exactly like a picture in my reader of a bugler boy, and the notes came flashing gallant through the night until the two of us went swinging along in step with them a hundred thousand strong. For this was another march that did march. It marched us miles. It made the feet eager and the heart brave. It said that life was worth the living and bright as morning shone ahead to show the way.

When he had finished and put the cornet away I said, "There's a field right behind the house that my father started cutting this afternoon. If you like we'll go over now for a few minutes and I'll show you how to stook. . . . You see, if you set your sheaves on top of the stubble they'll be over again in half an hour. That's how everybody does at first but it's wrong. You've got to push the butts down hard, right to the ground—like this, so they bind with the stubble. At a good slant, see, but not too much. So they'll stand the wind and still shed water if it rains."

It was too dark for him to see much, but he listened hard and finally succeeded in putting up a stook or two that to my touch seemed firm enough. Then my mother called, and I had to slip away fast so that she would think I was coming from the bunkhouse. "I hope he stooks as well as he plays," she said when I went in. "Just the same, you should have done as your father told you, and picked a likelier man to see us through the fall."

My father came in from the stable then, and he, too, had been listening. With a wondering, half-incredulous little movement of his head he made acknowledgment.

"Didn't I tell you he could?" I burst out, encouraged to indulge my pride in Philip. "Didn't I tell you he could play?" But with sudden anger in his voice he answered, "And what if he can! It's a man to stook I want. Just look at the hands on him. I don't think he's ever seen a farm before."

It was helplessness, though, not anger. Helplessness to escape his wheat when wheat was not enough, when something more than wheat had just revealed itself. Long after they were both asleep I remembered, and with a sharp foreboding that we might have to find another man, tried desperately to sleep myself. "Because if I'm up in good time," I rallied all my faith in life, "I'll be able to go to the field with him and at least make sure he's started right. And he'll maybe do. I'll ride down after school and help till supper time. My father's reasonable."

Only in such circumstances, of course, and after such a day, I couldn't sleep till nearly morning, with the result that when at last my mother wakened me there was barely time to dress and ride to school. But of the day I spent there I remember nothing. Nothing except the midriff clutch of dread that made it a long day—nothing, till straddling Clipper at four again, I galloped him straight to the far end of the farm where Philip that morning had started to work.

Only Philip, of course, wasn't there. I think I knew — I think it was what all day I had been expecting. I pulled Clipper up short and sat staring at the stooks. Three or four acres of them — crooked and dejected as if he had never heard about pushing the butts down hard into the stubble. I sat and stared till Clipper himself swung round and started for home. He wanted to run, but because there was nothing left now but the half-mile ahead of us, I held him to a walk. Just to prolong a little the possibility that I had misunderstood things. To wonder within the limits of the sane and probable if tonight he would play his cornet again.

When I reached the house my father was already there, eating an early supper. "I'm taking him back to town," he said quietly. "He tried hard enough — he's just not used to it. The sun was hot today; he lasted till about noon. We're starting in a few minutes, so you'd better go out and see him."

He looked older now, stretched out limp on the bed, his face haggard. I tiptoed close to him anxiously, afraid to speak. He pulled his mouth sidewise in a smile at my concern, then motioned me to sit down. "Sorry I didn't do better," he said. "I'll have to come back another year and have another lesson."

I clenched my hands and clung hard to this promise that I knew he couldn't keep. I wanted to rebel against what was happening, against the clumsiness and crudity of life, but instead I stood quiet a moment, almost passive, then wheeled away and carried out his cornet to the buggy. My mother was already there, with a box of lunch and some ointment for his sunburn. She said she was sorry things had turned out this way, and thanking her politely he said that he was sorry too. My father looked uncomfortable, feeling, no doubt, that we were all unjustly blaming everything on him. It's like that on a farm. You always have to put the harvest first.

And that's all there is to tell. He waved going through the gate; I never saw him again. We watched the buggy down the road to the first turn, then with a quick resentment in her voice my mother said, "Didn't I say that the little he gained would in the long run cost him dear? Next time he'll maybe listen to me — and remember the Sabbath Day."

What exactly she was thinking I never knew. Perhaps of the crop and the whole day's stooking lost. Perhaps of the stranger who had come with his cornet for a day, and then as meaninglessly gone again. For she had been listening, too, and she may have understood. A harvest, however lean, is certain every year; but a cornet at night is golden only once.

AUDREY THOMAS

Born Audrey Callahan in Binghamton, New York in 1935, Audrey Thomas was educated in the United States, Scotland, and Canada. Interrupting her formal education to spend two years in Ghana, she returned in 1966 to Vancouver, where she now lives. "If One Green Bottle . . . ," which was her first published short story, appeared in *The Atlantic Monthly* and was then collected in *Ten Green Bottles* (1967). (For the version printed here, the author has made several textual alterations.) Other stories followed, as did novels, novellas, and a radio play. Like "If One Green Bottle . . . ," her novel *Mrs. Blood* (1970) concerns a woman experiencing a difficult pregnancy; the one ends in miscarriage, the other threatens to, and both stories are told from the woman's own perspective. One of the key tensions in *Mrs. Blood* is that between the woman's two subjective identities: "Mrs. Blood," the visceral woman, unknowable outside herself, and "Mrs. Thing," the apparent "object" whom she and others can variously regard. That internal division mirrors various kinds of external schisms — most particularly those between men and women, in their attractions toward and misunderstandings of each other's nature. Such relationships, in entirely different forms, also constitute the overt subjects of her later story collections *Ladies and Escorts* (1977) and *Real Mothers* (1981), and her 1984 novel *Intertidal Life*.

A sense of isolation also pervades "If One Green Bottle. . . ." The rhythm of the story followed the narrator's experience, and the stream-of-consciousness style carries the associations of her mind, the leaps from fragmentary image to fragmentary image that retell part of her life. But nothing can erase the present — not myth, not philosophy, not knowledge of history and literature, not memories of her own childhood. The pressures of the here-and-now emphasize for her the inadequacy of ideas and systems. The writer's restraint in evoking those pressures makes the realization of solitariness into a painful discovery for narrator and reader alike.

FOR FURTHER READING

Interview with Audrey Thomas, *Capilano Review* 7 (Spring 1975).

H.J. Rosengarten, "Writer and Subject," *Canadian Literature*, no. 55 (Winter 1973): 111–13.

Audrey Thomas, "Basmati Rice: An Essay About Words," *Canadian Literature*, no. 100 (Spring 1984): 312–17.

IF ONE GREEN BOTTLE . . .

When fleeing, one should never look behind. Orpheus, Lot's wife . . . penalties grotesque and terrible await us all. It does not pay to doubt . . . to turn one's head . . . to rely on the confusion . . . the smoke . . . the fleeing multitudes . . . the satisfaction of the tumbling cities . . . to distract the attention of the gods. Argus-eyed, they wait, he waits . . . the golden chessmen spread upon the table . . . the opponent's move already known, accounted for. . . . Your pawns, so vulnerable . . . advancing with such care (if you step on a crack, then you'll break your mother's back). Already the monstrous hand trembles in anticipation . . . the thick lips twitch with suppressed laughter . . . then pawn, knight, castle, queen scooped up and tossed aside. "Check," and (click click) "check . . . mmmate." The game is over, and you . . . surprised (but why?) . . . petulant . . . your nose still raw from the cold . . . your galoshes not yet dried . . . really, it's indecent . . . inhumane (why bother to come? answer: the bother of not coming) . . . and not even the offer of a sandwich or a cup of tea . . . discouraging . . . disgusting. The great mouth opens . . . like a whale really . . . he strains you, one more bit of plankton, through his teeth. "Next week . . . ? At the same time . . . ? No, no, not at all. I do not find it boring in the least. . . . Each time a great improvement. Why, soon," the huge lips tremble violently, "ha, ha, *you'll* be beating *me*." Lies . . . all lies. Yet, even as you go, echoes of Olympian laughter in your ears, you know you will return, will once more challenge . . . and be defeated once again. Even plankton have to make a protest . . . a stand . . . what else can one do? "Besides, it passes the time . . . keeps my hand in . . . and you never know. . . . One time, perhaps . . . a slip . . . a flutter of the eyelids. . . . Even the gods grow old."

The tropical fan, three-bladed, ominiscient, omnipotent, inexorable, churns up dust and mosquitoes, the damp smell of coming rain, the overripe smell of vegetation, of charcoal fires, of human excrement, of fear . . . blown in through the open window, blown up from the walls and the floor. All is caught in the fan's embrace, the efficient arms of the unmoved mover. The deus in the machina, my old chum the chessplayer, refuses to descend . . . yet watches. Soon they will let down the nets and we will lie in the darkness, in our gauze houses, like so many lumps of cheese . . . protected . . . revealed. The night-fliers, dirty urchins, will press their noses at my windows and lick their hairy lips in hunger . . . in frustration. Can they differentiate, I wonder, between the blood of my neighbor and mine? Are there aesthetes among the insects who will touch only the soft parts . . . between the thighs . . . under the armpits . . . along the inner arm? Are there vintages and connoisseurs? I don't like the nights here: that is why I wanted it over before the night. One of the reasons. If am asleep I do not know who feeds on me, who has found the infinitesimal rip and invited his neighbors in. Besides, he promised it would be over before the night. And one listens, doesn't one? . . . one always believes. . . . Absurd to rely on verbal consolation . . . clichés so worn they feel like old coins . . . smooth . . . slightly oily to the touch . . . faceless.

Pain, the word, I mean, derived (not according to Skeat) from "pay" and "Cain." How can there, then, be an exit . . . a way out? The darker the night, the clearer the mark on the forehead . . . the brighter the blind man's cane at the crossing . . . the louder the sound of footsteps somewhere behind. Darkness heightens the absurd sense of "situation" . . . gives the audience its kicks. But tonight . . . really . . . All Souls' . . . it's too ridiculous. . . . Somebody goofed. The author has gone too far; the absurdity lies in one banana skin, not two or three. After one, it becomes too painful . . . too involved . . . too much like home. Somebody will have to pay for this . . . the reviews . . . tomorrow . . . will all be most severe. The actors will sulk over their morning cup of coffee . . . the angel will beat his double breast above the empty pocketbook . . . the director will shout and stamp his feet. . . . The whole thing should have been revised . . . rewritten . . . we knew it from the first.

(This is the house that Jack built. This is the cat that killed the rat that lived in the house that Jack built. We are the maidens all shaven and shorn, that milked the cow with the crumpled horn . . . that loved in the hearse that Joke built. Excuse me, please, was this the Joke that killed the giant or the Jack who tumbled down . . . who broke his crown? Crown him with many crowns, the lamb upon his throne. He tumbled too . . . it's inevitable. . . . It all, in the end, comes back to the nursery. . . . Jill, Humpty Dumpty, Rock-a-bye baby . . . they-kiss-you, they-kiss-you . . . they all fall down. The nurses in the corner playing Ludo . . . centurions dicing. We are all betrayed by Cock-a-Doodle-Doo. . . . We all fall down. Why, then, should I be exempt? . . . presumptuous of me . . . please forgive.)

Edges of pain. Watch it, now, the tide is beginning to turn. Like a cautious bather, stick in one toe . . . both feet . . . "brr" . . . the impact of the ocean . . . the solidity of the thing, now that you've finally got under . . . like swimming in an ice cube really. "Yes, I'm coming. Wait for me." The shock of the total immersion . . . the pain breaking over the head. Don't cry out . . . hold your breath . . . so. "Not so bad, really, when one gets used to it." That's it . . . just the right tone . . . the brave swimmer. . . . Now wave a gay hand toward the shore. Don't let them know . . . the indignities . . . the chattering teeth . . . the blue lips . . . the sense of isolation. . . . Good.

And Mary, how did she take it, I wonder, the original, the appalling announcement . . . the burden thrust upon her? "No, really, some other time . . . the spring planting . . . my aged mother . . . quite impossible. Very good of you to think of me, of course, but I couldn't take it on. Perhaps you'd call in again this time next year." (Dismiss him firmly . . . quickly, while there's still time. Don't let him get both feet in the door. Be firm and final. "No, I'm sorry, I never accept free gifts.") And then the growing awareness, the anger showing quick and hot under the warm brown of the cheeks. The voice . . . like oil. . . . "I'm afraid I didn't make myself clear." (Like the detective novels. . . . "Allow me to present my card . . . my credentials." The shock of recognition . . . the horror. "Oh, I see. . . . Yes . . . well, if it's like that. . . . Come this way." A gesture of resignation. She allows herself one sigh . . . the ghost of a smile.) But no, it's all wrong. Mary . . . peasant girl . . . quite a different reaction implied. Dumbfounded . . . remember Zachary. A shocked silence . . . the rough fingers twisting together like snakes . . . awe . . . a certain rough pride ("Wait until I tell the other girls. The well . . . tomorrow morning. . . . I won't be proud about it, not really. But it is an honor. What will Mother say?") *Droit de seigneur* . . . the servant summoned to the bedchamber . . . honored . . . afraid. Or perhaps like Leda. No preliminaries . . . no thoughts at all. Too stupid . . . too frightened . . . the thing was, after all, over so quickly. That's it . . . stupidity . . . the necessary attribute. I can hear him now. "That girl . . . whatzername? . . . Mary. Mary will do. Must be a simple woman. . . . That's where we made our first mistake. Eve too voluptuous . . . too intelligent . . . this time nothing must go wrong."

And the days were accomplished. Unfair to gloss that over . . . to make so little of the waiting . . . the months . . . the hours. They make no mention of the hours; but of course, men wrote it down. How were they to know? After the immaculate conception, after the long and dreadful journey, after the refusal at the inn . . . came the maculate delivery . . . the manger. And all that noise . . . cattle lowing (and doing other things besides) . . . angels blaring away . . . the eerie light. No peace . . . no chance for sleep . . . for rest between the pains . . . for time to think . . . to gather courage. Yet why should she be afraid . . . downhearted . . . ? Hadn't she had a sign . . . the voice . . . the presence of the star? (And notice well, they never told her about the other thing . . . the third act.) It probably seemed worth it at the time . . . the stench . . . the noise . . . the pain.

Robert the Bruce . . . Constantine . . . Noah. The spider . . . the flaming cross . . . the olive branch. . . . With these signs. . . . I would be content with something far more simple. A breath of wind on the cheek . . . the almost imperceptible movements of a curtain . . . a single flash of lightning. Courage consists, perhaps, in the ability to recognize signs . . . the symbolism of the spider. But for me . . . tonight . . . what is there? The sound of far-off thunder . . . the smell of the coming rain which will wet, but not refresh . . . that tropical fan. The curtain moves . . . yes, I will allow you that. But for me . . . tonight . . . there is only a rat behind the arras. Jack's rat. This time there is no exit . . . no way out or up.

(You are not amused by my abstract speculations? Listen . . . I have more. Time. Time is an awareness, either forward or backward, of Then, as opposed to Now . . . the stasis. Time is the moment between thunder and lightning . . . the interval at the street corner when the light is amber, neither red nor green, but shift gears, look both ways . . . the oasis of pleasure between pains . . . the space between the darkness and the dawn . . . the conversations between courses . . . the fear in the final stroke of twelve . . . the nervous fumbling with cloth and buttons, before the longed-for contact of the flesh . . . the ringing telephone . . . the solitary coffee cup . . . the oasis of pleasure between pains. Time . . . and time again.)

That time when I was eleven and at Scout camp . . . marching in a dusty serpentine to the fire tower . . . the hearty counselors with sun-streaked hair and muscular thighs . . . enjoying themselves, enjoying ourselves . . . the long hike almost over. "Ten green bottles standing on the wall. Ten green bottles standing on the wall. If one green bottle . . . should accidentally fall, there'd be nine green bottles standing on the wall." And that night . . . after pigs in blankets . . . cocoa . . . campfire songs . . . the older girls taught us how to faint . . . to hold our breath and count to thirty . . . then blow upon our thumbs. Gazing up at the stars . . . the sudden sinking back into warmth and darkness . . . the recovery . . . the fresh attempt . . . delicious. In the morning we climbed the fire tower (and I, afraid to look down or up, climbing blindly, relying on my sense of touch), reached the safety of the little room on top. We peered out the windows at the little world below . . . and found six baby mice, all dead . . . curled up, like dust kitties in the kitchen drawer. "How long d'you suppose they've been there?" "Too long. Ugh." "Throw them away." "Put them back where you found them." Disturbed . . . distressed . . . the pleasure marred. "Let's toss them down on Rachel. She was too scared to climb the tower. Baby." "Yes, let's toss them down. She ought to be paid back." (Everything all right now . . . the day saved. Ararat . . . Areopagus. . . .) Giggling, invulnerable, we hurled the small bodies out the window at the Lilliputian form below. Were we punished? Curious . . . I can't remember. And yet the rest . . . so vivid . . . as though it were yesterday . . . this morning . . . five minutes ago. . . . We must have been punished. Surely they wouldn't let us get away with that?

Waves of pain now . . . positive whitecaps . . . breakers. . . . Useless to try to remember . . . to look behind . . . to think. Swim for shore. Ignore the ringing in the ears . . . the eyes half blind with water . . . the waves breaking over the head. Just keep swimming . . . keep moving forward . . . rely on instinct . . . your sense of direction . . . don't look back or forward . . . there isn't time for foolish speculation. . . . See?

Flung up . . . at last . . . exhausted, but on the shore. Flotsam . . . jetsam . . . but there, you made it. Lie still.

The expected disaster is always the worst. One waits for it . . . is obsessed by it . . . it nibbles at the consciousness. Jack's rat. Far better the screech of brakes . . . the quick embrace of steel and shattered glass . . . or the sudden stumble from the wall. One is prepared through being unprepared. A few thumps of the old heart . . . like a brief flourish of announcing trumpets . . . a roll of drums . . . and then nothing. This way . . . tonight . . . I wait for the crouching darkness like a child waiting for that movement from the shadows in the corner of the bedroom. It's all wrong . . . unfair . . . there ought to be a law. . . . One can keep up only a given number of chins . . . one keeps silent only a given number of hours. After that, the final humiliation . . . the loss of self-control . . . the oozing out upon the pavement. . . . Dumpty-like, one refuses (or is unable?) to be reintegrated . . . whimpers for morphia and oblivion . . . shouts and tears her hair. . . . That must not happen. . . . Undignified . . . déclassé. I shall talk to my friend the fan . . . gossip with the night-fliers . . . pit my small light against the darkness, a miner descending the shaft. I have seen the opening gambit . . . am aware of the game's inevitable conclusion. What does it matter? I shall leap over the net . . . extend my hand . . . murmur, "Well done," and walk away, stiff-backed and shoulders high. I will drink the hemlock gaily . . . I will sing. Ten green bottles standing on the wall. Ten green bottles standing on the wall. If one green bottle should accidentally fall. . . . When it is over I will sit up and call for tea . . . ignore the covered basin . . . the bloody sheets (but what do they do with it afterward . . . where will they take it? I have no experience in these matters). They will learn that the death of a part is not the death of the whole. The tables will be turned . . . and overturned. The shield of Achilles will compensate for his heel.

And yet, were we as innocent as all that . . . as naive . . . that we never wondered where the bottles came from? I never wondered. . . . I accepted them the way a small child draws the Christmas turkey . . . brings the turkey home . . . pins it on the playroom wall . . . and then sits down to eat. One simply doesn't connect. Yet there they were . . . lined up on the laboratory wall . . . half-formed, some of them . . . the tiny vestigial tails of the smallest . . . like corpses of stillborn kittens . . . or baby mice. Did we think that they had been like that always . . . swimming forever in their little formaldehyde baths . . . ships in bottles . . . snowstorms in glass paperweights? The professor's voice . . . droning like a complacent bee . . . tapping his stick against each fragile glass shell . . . cross-pollinating facts with facts . . . our pencils racing over the paper. We accepted it all without question . . . even went up afterward for a closer look . . . boldly . . . without hesitation. It was all so simple . . . so uncomplex . . . so scientific. Stupidity, the necessary attribute. And once we dissected a guinea pig, only to discover that she had been pregnant . . . tiny little guinea pigs inside. We . . . like children presented with one of those Russian dolls . . . were delighted . . . gratified. We had received a bonus . . . a free gift.

Will they do that to part of me? How out of place it will look, bottled with the others . . . standing on the laboratory wall. Will the black professor . . . the brown-eyed students . . . bend their delighted eyes upon this bonus, this free gift? (White. 24 weeks. Female . . . or male.) But perhaps black babies are white . . . or pink . . . to begin. It is an interesting problem . . . one which could be pursued . . . speculated upon. I must ask someone. If black babies are not black before they are born, at what stage does the dark hand of heredity . . . of race . . . touch their small bodies? At the moment of birth perhaps? . . . like silver exposed to the air. But remember their palms . . . the soles of their feet. It's an interesting problem. And remember the beggar outside the central post office . . . the terrible burned place on his arm . . . the new skin . . . translucent . . . almost a shell pink. I turned away in disgust . . . wincing at the shared memory of scalding liquid . . . the pain. But really . . . in retrospect . . . it was beautiful. That pink skin . . . that delicate . . . Turneresque tint . . . apple blossoms against dark branches.

That's it . . . just the right tone. . . . Abstract speculation on birth . . . on death . . . on human suffering in general. Remember only the delicate tint . . . sunset against a dark sky . . . the pleasure of the Guernica. It's so simple, really . . . all a question of organization . . . of aesthetics. One can so easily escape the unpleasantness . . . the shock of recognition. Cleopatra in her robes . . . her crown. . . . "I have immortal longings in me." No fear . . . the asp suckles peacefully and unreproved. . . . She wins . . . and Caesar loses. Better than Falstaff "babbling of green fields." One needs the transcendentalism of the tragic hero. Forget the old man . . . pathetic . . . deserted . . . broken. The gray iniquity. It's all a question of organization . . . of aesthetics . . . of tone. Brooke, for example. "In that rich earth a richer dust concealed. . . ." Terrified out of his wits, of course, but still organizing . . . still posturing.

(The pain is really quite bad now . . . you will excuse me for a moment? I'll be back. I must not think for a moment . . . must not struggle . . . must let myself be carried over the crest of the wave . . . face downward . . . buoyant . . . a badge of seaweed across the shoulder. It's easier this way . . . not to think . . . not to struggle. . . . It's quicker . . . it's more humane.)

Still posturing. See the clown . . . advancing slowly across the platform . . . dragging the heavy rope . . . . Grunts . . . strains . . . the audience shivering with delight. Then the last . . . the desperate . . . tug. And what revealed? . . . a carrot . . . a bunch of grapes . . . a small dog . . . nothing. The audience in tears. . . . "Oh, God . . . how funny. . . . One knows, of course . . . all the time. And yet it never fails to amuse . . . I never fail to be taken in." Smothered giggles in the darkened taxi . . . the deserted streets. . . . "Oh, God, how amusing. . . . Did you see? The carrot . . . the bunch of grapes . . . the small dog . . . nothing. All a masquerade . . . a charade . . . the rouge . . . the powder . . . the false hair of an old woman . . . a clown." Babbling of green fields.

Once, when I was ten, I sat on a damp rock and watched my father fishing. Quiet . . . on a damp rock . . . I watched the flapping gills . . . the frenzied tail . . . the gasps for air . . . the refusal to accept the hook's reality. Rainbow body swinging through the air . . . the silver drops . . . like tears. Watching quietly from the haven of my damp rock, I saw my father struggle with the fish . . . the chased and beaten silver body. "Papa, let it go, Papa . . . please!" My father . . . annoyed . . . astonished . . . his communion disrupted . . . his chalice overturned . . . his paten trampled underfoot. He let it go . . . unhooked it carelessly and tossed it lightly toward the center of the pool. After all, what did it matter . . . to please the child . . . and the damage already done. No recriminations . . . only, perhaps (we never spoke of it), a certain loss of faith . . . a fall, however imperceptible . . . from grace?

The pain is harder now . . . more frequent . . . more intense. Don't think of it . . . ignore it . . . let it come. The symphony rises to its climax. No more andante . . . no more moderato . . . clashing cymbals . . . blaring horns. . . . Lean forward in your seat . . . excited . . . intense . . . a shiver of fear . . . of anticipation. The conductor . . . a wild thing . . . a clockwork toy gone mad. . . . Arms flailing . . . body arched . . . head swinging loosely . . . dum de dum de DUM DUM DUM. The orchestra . . . the audience . . . all bewitched . . . heads nodding . . . fingers moving, yes, oh, yes . . . the orgasm of sound . . . the straining . . . letting go. An ecstasy . . . a crescendo . . . a coda . . . it's over. "Whew." "Terrific." (Wiping the sweat from their eyes.) Smiling . . . self-conscious . . . a bit embarrassed now. . . . "Funny how you can get all worked up over a bit of music." Get back to the formalities. . . . Get off the slippery sand . . . onto the warm, safe planks of conversation. "Would you like a coffee . . . a drink . . . an ice?" The oasis of pleasure between pains. For me, too, it will soon be over. . . and for you.

Noah on Ararat . . . high and dry . . . sends out the dove to see if it is over. Waiting anxiously . . . the dove returning with the sign. Smug now . . . self-satisfied . . . know-it-all. . . . All those drowned neighbors . . . all those doubting Thomases . . . gone . . . washed away . . . full fathoms five. . . . And he, safe . . . the animals pawing restlessly, scenting freedom after their long confinement . . . smelling the rich smell of spring . . . of tender shoots. Victory . . . triumph . . . the chosen ones. Start again . . . make the world safe for democracy . . . cleansing . . . purging . . . Guernica . . . Auschwitz . . . God's fine Italian hand. Always the moral . . . the little tag . . . the cautionary tale. Willie in one of his bright new sashes/fell in the fire and was burnt to ashes. . . . Suffering is good for the soul . . . the effects on the body are not to be considered. Fire and rain . . . cleansing . . . purging . . . tempering the steel. Not much longer now . . . and soon they will let down the nets. (He promised it would be over before the dark. I do not like the dark here. Forgive me if

I've mentioned this before.) We will sing to keep our courage up. Ten green bottles standing on the wall. Ten green bottles standing on the wall. If one green bottle. . . .

The retreat from Russia . . . feet bleeding on the white snow . . . tired . . . discouraged . . . what was it all about anyway? . . . we weren't prepared. Yet we go on . . . feet bleeding on the white snow . . . dreaming of warmth . . . smooth arms and golden hair . . . a glass of kvass. We'll get there yet. (But will we ever be the same?) A phoenix . . . never refusing . . . flying true and straight . . . into the fire and out. Plunge downward now . . . a few more minutes . . . spread your wings . . . the moment has come . . . the fire blazes . . . the priest is ready . . . the worshipers are waiting. The battle over . . . the death within expelled . . . cast out . . . the long hike done . . . Arrat. Sleep now . . . and rise again from the dying fire . . . the ashes. It's over . . . eyes heavy . . . body broken but relaxed. All over. We made it, you and I. . . . It's all, is it not . . . a question of organization . . . of tone? Yet one would have been grateful at the last . . . for a reason . . . an explanation . . . a sign. A spider . . . a flaming cross . . . a carrot . . . a bunch of grapes . . . a small dog. Not this nothing.

ELIZABETH TROOP

Born in the English seaside resort of Blackpool in 1931, Elizabeth Troop was exposed early to the tensions and pretentions of lower-middle-class domestic life, both through the failed marriage of her parents and in the boarding houses where she helped her mother. After working for a time at Foyles, the London booksellers, and at the publishing firm of Pitman, she married the Canadian writer Robert Troop in 1957, and spent two years in Toronto. On her return to England she worked as a publisher's reader, and began her career as an author, finding particular success in writing plays and documentary features for radio. Her published novels include *A Fine Country* (1969), *Woolworth Madonna* (1976), and *Darling Daughter* (1981).

Troop's characters live in an England still marked by the distrust and alienation of the class system, but rapidly undergoing an uncomfortable process of change — a change that does not always seem for the better. Trapped by an inherited set of values, her heroines struggle to find a way of realizing their potential, whether through the liberating force of intellect or by the pursuit of a career; and in doing so they must exchange the stable and familiar, but inhibiting, world of the past for the uncertainties of the future. Though she writes from a feminist perspective, Troop is not a propagandist for women's issues; her characters must face not only the barrier of social attitudes, but also their own fears and weaknesses, and the inescapable realities of human life: sickness, age, and death. In "The Queen of Infinite Space" (*Shakespeare Stories*, ed. Giles Gordon, 1982), the protagonist is an ageing actress who must come to terms with her own mortality; the world around her has changed, and seems indifferent to her passing; but the story suggests that her life has not been without value. Troop's experience as a writer for radio is evident in this story, in which the reader obtains a sense of the characters' personalities and relationships through an interplay of voices, rather than through more conventional methods of narration and description.

FOR FURTHER READING

Simon Edwards, "Elizabeth Troop," *Dictionary of Literary Biography* 14 (Detroit: Gale Research, 1983): 730–35.

THE QUEEN OF INFINITE SPACE

She dreams she is in infinite space, on an endless stage. There is no audience, just a girl, sitting on a chair. She feels feral fear, the words will not come, Will's words, the words she has lived by — words that have sustained her over a lifetime. After a long run, when the soul shadows left her, each time she had felt voided, empty — a nothing. Between engagements she had hardly existed, bereft of an interior life she could but crawl through an ordinary day, mouthing and having to invent for herself the platitudes most people exchanged.

She feels the heat of the spot upon her; there is a vast white light. The male figure who bends over her is not Prospero, not Hamlet, not Orlando. She cannot make out who it is.

The spot blinds her, and the voice, her trademark, tries to rise in her plastic-tubed throat.

I am between roles again, she thinks. I have never been more empty. A void. I should have chosen one part to remain in, finally. To hide in for the rest of my days. Yet I am aware it is too late. Like a needle stuck in a record groove I must revolve in this eternal nothingness of myself. Nothing to hold on to — oblivion. No words. It is not, it had never been enough to be Laura Tate. *Her* face, my face, she tells herself, my face moulded by the grimaces and smiles of applied artifice, formed by a hundred passing parts, is now immobile, it has become the mask of tragedy. The mouth turns down, the sockets weep.

Machines, she is sure, are registering her functions, her bodily performance, as an audience used to do. It is an audience of a sort. They do not applaud, she thinks they might have rigged up a little studio applause. She does not mind her spirit and flesh being monitored by robots. She is no longer in control of her performance.

Interviewer:	Tonight we are honoured to have with us perhaps the greatest Shakespearean actress of our time, Dame Laura Tate. Dame Laura has just appeared as the Nurse in Romeo and Juliet with one of our national companies. Good evening and welcome, Dame Laura.
Dame Laura:	Thank you. Good evening.
Interviewer:	Your career, Dame Laura, started with Juliet, in the provinces, just before the War — now you have recently completed a run as the Nurse in the same play. How did it all begin for you?
Dame Laura:	Like a lot of little girls in England, I began at dancing class. Church hall, tap dancing — Miss Entwhistle's Academy.

Interviewer:	Amazing, amazing. A tap-dancing Lady Macbeth is hard to imagine.
Dame Laura:	Not these days.
Interviewer:	Soon after Miss Entwhistle's you played Juliet?
Dame Laura:	I could hardly have played Hamlet. Yes, you are right, one minute an ASM sweeping the stage, the next—Juliet. I was fourteen, which you must admit is nearer than most over-age juveniles are when they play it. Sheer luck — the leading lady got herself knocked up by a GI and rushed off to abort, silly old trout. I was ready with the lines, I have always been a quick study — and there I was. Wartime, you see. Emergency.
Interviewer:	You learned your craft as you went along. No drama schools for you?
Dame Laura:	Well, as you probably know, Sir Miles was my one-man drama school. After he read the reviews of my Juliet, he invited me to join his fly-blown touring company — all darned tights, orange make-up and bad verse-speaking. It took me years to undo what that man did to me—and I don't just mean on-stage.
Interviewer:	Quite. And then, Dame Laura —
Dame Laura:	Could we cut the "Dame Laura" business; it makes me feel like widow Twankey.
Interviewer:	Would it be correct to say that the review you referred to—er—Laura, was not only instrumental in your future success, but also gained a reputation for the young local journalist, Edwin Turner? He went on to become one of our major dramatic critics.
Dame Laura:	It would. But let's not talk about him. Whatever happened to him? Still fixated on little girls, I expect. Ruined him, you know.
Interviewer:	I have some cuttings here — he went into rhapsodies about your "corncrake voice and knock-kneed charm."
Dame Laura:	Besotted fool. I went into the cinema next, in spite of the knock knees.
Interviewer:	The ill-fated Hitchcock *Hamlet*?
Dame Laura:	Disaster. Korda chasing me around the set. Alfred hidden behind the arras.
Interviewer:	He saw it as a who-dun-it, I believe?
Dame Laura:	He did, but as everybody knows at the beginning, there was no way it would work. Unfinished masterpiece, they say, as they show it at the NFT. I believe they are putting music to it now. Don't go.
Interviewer:	Then there was your Miranda, to Sir Miles's Prospero. The critics found a touch of incest there, I note.

Dame Laura:	Damn right. Then his Petruchio to my Kate — what gall the man had. Did you ever see him in doublet and hose? Petruchio with a prostate.
Interviewer:	Then your scintillating Beatrice. The New Elizabethan Age — Festival of Britain time, and you its bright star.
Dame Laura:	I got a goitre from the ruff. I left Sir Miles and ran off with Benedick. I wonder what happened to young Benedick? Hollywood, I think.
Interviewer:	Cleopatra, that well-known hurdle for the mature actress — it was, if I may say so, a bit of a flop?
Dame Laura:	I could hardly be blamed for that. The director was in love with Antony. It was clear at rehearsal which way the wind was blowing. Not on the Serpent of Old Nile, I can assure you Still, we had some gaudy nights.
Interviewer:	And you found time to marry and produce a daughter — three times married, wasn't it?
Dame Laura:	Was it? Motherhood was a mistake. It happened when I was doing the Grotowski-inspired *Hamlet* for that Polish director . . . we were all being so acrobatic at the time. I was a plausible Gertrude, I think — it was hard to tell. I named my daughter Gertrude, for which she has never forgiven me. I think I was supposed to play Gertrude as Gertrude Stein. Hamlet was Hemingway. An interesting conception. My daughter bears the scar to this day. She is a structuralist critic, working on a study of sexual relationships in Elizabethan England with special reference to Shakespeare's heroines. As you know, they were all played by boys. She calls it ''The Androgyne Factor'' — you should have her on your show.
Interviewer:	We will, Dame Laura, we will. You, who have played nearly all Shakespeare's ladies, must be able to give her a great deal of help.
Dame Laura:	I would if she would speak to me.
Interviewer:	What is it like to live your life through the eyes of Rosalind, Beatrice, Desdemona?
Dame Laura:	A damn sight better than working in a department store, or scrubbing floors, I can tell you. But aren't all women Portias, Beatrices, Rosalinds?
Interviewer:	And start out as Juliet and end as the Nurse?
Dame Laura:	Exactly, but you didn't have to point it out.
Interviewer:	Thank you, Dame Laura, for a stimulating and outspoken interview.
Dame Laura:	Thank *you*.
Interviewer:	Next week our guest will be Geoffrey Boycott, cricketer in crisis.

Producer's Note:

This programme was shelved owing to the untimely death of Dame Laura Tate a few days after recording. A revised version may be shown at some future date. However, there may be legal problems owing to the extreme frankness of some of Dame Laura's remarks. Note to the interviewer: please contact the Head of Department.

The scene: an intensive care unit in a London hospital. The decor, white and stainless steel, is a set designer's dream for a futurist play.

A cast of two: the Nurse, Shakespeare's Nurse, Juliet's Nurse, beached like a white whale on the bed, festooned with plastic tubes in every orifice — and the nurse, small, neat and (almost as if for aesthetic effect) black against the white.

The patient breathes, just, activating instrument panels. The nurse breathes easily, relaxed, fully alive. There are black nurses, but no black Nurses — or indeed Juliets or Rosalinds. This does not bother the nurse. It will come, she is sure. She has in fact seen the Nurse, the patient, the beached whale, earlier in the month, but does not remember it. She yawned through Romeo and Juliet, and her boyfriend was annoyed with her. Tickets were expensive and hard to come by. He is trying to educate her.

"It's our story," he had nudged her to point out.

"Not at all," she had whispered back. Their mutual families approved of their future union, even though it was racially mixed. No drama there, just common sense. So much for silly plots, she thought. She prefers more ethnic culture, Fringe plays and reggae. A pragmatic female, she is geared to reality, which for her is interesting enough. It would matter little if she knew Dame Laura was a star; she treats all patients the same way. There are two forms of dedication in the room: one to fantasy, one to fact.

As her stomach rumbles delicately, reminding her she should be off-duty shortly, she notices with horror (in spite of her voodoo origins she is now an agnostic) that from under the oxygen tent's filmy curtaining, apparitions emerge. Women's faces are pressing against it; they resemble children peering through a window, willing to be released to play. One, younger than the rest, almost like the Juliet the nurse had viewed in that boring performance, edges out. It is not the Juliet she saw, but an old-fashioned one, with a frightful wig, and a nightdress dogging her tiny feet. She is pale as a surgeon's smock. The nurse puts out a hand to stay her, to question her, but just as suddenly as she appeared, she seems to melt into the sturdy rep curtains that keep the windows dark. From under the tent, voices rise, a cornucopia of words, rising and falling; it sounds, as far as she can gather, like speaking in tongues. But words rise, like ornate jewels, not the words of ordinary commerce, or the intricacies of medical obscurity, but the pure words of poetry. Golden, melancholy, honour, sullied, sumptuous, willow, hoar leaves . . . the nurse's head reels with the reiterated sounds. A red-haired girl/boy, in doublet and hose, long legs in white tights, bronzed shoes, and a cape of velvet beauty marches past and before the nurse can object, is out of the door and away. A wailing woman, rubbing her hands together, bends over the patient. There is an odour of blood, but not the blood smell familiar to the nurse. She crawls under the bed, but when the nurse peers down to see her, she is a mere shadow. The nurse bends and puts her head between her knees. She must be ill. She has never taken drugs, but she is suffering what she knows to be drug-induced hallucination. An imperious woman, who looks Egyptian, tears the film sheet. She moves out, like a barge in full sail — a queen. The nurse is awed. She rings for help.

"I'm unwell — why all these gliding ghosts?"

The young nurse, feeling incoherent, is off balance in front of her superior. Sister goes over to the patient, and then silently to the machines. She switches off, as if terminating a radio programme. Brain death, the young nurse knows they call it. It is as strange a phrase as any she has heard this night.

Sister guides her to the door and suggests coffee and an early return to the nurses' hostel. Sister too is black, but from a different continent. It seems odd to the young nurse that they, once-colonial sisters of a sprawling Empire, should be here, in Shakespeare's land, succouring and tending the sick. She shrugs off the thought. The forces of order are restored in the canteen with its bright clatter, its machines buzzing, its words describing only poor reality, which is enough.

They asked me to do *The Times* obituary, but I refused. I am surprised they remember who I am: Edwin Turner, the Fleet Street hack and collector of theatrical trivia — and, I thought, long-lost to them. I hide away in my South London bed-sit, churning out theatre notes for the local rag. Injured pride made me eager to turn them down, I hang on to my injured pride. It is all I have, it keeps me going, along with the meagre handouts from the State. By the time I changed my mind and rang them from the urinal they call a phone box, it was too late. Some slick Johnny who didn't know her had done his mediocre best, calling Laura Tate (my Juliet) the bridge between the old style Shakespeare production and the new, as if she had been a plastic prosthesis propping up decaying teeth. Yet I could not have done it — I have betrayed her in this as in everything else. I am no longer able to visit those palaces of dreams she inhabited; she, the epitome of every fine line the Bard ever wrote.

The suburb I inhabit has a lone theatre, a Victorian relic among the office blocks, all gilt and plush. It devotes itself to TV names who turn up there for pre-West End runs. I donate to them drops of acid from my pen.

I prefer the amateur groups in the church hall or social centre, fat house-wives essaying Elvira in *Blithe Spirit*; bank clerks getting their adolescent Adam's apples around the punning felicities of early Stoppard. With them I am gentle, for they have nothing to do with Laura, or with me.

Laura has won. I lost my faith years ago when we parted. I lost my religious passion for the theatre as surely as Mr Joyce lost his for the church. For me there was one church, the theatre, one god, Will Shakespeare, and one actress, Laura Tate.

Youthful theatre, the fringe brigade, leaves me cold, with its accent on social change and theatrical ignorance, its desire to change the world by playing to middle-brow intellectual converts. I am sometimes tempted to attend the new concrete cathedral complexes where the ritual is prac-tised these days, to genuflect in my old manner; but the heart has gone out of me.

What have I to remember of those days when I followed you like a cur (and was rewarded by you allowing Tynan to write your biography) and I moved towards self-hatred as surely as you moved towards self-fulfilment? Those were the years when my purple-tinted prose was praised, the mass of readers not realising it but a pale echo of what you inspired.

The first time, though; that is *mine*. A shabby theatre, a provincial rep. — a morning rehearsal, you with a mug of Ovaltine in your small hand. I, spotty and intense, promoted from funerals and jumble sales to the theatre column because old Perkins had piles — I was to take notes. And I did. As you began to speak, with that shrill-child yelp, marred by your nasal twang, my skin prickled. Magic had entered the arena. A virtual child had discovered herself, there on the bare stage, proclaiming the Master in a way all the touring hacks and has-beens could never do.

I went back and wrote my piece, and when the review of the actual performance came out (so inspired had I been) I was offered a better job, and then the *Manchester Guardian* beckoned. In your digs after the first night we had our first fumbling sexual encounter. You rhap-sodised about the leading man, who spoke the verse as if written by Ivor Novello, and wore his tights the same way. You had never heard of queers, and I informed you, while trying to get my dirty fingernails into your softer parts. "You are a fair viol, and your sense the strings; Who, finger'd to make man his lawful music, Would draw heaven down . . . to hearken."

I sit in the suburban park, filled with the lonely, the dogs and drop-pings. I watch the nymphets on their roller skates. I see in them, you, Juliet, as you were. The object of my latent (and fulfilled) desires. I have profaned with my unworthiest hand many holy shrines since then, Laura.

No, I'm afraid I wouldn't be of any use to you on *Kaleidoscope*. We didn't get on. It was rather like directing a talented cow. A deeply talented cow. Yes, only once, thank God — Antony and Cleo. Loved him, hated her. My dear, that voice, pure Bacup. Refined of course by Sir Miles. How she *shouted*. Of course in England old ladies can do no wrong. There is nothing like a dame, dear. Sorry I can't oblige. Kind of you to ask.

I heard the news flash on the car radio, driving to one of those old studios that are now devoted to TV movies. Off to do another *Bestseller*; they say my carefully studied grey hair over my unlined old face gives class to dross. We have to keep it up, here, Laura, cosmetically and sexually speaking, in the City of The Angels, Los Angeles.

I am to play yet another suave businessman with a touch of viciousness. I specialise, Laura darling, I specialise. Where did I go wrong, Beatrice? You may well ask. I was an adequate Benedick, wasn't I? I stayed you in a happy hour? I cannot imagine you dead, though you died so many times. Not meant as a joke, my love. I myself am got up each day like an Evelyn Waugh corpse from *The Loved One*, a living corpse. I can still move, play tennis, flop in a jacuzzi, and get myself around the set. I often take out a lacquered blonde. It is a life of sorts, but not your sort, witty Bea.

I think of Golders Green in the rain (it almost beggars my imagination to do so) and wish I could be there. I wonder which thespians will throng the pews. Sir Miles is too decrepit, no doubt, and a lot of your other swains defunct or scattered. Like me, who am both of those. You, I hope, had a Shakespearean death, to save us all. "Here comes Beatrice. By this day! she's a fair lady: I do spy some marks of love in her."

"Have a nice day, as they say here."

"Gertrude, could you speak to someone from the *Daily Mail*?"
"No."
"It's about —"
"I know what it's about. Tell them to get stuffed."
Gertrude tapped out a heading: "Woman and Ideality — Time, Change and Individuality in Shakespeare's Heroines."

It wouldn't do. She tippexed it out. She was, she supposed, in her own convoluted way, paying tribute. That wouldn't do at all. She had hated it all, the theatrical effusiveness, the false bonhomie, the ignoring of herself as the plain child of a talented mother. She had also had to admire the sheer integrity of the career. No one could accuse Laura, mother, of selling-out, of cheapness. It was the last straw, to have moral virtue, as well as all the others. It was impossible to live up to.

She would not mourn. She had work to do. It was as difficult to force out a word as a tear. She thought she heard behind her that glittering laugh, the scent of musk and Leichner goo. Just like *her* to try and get in on the act, playing Hamlet's father's ghost.

"Stay dead, mother — damn it," she said, and began again the staccato machine-gun rattle of the Olivetti, her only weapon.

Well, yes, dear child, I have outlasted you — if what I am doing can be said to be living. A vegetable, more or less, wheeled on and off this stage, the old actors' residence, by kind nurses. (I read the reviews of your Nurse; I always said your bawdy nature would out, in the end.) I never thought to see *you* out — I expected to exit first through that door whence no travellers return. I was old when we met, or you said so, in your rude child's way. True, I had one moth-eaten Elizabethan shoe in the grave even then. But you revived me, dear Shrew. "Is this the way to kill a wife, with kindness?" Do you remember? I tried to kill you with kindness (and overwork, and an old man's importunate libido). Forgive me.

What I gave you was all I knew, the tattered experience of a good craftsman — the pre-War squawkings of the Bard as he was done at the time, in the convention. What you gave me was indescribable. To bring one's own qualities to the conception of character and verse, to transcend, to transform, and bring delight.

They wheeled me in to the television lounge to see you on the box — a chat show. I was tranquillised, in case my old heart gave out at the sight of you. But I saw a Miss Shirley Bassey instead. Cancelled, they said. And then the news of your death. What could I do? Howl, howl, howl. They gave me a sedative. I shouted: "Wash me in steep down gulfs of liquid fire! O Desdemona! Desdemona — dead, oh, oh, oh . . ."

And then they gave me an injection.

Golders Green. A cold, blustery day. Not a bad turn-out. The ceremony, a stock one. The neat coffin sliding back behind the velvet curtains to a semi-religious muzak is an anti-climax. There is no great sense of occasion. The actors greet each other noisily, catching up on gossip. Those with matinée performances rush off, the ones "resting" pretend they have appointments to attend. There are, surprisingly, quite a few drama students.

"Who was the tall girl with glasses who cried?"

"Her daughter. Some kind of academic."

"Not like *her*, was she?"

"Did you see Sir Miles wheeled in? It was like seeing Irving."

"It was horrible. I want to be buried."

"Remember how she died as Cleopatra? Remember that."

"Or Juliet, on that ancient bit of film."

"I brought violets. But there is nowhere to put them."

"We should say something."

"You do it . . ."

"The barge she sat in, like a burnished throne, Burned on the water; the poop was beaten gold, Purple the sails, and so perfumed that The winds were lovesick with them, the oars were silver Which to the tune of flutes kept stroke, and made The water which they beat to follow faster, As amorous of their strokes. For her own person, It beggared all description."

"That's it, then."

"Let's go. I have a rehearsal."

JOHN UPDIKE

In a relatively short time John Updike has become one of the most celebrated writers in the United States. A product of the middle America which gives him much of his material, he was born in Shillington, Pennsylvania in 1932, and educated at Harvard and the Ruskin School of Drawing and Fine Art in Oxford, England. After a spell on the staff of *The New Yorker* from 1955 to 1957, Updike became a free-lance writer and journalist, developing a professionalism in his craft ("I would write ads for deodorant or labels for catsup bottles if I had to") which has led at times to a greater concern for surface than for substance, and earned him the charge of superficiality from some critics. Author of ten novels and nine volumes of short stories, as well as many poems and essays, he writes best (and most frequently) about domestic life, drawing the relationship between husbands and wives, parents and children, with a detailed vividness born of close observation; indeed, many of his stories have an autobiographical basis, and his novel *The Centaur* (1963) is centred on a character modelled after his father. His later work deals increasingly with the domestic crises and emotional traumas accompanying middle age, without any loss of the wit and eloquence characteristic of all his writing. In 1981 his achievement was rewarded with a Pulitzer Prize for his novel *Rabbit is Rich*.

Updike has summarized his major preoccupations as follows: "Domestic fierceness within the middle class, sex and death as riddles for the thinking animal, social existence as sacrifice, unexpected pleasures and rewards, corruption as a kind of evolution. . . ." Sex and death undoubtedly occupy the centre of his imagination, sometimes to morbid excess; *Couples* (1968) at times runs perilously close to refined pornography in its portrait of boredom and sexual decadence in suburban Massachusetts. But Updike is no pornographer; in his fiction he repeatedly shows the deadness of sex without love, and the frailty of domestic love in a society devoid of faith or purpose. In "Giving Blood" (*The Music School*, 1966) he depicts the strains of marriage with compassionate irony, and indicates how the selfish sensuality of contemporary human beings has blinded them to the ancient mystery of love, a mystery we can now apprehend only fleetingly.

FOR FURTHER READING

Robert Detweiler, *John Updike*, rev. ed. (Boston: Twayne, 1984).

Donald J. Greiner, *The Other John Updike: Poems/Short Stories/Prose/Play* (Athens, Ohio: Ohio University Press, 1981).

Charles T. Samuels, "The Art of Fiction XLIII: John Updike," *Paris Review* 45 (1968): 84–117.

GIVING
BLOOD

The Maples had been married now nine years, which is almost too long. "Goddammit, goddammit," Richard said to Joan, as they drove into Boston to give blood, "I drive this road five days a week and now I'm driving it again. It's like a nightmare. I'm exhausted. I'm emotionally, mentally, physically exhausted, and she isn't even an aunt of mine. She isn't even an aunt of *yours*."

"She's a sort of cousin," Joan said.

"Well hell, every goddam body in New England is some sort of cousin of yours; must I spend the rest of my life trying to save them *all?*"

"Hush," Joan said. "She might die. I'm ashamed of you. Really ashamed."

It cut. His voice for the moment took on an apologetic pallor. "Well I'd be my usual goddam saintly self if I'd had any sort of sleep last night. Five days a week I bump out of bed and stagger out the door past the milkman and on the one day of the week when I don't even have to truck the blasphemous little brats to Sunday school you make an appointment to have me drained dry thirty miles away."

"Well it wasn't *me*," Joan said, "who had to stay till two o'clock doing the Twist with Marlene Brossman."

"We weren't doing the Twist. We were gliding around very chastely to 'Hits of the Forties.' And don't think I was so oblivious I didn't see you snoogling behind the piano with Harry Saxon."

"We weren't behind the piano, we were on the bench. And he was just talking to me because he felt sorry for me. Everybody there felt sorry for me; you could have at *least* let somebody else dance *once* with Marlene, if only for show."

"Show, show," Richard said. "That's your mentality exactly."

"Why, the poor Matthews or whatever they are looked absolutely horrified."

"Matthiessons," he said. "And that's another thing. Why are idiots like that being invited these days? If there's anything I hate, it's women who keep putting one hand on their pearls and taking a deep breath. I thought she had something stuck in her throat."

"They're a perfectly pleasant, decent young couple. The thing you resent about their coming is that their being there shows us what we've become."

"If you're so attracted," he said, "to little fat men like Harry Saxon, why didn't you marry one?"

"My," Joan said calmly, and gazed out the window away from him, at the scudding gasoline stations. "You honestly *are* hateful. It's not just a pose."

"Pose, show, my Lord, who are you performing for? If it isn't Harry Saxon, it's Freddie Vetter — all these dwarves. Every time I looked over at you last night it was like some pale Queen of the Dew surrounded by a ring of mushrooms."

"You're too absurd," she said. Her hand, distinctly thirtyish, dry and green-veined and rasped by detergents, stubbed out her cigarette in the dashboard ashtray. "You're not subtle. You think you can match me up with another man so you can swirl off with Marlene with a free conscience."

Her reading his strategy so correctly made his face burn; he felt again the tingle of Mrs. Brossman's hair as he pressed his cheek against hers and in this damp privacy inhaled the perfume behind her ear. "You're right," he said. "But I want to get you a man your own size; I'm very loyal that way."

"Let's not talk," she said.

His hope, of turning the truth into a joke, was rebuked. Any implication of permission was blocked. "It's that *smugness*," he explained. speaking levelly, as if about a phenomenon of which they were both disinterested students. "It's your smugness that is really intolerable. Your stupidity I don't mind. Your sexlessness I've learned to live with. But that wonderfully smug, New England — I suppose we needed it to get the country founded, but in the Age of Anxiety it really does gall."

He had been looking over at her, and unexpectedly she turned and looked at him, with a startled but uncannily crystalline expression, as if her face had been in an instant rendered in tinted porcelain, even to the eyelashes.

"I asked you not to talk," she said. "Now you've said things that I'll always remember."

Plunged fathoms deep into the wrong, his face suffocated with warmth, he concentrated on the highway and sullenly steered. Though they were moving at sixty in the sparse Saturday traffic, he had travelled this road so often its distances were all translated into time, so that they seemed to him to be moving as slowly as a minute hand from one digit to the next. It would have been strategic and dignified of him to keep the silence; but he could not resist believing that just one more pinch of syllables would restore the fine balance which with each wordless mile slipped increasingly awry. He asked, "How did Bean seem to you?" Bean was their baby. They had left her last night, to go to the party, with a fever of 102.

Joan wrestled with her vow to say nothing, but guilt proved stronger than spite. She said, "Cooler. Her nose is a river."

"Sweetie," Richard blurted, "will they hurt me?" The curious fact was that he had never given blood before. Asthmatic and underweight, he had been 4-F, and at college and now at the office he had, less through his own determination than through the diffidence of the solicitors, evaded pledging blood. It was one of those tests of courage so trivial that no one had ever thought to make him face up to it.

Spring comes carefully to Boston. Speckled crusts of ice lingered around the parking meters, and the air, grayly stalemated between seasons, tinted the buildings along Longwood Avenue with a drab and homogeneous majesty. As they walked up the drive to the hospital entrance, Richard nervously wondered aloud if they would see the King of Arabia.

"He's in a separate wing," Joan said. "With four wives."

"Only four? What an ascetic." And he made bold to tap his wife's shoulder. It was not clear if, under the thickness of her winter coat, she felt it.

At the desk, they were directed down a long corridor floored with cigar-colored linoleum. Up and down, right and left it went, in the secretive, disjointed way peculiar to hospitals that have been built annex by annex. Richard seemed to himself Hansel orphaned with Gretel; birds ate the bread crumbs behind them, and at last they timidly knocked on the witch's door, which said BLOOD DONATION CENTER. A young man in white opened the door a crack. Over his shoulder Richard glimpsed — horrors! — a pair of dismembered female legs stripped of their shoes and laid parallel on a bed. Glints of needles and bottles pricked his eyes. Without widening the crack, the young man passed out to them two long forms. In sitting side by side on the waiting bench, remembering their middle initials and childhood diseases, Mr. and Mrs. Maple were newly defined to themselves. He fought down that urge to giggle and clown and lie that threatened him whenever he was asked — like a lawyer appointed by the court to plead a hopeless case — to present, as it were, his statistics to eternity. It seemed to mitigate his case slightly that a few of these statistics (present address, date of marriage) were shared by the hurt soul scratching beside him, with his own pen. He looked over her shoulder. "I never knew you had whooping cough."

"My mother says. I don't remember it."

A pan crashed to a distant floor. An elevator chuckled remotely. A woman, a middle-aged woman top-heavy with rouge and fur, stepped out of the blood door and wobbled a moment on legs that looked familiar. They had been restored to their shoes. The heels of these shoes clicked firmly as, having raked the Maples with a defiant blue glance, she turned and disappeared around a bend in the corridor. The young man appeared in the doorway holding a pair of surgical tongs. His noticeably recent haircut made him seem an apprentice barber. He clicked his tongs and smiled. "Shall I do you together?"

"Sure." It put Richard on his mettle that this callow fellow, to whom apparently they were to entrust their liquid essence, was so clearly younger than they. But when Richard stood, his indignation melted and his legs felt diluted under him. And the extraction of the blood sample from his middle finger seemed the nastiest and most needlessly prolonged physical involvement with another human being he had ever experienced. There is a touch that good dentists, mechanics, and barbers have, and this intern did not have it; he fumbled and in compensation was too rough. Again and again, an atrociously clumsy vampire, he tugged and twisted the purpling finger in vain. The tiny glass capillary tube remained transparent.

"He doesn't like to bleed, does he?" the intern asked Joan. As relaxed as a nurse, she sat in a chair next to a table of scintillating equipment.

"I don't think his blood moves much," she said, "until after midnight."

This stab at a joke made Richard in his extremity of fright laugh loudly, and the laugh at last seemed to jar the panicked coagulant. Red seeped upward in the thirsty little tube, as in a sudden thermometer.

The intern grunted in relief. As he smeared the samples on the analysis box, he explained idly, "What we ought to have down here is a pan of warm water. You just came in out of the cold. If you put your hand in hot water for a minute, the blood just pops out."

"A pretty thought," Richard said.

But the intern had already written him off as a clowner and continued calmly to Joan, "All we'd need would be a baby hot plate for about six dollars, then we could make our own coffee too. This way, when we get a donor who needs the coffee afterwards, we have to send up for it while we keep his head between his knees. Do you think you'll be needing coffee?"

"*No*," Richard interrupted, jealous of their rapport.

The intern told Joan, "You're O."

"I know," she said.

"And he's A positive."

"Why that's very good, Dick!" she called to him.

"Am I rare?" he asked.

The boy turned and explained, "O positive and A positive are the most common types." Something in the patient tilt of his closecropped head as its lateral sheen mixed with the lazily bright midmorning air of the room sharply reminded Richard of the days years ago when he had tended a battery of teletype machines in a room much this size. By now, ten o'clock, the yards of copy that began pouring through the machines at five and that lay in great crimped heaps on the floor when he arrived at seven would have been harvested and sorted and pasted together and turned in, and there was nothing to do but keep up with the staccato appearance of the later news and to think about simple things like coffee. It came back to him, how pleasant and secure those hours had been when, king of his own corner, he was young and newly responsible.

The intern asked, "Who wants to be first?"

"Let me," Joan said. "He's never done it before."

"Her full name is Joan of Arc," Richard explained, angered at this betrayal, so unimpeachably selfless and smug.

The intern, threatened in his element, fixed his puzzled eyes on the floor between them and said, "Take off your shoes and each get on a bed." He added, "Please," and all three laughed, one after the other, the intern last.

The beds were at right angles to one another along two walls. Joan lay down and from her husband's angle of vision was novelly foreshortened. He had never before seen her quite this way, the combed crown of her hair so poignant, her bared arm so silver and long, her stocking feet toed in so childishly and docilely. There were no pillows on the beds, and lying flat made him feel tipped head down; the illusion of floating encouraged his hope that this unreal adventure would soon dissolve in the manner of a dream. "You OK?"

"Are you?" Her voice came softly from the tucked-under wealth of her hair. From the straightness of the parting it seemed her mother had brushed it. He watched a long needle sink into the flat of her arm and a piece of moist cotton clumsily swab the spot. He had imagined their blood would be drained into cans or bottles, but the intern, whose breathing was now the only sound within the room, brought to Joan's side what looked like a miniature plastic knapsack, all coiled and tied. His body cloaked his actions. When he stepped away, a plastic cord had been grafted, a transparent vine, to the flattened crook of Joan's extended arm, where the skin was translucent and the veins were faint blue tributaries shallowly buried. It was a tender, vulnerable place where in courting days she had liked being stroked. Now, without visible transition, the pale tendril planted there went dark red. Richard wanted to cry out.

The instant readiness of her blood to leave her body pierced him like a physical pang. Though he had not so much as blinked, its initial leap had been too quick for his eye. He had expected some visible sign of flow, but from the mere appearance of it the tiny looped hose might be pouring blood *into* her body or might be a curved line added, irrelevant as a mustache, to a finished canvas. The fixed position of his head gave what he saw a certain flatness.

And now the intern turned to him, and there was the tiny felt prick of the novocain needle, and then the coarse, half-felt intrusion of something resembling a medium-weight nail. Twice the boy mistakenly probed for the vein and the third time taped the successful graft fast with adhesive tape. All the while, Richard's mind moved aloofly among the constellations of the stained cracked ceiling. What was being done to him did not bear contemplating. When the intern moved away to hum and tinkle among his instruments, Joan craned her neck to show her husband her face and, upside down in his vision, grotesquely smiled.

It was not many minutes that they lay there at right angles together, but the time passed as something beyond the walls, as something mixed with the faraway clatter of pans and the approach and retreat of footsteps and the opening and closing of unseen doors. Here, conscious of a pointed painless pulse in the inner hinge of his arm but incurious as to what it looked like, he floated and imagined how his soul would float free when all his blood was underneath the bed. His blood and Joan's merged on the floor, and together their spirits glided from crack to crack, from star to star on the ceiling. Once she cleared her throat, and the sound made an abrasion like the rasp of a pebble loosened by a cliff-climber's boot.

The door opened. Richard turned his head and saw an old man, bald and sallow, enter and settle in a chair. He was one of those old men who hold within an institution an ill-defined but consecrated place. The young doctor seemed to know him, and the two talked, softly, as if not to disturb the mystical union of the couple sacrificially bedded together. They talked of persons and events that meant nothing — of Iris, of Dr. Greenstein, of Ward D, again of Iris, who had given the old man an undeserved scolding, of the shameful lack of a hot plate to make coffee on, of the rumored black bodyguards who kept watch with scimitars by the bed of the glaucomatous king. Through Richard's tranced ignorance these topics passed as clouds of impression, iridescent, massy — Dr. Greenstein with a pointed nose and almond eyes the color of ivy, Iris eighty feet tall and hurling sterilized thunderbolts of wrath. As in some theologies the proliferant deities are said to exist as ripples upon the featureless ground of Godhead, so these inconstant images lightly overlay his continuous awareness of Joan's blood, like his own, ebbing. Linked to a common loss, they were chastely conjoined; the thesis developed upon him that the hoses attached to them somewhere out of sight met. Testing this belief, he glanced down and saw that indeed the plastic vine taped to the flattened crook of his arm was the same dark red as hers. He stared at the ceiling to disperse a sensation of faintness.

Abruptly the young intern left off his desultory conversation and moved to Joan's side. There was a chirp of clips. When he moved away, she was revealed holding her naked arm upright, pressing a piece of cotton against it with the other hand. Without pausing, the intern came to Richard's side, and the birdsong of the clips repeated, nearer. "Look at that," he said to his elderly friend. "I started him two minutes later than her and he's finished at the same time."

"Was it a race?" Richard asked.

Clumsily firm, the boy fitted Richard's fingers to a pad and lifted his arm for him. "Hold it there for five minutes," he said.

"What'll happen if I don't?"

"You'll mess up your shirt." To the old man he said, "I had a woman in here the other day, she was all set to leave when all of a sudden, pow! — all over the front of this beautiful linen dress. She was going to Symphony."

"Then they try to sue the hospital for the cleaning bill," the old man muttered.

"Why was I slower than him?" Joan asked. Her upright arm wavered, as if vexed or weakened.

"The woman generally is," the boy told her. "Nine times out of ten, the man is faster. Their hearts are so much stronger."

"Is that really so?"

"Sure it's so," Richard told her. "Don't argue with medical science."

"Woman up in Ward C," the old man said, "they saved her life for her out of an auto accident and now I hear she's suing because they didn't find her dental plate."

Under such patter, the five minutes eroded. Richard's upheld arm began to ache. It seemed that he and Joan were caught together in a classroom where they would never be recognized, or in a charade that would never be guessed, the correct answer being Two Silver Birches in a Meadow.

"You can sit up now if you want," the intern told them. "But don't let go of the venipuncture."

They sat up on their beds, legs dangling heavily. Joan asked him, "Do you feel dizzy?"

"With my powerful heart? Don't be presumptuous."

"Do you think he'll need coffee?" the intern asked her. "I'll have to send up for it now."

The old man shifted forward in his chair, preparing to heave to his feet.

"I do *not* want any *coffee*" — Richard said it so loud he saw himself transposed, another Iris, into the firmament of the old man's aggrieved gossip. *Some dizzy bastard down in the blood room, I get up to get him some coffee and he damn near bit my head off.* To demonstrate simultaneously his essential good humor and his total presence of mind, Richard gestured toward the blood they had given — two square plastic sacks filled solidly fat — and declared, "Back where I come from in West Virginia sometimes you pick a tick off a dog that looks like that." The men looked at him amazed. Had he not quite said what he meant to say? Or had they never seen anybody from West Virginia before?

Joan pointed at the blood, too. "Is that us? Those little doll pillows?"

"Maybe we should take one home to Bean," Richard suggested.

The intern did not seem convinced that this was a joke. "Your blood will be credited to Mrs. Henryson's account," he stated stiffly.

Joan asked him, "Do you know anything about her? When is she — when is her operation scheduled?"

"I think for tomorrow. The only thing on the tab this after is an open heart at two; that'll take about sixteen pints."

"Oh . . ." Joan was shaken. "Sixteen . . . that's a full person, isn't it?"

"More," the intern answered, with the regal handwave that bestows largess and dismisses compliments.

"Could we visit her?" Richard asked, for Joan's benefit. ("Really ashamed," she had said; it had cut.) He was confident of the refusal.

"Well, you can ask at the desk, but usually before a major one like this it's just the nearest of kin. I guess you're safe now." He meant their punctures. Richard's arm bore a small raised bruise; the intern covered it with one of those ample, salmon, unhesitatingly adhesive bandages that only hospitals have. That was their specialty, Richard thought — packaging. They wrap the human mess for final delivery. Sixteen doll's pillows, uniformly dark and snug, marching into an open heart: the vision momentarily satisfied his hunger for cosmic order.

He rolled down his sleeve and slid off the bed. It startled him to realize, in the instant before his feet touched the floor, that three pairs of eyes were fixed upon him, fascinated and apprehensive and eager for scandal. He stood and towered above them. He hopped on one foot to slip into one loafer, and then on this foot to slip into the other loafer. Then he did the little shuffle-tap, shuffle-tap step that was all that remained to him of dancing lessons he had taken at the age of seven, driving twelve miles each Saturday into Morgantown. He made a small bow toward his wife, smiled at the old man, and said to the intern, "All my life people have been expecting me to faint. I have no idea why. I never faint."

His coat and overcoat felt a shade queer, a bit slithery and light, but as he walked down the length of the corridor, space seemed to adjust snugly around him. At his side, Joan kept an inquisitive and chastened silence. They pushed through the great glass doors. A famished sun was nibbling through the overcast. Above and behind them, the King of Arabia lay in a drugged dream of dunes and Mrs. Henryson upon her sickbed received like the comatose mother of twins their identical gifts of blood. Richard hugged his wife's padded shoulders and as they walked along leaning on each other whispered, "Hey, I love you. Love love *love* you."

Romance is, simply, the strange, the untried. It was unusual for the Maples to be driving together at eleven in the morning. Almost always it was dark when they shared a car. The oval of her face was bright in the corner of his eye. She was watching him, alert to take the wheel if he suddenly lost consciousness. He felt tender toward her in the egg-shell light, and curious toward himself, wondering how far beneath his brain the black pit did lie. He felt no different; but then the quality of consciousness perhaps did not bear introspection. Something certainly had been taken from him; he was less himself by a pint and it was not impossible that like a trapeze artist saved by a net he was sustained in the world of light and reflection by a single layer of interwoven cells. Yet the earth, with its signals and buildings and cars and bricks, continued like a pedal note.

Boston behind them, he asked, "Where should we eat?"

"Should we eat?"

"Please, yes. Let me take you to lunch. Just like a secretary."

"I do feel sort of illicit. As if I've stolen something."

"You too? But what did we steal?"

"I don't know. The morning? Do you think Eve knows enough to feed them?" Eve was their sitter, a little sandy girl from down the street who would, in exactly a year, Richard calculated, be painfully lovely. They lasted three years on the average, sitters; you got them in the tenth grade and escorted them into their bloom and then, with graduation, like commuters who had reached their stop, they dropped out of sight, into nursing school or marriage. And the train went on, and took on other passengers, and itself became older and longer. The Maples had four children: Judith, Richard Jr., poor oversized, angel-faced John, and Bean.

"She'll manage. What would you like? All that talk about coffee has made me frantic for some."

"At the Pancake House beyond 128 they give you coffee before you even ask."

"Pancakes? Now? Aren't you gay? Do you think we'll throw up?"

"Do you feel like throwing up?"

"No, not really. I feel sort of insubstantial and gentle, but it's probably psychosomatic. I don't really understand this business of giving something away and still somehow having it. What is it — the spleen?"

"I don't know. Are the splenetic man and the sanguine man the same?"

"God. I've totally forgotten the humors. What are the others — phlegm and choler?"

"Bile and black bile are in there somewhere."

"One thing about you, Joan. You're educated. New England women are educated."

"Sexless as we are."

"That's right; drain me dry and then put me on the rack." But there was no wrath in his words; indeed, he had reminded her of their earlier conversation so that, in much this way, his words might be revived, diluted, and erased. It seemed to work. The restaurant where they served only pancakes was empty and quiet this early. A bashfulness possessed them both; it had become a date between two people who have little as yet in common but who are nevertheless sufficiently intimate to accept the fact without chatter. Touched by the stain her blueberry pancakes left on her teeth, he held a match to her cigarette and said, "Gee, I loved you back in the blood room."

"I wonder why."

"You were so brave."

"So were you."

"But I'm supposed to be. I'm paid to be. It's the price of having a penis."

"Shh."

"Hey. I didn't mean that about your being sexless."

The waitress refilled their coffee cups and gave them the check.

"And I promise never never to do the Twist, the cha-cha, or the schottische with Marlene Brossman."

"Don't be silly. I don't care."

This amounted to permission, but perversely irritated him. That smugness; why didn't she *fight?* Trying to regain their peace, scrambling uphill, he picked up their check and with an effort of acting, the pretense being that they were out on a date and he was a raw dumb suitor, said handsomely, "I'll pay."

But on looking into his wallet he saw only a single worn dollar there. He didn't know why this should make him so angry, except the fact somehow that it was only *one.* "Goddammit," he said. "Look at that." He waved it in her face. "I work like a bastard all week for you and those insatiable brats and at the end of it what do I have? One goddam crummy wrinkled dollar."

Her hands dropped to the pocketbook beside her on the seat, but her gaze stayed with him, her face having retreated, or advanced, into that porcelain shell of uncanny composure. "We'll both pay," Joan said.

KURT VONNEGUT

The writings of Kurt Vonnegut (b. 1922) are characterized by a Swiftian sense of despair at the extremes of human folly. His books are about the horrors of war, the dehumanization of modern men and women, the loss of humane values in a society dedicated to technological progress. Though these are now fashionable subjects, Vonnegut's insights derive from personal experience. After serving in the U.S. Infantry during World War II, and witnessing the fire-bombing of Dresden as a prisoner of war, he became a police reporter in Chicago; then he entered the field of public relations, working for the General Electric Company until 1950, when he devoted himself full time to writing. Such a background provided him with ample material for his satire.

Gifted with a Kafka-esque sense of the absurd, Vonnegut works through a mixture of fantasy and realism to depict the deep springs of irrationality which govern human conduct; and he shows how the intellectual genius of modern science has been perverted to base and violent ends by the moral stupidity of the masses and their leaders. A prominent feature of his work is his interest in science fiction, which provides him with images of an automated and impersonal universe, where the individual is of less and less significance. Vonnegut's first novel, *Player Piano* (1952), depicts an America in which government is conducted by computer, and people are of value only as consumers; the futility of human endeavor is set in an even bleaker perspective in *The Sirens of Titan* (1959), which presents human history as subject to control by the inhabitants of a distant planet. Vonnegut's vision is not totally pessimistic; his stories often include at least one character who, aware of the surrounding madness, seeks to restore a measure of sanity; thus the brilliant professor in "Report on the Barnhouse Effect" (1950; *Welcome to the Monkey House*, 1968) and his protegé, the narrator, are determined to turn their amazing discovery to good uses, much to the chagrin of their fellow citizens. But in the novel *Slaughterhouse-Five* (1969) Vonnegut is less hopeful, for in his treatment of the Dresden bombing, he suggests that individual effort is powerless to alleviate the misery and suffering of the human condition. The elements of fantasy and science fiction are less evident in his subsequent works, like *Jailbird* (1979), but he has continued his mordant satire of Western materialism and political corruption.

FOR FURTHER READING

D.H. Goldsmith, *Kurt Vonnegut, Fantasist of Fire and Ice* (Bowling Green, Ohio: Bowling Green Popular Press, 1972).

J. Klinkowitz and J. Somer, eds., *The Vonnegut Statement* (New York: Delacorte Press, 1973).

Stanley Schatt, *Kurt Vonnegut, Jr.* (Boston: Twayne, 1976).

REPORT ON THE BARNHOUSE EFFECT

Let me begin by saying that I don't know any more about where Professor Arthur Barnhouse is hiding than anyone else does. Save for one short, enigmatic message left in my mail box on Christmas Eve, I have not heard from him since his disappearance a year and a half ago.

What's more, readers of this article will be disappointed if they expect to learn how *they* can bring about the so-called "Barnhouse Effect." If I were able and willing to give away that secret, I would certainly be something more important than a psychology instructor.

I have been urged to write this report because I did research under the professor's direction and because I was the first to learn of his astonishing discovery. But while I was his student I was never entrusted with knowledge of how the mental forces could be released and directed. He was unwilling to trust anyone with that information.

I would like to point out that the term "Barnhouse Effect" is a creation of the popular press, and was never used by Professor Barnhouse. The name he chose for the phenomenon was *"dynamopsychism,"* or *force of the mind*.

I cannot believe that there is a civilized person yet to be convinced that such a force exists, what with its destructive effects on display in every national capital. I think humanity has always had an inkling that this sort of force does exist. It has been common knowledge that some people are luckier than others with inanimate objects like dice. What Professor Barnhouse did was to show that such "luck" was a measurable force, which in his case could be enormous.

By my calculations, the professor was about fifty-five times more powerful than a Nagasaki-type atomic bomb at the time he went into hiding. He was not bluffing when, on the eve of "Operation Brainstorm," he told General Honus Barker: "Sitting here at the dinner table, I'm pretty sure I can flatten anything on earth — from Joe Louis to the Great Wall of China."

There is an understandable tendency to look upon Professor Barnhouse as a supernatural visitation. The First Church of Barnhouse in Los Angeles has a congregation numbering in the thousands. He is godlike in neither appearance nor intellect. The man who disarms the world is single, shorter than the average American male, stout, and averse to exercise. His IQ is 143, which is good but certainly not sensational. He is quite mortal, about to celebrate his fortieth birthday, and in good health. If he is alone now, the isolation won't bother him too much. He was quiet and shy when I knew him, and seemed to find more companionship in books and music than in his associations at the college.

Neither he nor his powers fall outside the sphere of Nature. His dynamopsychic radiations are subject to many known physical laws that apply in the field of radio. Hardly a person has not now heard the snarl of "Barnhouse static" on his home receiver. Contrary to what one might expect, the radiations are affected by sunspots and variations in the ionosphere.

However, his radiations differ from ordinary broadcast waves in several important ways. Their total energy can be brought to bear on any single point the professor chooses, and that energy is undiminished by distance. As a weapon, then, dynamopsychism has an impressive advantage over bacteria and atomic bombs, beyond the fact that it costs nothing to use: it enables the professor to single out critical individuals and objects instead of slaughtering whole populations in the process of maintaining international equilibrium.

As General Honus Barker told the House Military Affairs Committee: "Until someone finds Barnhouse, there is no defense against the Barnhouse Effect." Efforts to "jam" or block the radiations have failed. Premier Slezak could have saved himself the fantastic expense of his "Barnhouseproof" shelter. Despite the shelter's twelve-foot-thick lead armor, the premier has been floored twice while in it.

There is talk of screening the population for men potentially as powerful dynamopsychically as the professor. Senator Warren Foust demanded funds for this purpose last month, with the passionate declaration: "He who rules the Barnhouse Effect rules the world!" Commissar Kropotnik said much the same thing, so another costly armaments race, with a new twist, has begun.

This race at least has its comical aspects. The world's best gamblers are being coddled by governments like so many nuclear physicists. There may be several hundred persons with dynamopsychic talent on earth, myself included, but, without knowledge of the professor's technique, they can never be anything but dice-table despots. With the secret, it would probably take them ten years to become dangerous weapons. It took the professor that long. He who rules the Barnhouse Effect is Barnhouse and will be for some time.

Popularly, the "Age of Barnhouse" is said to have begun a year and a half ago, on the day of Operation Brainstorm. That was when dynamopsychism became significant politically. Actually, the phenomenon was discovered in May, 1942, shortly after the professor turned down a direct commission in the Army and enlisted as an artillery private. Like X-rays and vulcanized rubber, dynamopsychism was discovered by accident.

From time to time Private Barnhouse was invited to take part in games of chance by his barrack mates. He knew nothing about the games, and usually begged off. But one evening, out of social grace, he agreed to shoot craps. It was a terrible or wonderful thing that he played, depending upon whether or not you like the world as it now is.

"Shoot sevens, Pop," someone said.

So "Pop" shot sevens — ten in a row to bankrupt the barracks. He retired to his bunk and, as a mathematical exercise, calculated the odds against his feat on the back of a laundry slip. His chances of doing it, he found, were one in almost ten million! Bewildered, he borrowed a pair of dice from the man in the bunk next to his. He tried to roll sevens again, but got only the usual assortment of numbers. He lay back for a moment, then resumed his toying with the dice. He rolled ten more sevens in a row.

He might have dismissed the phenomenon with a low whistle. But the professor instead mulled over the circumstances surrounding his two lucky streaks. There was one single factor in common: on both occasions, *the same thought train had flashed through his mind just before he threw the dice.* It was that thought train which aligned the professor's brain cells into what has since become the most powerful weapon on earth.

The soldier in the next bunk gave dynamopsychism its first token of respect. In an understatement certain to bring wry smiles to the faces of the world's dejected demagogues, the soldier said, "You're hotter'n a two-dollar pistol, Pop." Professor Barnhouse was all of that. The dice that did his bidding weighed but a few grams, so the forces involved were minute; but the unmistakable fact that there were such forces was earth-shaking.

Professional caution kept him from revealing his discovery immediately. He wanted more facts and a body of theory to go with them. Later, when the atomic bomb was dropped on Hiroshima, it was fear that made him hold his peace. At no time were his experiments, as Premier Slezak called them, "a bourgeois plot to shackle the true democracies of the world." The professor didn't know where they were leading.

In time, he came to recognize another startling feature of dynamopsychism: *its strength increased with use.* Within six months, he was able to govern dice thrown by men the length of a barracks distant. By the time of his discharge in 1945, he could knock bricks loose from chimneys three miles away.

Charges that Professor Barnhouse could have won the last war in a minute, but did not care to do so, are perfectly senseless. When the war ended, he had the range and power of a 37-millimeter cannon, perhaps — certainly no more. His dynamopsychic powers graduated from the small-arms class only after his discharge and return to Wyandotte College.

I enrolled in the Wyandotte Graduate School two years after the professor had rejoined the faculty. By chance, he was assigned as my thesis adviser. I was unhappy about the assignment, for the professor was, in the eyes of both colleagues and students, a somewhat ridiculous figure. He missed classes or had lapses of memory during lectures.

When I arrived, in fact, his shortcomings had passed from the ridiculous to the intolerable.

"We're assigning you to Barnhouse as a sort of temporary thing," the dean of social studies told me. He looked apologetic and perplexed. "Brilliant man, Barnhouse, I guess. Difficult to know since his return, perhaps, but his work before the war brought a great deal of credit to our little school."

When I reported to the professor's laboratory for the first time, what I saw was more distressing than the gossip. Every surface in the room was covered with dust; books and apparatus had not been disturbed for months. The professor sat napping at his desk when I entered. The only signs of recent activity were three overflowing ash trays, a pair of scissors, and a morning paper with several items clipped from its front page.

As he raised his head to look at me, I saw that his eyes were clouded with fatigue. "Hi," he said, "just can't seem to get my sleeping done at night." He lighted a cigarette, his hands trembling slightly. "You the young man I'm supposed to help with a thesis?"

"Yes, sir," I said. In minutes he converted my misgivings to alarm.

"You an overseas veteran?" he asked.

"Yes, sir."

"Not much left over there, is there?" He frowned. "Enjoy the last war?"

"No, sir."

"Look like another war to you?"

"Kind of, sir."

"What can be done about it?"

I shrugged. "Looks pretty hopeless."

He peered at me intently. "Know anything about international law, the UN and all that?"

"Only what I pick up from the papers."

"Same here," he sighed. He showed me a fat scrapbook packed with newspaper clippings. "Never used to pay any attention to international politics. Now I study them the way I used to study rats in mazes. Everybody tells me the same thing — 'Looks hopeless.' "

"Nothing short of a miracle —" I began.

"Believe in magic?" he asked sharply. The professor fished two dice from his vest pocket. "I will try to roll twos," he said. He rolled twos three times in a row. "One chance in about 47,000 of that happening. There's a miracle for you." He beamed for an instant, then brought the interview to an end, remarking that he had a class which had begun ten minutes ago.

He was not quick to take me into his confidence, and he said no more about his trick with the dice. I assumed they were loaded, and forgot about them. He set me the task of watching male rats cross electrified metal strips to get to food for female rats—an experiment that had been done to everyone's satisfaction in the 1930s. As though the pointlessness of my work were not bad enough, the professor annoyed me further with irrelevant questions. His favorites were: "Think we should have dropped the atomic bomb on Hiroshima?" and "Think every new piece of scientific information is a good thing for humanity?"

However, I did not feel put upon for long. "Give those poor animals a holiday," he said one morning, after I had been with him only a month. "I wish you'd help me look into a more interesting problem — namely, my sanity."

I returned the rats to their cages.

"What you must do is simple," he said, speaking softly. "Watch the inkwell on my desk. If you see nothing happen to it, say so, and I'll go quietly — relieved, I might add — to the nearest sanitarium."

I nodded uncertainly.

He locked the laboratory door and drew the blinds, so that we were in twilight for a moment. "I'm odd, I know," he said. "It's fear of myself that's made me odd."

"I've found you somewhat eccentric, perhaps, but certainly not —"

"If nothing happens to that inkwell, 'crazy as a bedbug' is the only description of me that will do," he interrupted, turning on the overhead lights. His eyes narrowed. "To give you an idea of how crazy, I'll tell you what's been running through my mind when I should have been sleeping. I think maybe I can save the world. I think maybe I can make every nation a *have* nation, and do away with war for good. I think maybe I can clear roads through jungles, irrigate deserts, build dams overnight."

"Yes, sir."

"Watch the inkwell!"

Dutifully and fearfully I watched. A high-pitched humming seemed to come from the inkwell; then it began to vibrate alarmingly, and finally to bound about the top of the desk, making two noisy circuits. It stopped, hummed again, glowed red, then popped in splinters with a blue-green flash.

Perhaps my hair stood on end. The professor laughed gently. "Magnets?" I managed to say at last.

"Wish to Heaven it were magnets," he murmured. It was then that he told me of dynamopsychism. He knew only that there was such a force; he could not explain it. "It's me and me alone — and it's awful."

"I'd say it was amazing and wonderful!" I cried.

"If all I could do was make inkwells dance, I'd be tickled silly with the whole business." He shrugged disconsolately. "But I'm no toy, my boy. If you like, we can drive around the neighborhood, and I'll show you what I mean." He told me about pulverized boulders, shattered oaks and abandoned farm buildings demolished within a fifty-mile radius of the campus. "Did every bit of it sitting right here, just thinking — not even thinking hard."

He scratched his head nervously. "I have never dared to concentrate as hard as I can for fear of the damage I might do. I'm to the point where a mere whim is a blockbuster." There was a depressing pause. "Up until a few days ago, I've thought it best to keep my secret for fear of what use it might be put to," he continued. "Now I realize that I haven't any more right to it than a man has a right to own an atomic bomb."

He fumbled through a heap of papers. "This says about all that needs to be said, I think." He handed me a draft of a letter to the Secretary of State.

> Dear Sir:
>   I have discovered a new force which costs nothing to use, and which is probably more important than atomic energy. I should like to see it used most effectively in the cause of peace, and am, therefore, requesting your advice as to how this might best be done.
>
>   Yours truly,
>   A. Barnhouse.

"I have no idea what will happen next," said the professor.

There followed three months of perpetual nightmare, wherein the nation's political and military great came at all hours to watch the professor's trick with fascination.

We were quartered in an old mansion near Charlottesville, Virginia, to which we had been whisked five days after the letter was mailed. Surrounded by barbed wire and twenty guards, we were labeled "Project Wishing Well," and were classified as Top Secret.

For companionship we had General Honus Barker and the State Department's William K. Cuthrell. For the professor's talk of peace-through-plenty they had indulgent smiles and much discourse on practical measures and realistic thinking. So treated, the professor, who had at first been almost meek, progressed in a matter of weeks toward stubbornness.

He had agreed to reveal the thought train by means of which he aligned his mind into a dynamopsychic transmitter. But, under Cuthrell's and Barker's nagging to do so, he began to hedge. At first he declared that the information could be passed on simply by word of mouth. Later he said that it would have to be written up in a long report. Finally, at dinner one night, just after General Barker had read the secret orders for Operation Brainstorm, the professor announced, "The report may take as long as five years to write." He looked fiercely at the general. "Maybe twenty."

The dismay occasioned by this flat announcement was offset somewhat by the exciting anticipation of Operation Brainstorm. The general was in a holiday mood. "The target ships are on their way to the Caroline Islands at this very moment," he declared ecstatically. "One hundred and twenty of them! At the same time, ten V-2s are being readied for firing in New Mexico, and fifty radio-controlled jet bombers are being equipped for a mock attack on the Aleutians. Just think of it!'' Happily he reviewed his orders. ''At exactly 1100 hours next Wednesday, I will give you the order to *concentrate*; and you, professor, will think as hard as you can about sinking the target ships, destroying the V-2s before they hit the ground, and knocking down the bombers before they reach the Aleutians! Think you can handle it?''

The professor turned gray and closed his eyes. ''As I told you before, my friend, I don't know what I can do.'' He added bitterly, ''As for this Operation Brainstorm, I was never consulted about it, and it strikes me as childish and insanely expensive.''

General Barker bridled. ''Sir,'' he said, ''your field is psychology, and I wouldn't presume to give you advice in that field. Mine is national defense. I have had thirty years of experience and success, Professor, and I'll ask you not to criticize my judgment.''

The professor appealed to Mr. Cuthrell. ''Look,'' he pleaded, ''isn't it war and military matters we're all trying to get rid of? Wouldn't it be a whole lot more significant and lots cheaper for me to try moving cloud masses into drought areas, and things like that? I admit I know next to nothing about international politics, but it seems reasonable to suppose that nobody would want to fight wars if there were enough of everything to go around. Mr. Cuthrell, I'd like to try running generators where there isn't any coal or water power, irrigating deserts, and so on. Why, you could figure out what each country needs to make the most of its resources, and I could give it to them without costing American taxpayers a penny.''

''Eternal vigilance is the price of freedom,'' said the general heavily.

Mr. Cuthrell threw the general a look of mild distaste. ''Unfortunately, the general is right in his own way,'' he said. ''I wish to Heaven the world were ready for ideals like yours, but it simply isn't. We aren't surrounded by brothers, but by enemies. It isn't a lack of food or resources that has us on the brink of war — it's a struggle for power. Who's going to be in charge of the world, our kind of people or theirs?''

The professor nodded in reluctant agreement and arose from the table. ''I beg your pardon, gentlemen. You are, after all, better qualified to judge what is best for the country. I'll do whatever you say.'' He turned to me. ''Don't forget to wind the restricted clock and put the confidential cat out,'' he said gloomily, and ascended the stairs to his bedroom.

For reasons of national security, Operation Brainstorm was carried on without the knowledge of the American citizenry which was footing the bill. The observers, technicians and military men involved in the activity knew that a test was under way — a test of what, they had no idea. Only thirty-seven key men, myself included, knew what was afoot.

In Virginia, the day for Operation Brainstorm was unseasonably cool. Inside, a log fire crackled in the fireplace, and the flames were reflected in the polished metal cabinets that lined the living room. All that remained of the room's lovely old furniture was a Victorian love seat, set squarely in the center of the floor, facing three television receivers. One long bench had been brought in for the ten of us privileged to watch. The television screens showed, from left to right, the stretch of desert which was the rocket target, the guinea-pig fleet, and a section of the Aleutian sky through which the radio-controlled bomber formation would roar.

Ninety minutes before H hour the radios announced that the rockets were ready, that the observation ships had backed away to what was thought to be a safe distance, and that the bombers were on their way. The small Virginia audience lined up on the bench in order of rank, smoked a great deal, and said little. Professor Barnhouse was in his bedroom. General Barker bustled about the house like a woman preparing Thanksgiving dinner for twenty.

At ten minutes before H hour the general came in, shepherding the professor before him. The professor was comfortably attired in sneakers, gray flannels, a blue sweater and a white shirt open at the neck. The two of them sat side by side on the love seat. The general was rigid and perspiring; the professor was cheerful. He looked at each of the screens, lighted a cigarette and settled back, comfortable and cool.

"Bombers sighted!" cried the Aleutian observers.

"Rockets away!" barked the New Mexico radio operator.

All of us looked quickly at the big electric clock over the mantel, while the professor, a half-smile on his face, continued to watch the television sets. In hollow tones, the general counted away the seconds remaining. "Five . . . four . . . three . . . two . . . one . . . *Concentrate!*"

Professor Barnhouse closed his eyes, pursed his lips, and stroked his temples. He held the position for a minute. The television images were scrambled, and the radio signals were drowned in the din of Barnhouse static. The professor sighed, opened his eyes and smiled confidently.

"Did you give it everything you had?" asked the general dubiously.

"I was wide open," the professor replied.

The television images pulled themselves together, and mingled cries of amazement came over the radios tuned to the observers. The Aleutian sky was streaked with the smoke trails of bombers screaming down in flames. Simultaneously, there appeared high over the rocket target a cluster of white puffs, followed by faint thunder.

General Barker shook his head happily. "By George!" he crowed. "Well, sir, by George, by George, by George!"

"Look!" shouted the admiral seated next to me. "The fleet — it wasn't touched!"

"The guns seem to be drooping," said Mr. Cuthrell.

We left the bench and clustered about the television sets to examine the damage more closely. What Mr. Cuthrell had said was true. The ships' guns curved downward, their muzzles resting on the steel decks. We in Virginia were making such a hullabaloo that it was impossible to hear the radio reports. We were so engrossed, in fact, that we didn't miss the professor until two short snarls of Barnhouse static shocked us into sudden silence. The radios went dead.

We looked around apprehensively. The professor was gone. A harassed guard threw open the front door from the outside to yell that the professor had escaped. He brandished his pistol in the direction of the gates, which hung open, limp and twisted. In the distance, a speeding government station wagon topped a ridge and dropped from sight into the valley beyond. The air was filled with choking smoke, for every vehicle on the grounds was ablaze. Pursuit was impossible.

"What in God's name got into him?" bellowed the general.

Mr. Cuthrell, who had rushed out onto the front porch, now slouched back into the room, reading a penciled note as he came. He thrust the note into my hands. "The good man left this billet-doux under the door knocker. Perhaps our young friend here will be kind enough to read it to you gentlemen, while I take a restful walk through the woods."

"Gentlemen," I read aloud, "As the first superweapon with a conscience, I am removing from your national defence stockpile. Setting a new precedent in the behavior of ordnance, I have humane reasons for going off. A. Barnhouse."

Since that day, of course, the professor has been systematically destroying the world's armaments, until there is now little with which to equip an army other than rocks and sharp sticks. His activities haven't exactly resulted in peace, but have, rather, precipitated a bloodless and entertaining sort of war that might be called the "War of the Tattletales." Every nation is flooded with enemy agents whose sole mission is to locate military equipment, which is promptly wrecked when it is brought to the professor's attention in the press.

Just as every day brings news of more armaments pulverized by dynamopsychism, so has it brought rumors of the professor's whereabouts. During the last week alone, three publications carried articles proving variously that he was hiding in an Inca ruin in the Andes, in the sewers of Paris, and in the unexplored lower chambers of Carlsbad Caverns. Knowing the man, I am inclined to regard such hiding places as unnecessarily romantic and uncomfortable. While there are numerous persons eager to kill him, there must be millions who would care for him and hide him. I like to think that he is in the home of such a person.

One thing is certain: at this writing, Professor Barnhouse is not dead. Barnhouse static jammed broadcasts not ten minutes ago. In the eighteen months since his disappearance, he has been reported dead some half-dozen times. Each report has stemmed from the death of an unidentified man resembling the professor, during a period free of the static. The first three reports were followed at once by renewed talk of rearmament and recourse to war. The saber rattlers have learned how imprudent premature celebrations of the professor's demise can be.

Many a stouthearted patriot has found himself prone in the tangled bunting and timbers of a smashed reviewing stand, seconds after having announced that the archtyranny of Barnhouse was at an end. But those who would make war if they could, in every country in the world, wait in sullen silence for what must come — the passing of Professor Barnhouse.

To ask how much longer the professor will live is to ask how much longer we must wait for the blessings of another world war. He is of short-lived stock: his mother lived to be fifty-three, his father to be forty-nine; and the life-spans of his grandparents on both sides were of the same order. He might be expected to live, then, for perhaps fifteen years more, if he can remain hidden from his enemies. When one considers the number and vigor of these enemies, however, fifteen years seems an extraordinary length of time, which might better be revised to fifteen days, hours or minutes.

The professor knows that he cannot live much longer. I say this because of the message left in my mailbox on Christmas Eve. Unsigned, typewritten on a soiled scrap of paper, the note consisted of ten sentences. The first nine of these, each a bewildering tangle of psychological jargon and references to obscure texts, made no sense to me at first reading. The tenth, unlike the rest, was simply constructed and contained no large words — but its irrational content made it the most puzzling and bizarre sentence of all. I nearly threw the note away, thinking it a colleague's warped notion of a practical joke. For some reason, though, I added it to the clutter on top of my desk, which included, among other mementos, the professor's dice.

It took me several weeks to realize that the message really meant something, that the first nine sentences, when unsnarled, could be taken as instructions. The tenth still told me nothing. It was only last night that I discovered how it fitted in with the rest. The sentence appeared in my thoughts last night, while I was toying absently with the professor's dice.

I promised to have this report on its way to the publishers today. In view of what has happened, I am obliged to break that promise, or release the report incomplete. The delay will not be a long one, for one of the few blessings accorded a bachelor like myself is the ability to move quickly from one abode to another, or from one way of life to another. What property I want to take with me can be packed in a few hours. Fortunately, I am not without substantial private means, which may take as long as a week to realize in liquid and anonymous form. When this is done, I shall mail the report.

I have just returned from a visit to my doctor, who tells me my health is excellent. I am young, and, with any luck at all, I shall live to a ripe old age indeed, for my family on both sides is noted for longevity.

Briefly, I propose to vanish.

Sooner or later, Professor Barnhouse must die. But long before then I shall be ready. So, to the saber rattlers of today — and even, I hope, of tomorrow — I say: Be advised. Barnhouse will die. But not the Barnhouse Effect.

Last night, I tried once more to follow the oblique instructions on the scrap of paper. I took the professor's dice, and then, with the last, nightmarish sentence flitting through my mind, I rolled fifty consecutive sevens.

Good-by.

ALICE WALKER

Alice Walker's parents were black sharecroppers in Georgia, a fact that has deeply influenced her life and her writing. Born in 1944, she attended Spelman College, Atlanta, and Sarah Lawrence College. She worked for the civil rights movement in Georgia and Mississippi, and in 1967 married a white civil rights lawyer (the marriage was dissolved in 1976). For a time she was employed by the New York City Welfare Department. In 1968 she became a writer-in-residence and a teacher of Black Studies at Jackson State College, and has subsequently taught at a number of universities across the United States. Her publications include several books of poetry, a collection of essays, and three novels: *The Third Life of Grange Copeland* (1970), *Meridian* (1976), and *The Color Purple* (1982), the last of which won a Pulitzer Prize and an American Book Award. Walker's short stories have been gathered in *In Love and Trouble: Stories of Black Women* (1973) and *You Can't Keep a Good Woman Down* (1981).

Walker writes from a background of racial, social, and sexual discrimination that has significantly shaped her career as an author. She is particularly concerned with the plight of the black woman in America, doubly oppressed by the sexism of her own race and the bigotry of white society. Walker's preoccupation with sexual politics has led some critics to accuse her of stereotyping male characters, but her work rises above simplistic denunciations of male chauvinism to plead for a fulfilment of human potential through a love and an understanding that cross sexual and racial boundaries. As a Southern writer, she has been compared to Faulkner in the evocative richness of her prose, and in her ability to dramatize the sensibility of a naïve or uneducated protagonist. In Walker's hands, the ungrammatical syntax of black Americans becomes a powerful, sometimes poetic expression of strong feeling, evoking a history and tradition that are deeply embedded in American consciousness, though often ignored or misrepresented. The uneasy relationship between blacks and whites is subtly explored in "Nineteen Fifty-five" (*You Can't Keep a Good Woman Down*), in which a white rock-and-roll singer (clearly modelled on Elvis Presley) achieves fame through a song written by a black woman, but searches in vain for the joy in life that the woman has expressed through the song. It may be noted here that Presley's 1956 hit record "Hound Dog" was first recorded in 1953 by Willie Mae ("Big Mama") Thornton.

FOR FURTHER READING

Barbara T. Christian, "Alice Walker," *Dictionary of Literary Biography 33: Afro-American Fiction Writers After 1955* (Detroit: Gale Research, 1984), pp. 258–71.

Mari Evans, ed., *Black Women Writers, 1950–1980* (Garden City: Doubleday, 1984).

Gloria Steinem, "Do You Know This Woman? She Knows You — A Profile of Alice Walker," *Ms* 10 (June 1982): 35–7, 89–94.

NINETEEN FIFTY-FIVE

1955

The car is a brandnew red Thunderbird convertible, and it's passed the house more than once. It slows down real slow now, and stops at the curb. An older gentleman dressed like a Baptist deacon gets out on the side near the house, and a young fellow who looks about sixteen gets out on the driver's side. They are white, and I wonder what in the world they doing in this neighborhood.

Well, I say to J. T., put your shirt on, anyway, and let me clean these glasses offa the table.

We had been watching the ballgame on TV. I wasn't actually watching, I was sort of daydreaming, with my foots up in J. T.'s lap.

I seen 'em coming on up the walk, brisk, like they coming to sell something, and then they rung the bell, and J. T. declined to put on a shirt but instead disappeared into the bedroom where the other television is. I turned down the one in the living room; I figured I'd be rid of these two double quick and J. T. could come back out again.

Are you Gracie Mae Still? asked the old guy, when I opened the door and put my hand on the lock inside the screen.

And I don't need to buy a thing, said I.

What makes you think we're sellin'? he asks, in that hearty Southern way that makes my eyeballs ache.

Well, one way or another and they're inside the house and the first thing the young fellow does is raise the TV a couple of decibels. He's about five feet nine, sort of womanish looking, with real dark white skin and a red pouting mouth. His hair is black and curly and he looks like a Loosianna creole.

About one of your songs, says the deacon. He is maybe sixty, with white hair and beard, white silk shirt, black linen suit, black tie and black shoes. His cold grey eyes look like they're sweating.

One of my songs?

Traynor here just *loves* your songs. Don't you, Traynor? He nudges Traynor with his elbow. Traynor blinks, says something I can't catch in a pitch I don't register.

The boy learned to sing and dance livin' round you people out in the country. Practically cut his teeth on you.

Traynor looks up at me and bites his thumbnail.

I laugh.

Well, one way or another they leave with my agreement that they can record one of my songs. The deacon writes me a check for five hundred dollars, the boy grunts his awareness of the transaction, and I am laughing all over myself by the time I rejoin J. T.

Just as I am snuggling down beside him though I hear the front door bell going off again.

Forgit his hat? asks J. T.

I hope not, I say.

The deacon stands there leaning on the door frame and once again I'm thinking of those sweaty-looking eyeballs of his. I wonder if sweat makes your eyeballs pink because his are sure pink. Pink and gray and it strikes me that nobody I'd care to know is behind them.

I forgot one little thing, he says pleasantly. I forgot to tell you Traynor and I would like to buy up all of those records you made of the song. I tell you we sure do love it.

Well, love it or not, I'm not so stupid as to let them do that without making 'em pay. So I says, Well, that's gonna cost you. Because, really, that song never did sell all that good, so I was glad they was going to buy it up. But on the other hand, them two listening to my song by themselves, and nobody else getting to hear me sing it, give me a pause.

Well, one way or another the deacon showed me where I would come out ahead on any deal he had proposed so far. Didn't I give you five hundred dollars? he asked. What white man — and don't even need to mentioned colored — would give you more? We buy up all your records of that particular song: first, you git royalties. Let me ask you, how much you sell that song for in the first place? Fifty dollars? A hundred, I say. And no royalties from it yet, right? Right. Well, when we buy up all of them records you gonna git royalties. And that's gonna make all them race record shops sit up and take notice of Gracie Mae Still. And they gonna push all them other records of yourn they got. And you no doubt will become one of the big name colored recording artists. And then we can offer you another five hundred dollars for letting us do all this for you. And by God you'll be sittin' pretty! You can go out and buy you the kind of outfit a star should have. Plenty sequins and yards of red satin.

I had done unlocked the screen when I saw I could get some more money out of him. Now I held it wide open while he squeezed through the opening between me and the door. He whipped out another piece of paper and I signed it.

He sort of trotted out to the car and slid in beside Traynor, whose head was back against the seat. They swung around in a u-turn in front of the house and then they were gone.

J. T. was putting his shirt on when I got back to the bedroom. Yankees beat the Orioles 10–6, he said. I believe I'll drive out to Paschal's pond and go fishing. Wanta go?

While I was putting on my pants J. T. was holding the two checks.

I'm real proud of a woman that can make cash money without leavin' home, he said. And I said *Umph*. Because we met on the road with me singing in first one little low-life jook after another, making ten dollars a night for myself if I was lucky, and sometimes bringin' home nothing but my life. And J. T. just loved them times. The way I was fast and flashy and always on the go from one town to another. He loved the way my singin' made the dirt farmers cry like babies and the womens shout Honey, hush! But that's mens. They loves any style to which you can get 'em accustomed.

1956

My little grandbaby called me one night on the phone: Little Mama, Little Mama, there's a white man on the television singing one of your songs! Turn on channel 5.

Lord, if it wasn't Traynor. Still looking half asleep from the neck up, but kind of awake in a nasty way from the waist down. He wasn't doing too bad with my song either, but it wasn't just the song the people in the audience was screeching and screaming over, it was that nasty little jerk he was doing from the waist down.

Well, Lord have mercy, I said, listening to him. If I'da closed my eyes, it could have been me. He had followed every turning of my voice, side streets, avenues, red lights, train crossings and all. It give me a chill.

Everywhere I went I heard Traynor singing my song, and all the little white girls just eating it up. I never had so many ponytails switched across my line of vision in my life. They was so *proud*. He was a *genius*.

Well, all that year I was trying to lose weight anyway and that and high blood pressure and sugar kept me pretty well occupied. Traynor had made a smash from a song of mine, I still had seven hundred dollars of the original one thousand dollars in the bank, and I felt if I could just bring my weight down, life would be sweet.

1957

I lost ten pounds in 1956. That's what I give myself for Christmas. And J. T. and me and the children and their friends and grandkids of all description had just finished dinner — over which I had put on nine and a half of my lost ten — when who should appear at the front door but Traynor. Little Mama, Little Mama! It's that white man who sings —— —— ——. The children didn't call it my song anymore. Nobody did. It was funny how that happened. Traynor and the deacon had bought up all my records, true, but on his record he had put "written by Gracie Mae Still." But that was just another name on the label, like "produced by Apex Records."

On the TV he was inclined to dress like the deacon told him. But now he looked presentable.

Merry Christmas, said he.

And same to you, Son.

I don't know why I called him Son. Well, one way or another they're all our sons. The only requirement is that they be younger than us. But then again Traynor seemed to be aging by the minute.

You looks tired, I said. Come on in and have a glass of Christmas cheer.

J. T. ain't never in his life been able to act decent to a white man he wasn't working for, but he poured Traynor a glass of bourbon and water, then he took all the children and grandkids and friends and whatnot out to the den. After while I heard Traynor's voice singing the song, coming from the stereo console. It was just the kind of Christmas present my kids would consider cute.

I looked at Traynor, complicit. But he looked like it was the last thing in the world he wanted to hear. His head was pitched forward over his lap, his hands holding his glass and his elbows on his knees.

I done sung that song seem like a million times this year, he said. I sung it on the Grand Ole Opry, I sung it on the Ed Sullivan show. I sung it on Mike Douglas, I sung it at the Cotton Bowl, the Orange Bowl. I sung it at Festivals. I sung it at Fairs. I sung it overseas in Rome, Italy, and once in a submarine *underseas*. I've sung it and sung it, and I'm making forty thousand dollars a day offa it, and you know what, I don't have the faintest notion what that song means.

Whatchumean, what do it mean? It mean what it says. All I could think was: these suckers is making forty thousand a *day* offa my song and now they gonna come back and try to swindle me out of the original thousand.

It's just a song, I said. Cagey. When you fool around with a lot of no count mens you sing a bunch of 'em. I shrugged.

Oh, he said. Well. He started brightening up. I just come by to tell you I think you are a great singer.

He didn't blush, saying that. Just said it straight out.

And I brought you a little Christmas present too. Now you take this little box and you hold it until I drive off. Then you take it outside under that first streetlight back up the street aways in front of that green house. Then you open the box and see . . . Well, just *see*.

What had come over this boy, I wondered, holding the box. I looked out the window in time to see another white man come up and get in the car with him and then two more cars full of white mens start out behind him. They was all in long black cars that looked like a funeral procession.

Little Mama, Little Mama, what it is? One of my grandkids come running up and started pulling at the box. It was wrapped in gay Christmas paper — the thick, rich kind that it's hard to picture folks making just to throw away.

J. T. and the rest of the crowd followed me out the house, up the street to the streetlight and in front of the green house. Nothing was there but somebody's gold-grille white Cadillac. Brandnew and most distracting. We got to looking at it so till I almost forgot the little box in my hand. While the others were busy making 'miration I carefully took off the paper and ribbon and folded them up and put them in my pants pocket. What should I see but a pair of genuine solid gold caddy keys.

Dangling the keys in front of everybody's nose, I unlocked the caddy, motioned for J. T. to git in on the other side, and us didn't come back home for two days.

1960

Well, the boy was sure nuff famous by now. He was still a mite shy of twenty but already they was calling him the Emperor of Rock and Roll.

Then what should happen but the draft.

Well, says J. T. There goes all this Emperor of Rock and Roll business.

But even in the army the womens was on him like white on rice. We watched it on the News.

> Dear Gracie Mae [he wrote from Germany],
>
> How you? Fine I hope as this leaves me doing real well. Before I come in the army I was gaining a lot of weight and gitting jittery from making all them dumb movies. But now I exercise and eat right and get plenty of rest. I'm more awake than I been in ten years.
> I wonder if you are writing any more songs?
>
> Sincerely,
> Traynor

I wrote him back:

> Dear Son,
>
> We is all fine in the Lord's good grace and hope this finds you the same. J. T. and me be out all times of the day and night in that car you give me — which you know you didn't have to do. Oh, and I do appreciate the mink and the new self-cleaning oven. But if you send anymore stuff to eat from Germany I'm going to have to open up a store in the neighborhood just to get rid of it. Really, we have more than enough of everything. The Lord is good to us and we don't know Want.
> Glad to here you is well and gitting your right rest. There ain't nothing like exercising to help that along. J. T. and me work some part of every day that we don't go fishing in the garden.
> Well, so long Soldier.
>
> Sincerely,
> Gracie Mae

He wrote:

> Dear Gracie Mae,
>
> I hope you and J. T. like that automatic power tiller I had one of the stores back home send you. I went through a mountain of catalogs looking for it — I wanted something that even a woman could use.
> I've been thinking about writing some songs of my own but every time I finish one it don't seem to be about nothing I've actually lived myself. My agent keeps sending me other people's songs but they just sound mooney. I can hardly git through 'em without gagging.
> Everybody still loves that song of yours. They ask me all the time what do I think it means, really. I mean, they want to know just what I want to know. Where out of your life did it come from?
>
> Sincerely,
> Traynor

1968

I didn't see the boy for seven years. No. Eight. Because just about everybody was dead when I saw him again. Malcolm X, King, the president and his brother, and even J. T. J. T. died of a head cold. It just settled in his head like a block of ice, he said, and nothing we did moved it until one day he just leaned out the bed and died.

His good friend Horace helped me put him away, and then about a year later Horace and me started going together. We was sitting out on the front porch swing one summer night, dusk-dark, and I saw this great procession of lights winding to a stop.

Holy Toledo! said Horace. (He's got a real sexy voice like Ray Charles.) Look *at* it. He meant the long line of flashy cars and the white men in white summer suits jumping out on the drivers' sides and standing at attention. With wings they could pass for angels, with hoods they could be the Klan.

Traynor comes waddling up the walk.

And suddenly I know what it is he could pass for. An Arab like the ones you see in storybooks. Plump and soft and with never a care about weight. Because with so much money, who cares? Traynor is almost dressed like someone from a storybook too. He has on, I swear, about ten necklaces. Two sets of bracelets on his arms, at least one ring on every finger, and some kind of shining buckles on his shoes, so that when he walks you get quite a few twinkling lights.

Gracie Mae, he says, coming up to give me a hug. J. T.

I explain that J. T. passed. That this is Horace.

Horace, he says, puzzled but polite, sort of rocking back on his heels, Horace.

That's it for Horace. He goes in the house and don't come back.

Looks like you and me is gained a few, I say.

He laughs. The first time I ever heard him laugh. It don't sound much like a laugh and I can't swear that it's better than no laugh a'tall.

He's gitting fat for sure, but he's still slim compared to me. I'll never see three hundreds pounds again and I've just about said (excuse me) fuck it. I got to thinking about it one day an' I thought: aside from the fact that they say it's unhealthy, my fat ain't never been no trouble. Mens always have loved me. My kids ain't never complained. Plus they's fat. And fat like I is I looks distinguished. You see me coming and know somebody's *there*.

Gracie Mae, he says, I've come with a personal invitation to you to my house tomorrow for dinner. He laughed. What did it sound like? I couldn't place it. See them men out there? he asked me. I'm sick and tired of eating with them. They don't never have nothing to talk about. That's why I eat so much. But if you come to dinner tomorrow we can talk about the old days. You can tell me about that farm I bought you.

I sold it, I said.

You did?

Yeah, I said, I did. Just cause I said I liked to exercise by working in a garden didn't mean I wanted five hundred acres! Anyhow, I'm a city girl now. Raised in the country it's true. Dirt poor — the whole bit — but that's all behind me now.

Oh well, he said, I didn't mean to offend you.

We sat a few minutes listening to the crickets.

Then he said: You wrote that song while you was still on the farm, didn't you, or was it right after you left?

You had somebody spying on me? I asked.

You and Bessie Smith got into a fight over it once, he said.

You *is* been spying on me!

But I don't know what the fight was about, he said. Just like I don't know what happened to your second husband. Your first one died in the Texas electric chair. Did you know that? Your third one beat you up, stole your touring costumes and your car and retired with a chorine to Tuskegee. He laughed. He's still there.

I had been mad, but suddenly I calmed down. Traynor was talking very dreamily. It was dark but seems like I could tell his eyes weren't right. It was like some*thing* was sitting there talking to me but not necessarily with a person behind it.

You gave up on marrying and seem happier for it. He laughed again. I married but it never went like it was supposed to. I never could squeeze any of my own life either into it or out of it. It was like singing somebody else's record. I copied the way it was sposed to be *exactly* but I never had a clue what marriage meant.

I bought her a diamond ring big as your fist. I bought her clothes. I built her a mansion. But right away she didn't want the boys to stay there. Said they smoked up the bottom floor. Hell, there were *five* floors.

No need to grieve, I said. No need to. Plenty more where she come from.

He perked up. That's part of what that song means, ain't it? No need to grieve. Whatever it is, there's plenty more down the line.

I never really believed that way back when I wrote the song, I said. It was all bluffing then. The trick is to live long enough to put your young bluffs to use. Now if I was to sing that song today I'd tear it up. 'Cause I done lived long enough to know it's *true*. Them words could hold me up.

I ain't lived that long, he said.

Look like you on your way, I said. I don't know why, but the boy seemed to need some encouraging. And I don't know, seem like one way or another you talk to rich white folks and you end up reassuring *them*. But what the hell, by now I feel something for the boy. I wouldn't be in his bed all alone in the middle of the night for nothing. Couldn't be nothing worse than being famous the world over for something you don't even understand. That's what I tried to tell Bessie. She wanted that same song. Overheard me practicing it one day, said, with her hands on her hips: Gracie Mae, I'ma sing your song tonight. I *likes* it.

Your lips be too swole to sing, I said. She was mean and she was strong, but I trounced her.

Ain't you famous enough with your own stuff? I said. Leave mine alone. Later on, she thanked me. By then she was Miss Bessie Smith to the World, and I was still Miss Gracie Mae Nobody from Notasulga.

The next day all these limousines arrived to pick me up. Five cars and twelve bodyguards. Horace picked that morning to start painting the kitchen.

Don't paint the kitchen, fool, I said. The only reason that dumb boy of ours is going to show me his mansion is because he intends to present us with a new house.

What you gonna do with it? he asked me, standing there in his shirtsleeves stirring the paint.

Sell it. Give it to the children. Live in it on weekends. It don't matter what I do. He sure don't care.

Horace just stood there shaking his head. Mama you sure looks *good*, he says. Wake me up when you git back.

Fool, I say, and pat my wig in front of the mirror.

The boy's house is something else. First you come to this mountain, and then you commence to drive and drive up this road that's lined with magnolias. Do magnolias grow on mountains? I was wondering. And you come to lakes and you come to ponds and you come to deer and you come up on some sheep. And I figure these two is sposed to represent England and Wales. Or something out of Europe. And you just keep on coming to stuff. And it's all pretty. Only the man driving my car don't look at nothing but the road. Fool. And then *finally*, after all this time, you begin to go up the driveway. And there's more magnolias —only they're not in such good shape. It's sort of cool up this high and I don't think they're gonna make it. And then I see this building that looks like if it had a name it would be The Tara Hotel. Columns and steps and outdoor chandeliers and rocking chairs. Rocking chairs? Well, and there's the boy on the steps dressed in a dark green satin jacket like you see folks wearing on TV late at night, and he looks sort of like a fat dracula with all that house rising behind him, and standing beside him there's this little white vision of loveliness that he introduces as his wife.

He's nervous when he introduces us and he says to her: This is Gracie Mae Still, I want you to know me. I mean . . . and she gives him a look that would fry meat.

Won't you come in, Grace Mae, she says, and that's the last I see of her.

He fishes around for something to say or do and decides to escort me

to the kitchen. We go through the entry and the parlor and the breakfast room and the dining room and the servants' passage and finally get
there. The first thing I notice is that, altogether, there are five stoves.
He looks about to introduce me to one.

Wait a minute, I say. Kitchens don't do nothing for me. Let's go sit on
the front porch.

Well, we hike back and we sit in the rocking chairs rocking until
dinner.

Gracie Mae, he says down the table, taking a piece of fried chicken
from the woman standing over him, I got a little surprise for you.

It's a house, ain't it? I ask, spearing a chitlin.

You're getting *spoiled*, he says. And the way he says *spoiled* sounds
funny. He slurs it. It sounds like his tongue is too thick for his mouth.
Just that quick he's finished the chicken and is now eating chitlins *and*
a pork chop. *Me* spoiled, I'm thinking.

I already got a house. Horace is right this minute painting the kitchen. I
bought that house. My kids feel comfortable in that house.

But this one I bought you is just like mine. Only a little smaller.

I still don't need no house. And anyway who would clean it?

He looks surprised.

Really, I think, some peoples advance *so* slowly.

I hadn't thought of that. But what the hell, I'll get you somebody to
live in.

I don't want other folks living 'round me. Makes me nervous.

You *don't*? It *do*?

What I want to wake up and see folks I don't even know for?

He just sits there downtable staring at me. Some of that feeling is in
the song, ain't it? Not the words, the *feeling*. What I want to wake up
and see folks I don't even know for? But I see twenty folks a day I don't
even know, including my wife.

This food wouldn't be bad to wake up to though, I said. The boy had
found the genius of corn bread.

He looked at me real hard. He laughed. Short. They want what you
got but they don't want you. They want what I got only it ain't mine.
That's what makes 'em so hungry for me when I sing. They getting the
flavor of something but they ain't getting the thing itself. They like a
pack of hound dogs trying to gobble up a scent.

You talking 'bout your fans?

Right. Right. He says.

Don't worry 'bout your fans, I say. They don't know their asses from
a hole in the ground. I doubt there's a honest one in the bunch.

That's the point. Dammit, that's the point! He hits the table with his
fist. It's so solid it don't even quiver. You need a honest audience! You
can't have folks that's just gonna lie right back to you.

Yeah, I say, it was small compared to yours, but I had one. It would have been worth my life to try to sing 'em somebody else's stuff that I didn't know nothing about.

He must have pressed a buzzer under the table. One of his flunkies zombies up.

Git Johnny Carson, he says.

On the phone? asks the zombie.

On the phone, says Traynor, what you think I mean, git him offa the front porch? Move your ass.

So two weeks later we's on the Johnny Carson show.

Traynor is all corseted down nice and looks a little bit fat but mostly good. And all the women that grew up on him and my song squeal and squeal. Traynor says: The lady who wrote my first hit record is here with us tonight, and she's agreed to sing it for all of us, just like she sung it forty-five years ago. Ladies and Gentlemen, the great Gracie Mae Still!

Well, I had tried to lose a couple of pounds my own self, but failing that I had me a very big dress made. So I sort of rolls over next to Traynor, who is dwarfted by me, so that when he puts his arm around back of me to try to hug me it looks funny to the audience and they laugh.

I can see this pisses him off. But I smile out there at 'em. Imagine squealing for twenty years and not knowing why you're squealing? No more sense of endings and beginnings than hogs.

It don't matter, Son, I say. Don't fret none over me.

I commence to sing. And I sound —— wonderful. Being able to sing good ain't all about having a good singing voice a'tall. A good singing voice helps. But when you come up in the Hard Shell Baptist church like I did you understand early that the fellow that sings is the singer. Them that waits for programs and arrangements and letters from home is just good voices occupying body space.

So there I am singing my own song, my own way. And I give it all I got and enjoy every minute of it. When I finish Traynor is standing up clapping and clapping and beaming at first me and then the audience like I'm his mama for true. The audience claps politely for about two seconds.

Traynor looks disgusted.

He comes over and tries to hug me again. The audience laughs.

Johnny Carson looks at us like we both weird.

Traynor is mad as hell. He's supposed to sing something called a love ballad. But instead he takes the mike, turns to me and says: Now see if my imitation still holds up. He goes into the same song, *our* song, I think, looking out at his flaky audience. And he sings it just the way he always did. My voice, my tone, my inflection, everything. But he forgets a couple of lines. Even before he's finished the matronly squeals begin.

He sits down next to me looking whipped.

It don't matter, Son, I say, patting his hand. You don't even know those people. Try to make the people you know happy.

Is that in the song? he asks.

Maybe. I say.

1977

For a few years I hear from him, then nothing. But trying to lose weight takes all the attention I got to spare. I finally faced up to the fact that my fat is the hurt I don't admit, not even to myself, and that I been trying to bury it from the day I was born. But also when you git real old, to tell the truth, it ain't as pleasant. It gits lumpy and slack. So one day I said to Horace, I'ma git this shit offa me.

And he fell in with the program like he always try to do and Lord such a procession of salads and cottage cheese and fruit juice!

One night I dreamed Traynor had split up with his fifteenth wife. He said: *You meet 'em for no reason. You date 'em for no reason. You marry 'em for no reason. I do it all but I swear it's just like somebody else doing it. I feel like I can't remember Life.*

The boy's in trouble, I said to Horace.

You've always said that, he said.

I have?

Yeah. You always said he looked asleep. You can't sleep through life if you wants to live it.

You not such a fool after all, I said, pushing myself up with my cane and hobbling over to where he was. Let me sit down on your lap, I said, while this salad I ate takes effect.

In the morning we heard Traynor was dead. Some said fat, some said heart, some said alcohol, some said drugs. One of the children called from Detroit. Them dumb fans of his on a crying rampage, she said. You just ought to turn on the TV.

But I didn't want to see 'em. They was crying and crying and didn't even know what they was crying for. One day this is going to be a pitiful country, I thought.

ALBERT WENDT

Albert Wendt is one of the most striking new writers to emerge from Polynesia. Born in Western Samoa in 1939, he attended primary school there, then in 1952 went to New Zealand on a scholarship, completing his formal education in New Plymouth, and at Victoria University in Wellington. He began to publish in New Zealand in 1962. Three years later he returned to Samoa to teach; and in 1974 he was appointed to the University of the South Pacific. "A Resurrection" comes from his first story collection, *Flying-Fox in a Freedom Tree* (1974); it has an organic connection with all the works that have followed: novels like *Pouliuli* (1977) and *Leaves of the Banyan Tree* (1979), and *Lali*, his 1980 anthology of South Pacific literature. Throughout his work, Wendt examines ways in which the rapid changes of twentieth-century life— "papalagi" (European) life at that—have affected the traditional community patterns of his island society.

"A Resurrection" addresses the subject both formally and thematically. While alluding to Christian belief and story, it manages at the same time to enact a ritual evocation of what the narrator at one point calls his "heritage of memories." The tone is ambivalent: it is a story of loss as well as of celebration. And the conflict is apparent in the textures of diction as well. There are Samoan words (a "fale" is a house; a "talie" is a large coastal tree) in a context of English ones. But the English is in a context as well: for all his appeal to historical and empirical exactness (the reference to "page five," for example) the narrator manages at the final outset to tell a modern story in the far more traditional form of an oral tale.

FOR FURTHER READING

K.O. Arvidson, "The Emergence of a Polynesian Literature," *Mana Review* 1 (January 1976): 24–48.

Jacqueline Bardolph, "Narrative Voices, Narrative Personae, in *Flying-Fox in a Freedom Tree*," *Echos du Commonwealth*, no. 8 (1984): 69–83.

John B. Beston and Rose Marie Beston, "An Interview with Albert Wendt," *World Literature Written in English* 16 (1977): 151–62.

Roger Robinson, "Albert Wendt: An Assessment," *Landfall* 34 (1980): 275–90.

A RESURRECTION

Tala Faasolopito died at 2:30 p.m. yesterday at Motootua Hospital: we heard about it over the radio. He died, so the doctors have diagnosed, of coronary thrombosis. He also died one of the most respected and saintly pastors of the Congregational Church (and of the whole nation therefore).

He was born in the Vaipe, oldest son of Miti and Salamo Faasolopito, both now deceased, and a brother to three sisters and two brothers, whose names I've forgotten. However, the Vaipe has not seen Tala for over forty years, ever since he walked out of it in 1920, at the age of nineteen. I never knew him. What I know about him I have gained from my father and other Vaipe people who knew him. Or, let me say, the Tala I know is a resurrection, a Lazarus resurrected from the memory bank of the Vaipe.

Tala did not kill the man who had raped his sister, he walked out of the Vaipe and into Malua Theological College to become an exemplary man of God. He never again set foot in the Vaipe. Not even when his father deserted his mother, not even when his mother died of a broken heart (so my mother has concluded) four years later, not even when his brothers and sisters disappeared one by one from the Vaipe in an attempt to escape his (Tala's) disgrace which had become *their* disgrace. The Vaipe was his cross, and he never wanted to confront it again. I once read an article about him in the "Bulletin," 12th September, 1959: his place of birth, the Vaipe, was never once mentioned in that article. Tala became, for most of our extremely religiously-minded countrymen, a symbol of peace and goodwill, a shining example of virtuous, civilised and saintly living. But to most Vaipe people he was still Tala, the nineteen-year-old who had refused to become a man, their type of man sprung free like elephant grass from fertile Vaipe mud. Not that they did not become proud of him when he became a "saint" (my father's description). They forgave him. But I believe that Tala never forgave himself. His choice not to avenge his sister's (family) honour determined the course of his life, the very sainthood he grew into. And he regretted that choice.

I possess copies of three of his now nationally-quoted sermons. The sermons are not very original; they reveal little of their composer or the heart of the religion he believed in; they are the usual-type sermons you hear over 2AP every Sunday night without fail. However, I also have the originals of two sermons which he composed a few months before he died and which he never made public. (My father, who grew up with Tala, got the originals from Tala's wife, Siamomua.)

The first sermon, dated Monday, 27th October, 1968, and written in an elaborate and ornate longhand (Tala went to Marist Brothers' School famous for such handwriting) on fragile letter-writing paper, is entitled: "A Resurrection of Judas." The second sermon, a typewritten script forty pages in length, is more a private confession than a sermon. It is dated 25th December, 1968, and under the date is this title printed in pencil: "On the Birthday of Man." A public perusal of these two sermons would have reduced Tala, in the fickle minds of the public, from saint to madman. For instance, in "A Resurrection of Judas," Tala offers us a compellingly original but disturbing conclusion: "Judas Iscariot was the Christ. He did not betray Jesus. Jesus betrayed Judas by not stopping him from fulfilling the prophecy."

I think that the key to the door into the endless corridors that were Tala's life was his choice not to avenge his family's honour.

As a child I used to play under the breadfruit trees surrounding the fale which belonged to Tala's family; this was after Tala had left the Vaipe for good. Tala's mother, who was a big woman with five chins (or so it seemed then) and long black hair streaked with grey, and an uncontrollable cough (they said she had Tb), and ragged dresses that hung down her like animal skins, sometimes invited me into the main fale to play with her children. They were much older than me but they condescended to play hopscotch, sweepy, and skipping with me. I sometimes ate with them, mainly boiled bananas and sparse helpings of tinned herrings. (They were poor, so my parents told me.) I really enjoyed those times. The fale and shacks are still there today, reminding me, every time I pass them, of a contented childhood, but the people (distant relatives of the Faasolopitos) who now occupy them are strangers to me.

I often ran over the muddy track, leading over the left bank of the Vaipe from the ageless breadfruit trees, to the home of the family of the man, Fetu, who, by raping Tala's sister, became the springboard of Tala's life. The track is still there, like a string you can use to find your way out of a dense forest, but Fetu is dead, he has been dead for a long time — he died in prison, stabbed to death by another prisoner who could have been Tala twenty years before because Tala should have killed Fetu but didn't.

Tala and his ill-fated family, and Fetu, and this whole section of the Vaipe are anchored into my mind and made meaningful by the memory of that awesome deed which Tala did not commit; by the profound and unforgettable presence of the ritual murder which Tala and his family and most of the inhabitants of the Vaipe committed in their hearts, and which has become a vital strand of my heritage of memories — a truth which Tala, by avoiding it, had to live with all his life.

"We are what we remember: the actions we lived through or should have lived out and which we have chosen to remember." Tala has written this in his sermon, "On the Birthday of Man," page five.

Tala's ordeal, his first real confrontation with the choice that separates innocence from guilt, occurred the night of 3rd March, 1920.

Behind the Vaipe, stretching immediately behind Tala's home up to Togafuafua and Tufuiopa and covering an area of a few uninhabited square miles, is a swamp. An area, into which a number of fresh water springs find their way turning the soil into mud and ponds, alive with crabs and shrimps and watercress and waterlily and wild taro and taamu and tall elephant grass and the stench of decay and armies of mosquitoes. Scene of children's war games: cowboys and Indians, massacres and ambushes and mudfights. Tala, so my father has told me, was the most skilful and adept crab and shrimp hunter in the Vaipe. His father (still remembered and referred to in the Vaipe as "that spineless, worthless failure") was incapable of supporting his large family. He despised work of any type or form. So the burden of feeding and clothing and keeping the family together was left to Miti and Tala. She worked as a house-servant for expatriots, while Tala, who had left school at standard four, stayed home during the day to care for the younger children, and to forage for food. The swamp became a valuable source of food: succulent crabs and shrimp, taro and taamu. Sometimes he sold these at the market to get money to buy other essentials, such as kerosene for the lamp, matches, sugar, salt and flour.

The children always looked clean and healthy and happy, so I've been told. (When I came on the scene five years after Tala's departure, the Faasolopito children I played with were dirty, unkempt and spotted with yaws.) "There was enough love and laughter and food to go around then," my father tells me. The eldest girl (and her name is of no importance to this story), a year younger than Tala, was extremely beautiful: a picture of Innocent Goodness, some Vaipe elders have described her to me.

The youth who emerged from the swamp that evening as the cicadas woke in a loud choral chant was on his way to meet a saint, a destiny he wasn't aware of yet. He was tired and covered with mud after a whole afternoon of digging for crabs; but now the thought of a cool shower and a hot meal and the smell and warmth of his family was easing his aching, as he went through the tangled bamboo grove on to the track that led to his home ahead — behind clumps of banana trees he had planted the Christmas before. Something brushed against his forehead, a butterfly? He looked up and saw through the murmuring bamboo heads a sky tinted with faint traces of red; the sun was setting quickly. Tomorrow there would be rain. As he moved past the banana trees the broad leaves caressed his arms and shoulders like the cool featherly flow of spring water. He saw the fale, oval and timeless in the fading light. (He took no notice of the group of people in the fale.) He veered off towards the kitchen fale expecting, at any moment, his youngest brother to come bursting out of the fale to greet him and inspect his catch. But no one came. He looked at the main fale again, at the silent group gathered like a frightened brood of chickens round the flickering lamp. Knew that something was terribly amiss. He dropped the basket

of crabs and ran towards the light; towards the future he would avoid —
to attain a sainthood that he would, on confronting the reality of old
age, deny — in order to *be* Judas.

Tala walked — more a shuffle than a walk — towards Fetu's fale, trying
to overcome the feeling of nausea which had welled up inside him the
moment he had pulled the bushknife out of the thatching of the kitchen
fale. The bushknife, now clutched firmly in his right hand, was a live,
throbbing extension of his humiliation and anger and doubts and fear
of the living deed which he had to fulfil in order to break into the strange,
grey world of men. His whole life was now condensed into that cross-
shaped piece of violent steel, a justification for Fetu's murder; "my murder," Tala has written in "On the Birthday of Man." Fetu's imaginary
murder was also his own murder, Tala believed. "There is no difference
between an *imagined* act and one actually committed."

He stopped in the darkness under the talie trees in front of Fetu's
house — a small shack made of rusting corrugated iron and sacking.
The clinking of bottles and glasses and the sound of laughter were coming from the shack. (Fetu operated what is known in the Vaipe as a
"home-brew den"; he had already served two prison terms for the ille-
gal brewing of beer.) Tala had never been in the shack before, even
when he had been sent by his mother to fetch his father, who sometimes came to Fetu's den to get violently drunk. He knew Fetu quite
well, as well as he knew most of the other men in the Vaipe. He went
up the three shaky steps and into the shack.

At the far corner, under the window and partly covered by shadow,
squatted an old man, still as an object. In the middle of the room three
youths were drinking at the only table. He knew them and they knew
him, but they said nothing, they just stopped drinking and watched
him. Tala saw no one else in the room. He went up and stopped in front
of the three youths. The mud had dried on his skin and it felt like a
layer of bandages throughout which blood had congealed. All the walls
of the room were covered with pictures clipped randomly from newspapers and magazines, and the one light-bulb that dangled from the
middle rafter gave the pictures a dream-like quality, ominous and unreal.
A few empty beer bottles lay scattered across the floor, glistening in the
harsh light.

"Are you looking for him?" one of the youths asked. Tala nodded. (Fetu
and his family lived in the back room, but no sound came from that
room.)

"He isn't here," the same youth said.

"I . . . have . . . I have to," but he couldn't say it; it was too difficult
and final a step to take into the unknown.

"To *kill* him?"

"Yes," he said.

"Yes, you *have* to kill him," the other two youths said. It was as if the youths (and the Vaipe) had resolved that he should kill Fetu, or die trying.

Tala turned slowly and left the shack. He told himself that he wasn't frightened.

No one in the Vaipe knows what happened next, for there was no one there to observe what Tala did before leaving the Vaipe forever. To the rich-blooded inhabitants of the Vaipe, a tale without an exciting (preferably violent) climax, no matter how exaggerated and untrue that climax may be, is definitely *not* a tale worth listening to. A yarn or anecdote especially concerning courage, must, in the telling, assume the fabulous depths and epic grandeur of true myth. And, being a Vaipean to the quick of my honest fingernails, I too cannot stop where actual fact ends and conjecture (imagination) begins; where a mortal turns into maggot-meat and the gods extend into eternity, as it were. So for Tala's life, for my Lazarus resurrected, let me provide you with a climax.

Tala waited under the talie trees until the youths had left the shack and the light had been switched off; until he glimpsed someone (Fetu?) slipping into the back room of the shack: until he thought that Fetu had fallen asleep; then, without hope (but also without fear), he groped his way round the shack to the back room and up into the room which stank of sweat and stale food.

A lamp, turned quite low, cast a dim light over everything. Two children lay near the lamp, clutching filthy sleeping sheets round their bodies. On the bed snored Fetu; beyond him slept his wife. Tala moved to the bed and stood above Fetu. He raised the bushknife. He stopped, the bushknife poised like a crucifix above his head. Mosquitoes stung at the silence with their incessant drone.

"Forgive me," he said to the figure on the bed which, in the gloom, looked like an altar. Carefully, he placed the bushknife across Fetu's paunch, turned, recrossed the threshold and went out into the night and towards an unwanted sainthood in our scheme of things.

In "On the Birthday of Man," page forty, second to last paragraph, Tala writes: "I believe now that to have killed then would have been a liberation, my joyous liberation."

My father, a prominent deacon in the Apia Congregational Church, is getting dressed to go to Tala's funeral service. (Tala's wife wants him to be one of the pallbearers.)

I'm not going to the funeral.

It is only a saint they are burying.

PATRICK WHITE

Winner of several literary awards including the 1973 Nobel Prize, Patrick White was born in London in 1912 to Anglophile parents, brought up in Sydney, Australia, and educated at a British public school and Cambridge University. In the late 1940s, after travelling through western Europe and the United States, serving in World War II, and living for a year in Greece, he returned to Australia to write. Dramatist, novelist, and short-story writer, he has produced eleven books, among which *The Tree of Man* (1955), *Voss* (1957), *Riders in the Chariot* (1961), *The Vivisector* (1970), *The Eye of the Storm* (1973) and *A Fringe of Leaves* (1976) won enthusiastic reviews, particularly outside Australia. In Australia itself he was something of an exotic, an observer of tragic depths and spiritual heights in a community that discouraged the display of excessive emotion. He rejected what he considered mediocre in much of Australian society and sought for alternative routes to meaning. Resulting from that confrontation were several hard-edged satires of bourgeois life — he created and populated a suburb he call Sarsaparilla, and could wittily orchestrate the events and perceptions that took place around it, as he does in "Willy-Wagtails by Moonlight" (*The Burnt Ones*, 1964). But beneath the brittle dialogues and surface ironies murmur White's more intangible assertions about the potential of the human spirit.

Deeply influenced by painting and music, he seeks for ways to make language communicate nonverbal understanding, to convey to a reader the insights of eye and ear. In the process he has developed in his novels a mannered and symbolic prose that is flexible enough to accommodate both his imaginative vision and his social criticism.

FOR FURTHER READING

J.F. Burrows, "The Short Stories of Patrick White," *Southerly* 24 (1964): 116–25.

Brian Kiernan, *Patrick White* (London: Macmillan, 1980).

Patrick White, "The Prodigal Son," *Australian Letters* 1 (April 1958): 37–39.

WILLY-WAGTAILS
BY MOONLIGHT

The Wheelers drove up to the Mackenzies' punctually at six-thirty. It was the hour for which they had been asked. My God, thought Jum Wheeler. It had been raining a little, and the tyres sounded blander on the wet gravel.

In front of the Mackenzies', which was what is known as a Lovely Old Home — colonial style — amongst some carefully natural-looking gums, there stood a taxi.

"Never knew Arch and Nora ask us with anyone else," Eileen Wheeler said.

"Maybe they didn't. Even now. Maybe it's someone they couldn't get rid of."

"Or an urgent prescription from the chemist's."

Eileen Wheeler yawned. She must remember to show sympathy, because Nora Mackenzie was going through a particularly difficult one.

Anyway, they were there, and the door stood open on the lights inside. Even the lives of the people you know, even the lives of Nora and Arch look interesting for a split second, when you drive up and glimpse them through a lit doorway.

"It's that Miss Cullen," Eileen said.

For there was Miss Cullen, doing something with a brief-case in the hall.

"Ugly bitch," Jum said.

"Plain is the word," corrected Eileen.

"Arch couldn't do without her. Practically runs the business."

Certainly that Miss Cullen looked most methodical, shuffling the immaculate papers, and slipping them into a new pigskin brief-case in Arch and Nora's hall.

"Got a figure," Eileen conceded.

"But not a chin."

"Oh, hello, Miss Cullen. It's stopped raining."

It was too bright stepping suddenly into the hall. The Wheelers brightly blinked. They looked newly made.

"Keeping well, Miss Cullen, I hope?"

"I have nothing to complain about, Mr Wheeler," Miss Cullen replied.

She snapped the catch. Small, rather pointed breasts under the rain-coat. But, definitely, no chin.

Eileen Wheeler was fixing her hair in the reproduction Sheraton mirror.

She had been to the hairdresser's recently, and the do was still set too tight.

"Well, good-bye now," Miss Cullen said.

When she smiled there was a hint of gold, but discreet, no more than a bridge. Then she would draw her lips together, and lick them ever so slightly, as if she had been sucking a not unpleasantly acid sweetie.

Miss Cullen went out the door, closing it firmly but quietly behind her.

"That was Miss Cullen," said Nora Mackenzie coming down. "She's Arch's secretary."

"He couldn't do without her," she added, as though they did not know.

Nora was like that. Eileen wondered how she and Nora had tagged along together, ever since Goulburn, all those years.

"God, she's plain!" Jum said.

Nora did not exactly frown, but pleated her forehead the way she did when other people's virtues were assailed. Such attacks seemed to affect her personally, causing her almost physical pain.

"But Mildred is so kind," she insisted.

Nora Mackenzie made a point of calling her husband's employees by first names, trying to make them part of a family which she alone, perhaps, would have liked to exist.

"She brought me some giblet soup, all the way from Balgowlah, that time I had virus 'flu."

"Was it good, darling?" Eileen asked.

She was going through the routine, rubbing Nora's cheek with her own. Nora was pale. She must remember to be kind.

Nora did not answer, but led the way into the lounge-room.

Nora said:

"I don't think I'll turn on the lights for the present. They hurt my eyes, and it's so restful sitting in the dusk."

Nora *was* pale. She had, in fact, just taken a couple of Disprin.

"Out of sorts, dear?" Eileen asked.

Nora did not answer, but offered some dry martinis.

Very watery, Jum knew from experience, but drink of a kind.

"Arch will be down presently," Nora said. "He had to attend to some business, some letters Miss Cullen brought. Then he went in to have a shower."

Nora's hands were trembling as she offered the dry martinis, but Eileen remembered they always had.

The Wheelers sat down. It was all so familiar, they did not have to be asked, which was fortunate, as Nora Mackenzie always experienced difficulty in settling guests into chairs. Now she sat down herself, far more diffidently than her friends. The cushions were standing on their points.

Eileen sighed. Old friendships and the first scent of gin always made her nostalgic.

"It's stopped raining," she said, and sighed.

"Arch well?" Jum asked.

As if he cared. She had let the ice get into the cocktail, turning it almost to pure water.

"He has his trouble," Nora said. "You know, his back."

Daring them to have forgotten.

Nora loved Arch. It made Eileen feel ashamed.

So fortunate for them to have discovered each other. Nora Leadbeatter and Arch Mackenzie. Two such bores. And with bird-watching in common. Though Eileen Wheeler had never believed Nora did not make herself learn to like watching birds.

At Goulburn, in the early days, Nora would come out to Glen Davie sometimes to be with Eileen at week-ends. Mr Leadbeatter had been manager at the Wales for a while. He always saw that his daughter had the cleanest notes. Nora was shy, but better than nothing, and the two girls would sit about on the veranda those summer evenings, buffing their nails, and listening to the sheep cough in the home paddock. Eileen gave Nora lessons in making-up. Nora had protested, but was pleased.

"Mother well, darling?" Eileen asked, sipping that sad, watery gin.

"Not exactly *well*," Nora replied, painfully.

Because she had been to Orange, to visit her widowed mother, who suffered from Parkinson's disease.

"You know what I mean, dear," said Eileen.

Jum was dropping his ash on the carpet. It might be better when poor bloody Arch came down.

"I have an idea that woman, that Mrs Galloway, is unkind to her," Nora said.

"Get another," Eileen advised. "It isn't like after the War."

"One can never be sure," Nora debated. "One would hate to hurt the woman's feelings."

Seated in the dusk Nora Mackenzie was of a moth colour. Her face looked as though she had been rubbing it with chalk. Might have, too, in spite of those lessons in make-up. She sat and twisted her hands together.

How very red Nora's hands had been, at Goulburn, at the convent, to which the two girls had gone. Not that they belonged to *those*. It was only convenient. Nora's hands had been red and trembly after practising a tarantella, early, in the frost. So very early all of that. Eileen had learnt about life shortly after puberty. She had tried to tell Nora one or two things, but Nora did not want to hear. Oh, no, no, *please*, Eileen, Nora cried. As though a boy had been twisting her arm. She had those long, entreating, sensitive hands.

And there they were still. Twisting together, making their excuses. For what they had never done.

Arch came in then. He turned on the lights, which made Nora wince, even those lights which barely existed in all the neutrality of Nora's room. Nora did not comment, but smiled, because it was Arch who had committed the crime.

Arch said:

"You two toping hard as usual."

He poured himself the rest of the cocktail.

Eileen laughed her laugh which people found amusing at parties. Jum said, and bent his leg, if it hadn't been for Arch and the shower, they wouldn't have had the one too many.

"A little alcohol releases the vitality," Nora remarked ever so gently.

She always grew anxious at the point where jokes became personal.

Arch composed his mouth under the handle-bars moustache, and Jum knew what they were in for.

"Miss Cullen came out with one or two letters," Arch was taking pains to explain. "Something she thought should go off tonight. I take a shower most evenings. Summer, at least."

"Such humidity," Nora helped.

Arch looked down into his glass. He might have been composing further remarks, but did not come out with them.

That silly, bloody English-air-force-officer's moustache. It was the only thing Arch had ever dared. War had given him the courage to pinch a detail which did not belong to him.

"That Miss Cullen, useful girl," Jum suggested.

"Runs the office."

"Forty, if a day," Eileen said, whose figure was beginning to slacken off.

Arch said he would not know, and Jum made a joke about Miss Cullen's *cul-de-sac*.

The little pleats had appeared again in Nora Mackenzie's chalky brow. "Well," she cried, jumping up, quite girlish, "I do hope the dinner will be a success."

And laughed.

Nora was half-way through her second course with that woman at the Chanticleer. Eileen suspected there would be avocadoes stuffed with prawns, chicken *Mornay* and *crêpes Suzette*.

Eileen was right.

Arch seemed to gain in authority sitting at the head of his table. "I'd like you to taste this wine," he said. "It's very light."

"Oh, yes?" said Jum.

The wine was corked, but nobody remarked. The second bottle, later on, was somewhat better. The Mackenzies were spreading themselves tonight.

Arch flipped his napkin once or twice, emphasizing a point. He smoothed the handle-bars moustache, which should have concealed a harelip, only there wasn't one. Jum dated from before the moustache, long, long, very long.

Arch said:

"There was a story Armitage told me at lunch. There was a man who bought a mower. Who suffered from indigestion. Now, how, exactly, did it . . . go?"

Jum had begun to make those little pellets out of bread. It always fascinated him how grubby the little pellets turned out. And himself not by any means dirty.

Arch failed to remember the point of the story Armitage had told.

It was difficult to understand how Arch had made a success of his business. Perhaps it was that Miss Cullen, breasts and all, under the raincoat. For a long time Arch had messed around. Travelled in something. Separator parts. Got the agency for some sort of phoney machine for supplying *ozone* to public buildings. The Mackenzies lived at Burwood then. Arch continued to mess around. The War was quite a godsend. Arch was the real adje type. Did a conscientious job. Careful with his allowances, too.

Then, suddenly, after the War, Arch Mackenzie had launched out, started the import-export business. Funny the way a man will suddenly hit on the idea to which his particular brand of stupidity can respond.

The Mackenzies had moved to the North Shore, to the house which still occasionally embarrassed Nora. She felt as though she ought to apologize for success. But there was the bird-watching. Most week-ends they went off to the bush, to the Mountains or somewhere. She felt happier in humbler circumstances. In time she got used to the tape recorder which they took along. She made herself look upon it as a necessity rather than ostentation.

Eileen was dying for a cigarette.

"May I smoke, Arch?"

"We're amongst friends, aren't we?"

Eileen did not answer that. And Arch fetched the ash-tray they kept handy for those who needed it.

Nora in the kitchen dropped the beans. Everybody heard, but Arch asked Jum for a few tips on investments, as he always did when Nora happened to be out of the room. Nora had some idea that the Stock Exchange was immoral.

Then Nora brought the dish of little, pale tinned peas.

"Ah! *Pet-ty pwah!*" said Jum.

He formed his full, and rather greasy lips into a funnel through which the little rounded syllables poured most impressively.

Nora forgot her embarrassment. She envied Jum his courage in foreign languages. Although there were her lessons in Italian, she would never have dared utter in public.

"Can you bear *crêpes Suzette*?" Nora had to apologize.

"Lovely, darling." Eileen smiled.

She would have swallowed a tiger. But was, *au fond*, at her gloomiest.

What was the betting Nora would drop the *crêpes Suzette*? It was those long, trembly hands, on which the turquoise ring looked too small and innocent. The Mackenzies were still in the semi-precious bracket in the days when they became engaged.

"How's the old bird-watching?"

Jum had to force himself, but after all he had drunk their wine.

Arch Mackenzie sat deeper in his chair, almost completely at his ease.

"Got some new tapes," he said. "We'll play them later. Went up to Kurrajong on Sunday, and got the bell-birds. I'll play you the lyre-bird, too. That was Mount Wilson."

"Didn't we hear the lyre-bird last time?" Eileen asked.

Arch said:

"Yes."

Deliberately.

"But wouldn't you like to hear it again? It's something of a collector's piece."

Nora said they'd be more comfortable drinking their coffee in the lounge.

Then Arch fetched the tape recorder. He set it up on the Queen Anne walnut piecrust. It certainly was an impressive machine.

"I'll play you the lyre-bird."

"The *pièce de résistance*? Don't you think we should keep it?"

"He can never wait for the lyre-bird."

Nora had grown almost complacent. She sat holding her coffee, smiling faintly through the steam. The children she had never had with Arch were about to enter.

"Delicious coffee," Eileen said.

She had finished her filter-tips. She had never felt drearier.

The tape machine had begun to snuffle. There was quite an unusual amount of crackle. Perhaps it was the bush. Yes, that was it. The bush!

"Well, it's really quite remarkable how you people have the patience," Eileen Wheeler had to say.

"Sssh!"

Arch Mackenzie was frowning. He had sat forward in the period chair.

"This is where it comes in."

His face was tragic in the shaded light.

"Get it?" he whispered.

His hand was helping. Or commanding.

"Quite remarkable," Eileen repeated.

Jum was shocked to realize he had only two days left in which to take up the ICI rights for old Thingummy.

Nora sat looking at her empty cup. But lovingly.

Nora could have been beautiful, Eileen saw. And suddenly felt old, she who had stripped once or twice at amusing parties. Nora Mackenzie did not know about that.

Somewhere in the depths of the bush Nora was calling that it had just turned four o'clock, but she had forgotten to pack the thermos.

The machine snuffled.

Arch Mackenzie was listening. He was biting his moustache.

"There's another passage soon." He frowned.

"Darling," Nora whispered, "after the lyre-bird you might slip into the kitchen and change the bulb. It went while I was making the coffee."

Arch Mackenzie's frown deepened. Even Nora was letting him down. But she did not see. She was so in love.

It might have been funny if it was not also pathetic. People were horribly pathetic, Eileen Wheeler decided, who had her intellectual moments. She was also feeling sick. It was Nora's *crêpes Suzette,* lying like blankets.

"You'll realize there are one or two rough passages," Arch said, coming forward when the tape had ended. "I might cut it."

"It could do with a little trimming," Eileen agreed. "But perhaps it's more natural without."

Am I a what's-this, a masochist, she asked.

"Don't forget the kitchen bulb," Nora prompted.

Very gently. Very dreamy.

Her hair had strayed, in full dowdiness, down along her white cheek.

"I'll give you the bell-birds for while I'm gone."

Jum's throat had begun to rattle. He sat up in time, though, and saved his cup in the same movement.

"I remember the bell-birds," he said.

"Not these ones, you don't. These are new. These are the very latest. The best bell-birds."

Arch had started the tape, and stalked out of the room, as if to let the bell-birds themselves prove his point.

"It is one of our loveliest recordings," Nora promised.

They all listened or appeared to.

When Nora said:

"Oh, dear" — getting up — "I do believe" — panting almost — "the bell-bird tape" — trembling — "is damaged."

Certainly the crackle was more intense.

"Arch will be so terribly upset."

She had switched off the horrifying machine. With surprising skill for one so helpless. For a moment it seemed to Eileen Wheeler that Nora Mackenzie was going to hide the offending tape somewhere in her bosom. But she thought better of it, and put it aside on one of those little superfluous tables.

"Perhaps it's the machine that's broken," suggested Jum.

"Oh, no," said Nora, "it's the tape. I know. We'll have to give you something else."

"I can't understand," — Eileen grinned — "how you ever got around, Nora, to being mechanical."

"If you're determined," Nora said.

Her head was lowered in concentration.

"If you want a thing enough."

She was fixing a fresh tape.

"And we do love our birds. Our Sundays together in the bush." The machine had begun its snuffling and shuffling again. Nora Mackenzie raised her head, as if launched on an invocation.

Two or three notes of bird-song fell surprisingly pure and clear, out of the crackle, into the beige and string-coloured room.

"This is one," Nora said, "I don't think I've ever heard before."

She smiled, however, and listened to identify.

"Willy-Wagtails," Nora said.

Willy-Wagtails were suited to tape. The song tumbled and exulted.

"It must be something," Nora said, "that Arch made while I was with Mother. There were a couple of Sundays when he did a little field-work on his own."

Nora might have given way to a gentle melancholy for all she had foregone if circumstances had not heightened the pitch. There was Arch standing in the doorway. Blood streaming.

"Blasted bulb collapsed in my hand!"

"Oh, darling! Oh *dear!*" Nora cried.

The Wheelers were both fascinated. There was the blood dripping on the beige wall-to-wall.

How the willy-wagtails chortled.

Nora Mackenzie literally staggered at her husband, to take upon herself, if possible, the whole ghastly business.

"Come along, Arch," she moaned. "We'll fix. In just a minute." Nora panted.

And simply by closing the door, she succeeded in blotting the situation, all but the drops of blood that were left behind on the carpet.

"Poor old Arch! Bleeding like a pig!" Jum Wheeler said, and laughed.

Eileen added:

"We shall suffer the willy-wags alone."

Perhaps it was better like that. You could relax. Eileen began to pull. Her step-ins had eaten into her.

The willy-wagtails were at it again.

"Am I going crackers?" asked Jum. "Listening to those bloody birds!"

When somebody laughed. Out of the tape. The Wheelers sat. Still.

Three-quarters of the bottle! Snuffle crackle. *Arch Mackenzie, you're a fair trimmer!* Again that rather brassy laughter.

"Well, I'll be blowed!" said Jum Wheeler.

"But it's that Miss Cullen," Eileen said.

The Wheeler spirits soared as surely as plummets dragged the notes of the wagtail down.

But it's far too rocky and far too late. Besides, it's willy-wagtails we're after. How Miss Cullen laughed. *Willy-wagtails by moon light!* Arch was less intelligible, as if he had listened to too many birds, and caught the habit. Snuffle crackle went the machine . . . *the buttons are not made to undo . . .* Miss Cullen informed. *Oh, stop it. Arch!* ARCH! *You're* TEARING *me!*

So that the merciless machine took possession of the room. There in the crackle of twigs, the stench of ants, the two Wheelers sat. There was that long, thin Harry Edwards, Eileen remembered, with bony wrists, had got her down behind the barn. She had hated it at first. All mirth had been exorcized from Miss Cullen's recorded laughter. Grinding out. Grinding out. So much of life was recorded by now. Returning late from a country dance, the Wheelers had fallen down amongst the sticks and stones, and made what is called love, and risen in the grey hours, to find themselves numb and bulging.

If only the tape, if you knew the trick with the wretched switch. Jum Wheeler decided not to look at his wife. Little, guilty pockets were turning themselves out in his mind. That woman at the Locomotive Hotel. Pockets and pockets of putrefying trash. Down along the creek, amongst the tussocks and the sheep pellets, the sun burning his boy's skin, he played his overture to sex. Alone.

This sort of thing's all very well, Miss Cullen decided. *It's time we turned practical. Are you sure we can find our way back to the car?*

Always trundling. Crackling. But there were the blessed wagtails again.

"Wonder if they forgot the machine?"

"Oh, God! Hasn't the tape bobbed up in Pymble?"

A single willy-wagtail sprinkled its grace-notes through the stuffy room.

"Everything's all right," Nora announced. "He's calmer now. I persuaded him to take a drop of brandy."

"That should fix him," Jum said.

But Nora was listening to the lone wagtail. She was standing in the bush. Listening. The notes of bird-song falling like mountain water, when they were not chiselled in moonlight.

"There is nothing purer," Nora said, "than the song of the wagtail. Excepting Schubert," she added, "some of Schubert."

She was so shyly glad it had occurred to her.

But the Wheelers just sat.

And again Nora Mackenzie was standing alone amongst the inexorable moonlit gums. She thought perhaps she had always felt alone, even with Arch, while grateful even for her loneliness.

"Ah, there you are!" Nora said.

It was Arch. He stood holding out his bandaged wound. Rather rigid. He could have been up for court martial.

"I've missed the willy-wagtails," Nora said, raising her face to him, exposing her distress, like a girl. "Some day you'll have to play it to me. When you've the time. And we can concentrate."

The Wheelers might not have existed.

As for the tape it had discovered silence.

Arch mumbled they'd all better have something to drink.

Jum agreed it was a good idea.

"Positively brilliant," Eileen said.

RUDY WIEBE

Born in 1934 to a Mennonite family in Fairholme, in the hilly wood-
lands of northern Saskatchewan, Rudy Wiebe notes in "Passage by
Land" that landscape and cultural heritage have always been important to him. Though he did not learn English until he went to school,
and did not see a mountain or a plain until he was almost thirteen, he
later found language and landscape indissolubly wedded to each other.
Encountering the world was a "wandering to find"; and paramount in
his work is the sense of wandering that derives from his early experience, expressing itself as a quest for knowledge about knowledge itself,
about ways of knowing. In this story, for example, he does not portray
a contrast so much as he enacts one, between the passivity of information and the activity of art.

His Mennonite background features significantly in two of his novels, *Peace Shall Destroy Many* (1964) and *The Blue Mountains of China*
(1970); the latter, a modern epic, probes the idealistic impulses behind
the sect, traces its spiritual and geographic journeys, and tries to come
to terms with the power of the commitment that has impelled so many
people to accept its invitation to individual action. His sympathy for
human beings takes a different form in *First and Vital Candle* (1966),
The Temptations of Big Bear (1973), about the Riel Rebellion, and
"Where Is the Voice Coming From?" which became the title story of a
collection which appeared in 1974. The Indians, Inuit, and Métis who
appear in these works are admirably realized characters, and Wiebe
has endeavored with great sensitivity to cross the cultural barriers that
lie between him and his subject. But he is acutely conscious of the
difficulty of being anyone but oneself, of the limitations that one's perspective erects against complete understanding, and of the problems
that face the artist and the historian when they try to convey their
perceptions of truth or reality. "Where Is the Voice Coming From?"
resulted, Wiebe writes, from personal encounters with museum displays and historical accounts of Indian and Royal Canadian Mounted
Police history, and from reading in nineteenth-century newspapers
and in volume 12 (*Reconsiderations*) of Arnold Toynbee's *A Study of
History*. On top of all that is his overpowering urge to "make story,"
for, as he writes in his introduction to an anthology, *The Story-Makers*
(1970), a good story seduces "both teller and listener out of their world
into its own," illuminating "the world in which teller and listener
actually are" and often proving "the more pleasurable as the seduction becomes less immediate: story worth pondering is story doubly
enjoyed."

FOR FURTHER READING

W.J. Keith, *Epic Fiction: The Art of Rudy Wiebe* (Edmonton: University of Alberta Press, 1981).

W.J. Keith, ed., *A Voice in the Land* (Edmonton: NeWest, 1981).

Rudy Wiebe, "Passage by Land," *Canadian Literature*, no. 48 (Spring
1971): 25–47; reprinted in *Writers of the Prairies*, ed. Donald Stephens (Vancouver: University of British Columbia, 1973), pp. 29–31.

WHERE IS THE VOICE COMING FROM?

The problem is to make the story.

A difficulty of this making may have been excellently stated by Teilhard de Chardin: "We are continually inclined to isolate ourselves from the things and events which surround us . . . as though we were spectators, not elements, in what goes on." Arnold Toynbee does venture, "For all that we know, Reality is the undifferentiated unity of the mystical experience," but that need not here be considered. This story ended long ago; it is one of finite acts, of orders, of elemental feelings and reactions, of obvious legal restrictions and requirements.

Presumably all the parts of the story are themselves available. A difficulty is that they are, as always, available only in bits and pieces. Though the acts themselves seem quite clear, some written reports of the acts contradict each other. As if these acts were, at one time, too well known; as if the original nodule of each particular fact had from somewhere received non-factual accretions; or even more, as if, since the basic facts were so clear perhaps there were a larger number of facts than any one reporter, or several, or even any reporter had ever attempted to record. About facts that are still simply told by this mouth to that ear, of course, even less can be expected.

An affair seventy-five years old should acquire some of the shiny transparency of an old man's skin. It should.

Sometimes it would seem that it would be enough — perhaps more than enough — to hear the names only. The grandfather One Arrow; the mother Spotted Calf; the father Sounding Sky; the wife (wives rather, but only one of them seems to have a name, though their fathers are Napaise, Kapahoo, Old Dust, The Rump) — the one wife named, of all things, Pale Face; the cousin Going-Up-To-Sky; the brother-in-law (again, of all things) Dublin. The names of the police sound very much alike; they all begin with Constable or Corporal or Sergeant, but here and there an Inspector, then a Superintendent and eventually all the resonance of an Assistant Commissioner echoes down. More. Herself: Victoria, by the Grace of God etc. etc. QUEEN, Defender of the Faith, etc. etc.· and witness "Our Right Trusty and Right Well-beloved Cousin and Councillor the Right Honorable Sir John Campbell Hamilton-Gordon, Earl of Aberdeen; Viscount Formartine, Baron Haddo, Methlic, Tarves and Kellie, in the Peerage of Scotland; Viscount Gordon of Aberdeen, County of Aberdeen, in the Peerage of the United Kingdom; Baronet of Nova Scotia, Knight Grand Cross of Our Most Distinguished Order of Saint Michael and Saint George etc. Governor General of Canada." And of course himself: in the award proclamation named "Jean-Baptiste" but otherwise known only as Almighty Voice.

But hearing cannot be enough; not even hearing all the thunder of A Proclamation: "Now Hear Ye that a reward of FIVE HUNDRED DOLLARS will be paid to any person or persons who will give such information as will lead . . . (etc. etc.) this Twentieth day of April, in the year of Our Lord one thousand eight hundred end ninety-six, and the Fifty-nineth year of Our Reign . . ." etc. and etc.

Such hearing cannot be enough. The first item to be seen is the piece of white bone. It is almost triangular, slightly convex — concave actually as it is positioned at this moment with its corners slightly raised — graduating from perhaps a strong eighth to a weak quarter of an inch in thickness, its scattered pore structure varying between larger and smaller on its perhaps polished, certainly shiny surface. Precision is difficult since the glass showcase is at least thirteen inches deep and therefore an eye cannot be brought as close as the minute inspection of such a small, though certainly quite adequate, sample of skull would normally require. Also, because of the position it cannot be determined whether the several hairs, well over a foot long, are still in some manner attached or not.

The seven-pounder cannon can be seen standing almost shyly between the showcase and the interior wall. Officially it is known as a gun, not a cannon, and clearly its bore is not large enough to admit a large man's fist. Even if it can be believed that this gun was used in the 1885 Rebellion and that on the evening of Saturday May 29, 1897 (while the nine-pounder, now unidentified, was in the process of arriving with the police on the special train from Regina), seven shells (all that were available in Prince Albert at that time) from it were sent shrieking into the poplar bluff as night fell, clearly such shelling could not and would not disembowel the whole earth. Its carriage is now nicely lacquered, the perhaps oak spokes of its petite wheels (little higher than a knee) have been recently scraped, puttied and varnished; the brilliant burnish of its brass breeching testifies with what meticulous care charmen and women have used nationally advertised cleaners and restorers.

Though it can also be seen, even a careless glance reveals that the same concern has not been expended on the one (of two) 44 calibre 1866 model Winchesters apparently found at the last in the pit with Almighty Voice. It also is preserved in a glass case; the number 1536735 is still, though barely, distinguishable on the brass cartridge section just below the brass saddle ring. However, perhaps because the case was imperfectly sealed at one time (though sealed enough not to warrant disturbance now), or because of simple neglect, the rifle is obviously spotted here and there with blotches of rust and the brass itself reveals discolorations almost like mildew. The rifle bore, the three long strands of hair themselves, actually bristle with clots of dust. It may be that this museum cannot afford to be as concerned as the other; conversely, the disfiguration may be something inherent in the items themselves.

The small building which was the police guardroom at Duck Lake,

Saskatchewan Territory, in 1895 may also be seen. It had subsequently been moved from its original place and used to house small animals, chickens perhaps, or pigs — such as a woman might be expected to have under her responsibility. It is, of course, now perfectly empty, and clean so that the public may enter with no more discomfort than a bend under the doorway and a heavy encounter with disinfectant. The door-jamb has obviously been replaced; the bar network at one window is, however, said to be original; smooth still, very smooth. The logs inside have been smeared again and again with whitewash, perhaps paint, to an insistent point of identity-defying characterlessness. Within the small rectangular box of these logs not a sound can be heard from the streets of the probably dead town.

Hey Injun you'll get hung for stealing that steer
Hey Injun for killing that government cow you'll get
three weeks on the woodpile Hey Injun

The place named Kinistino has disappeared from the map but the Minnechinass Hills have not. Whether they have ever been on a map is doubtful but they will, of course, not disappear from the landscape as long as the grass grows and the rivers run. Contrary to general report and belief, the Canadian prairies are rarely, if ever, flat and the Minnechinass (spelled five different ways and translated sometimes as "The Outside Hill," sometimes as "Beautiful Bare Hills") are dissimilar from any other of the numberless hills that everywhere block out the prairie horizon. They are not bare; poplars lie tattered along their tops, almost black against the straw-pale grass and sharp green against the grey soil of the plowing laid in half-mile rectangular blocks upon their western slopes. Poles holding various wires stick out of the fields, back down the bend of the valley; what was once a farmhouse is weathering into the cultivated earth. The poplar bluff where Almighty Voice made his stand has, of course, disappeared.

The policemen he shot and killed (not the ones he wounded, of course) are easily located. Six miles east, thirty-nine miles north in Prince Albert, the English Cemetery. Sergeant Colin Campbell Colebrook, North West Mounted Police Registration Number 605, lies presumably under a gravestone there. His name is seventeenth in a very long "list of non-commissioned officers and men who have died in the service since the inception of the force." The date is October 29, 1895, and the cause of death is anonymous: "Shot by escaping Indian prisoner near Prince Albert." At the foot of this grave are two others: Constable John R. Kerr, No. 3040, and Corporal C. H. S. Hockin, No. 3106. Their cause of death on May 28, 1897 is even more anonymous, but the place is relatively precise: "Shot by Indians at Min-etch-inass Hills, Prince Albert District."

The gravestone, if he has one, of the fourth man Almighty Voice killed is more difficult to locate. Mr. Ernest Grundy, postmaster at Duck Lake in 1897, apparently shut his window the afternoon of Friday, May 25, armed himself, rode east twenty miles, participated in the second charge into the bluff at about 6:30 P.M., and on the third sweep of that charge was shot dead at the edge of the pit. It would seem that he thereby contributed substantially not only to the Indians' bullet supply, but his clothing warmed them as well.

The burial place of Dublin and Going-Up-To-Sky is unknown, as is the grave of Almighty Voice. It is said that a Métis named Henry Smith lifted the latter's body from the pit in the bluff and gave it to Spotted Calf. The place of burial is not, of course, of ultimate significance. A gravestone is always less evidence than a triangular piece of skull, provided it is large enough.

Whatever further evidence there is to be gathered may rest on pictures. There are, presumably, almost numberless pictures of the policemen in the case, but the only one with direct bearing is one of Sergeant Colebrook who apparently insisted on advancing to complete an arrest after being warned three times that if he took another step he would be shot. The picture must have been taken before he joined the force; it reveals him a large-eared young man, hair brushcut and ascot tie, his eyelids slightly drooping, almost hooded under thick brows. Unfortunately a picture of Constable R. C. Dickson, into whose charge Almighty Voice was apparently placed in that guardroom and who after Colebrook's death was convicted of negligence, sentenced to two months hard labor and discharged, does not seem to be available.

There are no pictures to be found of either Dublin (killed early by rifle fire) or Going-Up-To-Sky (killed in the pit), the two teenage boys who gave their ultimate fealty to Almighty Voice. There is, however, one said to be of Almighty Voice, Junior. He may have been born to Pale Face during the year, two hundred and twenty-one days that his father was a fugitive. In the picture he is kneeling before what could be a tent, he wears striped denim overalls and displays twin babies whose sex cannot be determined from the double-laced dark bonnets they wear. In the supposed picture of Spotted Calf and Sounding Sky, Sounding Sky stands slightly before his wife; he wears a white shirt and a striped blanket folded over his left shoulder in such a manner that the arm in which he cradles a long rifle cannot be seen. His head is thrown back; the rim of his hat appears as a black half-moon above eyes that are pressed shut in, as it were, profound concentration above a mouth clenched thin in a downward curve. Spotted Calf wears a long dress, a sweater which could also be a man's dress coat, and a large fringed and embroidered shawl which would appear distinctly Doukhobor in origin if the scroll patterns on it were more irregular. Her head is small and turned slightly towards her husband so as to reveal her right ear. There is what can only be called a quizzical expression on her crumpled face; it may be she does not understand what is happening and that she would have asked a question, perhaps of her husband, perhaps of the photographer, perhaps even of anyone, anywhere in the world if such questioning were possible for an Indian lady.

There is one final picture. That is one of Almighty Voice himself. At least it is purported to be of Almighty Voice himself. In the Royal Canadian Mounted Police Museum on the Barracks Grounds just off Dewdney Avenue in Regina, Saskatchewan it lies in the same showcase, as a matter of fact immediately beside, that triangular piece of skull. Both are unequivocally labeled, and it must be assumed that a police force with a world-wide reputation would not label *such* evidence incorrectly. But here emerges an ultimate problem in making the story.

There are two official descriptions of Almighty Voice. The first reads: "Height about five feet, ten inches, slight build, rather good looking, a sharp hooked nose with a remarkably flat point. Has a bullet scar on the left side of his face about 1½ inches long running from near corner of mouth towards ear. The scar cannot be noticed when his face is painted but otherwise is plain. Skin fair for an Indian." The second description is on the Award Proclamation: "About twenty-two years old, five feet ten inches in height, weight about eleven stone, slightly erect, neat small feet and hands; complexion inclined to be fair, wavy dark hair to shoulders, large dark eyes, broad forehead, sharp features and parrot nose with flat tip, scar on left cheek running from mouth towards ear, feminine appearance."

So run the descriptions that were, presumably, to identify a well-known fugitive in so precise a manner that an informant could collect five hundred dollars — a considerable sum when a police constable earned between one and two dollars a day. The nexus of the problems appears when these supposed official descriptions are compared to the supposed official picture. The man in the picture is standing on a small rug. The fingers of his left hand touch a curved Victorian settee, behind him a photographer's backdrop of scrolled patterns merges to vaguely paradisaic trees and perhaps a sky. The moccasins he wears make it impossible to deduce whether his feet are "neat small." He may be five feet, ten inches tall, may weigh eleven stone, he certainly is "rather good looking" and, though it is a frontal view, it may be that the point of his long and flaring nose could be "remarkably flat." The photograph is slightly over-illuminated and so the unpainted complexion could be "inclined to be fair"; however, nothing can be seen of a scar, the hair is not wavy and shoulder-length but hangs almost to the waist in two thick straight braids worked through with beads, fur, ribbons and cords. The right hand that holds the corner of the blanket-like coat in position is large and, even in the high illumination, heavily veined. The neck is concealed under coiled beads and the forehead seems more low than "broad."

Perhaps, somehow, these picture details could be reconciled with the official description if the face as a whole were not so devastating.

On a cloth-backed sheet two feet by two and one-half feet in size, under the Great Seal of the Lion and the Unicorn, dignified by the names of the Deputy of the Minister of Justice, the Secretary of State, the Queen herself and all the heaped detail of her "Right Trusty and Right Well Beloved Cousin," this description concludes: "feminine appearance." But the picture: any face of history, any believed face that the world acknowledges as *man* — Socrates, Jesus, Attila, Genghis Khan, Mahatma Ghandi, Joseph Stalin — no believed face is more *man* than this face. The mouth, the nose, the clenched brows, the eyes — the eyes are large, yes, and dark, but even in this watered-down reproduction of unending reproductions of original, a steady look into those eyes cannot be endured. It is a face like an axe.

It is now evident that the de Chardin statement quoted at the beginning has relevance only as it proves itself inadequate to explain what has happened. At the same time, the inadequacy of Aristotle's much more famous statement becomes evident: "The true difference [between the historian and the poet] is that one relates what *has* happened, the other what *may* happen." These statements cannot explain the storyteller's activity since, despite the most rigid application of impersonal investigation, the elements of the story have now run me aground. If ever I could, I can no longer pretend to objective, omnipotent disinterestedness. I am no longer *spectator* of what *has* happened or what *may* happen: I am become *element* in what is happening at this very moment.

For it is, of course, I myself who cannot endure the shadows on that paper which are those eyes. It is I who stand beside this broken veranda post where two corner shingles have been torn away, where barbed wire tangles the dead weeds on the edge of this field. The bluff that sheltered Almighty Voice and his two friends has not disappeared from the slope of the Minnechinass, no more than the sound of Constable Dickson's voice in that guardhouse is silent. The sound of his speaking is there even if it has never been recorded in an official report:

hey injun you'll get
hung
for stealing that steer
hey injun for killing that government
cow you'll get three
weeks on the woodpile hey injun

The unknown contradictory words about an unprovable act that move a boy to defiance, an implacable Cree warrior long after the three-hundred-and-fifty-year war is ended, a war already lost the day the Cree watch Cartier hoist his gun ashore at Hochelaga and they begin the retreat west; these words of incomprehension, of threatened incomprehensible law are there to be heard, like the unmoving tableau of the three-day siege is there to be seen on the slopes of the Minnechinass. Sounding

Sky is somewhere not there, under arrest, but Spotted Calf stands on a shoulder of the Hills a little to the left, her arms upraised to the setting sun. Her mouth is open. A horse rears, riderless, above the scrub willow at the edge of the bluff, smoke puffs, screams tangle in rifle barrage, there are wounds, somewhere. The bluff is green this spring, it will not burn and the ragged line of seven police and two civilians is staggering through, faces twisted in rage, terror, and rifles sputter. Nothing moves. There is no sound of frogs in the night; twenty-seven policemen and five civilians stand in cordon at thirty-yard intervals and a body also lies in the shelter of a gully. Only a voice rises from the bluff:

We have fought well
You have died like braves
I have worked hard and am hungry
Give me food

but nothing moves. The bluff lies, a bright green island on the grassy slope surrounded by men hunched forward rigid over their long rifles, men clumped out of rifle-range, thirty-five men dressed as for fall hunting on a sharp spring day, a small gun positioned on a ridge above. A crow is falling out of the sky into the bluff, its feathers sprayed as by an explosion. The first gun and the second gun are in position, the beginning and end of the bristling surround of thirty-five Prince Albert Volunteers, thirteen civilians and fifty-six policemen in position relative to the bluff and relative to the unnumbered whites astride their horses, standing up in their carts, staring and pointing across the valley, in position relative to the bluff and the unnumbered Indians squatting silent along the higher ridges of the Hills, motionless mounds, faceless against the Sunday morning sunlight edging between and over them down along the tree tips, down into the shadows of the bluff. Nothing moves. Beside the second gun the red-coated officer has flung a handful of grass into the motionless air, almost to the rim of the red sun.

And there is a voice. It is an incredible voice that rises from among the young poplars ripped of their spring bark, from among the dead somewhere lying there, out of the arm-deep pit shorter than a man; a voice rises over the exploding smoke and thunder of guns that reel back in their positions, worked over, serviced by the grimed motionless men in bright coats and glinting buttons, a voice so high and clear, so unbelievably high and strong in its unending wordless cry.

The voice of "Gitchie-Manitou Wayo" — interpreted as "voice of the Great Spirit" — that is, Almighty Voice. His death chant no less incredible in its beauty than in its incomprehensible happiness.

I say "wordless cry" because that is the way it sounds to me. I could be more accurate if I had a reliable interpreter who would make a reliable interpretation. For I do not, of course, understand the Cree myself.

J. MICHAEL YATES

J. Michael Yates was born in Fulton, Missouri in 1938 and grew up in the United States, emigrating to Canada as an adult. There, he worked in a variety of jobs — writing, editing, and teaching creative writing (he was the founding editor of Sono Nis Press) — and he lived in a variety of places, from West Vancouver to the Queen Charlotte Islands. The range of backgrounds has had its impact on his writing, which transcends borders both political and generic. He writes poetry, drama, fiction, and meditations on existence which embrace features of several different genres. He does not write sociological documentary. Repeatedly, however, he uses the actual forms of literature to require his reader to see the world — and their roles in it — with abrupt clarity. He manages to do so, Andreas Schroeder writes, in his Introduction to *Stories from Pacific & Arctic Canada* (1974), while avoiding the "haven of straight metaphor or fable." Readers may have to suspend the laws of ordinary logic in order to follow Yates's stories, but in doing so they have the opportunity to discover — and surrender to — the inventive logic of the stories themselves.

Among Yates's books are two collections of fiction, *The Abstract Beast* (1971) and *Fazes in Elsewhen* (1977). "The Sinking of the Northwest Passage" comes from the first of these. It coolly portrays a universe of domestic ritual and suburban monomania, whose bizarreness is the more acute for its familiarity.

FOR FURTHER READING

George Bowering, "Introductory Notes" to his ed., *Fiction of Contemporary Canada* (Toronto: Coach House, 1980), pp. 7–9.

Geoff Hancock, "Magic Realism" in his ed., *Magic Realism* (Toronto: Aya, 1980), pp. 7–15.

THE SINKING OF THE NORTHWEST PASSAGE

So many of us, alas, were born with
no Northwest Passage to discover.
We spend our lives carrying that
poignant absence inside us wherever
we go, around and around the earth.

Commodore Eric F. F. Forrer stood in the bow of his sailboat, *The Northwest Passage*, near the base of the bowsprit (whose configuration was most personal, most abstract), arms folded over his still large-calibre chest and shouted: "Eric F. F. Forrer, Commodore!" And then he listened to his echo skittering away among the branches and boles of the scrub-pine.

There was no retort. But as if there had been one, as if there had been a challenge, he continued at the top of his basso: "I am Commodore because I say so. Let any man who doubts come forward and say."

The as-if: "In what navy do you serve, sir?"

The Commodore: "None. Such institutions are for ordinary men."

The as-if: "Such titles as 'Commodore' are earned with valor and conferred in formal and elaborate ceremony."

The Commodore: "Ordinary! Ordinary!"

The as-if: "Nevertheless."

The Commodore: " 'Nevertheless' hell! And nuts! Didn't great Caesar place the laurel on his own brow? And what of Tamburlaine? These were great men in history. I am greater than all history!"

The as-if: "Who says so?"

The Commodore: "I say so, you imbecile. Do you doubt it?"

The as-if: "Frankly, yes."

The Commodore: "Frankly, you are a quadrilateral incandescent ordinary gregarious afterbirth of a self-conscious bitch monkey. Why do I waste time talking to you? Name me one, among all past and present commodores, name me one who ever built his own ship with his own hands as I have."

The as-if: "I cannot."

The Commodore: "Of course you can't. I am my own navy, and as head of it, it is fitting and proper that I function as its commodore."

The as-if: "Hmmmmm."

The Commodore: "Further, mister, this may appear an innocuous sailing vessel, but, in fact, it is a cleverly-camouflaged submarine, and if you don't vanish, this instant, I shall cause it to dive, rig for silent running, and sink you with cleverly-concealed torpedos. Do we understand one another?"

The as-if: "Of course, sir. Right away, sir."

The Commodore: "Excellent. Once, while rafting on a lake near Terrace in the wilds of British Columbia, I sank an entire fleet of pleasure craft which annoyed me while I was sun bathing."

Out of the door of the house shuffled a woman hugging herself across her copious bosom against the chill of the northern morning; she yawned, then stood squinting at the tableau of Commodore Eric F. F. Forrer standing in the bow of his sailing ship which stood solid as a monument on its supports in the middle of the smooth asphalt driveway.

"Excellent sailing this morning (pointing to the asphalt of the driveway and the long winding asphalt road which led down the dome toward the town). Not a ripple. But I could wish for more wind, you know?"

"Why all the shouting? There's no one around."

"You'd be surprised, my dear, how many there are around us."

With that he stepped to the port railing and urinated noisily upon the pavement below.

"Oh, don't do that. Someone might see."

"But you just assured me there's no one about."

"Never mind."

He zipped up the fly of his "northern tuxedo" (overalls) with ceremony.

"Come aboard, come aboard, don't just stand there on the surface, can't you see I'm under way?"

She climbed up the ladder still shivering from the chill of the dew-soaked dome.

"Look at that view of Mount Forrer. You can see four hundred miles."

"Yes, its beautiful. Every day it's the same but not the same."

"Light. Things never look the same on successive days. It's all in how you look at a thing. And every day the light is changing. Wait till you see it up close. We're going to sail right to it, then right up to its summit before we turn north again into the Northwest Passage."

"There's no water straight to the mountain."

"Never mind that."

"And you know there's no longer a Northwest Passage to be found."

"Ordinary poppycock. You can come with me, or I'll set you ashore on an island and proceed alone, or leave you here. Whatever you prefer."

"Thank you. We'll think about it again after breakfast. Come on in now."

"Alright. I'll just anchor up now. I won't be a minute."

Over her shoulder she heard the clank of anchor and chain striking the dark asphalt. The boat secured, he followed her into the house.

After his third mug of sourdough wet breakfast (four fingers of overproof rum, honey, cinnamon, lemon juice, and strong black tea — never mixed in that order) he commented: "This is one of the best houses I ever built. It voyages well. Hardly keels at all in the wind."

"Yes."

"But it won't get through the passage. The passage is quite narrow, you know."

"No, I didn't know. How do you know, if it's never yet been discovered?"

"I know these things. It is my affair to know them."

"Yes, of course."

"We'll have to have just the right tide, woman, just the right tide. It may be necessary to wait days, days, or even months for just the right tide . . . and even then it'll be handy to have pikepoles starboard and port to push us off if she goes too close to the sides. But at the right tide, at just the right tide, with the big rollers behind us, we should surf right on through."

"I hope so."

"Probably we won't even need any canvas, much less the engine. No engine is really dependable anyway. Trust the natural stuff — wind and water."

"If you say so."

"I do. Truly."

It was a bright summer morning, light tentacles reaching in through the windows and curling about the legs of the furniture — brilliant as only mornings in the long-lit northern summers can be — when the first foreign, altogether indescribable, sound from the driveway filled their ears.

The Commodore leapt to the screen door and scowled out into the dazzling sunlight.

"What is it?"

"Nothing I can see. Ship's riding easily at anchor."

"What a strange noise."

". . . Yes . . ."

The sound again.

"It's coming from the boat."

"Is she breaking up?"

"I built it."

"Silly of me."

"Extremely."

"Why don't you go out and look around?"

"I guess I'd better."

He turned from the door and began placing dishes in a cupboard.

"Then go."

He first withdrew his pocket-watch from the upper left-hand pocket of his overalls and glanced at the time, then replaced it, then gazed slowly around the kitchen and through the doorway to the livingroom which framed a magnificent view of Mount Forrer, then pushed out the door and strode slowly down the asphalt driveway. She watched from the door and the house slowly filled with her ineffable dread. She could see nothing unusual — only the driveway with the boat on its supports filling it, and Commodore Eric F. F. Forrer nearing the source of the noise which was growing louder and continuous now.

"What do you see? Can you see anything?"

"The ship looks fine."

Then he was bending over examining the supports.

"Is it too heavy for them? Are they breaking?"

"No."

"Then what is it?"

"Eh . . . here!"

He was looking at the cross-members on the pavement.

"What?"

"The supports seem to be sinking through the pavement. Funny they've been here in this same position for such a long time . . . all these years . . . same weight, same conditions . . . why would they wait until this moment to begin sinking?"

She came up beside him and bent over too, examining. "I don't know. Maybe it's the heat."

"Can't be. It's not hot out."

"It's been much hotter than this on other days and it had no effect. Don't you remember the hot scorcher of a summer we had about nine years ago? If the supports were ever going to sink through the asphalt, they would have done so then."

"Well, it's right in front of your eyes, woman . . . sinking . . . there, look!"

As if on cue, the back cross-member vanished and the stern of the vessel settled to the ground. It gave the whole vehicle a strange lurching look — as if climbing a great swell on the high seas. The lines of the craft had become so familiar to them, and now the deck was almost at a thirty degree angle with the horizon.

"And look under here, the keel's more than halfway submerged."

"Yes."

"Blast it, blast the blasted luck!"

"What now?"

"Quick, help me put those planks over there under the hull."

Soon an assortment of weather-silvered two by sixes and two by eights were neatly formed into a protective bed beneath the middle and forward hull.

"We've got to keep her from keeling over; it'll smash the ribbing and ruin everything. I'll never find yellow cedar of that quality again. They don't even replant that stuff after they cut it."

They braced the boat from pavement to gunwales with four by fours.

"Where are you going?"

"To get jacks, jack her up, and build another platform under the stern."

"How did this happen? Do such things happen?"

"No."

The Commodore was fretfully pulling out hairs of his blonde moustache, a growth that couldn't be seen at a distance greater than a few feet. One could always tell when he enjoyed a book: its pages were full of hairs from his moustache.

"On the other hand, seamanship is a tricky science and a difficult art. There are strange currents, woman, strange currents which sink great ships even in the fairest of surface conditions. Tides change. Sea-floors rearrange themselves. A man can never know too much about navigation —although there are things a man can know far too much about. I'll get the jacks."

Behind him he heard the sound begin again, and even before he turned he knew the bow support and remaining keel had disappeared under the surface of the asphalt.

"Oh dear, now the bow is down."

"I have eyes. I . . . have . . . eyes."

"Will the planks keep it afloat?"

"Who can be certain of such things? No sense trying the jacks now. There's nothing forward or astern skookum enough to take leverage against that weight. I have no intention of cracking ribs and breaking off her railings to get purchase. Better *The Northwest Passage* go down just as I made her, than go down broken and maimed.

"But wouldn't it be better to save even . . ."

"No."

"Can't you do something?"

"Possibly I could tunnel in two places beneath the ship, run belts under, then hire a crane to yard her up while I build new supports under her."

"Yes, do that. But you would have to ruin the driveway, wouldn't you?"

"Yes."

He went in through the screen door then emerged a few minutes later carrying two kitchen chairs.

"What are those for?"

"We'll sit and keep a close watch. She's sailing high and easy now on the planks. Maybe something will occur to us."

"Did you call about the crane?"

"Yes."

"What did they say?"

"Either there is no elevation company listed in the yellow pages, or there is no crane this far north large enough for the job, or it would require two smaller cranes (and likely the two operators couldn't coordinate their lifting: suppose a bee flew into the cab of one of them at a crucial moment. And everyone knows that two machines cannot be perfectly harmonized . . . even by a third machine; there are too many variables). If one failed, not only would all that effort be vain, but much money would go for nothing; all our money is riding on the planks before us there. If one broke down in mid-lift (even without damage to the vessel, let us hopefully suppose), then where would we be? We would pay for men and machines alike by the hour nevertheless, if we could pay. They would have to send for a mechanic and then for parts which must be flown in from the outside. Or, since all of them are on tracks, it would take a long time to get up here from their present job-sites, if, indeed, they could be spared at all. This is the building season, and all things and all men are under contract. In fact, they wouldn't be allowed to come up here on tracks, they would scar the pavement, and there are ordinances. They would have to bring them on low-beds and it would be necessary to add the cost of the trucks and their drivers. If they came on trucks, there would be far too much weight per axle for the myriad small bridges between the city and this driveway. There are ordinances, always ordinances to protect the forms of civilization. They aren't fond, you know, of small and extraordinary jobs like this one and avoid them at almost all costs. Or the line was busy. Or out of order. Or they wouldn't believe me."

"I'd forgotten."

"Why do women forget such things?"

"I'm not women; I'm singular; and I don't know why I forget such things."

"Sit down. I'm sorry."

"Thank you. I'm sorry too. Can you use the ship's radio to call for help?"

"No, there are too many domes and ridges for sending signals from here. And there are no charts for this extremity of north; no-one sails here."

"How about sending up a flare?"

"Too dry. The forest fire hazard is too high. I won't risk burning the ship; too much of my life is in her seams."

"I suppose so."

"Believe it."

They sat, she still hugging herself, he with his left arm across the back of her chair, and both gazing at the soft line where the keel touched the pavement.

"Possibly it was only the night air. It might have somehow weakened the supports."

"There was nothing wrong with the supports. They sank without giving way."

"Ah, that's right. But it's not sinking now."

"I'm afraid you're wrong. Since the forward support disappeared, it's been sinking steadily."

"I can't hear it. And it doesn't look like it to me."

"Look closely. Don't you see how the planks we set underneath are gradually floating out beyond the sides?"

"Yes . . . I see it now. But why do we hear nothing?"

"Not all sinking is sensory. It sometimes goes on through the nights and days without our noticing at all. By the time we've grown cognizant of it, there is no bilge-pump strong enough to save us. Probably *The Northwest Passage* began to sink the moment I touched pencil to paper to design her."

"Do you think so?"

"Yes."

"And, knowing this, it made no difference?"

"No."

"I think I wouldn't have gone through with it, if such a suspicion occurred to me."

"I could have preferred things otherwise . . . but without boats to build . . . there wouldn't be anything."

The ship was settling evenly, gracefully, now, toward the waterline. Without sound. Not far away a grouse drummed. A ptarmigan strode across the asphalt road. And a black bear was nosing a blueberry bush absent of berries. High sun strummed through the well-strung rigging of the mast and cross-spars, then darted here and there among the polished brass fittings.

"Soon she'll hit the water-line."

"Yes."

"Then, who knows?"

"Say, I just thought of something. Maybe *The Northwest Passage* simply has a mind of her own and is trying to tell us something by launching herself. She'll stop at the water-line. I think I'll go inside for a bottle of champagne to christen her, just in case."

"That sparkling muscatel?"

"Don't be coarse. It's twenty a magnum."

"Ships should be christened with rum. Bring the rum."

"Where's your sense of ceremony?"

"In my insides — where that rum is going."

She brought the rum.

"There's the water-line!"

"Good. Now we'll see."

"I have the champagne near the door."

"Very well, if she stops at the water-line, you have my leave to ruin my stern varnish with that belly-rot."

"Later you'll be glad I christened her properly."

The mast stood like a sundial, wavering only slightly in the breeze and the almost imperceptible silent settlings below. It marked the passing of high noon and cast its crossed shadows in the direction of evening and the dark which never seems to arrive in the summer north, but suddenly is upon you.

"So much for my water-line." He tossed the empty rum bottle into the bushes which lined the driveway.

"Yes, nothing showing of it at all. I'll only have to pick up that bottle and discard it later."

"So you will. So you will."

Before she could protest, he leapt from his chair, raced to the ladder at the side of the vessel, climbed it, and drew the ladder up on the deck.

"What do you think you can accomplish from up there?"

No answer. He was drawing up the anchor. The anchor secured, he began pacing around the decks, the bill of his sailing cap pulled low against the vanishing rays of the strange northern sun. He paused to check this fitting, then that, gave a turn-buckle a couple of turns, then went inside to his compass, charts, and wheel.

"Don't you think you ought to come down?"

His head appeared around the frame of the cabin door. He glared at her with fraudulent anger.

"I mean, you never know what might happen."

"You never know."

He unlashed the mainsail and pulled it determinedly up the mast, secured the boom, then returned to the wheelhouse. A weak breeze over the dome-top began to luff the canvas erratically. He emerged again quickly, leapt to the bow, cupped his hands, and: "In the name of Boreas and all inspiration . . . MORE GODDAM WIND!!"

And you could hear it in the distant trees like a locomotive nearing.

"There's always breeze in the late afternoon and evening. You know it as well as I do."

"Never mind. Where's my line now?"

"About midway between water-line and gunwale, I guess."

The mainsail was full now. The Commodore went forward and ran up the jib which stiffened until it looked like the blade of a knife held aloft.

"Alright now, alright, we'll see what we'll see." And into the cabin we went again. Below on the driveway she paced round and round the craft, hugging herself against the chill and wind rising. The vessel heaved back and forth in the pavement and the noise had returned — grating and grating of the cedar ribs against the stone layers and permafrost into which it was sinking.

The Commodore again came out of the cabin, and, struggling against the winds mounting to gale force, managed to get the deep green spinnaker up. It required almost super-human effort. The canvas ballooned and burgeoned like the throat-sac of a monster frog.

The noise now was truly stupendous. It overwhelmed even the sound of the careering wind. She stood in the draft of the vessel, but not too close: it pitched now side to side and forward and aft, as if in the highest of seas. Anything might have happened — sails might have split, the boat might have broken up, or might even have rolled free. But these things did not occur; simply the violent motion accelerated the sinking.

Commodore Eric F.F. Forrer stood, legs rooted substantially far apart, knees bending rhythmically to absorb the shocks of the listing and pitching, there in the wheelhouse at the wheel until, at a dramatic moment toward late evening, the bowsprit nosed under and the wind expired as if there had never been wind, and the forward decks were awash with asphalt.

"You see? It didn't work."

The Commodore standing on the slant amidships, cap in his left hand, mopping his brow with his right sleeve: "On the contrary, woman, on the contrary."

Another lurch. The stern and aft decking sank from sight. He sprang to the roof of the cabin. The sails hung limp from their rigging.

"This is the best ship I ever made. See how she sinks evenly instead of going stern or bow first. You can tell the character of a boat by the way she dies."

"I see."

"Plenty of time for all hands to abandon."

"Plenty."

"Better stand back and clear. Sometimes the last suction can be fierce."

"Very well. Have all abandoned?"

"Yes, I gave the order some time ago."

"I didn't hear it."

"Doubtless it was the big wind and the sound of the sinking."

"Yes, I suppose."

The surface of the driveway was now level with the flat roof of the wheelhouse. No wind, and darkness closing like the shutter of a camera.

"I'll get a light."

She returned with a glass lantern, brilliant and hissing.

"Is there any more rum?" he asked as he began climbing the rigging toward the cross-spar.

"No. I'm sorry."

He sat, legs dangling on either side of the mast, and holding the tip of the mast near the flag with one hand.

The light of the lantern lit one side of his profile so brightly that his features seemed almost washed out. The other side of his face, like the moon which had now risen over the scrub-timber at the crest of the dome, erased itself in darkness. Up the mast crept the asphalt like mercury in a barometer. There was little sound now, so smooth was the surface of the mast, save the occasional crinkle of new canvas going under.

When the surface met the corrugated soles of his deck shoes, he stood upon the cross-spar, drew himself to his full height, inhaled the darkness deeply, and shouted:

"Eric F. F. Forrer, Commodore!"

There was no retort. Nor did he begin to polemicize as if there had been one.

She held the light closer as the asphalt gathered in his broad shoulders.

His last words were: "Blow that damn thing out."

She did.

And there was not a trace, not a ripple, not even a small indentation in the dark surface of the driveway. She spent some minutes looking after she re-lit the lamp (not difficult in the windless darkness; there was still plenty of pressure in it).

And then she went inside where the bottle of champagne still stood waiting; she replaced it in the liquor cupboard. She would fetch the empty rum bottle in the morning and throw it in the trash.

As she switched out the lights from room to room and began to prepare for bed, the house rolled a little . . . like a large boat at a calm mooring. But she hardly noticed the motion; miniature earth tremors are so very usual in that precinct of the world.

APPENDIX

HOW TO READ A SHORT STORY

There is no single form of short fiction; and there is no single acceptable way of responding to the art of this genre. Reading is a creative,
not a mechanical act; it requires imaginative participation, not passive
receptivity. But involvement of this kind does not permit us to decide
that a story may mean whatever we want it to mean. Writers arrange
their words to engage their readers in quite particular ways, and use a
variety of techniques — some familiar, some unusual or obscure — to
shape and guide our responses. One of the challenges facing the reader
is to sort out the *how* and the *why* of a story's structure: how is it put
together in order to create the effects it achieves? why did the writer
choose this way, rather than another? why did the writer select these
particular words, and arrange them in this particular order? Ideally,
finding answers to such questions adds to the pleasure of reading; we
end up, not merely with a grasp of the story's content, but with a greater
appreciation of the writer's verbal and architectonic skills, and of the
sophisticated art by means of which the writer has cast a fresh light on
human behavior.

You can identify many of the techniques of short fiction by asking particular questions about any story that you read, and the paragraphs that
follow attempt to suggest the kinds of questions that may be appropriate. However, two points should be borne in mind here: first, the use of
any given technique is no indication of a story's quality; a writer may
use a web of complex symbols or an intricate plot pattern, without producing a good story; and conversely, the absence of these or other techniques does not necessarily make a story weak. Secondly, not all the
questions or points listed below will be applicable to every story; the
artists have each made a choice and selected only those elements of
the storyteller's art that will most effectively render character, scene,
or action, and thus fulfil their purpose.

1.   What happens?
Answers to this question involve an understanding of the *plot*, the
sequence of events in the narrative. Who does what to whom? How do
the events that take place, and the order in which they occur, affect
the outcome of the story? (For example, in melodramatic stories dire
events often occur because something goes missing — a letter, a mort-
gage deed — at an inopportune time.)
   How does the story *begin*: at the beginning of the action or part-way
through? How does it *develop*: in chronological order or in flashback;

at one moment in time, or over an extended period? Is there a *climax*, a high point of the action when all the threads of the story come together? If the story has no discernible climax, why not? Is there any *suspense*, and how is it created? Is the outcome of the action a surprise? How does the story come to an *end* — does it close off the action with some kind of resolution, or leave it open and indeterminate? Does the ending offer a general comment about the world at large, or does it focus on the feelings of an individual character?

2. Where does the story happen, and when?

These questions ask about the *setting*, which involves both *place* and *time*. A story may make extensive use of scenic description, but in well-written stories such descriptions are never ornamental: they are a means of telling us something about the characters or the action. Some stories rely on your making either general or specific associations with details of setting: what comes to mind when you think of an Arctic winter, a day in May, the year 1867, the date 11 November 1918, a railway station, the American South, Middle Earth, a small-town diner, the starship "Enterprise"? Each of these is a "setting"; some are specific in their historical or geographical reference, others fantastic or imaginary; still others call on traditional associations common to human experience.

Why does the author set the action in a given place or at a given time? Are there political or cultural or social ramifications to the setting? What details of setting throw light on the actions or feelings of the characters? How are the characters formed or influenced by their physical environment? Does the writer want us to make conventional associations with a particular setting (a spring day suggesting possibility and hope, a crossroads pointing to a moment of decision)? Or does the story somehow subvert such conventional associations (the spring day leading to disaster, the crossroads offering merely an illusion of choice)?

In some stories, however, there may not be a conventional setting at all; the action may take place in a character's mind or imagination. Or the setting may be the printed page, itself a "field" on which words assemble, in patterns suggestive of action or meaning.

3. Who is the story about?

This question concerns both *character* and the techniques of *characterization* by which an author creates character. Who is the main character (the protagonist) in the story, and what do we learn about that character's identity, appearance, and background? How are the principal characters revealed to us: through what they say and do? through their thoughts? by the way that others react to them, or by what the author says about them? Do the characters undergo any kind of change in the course of the story? Do they come to some illumination or new understanding of the world (James Joyce called such a moment an "epiphany"), or are they unaffected by their experience?

Does the story include a "foil" for the main character — an enemy or "antagonist" who opposes the main character's progress or thwarts success? Such a foil does not always have to be human: it can be an aspect of nature (like a beast or a rugged landscape), imaginary (like a creature of nightmare), mythic (supernatural figures or deities), or even abstract and intangible (like the forces of time).

Does the story contain a "double" of the main character — that is, a character who in some way embodies or reflects an aspect of the main character's personality, possibly something that has lain hidden or suppressed? How do the experiences and problems of the minor characters reflect on those of the protagonist? Do they suggest alternative courses of action, or reveal options or solutions that the main character should, or should not, choose?

Some stories have first-person narrators. The "I" who tells a story may be the protagonist, or a minor character acting as observer, or a *persona* (Latin, "mask") of the author; whatever the case, the "I" is as much a character in the narrative as any of the other characters, and you should ask the same kinds of questions about this "I" as you would about the other actors in the story. (See the next section, on "Who tells the story?")

Characters are not "people" — that is, a story is not "real life," no matter how much it may create that illusion, and no matter how it may resemble the situations that we know happen in real life. Therefore we can know only as much about a character as the story reveals, and must form our judgments accordingly.

4. Who tells the story?

This question asks you not simply to give a name to the narrator, but to figure out the strategy of narration.

Is the story told in the *first person* by a participant in the action, or by an invisible narrator who records everything in the *third person*? Is the first-person narrator wholly reliable, or does that narrator betray some bias or prejudice that might slant his or her interpretation of events? If the story is in the third person, does the narrator intrude with comments or explanations, or does the story appear to unfold by itself, without any interpretive comment?

By the choice of narrative angle, the author can significantly influence our understanding of the story. For example, a story in which the narrator is *omniscient* — that is, knows all and tells all — will likely cast the reader in the role of observer of the action; readers may be sympathetic to the characters, but remain essentially uninvolved, sharing a viewpoint that distances them from the action. In a first-person narration, on the other hand, the speaker is likely to be limited in knowledge, and this very limitation may create a stronger bond with the reader: because we are forced to see things from one character's point of view, we are more likely to identify with that character's feelings and responses. In such cases, we should ask ourselves whether the narrator is telling us all he or she knows, or concealing something to mislead us. Sometimes narrators are unconsciously revealing something about themselves that they might not wish us to know, or showing us a side of themselves that they are unaware of.

In some stories the author may use the third person, but filter the events through the consciousness of the main character. What is the effect of such a strategy?

5. What is your reaction to the story?

The issue addressed by this question is that of *tone*. Tone is related to point of view, because it is a way of characterizing the attitude of mind conveyed by the style of narration. In conversation, a speaker's tone of voice helps the listener to interpret his or her meaning and feelings; similarly in fiction, the tone of the narration guides the reader's response and understanding. You will react differently to a story that you know is told in jest from one that is told angrily or sadly. How does a writer establish (and control) the tone of a story? Is the tone dependent just on the overt subject, or is it somehow linked with language (could you write a sad story about a comic event)? Is the story sad, funny, sarcastic, ironic, tragic, satiric, witty, playful, bitter, passionate, cool, or something else — and how do you know? What effect does the tone have on the way you respond emotionally or intellectually to the events of the story?

6. What form does the story take?

This is a question about the kinds and effects of various verbal patterns, and should really be thought of as three more specific questions, concerning (a) the *style*, or the shape, pattern, and rhythm of words, phrases, and sentences; (b) the design and function of separate *scenes*; and (c) the organization and shape of the story as a whole, its *narrative pattern*.

(a) *Style:* The questions to be asked about style in fiction are the same as those we use in the analysis of any kind of prose. Is the language *formal* or *informal*, or some combination of these? Is the vocabulary simple and direct, or complex and ornate? Why did the author choose these particular words, and arrange them in this particular order? (It can be instructive to substitute synonyms in a passage, to see the difference in effect that *word choice* can make.) The study of *syntax* (the way in which words are put together to form phrases and sentences) is equally important. Are the sentences short or long; *simple, compound,* or *complex*; cast in the *active* or the *passive*, the *affirmative* or the *negative*? Do they follow a standard order (subject-verb-object), or is this order altered in key places? Are any phrases, clauses, or sentences obviously parallel in structure, and if so does such *parallelism* imply any connections between characters, events, or ideas?

What contributions do word choice and syntax make to the story? The way that characters speak is an important clue to their social background, their attitudes, and their feelings. *Repetitions* of phrase or form can emphasize a particular attitude or reflect a speaker's obsessions; *fragmented* or *incomplete* sentences or *exclamations* may convey incoherent thoughts, sudden impulses, or strong emotions. In passages of narration or description, repetition may be used to suggest the cyclic nature of an event, or to draw attention to similarities between different parts of the story.

A writer may use *figurative language* to add layers of meaning to the narrative. *Symbol* and *metaphor* extend the literal meaning of an object or event by introducing another level of associations and enlarging the story's frame of reference. The use of *simile* is a means of stressing the likenesses between things. Another method of making comparisons is *allusion*; the story that makes repeated allusions to figures in history or myth, or to other works of literature, may be asking you to recognize the way it parallels, or echoes, or modifies some other work.

All writers use *images*, words or phrases that recreate the physical world by appealing to our senses (words, for example, like rose, flag, thunder, heave, gritty). Such images can take on figurative meaning, depending on their function and their context. An image that is used repeatedly in a story may acquire symbolic force, or become a kind of *motif* associated with a particular mood or setting or character.

(b) *Scenes*: Just as the structure of individual sentences can reflect aspects of character or elements of meaning, so the structure of individual scenes in a story can sometimes contain, in small, the issues and the tensions that the story as a whole explores on a larger scale. A scene which dramatizes an individual moment of temptation, for example, might constitute an intrinsic part of a story that concerns itself with the problem of moral choice in a fallen world. Or a scene in which is shown an act of petty cruelty might reflect the story's broader treatment of the injustices characterizing a hierarchical society.

Individual scenes play an important role in the development of plot and character. Some of the following questions may be relevant in considering the relation of scenes to overall plot structure: how does the scene contribute to the main action? Is it part of the story's exposition, laying the groundwork for what follows? Does it introduce a complication (the arrival of a new character, the announcement of some unexpected news, for instance)? Does it form the climax of the story, bring a conflict to a head, show the protagonist making a crucial decision? Does it form a conclusion to the narrative, embody a resolution of the central conflict, untangle any narrative knots (French, *dénouement*)? What aspect of the main character is revealed in the scene? If the scene occurs early in the story, does it offer clues about the main character's motives or future conduct?

(c) *Narrative pattern*: A writer may draw on any one of a variety of traditional patterns, or forms, to structure the narrative as a whole. The story can be constructed to read as a *memoir*, an *allegory*, a *documentary*, a *history*, a *fairy tale*, an *adventure*, a *romance*, a *character sketch*, a *journal*, a *myth*, a *fable*, a *parable*; each of these forms has its own set of conventions and associations. The critical reader must ask: what is the form that the author has chosen for the story, and what is the effect on the story of that choice? Clearly, the writer who casts a work of fiction as a documentary journal wants the fiction to give the illusion of being a faithful record of experience; the writer who presents us with a fable set in modern life may well be making an ironic comment on contemporary morality, drawing effects from an implicit comparison with traditional fables and their appeal to conventional virtues. Ask yourself whether the story you are reading follows a pattern of this kind. Is it presented as a tall tale? a heroic quest? a rite of initiation? a myth of death and resurrection, or of seasonal and cyclical return?

Some stories fall into the category of *metafiction*, fiction about the workings of fiction; such stories may include any of the forms noted above, or variants of these forms, in order to explore the character of verbal artifice itself.

7. Does the story have a central subject?

This is a difficult question, not least because it is often misleading. It sometimes takes other forms — "What is the story *about?*" "What does the story *say?*" "What is the *meaning* of the story?" Such questions suggest that hidden at the heart of a story, waiting to be sprung loose like a jack-in-the-box, is a secret "message." But good stories don't work that way; instead, they use narrative as a process to draw the reader into an appreciation of the complexities (and sometimes the simplicities) of human behavior, motivation, and value.

However, because they do select from and focus upon particular aspects of human experience, stories inevitably have *subjects* or *themes*; they concern themselves with politics and ethics, with life and death, youth and age, continuity and change, with war and peace, hate and love, science and nature, words and feelings — with everything that embodies or expresses our humanity. But simply to say that a story is "about war" or "about nature" is not enough. The effective reader seeks to discover how all the elements in a given story — character, plot, setting, language, tone — work together to create a sense of a whole. Though there may be times when you want to express a story's main concerns or themes in a sentence or two, by doing so you run the risk of oversimplifying the author's complex creation. The effective reader also looks for those occasions when a story isn't concerned so much with conventional "themes" as with the nature of language, the very process of storytelling itself; such stories are a reminder that fiction is artifice, and that however "real" it may seem to us, it can only take shape and meaning when writer and reader actively collaborate on the plane of the imagination.

FOR FURTHER READING

Helmut Bonheim, *The Narrative Modes* (Cambridge: D.S. Brewer, 1982).

Suzanne Ferguson, "Defining the Short Story: Impressionism and Form," *Modern Fiction Studies* 28, no. 1 (Spring 1982): 13–24.

Gerald Gillespie, "Novella, Novelle, Novella, Short Novel? A Review of Terms," *Neophilologus* 55 (1967): 117–27, 225–30.

Graham Good, "Notes on the Novella," *Novel* 10, no. 3 (Spring 1977): 197–211.

Susan Lohafer, *Coming to Terms with the Short Story* (Baton Rouge: Louisiana State University Press, 1983).

Charles E. May, ed., *Short Story Theories* (Athens, Ohio: Ohio University Press, 1978).

Mary Louise Pratt, "The Short Story: The Long and the Short of It," *Poetics* 10, nos. 2/3 (June 1981): 175–94.

Ian Reid, *The Short Story* (London: Methuen, 1977).

Hollis Summers, ed., *Discussions of the Short Story* (Boston: D.C. Heath, 1963).

1 2 3 4 5   135515   90 89 88 87 86